SPECIAL MESSAGE

THE ULVERSCROFT FOUNDATION
(registered UK charity number 264873)
was established in 1972 to provide funds for research, diagnosis and treatment of eye diseases. Examples of major projects funded by the Ulverscroft Foundation are:-

- The Children's Eye Unit at Moorfields Eye Hospital, London
- The Ulverscroft Children's Eye Unit at Great Ormond Street Hospital for Sick Children
- Funding research into eye diseases and treatment at the Department of Ophthalmology, University of Leicester
- The Ulverscroft Vision Research Group, Institute of Child Health
- Twin operating theatres at the Western Ophthalmic Hospital, London
- The Chair of Ophthalmology at the Royal Australian College of Ophthalmologists

You can help further the work of the Foundation by making a donation or leaving a legacy. Every contribution is gratefully received. If you would like to help support the Foundation or require further information, please contact:

THE ULVERSCROFT FOUNDATION
The Green, Bradgate Road, Anstey
Leicester LE7 7FU, England
Tel: (0116) 236 4325

website: www.foundation.ulverscroft.com

Born and raised in London and now living in Brighton with her four-year-old son, Charlene Allcott works part-time with young people in a residential care home. She writes a parenting blog at www.moderatemum.co.uk. *The Single Mum's Wish List* is her first novel.

THE SINGLE MUM'S WISH LIST

Martha Ross dreams of being a singer, but she's been working in a call centre far too long. She's separating from her husband, the father of her son. And she's moving back in with her parents, toddler in tow. Life has thrown her a few lemons, but Martha intends to make a gin and tonic. It's time to become the woman she's always wanted to be. At least her mum's on hand to provide childcare — and ample motherly judgement. Soon Martha realises that in order to find lasting love and fulfilment, she needs to find herself first. But her attempts at reinvention — from writing a definitive wish list of everything she wants in a new man, to half-marathons, business plans and meditation retreats — tend to go awry in the most surprising of ways . . .

CHARLENE ALLCOTT

◆

THE SINGLE MUM'S WISH LIST

Complete and Unabridged

CHARNWOOD
Leicester

First published in Great Britain in 2018 by
Bantam Press
an imprint of Transworld Publishers
London

First Charnwood Edition
published 2019
by arrangement with
Penguin Random House UK
London

A catalogue record for this book is available
from the British Library.

ISBN 978–1–4448–4277–7

Published by
F. A. Thorpe (Publishing)
Anstey, Leicestershire

Set by Words & Graphics Ltd.
Anstey, Leicestershire
Printed and bound in Great Britain by
T. J. International Ltd., Padstow, Cornwall

To Graham, for believing in me before
I believed in myself

1

I think it's appropriate to begin at the end. People say it's best to start at the beginning but I've never been a believer. I'm loyal to endings; I skip to the final page of every book I read. The end is where the truth is, and the end starts when Jacqueline opens her door.

I've never seen Jacqueline looking anything less than glamorous and even with sleep still clinging to her eyes and a silk robe replacing her starched, navy shift dress, she looks like an off-duty Marilyn Monroe. I feel inadequate in my workwear 101 outfit of black T-shirt, black trousers and flats.

'Martha,' she says carefully, 'are you OK?' Jacqueline says things like, 'Are you OK?' when what she really means is, 'What the fuck are you doing at my house at eight thirty in the morning?' That's why I need her. Jacqueline is my therapist.

She asks me in. 'Asks' is a strong word; she makes a gesture close to a shrug and steps to one side. I can't afford the luxury of socially acceptable behaviour, so I go through. Jacqueline ushers me past her magnolia-coloured therapy room and into a light, open-plan kitchen. I know this is her way of saying 'this is not official' but I don't mind because I've always wanted to see what goes on behind the velvet rope. I spend 40 per cent of every session with Jacqueline wondering who Jacqueline actually is — what she does at weekends; if she does Pilates; if she still has sex with her husband; if her husband is in fact a wife. I am not disappointed; the room looks like something from the pages of *Homes & Gardens*. I am transfixed by a huge, tartan-print three-seater. I have always fantasized about having a kitchen large enough to house a sofa. I take a few moments to imagine a sofa-kitchened life but then Alexander wanders into the fantasy with his bare feet and his ripped Diesel jeans, and I remember why I am there.

'I need you to tell me to split up with Alexander,' I say. Jacqueline shuts her eyes briefly and then gestures towards a high stool next to a granite-topped island. My mouth is dry but she doesn't offer me a drink and it doesn't seem appropriate to ask for one. Jacqueline doesn't sit, which I think is her way of saying she's only tolerating my visit, but why become a therapist if you don't want to invite crazy into your life?

'You said to contact you whenever I needed and I really need an answer today.' I don't know why today; today is no more significant than any other day: a Friday morning, mild with a threat of rain, no major events in the calendar. It is sinister in its mundaneness. Jacqueline makes a face that I have seen many times and previously taken to mean she is absorbing the significance of my words, but now I'm wondering if it means 'you are very irritating'. Perhaps it's the facial equivalent of one of those words that can mean two completely different things, like beat or tender or leaves. I've forgotten the name for those sorts of words. Alexander would know; perhaps that's another reason I should stay with him.

During the pause in which Jacqueline is thinking or praying or whatever she is doing, I try and predict what she will say. I am thinking: 'Why do you believe this is an issue for you?' Or maybe: 'Would it help if I reflected back to you what I just heard?' Or her favourite: 'I'm more interested in why you've posed the question.' She really loves that one; my money's on that.

She says, 'Yes, you should.' And I feel nauseous. I immediately understand that I came here because I thought she would not be allowed to give me the answer my heart already knew.

'Thanks,' I say as I stand. 'Sorry, I have to go to work.'

Jacqueline continues, 'We've spent a great deal of time discussing your relationship and it is obviously very flawed. In addition, your demeanour today suggests you may need some time to focus on yourself.'

'Thanks,' I say again.

'Also, before you go,' says Jacqueline, and I take a deep breath. She clears her throat. 'I can't see you again. I think some boundaries have been crossed here. I can recommend someone very good . . . very firm.' She turns and writes something on a handily placed book of notelets on the island and passes it to me. I have an urge to sniff it but I put it in my trouser pocket.

'Thanks,' I say and leave. This is the end.

Actually, this is not quite the end. The end is

twelve minutes later when I'm on the bus rumbling along the Brighton seafront towards the concrete prison that serves as my place of work. I send Alexander a text terminating our six-year marriage. It reads, 'WE ARE OVER.' Less than thirty seconds later he replies, 'OK.'

2

Why I stand by endings — beginnings are bullshit. Let me tell you about the start of Alexander and me. We were best friends but we weren't really best friends; I was the dumpy chick he tolerated hanging around. Everyone knew I was hopelessly in love with him but anyone with eyes could see I wasn't his type — I'm slightly above average height and more than slightly above average weight; I'm mixed race without any of the exoticism it claims to offer. My face is fine but forgettable. The only thing that stands out about me is my uncontrollable hair and I have spent a lifetime experimenting with products that might stop that being the case. So, I sat on the sidelines and I watched Alexander go through a series of petite, striking blondes, my favourite part being when they broke up and he would take me to the Twisted Yarn for a debrief. I would sip my dark ale (which made me gag at the time but now I actually quite like) and I would get to tell him all the things I had been secretly storing for a week, a month, or on one occasion, an entire year. To be honest, I was happy with that. OK, I was on the outskirts of happy; I could certainly catch the scent of happy if the wind was blowing in the right direction. And then one of the blondes broke his heart.

Her name was Jenna. She was impossibly and

impractically posh. She was one of those chicks that's done everything, but really how much can you experience in a rural, all-girls boarding school and then a small, top-tier university and then a cushy job, handed to you on a gold platter by your father? Still, when she spoke, Alexander listened. He was like a Labrador when he was with her. He looked at her the way I imagine I looked at him. Anyway, Jenna ended the relationship with very little explanation. I heard a rumour she had joined a bloke called Tristan on his boat in the Caribbean for the summer but I kept that nugget to myself. Jenna always seemed to have one eye on the lookout for something better, so the break-up came as no surprise to anyone but Alexander. I'm assuming he had been dumped before but on this occasion, it consumed him. I waited by the phone for him to arrange our usual post-break-up pity party, but the call never came. When I tried to contact him, he wouldn't answer and his voicemail message said he was 'taking time out from life'.

After a few days of this I did what any friend would do and went to his flat. I let myself in using a key I knew he kept hidden in a pot of dying lavender. The first thing that hit me was the smell — it was two parts gym locker room, one part that weird odour that haunts kitchen cupboards and always turns out to be rotting potatoes. Alexander was in bed and it looked like that had been the case for several days. The debris around him told a story — a broken photo frame, an over-flowing ashtray, three empty wine bottles and a pizza box.

'Alexander,' I said gently. 'Alexander, you have to get up.' He continued staring into the distance, so I quietly set about filling a bin liner with rubbish. When I had finished he was asleep and I gave the kitchen a thorough clean and then made soup out of the selection of sad-looking veggies in his fridge. When I walked in to tell him the food was ready he was awake but still huddled under his duvet.

'What's wrong with me?' he said.

'Oh my God, nothing,' I reassured him.

'It was different this time,' he said. 'I was gonna give her this.' He let his hand fall on to the bedside table, where lay a green velvet box.

'Is that . . . '

'Look,' said Alexander. I walked towards the box slowly, as if it might detonate. I picked it up carefully and checked if Alexander was watching me; he was not. Inside, safe in its satin nest, was an antique ring. Not exactly my style, except for the bold emerald stone — a unique rock for a one-of-a-kind girl. Much later I would get that ring and, fool that I am, instead of seeing it as some other woman's cast-off, I thought it meant I had won. At that point I didn't want it anywhere near me. Without saying anything I placed the box in Alexander's sock drawer.

'You have to try.' I sat on the edge of the bed and with some effort hauled him into a sitting position. 'See, not so hard.' Alexander gave me a weak smile.

'Not so hard with you,' he said. There was a pause in which I assume the room was silent but in my head I was screaming, 'Kiss me! Kiss me! Kiss me!' And he did.

★ ★ ★

When huge things happen, it feels like everything should change. The sky should turn purple and the laws of gravity should no longer apply. It's almost offensive how very much the same everything seems when I arrive at work. How can the security guy, Darryl, still be playing Candy Crush when I feel like every cell in my body has been altered? I'm thinking about this as I power up my computer and put on my headset.

Oh yeah, I work in a call centre. I never actually say I work in a call centre; I say I work in customer services. Not that there's anything wrong with working in a call centre, if that's what you want to do, but from my experience no one does. We're all waiting for our big break; even Darryl has shared his movie script with me. I want to be a singer. Slight problem — I've never sung in front of anyone. Well, I've sung in front of Moses. Moses is my son. Our son, mine and Alexander's. You wouldn't know it from their interactions. Alexander always looks mildly surprised when he sees him in a room — 'Oh, you again? Well, I guess you can stay for dinner.'

Moses is beautiful, though. I know that all parents are supposed to think their kid is beautiful but Moses actually is. When I was pregnant we played a game where we each got to pick the features we wanted our unborn baby to have; Alexander said he hoped he wouldn't get my chin and he didn't. He has my crazy black curls and his father's startling green eyes — eyes that I know from experience will bestow even the most mundane utterings with an intoxicating intensity. Women stop me in town and tell me he'll be a heartbreaker when he grows up, which is a creepy thing to say about a toddler, but I believe them.

I thought being a mother would make me a grown-up, that I would have no choice but to grow up. It was only after he was born that I realized how little adulting I had got around to doing. I watch other mothers carefully for evidence of how to stay calm and keep a child vaguely clean but I always end up Googling 'the dangers of eating cat food' or fishing electronics out of the toilet. Sometimes I share these anecdotes with people around me, in order to gauge exactly how close I am to becoming a *Daily Mail* headline. Like Greg, who sits next to me at work. He has two girls; I know this because he has a gigantic picture of them on his desk — pretty, blonde things with lopsided bows and the promise of mischief in their eyes. When I tell him my mishaps he always chuckles or says, 'It's like that.' Or, 'Tell me about it, buddy.' So I think I'm kinda on the right track.

I took the job at Fairfax Financial Services because Alexander said I needed to think about my future. I'd left a temp job to have Moses and had nothing to go back to. I told Alexander I was thinking about retraining and might start to do some singing auditions, but he told me he couldn't fund a dream-chasing lifestyle. The call

9

centre had two advantages — it offered shift work, so I would be able to fit it around childcare and singing gigs; and it was hellish enough that I wouldn't stay too long, six months tops. That was nearly a year ago. Now I wonder if even this job will fit my new life. Everything's fallen apart and it all needs to be put back together like a sadistic game of Jenga.

I try and make a start on constructing an image of what this new chapter will look like; I have a lot of time to do this because most of my job entails directing customers to yet another call centre where presumably someone will do something useful, by which I mean I say, 'Putting you through now . . . ' two million times a day; it doesn't take much mental energy.

We're allowed two breaks a day, one short and one long. Sometimes I would use the opportunity to call Alexander, not always but often. I feel bereft of this; it's like when I gave up smoking — it wasn't the nicotine I missed so much as the ritual of it, the way the process punctuated time.

'Do you smoke?' I ask Greg.

'Nah,' he says. 'It's bad for you.'

'So I've heard,' I say.

'I didn't know you smoked,' says Greg, as if we are life-long friends and I have intentionally kept this fact hidden.

'I've got a lot on my mind,' I say. He doesn't turn away.

'You OK, buddy?' he says. Every office has a Greg — you might know him as Steve or Dave, but they all share the same affable nature and inoffensive brand of charm. They're usually found offering to make the older women strong cups of tea or having intense debates about football team managership with the lads in the post room; their strength is in their consistency, and as I look at Greg's gentle, ex-boyband-member face, I'm hit by the fact that he is probably more reliable than the man I had pledged my life to. I nod my head. If I speak I will cry and if I cry I will be 'woman who cries at work'.

My phone rings and it's Alexander, as if he knows I need him. My break is officially over, and I'm not even supposed to have my phone on my desk. The lines are automated and if I'm not available the customer calls will go unanswered, but I accept his call anyway. I give Greg a hand signal, one that I hope he understands as, 'Cover for me, this is very important.' He seems to comprehend because he winks at me.

'Hello,' I say, as I scuttle out of the room to the only place of sanctuary in the building — the disabled loo.

'Thanks for answering,' says Alexander.

'Yeah, you too,' I say. 'I mean, thanks for calling.' I realize this is the only time he's called me during the day; he almost always sends a text and even then its content is of the practical, almost always instructional nature: 'Buy milk', 'Can you pick up dinner?', 'Where's the gas meter?' Nothing personal or intimate. Perhaps by forcing space on him he has realized that proximity is what he needs.

'It's brave of you to say what had to be said.' Alexander stops; I'm not sure if he's waiting for

11

me to speak or overcome with emotion but then I hear someone ask if he has a loyalty card and I realize he's in a supermarket. 'I've packed some of your stuff and I'll drop it at your mum's before you finish. Given that Moses has a room there, it makes sense if you both stay with her for a bit. I called and asked her to pick him up from nursery tonight.'

I lean against the wall. 'Alexander, I — '

'Don't worry,' he says. 'We can have a chat in a day or two, when the dust has settled.' I have a sudden urge to laugh, but instead I end the call. Then I don't feel like my legs will hold me, so I sit on the floor. I squeeze myself between the toilet bowl and the sanitary towel bin and sob.

*   *   *

I don't know how long has passed when I get up and brush myself off. My eyes in the mirror remind me of those of the white gerbil I had when I was seven — small, sad and pink. I try and make my face presentable with a blast from the hand dryer, and when I check myself again, my eyes fall on my rings. I wrench at my wedding band until it comes away, leaving a red, raw mark. I slip it in my pocket but I can't make myself do the same with the emerald. I tell myself it's too pretty but I think I'm not ready to let go of the knowledge that, at least one time, he chose me.

As I'm walking back to my desk Greg stands. He's on a call but he does a series of stretches, as if he's preparing for some sort of office-based

12

sport. As I get closer his gestures become more involved; it's almost like a dance. I wonder if he's unstable — the secret lives of call centre workers, eh? Too late I see that the title of Greg's contemporary piece is 'the boss is coming, stay out of sight for a minute' and the second I make it to my desk I am besieged by Bob.

Bob demands that I come to his office. I might be in serious trouble but I might not be as Bob demands everything. He manages to make every interaction feel aggressive; I swear even his sneezes are threatening. I don't know why Bob feels the need to be so macho about everything — he's tall, fit (on account of an apparent gym addiction) and he's good-looking if you like that artificially bronze, extra-from-*TOWIE* vibe, but obviously something has gone awry at some point. Rumour has it he's not even called Bob. He briefly dated Danielle in HR and after their break-up she revealed that he had chosen the name Bob because he 'did not feel his given name suited his present mindset'. Bob vowed never to date within the organization again following this indiscretion. He told me so during my interview: 'I don't shit where I eat, so don't get any ideas.'

Bob doesn't invite me to sit, so I end up standing with my hands in front of me like a kid being called before the headmaster. Actually, these days I bet the kid would be allowed to sit down; we're all so invested in children's welfare and treating them with respect. Bob is not a bedfellow with respect, so he leaves me hovering. He tells me I have dropped 36.5 calls over the past forty-six minutes and wants to know why. I want to know how it's possible to drop half a call but I'm not sure he would appreciate the question. I think about telling him the truth, saying, 'My heart feels like it's been ripped from my body and shredded on the fine side of the grater,' but then I look at Bob's impassive, possibly Botoxed face and say, 'I've been bleeding for twenty days.' Bob gives me the rest of the day off with strict instructions to 'find something to plug that up' by my next shift. I leave the office and head to Leanne's house.

3

Leanne opens her front door. She's wearing leggings covered in a brightly coloured geometric pattern and a long-sleeved top made out of shiny black material. 'Not that you aren't welcome,' she says, 'but this is a surprise.' Leanne takes Fridays off to spend 'quality time' with the kids and catch up with what she calls 'home admin'.

'Are you busy?' I ask. She pauses but says no.

'I was just about to take Lucas out with the running buggy.' Leanne heads to the kitchen and puts the kettle on, without needing to ask if this is the correct course of action.

I follow her and sit at the table. I start about twenty sentences in my head and go with, 'It's over.' And then, 'Oh God, it's really over. It's actually over.'

Leanne shoos her youngest, Lucas, from the room — she's clearly desperate to protect her children from legitimate human emotions for a couple more years. When he's safely out of earshot she says, 'What has he done?'

'It's not him, it's me!' I slap my hand against my breast-bone as if there's another contender for the title of me.

'What have you done?' Leanne asks patiently.

'I ended it. I had to end it. Jacqueline told me I should end it. Everyone knew it wasn't working, everyone. Oh God. Oh God.' Leanne stands up and pulls my head into her chest. I can

15

feel my tears creating a damp patch on her top and I try and pull away but she just tightens her grip.

'It's OK,' she whispers. 'It's OK.' We stay there in silence, both waiting for my breathing to return to a steady rhythm. Eventually my pace matches hers; there's something soothing about the synchronization of our exhalations. 'Martha,' says Leanne, 'who's Jacqueline?'

* * *

Leanne lets me hide within the bustle of her home. I follow her around like a puppy as she continues her daily routine. As we fold laundry and prep dinner, I play a canny game of avoidance — I avoid her gaze, I avoid my feelings, I avoid fourteen missed calls from my mother and a text message that says, 'CALL ME NOW!!!' After the fifteenth call, I text her: 'I AM FINE. WITH LEANNE. PLEASE PUT MOSES TO BED.' Then I turn my phone on silent. I know that if I hold my son I'll crumble; he'll have to watch his mother fall to pieces and won't understand why. And in addition, I don't need to hear 'All the Ways Martha is an Epic Failure: Volume 78' from my mother. Not today.

I accompany Leanne and Lucas to collect my god-daughter, Millie, from school. When she sees me at the gates she breaks into a spontaneous little tap dance and it is almost, but not quite, enough to lift my spirits. 'Auntie Marfa!' she cries when she reaches me. 'The truth came out!'

'It always does, beautiful,' I say.

'Look!' Millie carefully extracts a wad of tissue from the pocket of her pink coat and unwraps it carefully to reveal a tiny, white tooth.

'Well done, chicken,' I say. 'I'm so proud.' I pull her into a hug. 'I'm so, so proud of you.' Millie wriggles out of my arms and carefully places her treasure back in her pocket.

★   ★   ★

When the kids are in bed and Leanne's husband James is back from work and pottering about in that way only men can, it is no longer possible to avoid Leanne's slightly overwhelming concern. She makes me tea and then seats me on her sofa, where she paints my nails a shade of pearly pink. This is a throwback to our teenage years, when we would spend Saturday evenings getting beautified for parties to which we would never receive invites. We speak very little as she carefully coats each fingernail, although she gently probes into some of the pertinent details: Do I need somewhere to stay? (No.) Do I have enough money? (I don't know.) Do I need a good solicitor? (I hope not.) When she has finished she instructs me sternly not to smudge her work and then makes us both another brew.

'Is this definite?' she asks. I nod. 'When did you know?'

'Yesterday . . . Always,' I say.

'Will you go back to 'Ketch'?' Leanne asks. I am yet to give this thought but the answer arrives quickly.

'No. No, I'm still Martha Ross. I want to have

17

the same name as Moses.' Also, I need the reminder — not of Alexander but that, at one time, I belonged to someone. Leanne sips her tea. I suspect she is filling her mouth to prevent further comment. 'You can say it,' I continue, 'you can say whatever it is you're thinking.' For some reason, I think she's going to admit she thought I was too fat for him.

'I'm sorry,' she says.

Without introduction, my friend Cara walks into the room and falls heavily on to the sofa. Leanne must have sent a text requesting back-up. 'What do I need to fix?' she asks.

'How did you get in?' asks Leanne. A bird tweets from within Cara's bag and she ignores Leanne's question, retrieves her phone and starts stabbing at it violently. Leanne narrows her eyes at Cara as we both watch her scarlet-tipped fingers move deftly across the phone face. When it's apparent that Cara is oblivious to her silent judgement, Leanne switches back to concerned mode. She pats me on the thigh and tells Cara, 'Everything's under control. Martha's had a shock. It's over between her and Alexander.' Cara puts her phone away, tucks her spike-heeled ankle boots up beside her and pushes the sunglasses she's wearing on to her thick, inky head of hair.

'Thank fuck for that,' she says. 'He's a prick.'

'That's not helpful,' says Leanne.

'He is a bit of a prick,' I whisper.

'He's a lot of a prick,' says Cara. 'He could very easily go by Alex, but he forces everyone to say two pointless, extra syllables. Do you need

him hurt?' she asks. 'I know a guy in Rochester.'
I'm not sure if she's serious. Leanne pushes
Cara's feet off the sofa cushions.

'Martha doesn't need anything like that,' she
says. 'She needs some space and she needs us to
listen and be *here* for her.' Cara flares her
nostrils and places her feet on the coffee table.
Leanne lets her eyes rest on them for a second
and then asks, 'What happened?' And so, I tell
them.

You know those couples who are so perfect
they look like performance art? Alexander and I
were one of them. If you came for dinner, we
would make two courses and offer you
mid-priced wine and finish each other's jokes
and wave you goodbye at the door. Then it
would be curtains down. Alexander would
retreat to his office and I would hang out with
my lover, Netflix. Slowly we spent less and less
time with each other and soon, I was no longer
sure I wanted to spend time with him at all. The
saddest thing about a relationship that ends in
this way is the nagging feeling that it could have
been saved. It's like when you move into a house
and there's a crack in the wall and you say, 'How
ugly, we'll get that fixed right away,' but of
course you don't. There are far more interesting
things to do — tables to buy, prints to hang,
housewarming parties to host. For a few weeks,
your eyes fall upon that crack and you promise
yourself you'll address it but soon you grow
accustomed to it. The crack becomes a part of
the home; you don't even see it any more.
Except occasionally, in the middle of the night,

you can't sleep, and you think, I must deal with that crack. And then one day you're standing in your living room with a bloke called Mike and he's telling you that you have to give him five grand to stop your house from caving in. I don't know who Mike is in this analogy but I do know that the house fell down.

'I knew something was going on,' says Leanne. 'It was like you were getting smaller. He was extinguishing you. You're so brave. I have so much admiration for you.' I'm spared from saying anything by James walking into the room.

'I thought you might need this,' he says, and places three glasses and a bottle of wine on the coffee table before shuffling out backwards like some kind of geisha. I can tell Leanne is attempting not to beam with pride and I find myself resentful. Why does she think she can be so smug? I wouldn't go out with James if he were the last man on earth. OK, if he were the last man I would but only because if he were the last man and willing to date me, I would officially be the hottest woman on the planet. Other than this unlikely scenario, he would be a no. He's nice but wears terrible shoes and has too much gel in his hair and his mouth is too small for his face, which in my opinion gives him a slightly ratty appearance. It would be like being married to a devoted dormouse. Alexander is hot. Not movie-star hot, unless the movie was a low-budget, independent drama about a man reconnecting with his ailing father, but general-population hot. Cara leans forward and pours three large glasses of wine. She hands Leanne and me a glass each and then downs half of the third before topping it up again.

'To freedom,' says Cara, raising her drink. Leanne smacks her on the leg.

'To hope,' she says.

'To the hope of freedom,' I say, and we clink our glasses together.

'What are you actually going to do, though?' asks Leanne. I take a large mouthful of wine.

'Find someone new,' I say, 'something better.' Leanne places a hand on top of mine.

'I think it's a bit soon,' she says.

'It's not soon enough,' says Cara.

I can see Leanne gearing up to protest, so I say, 'I'm ready, I deserve to be happy. I want what you have, Leanne.'

Leanne colours a little and sips her drink. 'OK,' she says, 'what do you want? What wasn't Alexander giving you?' My mind is flooded with so many things — a kiss goodnight, a smile in the morning, a sense of safety.

'I don't know,' I say. Leanne stands and walks over to her solid oak bookcase. She pulls a notepad and pen from one of the shelves.

'If you're not clear on exactly what you need, you will never get it,' she says. Leanne sits back down and opens the pad to a clean page. 'My business coach got me to do one for work but I don't see why it wouldn't be the same for a bloke.'

'Totally did this last year,' says Cara, 'and the next day I met Rico.'

'What was on your list?' Leanne asks. Cara ticks the items off on her fingers: 'Young, fun,

21

not in town long and most importantly a really massive co — '

'The universe will receive your message and manifest it for you,' interrupts Leanne, turning her back on Cara's mockery, 'but you need to focus on what you want.' Cara crosses her eyes as she tips her head and lets her tongue fall out of her mouth. Sometimes I think Leanne and Cara don't like each other.

I met Leanne at school and we spent many Saturdays crying over Leonardo DiCaprio and perfecting our acne-camouflaging techniques. We drifted apart after university — Leanne worked hard, settled down quickly with James and pursued a parent-pleasing career path in accounting; I was mostly drunk. It was only when I was planning my wedding and realized that I couldn't trust any of my drinking buddies to rock up to the right place on the right day that I reached out to her and asked her to be my bridesmaid, and we rekindled our friendship. She has taught me a lot about being a wife and a mother, mostly about the stuff I'm doing wrong.

Cara, I met at a temp job. I was an admin assistant and she was the receptionist, or at least I think she was, but I never saw her do any work. She left suddenly amid rumours (which she has never confirmed or denied) of a mysterious pay-out. Then one day she called to ask if I would accept a package that was arriving at the office for her. When she came to collect it (thirty minutes late) I asked her what was in the box; it was very large and had taken some effort to conceal.

'Toys,' she said. 'You know, cock rings and such. You're a superstar. I need them for tonight.' She must've seen the shock in my eyes because she tutted and said, 'Not for me, for the talent.' The shock shifted to confusion and she sighed and said, 'Come on, I'll show you.' And she did.

'She's right, you know,' says Cara. 'You're not very good at focusing.'

'Remember the novel?' says Leanne.

'Which one?' says Cara, and they both snort-laugh simultaneously. I remember that even if they don't like each other they are united in the cause of trying to prevent me from continually fucking up my life.

With the aid of another bottle of wine we pull together a list, the summation of my hopes and dreams and values in human man form. It takes some time and negotiation but an hour or so later we are confident we have succeeded.

The definitive, non-negotiable — approved by Leanne, Cara and the universe — perfect man for Martha Ross official guidelines:

1) <u>Must have blue eyes and red hair.</u> (I have always had a predilection for redheads and I once heard that this combination of features is one of the rarest in the world. This man needs to be one in a million.)
2) <u>Must be intrigued by me.</u> (I never really felt I held Alexander's interest.)
3) <u>Has to work for himself but not be in it to make money.</u> He's got to do something useful to society. He has to spend

his free time doing something inspiring; not just inspiring but also worthy, e.g. deworming African orphans or similar. He can have little to no interest in developing strategies to excel at Championship Manager.

4) <u>Must be spiritually aware.</u> Not necessarily religious but have values and a belief system. He has to have done work on himself and be able to evidence that.

5) <u>Must be close to his family.</u> Not in a creepy way. He cannot under any circumstances live with his mother, but he must understand the importance of familial relationships (Alexander hates every last member of his family; Jacqueline had a field day with this).

6) <u>Has to like kids, but can't have kids.</u> He can't be childless because he can't commit or has some huge flaw that has prevented anyone wanting to breed with him. He has to have a legitimate reason for not having become a father, preferably tragic.

7) <u>Has to be confident in all senses of the word</u> — socially confident, sexually confident but especially confident about the fact that he's crazy about me.

8) <u>Has to be tall,</u> in exceptional health, has to like reading and long conversations.

9) <u>Has to like animals</u> and will have a cat called Hendrix.

10) His name will be George.

Cara tries to talk me out of George. 'George is a dead uncle name,' she says. I like George, though. George is solid; he sounds reliable. 'And why the cat thing?' she asks. 'You don't even like your cat.'

'I love my cat,' I say. 'As soon as I get a place for me and Moses, I'm gonna go get Moxie.' I don't love my cat that much — he's cranky and he pisses under the sofa when it thunders — but I don't see why Alexander should get everything. Leanne rips the page out carefully and hands it to me.

'There he is,' she says. I read it again. I already feel like I know him better than I know the man I married.

I didn't need a list when I met Alexander. I saw him, and I knew. The first time we met we were at a party in a pub garden on the edge of town. A girl called Petra was leaving for a three-month trip around South America; I remember I almost didn't go. I thought it was excessive to hold a party to mark such a short absence; I keep cheese in my fridge that long. As I walked into the room I whispered to myself, 'Why am I here?' And like an answer to my question, he fell into view. His sandy hair was longer then and when he laughed, as he was doing as I watched him, it fell forward, and he would push it back with his long, slender fingers. He had on black-rimmed glasses; somehow, I knew they were not prescription and this fact made him seem a little vulnerable. I asked three

25

separate people who he was, and no one seemed to know. To my relief after about an hour Petra pulled him over. Embracing her role as fabulous hostess, she placed him in front of me.

'Hey,' she gushed, 'you having fun?' Without waiting for an answer, she patted Alexander on the shoulder. 'This is Alexander, he was a freelancer on a project I did at work. He's so much fun. Alexander, this is Martha,' she said, grabbing my wrist to pull me closer. 'We go way back. We were in the Scrabble club together at uni.' As I silently thanked Petra for that little gem she rushed away to do more introductions.

'Hey,' said Alexander. I was conscious of the fact that I had to look up to make eye contact with him, something that doesn't always happen when I meet a guy.

'Hey,' I replied. It wasn't love at that point, but I had this visceral feeling that I needed to be near him.

'You have a bit of guac on your chin,' he said. I felt a heat build in my chest and rise steadily. I knew it would produce a colour on my cheeks so vivid even my tan skin wouldn't mask it. He smiled, reached out and gently swiped his thumb across a spot just under my lips. Then it was love.

If I had had a list back then, it wouldn't have mattered. I was a kid; I thought love was enough. Alexander has taught me that love is only the start. A man needs more than a cute smile and an endearing way about him. Even in my wine-and-adrenaline-fuelled haze I can see that if Alexander was what I wanted, *this* man — the

26

man from the list — is what I need.

'He's amazing,' I say. 'Where the hell am I gonna find him?' Cara reaches towards the coffee table and picks up my phone. Her thumb moves purposefully across the screen.

'What is this thing,' she mutters.

'An iPhone,' I say.

'Maybe it was five years ago, darling.' After a couple of minutes she passes me my phone. 'Here you go.' On the screen is a photo of a man I do not know.

'What do I do with him?' I ask. Cara rolls her eyes.

'Jesus, don't you have wi-fi under your rock? This, honey, is Linger. All the available totty in a ten-mile radius. You swipe left for no and right for the shag-worthy. Welcome to twenty-first-century dating.'

The man has a nice smile, but his eyes look cold. I swipe him left and he disappears and is replaced by a new face. I look to Cara and she nods encouragement. I swipe the next guy left and the next. No, no, no, not Alexander, not Alexander, not Alexander. I throw my phone on to the carpet.

'This isn't going to work,' I say. I can feel a tightness building in my chest. It's as if something is pressing down on me and even if I wanted to I don't have the energy to push it off. The girls are both silent for a few seconds and then Cara claps her hands together. She retrieves her tote from the floor and begins rooting around in it.

'I see we're going to have to do this the

27

old-fashioned way,' she says. 'Ladies, we're going out.' She holds up a bottle of tequila triumphantly.

'Why in God's name do you have that?' asks Leanne.

'Because,' says Cara, 'as this situation has just demonstrated, you never know when you're gonna need it.'

⋆　⋆　⋆

By the time our cab pulls up outside the Freaky Funk club, Cara's rejuvenating pep talks and lubricating tequila shots have convinced me that, if I cannot find the one, I can definitely find the one for tonight and sometimes the one for tonight can become the one. That totally happened to my cousin's best mate's sister. As we stand in the doorway of the club, Cara makes a sweeping gesture with her arm.

'Welcome to the land of the easy and the home of the desperate,' she says, and as if by celestial intervention, at that very moment the DJ drops 'It's Raining Men'.

4

As Leanne gets the first round in I give the room a quick survey. There's a stag party, or at least I hope that's their excuse for the T-shirts emblazoned with penises; what appears to be a quiet after-work drink that got away with itself; and a few stray groups of people who obviously have a penchant for sticky floors and eighties hits. I decide to approach the stags — they're all giving it some welly on the dance floor — and whilst the tequila means I don't need encouragement to join in, they offer it.

One of them, a short guy with unnervingly animated eyebrows, has a cowboy hat on. As I shimmy towards him he tips it and I accept this invitation and allow him to take me in his arms. He's not tall but he's solid and I feel safe enough to relax into his chest. There's something wonderful, yet slightly irritating, about how good his presence against me feels — despite all the finger waving and carping on about independence, it feels so delightful to have a man just hold you upright. As we're swaying vaguely rhythmically someone comes in behind me and so I reach back and place a hand on the unidentified hip. I'm really getting into being the ham in my man sandwich when Leanne comes over with a drink. I shuffle out, leave the two guys dancing together, and down the drink in one.

'Slow down,' says Leanne. I assume she's talking about the booze but she's looking at the men.

I say, 'I've been slow for a decade, I need to catch up.' I'm not sure that's exactly how it comes out because Leanne just stares at me from below knitted brows.

'I'm gonna go get you some water,' she says. 'Dancing Queen' comes on and I re-join the stags. I love this song. OK, right now I love every song but in this moment it feels like Benny and Björn and Agnetha and the other one are speaking directly to me. My body is the slightly saggy shell of a thirty-something woman but my soul, my soul is seventeen.

One of the cutest stags is watching my performance with quiet interest. He has lovely eyes, really warm and thoughtful, but when I wink at him he smiles and his smile is nothing short of wicked. His smile says, 'If you give me half a chance, I will ruin you' — and I love that. I walk slowly towards him and drape my hands over his shoulders, still moving my hips along with the jaunty beat. He leans in and whispers, 'We're all attached, love.' My hips halt. 'Well, all except Bryan.' He points to a chair at the edge of the room where Bryan, I assume, is asleep. Someone has scrawled the word 'BANTER' on his face. I thank the man and his smile and head to the bar.

'I will have three of your cheapest sambuca please, bar man,' I say.

'Sure thing,' he says, and lays out three glasses.

'And might I say you are quite handsome,' I

say, and as I say it, I realize he is. Like me, he's obviously of mixed parentage but he's not from common or garden black and white parents, as I am. I wonder if he has Asian heritage.

I lean over the bar in order to ask and he says, 'That's nice but I am so, so gay.' I stand up straight and bolt down one of the shots.

'I'll have another,' I say, and he pours out another sambuca.

I pay, drink a second shot, and then take the others and push past the revellers to find the girls. Leanne is standing close to the entrance, looking like she was just beamed down from her spaceship and is hoping that someone will help her phone home. 'I got you a drink,' I say, pushing one of the glasses into her hand. 'It might help dislodge that stick from your arse,' I add in my head. She places it on a table next to her and carefully wipes some escaped alcohol from her hand with the corner of her cardigan. She then offers me a glass of water, at which I shake my head vigorously.

'Do you wanna come home, honey?' she asks. I hate that voice she does. That 'I know what's best for you' tone. As she speaks she smooths an invisible crease out of her dress. Her outfit is cute but screams 'I'd rather be home with my husband'. I bet it's from Boden; it has to be from Boden.

'Where's your dress from?' I ask.

'Joules,' says Leanne. Same thing.

'I'm not ready,' I say, and give her my best 'I'm fabulous and I'm having a fabulous time' smile. 'Where's Car?'

31

Leanne nods in the direction of a dark corner where I see Cara on a sofa, perched on the lap of a gentleman who appears to be in his late sixties. When I reach her Cara is telling him he reminds her of her father.

'Is that a good thing?' he asks eagerly.

'No,' she says.

'I got you this,' I say, handing Cara the shot. She drinks it without breaking eye contact with her new friend.

'I'm striking out,' I tell her. Now I think of it, I do kinda wanna go home, I just don't have a home to go to. Cara turns to me.

'If you want to have sex, just go and have sex.'

'I don't just want to,' I say, 'I have to. I have to extract Alexander from my soul. I need to know that I haven't completely fucked up my only chance to have sex again.'

The man looks at me with open curiosity. Cara sighs and says, 'Sex for validation, so healthy.' And then a bit more kindly she says, 'So you need an orgasmic cleansing. We've all been there but you're not going to get it talking to me, so go.' She waves me away like I'm a puppy. 'Carpe dickem!' she calls as I walk away.

I pick the guy because of his shoulders, broad shoulders that make me think he could hold me up against a wall, although I would never let a guy hold me up against a wall because what if he couldn't take my weight? I would die of shame on the spot. Also, that's about all I have to go on as his back is to me while he talks to his companion. Just before I reach him, Leanne stops me.

'I was just outside on the phone to James. Apparently, Lucas woke up and couldn't find his blankie and I had to remind him that we gave it to the blankie fairy like three weeks ago.' She shakes her head in the way married women do when they are expressing how adorable but hapless their husbands are. 'I should probably get back, come jump in a cab with me. We could stop for pizza?'

I want to say, 'That's all good for you. You go home to your comfy house and have lacklustre sex with your mouse-faced husband; I have to find my self-esteem in someone else's orgasm,' but instead I say, 'Sorry, there's someone I have to say hello to.' And I step round her and continue across the room. When I reach Broad Shoulders, I tap him on his equally broad back and he turns around. His face does not quite match his shoulders in that his body says man and his face says little boy lost but it's a friendly face, one that doesn't erode my nerve to say, 'Hi.' 'Hi,' responds Broad Shoulders.

'Do you want to have sex?' I ask. Broad Shoulders makes the kind of face one makes when an air steward asks if you want chicken or fish before saying, 'OK.'

★ ★ ★

We leave almost immediately; there's a slight kerfuffle over the fact that the cloakroom attendant has lost my coat before I remember that I wasn't wearing one but soon we're standing awkwardly together on the street. The cold air is almost but not quite sobering.

'Where do you live?' I ask. I hope this makes it clear that the 'your place or mine' discussion is unnecessary.

'Not far,' he says, and starts to walk. I have to trot a little to catch up with him, but he doesn't protest as I fall into step beside him. Isn't it strange how the same act, depending on the context, can become something entirely different — walking in silence on a dark night with someone you have dated for some time is intimate, romantic even; doing the same with a man you have just met falls squarely into the category of sinister. Also, 'not far' is very subjective. I mean, Guatemala probably doesn't feel that far when you're flying in a luxury private jet; Broad Shoulders lives extremely far on a frigid, dark night. Far enough to make my nose run and my legs start to ache; far enough to make me lose all the courage I have, Dutch or otherwise. I'm about to bail; I'm literally considering how I will explain to Cara that I could not pull in a club where sex is so available they should offer the morning-after pill as a bar snack, when I realize Broad Shoulders has come to a stop.

'This is me,' he says. We're outside a row of stunning mansion flats. I used to walk Moses in his buggy along this road and try to peek through the windows at a life beyond my imagination. Broad Shoulders jogs up the steps to the building and puts his key in the door. Before he pushes it open I ask him his name.

'Rupert,' he says. He doesn't ask mine. Inside

he asks me if I want a drink.

'Yes please,' I say.

'Water or squash?' he asks. I pick squash.

He leaves me standing in the hallway as he goes to prepare it. From the sounds that emanate there is a lot of work that goes into the process. He returns with a pint glass and a mug and hands me the mug. 'This way,' he says, and guides me gently towards a room I assume is his bedroom, although only a mattress on the floor signifies this. There is no other bedroom apparatus — no wardrobe, no photos, no throw cushions. I suddenly miss my throw cushions. I got them from Homesense. They have navy stripes on them.

I'm trying to work out how to sensually mount a mattress on the floor when I notice that Rupert is taking off his clothes, all of them. Naked, he has strange proportions. His impressive upper body contrasts dramatically with his thick, short legs. Rupert gets into the bed, lies back and puts his hands behind his head. I put down my drink before taking off my shoes and joining him and it is then that he kisses me. The kisses are not exploratory or even sexy; he pecks away as if he thinks I have an access code. I let him think he has unlocked it and reach down to grab his penis. It is sort of hard but weirdly cold and damp. He makes a noise of encouragement, although I'm not really doing anything. I can't help but think about Alexander's penis. His penis was, and I assume still is, perfect. I actually gasped when I first saw it. He laughed so hard that he lost his erection but neither of us cared.

Rupert's penis is not perfect but it is here, and I am told that beggars cannot be choosers. He shifts his body on to one side and undoes my trousers with his free hand. Without further introduction, he shoves his fingers under my pants. I have a flashback to a party in Year 10. Adele Healey's mum went to the Canaries and I spent half the night with Kieran Nuttall in her younger brother's bedroom. He asked me if I knew that my lips were uneven; it took me a week to realize he wasn't talking about the ones on my face.

I'm not liking whatever Rupert is trying to do so I try and encourage him to move past the trailers.

'Do you have a condom?' I ask. He jumps up and leaves the room, still naked. I'm left feeling like I'm halfway through a particularly inept smear. I wiggle out of my trousers and knickers and leave them at the bottom of the bed. I'm thinking about removing my top when he returns. I can't stop imagining where he might have had to go to get the rubber. I picture the places one puts things to keep them safe — an empty Quality Street tin, an overfilled shoe-box. This turns out to be a good thing because it distracts me for the half a minute Rupert spends wrestling with the johnnie before returning his attention to the jabbing. I make a noise that I hope sounds positive but not too enthusiastic; I want the prodding to stop but I'm not sure what I want him to replace it with. In response he readjusts, straddles me and pushes himself inside me. It doesn't hurt. It doesn't feel good. It doesn't really feel like anything. It feels like exploring an ear canal with a cotton bud, only less satisfying. I feel my tears before I understand what they are. I've never been a silent crier — excessive snot production is the cause, I suspect. It takes around five strokes for Rupert to realize what's happening. He stops, puts a hand to my cheek and says, 'Is it all right if I finish?'

5

I spend the night, more for convenience than anything else. When I wake, Rupert is snoring gently; the little puffing noises he makes remind me of Moses. I roll on to my back and grab my breasts; I'm relieved to find my key and debit card still stashed in my bra. I locate my trousers under the covers and get out of bed and slip into them before stepping into my shoes. My phone lies on the carpet and I notice several missed calls before I put it in my pocket. I forgo my knickers because I'm scared I'll wake him whilst rooting around for them. I convince myself this is sexy, a lacy calling card, although I'm pretty sure I left a panty liner in them. As I make my way through the flat it becomes apparent that Rupert's home is in fact a squat. Under the spell of alcohol and anticipation, I had failed to notice some of the apartment's less charming features, specifically a life-sized mural in the hallway depicting Margaret Thatcher preparing to breastfeed what appears to be a bonneted Tony Blair.

When I get outside the crisp morning seems to magnify my own internal dankness. I speed-walk a few metres down the road, eager to put some distance between myself and the night before. How could I be a respectful wife and mother one day and a walk-of-shamin' hussy the next? I look at my phone and the calls are from Leanne. I know James usually gets up with the kids on a

Saturday, so it's safe to say she's not trying to reach me for a casual catch-up. I let my thumb rest on her name and she picks up after one ring.

'How the fudge could you be so irresponsible,' she says. 'I'm nearly dead with worry.' I love how even in the wake of trauma Leanne is mindful of innocent ears. Her concern hits me somewhere around my throat and I gasp for air.

'Can you come get me, please?' I ask.

'Where are you?' she says softly.

'I don't know,' I say.

'What can you see?' asks Leanne.

'A post box.'

★ ★ ★

Leanne finds me outside a Costa Coffee a couple of roads away from the squat. The bag that I left at her house is waiting for me on the passenger seat. She drives me back to my new but old home, in silence. It's a classic mum move, so much worse than the lecture I was prepared for. When we pull up at my parents' house she says, 'It will get better, you know. If Alexander wasn't the one, you'll find him.'

'Yep,' I say, and move to get out of the car.

Leanne grabs my hand. 'You deserve the one. Someone fit for the list,' she says with a smile. I give her a kiss on the cheek and climb out.

★ ★ ★

The energy of my mother's home — the hum of the fan oven; the enriching chatter of Radio 4

— makes me realize how hungover I am. Hungover doesn't cut it; my head feels like it's encased in amber. I just want a litre of Coke and a hole to crawl in and instead I get my mother.

Mum is in the kitchen with Moses. Despite the fact Ivy Ketch hasn't worked a day of my lifetime, she is dressed as though she is fresh from the office in slim navy trousers and a cream blouse. Her rich, brown skin is make-up free, aside from an ever-present coat of Fashion Fair's 'Ruby Plum' on her lips. I stand in the doorway watching her hold up a flashcard with a picture of a strawberry on it. Moses is in his high chair and has a plate of fruit in front of him. He is laughing at my mother's efforts, revealing the two little teeth that sit alone in the lower half of his mouth. 'Can you find the strawberry?' says Mum, enunciating each syllable carefully. She then shouts, 'Martha?!' As if I am not an only child and anyone else would be letting themselves into her quiet semi-detached home on a Saturday morning.

'I'm here, Mum,' I say — well, croak. 'Hey, baby,' I say to Moses. He scrunches up his fists and waves them in the air in excitement. I kiss him on the cheek and he makes a smacking sound in return. I can feel my mother's eyes on me.

'Good night?' she says.

'Not exactly,' I say, walking to the sink to get a glass of water. I lean against the counter to drink it; the cool liquid feels amazing in my mouth but seems unsure of itself in my stomach. Moses reaches out to me and I pull him from the high chair.

'Eskimo kiss,' I say, and he rubs his nose on mine, smearing crushed fruit on me in the process. His smile takes the edge off my hangover. If a man ever looked at me the way he does, it'd be game over.

'What will you do today?' I say, manoeuvring him so that I am holding him under each armpit. Moses wriggles in anticipation. 'Will you go up?' I say, lifting him in the air. He shrieks and kicks his legs. 'Will you go down?' I let my arms fall and Moses's eyes open wide. 'Will you go round and round?' I spin us both in a circle and Moses giggles throatily. Upon completing it I regret the sudden movement and I sit down on one of the kitchen chairs with Moses on my knee.

'Don't excite him, he's due a nap,' says Mum, taking my son into her arms. 'I take it you had a bit to drink then?' I don't answer and avoid her enquiring eye. 'Do you think this is an acceptable reaction to your marriage ending?'

I don't say anything because this is a rhetorical question. Almost all my mother's questions are rhetorical because for them not to be she would have to consider the possibility that someone knows more than her. Mum shakes her head almost imperceptibly; obviously not imperceptibly because then it wouldn't have the required effect of making me feel worthless. Mum then rubs at her right temple. This is her tell — this is the sign that she is about to deliver her killer blow. 'No wonder he ended it, if this is what he has to deal with.'

I love my mum — I mean, I would run into a burning building to save her life, even though I know she would scold me for not waiting for the fire service. I love my mum, but I don't like her. I don't dislike her because she is judgemental, and I don't dislike her because (particularly since the onset of menopause) she is unnecessarily spiteful; I dislike her because I will never become the daughter she wants me to be.

It started with ballet. Mum enrolled me when I was seven. I was many things as a child — spirited, inquisitive and uncontrollably talkative — but graceful I was not. I was curved where I should have been straight and stiff in places where the other girls bent easily. I did the work, though. I had a cassette tape that I would play on my Sony Walkman, practising the steps for hours at a time in our garage. On the day of my first recital I was so full of hope that I could be the type of little girl a mother would be proud of. I was faultless during the performance; around halfway through the butterflies escaped from my stomach and for a minute and a half I really believed I was a dancer.

After the show I waited backstage for my parents, watching as other children flew into the embrace of their mothers, waiting patiently for my turn. When Mum appeared, tears spontaneously came to my eyes. She stopped short of me; she had a look on her face I had seen many times before, one that seemed to say, 'Is this really my child?'

'Why did you keep picking your knickers out of your bum like that?' she asked, and I feel like

I have been picking my knickers out of my bum ever since. I want to tell her this. I want to tell her that all I have ever wanted is her love; all I have ever needed is for her to tell me just once that everything will be OK.

I'm not sure I convey this when I say, 'Fuck you, Mum.' I leave my mother sitting with her mouth open and head towards my bedroom. On the way I stick my head into the living room. My father is sitting on the armchair, to which I'm starting to wonder if he's surgically attached.

'You all right, love?' he asks, his gaze not shifting from the golf on the TV. His long, thin legs are stretched out in front of him and his hands rest on the small belly he has cultivated since his retirement.

'No, Dad. I'm pretty crap actually,' I say. He looks at me then, his hazel eyes full of questions that I know he will never ask me.

'I know, love,' he says, 'I know.'

★   ★   ★

I go to my room, which is no longer really my room but a spare room. My pale pink walls have been replaced with a hotel room grey. The bed is the same though, an antique piece with a wrought-iron headboard — Mum had insisted I would want it when I moved into a home of my own, but I didn't. Alexander favoured a more minimalist look; he was obsessed with Scandinavian chic.

From the bed, you can see into several of the upstairs windows of the houses across the quiet, tree-lined street, but the only one that ever concerned me was the house on the right-hand corner. That room, in that house, was the bedroom of Joseph Henchy, and Joseph Henchy was my first ever love. People often say that young people don't understand love, but I don't agree. Free of responsibilities, they have nothing to think about but love; I had whole weekends at a time when all I had to do was conjugate a few French verbs and be in love.

Joseph and I started out as buddies — well, young children aren't really friends; they just kind of occupy the same space and time — but Joe was a kind lad and, although I was a couple of years younger than him, he would often invite me to be one of the victims in whatever massacre he was re-enacting for the afternoon. Things changed abruptly when he went to secondary school. I guess he was too distracted to notice me, or maybe his growing independence allowed him to expand his social circle beyond our leafy avenue. Whatever the case, he was always friendly and polite, but he never again included me in his war games or brought me out a glass of Ribena and a slightly soggy rich tea biscuit. I imagine hormones played some part but it was at the moment of his withdrawal that I recognized the depths of my affection for him. On this bed I would watch the house for hours; I started to understand his patterns. He would arrive home from school at four, except for Thursdays when he would be given a lift home by someone at around seven. On Saturday mornings he left early, wearing shorts, and returned home late, later and later as the years went on. On Sundays I might catch several glimpses of him; he would nip to the sweet shop on the main road or sit on the front step and chat to his mother as she weeded the front garden.

Once I had entered secondary school myself, I grew braver. We were not at the same school, but I ensured that he would see me in my uniform and perhaps once again view us as equals. There are only so many excuses to find for loitering around in the front garden of a family home and after a couple of years of casual waves and unmet gazes, I thought that perhaps I should make a move. One Sunday I waited until he stepped outside and then bolted into the street.

'Are you going to the shop?' I called. 'Me too.' Joseph smiled and paused to let me catch up to him. 'Long time, no see,' I said, super casual like. 'What you up to?'

'Nothing much,' said Joseph.

'Have you got a girlfriend?' I asked, looking at my shoes whilst trying to suppress the hope in my tone.

'Yeah,' he said. 'You know Claire Baycock?' I did. Everybody did. She lived in the flats next to the park; from what I knew of her she was a rebellious redhead with a big fringe and an even bigger mouth.

I had one question: 'Why?' An abbreviation of the full question, why her and not me?

Joseph looked to the sky before saying, 'She's got big tits and a fit body.' It was so reasonable and so true that I couldn't really fault him.

'I forgot my money,' I said, and ran back to the safety of my bedroom, from where I continued my adoration until he left home at eighteen. I thought unrequited love was the saddest thing I would ever have to go through and I was right but I didn't yet know how right. Unrequited love when you have been promised absolutely nothing is painful, but unrequited love from someone who has promised you the world is a slow death.

I fish the list from my handbag. It's crumpled and smeared with something a little greasy but, even now I'm sober, it still makes a lot of sense. If I had kept it in mind I would not have ended up hungover and humiliated in Hove this morning; if I had written it earlier, I might not have a failed marriage. One thing is for sure: I can't rely on my own improvisation. I need a blueprint. I don't know how Joseph would have measured up to this list; I was so uninterested in details back then. All I wanted was to feel something; I had so much passion to give and no one and nothing to give it to.

I saw Joseph a few years ago, in a restaurant in London. Alexander and I had been to the theatre and Joseph was in the Pizza Express that we had stopped in for a quick bite. It took a few moments for him to connect me to the child he once knew but when he did he broke into a smile so genuine, I almost forgave him for the years of torment. He was eating with a woman I assumed to be his wife. He asked after my parents and talked animatedly about the crust of his pepperoni pizza. He spoke with such enthusiasm about his uninspired dish that I suddenly felt very sad.

When I was young, I would play incredibly maudlin indie music as I watched Joe from the window. Sometimes I would write embarrassingly overwrought love songs, which I imagined I might develop when I 'made it'. My CD player and discs are still stashed in a cupboard and so I plug it in and put on Radiohead. The haunting opening bars of 'Creep' take me to a familiar, lonely place. I turn to watch myself in the full-length mirror as I duet with Thom Yorke. I imagine Rupert seeing my album in a supermarket and trying to convince his companion that he once slept with me in a squat on the south coast. I see Broad Shoulders blend into the crowd at my intimate East London gig; I feel the band behind me and I open my arms to allow space for my chest to expand and the sound to flow from the bottom of my lungs. I see more and more faces in the crowd; it's full of all the boys and men that have ever let me down and all the girls with big tits and fit bodies and every teacher that has poked holes through my dreams and every cab driver that's driven past me in the rain and my mum and my mum's stuck-up friends and in the centre, at the very front, is Alexander. When I sing the final lines, I'm singing just to him and he's seeing me, really seeing me, as if for the first time.

My mother bangs on the ceiling with a broom just as she did twenty years ago. I turn off the music. I crawl under the lavender-scented duvet, in the clothes I have been wearing for a day and

47

a night. I have the sense that I want to cry but I can't. I am completely empty.

★ ★ ★

The sleep I have is dense and dreamless. When I wake it is dark and I'm disorientated for a few moments. My father is knocking on my door. I know it's him because the rapping is so tentative. I sit up in bed and shout, 'Yeah, Dad!' He opens the door a few inches and seems to slip in the room through the gap.

'Your phone's been making little noises,' he says. I must have left it in the kitchen. He hands it to me like it's a bird with a broken wing. 'Do you think you could come and sort it out with your mother?'

'Sure,' I say.

'Moses has been asking after you.'

'Yeah,' I say. My head still throbs but now I think it's from guilt. From what I understand every working parent feels as though they're on an eternal quest for balance; I can say conclusively that sambuca doesn't help. I sit up and try to look as if I'm ready to engage with the world. 'I'll be down soon,' I say. My father nods his head and retreats. I redo my ponytail so my curls look a little less chaotic and decide I'll make us all smoothies. Moses loves them and it might help replenish some nutrients for me. I'm about to get out of bed when I see an unfamiliar notification on my phone. It's from Linger and reads, 'You have a match!' I have a very broken memory of swiping wildly in the cab on the way

48

to the club, the girls cackling gleefully and the driver watching us apprehensively in his rear-view mirror. For a few moments, I think about deleting my account and all the potential for heartbreak it holds within, but curiosity gets the better of me. I open the app; it takes a few seconds for my match's face to appear but it's worth the wait. He has such an easy smile; it's like he's not just smiling at me but sharing something between us too. He's looking straight at the camera and his eyes are a truly dreamy shade of blue. His hair is mostly cropped out of the photo but from what I can see it's the perfect shade of strawberry blond. It's electrifying, it's mystifying; it's *him*. Below the picture is a message.

Undeterred83: I'm sorry. I haven't used this before and I can't think of anything to say but I had to contact you because I was so intrigued by your profile.

It's not clever or funny but that makes it better because it's real. He's real. The man of my dreams, and on my list, may have been within ten miles, all this time. I don't reply right away because I want to savour the feeling, a jittery light-headedness I have not experienced in many years. It's a complicated mix of thrill and comfort wrapped in a soft, warm blanket of expectation.

6

Although I spend Saturday doing my best impression of a pious daughter — being on hand to facilitate channel changes and offering weak teas hourly — the atmosphere between my mother and me remains slightly frosty. To avoid the chill and try to re-establish an image of responsibility, I offer to do an extra shift at the call centre on Sunday. I've never worked a weekend before — I've always reserved this time for poorly playing happy families — but I'm pleasantly surprised by how relaxed the atmosphere in the office is. Generally, there's a constant stream of people to pretend you have an interest in interacting with; today my whole bank of desks is empty apart from Greg and a girl called Tashi, a part-time worker also studying for a degree at the local university.

'Hello, stranger,' says Greg as I sit down.

'I saw you on Friday,' I say.

'Feels like longer, buddy,' he says. 'What you doing here on a Sunday?'

'I need the money,' I say. It's not until I say it that I realize it's true. I am officially a statistic: a poor, single mother in a dead-end job.

'Sorry to hear that,' says Greg, 'but it's a nice surprise.'

'What are you doing here?' I ask. 'Isn't there some sort of Disney On Ice you should be seeing?' Greg is always emailing me discount

50

vouchers to tedious-sounding children's events. After each one he tells me how much his girls enjoyed it and asks me what I ended up doing with my weekend; I always lie and say I was visiting friends as opposed to watching *Come Dine with Me* reruns.

'I work weekends when I don't have the girls,' he says. His words are like a glass of ice-cold water in my face. This hadn't occurred to me, that Alexander and I will need to split our time with Moses. It is heartbreaking and also exhilarating.

Bob is in the office too. When he sees me, he throws me a quizzical look and waves his hand around in front of his crotch. I give him a thumbs up in return. Greg looks at me with concern.

'Don't,' I say firmly. Tashi eyes me over the partition between us.

'I'm feeling there's a lot of stuck energy within you,' she says.

'It's probably the dodgy breakfast burrito I had,' I say.

'No,' she says brightly. 'You have this kind of cloud over you. I'm going to this retreat in a couple of weeks — it's an aura-cleansing camp, based on this wonderful meditation practice developed by my guru. I'll send you the details.'

'Please don't,' I say.

'It's run on donations and I'll drive, it won't cost you anything. Just think about it. Before I found Tula Shiki I was closed so tight, just like you.' I look at Tashi with her beaded hair and I decide I'm happy being closed. I yawn.

'I'm just tired,' I say, and I am. I was up late messaging my match.

Marthashotbod: Where did you go to school?

Undeterred83: Everywhere really. We moved about a lot when I was a kid. Even spent some time in Singapore. I moved to Brighton three years ago and it might be the longest I've been anywhere.

Marthashotbod: That's so interesting. It must have been an exciting childhood.

Undeterred83: It was actually kind of lonely a lot of the time. Always felt like I was on the outside looking in but it made me interested in people. What makes us different, what makes us the same.

Marthashotbod: What does make us the same?

Undeterred83: I think we're all trying to work something out.

Marthashotbod: What are you trying to work out?

Undeterred83: At this moment, you.

It was so wonderful to talk to someone clever and funny and curious, especially when most of that curiosity is about me. He asked me where I was born and what books I loved; he admitted that his favourite novel is Margaret Atwood's *Cat's Eye*, even though it's a female coming-of-age book.

Undeterred83: I sometimes tell my mates it's Catcher in the Rye. I do like it but I think Holden just needs some therapy and a talking to.

I felt that delicious wave of pleasure you experience when someone just gets you. When someone seems to reach in and access a private part of who you are. I am not alone in having overdeveloped feelings about fictional characters; I might never be alone again.

'It helps with tiredness too,' says Tashi. 'It helps with everything.' Bob walks past and gives an artificial cough so we all return to our calls.

★ ★ ★

After work I stop by Leanne's and give her a bouquet of lilies to apologize for being an even hotter mess than my usual level of hot messiness. 'You shouldn't have,' she says as she accepts them on the doorstep, but we both know I needed to. 'Come in,' she says. 'We should talk properly.'

'I can't,' I say. 'I want to run back to the flat.' Alexander did a decent job of packing my stuff but failed to include any knickers. Also, I want to see him. I'm not entirely confident about why this is. We have practicalities to discuss; I have questions I deserve answers to; but also I need to see him, because seeing him every day is natural. Not doing so feels like suddenly deciding not to brush your teeth — odd, rebellious, but also a bit gross. My marriage with Alexander had started to feel like a slowly shrinking box but now I was beginning to wonder if freedom was over-rated. Spending the night with Rupert made me think that perhaps one shit husband is worth a sea of unattached morons.

'If you're sure,' says Leanne. 'I'm sorry I let it get out of hand. We should talk things through.'

'You didn't let it get out of hand; that was Cara.'

Leanne laughs and then stops and nods her head.

'Actually, Cara and I had a chat and we thought we could go to the spa at the Queens Hotel after work tomorrow.' I'm both excited and perturbed by the idea of Leanne and Cara interacting without me as a buffer. I had considered them as the friend equivalent of two violently reactive chemicals, only able to coexist with me present to neutralize them. 'You should have a little chill-out and some self-care,' says Leanne. 'If your mum can't have Moses, I'll get James to stay in with the kids.'

'Sure,' I say, 'that would be nice.' Although I'm not sure it will be nice — self-care to Leanne means spending loads of money and I find it really hard to relax in spas; I never know when and where I should be naked.

'I'll call you tomorrow then. I hope it goes OK with Alexander.'

'Thanks. I'm sure it'll be fine,' I say, because I'm hoping the universe will hear me.

★ ★ ★

I walk to the flat slowly. The roads feel unfamiliar although I know it's me and not the streets that have changed. I'm surprised that I have to take a few fortifying breaths before I knock on the door, an alien act in itself. As I hear footsteps approaching, I curse myself for not putting on some make-up before coming over but then I think it might be better this way, for him to see me looking broken and drained. If men are visual creatures, perhaps Alexander needs to set eyes on my despair to comprehend it. It's not Alexander that answers the door, however; it's Poppy. Poppy with her low-waisted dark denim skinnies and then metres and metres of taut white skin before the hem of her cropped T-shirt. Poppy is Alexander's part-time PA and even though she knows who I am she looks confused to see me standing there.

'Is Alexander in?' I say. She doesn't speak so I walk past her and into the kitchen where Alexander is standing at the counter preparing two mugs of coffee.

'Martha,' he says when he sees me, 'what are you doing here?'

'This is my home,' I say.

'I mean, why didn't you say you were coming?'

'Do I have to?'

Alexander takes a sip of coffee and rage floods through me. How can he be casually concerned with topping up his caffeine consumption when this is the first time we have laid eyes on each other since our break-up?

'I'm not really in a head space to talk about stuff,' says Alexander.

'What's stuff?' I ask. 'Our marriage? Our child? Little stuff like that?' Alexander folds his arms and appraises me.

'You look tired,' he says.

'Yeah,' I say with forced lightness. 'I won't lie, I've had better weeks.'

Alexander makes a noise crossed between a scoff and a laugh. 'Can I remind you that you sacked me off,' he says.

'But you didn't have to take it so well.' At this point I notice Poppy hovering just outside my eyeline, all twelve pounds of her. She's like the world's most ineffectual bouncer. I turn to tell her to fuck off out of my flat and crawl back to her grubby little house-share and drink cheap rosé with her disillusioned twenty-something friends, when I notice her feet. On Poppy's feet is a pair of beige fluffy slippers — my slippers. I turn back to Alexander.

'Are you even gonna ask about your son?' I demand.

'Your mum's been texting me,' he says. Fucking treacherous bitch.

'And what about us? Did you not even want to ask why?!'

'I know why,' says Alexander, 'because I suck at being married, we suck at being married. You're clearly not happy.' I take a step towards him; he flinches as if I'm going to strike him and I stop.

'You never even tried to make me happy,' I say, but the last syllable gets caught up in a burped sob.

Alexander rubs the bridge of his nose before

saying, 'No one can make someone else happy, Martha.' I want to believe he believes this. It feels a little less traumatic to think that he saw our break-up as a hurtling train that even James Bond and all the X-Men couldn't stop. And then I see Alexander gaze over my shoulder. I follow his eyes to Poppy's reddening face and I can take it no longer. I fall to my knees and grab her right foot. After a couple of mortifying seconds, I am holding a slipper. Poppy removes the other one and hands it to me. I stand and clutch them to my chest.

'These are *my* slippers,' I say.

'I . . . I'm sorry, I just found them. Alex said it was cool.'

'Alex*ander*,' I whisper, and then more loudly I say, 'I'm gonna go.' I can buy knickers.

7

Leanne calls me ten seconds into my lunch break the next day. She skips the verbal canapés and gets to the meat.

'I've booked us in the spa for half six and I'm getting you a pedicure — no arguments. I called Ivy and told her we wanted to treat you, so she's picking up Moses.' Leanne has always been the only person able to tame my mother. I drank too much cheap vodka at our end of school prom and Leanne got me home and somehow managed to convince Mum I had eaten undercooked chicken; after that I started calling her The Ivy Whisperer.

'I haven't brought my swimming costume,' I say. Leanne makes an odd little noise — half sigh, half groan. Even when she's trying to do something nice for me I manage to make things difficult.

'Don't worry,' she says, 'you'll be given a robe. See you there.'

★   ★   ★

Fifteen minutes before the end of my shift, Bob corners me and tells me to induct a new member of staff. I've already tidied up and packed my bag and I'm reading an article Tashi left on my desk, about the benefits of meditation (weight loss!). Bob can clearly sense my resistance and reminds me that it's part of my job description. I have to show some bloke Jake how to log on to the system. Jake may be an intelligent fellow but, if so, he has chosen this day to keep it deeply hidden. I have to show him the set-up half a dozen times before he makes any indication he has retained even the slightest crumb of knowledge. Thirty minutes after the end of my shift, I lose patience and tell him he seems to have everything under control. Jake thanks me effusively before putting his headset on backwards.

Bob doesn't react to my words when I tell him I'm leaving. He's staring at his phone, biting his lip in concentration. I take a few steps closer. On his screen is a video of a well-endowed woman on a Space Hopper. 'Bob,' I say sharply. He slips his phone into his pocket.

'Yeah, thanks for that,' he says. Bob doesn't do thank yous — he even said that in a team meeting once — so his gratitude makes me suspicious.

'I don't remember it saying in my job description that I have to induct new staff,' I say.

Bob inspects the cuticles of his left hand. 'Yeah, it does at the end. You know, 'any other tasks your manager assigns you'.' I want to tell Bob exactly where he can shove his job description. The feeling gives me a thrill; I could do it. I could tell Bob exactly what I think of his job and his tan and never return. I could leave now and never say the words 'putting you through now . . . ' again, but I haven't had much luck with endings recently, so I don't.

When I find them at the Queens Hotel, Leanne and Cara are the best part of the way through a bottle of prosecco.

'We would have waited . . . ' says Leanne.

'But we didn't want to,' finishes Cara. I pour wine into the empty glass waiting for me and Leanne lifts hers in a toast.

'To our beautiful, brave friend,' she says. I drink deeply; the alcohol immediately loosens my muscles. 'How did it go?' asks Leanne. I shrug and drink again. Cara stretches out on the white sofa and appraises me squarely.

'Leanne tells me you had a crap shag.' I cough into my glass and look behind me. The spa is ridiculously chic and very quiet, not the sort of place you should say 'shag', unless discussing home decor. There's a woman folding towels but if she noticed Cara's lack of discretion she hasn't let on. Cara doesn't wait for me to confirm or deny. 'We need to get you drilled again — a bad lay will have you going back to A-hole.'

Leanne laughs in a manner that I know is forced. I keep drinking to stop myself from telling the girls how accurate Cara's assessment is. I can see now that going back to Alexander isn't an option. Even if we tried, it couldn't be a return. It would be a relaunch and a lifelong race away from the shadow of our failure.

'I'm not sure I want to have sex again for a very long time,' I say. Cara puts her glass down so heavily for a second I fear it will break.

'This is what I mean,' she says. She seems

genuinely cross. 'You can't let one dickhead and his little dick send you into hibernation.'

'It wasn't actually little,' I say. I gaze up to the ceiling as I pull together a hazy image of a naked Rupert. 'It was average-sized, I guess.'

'Little dick is a state of mind,' says Cara as she taps the side of her head knowingly.

'Martha's got to do what she wants to do,' says Leanne. She says this to Cara but she's smiling at me, a weak sympathetic smile, the kind you would give to a dog wearing a cone. Cara dismisses this with a rueful shake of her head.

'She's gotta do what she *needs* to do. My aunt Nina did that whole waiting-for-the-right-time shit. Died a couple of years ago with a cooch full of cobwebs.'

Leanne's dog smile collapses and she reaches out to pat Cara on the hand. 'I'm sorry about your aunt,' she says.

'S'all right,' says Cara. 'She was a bitch. Probably because she needed to get laid.'

Leanne's eyes narrow. 'It's not all about sex,' she says.

'Yeah, but it is,' says Cara. 'All of it — film, music, the fact that we're here to have our toenails painted primary colours. Everything is about sex.'

Alexander and I haven't had sex in one hundred and nineteen days. I know this because when I realized it had been two weeks I made a note in my diary. I thought that when we did the deed I could tell him the number and it would surprise him, perhaps shame him a little. I guess I can stop counting.

'Get on Linger,' continues Cara. I think of my match and am about to say something but she continues, 'Everyone's on there for sex, even if they pretend otherwise. That's why I advertised your wares in your profile name.' And like that another man has let me down, before I've even met him — a record. His messages seemed completely sincere and the realization that he could have other motives makes me feel exposed and I start to blush. I'm so focused on my own embarrassment that I miss the debate that has sparked between Cara and Leanne.

'He's great. He barely speaks English,' says Cara, 'so he *couldn't* upset her.'

'Sorry, who?' I ask. Leanne readjusts her robe; its thick folds drown her slim frame and for a second she looks incredibly young. When she speaks, however, it's clear she's a woman, one who knows her own mind and apparently mine.

'Cara has kindly offered to set you up with a personal trainer named Igor, but *I* was just saying that, *if* you're going to date, you should start as you mean to go on. In fact, I was telling James about your . . . uhm . . . encounter and he reminded me there's this guy he works with. He's called Tom. I met him at the summer barbecue and he's kinda cute. He's very polite. I think you could do with someone who will treat you like a lady.'

I wonder why Leanne has to share every last detail of every last thing with James? Someone needs to tell her he's her husband, not her journal. I'm unsurprised she has a solution to a problem I was yet to voice. Whenever I call her to say something's gone wrong, I can hear a shiver of pleasure in her voice. I'm a good friend to her in that regard, always flooding my kitchen or trying to work out how to get a new passport within forty-eight hours. When we were teenagers and I found myself distraught because I had completely forgotten about the existence of an exam she would arrive with sweets and flashcards and drag me through it. The thing is, I always slightly resented her for it; sometimes I just wanted to be her friend and not her renovation project. It didn't occur to me that I could resolve this by simply saying no.

'I don't know . . . ' I say.

'Of course, it's up to you,' says Leanne.

'Yeah, but cobwebs,' says Cara sagely.

A woman in a white tunic approaches us.

'Martha?' she asks. I raise my hand. 'Are you ready?' I finish my drink before standing up.

'Yes I am,' I say.

★   ★   ★

Leanne approaches the set-up of the date with the same attitude she does most things in life — methodically, thoroughly and extremely efficiently. Phone numbers and photos are exchanged; Tom looks happy and approachable in his picture, if a little stylistically challenged. Leanne also sends me a bit of background — almost exclusively his career achievements, but she also includes the fact that he ate a whole plate of king prawns at the barbecue. A few days later, Tom sends me a sweet message asking me to dinner the next evening and after waiting a couple of hours I reply positively; then I think about cancelling approximately every six minutes. Mainly because I think that even if Poppy, eater of men and destroyer of souls, has got her claws into Alexander I shouldn't settle for being courted by some desperado from the East Sussex council drainage department. But also because of this:

Marthashotbod: This isn't about sex, is it?

Undeterred83: No, not at all. I find you fascinating. I mean I'm sure I would like to have sex with you but I'm looking for much more.

Marthashotbod: I'm really pleased to hear that.

Marthashotbod: BTW my friend Cara picked my user-name :/

Undeterred83: I'm sure it's fitting :) Don't get me wrong you're gorgeous but I already know that's just the start.

Marthashotbod: You do?

Undeterred83: I know what I like and I like you.

Marthashotbod: I like you too.

Undeterred83: I really love talking to you. I can't believe the timing. I want us to meet but I'm leaving the day after tomorrow. Working on a children's project in Uganda for twelve weeks! We'll set something up the second I'm back though?

Marthashotbod: Of course. Your trip sounds amazing, so worthy. Do you mind if I ask if any of the kids have worms?

Undeterred83: Ha ha! I don't know if I'd call it worthy but I find it really inspiring. They do occasionally have parasites but we give them a treatment.

3) <u>Has to work for himself but not be in it to make money.</u> He's got to do something useful to society. He has to spend his free time doing something inspiring; not just inspiring but also worthy, e.g. deworming African orphans or similar . . .

My match tells me he's a freelance researcher and the things he examines — health, birth rate, education — they make a difference. Not in a casual, transient way but significantly and permanently. And the fact that he seems to possess so many of the qualities I need makes me believe that he can make that sort of difference to my life. I'm a romantic of sorts — I'm a fan of chocolates and love letters; my ultimate fantasy is that someone will race across a bustling city to stop me boarding a plane — but I have never believed in the concept of one great love. Even when I was mooning over Alexander for all those years, I didn't think he could be my one and only potential soulmate. How could it be logical, with over seven billion people in the world, that my one true love would happen to live in the same seaside town? No, I believed that there were dozens of people with whom I could build a life. Until I wrote that list.

I do wonder if I'm descending into madness and then I ask myself if the questioning of my sanity is a sign of my lack of madness and then I wonder if that thought is in itself mad. Would it be possible that, caught in the storm of grief, I have conjured up this man? It certainly wouldn't be beyond me to imagine a guy who represents everything I need; didn't I do that with Alexander? I re-read the list, forcing myself to appraise the situation objectively. It's undeniable — he's making the grade. I send a silent prayer to the universe that this person is simply a long overdue karmic refund.

So, I'm standing in my jeans and bra, to-ing and fro-ing between meeting Tom and slipping into my onesie and calling the whole thing off, when I decide I have to ask.

Marthashotbod: I can't believe I haven't asked you your name! I assume your parents didn't name you Undeterred83?

Undeterred83: :) No, it's Nathan but my friends and family sometimes call me George, because I was always asking questions when I was a kid.

George?! Fuck. Fuck, fuck, fuck, fuck, fuck.

I go on the date with Tom because I know now that there may be some truth in the concept of one true love and I will definitely need a dummy date before I meet mine, and also because there's still a chance I'm certifiable and crazy people don't go on dates.

I sneak into Moses's room to kiss him goodnight before going. He's still awake and pulls the covers over his face when I come in. I pull them down and tuck them around his body. 'It's not playtime, silly,' I whisper. He reaches out and I hold his hand. I stand in silence and after a minute I can feel his grip relax. I let his arm fall and watch him as he loses the battle to keep his eyes open.

As I leave, a floorboard creaks and Moses stirs and says, 'Mummy.'

'Shhhh,' I say. 'Mummy will be back soon.'

I try to get out of the house without my mum seeing me. I told her I was going to yoga with Leanne. I shout good-bye from the hallway but just before I can get out she calls my name. 'What time do you think you'll be back?' she says.

'Not late,' I say quickly. 'We might go for a drink afterwards.' I can feel her behind me and turn my head to say bye as I open the door.

'You're wearing heels to yoga?'

'You don't wear shoes, Mum, and like I said we might get a drink afterwards.'

Mum takes the door from me. 'Be careful,' she says.

'Yep, promise,' I say, as I walk away.

★   ★   ★

Tom picks Côte; this is good. Tom arrives wearing burgundy cords; this is bad. Tom pulls out my chair (despite my feminist protestations); this is good. Tom clicks his fingers at the waiter; this is very, very bad. I decide it's unfair to compile a catalogue of Tom's flaws before the first course and so channel my energy towards the story he has been telling me since we got settled. It's something about how you can work out how many people can fit on a boat by multiplying its length by its width, so I know that now.

Tom orders us both steaks, insisting they're divine. I don't really like eating steak — it feels like cardio — but I decide that I should save our first disagreement for dessert at least. I ask Tom how he knows James and he tells me that they both attend the same monthly meeting about sanitation and I think, so you don't really know him, and then I start to panic about how this date came to pass. Did James send out some sort of company-wide memo imploring anyone with a little time on their hands to take out his wife's crazy, loser friend?

'What do you do?' asks Tom, which is of course the question that everyone hates. What the hell does it even mean? The real answer is almost always, 'Barrel through life attempting to function as a semi-responsible human being and read the *Mail Online* more than I should.' The reason the question is so disconcerting is because it appears so innocent, but in reality it's quite aggressive. It's the small talk equivalent of folding your arms, leaning back and saying, 'Impress me.'

'I work in finance,' I say.

'Ah, that's cool,' says Tom. 'My uncle works in finance. Where do you work?'

'In Hove,' I say as I pick up the drinks menu. 'Another glass of wine?'

'Yes, but who do you work for?' asks Tom. I drain my glass.

'It's a small company, you wouldn't know them. We're basically the client support team.'

'So that means you do what?' asks Tom. What is this, a police interrogation?

'I answer the phone,' I say.

'I don't understand,' says Tom.

'Customers call and I take those calls,' I say.

'Right, so it's like . . . '

'A call centre. It's a call centre.'

Tom clears his throat. 'That must be . . . interesting.'

The waiter arrives with our steaks. 'Well done?' he asks.

'Here,' says Tom.

The waiter places the meal in front of him before putting the other plate down in front of me. 'More wine?'

'Yes,' I say.

As the waiter leaves Tom says pointlessly, 'Well, this looks well done.'

We eat our food in uncomfortable silence. After a few minutes Tom asks me how my steak tastes. It tastes like dead cow but I make some agreeable noises.

'Yeah, it's great here,' says Tom. 'My ex discovered it.' I want to tell him Côte is a chain, that his ex discovered Google, but he looks so pleased that I just nod. 'Yeah, she loved eating out. One of these girls that always wants to go places. To be honest it was exhausting. After a hard day's work the last thing you want to do is go dining . . . Sorry.'

I'm not sure what he's apologizing for — for bringing up his ex, for revealing himself to be a rubbish partner or for being terminally boring.

'Why did you break up?' I ask.

'I don't know,' he says. 'I think maybe we stopped trying.'

I catch his eye and we share a smile, one that says, we may hail from different planets but some things remain the same. I think this moment is what resuscitates the date — no longer restricted by the pressure to present a flawless facade, we commiserate about our overbearing mothers and swap stories about the not-so-hilarious-at-the-time bullying we endured at school. There's one uncomfortable moment when Tom discloses that he voted UKIP but he takes great pains to make clear that it was a protest vote. I think it helps that our waiter keeps the booze coming, perhaps sensing with his professional intuition that these two very out of practice thirty-somethings would need a helping hand.

I insist we split the bill since Tom didn't really ask me out and he tells me that that sounds 'very reasonable'. As he walks me to the bus stop he says, 'I would ask you to come for another drink but I think we've had enough.'

'I'm OK,' I say, but he doesn't ask again.

'I'm here,' I say at my stop.

'OK. I'm just round the corner so I'm going to walk back.'

'OK,' I say. He kisses me then and it's surprisingly nice. I could stand there for hours snogging under the gaze of all the passengers making their way home on the 21A.

★ ★ ★

When I get home I feel really positive for the first time in weeks, if not years. Perhaps I should not concern myself with a hypothetical future with a guy from the internet I have yet to lay eyes on, when I could be enjoying the here and now with a man who wants to kiss me goodnight in the moonlight. I can't help it; as I brush my teeth I imagine Tom doing the same beside me.

I'm unsurprised to find a text message from him as I climb into bed. But when I open it, it reads, 'THANKS FOR TONIGHT BUT I DON'T THINK WE SHOULD SEE EACH OTHER AGAIN. I'M SURE YOU ENJOY YOUR WORK BUT I THINK I NEED SOMEONE WITH MORE AMBITION.'

He works with James and I don't want to offend him, so I think I'm pretty restrained when I reply, 'YOU PRICK.'

One thing is certain: before I meet George, I need a new job.

8

Soft play centres sum up parenthood perfectly — loud, chaotic, a little bit musty and yet for some reason they feel safe. I appreciate its familiarity and the way I blend in there. It's more than a week since the date with Tom but the shame still feels fresh. Leanne, Lucas, Moses and I take up a spot in the corner of the ball pool. The boys entertain each other by throwing the brightly coloured plastic balls at each other's heads, and Leanne tries to help me make sense of my life as we work our way through the bag of Revels she has brought for us to share.

'Why were you seeing a therapist?' asks Leanne, before waiting for a moment when Lucas is distracted to slip another chocolate in her mouth and return the packet to its hiding place underneath a yellow ball.

'Do you think it's weird?' I ask in return.

'Of course not,' says Leanne. 'You see a doctor for your body and a therapist for your mind.'

'Have you been in therapy?' I ask. I watch Leanne watching our children and reconsider what I know about the world. Is it possible that my beautiful friend, with her picture-perfect life, has been struggling too?

'God, no,' she says. 'Like I said, I don't have anything against it but I tend to just get on with things.'

'Right,' I say, and then I shove a handful of

Revels in my mouth.

'We're all different, hun,' says Leanne. 'Seriously, no judgement. I guess I just wondered why you thought you couldn't come to me.' I finish my mouthful and release all the breath in my body.

'Because there wasn't anything I could come to you with really, nothing I could properly articulate.' I think about the nights when I couldn't sleep, my mind numb. I longed for tears or anger or something that could direct my sense of unease. 'I had everything I'd ever wanted but I was still so unhappy and I didn't even know how to be happy.'

'Did you talk to Alexander about it?' says Leanne. I know, for her, it would be this easy, that she and James would just speak about things, make time to work through it; have urgent, hushed conversations late at night as their children were sleeping. I try not to envy her for this.

'I tried but I just got . . . ' I sweep my palm in front of my face to indicate the invisible wall that Alexander had created between us. 'He didn't get it and he got frustrated with me. It was him who suggested counselling.' Leanne looks at me carefully, as if I am something fragile and the wrong words might break me.

'Did it help?' she asks.

'Yeah,' I say. 'Look at my life now.' I wink at Leanne to make clear that I understand how crappy my circumstances are; if I didn't then I would *really* need to be in therapy.

'I know it probably all feels a bit of a mess right now. That's why you need to take control,'

Leanne says. 'Don't let him make you feel like your life is over, he's taken enough.'

I start to bury my legs under the balls. 'It's not even about him,' I say. 'It's about me. I've forgotten who I am.'

Leanne turns to me sharply. 'It *is* about him. You can't let him get away with this. Why is he still living in the flat? He's probably shacked up there with some bimbo. I'm sorry to say it but that's what they're like.'

I asked Alexander about Poppy and he told me she was there to help him organize his end of year files. He told me he couldn't even think about another relationship yet.

'His office is there,' I say.

'You're still accommodating him!' Leanne snaps. 'He has your cat, for God's sake.'

'Why are you angry with me?' I snipe back.

'I'm not,' says Leanne. 'I'm angry *for* you. You need to make him step up to the plate.' I'm unsurprised by Leanne's attitude; she has a zero-tolerance stance towards exes in general. Her own former lovers are not even permitted to have names — they are known as the tall one, the stupid one and the one with no job.

'He's called me a couple of times, to make arrangements for Moses. We decided it's probably best we don't see each other for a while.' This is not strictly true. Alexander spoke; Alexander decided. His voice, at the time, had this stoic quality that I resented deeply. As if speaking to me was a heroic act. Moses crawls over to me and lies on his back before pushing his feet towards my face.

'Stinky,' I say, and he giggles. 'He's agreed to take Moses every other weekend.'

'How good of him,' Leanne says.

'And he's still paying for nursery,' I add in a rush. For some reason I feel the need to defend him; some habits are hard to break, I guess.

'Have you thought about a solicitor?' asks Leanne. Moses rolls towards Lucas, who is arguing over ownership of a lost sock with a vengeful-looking little girl. I lie down in the balls; they feel cool against my head.

'Can't. Too scary.'

Leanne grabs my hand and pulls me back up to sitting. 'Living with your mother for ever is far, far scarier.' I feel my face contort in horror. 'Right?!' says Leanne. 'Get the ball rolling. As soon as you take action you'll feel really empowered.'

'You sound like Tashi,' I say.

'Another therapist?' asks Leanne.

'No, this girl at work. She's trying to convince me to go on a retreat with her. You know, learning how to breathe and whatnot. She's always going on about empowerment.'

'She's right,' says Leanne. She claps her hands together several times and in response Lucas stops trying to drown Moses in the sea of plastic. 'I think it's a great idea to get some headspace. You need to get a serious plan together. You remember when I moved from audit to tax?' I don't want to lie so I keep my face very still. 'I had a week in Greece and it completely cleared my head. Do you want the details for my career coach?'

'What exactly did she do?' I ask. I imagine someone screaming at me as I type up covering letters.

Leanne shrugs. 'She helped me to identify my strengths and create a two-year plan.'

'Did you achieve it?' I ask. Leanne raises her right eye-brow and I laugh. 'OK, of course you did.' I notice Moses has a trail of snot hanging from his nose. I beckon to him but he's too busy trying to bend over and look through his legs. 'So, you think that could work for me?'

Leanne pulls a face I can't interpret.

'What? You don't think I can do it?' I ask.

'No,' says Leanne. 'I know you can. I got an orange-flavoured Revel — you know I hate them.'

I laugh again; it feels good. 'Why do you even buy Revels when you don't like half the flavours?'

Leanne wrinkles her nose as she considers this. 'I'm a realist. Life is like a bag of Revels: you have to put up with the orange ones because it makes it so much better when you get a nutty one.' I try and think of my marriage as one big orange-flavoured piece of confectionery. It helps. Leanne slips another chocolate in her mouth. 'See, nutty,' she says. 'I'm sorry,' she continues. Her gaze is lowered and she is speaking so softly, for a moment I am not sure she is addressing me. 'I'm sorry,' she says again, with more conviction, as if the first time she said it was a rehearsal. 'I shouldn't have set you up on that date.' She grabs my hand. 'You need to be working on you. I meant it when I said you were brave. You've done the hard part — now you'll make your life amazing, without him, without any man.'

I squeeze her hand and then pull my own away. I was going to tell her about George — I've already felt my phone vibrate twice in my pocket and I am desperate to see if it's him reaching out — but she looks so proud of me, so sure I can make it alone, that I hold back. I sort of want to believe her too. It's not that I don't think a single woman can have a happy existence; I'm just not sure that happy woman would be me.

'I'm gonna nip to the loo,' I say. I make my way out of the pit, carefully avoiding the limbs of small children, and then I hurry to the toilet. I want to savour the moment, so I don't look at my phone until I'm seated. The messages are from Greg asking me if I want to join the work Christmas party planning committee.

'IT'S GONNA BE EPIC', he's texted in a follow-up to the question. I relax my body, and pee and anticipation drain out of me.

'THE PARTY OR THE COMMITTEE?' I reply.

Greg immediately shoots back, 'HAR DE HAR.'

The thought of Christmas is like receiving a kick when I'm already in the foetal position, defeated by blows. I'm not a fan of the holiday as it is — the jolliness is overwhelming — but to help give Moses and Alexander a proper family Christmas, I could pretend. There would be no more pretending now; Moses will never have a real Christmas again.

Back at the pit the boys have started piling balls on to Leanne and she is doing a valiant job of pretending to enjoy it. I wade over and join in with their endeavour.

'No! Not you as well!' Leanne shouts. The boys squeal with delight.

'OK, truce,' I say. I grab Lucas, who has two balls poised above his head. 'Let's calm down and go for a walk.' We gather up our children and strap them into their push-chairs. They're too tired to put up a decent fight and within a few minutes of strolling along the seafront the two are asleep. Leanne and I keep walking and when we reach the pier I suggest we get some soft scoop. Even though it's October and chilly, it's bright and if you look towards it you can feel the sun on your face; so we park the children next to a couple of deckchairs and look out to the water as we slowly work through our ice creams. Leanne bites the end off her cone and sucks the last of the ice cream out, just as she did when we were kids.

'Do these taste better than I remember?' she asks.

'Yes,' I tell her. 'I think they do.'

9

Leanne sends me the details of her career coach. Her glossy website outlines the achievements of her former clients in intimidating detail. In a video introducing herself, Grace Fermin explains how she will help me to 'rise through the ranks of my current career'. Rising through the ranks of my current career would mean becoming Bob; I don't know what I want but I know I don't want that. Grace also says a lot about investing in yourself, which I understand as code for spending money that I don't have. I'm not willing to give up, though; I know Leanne believes in me and Moses needs me and that knowledge gives me enough motivation to scour the internet for careers advice deep into the night. Just before my brain bails out on my enthusiasm, I come across an ad that reads, 'Are you stuck? Are you unmotivated? Worried you'll never achieve the life of your dreams? We can help.' I think yes, yes and resoundingly yes and so I use the online booking system to claim an appointment for the next morning.

★　★　★

The Live the Life You Love business mentor scheme's office is located above a hot yoga studio in the centre of town. I climb the stairs, squeezing past a couple of dozen Lycraclad yogis on their way out of class; I can't quite believe that so many people would *pay* to start their week that way. At the top I reach a tiny stairwell/waiting room with a grey polypropylene chair and a very artificial-looking plant. I sit and look for a mint in my bag. Before I locate one, a short woman with a generous bosom opens the door. She has a very sharp, expensive-looking bob, underneath which is a face so round it verges on spherical. She introduces herself as Patricia.

'I'm the scheme's founder and chief mentor. Welcome.' She offers up her hand and, still seated, I receive a firm but clammy handshake.

'Thanks for meeting me,' I say.

'Come in,' she says, before leading me into a windowless office. As she clears several carrier bags of groceries from the desk, Patricia says, 'When I say welcome I mean welcome to the rest of your life.' She gestures for me to sit before doing the same. Patricia rests her elbows on her desk and builds a little steeple with her fingers. 'What brings you here?' she asks.

'Uhm, I guess I'm going through a transition and I need some support to, uhm, support me through this, well, transition.'

'Quite,' says Patricia.

'I'm on my own for the first time in a long time and I need to start bringing in more money. I work part-time because I've got a little boy, so I want my work to be flexible. I thought starting a business could make that happen.' I know starting a business isn't easy — I watched the whole ugly process up close and personal when

Alexander started his design company — but whilst I know it will be hard, life already feels hard, so what's a little more?

Patricia glances up at the ceiling before pulling a wad of tissues out of her cardigan sleeve and blowing her nose heavily. 'Sorry,' she says, 'allergies. Anyway, let me tell you some more about me. Three years ago, I had nothing.' Patricia opens her hands suddenly; I guess in case I'm not sure what 'nothing' consists of. 'Nothing at all except this' — she taps her head — 'and this.' Patricia then places her right hand over her heart. 'Then I launched and I realized I had this business inside me all along and so do you. So why don't you tell me about your business plan.' My armpits prickle. I kind of thought she would be giving the plan to *me*.

'Well, it's not quite outlined yet . . . '

'Of course,' says Patricia. 'That's why we're here.'

'I guess I want to help people.' Patricia smiles. 'People like . . . women.'

'It's an under-resourced market,' she says. We sit in silence for a couple of seconds, until I understand that Patricia expects me to continue.

'I want to help women . . . '

'A business should always be of service. Help them with what?'

I figure that what I need is probably true of everyone else, so I say, 'I want to help them meet their ideal partner, if they haven't already. Which in my experience is rare.'

Patricia chuckles. 'I hear you, sister,' she says.

I make my face smile. I think, if I can connect

with this woman, with whom I can already tell I have little in common, I can do it with women like me.

'I've been invited to a retreat this weekend,' I say, 'and I think I could use the experience to work out how to set up one of my own, or maybe I could do coaching.'

I hope that Tashi can still get me a place on the retreat and that she isn't suspicious of my sudden turnaround.

Patricia opens a new notebook at the first page. 'Well, your business plan sounds like a simple subscription model: sign them up and sell them something! And of course the dating arena is ripe for the picking. What's your social media presence?'

'Limited,' I say.

'That's no problem,' says Patricia, scribbling 'limited' in the notebook. 'I can help you develop a really clear company message. I'd suggest you start with your market research and then come back to me and we can pull together your avatar.' I didn't even see that film, so I have no idea what she is referring to, but I'm excited I'm winning her over.

'So, shall we get started?' asks Patricia.

'Sure, yes please,' I say.

'Yes!' says Patricia, making a fist.

'Yes!' I say with more conviction, but I can't bring myself to mimic the gesture.

'OK,' says Patricia, turning to a desktop computer to her right. 'I just need to take a few details and then we can get you up and out there.' She spends a minute or so tapping on the keyboard before telling me, 'The entire year costs eleven hundred pounds, which is the best value you will find for this level of input.'

I want to pick up my bag and run. I came here with the hope of making money, not losing funds I don't yet have. 'I can see some hesitation,' says Patricia, raising a finger, 'and let me tell you that's just because you don't yet believe in your vision . . . but you will. Every flight starts with a leap.' I nod. 'I can see you still have reservations, so here's what I'm gonna do for you. If you pay a non-refundable deposit of two hundred pounds today, you can pay the rest off in two instalments. Let me offer you this.' Patricia places her hands flat on the desk. 'You can think if you need to but thinking has got you where you are today; wouldn't it be nice to stop thinking and just feel?'

I'm not sure how much Patricia is right about but she's right about that. I open my bag and get out an old debit card. As Patricia merrily taps the information into her computer I say a silent prayer to the money gods. The last time I used the card a man called Kalpesh called to tell me that I was in my *overdraft's* overdraft, and pretty much implied that if I used it again, the thing would self-destruct.

'All gone through,' says Patricia, and I release the breath that I didn't realize I was holding. 'Why don't you go home and email me through a basic business plan and we can start from there.'

'That's it?'

'Oh, of course,' says Patricia. She roots around in her desk drawer and pulls out a hot pink folder, which she hands to me. The words 'The Life You Love Starts Today' are printed on the front.

'So, I should just go?'

'Yep, to wherever you feel most inspired. Here's the thing: it's really more simple than you think. Every action begins with a thought. Have you ever thought something' — Patricia clicks her fingers — 'and just like that it appears, just as you imagined it?' For the most part I have a thought and the outcome isn't even in the same family as what I had hoped. I have *never* imagined something and had it come to pass, until George.

I pop into a coffee shop on the way to work and order a latte with extra foam and expensive syrupy stuff. As I wait, I look around at the other patrons and consider Patricia's words. To these people there is no reason why I couldn't be a successful entrepreneur, taking a self-directed break at the start of her amazing day. I decide that if I think it, it is so — what is reality but a construct of the mind?

★   ★   ★

I walk into the office and straight into Greg. A little of my coffee spills on to his shirt sleeve but he tells me it's fine as I dab at the stain unsuccessfully with my napkin.

'How are your teeth?' he asks when I cease my efforts.

'My teeth?' I echo, forgetting momentarily that I fabricated an emergency trip to the dentist in

84

order to meet Patricia. 'Yeah, good. Great.' For some reason, I feel guilty lying to Greg. He always looks so earnest. As he smiles at my response, I feel like I'm tainting him with my deceit.

'You coming to the meeting?' he asks. I nod. 'You don't know what meeting I'm talking about, do you?'

'Busted,' I say.

'It's the first Christmas party planning committee meeting.' I wasn't even planning to attend the party but I let him lead the way to the conference room.

Lisa, an administrator in the training department, is standing authoritatively at the front of the room.

'Take a seat, Greg,' she says. 'We're just talking about refreshments.' She says nothing to me. We sit down and Lisa continues, 'I'm committed to making this the best party we've seen in years, so no suggestion is too crazy, guys.' I look over at Greg but he doesn't look back at me; he's watching Lisa with a fierce concentration. I take her in properly for the first time. She has an elaborate braid in her hair and her blue shirt is precisely the same shade as her kitten heels. Everything about her screams enthusiasm. It looks exhausting.

'Salsa,' says someone to the left of me.

'Great,' says Lisa, writing the word on a whiteboard behind her. 'Everyone loves dips and we'll need something that can last the night.' She turns back to us, her face flush. 'Any more?' The room becomes a cacophony of snack foods; Lisa looks unsettled. 'Guys! Guys! One at a time, please.' Her plea goes unheeded; two lads in the customer retainment department start chanting 'Monster Munch'. Lisa looks a little as if she might cry.

Greg stands up, cups his mouth with his hands and shouts, 'Oi! Put a lid on it!' The room falls silent.

'Thanks, Greg,' says Lisa. He winks at her in return and she appears flustered. 'Let's get into pairs and come up with a bunch of ideas,' she says. As I turn to tell Greg how stupid it all is, she reaches out to him. 'Greg, join me.' He goes to her without even acknowledging me, and then, when I look for someone else to pair with, it seems that everyone has already coupled up. I leave quietly and head to my cubicle. I have bigger things than dip to think about.

Marthashotbod: I've just had a really exciting meeting about the new business I'm starting.

Undeterred83: Awesome! What's the business?

Marthashotbod: I'm working on the vision now so I'll let you know when I've really got it down.

Undeterred83: I'm so impressed by your work ethic, I'd love to start my own thing. Can't wait to chat to you about it. Only eleven weeks till I'm back on British soil!

Marthashotbod: I know! What's stopping you? From starting your own thing.

Undeterred83: You always know exactly what to say. There's nothing stopping me. I had a challenging time a few years ago but I did the work, cut out some shit, started meditating and I feel really confident now.

Marthashotbod: It's so important to work on yourself. I'm going on a meditation retreat next week.

I'll confirm with Tashi when she comes in for the evening shift. I won't mention that when she sent me an email to let me know she had reserved me a place, I sent it to junk.

Undeterred83: Man. I swear you are perfect for me.

I don't reply because there is nothing more to say. I can't remember the last time someone wanted me, no strings attached — no trial period, no training necessary.

10

About once a month I take my mother out for coffee. I think for her it's a tangible representation of a legitimate mother — daughter relationship and for me I get to have all my wrongdoings outlined in one contained hour. Nine times out of ten she picks a tearoom on the seafront; I think she likes the high footfall. It means she gets to show her friends and acquaintances what a wonderful bond we have and if I'm lucky, after subtracting all the pleasantries she stops to exchange, she only spends ten or twenty minutes engaging with me.

I really don't mind my mother's commitment to community cohesion because I love being around her when her attention isn't focused on me. She's the sort of person who draws you in from across a room; she just has this wonderful, uplifting presence that makes people (and small dogs) want to be around her. Conversely, ten seconds into any interaction with a new person, I become convinced I have a bogey on my face and then spend the entire conversation focused on how quickly I can get away to rectify this. My extraction is always forced and awkward and more than once it's been the case that my suspicions have been confirmed.

I suggest that we go and collect Moses from nursery together and stop on the way for a catch-up. In the tearoom, I buy my mother a symbolic slice of chocolate cake. It is symbolic because my mother will not touch it. Ivy Ketch claims to have no prejudices; in fact she is fond of saying, 'I am against nothing,' and then pausing to allow any onlookers to glory in her beatific aura. She's almost right; my mother is against nothing — she is against everything and everyone. There is one thing, however, that she reserves a special kind of hatred for, the kind of disgust that one would usually find aimed at the far right or perpetrators of child abuse: fat. Fat on herself, fat in her line of vision and most of all fat, actual or potential, on her only daughter. My mother's personal attitude to fat is to head it off at the pass — she eats little and not very often; one of my earliest memories is sitting in a high chair watching her bob along to a callisthenics video. Over the years her methodology may have changed — power walking, aerobics, Zumba — but the aim remains: avoiding fat, avoiding even the merest implication of fat, at all costs.

I always found it slightly odd, this anti-fat stance. She was born into a Jamaican family that was large in all senses of the word. Ample curves weren't just the norm, they were positively coveted. As a child, one of the places I felt safest was in my grandmother's tiny kitchen in her retirement flat in south London. She would pile steaming white rice into a bowl before adding a generous knob of butter; this would melt into the grains, creating a satisfying glaze which would coat my lips as I ate. Sometimes my mother would tut as I scraped the bowl clean but my grandmother would simply offer me a refill, to which I always said yes. Partly because, then and now, I exist in a permanent state of hunger, but mostly because I loved to see the joy in her eyes. She would pinch my cheek and say, 'What a way you fat and roun' and pretty,' and her words were like clutching a hot water bottle to my stomach.

Being with Alexander didn't do a lot to curtail my body issues. He was always very supportive of my endeavours to lose a few pounds but perhaps a little too supportive. He saw my body, obviously — how could he miss it? — but I never got the impression that he held an opinion on it, negative *or* positive. I've noticed it's become a trend for young women to complain about comments on their figures received from men in the street. I always read another article and think, it's all right for you with your peachy face and your high breasts, 'cause the thing that no woman ever admits is that they don't want men to talk about their bodies, but then again they really, really do.

Before James, Leanne briefly dated a guy (the stupid one) who was entirely unsuitable for her. Wally (I never discovered if this was a nickname or his given one) was a walking, breathing stereotype of the British working-class man. He had a job in construction and a potty mouth. Whenever the conversation became too involved he would procure a dirty, crumpled edition of the *Sun* from somewhere and become immersed in the copy until the discussion returned to safer ground. I didn't get it; I didn't want to get it. My friend was bright, refined and disciplined, and he was an oaf. Then one day we were out for a pint and apropos of nothing he said to Leanne, 'You've got such a great arse.' As I watched her pretend to be embarrassed I understood.

Not for the first time I worry that when George first lays eyes on me, he isn't going to like what he sees. The only dating advice my mother has ever given me is that 'men decide with their eyes'; she said this as she gifted me a girdle. Irritated as I was by her crassness at the time (the girdle went directly from the bag to the bin), I have to admit my father, a man whose only passion in life is the dunkability of his evening biscuit, unreservedly adores her. Whatever Mum might say, I don't think his dedication is based solely on her waistline. I was around ten when I became fully aware of the fact that my parents had a relationship outside of raising me. As much as it grossed me out, I took note of the way my father would kiss my mum as soon as he stepped in the house, before removing his coat; I would see him watching her in crowded rooms, smiling as though he had a secret. Whilst I can't imagine a life without cake, I would give it up for love like that.

A woman wearing a canary yellow tracksuit stops at our table. 'Heeeellllo, Ive,' she coos. 'That dessert is divine! You're in for a real treat.'

Mum gives a little laugh. 'I'm sure,' she says. 'We missed you at bums and tums last week.'

'Oh, I haven't got time at the minute,' says the woman. 'I'm in training for a 5k.' She bends her arms at the elbow and swings them back and forth by her sides several times.

'Oh, good for you, honey,' says Mum. 'Let me know if you want sponsors or anything.'

'Thanks, I will! Enjoy your cake.' She marches out of the cafe. As soon as her yellow posterior is out of sight Mum tuts.

'These people, you'd think she was doing a triathlon — such a bloody fuss. I do 5k round the supermarket.'

'At least she's trying,' I say. I dip my finger into the icing of the slice of cake and pop it in my mouth. Big Bird was right, it is delicious.

'Barely,' says Mum, her face briefly contorting in disgust.

'Well, I'm doing the half-marathon,' I say. I have no idea why. The closest I've ever got to a marathon is watching an entire season of *Grey's Anatomy* in one weekend. Then I see my mother's face; confusion gives way to something approaching pride and I decide that I *am* doing a half-marathon. I know at least that I want to be the kind of person who does a half-marathon.

'A project is just what you need! And with all that training, when you see Alexander he won't know what's hit him.' I open my mouth to protest but stop myself; she's actually right. I can't wait to feel lean and comment-worthy and accomplished and spiritually superior, but the person I want to impress is not Alexander but George.

11

'What do you take to a retreat?' I ask Tashi as I climb into her green Nissan Micra on Friday morning.

'Just an open heart,' says Tashi.

'So, I won't need my hair straighteners?'

'No,' says Tashi, 'I don't think so.'

I smack my left hand on the dashboard. 'Then I'm good to go.'

Tashi tells me she has been meditating twice a day in preparation for the weekend. 'You have to train your brain,' she says. 'Being present is like a muscle. Have you ever meditated before?'

I scour my brain. I am rarely present; I'm always thinking about how things will be better in the future, or about how I've fucked up in the past.

'I did some hypnobirthing classes when I was having Moses. I had to pretend my vagina was a flower. Is it something like that?'

'Erm, I'm sure there's some overlap,' Tashi says.

As Tashi drives, I fiddle with the radio until I find a station playing old classics. I don't think Tashi knows any of the songs but she hums along companionably. Tashi is concerned that her car won't make it up to motorway speeds so we drive on small country roads. Although I barely know Tashi, I suddenly feel very connected to her. I just know the trip will be life-changing; we'll be like Thelma and Louise but with less murder and more snacks.

I've never learned to drive. Living in Brighton, where most things are walking distance, there didn't seem a point. That's what I told myself and anyone who questioned my avoidance of such a common rite of passage, but now I wonder if, on some level, I chose not to learn because I loved the experience of having Alexander drive me. He's a great driver, never more comfortable than when on the road — distance, traffic, nothing fazed him. In the early days he would often give me a ride to work or drop me off on a night out. Once, I had gone to a festival a couple of towns over with Cara. She'd hooked up with a guy, a bassist in a Danish death metal band, and being the good friend I am, I gave up my space in our two-man tent and told her I would get a cab home.

Of course, every taxi in the area had been booked weeks in advance and I was faced with a very long wait or an even longer walk home. I called Alexander with the dying embers of my phone battery; gave him sloppy directions to the edge of the field I was standing next to and somehow, through sheer will or possibly an intangible connection, he found me. I don't remember what he said to me on the drive home — I was more concerned with the way my brain seemed to be running laps within my skull — but I remember the feeling, the warmth of knowing he had been there to save me.

When 'Young Hearts Run Free' fills the car, I feel compelled to join in. I've always loved the song, mostly because so many people think it's fun and upbeat, when in fact the lyrics are desperately sad.

'I didn't know you could sing,' says Tashi. I feel myself blushing.

'I can't, not really,' I say.

'Oh, OK,' she says.

I ask Tashi how she got into Tula Shiki and request a little more information on where she's actually taking me. 'Tula is a philosophy,' she says. 'Its basis is in minimalism and self-contemplation. The retreat is based at its main centre. My ex, Guido, got me into it. He's such a centred man, so introspective. He taught me a lot.'

Tashi explains that she met Guido when he was running a workshop on her university campus entitled 'The Fast Path to Simple Living'. 'I needed to pay off, like, five credit cards but I got so much more.' Tashi tells me that she found herself blown away by Guido's presence and intensity; apparently his lack of investment in material objects gave him a sense of freedom she found highly desirable. Guido was a former model and having experienced a life of excess, he understood its limitations. Hearing about his previous profession, I wonder if it was just his freedom she desired.

'So why did you break up?' I ask. Tashi inhales slowly through her nose and then exhales loudly from her mouth.

'I guess he had too much love to give,' she says.

'Is that possible?' I ask.

95

'Sure,' says Tashi. 'When you have so much you need to share it around several people, it's too much.'

Tashi tells me, as though relieved to unburden herself, an age-old story of empty beds and unanswered calls and how women are so ridiculously adept at ignoring the patently obvious. She tells me that a few weeks into their courtship he had taken her to a party. She remembers taking great care over her outfit — she wanted, so very much, to live up to the moniker of his girlfriend. The party was the sort that Tashi found intimidating — a crowd of older people with interesting stories — but Guido's friends were warm and inclusive and she quickly found herself having a good time. She was listening to a guy tell her about a recent trek through Peru when she got the sense that Guido was no longer with her, not emotionally, but physically. She excused herself from the conversation and searched the apartment. She remembers opening a door to find an empty broom cupboard before she started to panic. She wanted to leave. She wanted to go home and eat ice cream and cry but to do so would be to accept the fact that he had abandoned her. When Guido returned two hours later, she confronted him. He told her she was being hysterical and that he had just stepped out for a cigarette, and she accepted this despite the fact that he didn't smoke.

When she was forced to face the truth, it was on the screen of Guido's open netbook. An email from a girl stating in uncompromising detail what he had done to her and what she would very much like for him to do to her again. The time stamp offered no escape route for him. The message, read but not deleted, was offered up to her so carelessly that it was clear that Guido either wanted to get caught or did not care if he was. When she asked him, calmly and clearly, what his explanation was, he said, 'We didn't say we were exclusive.' Tashi had given up her room in a shared house just three weeks prior to move in with him.

I sympathize with Tashi and reassure her that we've all been there because it's true. Alexander never cheated on me, not that I know of, but he had shown me in many ways that he was biding his time, and even if he was not with someone else he was certainly not with me.

Once we had taken a holiday to Ibiza. I had obsessed over it for weeks. I was so determined to make the trip perfect I even went to a travel agent, rather than picking it on some low-cost website, and had been bedevilled into paying for a load of unnecessary, barely noticeable extras. As holidays often are, it was a disappointment — we were too old for the party scene but not old enough to admit it. We spent most nights pretending we were going to hit the clubs and then getting drunk in the hotel bar. There was one day, though, that we made it to the old town. We wandered the cobbled streets for hours and I kept imagining that other tourists would look at us and marvel at how beautiful and in love we were. We found ourselves at Café del Mar, a stunning waterside bar known for its amazing atmosphere. It was one of the few places I've been to that has lived up to my expectations. The bar is the place to be at sunset, when the resident DJs play ambient sounds to complement the unbelievable view. Thirty minutes before the sun went down I asked Alexander if he wanted another beer. 'I'm kinda hungry,' he said. 'I fancy paella.' I placed my hand on his knee.

'Let's hold off,' I said. 'I think I'm happy here.'

'Sorry, babe,' said Alexander, sounding anything but. As we left, another couple eagerly scrambled into our seats. How could I have imagined I would make him stay for a lifetime if I couldn't get him to commit to a sunset?

My phone stirs.

Undeterred83: Are you OK?

I decide it's time to start being open.

> **Marthashotbod: I am now I've heard from you.**
> **Undeterred83: That's great. That's exactly what I wanted to hear. What you up to?**
> **Marthashotbod: I'm going on a journey.**
> **Undeterred83: I'd love to be coming with you.**
> **Marthashotbod: Maybe next year?**
> **Undeterred83: If I play my cards right?**
> **Marthashotbod: You're holding aces right now.**

'You wanna stop for supplies?' says Tashi.

We stop at a shop in a tiny village, run by a woman who clearly wants it to stay that way. She serves us with such open hostility I start to reassess my hair, my clothes, even my gait for evidence of their contemptibility. Tashi seems oblivious to her blind hatred and babbles happily as she buys toilet roll, water and nuts.

'Hi, Mary,' she says. 'Had a lot of us coming through?' Mary's face offers nothing. 'I'm so excited to see you again; you're like the start of my awakening every time I arrive.'

I think Mary is going to comment but she simply coughs productively, leaving her mouth uncovered as she does so. I replicate Tashi's shopping, although as she leaves the shop, stating plans to warm up the car, I add three Bounty bars, and then just before paying I ask the woman to get me four of the miniature brandies she has behind the counter. This seems to defrost her, and she winks at me before slipping the bottles into the bottom of the bag. I thank her and hurry back to Tashi. As I'm leaving, Mary speaks for the first time. I can't exactly be sure what she says but it sounds like, 'You're gonna need it.'

★ ★ ★

The Tula Shiki Education and Resource Centre is located behind a small copse of fir trees. From the road it looks like an outdoor centre, the kind Scouts might frequent to learn skills they will never require in a modern world, but as we drive closer to the collection of buildings I see figures

99

dotted about in the trees and pathways. Adults, some dressed in robes, others in fun, stylish clothes; but all wearing the same 'ready for Armageddon' smile that Tashi also sports. After parking the car, we are met in reception by a woman with waist-length grey hair who introduces herself as Sunbeam.

'Welcome, welcome,' she says breathily. She shuts her eyes for several seconds and, just as I am growing concerned she is having a stroke, she leaps back to life, like a mechanical doll. 'I've just got some medical forms for you to fill in and then I'm pleased to tell you you can have a sitting with Larry.' Sunbeam offers us two wooden chairs as she goes to fetch the paperwork.

'Who's Larry?' I whisper to Tashi.

'The guru!' says Tashi.

'A guru . . . called Larry?'

'Yes,' says Tashi, 'and we're really lucky that we get to see him so early on!'

Sunbeam comes over with the forms. It's mostly standard health stuff; I try to make myself sound like a functioning human. I pause at the emergency contact section, a place where Alexander's name used to live. I shake my head to see off any burgeoning tears and write 'I need nothing and no one' in the space, but then I cross it out and put down my mum. Sunbeam returns to take our forms.

'Can I also have your phones,' she says. Tashi is busy rooting around in her bag and so cannot see me staring at her in stunned silence. When she hands her mobile to Sunbeam I still haven't moved. Sunbeam watches me with a fixed smile.

'I can't,' I say. 'I . . . I have a son.' Yes, the child card, I think. No one can argue with that one.

'It's fine,' says Sunbeam. 'All the calls are monitored and if there's an emergency we'll get you immediately.' Very briefly I consider running and then I feel a bit ashamed about how ridiculous I am being. For the first half of my life I didn't have a mobile phone; I will be fine. I hand my iPhone to Sunbeam and in return she gives me a small bow. 'Leave your bags here and someone will take them to your room. Larry will see you now.' She gestures for us to head to a door across the reception. Tashi gives Sunbeam a bow of her own before rushing over and I quickly follow, unsure of what is scarier — going with her or being left alone.

Inside the room heavy curtains block most of the light but a few candles illuminate Larry's brown, lined face. Although it is cold he is wearing a light tunic and sandals. He nods very slightly to us as we enter. Tashi sits cross-legged on the floor in front of him and I follow suit. 'Welcome back,' Larry says towards Tashi.

She claps her hands over her mouth. 'You remember me,' she squeals through her fingers.

'All my students have a piece of me in them,' he says.

I know the enlightenment process has already started; otherwise how is it that I'm able to resist giggling at this unfortunate statement?

'You,' says Larry, his head whipping in my direction, 'you have lost something.'

'No, I don't think so,' I say.

'Yes, I think you have.' I can actually feel Tashi's eagerness radiating on to me. Clearly, she has something to contribute to the conversation. She doesn't know about Alexander so I'm keen to know why she is so confident that I'm a loser. I glance at her.

'You lost your key, remember,' she whispers.

'Right, yeah, but I found it again.' I turn to Larry. 'It was under my bed.'

'It always is,' says Larry. 'I think there's more, though.' I can feel myself colouring. 'Not to worry, you will find something here, even if it is not what you have lost. Be open.' I nod.

'Can you show her the way?' he says to Tashi.

She grabs my hand. 'Of course,' she says.

'You should probably eat less meat,' he says. 'Your energy is stagnant.'

Tashi squeezes my hand. I look at her and she raises her eyebrows. Her eyes say, 'I told you so.'

'I must encourage you to go for replenishments now.' It takes a few seconds for us both to understand we have been dismissed and we stumble a little as our bodies try to catch up with the realization.

★   ★   ★

'He likes you!' cries Tashi as we walk towards an outhouse that serves as the kitchen.

'How can you tell?'

'I can tell,' she says. 'My first meeting with him, he didn't even speak.'

I grab Tashi round the waist. 'The problem is,

102

I'm not sure if him taking a shine to me is a good thing or a bad thing.'

'Oh, it's the best thing,' says Tashi, reciprocating my gesture.

When we reach the kitchen Tashi asks Brett, a bearded Welshman with a gentle manner and questionable tattoos, for our 'assignment'.

'You're on potatoes,' he says. He hands each of us a small raffia sack. I follow Tashi into a vast vegetable patch.

'Just fill it, you're not supposed to talk,' she says before falling to her knees. I think about my Bounty bars. I wonder if I say I'm going to use the toilet I'd have time to go and snaffle one. I look at Tashi pulling away soil, the wind licking her hair into her face, and I decide to try to be open and embrace the process. I start digging tentatively but I quickly discover that my bag will never be full this way and so I increase my fervour, pushing my fingers into the cool mud, fearless in the face of earthworms and other mini beasts. After a few minutes some more people join us. I look up and acknowledge them but I don't break the rules by saying hello. When I've filled my bag, rather than returning my haul to Brett, I help the others fill theirs. One woman appears to be in her seventies; when her bag is full she grabs my hand and kisses it. Her lips are so cold and so rough and yet so comforting.

We all carry our potatoes back together. 'You've definitely earned your supper, sweetheart,' says Brett, taking my sack. He exchanges it for a steaming bowl of vegetable stew. Tashi, the rest of the potato pickers and I sit together on the wooden benches that line the kitchen. We eat in satisfied silence. The meal, though small and lacking in seasoning, tastes wonderful. When I try to work out why, it occurs to me that I may never have been truly, physically hungry before.

★　★　★

Tashi and I have been put in a room on the first floor of the centre, from which you can see miles and miles of unbroken green from the window. I could not live more than five miles from the nearest Marks & Spencer but it's nice to step outside your own life from time to time. Our room has three single beds; one is already occupied by a woman with cropped, grey hair. She is lying on top of the covers and dressed completely in white — even her socks. I cannot tell if she is sleeping or meditating but either way it does not seem like the right time to make introductions.

Tashi and I brush our teeth in the small sink in the corner of the room before getting ready for bed. As I change into my pyjamas I sneak a glimpse of Tashi doing the same. Her legs are thin and undefined, almost colt-like. The little weight she carries has settled around her middle and although not overweight she has a rounded tummy. It's nice; it's womanly and also sort of childlike. I can tell by the way she wiggles quickly out of her clothes and aggressively pulls on her oversized T-shirt that she has no idea how beautiful she is.

We lie in our beds facing each other. 'How are

you doing?' asks Tashi.

'I'm good. No, I'm really good,' I say.

'That's wonderful,' says Tashi, 'I knew this would move you.'

'I kinda feel like I'm on a school trip.' I can't quite make out Tashi's face but somehow I can feel her smile. 'Which isn't a bad thing.'

'Mmmmm,' says Tashi.

I can hear that she's only clinging to the edge of consciousness; perhaps that's what gives me the courage to pause and say, 'I wasn't honest earlier. I have lost something . . . someone. I'm getting a divorce.' It's the first time I've said this word out loud in relation to Alexander and myself. I'm relieved to find the experience is like getting a jab; all the pain is in the anticipation. 'I thought I had lost my husband but I'm starting to think that maybe I had already lost myself a long time ago. Maybe he was just, I don't know, collateral damage or something . . . Tashi . . . Tashi?'

A voice that does not belong to Tashi says quietly but firmly, 'Shut the fuck up.'

12

I dream that Alexander and I are getting married and it's our wedding day, but I cannot find one of my shoes. I search frantically for it, mussing my hair and snagging my dress in the process. I beg my friends and family to help me look but they dismiss me. The church bells chime. I stop my search, take off the other shoe and start running. My anxiety is eased by the sound of the bells fading into the distance. I can hear the wedding guests calling after me but I ignore them until . . .

'Martha, you've got to get up!' It's Tashi; I'm not getting married, I'm the furthest thing from it. When I open my eyes, she's leaning over me grinning. 'We have yoga.' Yoga, I can handle yoga, it's just lying down with good PR. I sit up. Our roommate has already gone to spread her positive karma elsewhere.

'What time is it?' I ask.

'Five,' says Tashi. I lie back down.

'That's the night, Tashi,' I mumble. Tashi pulls the duvet off me.

'It's not,' she says, 'it's the beginning of a brand new day!'

★　★　★

Yoga is led by Sunbeam. She sits at the front of the hall, her eyes closed and her legs folded into

106

a pretzel. Tashi immediately takes a position at the front of the room but I hang back — I don't need a room full of people staring at my arse. Sunbeam rings a little bell which seems to be the signal for everyone to assume the same position and I do the same. She starts making a series of moaning sounds; I look round to see if anyone else is trying not to laugh but they all appear to be going to their happy places. After a few minutes Sunbeam stands and raises her arms, followed by everyone else. She then starts a series of movements accompanied by foreign phrases. Everyone else joins in with her without question and I try to recall the details of an article I once read about cults.

I stay sitting on the floor cross-legged, hoping to find a moment when I can join in successfully. I try to put together an expression that looks peaceful. I don't feel at peace, though, I feel out of step with everyone there and that's a familiar feeling. It's tense and awkward and seems unfair but I recognize it and that knowledge makes me feel unsettled and frustrated, which in my opinion is the worst combination of emotions one can experience. I know I need to cry but not sad tears; sad and angry tears, which are much uglier and generally louder. I close my eyes to try and halt, or at least delay, the process.

After a few seconds I feel a presence behind me. Above my head I hear Sunbeam: 'Carry on with the sequence, everyone. Whatever stage of your yoga journey you are in, remember that yoga means breath. As long as you're inhaling, you are in touch with your yogi.' Without request for consent, two hands clasp my belly. I have to swallow an instinct to start elbowing her in the ribcage, a move I was shown at a self-defence class at university. Her breath is on my neck. 'Just exhale all the negativity you're storing,' she whispers. 'I can feel the tension in your body, it's like it's full of static.' I'm not sure what she expects; she is essentially trying to mount me and she hasn't even bought me a drink. 'Breathe with me,' she says, and the whole thing levels up from creepy to creepy as all hell. I open my eyes and everyone is on all fours and I think I will feel marginally less self-conscious if I attempt to join in.

I wriggle free of Sunbeam, who takes the hint and continues her journey round the class. As the group moves, I try to move with them. The woman to the left of me looks very pleased with herself but if I could put my forehead to my knees, I would also feel smug. The man to my right seems to be struggling with the positions but he is enjoying his struggle, sometimes chuckling to himself as his body fails to meet up with his ambition. The class is much faster than I anticipated; no lying down at all. I have to keep looking up to see what everyone else is doing and as a result I am always a few seconds behind. At one point I stand up to see that everyone else is on all fours again and I feel like crying. The class seems like an analogy for something, something I don't actually want to think about right now. I get down on the floor just as everyone else glides into the next position and I give in. I stay where I am, heavy-limbed and cow-like.

There was a moment during my labour with Moses when I found myself in the exact same position. It did nothing to ease the searing pain of contractions but for some reason I felt safe down there. I could smell the disinfected floor and feel it cool against my palms. The midwife was trying to convince me to stand but I was immovable. Alexander returned from getting a coffee and she said, 'You're gonna have to get her up.'

'I don't know how,' he said.

Sunbeam comes over to me and places her hand on the small of my back. 'That's right,' she says, 'just stay in the moment and breathe.' I can do that; breathing is about all I can do.

★　★　★

Sunbeam announces a five-minute break before chanting begins. I know that I will be tempted to chant, 'You are all frickin' loopy.' So, as the others are milling around, getting water and bowing to each other, I slip out. My intention is to sneak back to my room and eat my contraband and catch up on the four hours' sleep I was robbed of this morning, but as I approach the stairs I'm halted by a little girl, sitting on the bottom step in tears. She's a pretty, skinny thing. Her shiny, brunette curls are in sharp juxtaposition to her muck-strewn overalls. I crouch down in front of her and ask if she's OK. She collapses on to my shoulder and sobs energetically. 'What happened?' I whisper.

'He took my roooooock!' she wails. I hold her at arm's lengths in an effort to protect my eardrums.

'Ah, I see,' I say. Not seeing at all.

'I was playing with a rock and Jack, to — , to — , took it.'

'Where's your mummy?' I ask. The girl points towards the hall door, where the groans of Sunbeam and her followers can be heard.

'OK then. Should I go and talk to him?'

'Yeah,' she says, whilst nodding violently. I stand up and hold my hand out. She grips it with a surprising force for such a small hand. My new friend pulls me into the garden and then behind the kitchen, where, in a clearing surrounded by thicket, is a small crowd of children; it looks like a scene from *Oliver Twist*. The children — a variety of ages and sizes — are shouting and chasing each other and seemingly trying to cover themselves with as much debris as possible. Sitting at some distance is a long-limbed teenage girl, tapping industriously on a mobile phone; I assume she is the allocated supervisor. Watching her, I feel a wave of irritation, partly because she has such a lax attitude to her responsibilities but also because of her access to social media. I also feel sad for the kids, left to fend for themselves as their parents chase enlightenment. I look down at the little girl. Her expression is fearful and something about her vulnerability reminds me of Moses. She deserves more than a rock.

'Is there a tiger here!' I yell. The children stop and stare at me; they look like startled woodland creatures, awaiting further gunshots. I see their shock turn to confusion and morph again to mirth. 'I lost my tiger,' I say, 'have you seen him?'

'Nooooooo!' the children chorus.

'Oh dear, oh dear,' I say, and scratch my head in pantomime fashion. 'If I don't find him, he'll get hungry and you know what he eats . . . ' Some of the children giggle nervously. 'Children,' I say with a growl. The kids scream and scatter. I hold my hands up and shout, 'I'm kidding! He's a vegetarian. He eats vegetables but he'll eat absolutely everything, the whole garden, and then we'll have nothing for dinner.' The children stop and come towards me. 'But you know what he likes? Singing! Especially children singing. Do you want to help me?' The supervisor breaks eye contact with her phone screen and looks up just long enough to roll her eyes at me, but the other children come together and sit on the grass in front of me, my little audience. I sit down with them. My new friend nestles next to me, her rock seemingly forgotten. 'Are all your parents doing yoga?' I ask. They nod. 'What are your names?' All the children shout out their names at the same time. 'OK, OK! One at a time. You start,' I say to the little girl with the curls. 'Tell me your name and something you're really, really good at.'

⋆　⋆　⋆

I teach the children how to sing a round and we manage to produce a pretty rockin' version of 'London's Burning'; the supervisor is even inspired to record a performance of it on her

111

phone. When we hear the breakfast bell ringing, the children beg me to stay and teach them another song. I remind them we should get to breakfast before the tiger does and they scatter. I feel lighter than I have in a long time as I walk back to the main building to find Tashi. Being with the children made me think of Moses and miss him even more but it also made me realize I can be something other than his mother. I had feared that without him to think about I would feel even more lost, but for twenty minutes I had felt more in control than I have in a long time.

I find Tashi in the hall, her face flush with excitement. She disengages from the man she is talking to and rushes over to me. 'Are you OK?' she asks. 'You didn't stay for chanting. Was it too emotional?'

'Yeah, I think it was all a bit much for me. I won't lie, I felt like a bit of a prat,' I say. I start towards the kitchen; everything is better with carbs. Tashi tries to reassure me that it's all just part of the process but I'm concerned it's a process I no longer want to go through. I'm feeling a little embarrassed; I had visions of massages and sitting in window seats reading. My mind flits to my brandy stash.

'It will get easier,' she says. 'When I started yoga, I couldn't even touch my toes.' She says this as if I should find it shocking, as if touching your toes is a thing you're *supposed* to be able to do. As we reach the kitchen Tashi suddenly stops.

'Uhm, go without me,' she says.

'No way!' I counter. I'm not going in alone, but also my stomach is growling an angry protest. I grab her arm and we wrestle a little in the doorway. I'm about to abandon the cause when I turn to see the source of her distress, all six feet of him. The man walks over to us and places his hands in prayer position.

'Namaste,' he says.

'Sure,' I say. Tashi says nothing. I give her arm a little tug but she doesn't respond.

'Tashi, is this . . . is this him?' Tashi nods. 'Excuse us,' I say to the man before pushing Tashi back into the garden. 'Did you know Guido was going to be here?' I say from the safety of behind a tree.

'No, no. Of course not. I thought he was in Kerala,' says Tashi, her eyes still trained on the kitchen.

'You still talk to him?' I ask.

'God, no. I just check his Facebook . . . and his Instagram and stuff.' I place my hands on Tashi's shoulders.

'Well, maybe he's here for a reason. Maybe he's been sent here so you can finally have closure, so you can be at peace with him.'

'I feel sick,' says Tashi.

'Tashi,' I say, 'you are ten times the man he is. Well, you're not a man but you know what I mean. You are so much better than him and so much better than this.' I mean the whole hiding-behind-a-tree thing but a little bit of me means the whole retreat, the whole charade. It's all starting to feel like cheap theatre and if anyone knows about pretending it's me.

'I can't do this,' says Tashi. She breaks away from me and runs back in the direction of the main lodge. I can taste my anger and, propelled by the sense of injustice, I turn and march back to the kitchen.

Guido is standing in the centre of the room, his hand placed on the breastbone of a tall blonde woman. As I approach I hear him say, 'I can feel your prana expanding . . . '

I tap him on the shoulder. 'So you're Guido?'

'Excuse me,' he says to the blonde, who bows prettily and walks away. 'I am honoured to be in your presence,' he continues. 'How can I aid you?'

'You can't,' I say. Momentarily he looks irritated, and in his face I can see the petulant little boy he once was. 'What you can do is wipe that smirk off your pretty face and go and apologize to my friend.' It *is* a pretty face, so attractive it almost becomes boring — almost.

'Who is your friend?' he asks. It is this comment that tips my anger into full-blown rage. Tashi *is* my friend — somehow this ridiculous trip has sealed us — but also she is every woman who has been dismissed by a man. Tashi is my friend but she is also me.

'My friend is someone who you should never have had the privilege of breathing the same air as, let alone been allowed to have anything close to a relationship with. She is a person that if you are clever you will remember as the best thing you never had and who will remember *you* as a brief and regrettable footnote in her otherwise amazing life. My friend is someone who is so beautiful you were blinded by her light, which must have been why you tripped and let your

114

dick fall into some other hippy tramp. My friend is wonderful and graceful, and her name is Tashi.'

Guido lets his mouth fall open for a few seconds. He then shakes his head and says, 'You are filled with so much anger.'

'You bet I am,' I say. Then I pick up a glass of something algae-coloured from the table next to me and throw the whole thing in his face. I think it best to quit whilst I'm ahead, so I leave to look for Tashi. I won't lie; as I walk I hear Beyoncé in my head. At the door to the kitchen a petite Asian girl smiles widely and holds her hand up, and I raise mine to meet hers in a very unzenlike high five.

★ ★ ★

Tashi is huddled on her bed in our cell. Her face is damp and blotchy, and she wipes her nose messily on her sleeve when she sees me come in. 'I'm sorry,' she says.

'For dating that nimrod, you should be.'

Tashi gives me a weak smile. 'I don't know why I let him get under my skin; we only saw each other for a couple of months.'

I sit on Tashi's bed and tuck a piece of her hair behind her ear. 'Tashi, there are some people that are put on this earth simply to steal part of our soul.'

Tashi sighs. 'I guess if I hadn't met him I wouldn't have found Tula Shiki.'

'Yeeeeah,' I say.

'At school I was such a geek,' Tashi says. 'The

idea that someone like him would even look at me . . . ' I want to slap her — affectionately.

'He is clearly riddled with insecurity; he sweats the stuff. You deserve so much better,' I say. 'You know that, right?'

Tashi shuffles towards me and gives me a hug. 'I'll meet someone else?' she asks as we untangle ourselves.

'You can't be serious,' I say, giving her a playful prod. 'It could be worse — you could have married him.'

Tashi laughs. 'Can you imagine?' Sadly, I can. 'I can't go back out there,' she says.

'I don't think he's gonna be bothering you,' I say. I tell Tashi about the smoothie facial I gave Guido.

'Oh my God, I love you,' says Tashi.

'I know,' I say. 'Do you want a Bounty?' Tashi nods.

★   ★   ★

Tashi and I share her bed and my chocolate until she feels ready to face the world, or at least the world of the retreat. 'I think you're right. He was sent to test me,' says Tashi. 'I'm so ready for the meditation now.'

'What does that consist of?' I ask.

'Just being,' she says.

We return to the same room we did yoga in except it's been filled with candles and cushions. Tashi encourages me to take a seat next to hers. The cushion seems to be primarily decorative because I can feel the floorboards through it. The room is filled with quiet chatter; there's definitely an air of anticipation. It amuses me a little that everyone is so excited about essentially doing nothing. The elderly woman I helped in the garden is at the front of the room; she waves at me and I smile back. I probably wouldn't admit it to anyone but I am feeling very peaceful.

Larry walks in and the room falls silent. He sits on the floor facing us all; he does not use a cushion and no one offers him one. Once settled he makes a loud moaning sound and then nothing. No one moves, no one speaks, no one does anything. I sort of want to scream. This is a habit I have — finding myself wanting to do the most inappropriate thing at particularly sombre moments; I can't even see a church without wanting to shout an obscenity. I find myself wondering what George would be doing on a Saturday morning. I picture him sitting on a sofa, flicking through the weekend broadsheets, but this is not really George; this is something Alexander would do, is probably doing, commit-ted as he is to carrying on with his life as if nothing has happened. My leg gets an itch. I try to ignore it but it yells at me urgently. I wiggle around trying to find a more comfortable position but doing so seems to make the itch worse as well as draw the attention of the people around me. Then I want to pee — does nobody else need to pee? I cave and get up, avoiding Tashi's gaze as I creep out backwards.

Sunbeam is in the reception. 'Is everything OK?' she asks.

'Just need a water break,' I say. Sunbeam gives

me another of her bows, as if she's blessing the emptying of my bladder. I examine her properly. Her face is dramatically and irreversibly sun-damaged. Her long hair, naturally high-lighted with white streaks, is starting to dreadlock in the lower half. It's difficult to tell if this is intentional or the result of chronic mismanagement. If I saw her on the high street outside a Tesco Metro, for example, I would think she was deeply troubled. I would assume she was a woman rejected by a society insensitive to the needs of the traumatized or addicted; but here she looks very serene. Trite as the word seems, she appears happy.

'Can I ask you something?' I ask her.

'Of course,' she says.

'Why are you here?'

Sunbeam doesn't miss a beat. 'I'm here to welcome new followers and help them commit to their path.'

'Yeah, sure,' I say, frustrated at what I see as her avoidance of my enquiry, 'but how did you end up here; what was your life like before?'

Sunbeam laughs. I know she's not laughing at me; she's amused by a previous iteration of herself. 'I had a life,' she says, 'of sorts. By anyone's standards, I was successful.'

'What do you mean?' I ask.

'House, husband, friends . . . ' Sunbeam waves her hand dismissively, as if these things are mere trinkets on the charm bracelet of life.

'And you gave it up?' I ask. 'For this?'

Sunbeam pauses. She looks up at the ceiling, searching for the right words there. 'I was playing a game,' she says, 'and I didn't know the rules; no one did. My husband, the one I had dedicated my life to, given up almost everything for, just left me. No word, no explanation. I realized that nothing in life is guaranteed; everything is so transient. What Larry and the group showed me is the only thing you can rely on is the present. You can never hope for more than this moment.' She clasps my two hands in hers. 'This very moment.'

'How long does it go on for?' I ask.

'Who knows? Time is a man-made structure. A moment could be a lifetime, if we wish it.'

I pull my hands away and try not to look afraid. 'No, I mean how long is the meditation?'

'We meditate for the morning,' says Sunbeam. She offers this as if it's a gift. I feel like a ten-year-old who's just found a book voucher under the Christmas tree.

'What's the morning?' I ask.

'Around three hours.'

'Right . . . OK . . . And how long have we been going?'

Sunbeam looks at her wristwatch. 'Nineteen minutes.'

'I feel really uncomfortable,' I say. 'It's a bit hot in here — are you hot?'

'The growth is in the discomfort,' says Sunbeam. 'We all live in a personal hell. Enduring this is the key to your awakening.'

I don't want to endure a single second more of discomfort. I hastily scribble an apology note for Tashi and tell Sunbeam to book me a cab. I don't leave her side until she confirms that it's on its way. I'm getting the hell out of hell but not before getting my phone back.

13

'You're back early,' says Mum as I fall on to the sofa.

'I got let out for good behaviour,' I say.

'I don't understand,' says Mum angrily; she hates feeling like someone is getting something over on her. I start to describe the weekend's events but Mum has already started busying herself packing Moses's change bag, so I stop talking.

Moses comes over to me waving a plastic horse. I pull him on to my lap and make the horse dance up and down his leg, causing him to laugh uncontrollably. 'You might as well come with us to Stanmer Park,' says Mum. I don't really want to — I've just endured a cab, a train and a bus back from the middle of nowhere — I want to have a bath and some recovery time from my so-called retreat, but this isn't an option; Mum is giving me her 'dare to defy me' face and Moses is bouncing like a spaniel that's just heard the word 'walkies'. Before we leave I stop to coat my lips in red. 'Who's that for?' says Mum.

'For me,' I say.

★   ★   ★

Stanmer Park is just a few miles outside town but it feels like a different world. I have always intended to take Moses but other things seemed to come up. On the journey Moses waves his horse enthusiastically as Mum tells me what he's been up to. She insists that he knows his colours on the basis that she asked him to pick out red socks that morning and he did. I tell her that he just loves red socks. 'He is my child, you know. I know what he can and can't do.'

'Yes,' says Mum, 'but you've been distracted lately. I think he's benefited from the consistency of being with me.'

'I've been distracted by the breakdown of my marriage, Mum,' I say. Mum snorts incredulously; I'm not sure what part of my claim this is in reference to.

Mum pulls up outside Stanmer House, the stately home in the centre of the park. I love old buildings like this; I'm always fascinated by the idea people once actually lived here — that we are taking a casual Saturday stroll through what was someone's life. As I take Moses out of his car seat he makes little whinnying noises, and the simple pleasure he takes in this makes me feel a burst of joy that I had a part in creating him. 'I love you,' I say. He whinnies in response.

'We better get him to those horses before he explodes,' says Mum. We walk together through a wooded pathway, stopping regularly for Moses to pick up a stone and examine it before throwing it back to the ground.

'You used to like coming here when you were a kid,' says Mum.

'Yeah,' I say.

'You used to like playing hide and seek. You'd

put your hands over your eyes and think no one could see you.'

'Fancy a game now?' I ask, smiling at her.

She looks at me and frowns. 'Why didn't you wear a coat?' she says.

When we reach the horses, it's clear that the fantasy has not lived up to the reality for Moses and he quickly becomes restless. I try to engage him by holding him up to the fence to get a closer look at a white mare but he just wriggles furiously until I put him down; even the horse seems to be looking at me in a way that says, 'Nice try, love.'

'He enjoyed it last week,' says Mum. The mare sticks her nose over the fence and starts to sniff in my direction. I want to pet her but I can't remember how you should approach a horse; I recall something about a flat palm but nothing else. The horse sticks her tongue out and I quickly step back. She tips her head to the side, which, if there is one, I decide is the equine equivalent of a shrug, and then she backs up a little before galloping across the field. I look down, where Mum is crouched beside Moses, showing him a ladybird.

'Let's go get a scone,' I say. Mum looks up at me and rolls her eyes but she doesn't protest as I start to walk back towards the house.

* * *

We are seated at a table next to an amazing open fire. I order a scone and a slice of carrot cake for Moses and me, while Mum has an espresso.

123

After it all arrives Mum says, 'Are you going to tell me what happened with you and Alexander?'

'Nothing happened, Mum. We got married, it didn't work out, we broke up.'

'Do you think he had someone else?' she said. Oddly this comment doesn't upset me but it offends me. It doesn't occur to her that it could have been me that had someone else, that I could have been the desirable one.

'There was no one else involved, Mum.'

'You don't know, though,' says Mum, 'men can be very sneaky.' I think about Dad shining his shoes at exactly ten o'clock every evening.

'I think you young people give up too easily; as soon as it gets tough you're looking elsewhere,' says Mum as she brushes cake crumbs from around Moses's mouth. When she has finished, I give him another piece.

'I don't know why you're so bothered,' I say, 'you never even liked Alexander.' She doesn't correct me.

'If you had listened to me and delayed the wedding I think things would have been different,' says Mum.

To my mind the wedding was not rushed. I had been wanting it since the day we met, or perhaps the day after; Alexander had not been as sure. He had told me more than once that marriage was an institution and he was not ready to be committed to one. His escaped engagement was a sign, he felt, that marriage was not the right choice for him. I would have been happy with that, to be together but not shackled together, for an eternity. I had made the decision to be happy with that and then I got pregnant.

I knew I wanted children and Alexander had not resisted the idea. Our discussions about a family were always cut short by him making a vague statement about the right time. I think on some level I feared that that time would never come and this was probably why I took such a cavalier attitude to contraception. When the two lines appeared, it felt like a magic trick. I kept closing my eyes and thinking that when I reopened them the test would say something different. I carried the pee-soaked stick through to Alexander in his office. He stared at it for several seconds before saying, 'I'll do whatever you want.' What I wanted was to get married. Never in my life had I described myself as a traditionalist but I was a sucker; I had been sold a lie of fairy tales and Barbie princesses and I wanted my turn. It was the first time in our relationship that I had been insistent on anything and I think it may have been this, rather than the pregnancy or the marriage, that caused Alexander such concern.

I went about choosing invitations and planning guest lists, unperturbed by the anxieties he voiced. One evening I asked him to help me pick colours and it seemed he had reached his limit; he told me he didn't care, he didn't even want to care and he was going out to meet Matt. Matt is the man that every woman loves until he is friends with her partner — good-looking, charismatic and unnecessarily wealthy. The only thing matching the size of his bank balance is his ego. Matt and Alexander went to school together and appeared to have retained a childish sense of rivalry from their youth; they were always pushing each other to go faster and further, and more than once it resulted in physical or emotional injury. The first time I met Matt we were two champagne bottles into the evening when he began telling me that he could have any girl he wanted because he had the cash and connections to meet any woman's needs.

'What do you want?' he asked. 'I can get you anything.' My mind battled to come up with something suitably cool to ask for. 'I can have coke here in twenty minutes,' he suggested. I didn't want cocaine but I said yes just to see if he could actually come through, and he did. An hour later, when half of the supply had been 'tested' by the boys, Matt leaned across our small table and said, 'If Al ever fucks up, I've got a seat for you right here.' He indicated his lap. I turned to Alexander to see how he was reacting, what he might say or do to defend my honour; I'm not sure I had ever seen him look so pleased.

The night that Alexander left me at home with my aquamarine napkins he was anything but pleased. I don't know where he went that evening because I did not hear from him or see him until three the following afternoon. I was lying on the sofa, queasy from hormones and worry, and he knelt on the floor beside me.

'OK,' he said. 'I'll marry you. If you think it best, I'll marry you. Just let's do it without all the crap. Let's do it the way we want it.' The next day he gave me Jenna's emerald and I booked the soonest available wedding date at the town hall.

It wasn't perfect but it doesn't put me off it all; if anything my previous failure has reinvigorated me — how many chances do you get for a do-over of one of life's key events? As soon as I have disposed of this marriage, I want to get married again but I want to do it the right way, with the right man. I look up at the six-foot fireplace and imagine it covered in peonies. I decide that I want to be married right here with someone who knows, to their very core, that marrying me is the right thing for them.

'Excuse me,' I say to Mum. I go to the ladies' toilets, lock myself in a cubicle and pull out my phone.

> **Marthashotbod: Do you want to get married?**
> **Undeterred83: To you? :)**
> **Marthashotbod: :) Generally.**
> **Undeterred83: Yes. Definitely.**
> **Marthashotbod: I'm spending the afternoon with my son. Do you want kids?**
> **Undeterred83: That's brilliant. I really want kids.**
> **Marthashotbod: Why haven't you had them already, if that's not too forward?**
> **Undeterred83: It's not at all. Can I call you later? I would rather tell you over the phone and anyway I think it's about time we spoke, don't you? What's your number?**

I type the digits into the screen with unsteady fingers. Suddenly I'm nervous. Within the next few hours my list will start to become my reality.

14

Mum tells me she needs to go to Waitrose on the way home. I cannot endure a turn round the supermarket with my mother right now; there's a legitimate chance I might brain her with a frozen leg of lamb. In the carpark, she asks me to fetch a trolley and as I do I call Cara.

'Can we meet?' I ask.

'Sure,' she says.

'When are you free?'

'It depends what you need,' Cara says.

'I need to get pissed,' I say.

'Meet me in Neighbourhood in twenty,' she says. I push the trolley over to Mum and she sets about strapping Moses in.

'I forgot there's something I have to do,' I tell her. She doesn't respond. 'I could take Mosey with me but . . . '

'It's fine, you go,' says Mum. 'He'll be ready for a snack soon anyway. I'll see you at home.' I don't wait for her to change her mind. I practically run to Neighbourhood, a small bar squeezed in between the charity shops on the high street. Cara and a strongly mixed drink are waiting for me.

★　★　★

'What's the update on A-hole?' says Cara. I take a swig of my drink.

'Well, first of all, we don't call him that because we're doing a thing called respect and focusing on productive co-parenting,' I say. Cara does the face you make when someone farts.

'I've heard about this co-parenting — isn't it where you don't think about yourself all the fucking time? How's A . . . sorry, it's Alexander right? How's he getting on with that?'

'It's an adjustment,' I say, 'but I'm hopeful. We've agreed the days he'll have Moses and how we'll do the exchange. He's being reasonable.' I don't tell Cara that these arrangements were made over a series of sinisterly formal text messages and that Alexander has engineered things so that he always collects and delivers Moses to nursery and there is no risk of us having actual, human contact.

'Hmm,' says Cara, 'so he's getting his dick wet.'

'That's not relevant,' I say, as I push unwanted images from my mind.

'It's totally relevant,' says Cara. 'Speaking of which, how are you getting on with Linger?' I have a short debate in my head. Just say it, I tell myself, say you've found the man of your dreams and you're working towards becoming the best version of yourself so that you can meet him and fall in love and live your days out together like that couple in *The Notebook*.

'I'm a bit confused by how it works; do you have to swipe right to get a match?'

'Aren't you the one with the degree?' asks Cara. 'It could not be simpler: right for the treasure, left for the trash.'

'But it's random. You can't just get sent a match, based on your profile or something?'

'Give it here,' says Cara, reaching for my phone.

'No, no, it's fine!' I say, snatching it out of reach. 'I'm probably just not ready for it.'

Cara rolls her eyes. 'You don't have to be ready for it, it's not a German invasion. It's not like you have to marry the guy.'

I sip my drink. 'Cara,' I ask, 'have you ever been in love?'

'Sure,' she says, 'I fall in love once a week. I'm in love with the guy that made this drink. I *am* fucking love.'

'But you know,' I say, 'love, love. Can't-live-without-you love.'

Cara examines me carefully. 'Why on earth would I want to put myself in a situation where I can't live without someone?'

'Because it feels good,' I say.

'It feels good to feel like your very existence is tied up in someone else's regard for you?' She doesn't sound like she's judging me; she sounds like she genuinely wants to understand. I don't know how to explain it — it does feel good; even the lows feel good because the lows are proof that the highs are real.

Cara leans in towards me. 'You know what feels good? Knowing that your happiness is a product of nothing but your own damn awesomeness.' Her eyes are intense. I try to turn my head away from their glare but Cara gently pulls my face back towards her. 'When you get,' she says, and I have never heard her sound so serious, 'that no man or child or beast or fucking face cream will make you feel like enough; that being you is enough. That feels really bloody good.'

My throat starts to get hot. 'It's not that I want a man to make me feel good, it's that . . . I don't know . . . '

'You want a man to make you feel good?' suggests Cara and we both laugh.

I throw my hands up and say, 'Is that so bad?!'

'It's not bad,' says Cara, 'it's just too easy.' She reaches out and stops a man walking past our table. 'Would you like to have sex with my friend?' she says.

I say, 'Sorry,' at the same time as the guy says, 'Yeah, all right then!'

Cara turns to me. 'You see? Where was the creativity, the hustle, the magic?' The man clears his throat and Cara turns back to him. 'Did you want something?'

'Err, no,' he says before walking away.

'I believe in magic,' I say. I touch my phone before I realize what I'm doing. Cara downs the rest of her drink.

'Oh God, I can't believe you're gonna make me go all Oprah on you. You *know* how much I hate that shit.'

'What do you mean?' I ask.

She sighs. 'What have you done for *you* since the break-up?'

'Loads,' I say. I tick the points off on my fingers. 'I've signed up for a half-marathon, I've just come back from a retreat . . . ' Cara makes a face like she ate something rotten. 'Also, I've got

132

a business coach.' I try not to smile too widely but I do seem to be on a bit of a roll.

'For what business?' asks Cara.

'The one I'm starting,' I say.

'Why are you starting a business? I thought you wanted to be a singer?'

'Yes, but I'm not sure how practical that is. I mean, singing would be great but I don't have any access to that world; this way I can build the life I want.' As I'm talking Cara raises her arm in the air and holds a peace sign above her head. When I see the barman spring into action behind her I realize she's ordering us fresh drinks.

'I'm an events organizer, babe; if you want a link into performing, I'll get you one. I haven't before because I thought you were kinda committed to the old married lady vibe.' Cara starts to look through the contacts on her phone.

I wave my hand no. 'It's OK — '

'I'm gonna send you to Marc,' says Cara. 'He'll look after you — besides, he owes me.'

'The thing is I'm not sure it's what I want . . . ' The barman places two tall rum and ginger ales in front of us.

'Thanks, darling,' says Cara, and then she says to me, 'If it's not what you want, sack it off. You've had some practice at that recently.' I'd like to be enthusiastic but singing means travel and late nights, something that's tough to do as a single parent, and more to the point not the best plan when you're about to meet the love of your life.

I try to distract Cara: 'What's going on with you, anyway, what are you working on?'

'Don't try to distract me,' says Cara, still fiddling with her phone. 'There, I've sent Marc your details, I've told him you're kinda funky, kinda jazzy, kinda rocky cause I wouldn't know.' She swallows half her drink. 'I'm good, thanks for asking. I've not picked up any new projects 'cause I'm going abroad for a bit, see if I can get anything going in Stockholm.'

'Why?' I say.

'I've always preferred the cold and would you believe I've never been with a blond?' Cara says.

'No, I mean why are you going away and how? I mean, how can you afford it?' I ask.

'Because why not, Martha. You need to start asking yourself that more. I've got some savings but I'll probably rent out my place — actually I was going to give you first refusal.'

'Wow,' I say, 'I don't know — '

'I'll take down the pole,' says Cara.

'No, it's not that, it's just . . . I hadn't thought about where I'm gonna live or anything like that,' I say. Thinking about it now feels like turbulence on a plane; sort of exciting but also like you're possibly going to die.

'Course, I'm sure you've had more important things to think about.' As if in answer to the question my phone rings.

'I'm sorry, I have to take this,' I say.

'No probs,' says Cara, 'gotta see a man about a dog anyway.' Cara leans over and gives me a quick kiss on the cheek before dropping a twenty-pound note on to the table and sliding out of her chair. I make sure she's out of earshot before I take his call.

15

'Hello?'

'Hey,' says George. 'How you doing?' I had expected his voice to be faint, distorted and eroded by distance but it's strong and clear and very sexy — he could do voiceovers for luxury car adverts.

'I'm good,' I say. 'Thanks for calling. Does it feel weird?'

'A little,' he says, and he sounds relieved, 'but in another way not weird at all.' It's what I've been waiting for my whole life, someone who knows exactly the words to make everything OK.

'Where are you?' I ask.

'It's gonna sound crazy but I'm sitting overlooking a waterfall.'

'Wow,' I say.

'Yeah,' says George, 'it's pretty amazing but it would be better to share it with someone.' I feel my face grow warm. 'What you been up to, you've been quiet.'

'I was on my meditation retreat,' I say.

'Cool,' says George. 'The ten-day silent retreat I did was intense. I learned a lot about myself though.'

I think about telling Guido where to go and say, 'Yeah, me too.'

'I can't believe how much we have in common,' says George.

'I know,' I say. 'It's like — '

'Fate.'

'Or something.' We are silent for a few seconds.

Finally, George says, 'How was your day with the boy?'

'Boy?'

'Your son.'

'Oh, of course,' I say. 'It was great.' I tell him a little bit about Moses, about how funny and crazy he is. George makes appropriate noises in response, noises that Alexander couldn't even muster up.

'What did you want to talk to me about?' I ask when I've finished.

'Oh, the children thing; a message seemed a bit impersonal.'

'That's OK,' I say.

'I was engaged a few years ago. We wanted to have children.' And here it is: after all the messages and all the longing, he's going to tell me that he's scared of commitment because he had his heart broken by some tramp. 'She died,' he says.

'Oh,' I say, 'I'm sorry . . . How?'

'She was sick,' he says. 'I knew when I met her but I was hopeful.'

'That's so sad,' I say. In fact, it's tragic. 'Thanks for telling me.'

'It's OK,' says George. 'I wanted to. You know, talking to you I feel so much less alone.'

'I know,' I say, 'it's weird.' I'm annoyed I've said 'weird' again; I'm no poet but my vocabulary is more developed than that. 'I'm sorry,' I say. 'I'm a little tongue-tied — you make me feel like I'm a teenager or something.'

'I couldn't have put it better,' he says. 'I feel like I'm about sixteen but that's the way I want this to feel.' He doesn't define 'this' because he doesn't have to. We both know what 'this' is; this is the start of our story. 'It kinda feels like our first date,' he says.

'A waterfall is quite an impressive first date destination,' I say. 'How will you top it with our second?'

'Where would you like me to take you?' he asks.

'Well, if I get a free choice, The Salt Room,' I say. The Salt Room is a beautiful restaurant on the seafront. I had dropped hints for Alexander to take me there for months and when the hints did not prove effective, I simply begged. He said it sounded pretentious, which is not something he had ever seemed to have a problem with before.

'I can do better than that,' says George. 'How about Paris?'

I don't like France. I know that's a ridiculous statement, like those people who say, 'I don't like music,' as if music is a singular thing. I know that France is a tapestry of people, cultures and climates but I have been several times and on each occasion I've felt as if everything — the people, the food, the architecture — was silently judging me. I like that George has chosen Paris, though, because of what it represents; nothing says 'I choose you' more than a stroll along the Seine.

'I could deal with Paris,' I say, and George

137

laughs. I love the feeling of making him laugh.

'So, we've been to a waterfall and to Paris — what next?'

'A walk along the beach, obviously,' I say.

This is the sort of thing I would suggest to Alexander from time to time, lightly; very, very casually. He would snort as if I had made a wry joke. Once I described to him how a colleague's boyfriend had sent her a huge bouquet of long-stemmed roses to the office, with a note that read, 'Because it's Tuesday.' Alexander, who was watching *Top Gear* at the time, did not remove his eyes from the screen as he said, 'I'm so glad we aren't one of those couples that go in for all that obvious stuff.' It's not that there was no romance in our relationship, it's just that, as Alexander said, it wasn't obvious — you had to seek it out; you had to remain aware at all times, or risk missing it.

George says a walk on the beach sounds perfect, so I leave the rest of my drink and Cara's money on the table and walk down to the seafront.

'It's cold,' I say.

'We better get coffee then,' says George. He's quiet as I buy an instant coffee in a plastic cup from a hatch on the seafront. I settle on to the pebbles to drink it.

'This is romantic,' I say.

'It sort of is,' says George. 'I'm supposed to ask you about your hopes and fears now, right?'

'Oh God, no,' I say. 'Don't kill my buzz.'

George laughs. 'But seriously,' he says, 'what do you want?' The question shouldn't be as complicated as it is but I've spent so long denying or ignoring what I want that I struggle to find a definitive answer.

'I want to stop running,' I say. 'I feel like I've lived every day of my life waiting for it to begin.'

'I know how you feel,' says George. 'I felt the same way until Cass died. Then I realized that what I was running to or from probably didn't matter.'

'Is it time to stop running then?' I ask.

'I think it is,' he says.

'I'm really cold now,' I say.

'OK, I'll let you go,' says George.

'No, no,' I say. 'Walk with me.'

'OK.'

I get up and start to stumble across the pebbles. 'I'm walking towards the pier,' I say. 'Did you know Brighton Pier was erected in 1903?'

George laughs. 'Was it?'

'I have no idea,' I say.

'Tell me the real story,' says George, 'your story.'

'All right,' I say. 'I had my first snog under the pier; it was with a boy called Tyler. He lived in a caravan.'

'He lived in a caravan? How old was he?'

'With his dad!' I say. As I walk under the pier the smell of stale urine takes me back to the moment, the highlight of one of those endless summers of childhood. I tell George all my pier stories: Leanne and I trying our first cigarettes followed by her vomiting violently; a guy I once met and spent the afternoon with, who told me about all the adventures he had had, and only years later did I realize he had been homeless.

'Where are you now?' asks George.

'I'm walking in front of OhSo, it's my favourite bar.' OhSo is right on the beach, and in the evenings they set up environmentally evil heaters. When I drink there I always forget to go home.

'I love it there too,' says George. 'I can't wait to take you.'

I smile. 'I'm smiling,' I tell him.

'Me too,' he says.

We walk the length of the beach. It's dark by the time I get to the end and I realize I'm going to need to take a bus home.

'I should go,' I say, as I make my way back up to the road.

'I hate shoulds,' says George.

'Me too, but this is a real one,' I say.

'Thanks for a lovely date,' says George.

'Thank you.'

'I think this is where I kiss you,' says George.

'It absolutely is,' I say. We end the call. My fingers are so cold I can barely work the buttons on my phone but inside I'm burning up. That was the best date of my life and he wasn't even with me; I can't help but imagine how good it will be when he is.

★ ★ ★

'What have you been up to?' says Mum as I walk into the living room with a smile still plastered on my face.

'Walking,' I say.

'You've been drinking,' she says, narrowing her eyes, 'your face is all red.'

'No, I've just been walking.' I sit down beside her on the sofa. Mum shifts as if to make space for me, although there is plenty.

'Moses is in bed,' she says. 'You've missed him.' It's early still; I imagine her drugging him to prove a point.

'I'll see him in the morning,' I say. I pick up the remote control and start to flick through the channels, although I can't really concentrate on what is on each one. Mum takes the remote from my hand and places it on the coffee table.

'Your dad and I are worried about you,' she says. I look at Dad in his chair; he looks like a dog caught with a chewed slipper.

'You don't have to be worried about me, I'm fine. I'm better than fine.'

'OK,' says Mum, 'we're worried about Moses.'

'Why?' I ask, elongating the word with practised insolence.

'You just seem to have, what do they call it, checked out. Motherhood is not a part-time thing.'

'I know that, Mother,' I say.

'Great. What are you planning to do about it?'

'What do you mean?'

'Well, you can start by getting up with him in the morning.' I *am* up in the morning but I hear her fussing around with him and I worry about being the extra cook that spoils the broth. I can tell Mum is preparing to unleash a full litany of my errors and I don't want to give her the satisfaction.

141

'I agree,' I say. 'I'm on it; in fact, we've got a lovely day planned tomorrow. I'm going to get ready for bed so we can start early.' Mum purses her lips; I feel a fizz of satisfaction at having sabotaged her intervention and leave before she can come up with a response.

I go up to my room and lie on the bed. The frustration I feel with my mother becomes wrapped in a layer of anger, like one of those turkeys stuffed in a duck. The anger is directed towards Alexander, or more specifically the question, what is his part in this parenting fail? Perhaps Mum is right — I should be spending more time with my son; but I also deserve a decent break, a break that should be given to me by his father. It has always been this way, as if Alexander was just an innocent bystander in the car crash of parenthood. I remember when Moses was little, I would do all the feeding and the burping and the bouncing whilst Alexander would just eye him suspiciously. If I asked him to do anything he would express complete incredulity. Sometimes he would offer that the baby was 'too small' for him to handle. Of course, if there were ever witnesses he would be chucking Moses around like a beach ball.

One evening, completely floored by the combination of exhaustion and responsibility, I told Alexander I was taking a bath and asked him to watch Moses for an hour or two. Twenty minutes into my soak I felt like I was beginning to regain access to who I was before my labour and Alexander knocked on the door.

'Where do we keep his pyjamas?' he said. I

heaved myself from the tub, dripping water through the flat as I got a fresh Babygro from the chest of drawers in the nursery. I can't believe I handed it to Alexander and didn't shove it down his throat. I think about ringing my ex and telling him I'm dropping off his son for a week but the thought of doing it makes me feel outraged on Moses's behalf. Alexander can disregard me if he wants to but my child should never feel anything but wanted. Instead I ring Greg.

'Hey, buddy!'

'Are you doing anything fun with the girls tomorrow?' I ask.

'Yeah, we're going to the zoo. Wanna come?'

'Yes please, we'd love to.'

'That's great,' says Greg. 'Have you got a car seat? We'll pick you up.'

I give Greg our address and he says he'll be with us at ten. Moses needs two parents, and if necessary I'll parent for two.

16

Greg honks his horn at precisely ten. I tell Mum to watch Moses for a second whilst I run out with the car seat. Greg gets out of the car to meet me. We haven't seen each other outside the office before and it feels slightly wrong; I don't know how to greet him. I lean in to give him a kiss on the cheek and, at the same time, he tries to give me a hug; immediately I try to convert my kiss to a hug and he tries to redesign his hug into a kiss. We untangle and smile at each other stupidly.

'Need help with that?' asks Greg. He nods to the car seat on the pavement.

'Nah, it's tricksy,' I say. I open the car door and heave the seat inside. Greg's two daughters stare at me as I do so.

'Hi,' I say, 'I'm Martha.' They remain silent. I strap the seatbelt into the car seat but I struggle to latch the belt into the clip.

After watching me grapple with it for some time, the bigger of the girls says, 'You're doing it wrong.' She takes the belt and smoothly clips it in.

'Thanks,' I say. She returns to silence.

Mum carries Moses out. 'Have you got extra clothes in the bag?' she asks.

'Of course, Mum,' I say. Greg extends his hand; Mum hands Moses and the change bag to me before shaking it.

'Lovely to meet you,' Greg says.

'Hello,' says Mum. She has this ridiculous coquettish look on her face. Mum thinks every man is a heartbeat away from falling in love with her.

'Let's move!' I shout. I bundle Moses into his seat. He chuckles at the girls who, unable to resist his charm, laugh back at him. Greg tells Mum to have a nice day and climbs back into the driver's seat. As I go to get in myself, Mum gives me an awkward and unaccustomed hug.

'Have a lovely day,' she says. 'If he likes it maybe we can go next week?'

'Sure,' I say.

In the car I clap my hands together. 'Where are we going!' I cry. No one says anything. 'To the zoo!' I answer myself.

Greg laughs and pulls away. 'The zoo it is,' he says.

Greg introduces me to the girls. 'This is Charlotte and Lyra,' he says. They don't say anything. He makes pleading faces at them in the rear-view mirror but they won't concede. 'They're shy,' he says. I twist round in my seat to look at them. They don't look shy, they look mean. 'Charlotte just lost a tooth so she's self-conscious,' says Greg. Charlotte folds her arms and breathes out heavily. I can tell she is furious at her father's indiscretion; I fear for her future partners.

'Ugh, is it sore?' I ask. She looks at me but doesn't respond. 'You know what helps with that,' I say. She doesn't speak but I sense a slight shift in her energy. 'Singing.' I turn up the radio and Taylor Swift's 'Shake It Off' fills the car. 'The bakers gotta bake, bake, bake, bake, bake,' I sing.

'Noooooo!' squeals Charlotte. 'That's not how it goes.' She is smiling broadly now and I can see the space where her front tooth used to be.

'Oh no, how does it go?'

Charlotte sings along with Taylor. Her sister joins in for the last part of the chorus. I love watching them express themselves so freely and joyously. Moses tries to join in, clapping and wiggling from side to side. I look over at Greg and he looks back at me for a second and winks.

★　★　★

Even though it's drizzly the zoo is quite crowded. By the time we get to the front of the queue the kids are fractious and eager to get on with it. Greg chats to the guy at the ticket booth for a couple of minutes and then waves us through. 'How much do I owe you?' I say.

'It's OK, I had a voucher,' says Greg. 'What first, girls?'

'The monkeys!' they shout in unison.

It's only when we're standing in front of the primate enclosure that I remember that sometimes zoos depress me. They're so sad. I imagine the animals all knowing that their peers are somewhere living it up in the jungle or wherever. I find the attempt to recreate their natural habitat the most upsetting part. The concrete rocks can't compare to anything in the great outdoors; it kinda makes me think they should just give up and go in a completely different direction — base the enclosure on a New York cityscape or something. The girls press their noses up against the glass, and the apes look back at them with very human expressions of tedium.

'They're not monkeying,' says Lyra. She thrusts her bottom lip out and looks to her father. Oh, how I miss those days, when I still held the belief that my dad could fix anything.

'Oh no,' says Greg, 'do you think they've forgotten how to monkey?' Lyra nods sadly. 'I better show them then,' he says. Greg takes on an ape-like stance and starts to side-step along the glass, scratching his head and his armpits and making monkey noises. Lyra begins to giggle. Greg exaggerates his actions further, pretending to sniff other families and beating his chest. Both girls and Moses are in hysterics.

Lyra looks up and points. 'Look, Daddy, you showed him how to monkey!' A large ape is swinging down from a branch at a pace that its size belies. Once on the ground it picks up even more speed, charging towards us with bared teeth. When it reaches the spot where Greg is putting on his show, the ape stretches up to full height and bangs on the glass. The girls both jump back, and the crowd takes in a collective breath.

'Hmm,' says Greg, 'maybe he's not in the mood for a lesson today.' He gathers up one girl in each arm. 'Shall we go, ladies?' The girls nod yes. 'Good day to you,' says Greg to the ape before leaving the enclosure. Once outside we all look at each other and dissolve into laughter.

'Remember when the monkey ran, Daddy?' asks Lyra.

'Yes, princess,' says Greg, before giving her a kiss on the forehead. He then crouches down so that he is eye to eye with Moses and says, 'I think you should choose what's next, buddy.'

Moses throws his hands up in the air and says, 'Fish!'

'The master has spoken,' says Greg.

★　★　★

The aquarium houses not only fish but also a collection of intimidating-looking lizards and snakes, which the girls take turns pushing each other towards while squealing. 'They're pretty rad kids,' I say to Greg as we watch them.

'Aren't they,' says Greg. 'They're the best thing I've ever done.' I feel like if anyone else had said this it would sound cheesy but he really means it.

'It's hard being a single parent, though?' I ask.

'It gets better,' says Greg. 'You'll be OK.'

'How do you know? I . . . I mean, what makes you think I need to be OK?' I think I ask this a little too aggressively because Greg holds his palms up in a gesture of surrender before speaking.

'You've just been out of sorts lately and then the change in shifts and the whole retreat thing and picking you up at your mum's. I assumed . . . '

I almost tell him to mind his own business but

I look at how much fun Moses is having chasing the girls round a pillar and I say, 'It's shit, isn't it.'

'It's the worst kind of shit,' says Greg, 'but then it's a little less shit and then it's even less shit than that and then one day you wake up and realize it's only slightly shit.'

'A soupçon of shit,' I say.

'Just a light smattering of shit,' says Greg, and we smile at each other. The girls run over to us, with Moses following, and proclaim abject boredom.

'Ready for some grub?' says Greg to cheers all round.

⋆ ⋆ ⋆

The restaurant has an animal theme and a menu of basic foods with exotic names — crazy cobra chocolate cake and lion's tail pasta. Greg tells the girls to pick a sandwich each but they have already caught the scent of chips and make it clear that they are unwilling to compromise.

'Come on, girls,' says Greg. 'We've had a lovely day, let's not ruin it. We had chips yesterday and chips aren't a healthy food.' I recognize his voice as a 'parenting in public' one. To many people it might sound like a calm, reassuring tone but other parents can detect the slightly sinister edge to it. Sadly, Charlotte and Lyra don't. Lyra starts to wail and Charlotte begins kicking a wall with a surprising amount of ferocity.

Greg starts to blush. 'If you keep behaving like

this we will have to go home and you will not like that and it won't be fair on Moses,' he says. I look at Moses; having forgotten his buggy he has done more walking than he's ever done in his life and he looks like he'd be well up for going home, but I don't say anything. 'Girls, I mean it,' he says.

I step forward and place my hand on Charlotte's shoulder. She stops kicking the wall and I think for a second she's going to redirect her aim at me but she simply looks at me. Her sister stops crying and does the same.

'Your dad's right,' I say, 'chips aren't healthy. So if you want them you have to eat something healthy with them to balance it. How's this for a deal? If you want chips, you have to have a serving of vegetables first, a big one.' The girls both tip their heads to the side to ponder my offer. I steal a glance at Greg; I'm worried he might be offended at my heavy-handedness but he looks as if he might kiss me.

After a couple of minutes of deliberation and several rounds of eeny meeny, Lyra decides to play it safe with a ham sandwich and Charlotte chooses chips along with a serving of broccoli. We find some seats and settle down to eat. Charlotte immediately starts shovelling broccoli into her mouth, eager to get to the main attraction. Greg tells her to slow down but she shoots him a look that makes clear that eating slowly was not in the contract.

'When we've finished this, I've got a great idea about what we should do,' I say.

'What?!' shouts Lyra.

'Go and watch the penguins have *their* lunch!'

Lyra cheers and her sister nods, her mouth still filled with greenery. Greg reaches a fist across the table and I give it a little bump with my own.

The penguin enclosure is quite a walk from the cafe so Greg offers to put Moses on his shoulders. Moses finds this to be the most exciting thing that's happened all day and I wonder if taking toddlers on day trips is a waste of time and effort. When we reach the pool I lead the way to the best spot, a small ledge on the far side, from where you can see every angle. I remember my dad bringing me here when I was a kid and sitting with him for hours watching the birds. Every now and then he would say, 'You ready to go, love?' And I would usually say no and we would sit in silence for another twenty minutes. When I was around twelve my mum adopted a penguin in my name, which I think meant I had my name on the wall somewhere and I paid for his fish for the year, but by that time I was kinda over penguins, so I never went to visit him.

The zookeeper is telling us about how penguins hunt in their natural habitat. 'This bit's rubbish,' I whisper to Charlotte. She wrinkles her nose with pleasure at an adult saying something naughty. The zookeeper picks up her bucket and the penguins all do their little Charlie Chaplin waddle over to her. She then starts to throw the fish into the water and they dive after them. I remember why I loved the penguins so much; on land they seem silly and ungainly but then they hit the water and they're so agile and graceful you realize you were wrong to laugh at them, because underneath it all, they're badass.

Lyra tugs at my hand. 'I can't see,' she says. I put my hands under her armpits and haul her on to my hip. There, she wraps her legs around me and nuzzles her head into my shoulder.

After the penguins, we decide to call it a day. Greg carries Moses back to the car and Charlotte and Lyra each hold one of my hands. On the drive back the kids all fall asleep so Greg and I sit in silence so as not to wake them. I watch him drive, shifting smoothly between gears and lanes; it feels nice to be with someone so in control. As I watch Greg's broad, smooth hands work the steering wheel I am reminded of the phrase 'a safe pair of hands'. I think with Alexander I just wanted to feel safe. Not feeling safe is exhausting. I message George.

Marthashotbod: I miss you.

My phone rings out an alert when he replies and I whisper, 'Sorry,' to Greg.

Undeterred83: I miss you more.

17

Leanne knocks on Mum's door at 7 a.m., a plan that I felt so positive about the night before but now every cell of my body is rejecting. I try to lure her in with coffee but she won't be distracted; she stays bouncing up and down on the doorstep, her bobbing ponytail exhibiting more enthusiasm than I can muster. 'Have you got those endorphins I keep hearing about?' I ask as I shrug into my hoodie.

'Honestly, babe, it feels like shit for a bit but then there's this point you just break through and get this rush.' She stops bouncing and pulls her left foot up to her bum, and then repeats the move with the other leg.

'It sounds like losing your virginity,' I say.

'Only so much better,' says Leanne, returning to the bouncing.

'It'd better be better than that German exchange student slapping my arse like I'm a horse struggling up a hill,' I say.

'Exactly,' says Leanne. 'If you could pretend to enjoy that, this will be a piece of piss.'

It's not. By the time we get to the newsagent's round the corner, my shins feel like they're on fire. Leanne tries to tell me about warming up and lactic acid but I can't run and listen and breathe so I don't take it in. I think about stopping and getting a Cherryade and a packet of Flamin' Hot Cheetos from Mr Chaudry, the ever-present proprietor, but as Leanne pulls ahead it occurs to me that this experience is like so many others I have had. So many times I've had a goal or an opportunity and I've given it up before I've really got going; I've watched everyone else get ahead as I sat at home and ate Cheetos.

We reach the park and I think this seems like an apt juncture to turn back but Leanne is just getting started. 'We'll only do two laps of the park,' she says. 'At this stage it doesn't matter how fast you go, just don't stop moving.' Leanne sets off at a pace I would use to flee a pursuing assailant, and even if I wanted to try and stay with her I know it wouldn't be physically possible. Instead I move at a speed that isn't walking but could not truthfully be called running; it's a kind of trot and I'm sure it looks ridiculous. It doesn't feel completely ridiculous, though; it feels kind of good. I'm enveloped in a peculiar feeling, a kind of fizziness in my tummy, and it takes me a few minutes to recognize it for what it is: excitement. The second lap feels harder; the knowledge that I am only halfway through becomes a weight on my back. I repeat Leanne's words in my head — don't stop moving. This seems to help and I speak them quietly; then louder, the rhythm of the words matching my steps.

When I finish the lap, Leanne is sitting on the ground with her legs stretched out in front of her and her head bowed forward and resting comfortably on her knees. I fall on to the ground beside her, breathing heavily and trying to focus on the cartoonish, fluffy clouds above my head. Leanne sits up and looks down on me. She has a slightly troubled expression. 'How you doing?' she asks.

I close my eyes for a second and when I open them she's leaning in towards me. I give her a weak smile and say, 'I feel all right.'

Leanne springs up and holds out her hand. 'That'll do for me,' she says.

★ ★ ★

When I get home I can hear that the flurry of morning activity is well underway. I sit on the stairs and message George.

Marthashotbod: Just completed a few laps of St Ann's.
Undeterred83: I love running there.

This makes me decide I'm going to do it again tomorrow and it's the first time I feel grateful that I'm living with Mum and Dad. Moving back to your parents' in your thirties would be a soul-destroying experience were it not for all the free childcare. When I was in a partnership I thought single parenting would be nothing but toil and turmoil, but compared to the casual efforts at fatherhood made by Alexander on a day-to-day basis, and having Mum to get up with Moses, ferry him to nursery and make him nutritious meals, single parenting feels quite freeing.

It also means I've had no further encounters

with my soon-to-be ex-husband. It's not that I don't want to see him; I do. At least, I think I do, but I want him to come to me. I want him to realize the colossal hole I have left in his life and seek me out. We've still managed to avoid contact with each other. He's collected Moses from nursery or I've asked Mum to drop him off. Mum always gives me a little description of Alexander after an encounter, however brief — he looks so tired; he's a broken man; he didn't say it but he misses you. That I believe, but I'm sure what he misses most is the way I magically created clean, folded laundry from dirty clothes. My mother's continued advocacy for Alexander angers me no end; what happened to being on my side? Moses would have to murder several innocent strangers in cold blood before I would even think to utter anything that suggested that I was not completely on his team.

Mum comes into the hallway and pours some water into a flower arrangement on the sideboard. I think I may have let my frustrations with her show, that they may have seeped out, despite my best efforts, through the suspiciously loud crunch of toast or a smile held for just not long enough. I think this is why, as I sit on the stairs, clammy but triumphant, she casually informs me that she has landed me right in it.

'I've agreed to go and visit Mrs Jenson — you know, the lady that lived next door but one? Now she's in one of those wretched facilities. I mean, would you ever do that to me?' She stares at me as I pull off my trainers. When I look at her, it's clear she's waiting for me to respond.

156

'No, Mum.' She wrinkles her nose. Right answer but too late, so still wrong.

'She hasn't got anyone to see her there. I mean, she's got children and grandchildren, but the son is so cold; he was always giving me those stiff little waves. I've made her some of my famous banana cake.'

I rub my feet. I can already tell I'm going to get a blister on the back of my right heel. 'That's nice of you then, Mum.'

'Are you being sarcastic?' she says.

'No,' I say clearly, careful to ensure an even tone.

'Well, I can't tell with you. Everything sounds like you're taking the mickey. Some things in life are serious, you know.'

I stand up quickly and turn to go up the stairs as I say, 'That, I know.'

'Anyway,' she says. She speaks quickly, sensing she's losing me. 'You can't stay late at work as you'll have to be here when Alexander collects Moses. He said he'll keep him and take him to nursery in the morning.' I've already started up the stairs and it's as if my brain takes a few seconds to translate the sound to words. By the time I've understood I'm halfway up. I rush back down to the bottom, so that I'm eye to eye with my mother.

'Can't Dad watch Moses?'

'Don't be silly, he's driving me. What, do you think I'm going to drive there on my own?'

I want to shout, 'Yes, Mum, do something on your own, it might be good for you, you might learn something. Some of us don't have the choice!' Luckily, I'm exhausted by the exercise, or my circumstances, or both, and instead I say, 'You should have checked with me; I can't just tell them I'm not working late.'

'For God's sake, you've put in loads of hours there recently, don't they owe you? Anyway, you're one of the ones in charge — just give yourself some time off.'

I may have let my mother think I have more responsibility at my job than I do. I may have intimated to her that I manage some things and possibly some people. I've never said it outright, but I've never disabused her of any beliefs she may have had along these lines and now does not feel like the time for honesty. Mum takes my silence as acceptance, which I suppose it is.

★   ★   ★

I arrive in the office ten minutes early rather than with seconds to spare. The knowledge that I am going to be face to face with Alexander again has given me a burst of adrenaline. I power walk from the bus stop, then become impatient waiting for the lift's slow descent and take the stairs, two at a time. When I reach my floor, I see Greg standing in the little square of carpet between flights. His eyes are trained on his phone and both of his thumbs are working across the screen. He is so engrossed in the task he doesn't seem to hear me coming and doesn't look up until I'm inches away from him. When he does he breaks into a smile and shoves his phone into his pocket. 'You shit the bed?' he asks.

'What?! No!' I say sharply. This day is stressful enough without my workmates accusing me of incontinence. Greg looks shocked and reaches out as if I might trip and he wants to be there to steady me.

'Sorry,' he says, 'just something my mum used to say. You're not usually early.'

'It's hardly early,' I snap. 'And it's not like I'm always late, not all the time anyway. And just because someone behaves one way for a long time, doesn't mean that that's how it's gonna be for ever, you know.' Greg withdraws his hands and opens his mouth but doesn't speak. He takes a step back and gestures towards the door, like a butler. I feel a prick of anxiety that I have treated Greg — who is always on time, always helpful, possibly (very sadly) the most reliable thing in my life — in such a derisory way, but I also feel completely justified. As a woman, as a mother, I'm expected to be soft and nurturing and agreeable all the time. Not any more.

I sit down at my desk. I've never been here with time to spare before and I feel a bit at a loss. I straighten up the stationery and give the grooves of my keyboard a quick excavation with the tip of a pen; as I'm doing so a mug slides into my peripheral vision. I look up and see Greg with a drink of his own and, even though I still feel a bit indignant, I offer him a closed-mouth smile. It's not just Greg I'm angry with; it's all men, every one that gets to wander about the earth basking in his own privilege, but especially Alexander. I want to know that he's as agitated by the thought of seeing me as I am of seeing him. I want to know that he is affected by me and not just inconvenienced. I deserve that.

On the inside of my handbag is a small pocket. I've never been clear what it's for. It's too small for my phone and until recently had served as a stray-gum-and-pennies receptacle. However, now it holds The List. I pull my bag up from its home next to my feet and smooth the list out on the desk in front of me. As I read I pause at 'long conversations'.

I think I've avoided looking at the fact that these guidelines, as well as being a representation of what I need, are a reminder of a lot of the things I didn't have. Alexander has always been conservative with his words. One day I told him about an article I had read which reported that the average woman says three times more than the average man on any given day, and he responded, 'OK.'

When I first knew him, I was naive enough to think this trait made him enigmatic and that his silence — as counter-intuitive as this may seem — was because he was *more* thoughtful than most. Once, not long after we had met but before we were a couple, I told Cara that we had an understanding that was unspoken. We were at a gig, so I had to shout a little. I told her that so much of what was said between us was in gestures and mirroring and just a connection that wasn't entirely understandable. Cara's face bunched up. I remember thinking she hadn't heard me and was going to ask me to repeat myself, so I leaned in and as I did laughter exploded out of her like a misfiring machine gun. The people around us started to stare and I pulled her towards the side of the room to minimize my embarrassment. Even with my hand vice-like on her arm, she maintained a steady stream of mirth. Once at the side of the room, she managed to regain control of herself. She pushed her hair from her face and met my eyes. I looked at her steadily. I wanted her to know it hadn't been a joke, that just because she hadn't experienced it with anyone, it did not mean it wasn't real for me. She wiped a couple of stray tears from her eyes and patted me on the shoulder gently, like she was offering sympathy to a recently fired colleague. I never really forgave her for that but she was probably right; perhaps Alexander didn't share his thoughts with me because he had nothing to share, or worse, nothing he wanted me to hear. I won't make that mistake again.

'What's that?' I hear Greg say from beside me.

'Nothing,' I say, and quickly fold up the bit of paper.

'I've not got a lot of education but I know what nothing looks like,' he says. 'Is it a secret plan to kill us all?' He sits down in his chair and loads up his computer. 'Actually, don't tell me 'cause then I'll be forced to push the button.' I'm still a little annoyed with him but I can't resist biting.

'What button?' I ask.

'You know, the button you press when you find out people are doing something untoward. We did that training.'

I laugh. 'It's a whistle, Greg, you blow the whistle.'

'Yeah, but that's a bit naff, innit. Makes me feel like a Boy Scout leader or something. Pressing a button, that's more dramatic. You know, like, boom!' He slams his hand on his desk.

'Shut up, Greg,' I whisper. 'You'll get us both in trouble and you better know that before that happens I will throw you under the bus so fast.' Greg turns to me and narrows his eyes as if he's trying to measure a distance.

'Really?' he asks. 'Just like that?'

'No question,' I say lightly.

'Really?' repeats Greg. His face looks searching now and, unexpectedly, I feel self-conscious. 'Are you gonna blow my whistle, Martha?' He holds my gaze for a couple of seconds before his mouth betrays him with a twitch that is clearly an effort to conceal a smirk. I smack him hard on the arm. He bats my hand away with his, ineffectually — an imitation of schoolgirl fighting. I pull my hand back and take a sip of the coffee he brought me; it's good. I put on my headset.

'You know I wouldn't push the button though, Martha,' says Greg. 'I mean, I know we're supposed to but you might have a good reason to want to top us all. I feel like you'd rather I asked you about it, right? Sat you down and said, 'Martha, you seem a little maniacal. Is there any way I can help?''

Just as he finishes speaking my first call comes through, so my response to him is, 'Hello,

162

Martha speaking, how can I help you today?'
Greg winks at me and puts on his own headset.

'I want to know why I keep getting all these charges when I int bought nuffin?' says a gruff Bristolian voice. And so it begins.

★ ★ ★

The day goes by quickly and for once this doesn't feel like a good thing. At lunch Greg asks if I want to go and grab a sandwich with him. He tells me he's planning a trip to Peppa Pig World with the girls and that Moses and I should come. To be honest, it's bad enough having to experience that wretched, porcine brat for five minutes every day; a whole afternoon sounds like a pig-themed hell, but also, I'm not completely sure when I will be free to go with him; what my long-term co-parenting arrangement will be. I tell Greg I'll take a rain check on the sarnie because I have to run to the high street. I need something — a crutch, a talisman — that will give me the strength not to blurt out all the questions in my head when I see Alexander.

In Boots, I wander up and down the make-up counter, waiting for something to jump out at me, some magic fix that I've missed despite a twenty-year commitment to women's magazines. The woman behind the counter offers me her counsel and I tell her, 'I need something that will make me feel like myself again.' She ducks behind the divide for a few seconds and then stands holding a gold tube, a lipstick.

'It's just been released,' she says. 'It's really

natural but it's got these little gold flecks that make it shimmer just the right amount. It's basically you but better.'

'That's exactly what I need,' I say, and put it on my credit card.

★ ★ ★

I can tell Moses is a bit confused when I change his clothes after nursery.

'I know,' I say. 'I'm confused too.' I put him in a clean pair of jogging bottoms and a polo shirt that Mum bought but I've never put him in because I think it makes him look like a tiny golfer. I want Moses to look like he is being parented by someone strong and capable, someone who owns an iron.

As my parents leave, Mum tells me she didn't cook but there's pizza in the freezer. I feel irritated that she thinks I can't fend for myself and simultaneously annoyed that I have to, so I mumble goodbyes to her and Dad and pretend to be preoccupied with packing Moses's bag, even though I can tell she's waiting for more from me. When I don't supply it she leaves wordlessly, and I go to the big mirror in the hallway to apply my new lipstick. It doesn't look like me but better; it looks like me with some slightly shimmery, beige stuff on my lips.

Alexander rings the bell at exactly ten past the hour. His lateness was one thing I couldn't bear about him, even when I was tits over arse, can't see the wood for the trees in love with him. He is never anywhere on time; it's as if he's physically incapable of it. Even on our wedding day I had to circle in the car, which was in fact a taxi clocking up minutes on the meter, so that I could arrive after him. At times it felt like a message, never to forget that, whatever the occasion, his time was more important than mine. Not any more — he is no longer entitled to any of my time and I open the door prepared to let him know that.

'If you can't be on time, you're gonna have to be early,' I say. 'Don't ever keep our son waiting.' I finish before the door is even fully open. Alexander's face is crimson and he nods his head with a nervous energy.

'I know,' he says. 'I'm sorry. I was in this meeting and the director kept banging on. I should have just said something but you know what I'm like, I was being all British about it and just sliding my chair across the room, hoping no one would notice.' I really don't want to but I smile because I know this is exactly what he would do. I recall all the dinners where he battled his way through over-cooked meat or stone-cold vegetables, never willing to draw attention to his unhappiness. 'It won't happen again.' I believe him and I don't know if it's because I don't have all the doubts about our relationship clouding my thinking or because he's started being honest.

'It's OK, come in,' I say, and step aside to allow him space to walk through. Moses waddles up to him and Alexander picks him up and holds him over his head. Moses giggles and kicks his feet and I feel a spark of joy that is quickly extinguished with a bucket full of cold grief. From now on Alexander and I will each revel in Moses's happiness but we will never share it. Alexander settles our son on to his hip and pulls at the collar of his shirt.

'What's this,' he says, 'channelling Tiger Woods's son?' Alexander smiles at me but I don't return it.

'Bring it back, it's new,' I say.

'No problem,' says Alexander in a businesslike tone. 'Anything I should know?'

My stomach jolts. 'About what?'

'Food, poos, you know, the usual.' I feel a bit disappointed. The moment, the one where Alexander tells me all the ways he's hurting and why not having me in his life is tantamount to torture, is not coming. Not today, not ever.

'No, he's been great. How are you?'

'Yeah, good,' says Alexander. 'I've got this new account and they are sucking me dry but they've got three offices in the UK so I'm hoping if I can get my foot in the door . . . ' It's like a time machine, Alexander banging on about his work as if it's the most significant thing going on in the world. I swear there could be a sudden outbreak of war and all Alexander would care about would be submitting his invoices before getting to the bunker. 'I'm bringing in someone part-time,' he continues. 'I've got help, obviously, but I'm getting a freelancer to do some of the artwork.'

I grip the sideboard and focus on not screaming, 'I don't care, no one fucking cares!' I hate that he wants to just pick up where we left off and the hate is glazed with a coat of rage, that

166

in mentioning 'help' he is referencing Poppy the anorexic intern, however obliquely. I pick up the backpack that gets passed between us along with Moses and say, 'That's brilliant, just wonderful. Have a good night.'

'Hey, you asked me,' says Alexander, with the audacity to look wounded.

'Right, but you were late and I've got stuff to do. I don't have time for the whole song and verse.' Alexander looks at me with an expression en route from confusion to amusement.

'What stuff?' he asks.

'Stuff, stuff. My stuff. Stuff that's none of your business.' Alexander doesn't move and I'm forced to walk past him and open the door.

'OK, OK, I'm going,' he says. 'I'll let you get on with your stuff.' He says this with a half smile he does, a smile that has always been an instant aphrodisiac. I'm horrified to discover that even though I hate him in this moment (I hate him in the way a proud, retired man hates the foxes that shit on his lawn) if he kissed me, I would kiss him back.

Alexander moves past me and I shout to his retreating back, 'I will! I'll enjoy doing my stuff a lot, thank you!' And then I throw the door closed behind him. Afterwards, I feel like the door slamming might have been a bit much.

When I'm alone I can feel my tears are close to the surface and I dig out the list to remind myself of what I'm waiting for, because despair can't live in the face of hope.

I message George hello and a few minutes later he replies:

167

Undeterred83: HOW ARE YOU? WHAT ARE YOU DOING? TELL ME, I WANT TO BE ABLE TO SEE IT. SORRY DON'T KNOW WHY MY PHONE IS DOING CAPS.

2) <u>Must be intrigued by me.</u>
His words are like a virtual hug. I swear, if men asked women how they were doing seventeen times as much as they currently do, the divorce rate amongst heterosexual couples would plummet.

Marthashotbod: Just getting ready to go out.

It's a small lie, a white lie, because God help me, I'm going to find something to do. Alexander thinks I have nothing in my life because I gave up what little life I had to cater to his needs. If a man is going to be intrigued by me, I must do some stuff that makes me intriguing. So I put on another coat of my more-me-than-me lipstick and make a call.

18

Is it ironic that I work in a call centre but hate making phone calls? If it's someone I know and trust, I can cope, but when I have to reach out to someone new and by default intimidating, I always imagine they're in the midst of something terribly important and my interruption only serves as an irritant. Unfortunately, Cara's gig contact 'doesn't do internet' so ringing is my only option. And however much my pits are sweating, I'm going to call him because people with stuff to do pick up the phone and make that stuff happen.

'Marc Billingsworth,' he says after a lifetime of rings.

'Hi,' I say. 'This is Martha Ross.'

There are several seconds of silence in which I think we may have been disconnected and then he suddenly barks, 'Good for you, love. What do you want?'

'Oh,' I say. I hadn't really planned beyond this point. 'I think Cara messaged you about me ... ?' Marc coughs, seemingly without moving his mouth away from the phone. 'I'm ... are you there?'

'Yes, love, spit it out.'

'I'm ... I'm a singer.' Now I've said it, I suppose I am.

'I gather that. Yeah, all right, anything jazzy will do. You'll have to do all the standard stuff but at the end of the night we mix it up a bit. Can you come down about half nine and let me hear a number? If it goes all right I can get you on for a full set next week.'

'Tonight?' I manage to squeak.

'No time like the present, darling,' he says.

★　★　★

After our call I go into what can only be fairly described as complete meltdown. The problem with my singing goals is that they have pretty much only manifested in my head. When I was eight my mother, father and I stayed at a self-catered apartment somewhere in Greece. The holiday itself was a bit of a disappointment; the resort appeared to have a concrete theme and my father got second-degree sunburn on our first afternoon there. On our final evening, in a desperate attempt to rescue our disastrous trip, my mother made us all attend the dinner and cabaret put on at a local restaurant each night. As we sat in front of rubbery chicken and watched a string of failed musical theatre students leave their souls on the stage, I felt increasingly tired and fidgety and full to bursting of that end-of-holiday feeling when all you want to do is return to the damp comfort of home.

Maybe it was because I was feeling so despondent that the headline act had the impact that she did. She was tiny, so small that at first glance I thought she was my age or even younger. Then I clocked her tight purple dress and deep red nails and, to me, she was the

170

epitome of womanhood. Little as she was, her presence filled the room and had she simply stood there I would have been in love. But she didn't only stand; she released the purest, most moving sound I had ever in my short life experienced. She sang an old Whitney Houston song, and the themes it covered — sex, infidelity — I knew nothing of but the feeling she sang it with, that I knew. That was universal. I told myself that when I was a grown-up, I would be *that* woman, or as close to her as I could be.

It might seem strange but from that evening forward I knew singing was something I would eventually do; it was only a matter of when. According to Marc, my when is now; the panic I feel is induced by years of longing and not an ounce of preparation. I don't even have a song ready, and more importantly, what will I wear? I spend thirty minutes pulling all my clothes out of my wardrobe and rejecting them as too old or too sad or too trashy. Eventually I settle for a black dress I bought for a funeral — not that exciting but clean and vaguely flattering. I find an old songbook from my piano lesson days in a cupboard. It's filled with wartime songs but I figure I can jazz them up a bit. I sing the opening lines of 'A Sentimental Journey' but it doesn't feel right. I think maybe it's because I don't have music, so I find a video of Doris Day singing the song on YouTube and try to duet with her. This only serves to emphasize how far from competent I am and my head starts to itch as the sweat collects in my hairline. I call Cara and tell her about the audition.

'I can't do it,' I tell her.

'Sure you can,' she says. 'You book an Uber and get your butt into it.'

'No, no, I mean I'm not ready,' I say.

Cara tuts. 'Martha, I do not have time for your histrionics.'

'I just need to relax a bit. I can't curb my nerves.' I hear what sounds like Cara getting into a car.

'Relaxing I can do,' she says, 'gimme five.' And then she ends the call. I sit on my bed, staring at my phone. The problem with having a soon-to-be boyfriend in Africa is it's not really convenient to ask him for a hug.

A number I don't recognize flashes on the screen and when I answer a voice says, 'You want a twenty-five bag or a forty?'

'Uhm, I think you have the wrong number,' I say.

'Nah, Martha, right? Cara said you needed me to hook you up.'

'Hook me up how?' I ask.

'With weed, right? It's good stuff. So, twenty-five or forty?'

'Twenty-five or forty what?'

'Pounds, lady.' I'm silent for a few seconds whilst I contemplate the madness of this call. Like many things Cara does, it's crazy but also a little genius. I realize that being a single parent could be kind of like living a double life. I can spend part of my time being a responsible parent and my child-free evenings enjoying a life of glamour and debauchery.

'Twenty-five, I guess,' I say.

172

'Safe, let me know your address and I'll be over in thirty.'

I stand up. 'No, no, no.' I imagine my parents' neighbours watching me open the door to the friendly local drug dealer. 'Can I meet you somewhere?'

'Whatever you want, lady. Meet me outside the cinema on London Road in thirty.' He hangs up.

'OK,' I say to no one in particular.

★   ★   ★

I am completely clueless as to what one wears to meet a drug dealer so I put on the funeral dress. When I reach the cinema, there is no one to be seen and then I realize I don't know who I'm looking for anyway. What does a drug dealer look like? It's not as if they can wear a company T-shirt. I'm starting to think the guy's not coming when I hear a voice behind me call my name.

'Oh, hey Martha!' shouts Greta as she waves energetically.

Greta attends the same mother and toddler group as I do, when I have the mental strength to attend. Her partner goes for the odd pint with Alexander and we've had dinner at their elegant Victorian terrace on several occasions. Greta has sharp but beautiful features and always looks harassed but in a smug way, as if she's only flustered because she is consistently running from one fabulous thing to another. When Greta reaches me she briskly kisses me on each cheek.

As she withdraws she slowly looks me up and down and says, 'You look good,' because what else are you supposed to say after you've examined someone in this way?

'Thanks,' I reply.

I'm about to return the compliment when she says, 'I'm sorry about you and Alexander.' It's strange, hearing about the split from outside my own head. Whenever someone else brings up the separation, the outline of the concept becomes more solidified.

'Oh, thanks. It's OK, though,' I say.

'Between you and me,' Greta says conspiratorially, 'I think it's really tacky, him taking up with that Poppy girl. Men are so lazy sometimes, they'll just take the first thing in front of them.'

I nod voicelessly. It becomes very important in this moment not to convey that this is the first time I am hearing this information. It comes as a blow, even though, if I'm honest, it was knowledge I already had on some level. I knew it the way that suspicious partners know the truth before they check their lover's phone; my heart knew it but my head was holding out until the bitter end. Before I can think of a response we're interrupted by a short, pale young man wearing wire-rimmed spectacles.

'We speak earlier?' he asks.

'Excuse me?' says Greta, with haughtiness practically oozing from her pores. 'Are you lost?' The guy looks from her face to mine quickly.

'Who's Martha?' he asks.

'I'm Martha,' I say quietly.

'So are we doing this?' He begins tapping his

foot self-consciously. I look at Greta.

'You want the weed, lady?' he says.

'Drugs!' shouts Greta, as if she wasn't gurning her tits off every Friday in her pre-baby days.

'I'm sorry, I — ' I say.

'Lady, this ain't how I like to do business,' says the boy.

'I'm sorry . . . '

'I'll see you around,' Greta says, still looking at the boy. Then she grabs my forearm and says to me, 'Look after yourself.' She speeds off, clearly eager to find someone with whom she can share this stellar piece of gossip.

'Here.' He looks around before handing me a small plastic bag full of what looks like dead parsley. 'Get me next time. I don't usually run tabs but, yunno, it's Cara.' He turns and jogs out of sight. I stuff the package in my bra and walk home quickly.

★   ★   ★

Back at home I lock myself in Dad's office, which is actually a very large shed in the garden, and since he recently retired, is more or less functionless. In the shed I set about rolling my first joint. I've smoked cannabis before — there was a semester of university when I was more often stoned than not — but it was always a guy procuring the drug and preparing it for consumption. I'm not sure how much to put in and I forgot to purchase tobacco when I self-consciously asked Mr Chaudry for Rizlas, certain my intentions were clear on my face. I take about a quarter of the bag and pack it in to the paper. I look back at the house to check my parents haven't come home before lighting up and taking the first drag. I'm hit by a familiar light-headedness and almost immediately I think that maybe, possibly, I can do this audition; so I take another deep inhalation.

I hold my breath for as long as I can and when I finally release it the sensation takes me back to a moment with Alexander. Shortly after we became a couple he convinced me to go to a world music festival in Spain. My taste in music falls more into the category of pop than progressive but at the time I carried a feeling that having snagged Alexander I should not let him out of my sight. On day two of our trip Alexander managed to buy a batch of brownies, baked with an extra special ingredient. We spent the afternoon sitting on the grass, chasing our treats with warm beer. By the time the evening had set in, I was done. Alexander tried to encourage me back to the tent but I just settled down on to the cool grass. I felt very sure that if I attempted anything vertical I would vomit or worse.

'It's OK,' I murmured. 'I'll just stay here.'

Alexander tugged at my vest top. 'You can't stay here, baby, we have to go to bed.'

'We don't have a bed,' I said very logically.

'Well, tent then.'

'No,' I said firmly, 'here.'

Alexander lay down and spooned me on the grass. 'You are so mashed, my beautiful, so very mashed.'

'Hmmmmm,' I said.

'Whatever my little mashed princess wants she will receive. We will make our bed on this Spanish soil and I will protect you from the beetles.' I know he said that last bit to inspire me to move but I didn't care, I kinda liked the idea of it. When my only response was to pull his arm tighter around me he laughed.

'So we're really gonna stay here then?' he asked.

'If that's OK.'

'Whatever you want; we'll stay here all night,' he said. I think he was trying to be dramatic but that's what we did. I woke in the morning to discover that my neck no longer had a full range of motion and my mobile phone had been stolen but I was so very happy.

After my second toke everything starts to feel a bit furry. My body feels too heavy, particularly my head. I lie down on the tatty two-seater sofa Dad rescued from Mum's last home makeover and close my eyes. That feels terrible so I open them. It's times like these that you need a boyfriend, for when you get disastrously stoned by accident and need someone to remind you that you're probably not dying. Also for when you can feel something strange on your back and you need someone to check if it's a zit or something more sinister; or for when you want to call in sick but you know if you do it yourself you'll fake-cough a suspicious number of times; or for when you bump into Chloe Leonard, who used to terrorize you at school, and you want her to believe that you are loved, that you are capable of being loved.

Apart from these things, being single isn't as bad as I thought it would be; it's like a whole drawer of my brain has been cleared out of Alexander and is now available to hold so many other cool things. Like maybe I will learn to waterboard or maybe I will keep bees. I think maybe I have confused waterboarding with something else but it's the concept and not the details that is important. The freedom to explore who I am, without the annoyance of having to manipulate the experience to accommodate someone else's wishes. Not having to consider someone else's feelings every minute of every hour is good, but I must admit it is nice to know there's a person thinking about you. Little updates from George are what get me through the day at the moment; for example, he'll message me to say he had some chicken and he didn't think it was cooked through. It's uplifting to know that I am the one he needs to tell him he might get the shits.

This, I realize, is a brilliant idea for a business. I'll provide a service that messages single women with cute, affirming messages throughout the week. I'll get them to create their own list of the perfect man's attributes and base my communication on it; a kind of virtual boyfriend. He will tell you he loved last night's dinner and he thinks you're beautiful; he will never forget your anniversary or start sleeping with his barely legal personal assistant. I haul myself to sitting and grab a piece of paper and pencil from Dad's desk to scribble down my business idea. I can already see the logo — an outline of a man sitting on a moon. Maybe I will call it Man in the Moon or maybe To the Moon and Back. Maybe I won't go with the whole moon thing but the rest is gold. I sink back on to the sofa. I'll just have a little nap, go to my audition and then take over the world.

I wake up an hour later, fifteen minutes into my audition. A piece of paper beside me says, 'Fake . . . Messages . . . All the pretty things . . . ' I call Marc and tell him my son is unwell and I can't leave him.

'Little fuckers,' he says. 'No worries, I trust Car. She knows her talent. I'll put you in for a full set in a couple of weeks.' I can't feel my legs but I have my first singing gig.

19

When I read the email, I think I'm still high. It's so unreal I print it out so that I can actually hold it. I then keep it in my pocket for the entire afternoon and it plays on my mind like a backing track throughout the day.

Collecting Moses from nursery, I take on the role of an engaged parent. I ask about his day and praise the artistic talent displayed in his haphazard splodges, but despite my efforts I pull on his coat a little too briskly and push him into the buggy hurriedly because I know my mind will not quieten until I have addressed the contents of the message, which reads:

Martha,

I want to apologize for how things with us ended. Don't feel bad, it was absolutely my fault. I thought I was ready to move on but being with you made me realize that I was still in love with Rhiannon.

We've reconnected and I knew that I couldn't let her get away from me again so I'm pleased to tell you we're engaged.

We'd both like you to come to our engagement party on 4 November, at OhSo from 8 p.m. You are an important part of why we are able to celebrate the occasion.

I hope you are well and have been able to make positive decisions of your own.

Kind Regards,
Tom

I must have read it a dozen times and at every reading the structure and content is the same. It's enraging and also completely baffling — for a start, how did he get my email address? I guess it's true that with a little time and effort he could have investigated me online but Tom is not that guy. Tom would only have my contact details if they were right in front of him.

★   ★   ★

Leanne opens her front door. I have Moses in one arm and with the other I hold up the email like it's a search warrant. 'What the hell is this?' I demand.

Leanne lifts her left eyebrow. 'A piece of paper,' she says.

'Where's James?' I say. I hand Moses to Leanne and push past her, leaving the buggy on the porch.

I walk straight through to the kitchen and Leanne follows me with Moses, saying, 'Hi, Leanne, how are you doing? Oh, I'm fine, yeah the kids are great.' I ignore her; I have no time for pleasantries. James is sitting at the kitchen table, his slippered feet resting on a chair. When he sees me, he swallows the biscuit he's eating guiltily.

'Hi, Martha,' he says, but his greeting is a question. I give him the answer.

'What moved you to talk about me to Tom?'

'Huh?' says James. I slam the email down on the table. James looks at it and then back at me and then behind me to his wife. I push James's feet from the chair so that I can sit down and force him to look me in the eye.

'This is an invitation to Tom's engagement party. One that he has sent me as some sort of charitable act.'

'Right,' says James. Leanne places Moses in front of a wooden toy kitchen in the corner and comes and stands between me and her husband. She puts her hands on her hips, fully embracing the role of referee.

'James,' she says. 'Did you and Tom talk about Martha after their date?'

'No,' says James. 'Well, not really.'

I slam my palm against the table, sending the family hamster into a flurry of activity in his cage. 'You did or you didn't: there are no 'not really's in this scenario,' I say.

'Erm, OK, so yes.'

Leanne covers her face with her hands.

'I mean, barely,' continues James. 'Obviously he asked me if you were OK — he said you seemed a bit angry after your date.' James's eyes flit wildly between the two women before him.

'And . . . ' says Leanne.

'Well, I said no,' says James. 'I said you were having a hard time, you . . . with . . . you know, stuff. I thought it might help to explain things . . . '

I smack my forehead with my hand several times. I consider that if I seriously injure him right now I could offer a very reasonable defence. Leanne crouches down beside her husband.

'Honey,' she says, 'it almost never helps to explain things, OK?'

'OK,' says James. 'I'm sorry — '

'Just stop talking,' I say. Millie comes into the kitchen. She's wearing a Batman costume and holding a small plastic handbag.

'Mummy, can I have a snack?' she asks.

'Yes, darling,' says Leanne. She prods James in the thigh. 'Go get them something to eat.' James gets up and pats me on the shoulder before rounding up Millie and Moses. Leanne takes his chair.

'Don't worry, if Tom mentions you at the party I'll set him straight,' she says.

'Oh, I'm going to the party,' I say. 'Thanks to your husband I have to.' I look at James, who has the grace to look embarrassed.

'But . . . I don't understand . . . ' says Leanne. I hope I wasn't this ignorant when I was in a relationship.

'I have to go to show him that I am, and look, amazing,' I say.

'Let's go see if Dora is on,' says James, ushering the kids out of the room.

'Why do you care what he thinks?' asks Leanne. 'Move on with your life; he clearly has.'

'Ouch! Let's just run that one in a little deeper,' I say, and then, 'Whatever. I don't care what he thinks.'

'You clearly care what he thinks,' says Leanne.

'OK, I care, but only in the most time-sensitive, transient way.' Leanne gives me an unconvinced face. 'Really, I just don't want him to think all women are helpless little walkovers

— it's a feminist act really.' Leanne opens her mouth to say something, something I know will be a chastisement, so I interrupt her and say, 'Anyway, I'm kinda seeing someone.'

Leanne closes her mouth then asks, 'Who?'

'His name is George,' I say.

'Like the list George?' Leanne asks.

'Exactly like the list George. He's got red hair and everything.'

'Where did you meet him?' she asks.

'On Linger,' I say. I can feel my blood pumping faster as I gear up to spill the beans. Leanne stands up.

'I'm gonna need wine for this,' she says. Leanne pours out two large glasses of shiraz and I tell her all about him. I downplay the overwhelming sense that we are destined to be together but she clearly feels the significance because when I finish talking she remains silent for a few seconds.

'So his name isn't George, it's Nathan,' she says. I understand this is why I didn't want to tell people about him; because it's human instinct to want to taint things. I remember going to visit a butterfly house at primary school. Before we went in we were told under no circumstances were we to touch the butterflies and we all nodded our heads solemnly, but of course as soon as we were ushered in, those beautiful but forbidden wings were far too inviting.

'Well yes, but you're missing the important bit!'

'Which is?' asks Leanne.

I smile. 'That he gets me, that he wants me.

184

I'm so excited about meeting him and I'm nearly ready, I just need to lose a few pounds and get the work thing sorted . . . '

Leanne shakes her head as if she's trying to empty it. 'What's the point of him wanting you if you're just going to change who you are?' she asks. Leanne is really annoying sometimes.

'You know, you're really annoying sometimes,' I tell her.

'Annoying or right?' Leanne asks.

'Definitely annoying,' I say.

20

Lisa has procured a clipboard from somewhere. I've never noticed one in the office before, so I suspect that she has purchased this specifically for her role of Unpaid Christmas Party Planning Dictator. Lisa informs us that the theme of the party will be tapas and almost everyone nods agreeably. Lisa's hair is styled in a very intricate arrangement. Waves muddle with plaits and meet in a glossy ponytail at the nape of her neck. It's the sort of style that should be impressive but makes me feel a little bit of second-hand embarrassment, because I know it has taken three YouTube videos and a can of hairspray to achieve the look and that the whole thing was contrived in the hope that just one person would say, 'Ooh, that looks nice.' That makes me feel a little sorry for Lisa because it's a hope I recognize — that something I have achieved, however minor, will be acknowledged. That's why I feel a little guilty when I raise my hand.

'Yes?' asks Lisa, with a glare that says, 'Who let you in?' I lower my hand, conscious of the other people in the room waiting for my response.

'Uhm, it's just I'm pretty sure tapas isn't a theme.' Lisa rolls her eyes and throws me a smile that could be given no other description than patronizing.

'A theme is just a feeling, Marsha,' she says.

'Yeah, Marsha,' says Greg from beside me, 'it's just a feeling.' I can hear the catch in his voice, where I know a laugh is lurking. I stare at my knees so that I can't look at him and fail to keep my composure.

'See,' says Lisa, 'Greg gets it.' I raise my head, expecting to see him pulling a face or sneaking me a sideways look, but he is winking at Lisa and for a minute I'm unsure if he was joking and that uncertainty makes me feel uncomfortable.

'Let's all decide what area we're going to cover,' says Lisa enthusiastically. I am given olives. I think it's a punishment. I decide not to care. As we're leaving Lisa asks me to stay behind, as if I've been caught passing notes in the back of her class. I really want to walk out but my feet are politer than my mind.

'Everything OK?' I ask. 'I really got behind the tapas thing in the end.'

'Don't worry about it,' says Lisa, and I'm annoyed she thinks I was. 'I just wanted to ask you something.' She stops and her mouth twists to one side. She's assessing me, checking if I'm a worthy source of information.

'Of course,' I say.

'You sit next to Greg, right?'

'Right,' I say. For a second I think she's going to make a complaint about him and I want to run. The thought of pushing the button on Greg makes me nauseous.

'I was wondering if he's single?' She lowers her eyes bashfully as she says this and I'm glad because it means that she doesn't see my own widen with surprise.

'Yeah,' I say, after too long a pause. 'I mean, yeah, I think so.'

'And you'd say he was a good guy?' she asks.

'He's the best guy,' I say, and I mean it. Her body relaxes and she lets out a pretty laugh.

'I know he's not the tallest but he's so funny and, I don't know, he's sorta got something about him. He's really kind, you know.' I do know this and I feel embarrassed because I realize that, in a vague, unformed way, I had believed his kindness had been inspired by me.

'He's tall enough,' I say, a bit offended on Greg's behalf. Lisa smiles.

'I guess so. I mean, I usually wear flats so it'd be OK.' Even in her kitten heels, the top of Lisa's head only reaches my nose. I don't know why she would want a tall guy. What exactly would she do with all those extra inches? Put them into storage? Share them with her friends? Lisa's response is jarring; I didn't intend to communicate that he was tall enough for her — I meant tall enough for someone, tall enough for anyone — but I can tell that my throwaway comment has greenlit whatever fantasy Lisa has been concocting in her head.

'OK, thanks then,' says Lisa, and then she turns to start tidying the room, carefully collecting abandoned pieces of paper with sketches of sombreros and lists such as 'Best Cheeses'. I don't say anything to her before leaving, which is my way of expressing disapproval, but by the time I reach my desk I worry that leaving without speaking might be like a disgruntled customer not leaving a tip. The waiter doesn't understand you're unhappy, they just think that you're a twat.

Greg is packing up and doesn't stop as he says, 'The theme is definitely not cultural sensitivity, then?'

I laugh and feel a rush of relief. 'You know what's really awkward?'

Greg looks up. His face is eager and I wait a beat, so I can enjoy this.

'Lisa just asked me if you're single.'

Greg's eyes widen for a second and then he does a little swaggery jig. 'Still got it,' he says in an American accent. He returns to packing his bag with no further comment and I worry that I've made a faux pas by informing him of Lisa's crush.

'Sorry,' I say. 'I didn't mean to embarrass you or anything.'

Greg removes his jacket from the back of his chair and slips it on. 'No problem,' he says. 'Why would I be embarrassed? Lisa's a cracker.' He grabs his backpack and swings it over one shoulder.

'Catch you soon, amigo,' he says with a chuckle.

'Bye,' I say, and then watch him walk away, his bag bouncing with every step.

8) Has to be tall.

Lisa's comment about Greg's height makes me think that it might be wrong to have a personal requirement based on physicality but then I recall a string of messages in which I asked George to describe himself and he told me he is tall, so tall he rarely fits completely on a standard-sized bed, and he told me that he had been on the rowing team at university and that the discipline had left him with defined arms, even though he no longer found the time to train that much. I could not resist — although I admit I did not try — imagining myself being enveloped by him, for once feeling dainty and for ever feeling protected.

Rather than getting ready to leave work myself, I message George.

> **Marthashotbod: I can't wait to feel your arms around me.**
> **Undeterred83: Be careful what you wish for. Once I get hold of you I might not let go.**

To myself I say, 'I think I'd like that,' but I reply:

> **Marthashotbod: What're you up to?**
> **Undeterred83: Setting up camp. Climbed a mountain today. The altitude effect is crazy.**

What's crazy is that he climbed a mountain. For fun.

> **Marthashotbod: Mountain?! That's awesome.**
> **Undeterred83: Maybe we can bag a peak together some day. I love Grasmoor.**
> **Marthashotbod: Sure.**

And I feel, as I often do when I interact with George, a sense of optimism that makes me a little breathless. He is healthy! He is mountain-climbing healthy, which by my standards is exceptionally healthy. The idea of hiking and climbing and exploring with him is wonderful in theory, although it doesn't jibe with my lifestyle to date. When I wrote the guidelines I failed to take into account that a successful, tall, exceptionally healthy man may want a mate who matches that. It doesn't seem fair to offer this perfect specimen of a man a woman made of poorly stitched together scraps. I want him to meet someone whole and happy, someone who deserves to be his equal.

Even though I'm getting concerned looks from the rest of my shift teammates, who are racing to the exit, I remain at my desk and pull the list from my bag. I can recite it from memory but I read it again and then I turn it over and start another list on the back. A list of what he might want, but more importantly a list of what *I* want — for me.

1) Must be healthy in mind and body and have an outside form that is representative of her inner worth.
2) Has plans and ambitions and must be taking steps to ensure they are achieved.
3) Always bold, assertive and unwilling to accept bullshit in any of its presented forms.
4) Speaks French.

I cross out the last one. Even a woman with ambition can't commit to learning French in a few weeks. I feel like I should write more, create a list for myself that equals the one I have outlined for my mate, but it's so much harder doing it for yourself. Still, I like this girl I've described. And I know that a girl like her wouldn't slug home and watch two episodes of *Hollyoaks* and feel sorry for herself. She would play with her son, eat dinner with her loved ones, go for a run and reward herself with a long bath. So that's what I choose to do.

21

It clears my head hearing the thump of my feet on the pavement. I can't really think about anything except the burning in my throat and that comes as a bizarre reprieve. I feel a bit of empathy for the crazies I met at the retreat; pain is a short holiday from the incessant whirring of my mind.

When I get home and go inside, I fall back against the front door and wait for my legs to remember what they're for. Mum pokes her head around the living room door and eyes me with a mixture of suspicion and contempt. 'Be quiet,' she hisses, 'you'll wake Moses.' Any warmth created by our family dinner earlier flies out of the building.

'He's my son,' I remind her firmly, assertively, 'I know what level of noise would wake him.' Mum retreats without comment. I slowly climb the stairs to take my bath and I hear Moses making the low groaning sound that's usually a prelude to crying. I swear under my breath and creep into his room. His blanket has been kicked from his body. His eyes are closed but he is twisting his head from side to side; he's on the edge of awakening but putting up an admirable fight. I carefully place my hand on his chest and start to sing, slow and very low. It's a Stevie Wonder song that I have used as a lullaby since Moses was safe in my belly and would keep me up with his nocturnal disco dancing. After a few bars I can feel his breathing start to slow and then return to his little snorting snores.

As I take off my clothes, I catch myself in the mirror. I have a body that would be aptly described as sturdy. It would probably be good for living on a farm in 1923 but it doesn't fit with any modern-day goals of woman-hood. After I had Moses my body didn't, as they say, 'bounce back' — my stomach hangs lazily over the waistband of my pants and my breasts have been left sad and empty. Exercise is several steps in the right direction but, obviously, I have to go on a diet. I have a gig, an ex's engagement party and a real-life date with the love of my life to prepare for.

Diets and I have a weird relationship; we're sort of frenemies. I hate them, I talk endlessly about removing them from my life, but then as soon as I'm in trouble I run right back to them. I have been on various iterations of the following diets: low calorie, low sugar, low fat, low carbs, no carbs, no meat, no wheat, no dairy, no food, no fun. I have failed at them all, evidenced by the fact that I have to keep going on a new one. This time will be the last time, though; I'm ready to start a new life at a new weight. I think in the past it wasn't that I didn't have the right diet, but the right motivation.

After my bath I write out a diet plan of one thousand calories a day. It includes a couple of treats a week but most of the good stuff has been removed. I kind of like that, though; I don't deserve good stuff right now. I never understand it when people try to sell diets by saying they don't feel like a diet. I think the punishment is part of the process. If I don't feel like I can never go through this again and want to die, what will prevent me from putting on all the weight again? When I'm done, I feel a bit more at peace. I have a plan for my body, for my life and for love.

I gather a family bag of crisps, two Kit Kats, a slice of Victoria sponge cake and a bottle of pinot grigio, because before every diet there must be a really big blowout. You have to eat so much of the wrong kind of stuff that when you wake up in the morning you don't actually want to eat again anyway. As I work my way through my stash, I do what I always do — I revisit all my Facebook photos, analysing my body throughout the years. There's a period in 2012 when I definitely look a lot thinner than I thought I did. As I scroll I get a message from George.

Undeterred83: I'm bored. Entertain me.

I pour myself another glass of wine before replying.

Marthashotbod: How can you be bored, you're in Africa.
Undeterred83: I'm bored because I don't have you.
Marthashotbod: Good point. What are you doing?
Undeterred83: Nothing. In my cabin,

having a beer. What you wearing?

There it is. The text message that every guy sends at some point and every girl, depending on how drunk or horny or needy she is, can choose to embrace or ignore.

> **Marthashotbod: Wouldn't you like to know?**
> **Undeterred83: I would actually. That's why I asked.**

I am wearing a pair of my dad's old pyjamas. The elastic is all but gone from the waistband, which is partly why they were chosen.

> **Marthashotbod: Knickers. Black ones.**
> **Undeterred83: And?**
> **Marthashotbod: A smile.**
> **Undeterred83: Awesome.**

I relax now as I realize there isn't much to this sexting business, just suggesting you're semi-naked and up for it. Alexander and I started dating at a time when mobile phones were basically a tool for logistics and not the actual method of dating.

> **Marthashotbod: What are you wearing?**
> **Undeterred83: Cargo shorts. I'd rather be wearing you though.**

OK, I recognize this juncture. This also happens in the physical realm. The moment when the man tries to push his luck and the woman grants or denies him access, a dance performed since the dawn of time.

Marthashotbod: I have a feeling you would wear me well.

Access granted.

Undeterred83: I would. I would wear you out.
Marthashotbod: How long would that take?
Undeterred83: As long as you needed.

I unwrap a Kit Kat whilst I think about my reply. It could be a good opportunity to educate him, but if the universe has listened he won't need direction and men hate being told what to do in bed. I eat a finger of chocolate to see if the sugar helps to kickstart my creativity, and he writes:

Undeterred83: And as long as you needed again.

OK, that works for me. To the point, without being totally, obnoxiously obvious about it. There was a guy in my university halls like that; we called him the cheerleader because he would announce every act as if you both hadn't just been there to experience it — 'Yeah, grab my arse! Whoo, condom on!' I lick some chocolate off my fingers before typing:

197

Marthashotbod: I can't wait to get you out of those shorts.

Undeterred83: You can't! I can't wait, I think you're lucky I'm not there now.

Marthashotbod: Not long to wait though.

Undeterred83: Too long, please let me have a preview.

And here we have it: the question every girl must also answer. To send pictures or not to send pictures? I've heard all the horror stories and I know all the rules — no identifying features, nothing too graphic — but still, I've never sent a risqué picture to a guy, not even Alexander. The concept doesn't offend me; I get it — the teasing, the anticipation. It's like how I sometimes look up a restaurant's menu online and choose what I want to eat the day before I visit. What scares me is offering a guy solid, undeniable evidence of my flaws, something he can refer back to. The mind is fluid and creative; it will airbrush cellulite and stretch marks from a memory. A picture does not lie.

Everything with George feels like an adventure, though. I get the sense that if I do everything differently maybe this time will *be* different. I take off the pyjamas and then wrap myself in a bath towel. I take twenty-four different pictures of myself lying across the bed. It takes me quite a few minutes to find one that has enough skin showing to be considered sexual, if not sexy, which also hides enough of my body for me to feel OK sending it. Once I have selected the shot, I crop and edit it to the point where I can almost look at it comfortably, and then I send it before I lose my nerve. George doesn't reply for four terrifying minutes but when he does he says the only thing I wanted to hear.

Undeterred83: Wow.

22

After the engagement invitation from Tom, I have been avoiding my emails, which is why I missed three from Patricia. Three on top of the two I had previously ignored. When I still don't respond, she switches her weapon of choice to the phone and I slip up one morning when I answer a call from a withheld number.

'I'll assume that it's because you're off living your best life that you haven't been in touch,' says Patricia. Her tone is curt, rather than full of its usual frothy exuberance.

'I'm sorry,' I say, 'my kid's been sick.'

'Kids get sick all the time,' she says. 'The world of business doesn't stop for a head cold.' I tell her I'll be in to see her as soon as I can. I take the folder she gave me and also a leather-bound notebook I bought to fill with all my business ideas, which both remain empty.

When I arrive at her office Patricia starts speaking before I even sit down. 'You're late on your next instalment, so I'm sorry but I'll have to charge you a fee,' she says. When she says this she does actually sound sorry, as if she has no control over the appearance of this fee; the fee, capable of independent thought, has simply turned up, determined to ruin my day.

'I guess I've spent longer on the research period than I thought I would.'

'OK,' says Patricia, the bounciness back in her

voice, 'what have you got so far?'

I fumble with the hem of my T-shirt. 'I guess I'm not much further than where I was.'

'Right. Let me just pull up your details.' Patricia taps briskly on her keyboard. 'OK, you want to set up a support service for lonely women.'

I wince. 'I want to help women. I guess I want to support women to find something better than they have had in the past.'

Patricia types as I speak. She hits the 'enter' button with a flourish and then turns back to me. 'And what experience do you have of this?'

'Of what?' I ask.

'Well, what have you experienced in past relationships?' This is the big question; moving forward is not just having a list of what you want but having a sackful of non-negotiables too, all the things you will never again tolerate.

'Nothing,' I say. Patricia looks confused. 'I mean, no passion, no joy. A relationship should be two amazing people coming together to become two really amazing people together. In my past relationship it was like two average people coming together and making the other less than average.'

Patricia nods slowly. 'So you're saying you have to work on yourself before you commit to a relationship?'

Am I saying that? 'Yeah, I guess so.'

Patricia takes off her glasses and smiles at me conspiratorially. 'Let me tell you a little secret. My partner, Phil, adores me.' As Patricia says the word 'adores', she elongates its vowels and rolls her eyes. 'I mean, he literally worships the ground I walk on. That definitely happened because I had my house in order before I took up with him.' I glance down at Patricia's chest. On her red blouse is a small stain, toothpaste I think. 'Also, he gets a bit of the other, whenever he wants. No questions asked.' I have questions, but this is not the time. 'So, tell me about your current relationship,' says Patricia.

'I'm not in a relationship right now.' I think of George. 'Not quite.'

Patricia puts her glasses back on. 'Well, this is a problem,' she says. 'How can you educate others on something you have not done yourself? I mean, where's your test model?'

'That makes sense,' I say. I feel a familiar hot sensation behind my eyes, and noticing what is threatening to occur, Patricia hands me a couple of tissues from her sleeve. I take them and dab at my eyes before blinking a few times to try and stem the flow.

'Listen, this is what I'll do,' says Patricia. 'Just get me this instalment and I'll put your account on pause. You need to invest in yourself right now. Get some therapy, get a bit of a makeover, find your dream guy and then teach other women how to do it.' Patricia is smiling and nodding as if this is the most revolutionary idea ever conceived.

'I don't know. I've already tried therapy . . . ' I say.

'OK, I see what's happening here: you need a clear-out. A soul clear-out. You can't become the phenomenal businesswoman I know you can be without saying cheerio to this scared little creature.' As Patricia says this she waves her hand in my direction. I think the comment is sort of mean but I'm pleased that she referred to me as little. 'Let's go on a field trip — this one's on the house.'

Patricia takes a minute to pack her belongings into a vast tapestry bag and apply another layer of lime green eyeshadow. She leads me out on to the main road and sets off purposefully.

'Can I ask where we're going?'

'You should always ask where you're going,' says Patricia, 'but I'm not telling you.' Patricia and I weave through tourists in the Lanes as we walk; she seems to be giving me a guided tour of the city. 'I got my engagement ring fixed in that jeweller's. Phil gave me something that belonged to his mother; they got me a new stone and a new band and now it's perfect ... The empanadas there are literally to die for; I mean, you have to take a first-aider with you because it's literally to die for.'

I feel like telling her that I've lived in Brighton almost my entire life and that if you tried to tell a Spaniard that the food in that restaurant was to die for, they'd probably kill you. I don't say anything because I'm not sure that Patricia would care. I wonder what it takes to be so sure of yourself and if, after I have finished being mentored by her, I too will have this self-assurance.

Patricia leads me to a groyne on the seafront. A doughnut-shaped piece of art sits on the end of it and it is a place I have always loved. I harboured a secret hope that Alexander would ask me to marry him here, as it would be such a romantic spot for a proposal; perhaps hope is not lost. I say a silent prayer that Patricia won't ruin the place for me. She leads me to the edge of the groyne. The wind crashes against us and I have to concentrate on staying upright.

'OK,' says Patricia, 'let her go.' I feel a little bit anxious; I mean, I really don't know this woman. 'Send everything you no longer need out to sea. Scream it into the surf and let it carry it all away.' When I don't react Patricia faces the water and shouts, 'A belief in scarcity!' She then turns and looks at me. After a couple of seconds I shout the same.

'Very good, but you have to choose your own things and also you need to be about ten times louder.'

I think for a few seconds and then I shout, 'Fear!'

'Good,' says Patricia.

'Low self-worth!'

'Yes. Good, good.'

I glance behind me. 'People are looking,' I say.

'People will always be looking,' says Patricia.

I exhale deeply and shout, 'Disconnection from the world! A feeling of inadequacy! Alexander Eric Ross! Shame!' I'm on a roll now. 'Disorganization! Procrastination! Self-loathing! Unhealthy habits! Low motivation! Indecisiveness! Bullshit!' I stop. I'm smiling. I feel free.

Patricia pats me on the shoulder. 'Excellent. Now does that sound like a woman who doesn't pay her debts?'

I promise Patricia that I will get her money to her as soon as I can, and she leaves me standing looking out to sea. I really want to be a woman without all those negative things — my biggest fear is that George thinks I'm already that woman. It would be nice to think he would love me *and* my flaws but I've tried that and it didn't work out so well.

I lost my baby before the wedding. Not 'lost'. Before my wedding day, my baby died. I remember the precise moment my symptoms shifted from 'commonplace' to 'concerning'. Alexander said something along the lines of 'what will be will be', definitely something that belonged on an Instagram post and not in the mouth of my soon-to-be betrothed. The wedding day was a haze of pain, both physical and emotional; the only bit I really wanted was to fall asleep with my new husband but sadly I was unconscious before he made it up from the bar.

My parents sent us to the Algarve on honeymoon. The first morning we had tea and toast on our balcony overlooking the coast and I thought, I might be willing to try again, or at least to take the risk of looking forward and not back. Apparently, Alexander was thinking the same. He told me he'd been considering it for a while and he wanted to give birth to something big.

'When we get home,' he said, 'I'm going to set up my own business.' Alexander had been working for a small design company for years, but like every employee on the planet he thought he was ridiculously undervalued and woefully underpaid. I wasn't sure it was the best idea; you can throw a stone in Brighton and hit a graphic designer. Also, new businesses and newborns don't really mix.

'It means you're gonna have to hold the fort for a while,' said Alexander. I agreed because sitting in that gentle morning light I didn't know what that meant; I didn't know that it meant a year of anxiety as I fell deeper into debt.

As soon as we got back on British soil, Alexander Ross Design was born. To his credit, he made it work. He sought new clients with a determination I had never seen in him before; I took this to mean he was committed to building something for us. Almost exactly a year to the day after Alexander told me his plan, his business was turning a profit and he celebrated by buying a classic MG — soft top, two seats. Now it's my turn. I'm going to create something out of nothing, and I may not have someone supporting me financially but I have someone behind me emotionally, which is priceless.

Marthashotbod: Just had an amazing session with my business mentor.
Undeterred83: Because you're amazing.

23

However quirky I find Patricia to be, I respect what she is saying. I want to invest in myself, I'm desperate to create change, and desperate times call for desperate measures. It's out of pure desperation that I offer to work a night shift. I hate them. The office is full of the lost and lonely, the people with no one who cares where they are at three in the morning. It's like corporate purgatory. You get time and a half for working after ten but you pay for that with a little bit of your soul. You have to man the phones even when no one calls and the majority of the time no one does. When you do get a call the customer falls into one of two categories — drunk or mad.

My line is particularly quiet tonight. It leaves me alone with my thoughts, which is not always a fun place to be. When my phone rings I'm relieved. I ask how I can help and I mean it.

'Where's Darren?' asks a woman.

'Hi,' I say. 'I'm Martha, I'll be helping you today.'

'Well, I don't want you. I want Darren.' Mad.

'I'm not sure who you spoke to earlier but I'm sure I can help you.' I hear some shuffling, after which the woman recites the customer hotline.

'Is that the number?' she asks.

'Yes, it is,' I say.

'Well, it's supposed to be Darren.' She says

this as if she has caught me out in a lie. 'Can you get me him?'

'What is it you would like to discuss?' I ask.

'None of your beeswax,' snaps the woman. 'Darren told me I could have all this stuff but I ain't got no stuff.'

'What were you expecting, Madam?' I ask.

'I don't know — that's why I need to talk to Darren. He told me with the gold plan I get all this stuff . . . '

'Well, the stuff isn't actually physical,' I say. 'I mean, it's not tangible stuff.'

'Eh,' says the woman, 'you calling me a liar?'

'Listen, lady,' I say, 'I don't know what's going on here but it feels like you've got more problems than your preferential customer plan.'

There is silence on the line and then the woman says, 'I have half a mind to — ' I cut off the call. I have no desire to hear what she plans to do with her half a mind. When I'm angry I want to cry; it's one of the traits I like least about myself. It's so ineffective, and you end up communicating completely the wrong message. Often it results in an awkward hug with someone I hate.

I escape to the break room before the tears arrive. When Greg comes in shortly after me my head throbs with irritation. I really want to be alone but then he hands me a Twix and I soften. I'm probably more hangry than angry. I thank him and experience a brief moment of guilt about the chocolate's impact on my diet before cramming both fingers in my mouth at the same time.

'Yeah,' says Greg, 'You just had this kind of wild, low-sugar look in your eyes.' I hope that my face tells him I'm not amused, because my mouth is too full of biscuit and caramel to speak. 'And from what I understand chocolate solves every female problem, right?' I finish my mouthful.

'With beliefs like that I can see why you're divorced,' I say.

Greg laughs. 'That's not why I'm divorced.'

'Why then?' I ask, popping the last bit of Twix in my mouth.

'It's a long story,' says Greg. 'We didn't appreciate each other and wanted different things, et cetera, but the radio edit is she started shagging the guy upstairs.'

I make a noise like I've been punched in the gut. 'That's harsh, Greg.'

'Yeah, I know,' he says, 'I was there.' Greg clocks my astonished expression and clarifies: 'Not literally there but, you know, I experienced it. The weird thing is the long story is true too, but I don't know if it happened before or after she . . . you know.'

I lean forward and pat Greg on the knee. 'It's obvious you wanted different things,' I say. Greg smiles weakly at me. 'She wanted to shag the dude upstairs and you didn't want her to.' There is a moment of silence before Greg collapses into laughter. Watching him makes me feel much less tired. 'What about Lisa then?' I ask, keeping my voice light, letting the words slip out quickly. I've seen them a couple of times having earnest-looking conferences in the hallways. When I walked past them once, Greg stopped and said hello, feigning politeness to keep their conversation under wraps. He never mentioned it afterwards and for some reason I hadn't wanted to bring it up until now. Greg's face grows serious. He's quiet but I can tell he's not being evasive, just seeking out the most honest response.

'I've only really been in relationships. Even at school I didn't do dates; I was committed. I'm not sure I know how to play the game. It's not about my ex — honestly, I'm over it. It's just that sometimes the idea of dating seems tiring.' I smile, even though Greg isn't looking at me as he speaks.

'Do you want a coffee?' I ask. 'I brought in the posh instant.'

'Yes, definitely,' Greg says.

'On another double shift?'

'Bills to pay, yunno,' he says with a tired smile.

I go and make us two milky coffees. As I make them I realize I don't know how Greg takes his so I don't put in any sugar. I tell Greg this as I hand him the mug and he insists he is 'sweet enough'.

'So how did you get over it?' I ask, clutching my hands around my mug like I'm sitting beside a camp fire.

'If I'm honest, I didn't really,' says Greg. 'Maybe I won't ever. It wasn't even the sex. I mean, some guy putting his penis in my wife: *not* on my bucket list, obviously, but I think I could have dealt with that. It was all the lying; all the messages; all the bullshit that went with it.' I nod. 'She didn't even tell me — he did. He came straight up to me one day when I was bringing in the shopping. I felt like such a prick. Her face when I confronted her. I almost laughed — she looked like a cartoon character, you know.' Greg uses his index fingers to mime his eyes coming out on stalks. I laugh, and he smiles.

'So you didn't end it straight away?'

Greg takes a sip of coffee and shakes his head. 'I couldn't. My dad left when I was eight; I couldn't do it to the girls.'

'What changed?' I ask.

'Me,' says Greg. We both drink our coffees in silence for a bit before Greg asks, 'What's happening with you?'

I wave my hand dismissively. 'It was done before it was done.' Greg nods. 'I'm just looking to do it again and do it right this time.'

'How will you know when it's right?' asks Greg.

'When I can relax,' I say. 'When I know I have what I've been waiting for.'

'Which is?'

'Everything,' I say.

'Obviously,' says Greg.

'I mean all of it: the mixtapes, movies in bed, homemade soup when I'm ill and giving me his coat even when it's not that cold, even when I've already got a coat on.' Greg laughs but it's not a 'you're hopeless, I'm so glad I'm more evolved than you' laugh; I think it's a laugh of recognition. 'If I can't have all that, I just want someone who would step in front of a train for me. You know, your standard to-hell-and-back,

211

dragon-slaying stuff.'

'You don't want much then,' says Greg, 'just your standard dragon-slaying stuff.'

'Right,' I say, and he winks at me.

'I know what you mean,' says Greg. 'You'd think we'd be more cynical after divorce.'

'I'm not divorced yet,' I say.

'Aww, well maybe when it comes through you'll wanna forget all this romance business. You'll probably just want to stick all the men on an island and forget about us.'

'Could I visit the island?' I ask him. Greg grabs a flyer for the inter-office football team from the coffee table, screws it up and lobs it at my head. It bounces off and lands in my lap. I pick it up and raise my hand.

'Don't even think about it,' says Greg. 'You don't know what you're starting here.' Before I retaliate, Anekwe, the IT supervisor, walks in.

'Having fun?' she asks, raising her eyebrows.

'We'd better get back to work,' I say. Greg has his back to Anekwe and makes a face at me. 'Come on,' I say, before pulling him up from his seat. 'You can stop me from traumatizing any more customers.'

24

I only manage to grab a few hours of fitful sleep when I get back after the night shift before Mum walks in unannounced with my fractious toddler in her arms. She deposits my son on my stomach and says, 'I know you've been working but, may I remind you, motherhood is a full-time job and I've got water aerobics.' I grunt in response. Moses starts to smack me in the face so I sit up and give him my phone to play with.

'Morning, baby,' I say to Moses. At the same time the phone rings out an alert. I prize it from his fingers and he looks like he might cry so I get my laptop from the floor and put on *Thomas the Tank Engine*.

Undeterred83: Hey! How are you?
Marthashotbod: I'm OK.
Marthashotbod: Can we talk again? It's
important.

George tells me he'll try me in half an hour, which leaves me with thirty long minutes to fill. I run a bath with loads of bubbles for me and Moses. I set Moses between my legs and as I do I notice the pedicure Leanne got me a month ago has grown out and chipped. I scoot down so that the warm water can start to work on the tension in my back.

'Duck,' says Moses. I forgot his bath toys. I

give him a loofah sitting on the side of the tub.

'Duck,' I say. He looks at it, only slightly doubtful, before pushing it under the water.

'Quack! Quack!' he shouts as it bobs back up again. If only all men were so easy to please.

I was so anxious about becoming a mother. I probably spent more time on the internet researching childhood diseases than asleep that first year. It's strange because the reality of babies is that they're very easy. They need to be warm, they need to eat, and they need to be cuddled. Everything else is just frills, stuff to make you feel good. I wonder if things would have been different if I'd invested more time into what Alexander needed? I was so worried about whether I could be a mother, the most natural thing in the world, but a relationship with another adult I expected to just excel at. I believed it was my right to be in a happy marriage. I wanted a singing career, I wanted a baby, but I never believed it was guaranteed that I would have those things. A relationship, on the other hand — of course I would because, well, everybody gets that.

'You have me,' I told Moses. 'Don't assume you'll get more than that unless you work really hard on being a really good person who deserves it.' Moses tries to eat the loofah. 'Don't eat that,' I say, and take it from him. He looks like he might cry so I give it back.

I pull myself out of the bath and dry off. When I've finished I look at myself in the full-length mirror. I have no memory of looking at my body and being happy with what I saw. I often hear women talking about their favourite and least favourite parts of their bodies but I don't have either; I hate it all just a little bit. I think I was one of the only women in the world to actually look forward to having a post-baby body — at least then I had an excuse. I put on Dad's bathrobe and as I am lifting Moses out of the bath I hear my phone from the bedroom. I run down the stairs, clutching my son under my arm like a sandbag. In the kitchen, Dad is watching a programme about people trying to buy houses in Spain; I shove a dripping Moses in his lap.

'Can you take him? I have a call,' I say, and I don't stop to hear his reaction. In my room, I fall on to my phone, convinced the ringing will stop as soon as my hand reaches it; when it doesn't I'm surprised and I fumble as I try to take the call.

'Hello?' I hear George say.

'Hi! Hi! Hello.' My breathing is heavy; I hope it sounds sexy.

'It's good to hear your voice,' he says.

'You too.' It feels like we've never been apart, rather than on two separate continents.

'What was it you wanted?'

'Oh yes, that.' I sit on the bed. 'This is the thing. I'm concerned you don't realize . . . I mean . . . The thing is . . . I need you to know I'm a bit fucked up.'

'Aren't we all?'

'No, but like, I mean . . . I'm worried you don't understand I'm a mess. I mean I'm going through a divorce, I think.'

'You were married?'

'Well yes, exactly!'

'Don't worry — we all have stuff going on, just ask my therapist.'

I play with the cord of the dressing gown. 'I know, it's just . . . I'm not quite the person I want to be, maybe not the person you want to be with, if you want to be with me.'

George pauses. 'I'm pretty sure I do,' he says, and it feels like I've solved a riddle. I've done the one thing I've always avoided doing when getting to know a guy — told the truth.

'As long as you know that things are kind of up in the air right now. I'm in transition at work. My ex isn't great, he hasn't really stepped up with childcare. He's kinda left me to work things out. I'm doing all the hard work and nothing's changed for him — he's still got his work, he's living in our flat, he still has my cat, for God's sake.' George doesn't respond; maybe I got carried away with the honesty thing. 'I'm sorry,' I say. 'I shouldn't offload on you like this.'

'You should,' says George. 'I want to know what you're thinking. He sounds pretty pathetic — who keeps someone's cat? That's just evil.'

I laugh and I swear I can hear him smiling. 'Well, he was our cat, Moxie, that's his name, the cat. He was our cat but, you know, not really. He was *my* cat, you know.'

George laughs softly. 'Break-ups are hard. Don't worry about it. You can tell me anything.'

I lie back on the bed. I feel like I'm a teenager again, or I guess what I would have felt like if any boys had called me.

'I guess I just don't want to feel like I'm

216

overburdening you.'

'But isn't that what I'm for?' An interesting concept. I spent a lot of time with Alexander trying to make sure that I didn't burden him in any way. I kind of thought that was my job; I never considered another option might be to share the burdens.

'OK. Actually, that sounds really good.'

'So hit me . . . '

'What do you mean?'

'What's the worst thing you've ever done? Burden me.'

'Ha ha!' This seems so wrong; this goes against everything I know about being a woman trying to attract a man, but I guess this is the ultimate test. If I give him my worst and he can take it, then maybe he deserves my best.

'I went through a period when I was in my teens of stealing stuff from shops. Nothing big, stationery mainly, but then I felt too guilty to use it and stashed it all under my bed.'

'Ha ha! So you didn't commit to a life of crime?'

'Also, I once told a bride she looked fat on her wedding day.'

George laughs again. His laugh is so deep and even. 'Who?'

'My cousin.'

'How old were you?'

'Six.'

'I think we'll let that one slide.'

'OK, also' — I'm sort of warming up now; I think I'm kinda getting the whole Catholic confession thing — 'I let someone take the blame for setting the chemistry lab on fire at school.'

'And arson. Nice little catalogue of evil there. I'm going to have to take all this under advisement.'

'OK, fine,' I say. I feel a bit foolish for starting it all but I also feel wonderful that I did. 'What's the worst thing you've done?'

'I killed a man once.' For a second, time stops, until I hear him chuckle down the line. 'No, the worst thing I've done is let too many opportunities pass me by.' We both pause to let his words sink in. 'Don't worry about not being whole; it's a journey. And go get your cat. I'd never let someone keep Marley from me.'

'Who's Marley?' I ask.

'My cat — she's with my mum at the moment.'

9) <u>Has to like animals</u> and will have a cat called Hendrix.

Marley. Close enough.

25

Details matter. The fact that George has a cat might seem trite, a bit silly, but it says so much. It says that he's kind and nurturing and that he can commit to something. I see now that I've been approaching the task of changing my life in a big-picture way, when I need to be working on making each day different, working on the individual minutes. I find a running schedule online, one that outlines a weekly target of circuits. The first session is walking for twenty minutes at a steady pace. I know I can walk; I do it every day. I just need to walk with intention.

When I go out for the first time, the park is almost empty. A woman with an overexcited terrier says hello as we pass and I love the interaction — two independent women, doing something productive with their evening. As I walk away I imagine she is saying to herself she might do a bit more tomorrow — put on her trainers, take Fido for an extra-long run. I see her reasserting her promise to herself that she will finally get started, because she has seen me and I already have.

I sit down with Mum and work out a proper routine for our new living situation. I let her know I'll be getting up with her and Moses in the morning and will give her and Dad some money for keeping us. To my surprise she's accepting of this and when we've finished our chat she leaves the room and returns with a large cardboard box.

'I've saved some of your books,' she says. I wonder why she has waited until now to bestow them upon me, but as I pull out the yellowing hardbacks, I am taken back to long afternoons curled up on the sofa with my dad and I push aside any analysis of my mother's motivations.

'You loved that one,' she says, as I flick through *Fanny and May*. It's the story of two elephants who build a house out of cake and then one of them eats it and they are left homeless. I recall the fear I felt as the young elephant couldn't stop herself from eating the roof and the walls, a helpless victim of her own gluttony.

Moses is playing with some bricks on the kitchen floor and I take him and the book into the living room. We settle together into the armchair and I tell him a story I know by heart and my heart knows. He's so still as I read, and even though I'm not sure if he understands what's going on, he's with me every step of the journey. When I finish he shouts, 'Again!' and it's music to my ears.

I decide to spend half an hour reading with my boy every day. Together we rediscover my old friends. He loves the playfulness of Dr Seuss and the naughtiness of Peter Rabbit. Often, he comes home from nursery and calls out, 'Book! Book!' as if he is summoning a pet. If I am not too tired after I have put him to bed, I go for a walk around the park. I can feel it getting easier, feeling less like something *other* people do.

'I'm doing really well,' I tell Leanne over coffees and babycinos with the boys one Friday. 'I'm moving past stuff. I'm just . . . moving.'

'I'm really pleased for you,' she says. 'I want nothing but the best for you.'

'You sound like a greeting card,' I say.

'I don't mean to,' she says, and then takes a sip of her coffee. 'I'm just wondering what's got you so fired up?'

'If I'm honest, I think it's George,' I say. 'You were so right about the list thing. If you ask the universe, it will give you what you need.' I pick up a biscuit that Moses has abandoned and then change my mind and place it back down.

'I was sort of worried you would say that,' says Leanne.

'Expand,' I say, maintaining my smile in an effort to hold on to my positive outlook.

Leanne licks her lips and says, 'You invested so much of your happiness in Alexander. I don't want you to be let down by another man.'

'I'm not going to be let down. That's the point. He's not the sort of guy who would do that. The list was your idea, Lee. Why would you build me up just to shit on my disco?'

Leanne gently places her cup on its saucer. 'I'm not' — she clears her throat and glances at Lucas — '*pooping* on anything. We were drunk; coming up with that list was a laugh. I don't want you to think it means anything.'

'Everything has meaning,' I say, and I realize I sound like Tashi.

I don't try to convince Leanne but I don't let her doubt derail me either. If I have found a fire within me, what does it matter who created the spark? I still check in with George most mornings. He continues to be the first thing I think about but now I have something to share, little titbits from the previous day — things that have lifted me up. I start to feel closer to being a whole person and not a fragile Kinder Egg, with a missing toy. Having George to share my day with helps me to think about my actions. I don't want to tell him that I stayed in bed all day, that I ate a ready meal and cried myself to sleep, so I don't. I keep my head down at work, I read to Moses, I call Marc and confirm my gig. I work on the minutes and change my days.

26

The day of Tom's engagement party I go to a boutique just off the high street. I need to find a dress, specifically the most fabulous dress I have ever worn in my life. My dream is that Tom will see me and wonder why he ever let me go. Failing that, I want him at least to wish he'd had the chance to spend the night with me before he did so. I'm greeted enthusiastically by the saleswoman, who asks me if she can help. 'I need something that's going to make me feel amazing,' I say.

'Amazing I can do,' she says. 'What size are you?'

'A fourteen,' I say. She pauses — not for long but long enough that I know she is reconsidering whether making me look amazing is something she can achieve.

'I have the perfect thing,' she says. She goes out back and returns holding an emerald green dress in front of her. I take it into the fitting room. It's a great choice — knee length and close fitting with a large bow at the neck. I take off my clothes and wiggle into it. It takes some effort. Standing in it I still think it's a great choice but perhaps for someone else's body. There is some ruching around the stomach that is definitely not part of the design and I don't usually go for sleeveless because I've always thought my arms are a little sausagey. I stand on my toes to try and simulate heels and turn slowly from left to right. When I inhale the dress looks better; can I hold my stomach in for two hours?

'How are you getting on?' asks the saleswoman. I open the curtain and look at her questioningly. 'Oh,' says the woman, and then claps her hand over her mouth. She adjusts the bow a little and steps back to review me again. 'It looks perfect,' she says. I like how the dress looks through her eyes, so I go back into the changing room, put my clothes back on and take it to the till.

'It doesn't have a price on it,' I say.

'Yes, it's just come in, literally this morning. It's a hundred and eighty-nine pounds.'

I don't speak. I have to pay Patricia. I have to think about finding somewhere to live; I can't spend that much money on a dress. I also can't say no now; I can't have this woman look at me and see me for the failure that I am. I get out my debit card and force a smile on my face as I place it in the machine. As I head home, I console myself that a woman in a dress like this couldn't possibly have a bad night — and also that, as it has no price tag on it, I can wear it and return it.

*   *   *

Mum has taken Moses to a miniature railway, so I sleep for an hour before throwing back a fortifying vodka and forcing two pairs of Spanx over my thighs. On the way to the party I stop by Cara's flat. I had tried to persuade her to come

224

with me — crashing the engagement party of the guy who rejected your mate seemed like the kind of subversive act she would enjoy, but she refused. I hope that I can convince her — Cara would make it fun; she'd help me to find the punchline to this joke — but as she leads me to her living room, she repeats what she told me on the phone: 'I won't be part of this sadness.'

'Not everything has to be achingly cool, Cara.' She pours us both a glass of rum from her drinks trolley and tops each of them with a splash of ginger ale.

'Not that kind of sad,' Cara says as she hands me my drink, 'although I do find the concept of an engagement, let alone a party for it, pathetic. The literal sadness. Whatever sadness is in your soul that makes you think this is a good idea.' I take a sip of my drink and Cara's generous measures make me cough a little. Cara drinks half of her own glass and waits for my response.

'It's not that I think it's a *good* idea,' I say. 'It's just something I have to do.' Cara dismisses this idea with a shake of her head.

'That's the thing. You don't have to *do* anything. I guess besides raise your kid, but that's your fuck-up.'

'I suppose I want to feel empowered. I want to show him that he doesn't affect me.'

Cara looks thoughtful. 'He doesn't affect you but you're going to celebrate him shackling himself to some other human?'

'OK, that he doesn't affect me, like, negatively.'

Cara finishes her drink and says, 'Why don't

you show that by coming with me to a house party at Julie's? I won't try and force you to play naked Twister this time.' She nods towards my glass. 'Top up?'

'No, Cara, I'm going. I bought a dress.' Cara takes in my outfit without comment and shrugs. 'It's going to be good. I'm going to show him what he missed out on.' I hand Cara my glass and prepare to leave. She shakes her head.

'Don't say I didn't warn you,' she says as I gather my things.

'I appreciate it,' I say, 'but I know what I'm doing.'

Cara lifts my half-full glass in a toast. 'I'm glad someone does, babe.'

★ ★ ★

On the walk, I repeat uplifting mantras to myself — I am beautiful, I am confident, I am free. It sort of works and then I arrive at OhSo. Fairy lights are strung up and jazz music is playing and it is exactly as I would have had it. A woman ushers me in.

'Hello, my darling,' she says. 'Green is obviously in fashion.' I look at her lime green skirt suit and nod wordlessly. 'Are you a friend of the bride or groom?' she asks. I can tell that saying this tickles her.

'The groom, I guess,' I say.

'I didn't think I recognized you,' she says. 'I'm Rhiannon's mother.'

I need another drink. We stand in silence and the awkwardness starts to set in. When another woman approaches us, I am relieved at first but then I see the joy on the face of my companion, and I want to cease existing.

'Rhi, Rhi!' My new friend squeezes her daughter around the waist. 'I'm going to go and powder my nose. This is one of Tom's people.' As her mother leaves, Rhiannon gives me a hug and flashes me a model-perfect smile. She is wearing a dress of ivory lace that embraces every inch of her body and I can't take my eyes away from her perfect stomach, a stomach that looks like it has never held more than a salad, let alone a baby.

'Thanks for coming. Do you work with Tom?'

I am too wounded to lie. I say no. 'I'm Martha,' I tell her. I think she will look angry but her smile becomes even more pronounced.

'Thank you for coming and *thank you*,' she says again. She gives me a wink, as if we are co-conspirators.

'Well, I never turn down a drink,' I say. Rhiannon throws back her head and laughs wildly. As she does so her waist-length auburn curls bounce around her face. I have a vision of cutting the lot off in her sleep.

'There's plenty of that,' says Rhiannon, 'and if you don't mind me saying, lots of lovely single guys.' I search her face for evidence that she is aware of the cruelty of her comment. I find none and decide that she is simply an imbecile.

'That's fine,' I say. 'I'm seeing someone.'

'Oh, great!' she says. 'Where is he?' She looks behind me as if my boyfriend could have been hiding behind me all this time.

'He's not here,' I say. 'He's in Africa.'

'Cool,' says Rhiannon. 'Where's he from?'

'Uhm, Brighton,' I say.

'Oh right, why is he in Africa?' Her brow furrows and I realize that because I am black and my boyfriend is in Africa, she has completed a mental equation that results in him coming from the motherland.

'He's not African,' I say. As I say this I hope she will look a little embarrassed. She doesn't, though; she's either too confident or too happy for such a negative emotion to touch her. More people arrive and she looks distracted.

'The bar is over there,' she says, indicating behind her. She doesn't have to tell me twice. The bar is staffed by two young guys wearing bow ties. They're probably students; they look like they're in fancy dress in their starched, white shirts. One asks me if I want a cocktail or some prosecco.

'What's in the cocktail?' I ask.

'Pretty much vodka and pomegranate juice,' he says.

'Yeah, but how much alcohol?' The bartender shrugs.

'Maybe one shot.'

'OK, give me prosecco,' I say. 'Two glasses.' The barman dutifully does so and I down the first glass. I'm about to start on the second when I feel a tap on my shoulder. When I turn Tom is standing there. He's red-faced and breathing audibly; he looks like he's been running.

'Hiiiiii!' he says. He tries to draw me into a hug but I'm still holding my drink and he ends up just crashing into me. 'Thanks so much for coming,' he says. He's actually smiling at me, smiling as if we're friends.

'No problem,' I say. 'I wasn't doing anything anyway.'

'Good, good,' he says. 'You look . . . great.' I can feel my dress bunching around my waist and I'm not sure I believe him.

'Whatever,' I say, and finish my drink.

'Two more,' says Tom to the barman. 'It's a free bar,' he says to me. The barman places them in front of us. Tom holds up his glass; I assume he wants me to toast.

'What am I doing here?' I ask.

'You were the one who made me realize what I had lost,' says Tom, still smiling like a loon.

'Well, that's great. That's dandy. Good for you.'

'I just wanted to make things right between us,' he says.

I laugh and then Tom laughs and I say, 'You're a psychopath.'

Tom stops. 'I think you need to relax,' he says. He puts a hand on my shoulder. It feels like a lead weight resting there. I down my drink and reach for another glass, shrugging my shoulder as I do so, so that his hand slips off. 'I'm not that great a catch,' says Tom. He smiles again; I guess that's his way of apologizing.

'I'm fine,' I say. 'I'm relaxed. Thanks for this.' I tip my glass at him and walk away. I try to move in a way that looks purposeful, although I have no idea where I am going. I walk towards the toilet but before I get there I spot Leanne arriving. She looks amazing; her blonde hair is in a neat bun and she's wearing a yellow shift dress and nude heels, the quintessential colleague's wife.

'You were supposed to be here before me,' I hiss at her.

'Lucas wouldn't settle,' she says. 'You OK?'

'Yeah, yeah,' I say, but I feel really light-headed. In part because of the booze and the lack of food and the underwear cutting off my circulation, but also because of the injustice of it all. 'How does it work?' I ask Leanne. 'How do some people get this?' Leanne looks confused but before she can speak James pulls me in for a hug.

As we part he looks at my face and says, 'Let's get pissed, eh?'

James gets us all fresh drinks and we sit together as he tells us stories about his colleagues. Apparently Tom doesn't have any friends outside work, so almost the entire office is there. 'That's Mike,' says James, pointing to a tall, thin guy with acne scars and a scowl. 'We call him Crazy Mike because he eats the same lunch every day — one egg sandwich and a packet of salt and vinegar crisps. Never plain, God forbid smoky bacon.' Although there is no way Mike can hear us he looks over and we all giggle. James tells us off. 'You two are gonna get me in trouble,' he says. It occurs to me that I'm starting to have fun. I probably shouldn't have waited this long to go out with Leanne and James. I hope that George and James get on and we can go on double dates and then on holiday together.

The jazz has been replaced by a DJ playing nineties music and Pulp's 'Common People' comes on.

'Oh my God,' says Leanne. 'We have to dance!'

'I can't dance,' I say; I literally can't in this dress.

James holds out his hand. 'Can I have this dance?' he asks his wife. She accepts, and he leads her to a small clearing between the tables. Soon most people are dancing, including Tom and his wife-to-be. Although the song is uptempo they have their arms wrapped round each other and are swaying gently. A small pit of loneliness starts to jostle around in my stomach and I look for someone to distract me from it. A few chairs away I see Crazy Mike sitting alone. Although ale is not being served, he has acquired a pint from somewhere. I admire his resourcefulness and I go and sit next to him.

'You having a good time?' I ask.

'Does it look like I'm having a good time?' he asks back. He says this in a friendly way, though. He has a nice Yorkshire accent.

'Not really,' I say.

'Shit, and I was trying so hard,' he says.

'Why have you come then?' I ask him.

'That's what I've been trying to work out,' he says.

'Well, you've met me now,' I say. He smiles a little. 'You have no excuse; this is my ex's party and I'm having a great time.'

He studies me closely. 'No, no,' I say, 'I've found someone else now. He's perfect, literally perfect. I asked the universe for what I wanted.' Crazy Mike looks a bit concerned. 'I know it sounds mad, no offence. You should try it, though, if you want someone who will accept you for you; who won't ask you to change.' Mike takes a sip of his pint. I put my hand over his. 'If you like egg sandwiches you will find someone who appreciates that.'

Mike removes his hand from mine and says, 'There's someone I've got to say hello to.' He gets up and crosses the room and takes a seat next to no one. Whatever, I think.

Marthashotbod: What're you doing?

No response. I head back to the bar and sample the cocktail. It goes down like squash. I tell the bartender to keep them coming and, although he looks at me suspiciously, he obliges. The music stops and Tom's voice fills the room. I look round and see him standing by the DJ booth.

'Thank you all for being here,' he says. 'My wife-to-be and I — ' His words are then drowned out by a drunken cheer from the crowd and he starts again. 'My wife-to-be and I want to thank you for being a part of today and of our future. I'm so happy I've found her.' He gestures to Rhiannon, who walks over and stands beside him. He wraps an arm round her waist and says, 'Now that I have her, I'm never letting her go.' The crowd cheers again. An elderly version of Tom walks over to him and takes the microphone.

'Hello, hello,' he says into the mic and

everyone laughs. 'For those of you I haven't met, I'm Thomas's father. I want to say I hope you're all enjoying yourselves and I hope Rhiannon and Tom have a long and happy life together. I'm so pleased to have her in my family. She really is the most elegant, beautiful girl I have ever known.'

'Why don't *you* marry her then,' I mumble, and a couple of people turn to look at me.

'I don't know how Tom has done it,' he says. Everyone laughs, I think in agreement. 'I hope everybody here can have what they have.' He raises his glass and everyone copies his action. 'To Tom and Rhiannon,' he says, and the crowd parrots it back before giving applause. When the party is quiet again Tom's father asks if anyone else has any words to say. I have a lot to say. As I approach him I can feel the anticipation of the crowd. I can hear whispering voices questioning who I am as I take the microphone.

'Hello,' I say to a rapt audience. 'I just want to say that everyone deserves love, whether they're young, old, thin or a little bit chubby but more or less in proportion.' At this point I catch sight of Leanne in the crowd. Obviously, I have no definitive proof of this but I'm pretty sure her eyes are the widest they have ever been. Her face sobers me a little. I glance at Tom and Rhiannon, who are looking at each other with similar expressions. 'Anyway, to Tom and Rhiannon,' I say to continued silence. I hand the microphone back to the DJ and he quickly starts playing 'Build Me Up Buttercup'.

Leanne rushes over to me.

'What the hell was that?' she asks.

'My speech,' I say. I decide I will just brazen it out, I will brazen the whole thing out.

'You need to go home,' she says. As she says this she links her arm with mine and starts to move towards the door. I wrestle from her grip, causing us both to stumble a little in the process. Leanne looks upset.

'What I need is another drink.' I march back to the bar, leaving her alone.

'More prosecco,' I tell the barman.

He folds his arms. 'I think you've had enough,' he says.

'I'm so sick of people telling me what to do,' I spit at him. The barman starts serving someone else; my body feels almost overwhelmed by the shame of his dismissal. I walk away from the bar and I decide to keep walking, to walk away from the whole thing. I leave OhSo, struggle up from the beach on to the road and hail a cab.

'Where you going, love?' says the driver. And I give him the address. My address with Alexander, the address my bank statements still get sent to.

27

As the cab pulls away from the apartment building it seems like an appropriate time for me to work out why I'm there, what it is I hope to gain, and then I see it, crouched underneath a fir tree — Moxie. I walk towards him and he mews softly. I feel a stab of guilt that he may have been missing his mummy. I put my hand out and he licks it but when I try to pick him up he struggles. 'Shhhhh,' I say. 'We need to go home.'

He does not comprehend my Human and hooks his claws into the front of my dress. I sit down on the damp grass and try to wrap him up in my cardigan. He does not like this. I don't know if it's my wailing or the cat's that wakes them but I suddenly find myself bathed in the glow of the security light, and standing silhouetted in the doorway of the flat entrance are Alexander and Poppy. Poppy is wearing one of Alexander's T-shirts. I remember he bought it from a market in south London and I laughed at him for paying forty pounds for a crappy T-shirt. I still think it's crappy but Poppy does not look crap in it; even tousled hair and a scrunched-up sleep face can't detract from her long tanned legs and flawless complexion. Alexander has on his dressing gown. I know he has nothing underneath it because that's how he sleeps. When we first got together he would walk round the flat naked in the mornings, making toast and tea and swinging his penis to make me laugh. At the end he was always in that tatty dressing gown and there was no penis swinging of any kind.

Alexander returns indoors briefly and comes back wearing a pair of trainers. He stops at the door and says a few words to Poppy. She looks over at me sadly and nods. Alexander kisses her on the nose and she disappears inside. He then walks over to me. Without helping me up or bending down he says, 'Martha, what the fuck are you doing? I mean, seriously, what the fuck are you doing?'

'This is my cat,' I whisper.

'What?' asks Alexander.

'This is my fucking cat!' I shout.

★   ★   ★

Alexander gives me a lift back to my mother's, Moxie huddled with me in the passenger seat of the MG. We drive in silence; even the cat seems to understand that now is not the time for conversation.

After he's parked Alexander says, 'What is going on with you?'

I stare out of the passenger window of the car. 'I'm getting a divorce,' I say.

'And what about me?' says Alexander. 'You act like this is a good time for me.'

'Isn't it?' I say. 'Shacking up with your child bride. You look like you're having fun to me.'

Alexander smacks his hand against the steering wheel. 'You dumped me!' he shouts. 'You decided on a whim you were over being married to me and now what? I'm supposed to support you through it?' I look at Alexander. He looks hurt and angry.

'We're supposed to support each other,' I say. 'And Moses, what about him? He needs to see more of you.'

Alexander closes his eyes. 'Yeah, I want him to stay more often but I don't want to confuse him. I worry I'm not good to be around him. I'm feeling pretty shaken up.' I look at Alexander, strong and sober in the driver's seat, always in the driver's seat.

'He needs you,' I say, and then quietly, 'I need you.'

Alexander rakes his hand through his hair. 'Don't say that,' he says. 'It doesn't help. We both need space.'

I look at Alexander's profile as he leans back against the headrest. When Moses was born, I was taken aback by how much he looked like his father. When I was pregnant I would imagine my tiny, new child and in my mind he was a smaller version of me, but from day one I could see Alexander's big eyes and strong chin. I don't get to have space; I see Alexander every day. I begin to cry.

'I'm sorry,' I say. 'Can we just start again?'

Alexander laughs bitterly. 'From when? From tonight? Yes, let's do that and try you not turning up in my garden, mad and drunk.'

'What about from the beginning?' I ask. 'If we could start again from the beginning what would you have done differently?' This is what I would have done differently: I would have told him how

I felt about him sooner; we would have gone travelling; I would have worked harder; we would have danced together more often; I would have asked him what he wanted; I would have told him what I needed; I would not have had the calamari that time; I would have told him I loved him every day, even if I didn't feel it, but I *would* have loved him every day because love is about actions and not words.

'I wouldn't have married you,' says Alexander.

I get out of the car. It takes some time because I must negotiate keeping hold of Moxie as I do but after I succeed, I slam the door behind me and I don't look back.

28

I open my eyes and try to put together the pieces of the previous evening but they won't fit. Mum comes in carrying Moses. 'Do you plan to lie in bed all day?' she asks.

'No,' I say. I can't. In my wisdom I confirmed my gig for today, believing I would be boosted by my triumph at the party.

'Why is there a cat in my kitchen?' asks Mum.

'I'll sort it,' I say. Mum looks like she has more to say but thankfully she leaves and takes Moses with her.

After I drag myself from the comfort of my bed, I spend the afternoon curled up on the sofa watching cartoons with Moses and drinking Dad's secret stash of full-fat Coke. I text Leanne an apology and a carefully selected 'I'm sorry' GIF but she doesn't reply; maybe she wishes she didn't know me too.

As the evening draws in the last thing I want to do is sing and only the thought of George makes me feel like I can do it. I know you're not supposed to say that; you're supposed to pretend that all your strength comes from within, manufactured from a little inner strength factory located in your gut — but that's bullshit. Everything good I've ever done has been with the encouragement or approval of someone else — my mother, my friends or a man. That's why I achieved so little with Alexander; he never gave me strength. I think he was scared of what I might do with it. Once I told him I was thinking about a career in talent management. I thought I could partner with Cara; we could manage artists and put on events. He didn't say, 'That's great!' or, 'Tell me more!' He said, 'Why?' George knows that it doesn't matter why; what matters is me. I know it is this thought that gives me the motivation to put on my make-up and iron my funeral dress. I even manage to push my anxiety to the edge of my consciousness as I walk to the club, until I see Cara. She is standing with someone who must be Marc in the club's dressing room and seeing her familiar face makes everything real. She gives me a kiss on each cheek.

'Ready, darling?'

'I think so,' I say.

'Not quite,' says Cara. She gets a lip gloss out of her bag and indicates that I should open my mouth. I do so and she carefully applies it to my lips.

'Now you're ready,' she says.

Marc pats me on the bum. 'Looking good, darlin', I hope you sound as good as you look.' Marc is at least three inches shorter than me and from my vantage point I can see the light bouncing off his head through his thinning hair. Despite our obvious incompatibility he is looking at me like I'm a plate of baby-back ribs. I guess having the power to offer people what they want gives a man a decent dose of self-confidence.

'What have you got?' he asks.

I give him my sheet music and he looks over it.

'It'll do — a little vanilla but we can work on that. As soon as you're settled can you come and sound check?'

'Sure,' I say, and he leaves. 'I didn't know you were coming,' I say to Cara.

'How could you think I wouldn't come?' she asks.

'I guess I just thought you might have something better to do.'

'Something better than this? You're ridiculous.' She turns to face the mirror and pushes her fingers into her hair, wiggling her hands around to lift her roots. 'Besides, have you seen Curtis on the drums? Hands off.'

I laugh and say, 'Don't worry.' I take off my coat and as I slip it on to a coat hook I say, 'Actually, I'm seeing someone.' I try to say this casually. I hope my tone makes clear that this is just an aside, nothing to dwell on. Even though I want to tell her about George, I instinctively know I don't want Cara to ask any questions. Cara, however, is very skilled at doing the exact opposite of whatever someone wants her to do.

'No, you're not,' she says. 'So what's really going on?'

'What do you mean?' I ask.

Cara straightens out the hem of my dress before saying, 'You're not seeing anyone because if you were you would have told me already. You wouldn't have been able to resist reliving the romance and regurgitating all the tawdry details. So what are you really telling me? Are you back with A-hole?'

'No, God no. I actually have a boyfriend.' We

241

haven't confirmed this officially but it's one of those unspoken things we both know.

'How did you meet him?' asks Cara. She does not sound happy; she does not sound like a friend eager to share in her buddy's joy. She sounds dubious.

'I met him on the app. On Linger.'

'Right, so you met him on the app and now . . . he's your boyfriend?'

'Yes,' I say. I say it with a finality that Cara ignores.

'Has he met Moses?' she asks.

'No, not yet,' I say.

Cara's face relaxes. 'Is he good in the sack?' she asks.

'I . . . er . . . I don't actually know yet.'

'Ooh,' says Cara, 'playing coy.' She shrugs as she says this and then leans in towards the mirror to check her eye make-up. 'Good kisser, though?' she asks.

I watch her for a few seconds before saying, 'I don't know that either.' Cara stops preening and looks at me via my reflection in the mirror. 'We haven't met yet.' Cara stands up straight and turns around so she is facing me.

'So you *don't* have a boyfriend,' she says.

I shake my head. 'You have no idea what you're talking about,' I say.

'Mate, you're the one with the make-believe boyfriend.'

I feel my arms get tense. 'Can't you just be supportive or pretend to be supportive or does that go against your moral code or something?'

Cara presses each thumb and forefinger

242

together and moves them up and down to emphasize each word, as if she is conducting a tiny orchestra. 'You. Have. An. Imaginary. Boyfriend,' she says.

'What is it?' I ask. 'It's like if you're not being a bitch you don't have a reason to exist.'

Cara narrows her eyes. 'You're right, babe, I don't have time for this.' She gives me a kiss on the cheek and leaves the dressing room, but just before she closes the door she says, 'Break a leg.'

★ ★ ★

Having Cara go like that is something of a relief. I'm tired of having to hold on to things. In truth I think I prefer doing things on my own — being with other people, even people you like, requires constant assessment of their wants. It's not possible to keep doing that without damaging yourself in the process. I don't have the energy any more. I have a little cry and then I redo my make-up. It's time to accept that I need to start doing stuff without anyone to support me.

Marthashotbod: I have a gig tonight, wish me luck.
Undeterred83: That's hot. What sort of gig?
Marthashotbod: A little jazz club.
Undeterred83: Wow, you have so many talents, I'm feeling inadequate.
Marthashotbod: You are anything but that.
Undeterred83: Well, good luck. Not that

you need it, you're amazing.

The club is small and made to look smaller by the black and red decor. There's a handful of patrons dotted around the room, along with a full table at the front. Marc is at the bar drinking a short. 'Was that as quick as you could be? Women for you, I guess,' he says. He slips an arm round me and rests his hand on my hip. 'If you don't mind, can you go straight into your set? I have some special guests in.'

'Uhm, the band — ' I say.

'Don't you worry yourself about the boys, they're tight. These folks have just signed up for my premium member scheme — the stuff people will pay if you include a glass of cheap fizz, eh. I want you to charm them a little for me.' He leads me over to a table at the front of the room. Two men and two women, I assume couples, sit looking pleased with themselves.

'Meet the talent,' says Marc to the table. They smile and nod. Marc turns to me and I realize I'm supposed to say something.

'Have a wonderful evening,' I say. It takes Marc a few seconds to work out that I don't have any more. He shakes hands with the gentlemen and then leads me to the side of the stage.

'Take it easy on this set,' he says. 'You can go on again later and bring it home.'

'Definitely,' I say. My throat feels tight, as if it's fighting to keep hold of my voice. I know that professionals do vocal exercises and, since I'm getting paid, I'm a professional now too. I stand at the side of the stage and gently run up and down a scale.

'Fuck, fuck, fuck, fuck, fuck, fuck, fuck, fuck, fuck,' I sing. The room around me goes into soft focus. I understand that it's just a tiny club with an audience smaller than the average coffee shop line but, however low-key the event is, its symbolism is huge. It's a gig, a real solo spot. It's the first step in the direction of a new life.

I've never even performed in public before, but there was another occasion when I was supposed to. Aged ten I was cast as Mary in Stanford Junior School's musical version of the nativity. I don't remember how I was given the role; I can't imagine I put myself forward for it. Perhaps a bright-eyed teacher was hoping for her *Dangerous Minds* moment and tried to give the shy, awkward girl her day in the spotlight. However it came about, the decision was controversial. I was the first Mary of colour Stanford had seen and my classmates made it clear I was not the popular choice.

The scene is tattooed on my mind, Mrs Baker playing my introductory chord over and over until it rang in my ears, and even then I think I might have been OK, but then I caught my mother's eyes, narrowed in anticipation, and I did the unthinkable. I wet myself. The warmth of the liquid was almost comforting and Mary's robes were concealing most of the evidence. Mrs Baker skipped to the next song and it would have been fine — my humiliation might have remained personal — if Christopher Nagle, my nativity husband, had not noticed the puddle and shouted, 'She pissed herself!'

There was an impromptu interval whilst I was cleaned up and bundled into our car. My mother didn't even comment on the event; it was obvious to all that her judgement was not necessary. When I ended up attending secondary school across town, the official reason was because of the school's excellent GCSE results, but the move was really to escape the ghosts of Christmas past.

Standing next to the stage now, I'm taken back to that moment. I can even smell the hall — wood polish and boiled veg.

'Ready?' the drummer mouths to me. Cara was right, he is good-looking. He's got a shaved head and two full tattoo sleeves; he looks like he might keep me safe up there. I lift a finger to indicate that he should give me a second. Then I walk slowly to the bar and ask for a glass of water. As I drink I scan the room. I can see Marc still sweet talking his golden table but his eyes are trained on me. Bile rises to my mouth — nerves with a side of hangover. I ask for a second glass and drink this one more slowly. I concentrate on the sensation of the liquid sliding down my throat and on the cold firmness of the glass. I place it on the bar and turn to face the stage. The six band members are looking at me with a variety of 'what the fuck' expressions. I walk over to them and as I climb the steps they seem to shake. I look at my knight on drums and he just looks bored; none of the band members speak to me. I stand at the microphone and as I adjust it I survey the crowd. There's a handful of people either deep in conversation or smiling at me encouragingly; I should be fine.

From behind me someone says, 'Shall we go from the top?' I nod and the band starts to play without even counting me in. As Marc promised, they're tight, so tight I can't breathe. I clear my throat and hear the sound ringing around the room. I open my mouth to sing the first words of 'My Baby Just Cares For Me' and nothing emerges but a croak. The band keeps repeating the intro; I try to start again and the same thing happens. One of the ladies at the front table holds out a glass of water. My bladder couldn't take any more liquid and that thought drags me back to that terrifying school stage and a hundred tiny heads bobbing with laughter. I reach out to take it anyway but my hand is shaking so much I can't be sure I'll be able to hold it. I stand with the mic to my mouth and my hand out-stretched, like a confused zombie. The band keeps playing. I try to smile but moving my face unleashes the tears that have been working their way to the front of my eyes. I apologize and drop the microphone. It shrieks in protest as it hits the ground. I apologize again even though no one can hear me now and walk carefully off the stage.

★   ★   ★

I try to pack my things up quickly but I'm not quick enough. As Marc enters the dressing room his face glistens from the effort of coming to find me, or perhaps from rage. 'What the fucking fuck was that, missus?' he asks.

'I'm so sorry, I've had a lot on my mind,' I say.

'You've lost your mind, more like,' he says.

I put on my coat. 'I'm not feeling well,' I say. 'I'm sure I could do better a bit later or maybe tomorrow.'

'There ain't no tomorrow for you, love, you're dead to me.' That seems slightly dramatic.

'I'm sorry,' I say. He seems to soften; perhaps this happens to a lot of people. 'I won't expect full payment.'

Marc laughs. He actually clutches his stomach as he leans over and lets the mirth overcome his body.

'Payment! Payment? You've got some cheek. You should be paying me!'

'OK, I'm gonna go then,' I say, and walk past him towards the door.

'I thought Cara was your mate,' he says, without turning round. 'You've made her look like a dick.'

I don't respond. I think, no one can make Cara do anything.

29

The next morning I call in sick. I don't even have to do the calling-in-sick voice because I feel so despondent that every word I speak sounds like I'm in pain. 'Try an enema,' says Bob, 'works wonders.' I promise to look into his recommendation.

I manage to sleep through most of the day and my lethargy convinces Mum I have a lethal strain of flu she read about in the local paper. She leaves me to myself, save to pop into my room in the late afternoon with a bowl of chicken stew in her hand and a floral chiffon scarf wrapped around her mouth and nose. 'I'll go and collect Moses and keep him away from you,' she says. I want to say no because I think that Moses is the only person who won't judge me right now, but I don't want to blow my cover and have to explain that I'm not physically sick, just sick of life.

Leanne calls me shortly after seven. I can hear a car door slam and the start of the engine and I know that she's just left the office. 'How's things?' she asks. 'Sorry we didn't get a chance to catch up properly after the party.'

'I feel shit,' I say.

'Hmmmm,' says Leanne, 'is it work?'

'No, work is always shit, it's a bit of everything, a smattering of shit.' I leave a gap for Leanne to laugh but she doesn't. 'I don't know. I've just got a lot going on.'

'I know, babe,' says Leanne, 'but we all have.' I hear the clicks of her indicator. 'How's the running going? That usually clears my head.'

'Yeah, I'm not in the mood.'

'You've got to push through that, hun,' says Leanne. I recognize her tone. It's warm but distracted; it's a voice she uses with her children. 'They have been busting my arse at work but I can't take it home. I don't have a choice.' I'm not sure how supportive this is, bringing up her cosy home life when I'm clearly struggling.

'You wouldn't understand, Leanne,' I say quietly.

'I understand tough times,' she says sharply. I feel like she's telling me off and I don't know why. 'Anyway, you've got good stuff going on — how was the gig?' I just can't say it; she's my best friend but I feel as though telling her how horribly and suddenly I watched my dream fall to pieces would break me.

'It was fine,' I say.

'Well, practice makes perfect,' says Leanne. The sentence makes me wince. I want to tell her that not everything has to be perfect. 'I'd stop by but I really need to go straight home tonight.'

'No, that's OK,' I say.

'I better run, I'm at the gym now. Speak soon, yeah?'

'Course,' I say.

⋆ ⋆ ⋆

Honestly, I think it was because of Leanne that I first went to Jacqueline. Motherhood was and is wonderful but it can be bloody hard. The initial fuss and excitement was so intoxicating but then everyone went back to their lives and I was left to try and understand mine. The ads for mild washing powder and unperfumed shampoo, featuring plump, laughing babies and clean-haired mothers — they lied to me. Finally, I was playing a role I had coveted for so long but I felt guilty every moment my heart wasn't filled with gratitude, and there were a lot of those moments. What hurt the most was how untouched Alexander's life seemed to be. He still took on new projects and went out with his friends; if anything he went out more as he always assumed I would want to stay home with Moses and go to bed early, and the fact that he was right didn't make it any less annoying.

One evening he had gone to a really important five-a-side meet-up, and no matter where I went in our home, I couldn't run away from the feeling of loneliness. I called Leanne and begged her to come over and she did. She arrived twenty minutes later with fresh cream cakes and even fresher highlights and seeing her, polished and in control, contentment leaking from her invisible pores, I felt more isolated than ever. I held it together for her visit. She talked me through a list of courses and activities that she was sure Moses and I would 'absolutely love' and to say otherwise would have seemed like a betrayal of my boy. I clutched him to my chest because he served as a reminder of why I should bother to keep going; Leanne cooed over him and told me that he was making her think about having another. Her admission was overwhelming — how could she possibly think about having three young children; why did she believe she would cope?

Leanne left and I couldn't stop my grief escaping. Alexander returned, flushed and loose-limbed, and found me lying in a damp patch of tears on the sofa. He sighed. I could tell he was irritated that I was killing his vibe, but as a wife, wasn't that my right? He sat gingerly next to me and told me about his day. I knew he was avoiding asking me what was wrong. I interrupted his chatter to say, 'I don't know who I am.'

Alexander squeezed the bridge of his nose. 'OK,' he said.

'OK, just OK? That's all you have to say?'

Alexander threw himself back on to the sofa. 'What else can I say? I can't tell you who you are.'

'Who can?'

'I think you need to talk to someone,' Alexander said.

'I'm talking to you!' I cried, pulling my knees up to my chest.

'Someone who can help you,' said Alexander, gently but firmly.

The following morning I still feel like a pile of crap that's been put through a NutriBullet but I make the decision to go to work. At least there, I know who I am and what I'm doing, even if I don't like it.

When I arrive, Bob is giving the room one of his 'motivational' speeches.

'... and some of you may not be used to winning, but let me tell you, when you get into the mindset you don't want to stop, and that's why I want this team to be top performing for the second year running.' As I take a seat Bob starts to walk up and down the room, sporadically tapping the back of someone's chair. 'You wanna know what I do? I look at myself in the mirror every morning and say, you are amazing. Not you — you lot need to pull your socks up if you wanna get back on track before end of year. *I* am amazing. Try it tomorrow. 'I am amazing.' It'll put a rocket up your arse.' No one responds, and Bob leaves us to take in his words.

'Don't know about you, but I'm feeling pumped now,' says Greg.

'What do we even get if we win?' Tashi asks him from across the desk divider.

'That,' says Greg, pointing towards the wall behind her. Tashi turns to look at the glass plaque awarded to the team last year. She turns back to face Greg and nods her head.

'I better get to work then,' she says.

It's a slow morning — thankfully, because I can't focus. A customer even manages to come through to me a second time, his voice full of indignation that he had been passed to 'entirely the wrong person'. Even though I start each call by stating my name, I pretend to be someone else and ignore his protests.

I plan to use my break to hide in reception and eat at least two Mars bars, and so as I see Lisa walk towards me as I end my last call, I think momentarily about ducking under the table. I know she's going to want to engage me in some inane prattle about paper plate colours or tapas-themed music. I prepare myself to be polite but boundaried or at the very least not to tell her to piss off. Lisa doesn't start with her usual pleasantries, though; she licks her lips before saying, 'I need to know if you've done any work on the olives?'

I look at Lisa. She's maybe twenty-two, twenty-three, and I understand that olives are the sum of her problems.

'What exactly did you want me to do with the olives?' I ask.

Lisa lets out a noise of complete exasperation. 'Well, work out numbers, ask about preferred colours, think about bowls . . . ' She marks each item by tapping a finger of her left hand with her right forefinger. I understand I have drastically underestimated the amount of olive-based admin there is.

'No, Lisa. I haven't had time.' Lisa glances at my desk, perhaps thinking it will reveal the source of my lack of focus. I am aware that a half-eaten packet of Jelly Babies lies there and I'm too tired to even work up the energy to feel embarrassed about it.

'If this is too much for you, let me know so I can hand it over to someone else.'

I let my eyes drop. 'Yes, I think it's too much.'

Lisa doesn't speak and when I look up I expect to see her angry, but what I see is worse: she's staring at me sympathetically.

'It's not a problem', says Lisa, in a tone an octave higher than her standard speaking voice.

'I'm sure it can be reassigned.'

Greg, who has clearly been listening, although he has given no indication of this, stands up. 'I can help, Lisa. To be honest we can probably knock it out over break.'

'God, thanks G!' cries Lisa. She reaches out and for an awkward second I think she's going to kiss him but she simply places her hand on his forearm. They walk away together, already deep into olive chat.

I'm still watching them when Tashi says, 'Do you want to try a healing mantra with me?' And I feel so desolate, I agree.

★ ★ ★

Tashi and I go to the multi-faith prayer room, which as far as I know has never been used in any spiritual way, although a temp once claimed she had sex there with a guy who works in the canteen, which is pretty close. Tashi opens the blinds and the light that streams in throws a spotlight on hundreds of pieces of fluff dancing through the air. She clears up a few Styrofoam cups and tosses them in an already overflowing bin.

'Not the most inspiring environment,' she says, 'but that's good, that will show you that it's about using your mind to transcend your circumstances.' I smile weakly at her. I know that the only way my mind will be able to transcend my circumstances is if I help it along with a litre or two of vodka. 'OK,' continues Tashi. 'We just need to make an altar out of something.'

'Like in church?'

'Similar, but, like, less Goddy. Just something to focus your mind.' Tashi pulls a chair into the centre of the room and then removes a string of beads from around her neck and places them on the seat. 'I had this made to attract more creativity into my life.' I make an agreeable noise but I'm thinking it looks like something gleaned from a cut-price Christmas cracker. 'Now we need something from you.'

'My cardigan?' I suggest.

Tashi shakes her head. 'It's got to be more personal.'

'This is personal, it's on my body. You can't get more personal than that.'

'Yes, but it doesn't really mean anything to you.'

'I disagree, it means I haven't frozen my tits off today.'

Tashi's face wrinkles in concentration. 'What about that?' she asks, and grabs my left hand.

My engagement ring. I pull my hand away and at first I think about refusing but I can't come up with an honest reason why. I ease it off my finger and put it on the chair next to Tashi's beads. Tashi grabs her long, dark-blonde curls and twists them into a rope over her shoulder. We both sit on the floor in front of the chair. Tashi says, 'Let's do 'ra ma da ma', it's totally cleansing.' She then begins to chant the phrase in a low, sinister voice. She sounds possessed; perhaps this is the explanation for the fact that she is completely bonkers. After a minute she stops and looks at me.

'Is it not working?' she asks. 'Do you not feel anything?'

I feel my knees starting to ache. 'It's just the chanting. It's a bit . . . ridiculous.'

'It might be a bit advanced,' says Tashi, and I know she doesn't intend to sound offensive. 'Just tune into what's happening outside you. Listen to the sound of a silent room.' Tashi closes her eyes; I do the same and for fifteen minutes I listen to the sound of my growling stomach.

⋆　⋆　⋆

I decide to walk home from work; not for exercise, just to lengthen the amount of time between being in one place and another, to have some space to be nowhere. As I walk, I think about Tashi, how serene she looked sitting on that scratchy carpet. Perhaps I'm the one who has it all wrong. I used to describe myself as a spiritual person but what I think I meant by that was my life was kind of OK and I was content to attribute that to some unknowable force in the world. When my life began to lose the shape I was comfortable with, any affinity with the universe was lost. When I was a child my grandmother would sometimes take me along to her church. My mother would take me to her flat the day before and I would sleep alongside my grandma, staying awake as long as I could so I could listen to her snoring, loud and strong. In the morning we would take two buses to attend the service in a chapel that looked not dissimilar to three others we would pass along the way.

One Sunday I asked my grandmother why she went so far. Was the word of God not the same word at the church round the corner? Grandma said she liked the pastor's sermon, which was only more baffling because his weekly offerings were so dark — full of sin and damnation, never failing to remind us all that we were one misstep from the fiery pits of hell. 'Remind me why I need 'im,' she said. I guess I get it now; she wanted to be assured that she had something to protect her from all the fucked-up shit in the world. I wish I could go to her now, so she could protect me.

Mum and Dad are watching a show set in a hospital when I arrive back, neither of them looking up when I enter the room. I watch them for a few moments, enthralled by a clumsy romantic scene. I'm struck by how comfortable they are, with their lives and themselves. I chastise myself for wanting more, for harbouring such ridiculous dreams for so long and letting the inevitable implosion shake me so much. I should have aimed for so much less — trust and companionship. So much less but so much more. I whisper that I'm going upstairs and close the living room door behind me.

4) <u>Must be spiritually aware.</u> Not necessarily religious but have values and a belief system.

Marthashotbod: Do you believe in God?
Undeterred83: Nah.
Marthashotbod: What do you believe in?
Undeterred83: I've never thought about it.

Marthashotbod: No time like the present.
Undeterred83: Maybe but I'm a bit pissed.
Marthashotbod: OK, have a great night.
Undeterred83: :) :) :)

I can't judge him for that. We can't always be in touch with our spiritual side and who doesn't like a drink? In fact, I would quite like to be drunk right now. Dad has a pretty decent collection of whisky stashed in the back of the larder. I can't find anything to mix it with so I chuck a good few measures and a carton of apple juice into a pitcher and discover it makes a reasonably palatable cocktail. On an empty stomach I feel the effects quite quickly and I wonder if this dinner choice means I have a 'problem'. I decide that I'm the problem and within this jug lies the solution. I once read that drug addicts of any variety aren't seeking oblivion but connection. And if this is true it makes sense that ever since the invention of the telephone excessive drinking results in one common occurrence — drunk dialling.

He answers just as I am making the decision to end the call.

'Hey,' I say.

'You good?' Alexander asks.

'Yes, I'm fine,' I say carefully.

'Why are you ringing?' he asks, and I remember I have to have a reason to now.

'I'm just ringing to check on Moses. I miss him.' It's true.

'Yeah,' says Alexander, and I hear his voice

259

relax, 'took ages to get him off. He kept saying horsey.'

I smile even though he can't see me. 'That's the little plastic one; it's in his bag. He takes it to bed now.'

'Really? That sounds uncomfortable.' I am enjoying Alexander's amused confusion. I can imagine him scrunching up his nose as he does when he's trying to understand something or someone.

'If it ain't broke,' I say.

'Whatever the man wants,' says Alexander. 'I'll get one for mi — , here. In case we forget it one day. You were right about him staying over more often. We'll make it happen.' I nearly miss the last part, I'm so floored by the fact that he nearly said 'mine' for our flat, by how easily it came to him.

'I feel a bit lost,' I say. Alexander is quiet and I want to take the words back. I'm reminded of trying to pour wine back into a bottle and then I remember my cocktail and serve myself another glass.

'You'll find your way,' he says eventually. I'm happy he has faith in me. 'I think you can do anything you can put your mind to. You just have to put your mind to something.' I laugh and Alexander says, 'Anything,' and I know he's taking the piss out of me and it feels really good because he's taking the piss out of me in a way that only someone who really knows you can. 'I'm sorry about what I said in the car the other day,' he says. 'I didn't mean it.' I nod, forgetting for a second he can't see me.

When he doesn't fill the silence, I whisper, 'Yeah.'

'I mean it,' he says, 'I wouldn't change anything.' My breath shortens but then he adds, 'Moses is the best thing that ever happened to me.'

'Yeah,' I say, 'Moses, yeah, of course.'

'I better go, though,' Alexander says. It takes me a few seconds to understand the conversation is over because nearly all our conversations are over. He's there for me but he's very much not.

'Is it Moses?' I ask.

'No, he's fine. Gotta go.'

'Bye,' I say, long after he has disconnected.

I have a sensation, sort of like I'm falling. I lie down to try and steady myself. I had been so focused on the ending of our relationship that I didn't realize the magnitude of what I would have to take on — creating a new home; forging a stable career. Had I truly understood the path I was setting out for myself, I can't be sure I would have made the same choice.

I am unaware of the process of completing this thought, falling asleep and then waking up again, but this must be what has occurred because I find myself lying in the dark, my clothes twisted uncomfortably on my body and my stomach calling for attention. I change into Dad's old dressing gown and creep downstairs. I think I spotted a pavlova in the fridge earlier. The light switch isn't quite where I remember it to be and it takes me a few tries to illuminate the room. When I do, thoughts of pavlova vanish and all the air leaves my body to force out a noise in the same family as a scream.

'Bleurrrrrgh! Yeurgh! God! Why?' Sitting at the kitchen table, face calm, rollers still in, is my mother. 'For fuck's sake, Mum, are you trying to kill me?' My mother doesn't move.

'You'll wake your dad, and don't say fuck,' she says. I sit opposite her. She looks so much older than I remember. I feel a flutter of fear that I've been asleep a very long time.

'Mother, neither of those things would be an issue if you weren't hiding in the dark like a deranged person. What's going on? Is this early dementia? Sorry, I mean, you can't ask a person with dementia if they have dementia.' I feel sick. I'm not in a position to take on the care of my deteriorating mother, although it would explain some things. Mum tuts.

'I'm not mad or senile. I just couldn't sleep.'

'Why not?' My mother is so happy, at least with herself. I can't think of a reason why she wouldn't be able to fall into a tranquil, dream-filled sleep each evening.

'I don't know. It's been that way since you were born.' Fabulous, I think, another thing I've fucked up. Mum reaches across the table and squeezes my hand. 'Nothing to do with you. You were perfect, slept through from about six weeks, but I still couldn't rest. Felt I always had to be ready for something.'

'What?' I ask, hoping perhaps she will impart something that will give me wisdom or at least understanding.

'I don't bloody know,' she says. 'If I knew I'd be ready for it.' I feel so tired I want to weep.

Even my mother, a woman who makes an art form out of self-satisfaction, is looking for something. I'm devastated by the possibility that maybe I'll never find the answer; maybe there is no answer. It might just be the case that life, love and all the rest of it is just some omnipotent force's huge practical joke.

'Are you happy, Mum?' I ask.

'Yes,' she says. 'What other choice do I have?'

I pull my hand away from her. 'Loads,' I say, 'life can be really, really shitty.' As I say it, I feel it, and a hard knot forms in my throat.

'I know,' Mum says softly. 'You know what I do when I think that?' She leaves her chair and goes to the little digital radio that lives by the sink. I watch her play with the buttons until she is satisfied and I hear a man, with the low, smooth voice that all eighties DJs were required to have, introduce, 'Another great tune from the time when tunes were great.' Cheryl Lynn's 'Got To Be Real' starts to play and Mum walks towards me with her arms out-stretched. I shake my head, embarrassed, even with an invisible audience. Mum refuses to accept my protest. She grabs my hands and pulls me to my feet. Still holding my hands, she starts to step from side to side, pulling me into her rhythm as I remember her doing with me when we would attend family weddings in my childhood. It doesn't take long for me to succumb to the music and her mood and I start to match her pace before spinning her under my arm, causing her to laugh and lose her balance and cling on to me for support. Mum regains her composure and starts to roll her shoulders and tap her heels; I can imagine her thirty years ago, lost in music, owning a dance floor in a sweaty club. I do a few body rolls and Mum cocks her head at me.

'Oh, you got moves, have you?'

'Looks like it,' I say. She clicks her fingers along to the beat and I join in. Then we both strut around the kitchen, pulling poses when the lyric inspires it. For a few minutes, it's just my mother, the music and me. And that's how the sunrise finds us, barefoot in the kitchen, dancing to funk in our dressing gowns.

30

Patricia has restarted her phone campaign. She leaves me several voicemails reminding me that I can only have my mentorship deferred if I stump up the cash and finally she sends me a text message that reads, 'UPDATE ME ON YOUR PERSONAL DEVELOPMENT. HAVE YOU GONE BACK TO BEING THE TYPE OF GIRL THAT DOESN'T PAY HER DEBTS?' I call Tashi and beg her to swap a shift with me. She tells me that she needs the cash to attend a karmic cleansing workshop but I convince her that her karma will be far improved by giving me her shift.

The evening shift is much livelier than any other; many of the staff in are students making extra beer money, and you can tell they're under the misguided belief that amazing things await them. It helps being somewhere where I know what I'm doing, and I breeze through the clients and even manage to sound something approximating chirpy. Towards the end of my shift Bob comes over to tell me he has noticed the additional hours I've been putting in. 'It's great when staff don't have a social life,' he says, which I think is the closest I will ever get to a 'well done' from him.

After he has strolled off to find someone else to torment, Greg says, 'Let's show him who doesn't have a social life — wanna go for a pint?'

'You don't have a social life, Greg; you're always here.' Greg colours a little. 'Anyway, I'm exhausted,' I say. I am and also I haven't heard from George for three days. This fact is like a toothache, taunting me throughout the day.

'Just one,' says Greg. When he says this he bats his eye-lids in an exaggerated way that makes me laugh.

'OK,' I say, 'let me clean up.' I go to the ladies' and send George a quick message asking how he is. I don't get a response, so I wash my hands and leave. Greg is waiting in the hallway with his head leaned back against the wall and his eyes closed; he looks as tired as I feel. I tap him on the arm and he springs to life.

'Are you sure you wanna go? You look knackered.'

Greg rubs his face. 'I'm a dad. This is how I look.'

I link arms with him. 'Right, let's do this.'

We walk to the Foragers, where a pub quiz is in full swing. 'We should start a team,' says Greg. 'Stop us from going brain-dead.' I think about how pedestrian it would be to finish up at the call centre and then go to a pub quiz every week and shudder. 'What you drinking?' asks Greg.

'Surprise me,' I say.

Greg goes to the bar. I can't hear the conversation he has with the bar lady but at one point she reaches over the bar and slaps him playfully on the arm. She looks happy. I don't know her, I've never seen her in my life, but I'm envious of her ease. She may be crawling through the depths of a metaphorical hell but if she is it's not evident. Maybe it's that simple. I make a little promise to myself that I will be happy and if not *be* happy, look it.

Greg comes back and puts a drink in front of me.

'What is it?' I ask.

'Gin and tonic,' he says.

'That's not much of a surprise,' I say. I rest my chin against my hands. 'Is that how you think of me?'

'What do you mean?' asks Greg as he settles in his seat. He looks pleased; I can tell he's gearing up for a debate. I recognize the excitement — when you spend a lot of time conversing with children some adult banter is light relief.

'Well, gin and tonic, it's so, I don't know, so obvious. It's predictable.'

Greg takes a sip of his own gin. 'Sometimes that's nice though, right? Sometimes it feels good to know what's coming.' I think about this as I have a bit of my own drink. It tastes good — familiar.

'I want a combination, I think. A bit of the expected but something to keep you on your toes.'

'All right, gin and Coke next time?' asks Greg.

'Bleurgh, no way.'

'See,' says Greg, 'unpredictable isn't always as good as it sounds.'

'Is that why you work at Fairfax?' I say. 'You like saying the same thing over and over again?'

Greg makes a face like he's smelt something really bad. 'Sometimes I have to count the minutes in pounds. Like, two hours: that's school lunches for the week.'

'But you always sound so into it,' I tell him.

Greg shrugs. 'It's not the customers' fault I don't know what to do with my life.'

'What did you plan to do?' I ask.

'I never really had a plan,' says Greg. 'My mum was — still is — an alcoholic. I was focused on making sure the younger ones were OK and then as soon as I could get out, I got out.'

'I'm sorry,' I say. I am. Greg's a nice guy, the sort of guy that deserves to have a dream. 'What would you do if you could do anything in the world?' I ask.

'Be Beyoncé's foot cushion.'

'Foot cushion? Aim higher, love! Not even pillow?'

'Thanks for your encouragement,' says Greg.

'Any time,' I say.

'What about you?' asks Greg. 'What would you do if I could wave my magic wand and make it happen? Hang on.' Greg pats his pockets. 'Shit, I left it at home.'

My car crash of a gig comes back to me in high definition. 'I have no idea,' I say.

'Well, you know that's the best place to be,' says Greg. 'You're free to do anything. I could put a word in with Beyoncé; you could be her flannel or something.'

'Not sure I have the skills,' I say.

'Aw well, you'll work it out,' says Greg, in a way that makes me think he believes it. We both fall silent and after a few seconds Greg leans over to a guy on the next table and says, 'Aha, mate.'

'What?' says the man, which is exactly my sentiment.

'The answer. It's a-ha, the band.'

'Oh, right. Of course it is. Obvious when you know it,' says the guy. 'Cheers!' He turns and tells the other men at his table and they all smile and give Greg thumbs up.

'Maybe you could build a career out of knowing obscure pub quiz answers,' I say.

'Been there, done that,' says Greg. The next question starts a furious debate from the guys at the next table, and it's my turn to lean over.

' 'Fight For This Love',' I say, and the men turn to me. 'Cheryl Cole's first number one single.' The men cheer.

'We need you,' a large blond guy says to me. 'If we get all the answers from you and you don't join our team, we'll be cheating.' Greg and I look at each other and silently agree. The blond pulls out a chair for me and the two other guys pat Greg on the back as we sit down.

'I'm Jimmy,' says the blond. 'We've been coming here for years and haven't won so much as a lollipop.'

'Come on then,' says Greg. 'Let's do this!' He puts his hand in towards the centre of the table; we each pile one of our own on top of his and, instinctively, all make a caveman-like grunt.

We storm the music round; Greg has an encyclopaedic knowledge of the eighties and I have the cheesy pop artists covered. Up next is sport so I offer to get the drinks in; when I get back from the bar our new teammates are all completely entranced by Greg, who's telling them a story about a time he performed a citizen's arrest on a cricket team mascot. 'I had to keep smiling so the kids would think I was hugging Fergy and not catch on that he was a violent cokehead.' The guys all laugh; I can tell they really like Greg.

For the first time I consider Greg as a potential romantic candidate, or more specifically I wonder if he finds me attractive. I subtly undo another button on my shirt. The guys all say thanks for the drinks and Greg winks at me. The final round is about Brighton. Greg and I are both born and bred, an anomaly in this transient town, and we impress the table with our local know-how. It feels good to be the one in control for once.

There's a buzz of excitement as we wait for the results and I find myself caught up in it; maybe all this time a good pub quiz was what I needed. The quiz master draws out the announcements and each time he says a team name that's not ours we cheer.

'Annnnd the second runners-up . . . The Accrington Stanleys!' Jimmy stands and beats his chest. Greg reaches over and gives me a high five and one of the other guys hugs me.

'We couldn't have done it without you,' he says. Our prize is another round of drinks, which we claim immediately.

'To victory,' says Greg, after the bar lady brings over five brimming pints.

'To victory!' we chant together.

★ ★ ★

270

Greg offers to walk me home. 'I'll get the bus,' I say.

'You sure?' asks Greg. 'You seem pretty squiffy.'

'I'm fine,' I say, and then a few steps down the road, I trip on a bit of cracked pavement. Greg catches me by the elbow. 'I'm fine,' I say again, and laugh.

At the bus stop Greg says, 'We showed Bob, then?'

'What do you mean?'

'We were social.'

'We were totally social,' I say.

'We're fun,' says Greg. 'Our exes are idiots, right?'

'Well, *I* dumped *him*,' I say to Greg.

'Aw, he still let you go,' says Greg.

My bus arrives just as we reach the bus stop and I'm still smiling as I take my seat. Even when life chucks you a load of lemons, you can take a slice and make a strong gin and tonic.

31

When I was really little, I would wake up almost everyday feeling excited. Most days I wouldn't even know why. I'd have to claw through my memory for the source of my joy until eventually I'd locate it: ah yes, chips for lunch! And the excitement would then be amplified. I wake up today feeling a fuzzier version of that but it's a good fuzzy, a feeling I want to sink into. It's so nice, I'm a little irritated when my phone alert sounds, but when I look and see it's George this dissolves.

Undeterred83: Sorry for the gap, I was moving between cities and had no reception. Good luck for today!
Marthashotbod: No problem, no problem at all. Good luck with what?
Undeterred83: The half marathon.

I shuffle downstairs; somehow I think moving quietly and slowly will make the situation less real. I hear my mother in the kitchen and brace myself before going in.

'You're up!' she cries. 'I've made you porridge — it's got these seeds from the health shop. I read they're good for runners. I don't think you can taste them.' She places the bowl on the table and looks at me. Her face is questioning; I know she wants me to say I'm not doing it, that I'm

272

failing at yet another thing. I won't.

'Thanks,' I say, 'this is perfect.' Mum waits until I start eating before making breakfast for Moses.

'Mummy run!' cries Moses.

'Yes, honey,' I say.

★ ★ ★

My sports bra and leggings are in the bottom of the wash basket where they were abandoned, so I pull on a tracksuit I bought for sleeping in on cold nights. Dad finds a parking space near the start line in Hove Park. Mum is full of advice.

'Remember to pace yourself at the beginning,' she says.

'I will,' I say. I stare out of the passenger window. I'm looking for a sign but I'm not sure what I want it to say.

'I haven't seen you doing much training,' says Mum.

'I've been using the treadmill at the gym in my lunch hour,' I tell her. This seems to please her.

'You know, it's very different running on the road. I hope you don't get injured.' I try to distract myself from my frustration with her by reading the event welcome letter again. It doesn't say much — basically, run. Run really far. 'I read about a woman who did a marathon and tore something in her ankle so badly she couldn't walk again.'

'That's not very useful,' I say, 'pointing out the potential for terrible injury just before I do something.'

'I'm just trying to help,' says Mum. 'That's your problem, you always want to have your head in the sand.'

We pull into the allocated parking and I watch the other runners, clad in Lycra and dripping with anticipation. I can feel a knot starting to tie itself in my stomach. I go to the registration tent and a woman talks me through the process. I recognize what is coming out of her mouth as words but I don't take in the content. I'm fairly sure it's just run, run really far.

Mum tells me that she and Dad and Moses will wait for me at the finish line and then I'm by myself. I mean, I'm not, I'm surrounded by hundreds of people, but I feel set apart from them. This isn't a new experience; I often feel as though everyone else has had an email that I missed. I make my way to the centre of the crowd of runners, where they look a bit more light-hearted than the steely-eyed people at the front. Around me people are folding themselves forward and jumping up and down, so I imitate them, more to blend in than because I believe it will have any benefits.

'Hey,' says a petite Asian girl beside me, 'you ready?' I recognize her voice but I can't place her face. She obviously sees my hesitation and explains: 'I work on reception. You're in customer care, right? I've seen you in town with your son, he's so cute.' As she says this she is bouncing from one foot to the other.

'Yeah, right . . . uhm . . . '

'Nisha,' she says. 'Martha, right?'

'Yeah, sorry,' I say. 'I'm pretty nervous.'

'Me too,' she says, although she doesn't look or sound it. 'Is your boy gonna be at the end?'

'Yeah,' I say.

'How cute!' I don't think it will be cute, for a boy to see his mother limp towards him, her fat face contorted with exertion. I think it may well be traumatizing and I wish I had my phone to tell my parents to save him from the horror. 'It's really good for him to see you doing stuff like this. What's it called, modelling?' Nisha prattles on. I can't respond to her words because of the screaming in my head. 'When he goes to school, you'll be like, 'I'm not a regular mom, I'm a cool mom.'' Nisha looks confused at something she sees in my face and says, 'Haven't you seen *Mean Girls*? It's great.' I'm in awe of her ability to casually reflect on teen movies in the face of such a personal trial. 'Anyway,' she continues, 'see you at the finish . . . probably.'

She bounces away through the crowd and as I watch her disappear I know that I won't make it with my current mindset. I can't see this as a torturous, ridiculous mistake; I must view it as a rebirth. As I stand I am scared, lost Martha Ross, but I will emerge as a cool, single mother who runs half-marathons. Nisha believes this already so there's no reason why I shouldn't.

★ ★ ★

It's a disarming feeling as an adult to realize that you can't do something extremely basic, some would say ingrained. I realize, at perhaps the most inopportune moment ever, that I don't

275

know how to run because I've never truly run, not even for a train. I assume I ran in childhood but I don't recall it. As soon as what I was informed would show up as buds appeared as fully blown breasts, I unofficially retired from running.

In secondary school we had a sadistic physical education teacher who would force us to jog the length of the sea-front. We would set off from school and be collected three miles along the coast. If I hadn't found a creative enough reason not to partake I would duck out early on and use my dinner money to get a bus to the end of the course, such was my commitment to not breaking a sweat; that was when I thought you could get away with taking shortcuts.

I take Mum's advice to pace myself and move only slightly faster than walking pace. I think of my tentative park runs and Leanne's words to just keep going. This, I tell myself, is just an extension of that. I think if I stay at this pace, I'll make it, and I repeat the phrase under my breath — I'll make it, I'll make it. I start to believe I can do it; these strangers lining the route believe I can. But dozens of people overtake me — young, old, inconceivably old and at one point a camel. I imagine myself finishing behind such a ragtag bunch and increase my speed. Maybe I accelerate too quickly — maybe every individual has a definitive ceiling to their physical capacity and I have reached mine — because alarmingly quickly my chest starts burning. I stop and lean over, hoping it will ease the pain, but it seems to make it worse. As I straighten up I see a small child waving. He gestures for me to come towards him. When I do, he hands me a sweaty little pile of Jelly Babies.

'You can do it!' he shouts. I hobble away with my head held high; I don't want to let the little tyke down. I try to distract myself from the pain in my thighs by thinking about George. I believe strongly that there is a finite amount of love in the world and the reason he has come into my life now is because I have created room for him; I have stopped giving myself to people and things that don't deserve me, like Alexander and Cara. I was just a mirror in which they could see themselves reflected; neither of them really wanted me to succeed because if I had my own life I could no longer be their adoring audience. I feel a burst of anger which helps to power me along for some time. I love the energy that surges from the spectators; I feel more support from them than I have felt from my friends and family in a decade.

I feel like I'm flying. I can hear the blood pumping in my head and little flashes of light appear before my eyes. Trees and people blur into a Monet beside me. I try counting my paces and for a while it makes me feel calmer. The landscape starts to become less green, more urban; I can't remember the route but I think it means I'm making progress. Then I see a sign that says we have gone four miles, only four miles. I feel all the exuberance drain out of me, exiting through my feet. Also, I really need to pee. I had noticed several toilets along the course but now, obviously, there isn't one to be seen.

Everything I look at is assessed as a receptacle to hold the contents of my insistent bladder.

When I spot the next set of toilets I relax in anticipation a little too soon. I make it, but only just. It's a desperate scramble to get my tracksuit bottoms and pants past my knees. As I do, relief floods through me. Most of that relief is down to the fact that I am no longer running. I think it might be feasible to stay right here, to sit on this chemical toilet until the whole thing is over, and then there's a pounding on the door. The urgent banging of someone clearly worried about getting a good time, as opposed to just surviving. 'In a minute!' I shout. I hear the hushed, clipped tones of British people grumbling from outside. I get up and straighten myself out. I open the door to a tiny pensioner, still jogging on the spot. She beckons for me to hurry and the instant I'm out, she scrambles up the steps without a second glance at me.

Starting again is even harder than getting going in the first place. I wonder if Mum and Dad and Moses have got to the finish line early to get a good place. When I first signed up I had meant to tell Leanne to come down with James and the kids. For once my flakiness has been to my advantage. Thank goodness for small mercies. Whatever miracle seed was in my porridge has worn off because I'm extremely hungry and my legs feel like lead. I've no idea how long it will take me to run the remainder of the course and that thought makes me feel like I'm having one of those dreams in which you're falling and falling yet never reach the ground.

Sweat is pouring in a sheet down my face; I try to claw the moisture from my eyes with my hands and somehow manage to impede my vision further.

'You all right?' asks a man passing me. I don't have the voice to respond and he seems to take this as confirmation that I'm OK. I'm not OK. I'm fairly sure I'm going to have to stop, certainly within the next five minutes. I decide I'm definitely going to stop, I'm making the decision to stop. And then I look up, and leaning over the barrier about a hundred metres ahead I see George. He's wearing a blue beanie and waving at me. He's showed up for me in a way that even the list could not predict. I keep going; the moment I am in his arms will make it all worthwhile. As I get closer I speed up and start to push my way past other people. The crowd notice my triumphant return to form and egg me on. This is not how I wanted to meet him — damp, exhausted and wearing a lumpy tracksuit — but even so, he's the only thing I want to see. I'm less than a few feet away when I understand it's not him, it's not even close to him, and it's the final blow to my psyche. I stop, my body folds in on itself and I find myself heaving forcefully. Everyone around me jumps away in horror, but they needn't bother because I don't have enough in my stomach to bring anything substantial up. A light pebble-dashing of oats leaves my mouth before I collapse on to the road.

32

When people say their life has flashed before them, you imagine this montage consists of poignant moments — wedding days, the birth of a child — but it's not like that at all. You start thinking that you definitely left your winter jacket at the dry cleaner's and about how you never got round to watching *The Wire*. I must have lost consciousness because when I regain awareness of my surroundings I can make out people already in the throes of conversation.

'Just get her out the way, she's gonna get trampled on.'

'We're not supposed to move them until the paramedic gets here.'

'Stop being such a jobsworth, Caroline. We're *supposed* to make the area safe — having her sprawled out like this definitely isn't safe.' I try to speak to reassure them that I'm more or less OK, but I just feel a stream of drool trickle from the corner of my mouth. I sense several sets of hands pulling on me; even in my semi-consciousness I cringe at the sound of the effort they have to make. The hands are removed.

'Yeah, leave her here,' says one of the voices. The next voice I hear is one I recognize, that of my mother.

'No,' I hear her telling someone. 'She doesn't have any health problems, she's been training for weeks. Someone needs to find out why this happened. Do you think she may have had a heart attack? I've read about that.' I think I probably could open my eyes at this point but I decide against it.

'She's unresponsive,' says a new voice. 'We'll have to take her to general.' They shift me on to something soft and I feel myself rise before being wheeled away. As I move I can hear Mum shouting instructions, I presume to Dad. It feels nice to have someone else in charge of what's happening to me and where I'm going. I love listening to the paramedics discuss my condition in calm whispers.

★   ★   ★

The smell of the ward is so familiar. This hospital is the site of my most immense pain and my greatest joy. Perhaps it's fate that I find myself here, and I'm supposed to come out the other side as yet another incarnation of myself.

'I'm going to help you move now,' says a soft voice. I open my eyes and look into the gentle, shining face of a nurse. For no reason I can identify, the African lilt in her voice is a comfort to me. She stands ready to catch me as I shift awkwardly from the gurney to the bed. Even though I'm still in my tracksuit bottoms the nurse pulls the covers over me, tucking the stiff sheets into the sides of the bed so that they stretch across my legs in a tight embrace.

'I'm Precious. Do you want a cup of tea?' she asks, and I have never wanted anything more in my life.

281

Precious leaves and is replaced by my mother. She has a concerned expression and fresh lipstick on her face. 'They have no idea when you will see the doctor,' she says. 'Did you get that private health insurance I sent you the details for? We can have you moved within the hour.'

I shake my head no. 'Where's Moses?'

'Your father has taken him home. I didn't want him to see you like this.'

I close my eyes again. 'That wasn't your decision to make, Mum.'

She tuts. 'I think it was, because I made it. It was bad enough that he had to see you rolling around on the ground like that, in front of everyone.' I look at her now and search her face for the warmth I imagine I would exhibit if my child was in a hospital bed before me.

'I'm sorry I didn't think to collapse more privately,' I say. Mum looks around, clutching her bag to herself as if the ward were a city centre underpass.

'These places are full of disease,' she says. 'You know you'll come out worse than when you came in.'

Precious returns with a plastic cup, which she hands to me. I take a sip and it's grainy but hot and very sweet.

'I just need to take your blood pressure, dear,' she says. She helps me out of my tracksuit top and straps the gauge to my bicep. We all stare at the reading as the numbers rise and fall before settling on something that means nothing to me. 'It's a little high,' she says. 'How do you feel?'

'Tired,' I say, and glance at my mother. Only very briefly but long enough, it seems, for Precious to understand my plea.

'I think we should leave her to have some rest, Mum,' says the nurse.

'No, I — ' says my mother.

Precious places a hand on her back as she says, 'I need your help with some information about her medical history — it would speed things along.' Mum allows herself to be led away. I feel that surge of appreciation you only experience when you witness someone being really good at their job. A lot of people don't like hospitals and I understand this; they house so much suffering. But sitting in this bed I feel sheltered from the world; it's a similar sensation to the one I have each time the door closes after I've boarded an aeroplane. The sense of calm that comes from knowing that no one can expect anything of me is reassuring. I adjust my bed and fall back into the pillows. I am hungry and sore but, for the first time in weeks, I feel safe.

★   ★   ★

'Hey,' someone whispers. I open my eyes and see Greg poking his head through my curtains. 'Is the coast clear?' he asks.

I shuffle up in the bed. 'Sure,' I say. 'What do you mean?'

Greg steps in and shuts the curtains behind him. 'I came earlier and your mum started quizzing me about how hard we're pushing you at work.'

I laugh. 'I think you're safe.'

Greg holds out a bright pink gift bag, inside which is a copy of *Grazia*, a bag of white chocolate buttons and some posh hand cream.

'The girls wanted to get you flowers but I wasn't sure how useful they would be.'

'This is wonderful,' I say.

'Yeah, you're always using that goop on your hands at work,' he says. Greg sits in the chair beside the bed and starts to help himself to the chocolate buttons.

'How did you know I was here?' I ask.

'Your mum rang to say you wouldn't be back on shift for a while. What's wrong?'

I lean back against my pillows. 'I'm dehydrated and very, very stupid.'

Greg smiles and says, 'How do they treat stupid?'

'With lots of rest,' I say.

'It's not contagious, is it?' he asks.

'Yes, I'm afraid it is,' I say. 'How was work today?'

'Same old,' says Greg. 'People called, I put them through, yunno, life and death stuff. Something's going on with Bob, though.'

'This is news?'

'Nah,' says Greg, leaning forward and lowering his voice, 'I mean he's weirder than usual. When I told him I was leaving to come see you, he said something about changing company policy. I thought he meant about me taking time off but he started muttering something about employees not being allowed to get sick.'

'Bloody hell, I need to get out of there.'

'Is that what this was all about? You didn't want to come to work? You know they have annual leave for that.'

I lean over to try and swipe Greg but he moves back quickly and I miss. 'I'm trying to change my life. I need to. I know it might sound stupid but I just wanted to do something impressive.'

Greg gives me a chocolate button. 'It doesn't sound stupid. I get it. I mean, that happens to me all the time. I meet someone who kitesurfs or climbs mountains or whatever and I think, I want to be like them. I don't want to *be* them because they're usually smug twats, but I want to have something they have.'

'Money, usually,' I say.

'Wise words.'

I shift so that my body is turned towards him. 'Do I just need to grow up? You can tell me. Is it too late; should I just be happy with my lot?'

'No way,' says Greg, and there's no trace of his usual joviality. 'It's never too late, never.'

'I don't know,' I say. 'I'm feeling really, really old.'

'You don't look old,' says Greg.

'How old do I look?' I ask.

'Not a day over forty,' says Greg. I reach into the bag of buttons and throw one at his face.

'I'm starting to think you have a problem with violence,' says Greg solemnly.

'I assure you, it's a Greg-specific problem.'

'Maybe that's my thing,' he says, 'protecting others from all your seething rage.'

'You're doing a very good job,' I say.

Greg stays for another half an hour. He tells

me about his daughter Charlotte's school play. It's great watching him talk about his kids; his love for them fills the room. Eventually Precious appears and tells me I have to see the doctor, so Greg says he'll leave me to it. 'Don't run any more marathons,' he says before he goes. I promise him I won't.

The doctor says I'm fine but it's too late to discharge me. They'll give me fluids and let me rest overnight. I'm not unhappy but I try to look like I am. When he leaves I sit and listen to the sounds around me, families whispering news from home and nurses offering reassurance. What I love about hospitals is how everything is stripped back to the basics. You only receive what you need; you only see the people who truly care. When Moses was born I lost a lot of blood; they made the two of us stay until I was strong enough to be a mother at home. On my second day, I called Alexander, crying.

'How am I supposed to get better when they're feeding me this crap?' He arrived thirty minutes later with a Subway sandwich and a thermos of coffee, the really good kind. He climbed on the narrow bed with me and we shared the food together and watched our baby sleep in his little Perspex cot. Just the three of us and processed meat; it was everything I needed.

★ ★ ★

I must have drifted off because I am suddenly aware of Leanne standing beside me. 'Visiting time has just finished. They let me come in as long as I promised to be five minutes,' she says. Leanne is the type of woman people want to give five minutes. She sits on the edge of the bed and strokes my leg through the hospital blankets. 'What were you doing?' she asks.

'Running a marathon,' I say. 'Well, half of one.'

'I know, but why?'

'Why not?' I ask. 'Why can't I be a woman who runs half-marathons?' And then I start to cry. Leanne hands me a tissue from a box on my bedside table and I use it to mop up my face.

'You can be a woman who runs half-marathons; you can't *wake up* and decide to be a woman who runs a half-marathon without proper preparation. You just ran round the park with me for the first time the other week. Are you doing all this to avoid the separation?'

'No,' I say. 'This is nothing to do with Alexander, I almost never think of him. I had already let go of him long before we broke up.'

'Even if that's the case,' says Leanne, in a tone that suggests she doesn't believe this for a second, 'maybe you're not over the idea of him, the fantasy of being in a perfect couple.'

'Why would I get over that? You're in the perfect couple. Are you saying I'm not good enough to have that too?'

Leanne laughs. 'James and I are far from perfect — there is no perfect. There's basically trying as hard as you possibly can every day.'

'That's what I don't think you understand,' I say, grabbing Leanne's hand. 'I am trying, I'm trying so hard. I'm so, so sick of trying.'

287

Leanne squeezes my hand. 'I know you are, honey, I know.'

33

Hospitals are so easy to get into and so terribly hard to get out of. I need to wait until the doctor discharges me but all the next morning there's not a doctor to be seen. I don't mind it except that the longer I stay the more stupid I feel for ending up here, and Precious has been replaced with a stern Irish woman called Anna, who consistently makes me feel like I'm interrupting her Sunday dinner. When I call her to ask yet again when I will be seen, she tells me to be a patient patient. 'There are sick people here, you know.'

I go to the TV room for a change of scene. There's no one in there save for an older woman watching *Jeremy Kyle*. She's wearing two cardigans and a felt hat.

'Hello,' I say.

'All right, you waiting for someone to pick you up?'

'Yeah,' I say, 'are you?' The woman laughs as if I have said something extremely funny.

'I'm not getting out for a long time, if at all. I just like to get up every day. Even if I did get out, got no one to pick me up. Got no one.' She laughs again; I can see the gaps where her teeth should be. I sit in one of the plasticky chairs and message George.

Marthashotbod: Hey, are you there?

Marthashotbod: I really need to talk to you.
Undeterred83: It's tough today.
Marthashotbod: Please.
Undeterred83: I'll do my best.

I rest my phone on my lap.

'Are these people for real?' asks the woman, I think to me, but her eyes don't leave the screen. I scroll through my contacts to avoid engaging with her. I pause at Cara's name. I should message her; she would force me to see the funny side. I know she'd say something about the dangers of cardio but I'm still upset with her — for leaving me, for not believing me or believing in me. 'Of course 'e's lyin',' the woman says, 'they're always lyin'. Men, who'd 'ave 'em?'

I feel relieved when my phone rings.

'Yeah, what's up?' asks George.

'Nothing really. I just wanted to hear your voice.'

'Ah,' he says. 'It was quite difficult to call you.'

'Oh right, sorry. What are you up to?'

'I'm rafting today,' he says. He sounds happy. I wonder who he is rafting with.

'I've been ill,' I say. 'I'm in hospital.'

'Oh wow, sorry,' he says. 'Hang on.' I hear him moving. 'What happened?'

'I kind of collapsed at the half-marathon.'

'After?'

'During.'

'Crap. You OK now, though?'

'Better for speaking to you.' George doesn't say anything and then I hear him talking to someone. It's muffled, as if his hand is over the phone.

'Sorry, they're calling me,' he says.

'No, it's OK. I just wanted . . . I wanted to know if we could get a date in for when you're back?'

'Yeah, of course. I don't have my diary on me at the minute though.'

'Oh right, I guess you don't need it on a raft.'

George laughs but it sounds a bit forced. 'I've really gotta go,' he says.

'OK, have a great time and let me know how it goes.' I hold the phone to my ear long after he has gone.

'Man trouble?' asks the woman.

I put my phone in my pocket. 'No, not really,' I say.

She laughs again — I wonder if she's on drugs.

'I 'ad an 'usband once. You know what 'appened?' I shake my head. 'I killed 'im.' I glance at the closed door of the room. The woman waits for me to make eye contact with her before saying, 'I did, though, I picked, picked, picked until 'e was dead.' Each time she says the word 'picked' she jabs at the air with her forefinger. 'This is what I know. I don't know much but I know this: 'ave a man an' leave 'im be or don't 'ave one at all.' She says this with a nod of her head; this is the final word on the subject as far as she is concerned. Times have probably changed since she was a young woman; husbands have changed.

I remember my father's mother talking about her husband as if he wasn't in the room. 'Tell

Grandad his tea will get cold,' she would say, and I would walk over to him and repeat it, worried that my mother's whisperings that she would 'lose her marbles' had come to pass. This wasn't the case, though; she had every last one of her marbles until the bitter end and each and every one rolled around in a small pool of bitter resentment. I don't want that; I don't want to leave my man be or have him leave me be. I want to exist together; I want us entwined irreversibly even when it's boring, even when it's hard — especially when it's hard.

Anna the nurse bursts into the room. 'You're here!' she scolds. 'You're at me all morning and as soon as the doctor appears you're nowhere to be found.' I stand up to go with her. Before I leave I look back to the woman, who's engrossed in her show again. To be honest, she looks perfectly content.

34

Returning to Mum and Dad's from hospital is like arriving home after a holiday, both a relief and a disappointment. Mum tells me she has made me some soup but all I want to do is get out of my tracksuit, burn it and have a long shower. When I get to my room my stuff isn't there. It's as if I have been the victim of an extremely orderly robbery.

'Mum!' I shout, and she appears behind me.

'I've moved you to the extension, so you won't be disturbed by Moses,' she says. A small bead of pain forms at my temple.

'I want to be disturbed by Moses,' I say carefully, 'because he's my son. Where is he?'

'Alexander came and got him; I wanted the time to get you settled.'

I sink down to the floor and lean back against the wall. 'How hard is it to call me and ask? How hard is it to treat me like an adult?'

Mum goes over and sits on what used to be my bed and says, 'I do want to treat you like an adult but you don't always act like one.'

'How am I supposed to do anything?' I whisper. 'How am I supposed to do anything if the one person who's meant to be behind me every step of the way isn't there at all?'

'What are you talking about?' asks Mum. She sounds impatient. Whenever I have a conversation with her I get the sense that she's eager to get off and do something more interesting. Even as a small child I felt this. I think this is why people often comment on how quickly I speak; I was always aware that I had to get out as much as I could before I was dismissed.

'Could you not *ask* me what I need rather than patronizing me and stealing my son?'

'I'm not trying to steal him. I did not see myself raising a child at this stage in life but you need to get yourself together.'

'I'm getting a divorce, Mum,' I spit at her. 'It's one of the most stressful life events you can experience; I'm doing pretty well. I'm working, I'm looking into new opportunities, I'm seeing someone . . . '

Mum looks up at the ceiling, where I assume she believes God is hiding. 'You can't be seeing someone already. This is how you get a reputation.'

'Mum, it's not 1803, and Alexander is already shacked up with someone!'

'It's different for men,' says Mum unapologetically.

'Why can't you just want me to be happy?' I say. I look towards her but not directly at her, and in my peripheral vision I can see Mum fold her arms.

'Because happiness is a cop-out. Any idiot can be happy.'

I roll my eyes. 'Apparently not.'

'Do you know how hard your grandmother worked? On weekends, I used to go with her. I'd watch her iron piles and piles of white people's clothes. She never let me help; she always told me to read my books. When I met your dad and he earned enough to keep us both, I thought I had won but . . . ' I wait. The moment feels so heavy. I understand that what is said next could change things for us for ever. 'I know you can do better than this,' Mum says finally. She waves her hand in my direction on the last word.

My emotional scale teeters between anger and acceptance. On one hand I'm so sick of her constant criticism; on the other I am sitting on the floor of my childhood bedroom, a failed half-marathon runner and almost divorcée.

Mum says, 'I know *I* didn't raise you like this.' And the scale tips. My rage propels me from the floor and I am quickly standing looking down on her. She tries to hide it but I can see she's shocked; I might give her some lip now and then but I've never stood up to her in a real or metaphorical sense.

'This is *precisely* how you raised me. What? You think your gold star parenting gave me all the tools I need to excel but I, stubborn little wretch that I am, was just determined to be a fat fuck-up?' Mum opens her mouth to respond but I continue, 'Newsflash: that's not the case. In fact, I'm starting to think living with you might be a big part of the problem.' I turn and walk away and formulate my plan as I do so.

My stuff has been put away neatly in the loft conversion. I repack it into the bags that Alexander sent it to me in and then haul each bag downstairs, one by one. I allow every load to bounce heavily on all the steps of the two flights to the entrance hall. When I'm finished I'm sweating but I feel good; perhaps these are those endorphins that they talk about. I walk into the living room, where my mother and father are sitting in silence. Mum turns away as she sees me enter the room so I leave her to it. My father looks at me, his face full of apprehension.

'Dad,' I say. 'Can I get a lift?'

35

Leanne reacts to me, my cat and all my bags showing up at her door with an admirable level of calm. Most friends say that you can always call on them. They clutch your hand and murmur, 'If there's *anything* you need.' But they say this safe in the knowledge that you will never, ever actually call on them. Leanne isn't this person. If Leanne says she'll be there for you, she'll be there, early, with muffins. She puts me in her guest bedroom, which is always ready for guests. It's quite small and it's only after I bring up my belongings that I remember that I will need to fit Moses and all his toddler paraphernalia in here too. I sit on the bed and look at the contents of my life in holdalls. I have so very little and it still has nowhere to belong. Moving to Leanne's is like unwrapping another layer of pain; I actually feel a dull ache in my belly. The little nicotine-like hits I had been getting from George's increasingly sporadic messages are no longer enough.

Leanne comes in with extra blankets and joins me on the bed. 'Wanna tell me what's going on?'

I pull one of the blankets over my legs. 'I just reached the end of my rope with Mum.' I don't have to say anything else. As a teenager I would spend many a weekend hiding from my mother at Leanne's family home. I loved her mother Tanya so much — a wiry redhead who, contrary to the stereotype, was always quiet and measured. She rarely offered more than the blandest of small talk. After which she would make us chip sandwiches and huge mugs of tea and sit in the kitchen as we lay sprawled in front of her television, watching soaps for hours. Leanne always swore that her mother's passivity came with its own disadvantages but I just think she was trying to make me feel better.

'So, shall we talk about boys?' asks Leanne. I smile. Leanne and I have clocked up hours and hours lying on her bed discussing boys over the years; usually boys who didn't know we existed.

'I feel like he's pulling away,' I say.

'I didn't know you were talking,' says Leanne.

'Not *talking* talking, but we message every day.'

'About Moses?' We both look at each other in confusion. 'We're talking about Alexander, right?' Leanne asks.

'No! Of course not. George.'

'Oh,' says Leanne. 'Nathan George.'

'Shut up,' I say. I show her our conversations on my phone. This is something we used to do years ago, analyse the syntax and frequency of his messages in order to ascertain just how quickly a guy was falling in love.

Leanne reads in silence. When she's had her fill she says, 'He sounds nice.'

'Don't get too excited,' I say, snatching my phone back from her.

'I'm worried it's too soon.' George's profile says he's online but I decide to wait to see if he sends me a message first.

'Weren't you the one telling me to ask the universe to hook me up and setting me up on hideous dates?'

'I still want that for you — not the hideous dates, but finding the right guy,' says Leanne. 'Anyway, what do I know?'

'Exactly,' I say, 'what do you know with your amazing marriage and your beautiful house and your adorable kids?'

Leanne purses her lips and then says, 'Yes, but you know I'd give it all up for your eyebrows.' I scoot across the bed and rest my head on her shoulder. I'm shocked at how good it feels to have her body against mine. I wonder how long it would take to get used to not being held — a month? A year? A decade? Sometimes I see this old woman in the Co-op. As I queue up behind her, I watch her fumble for exact change in a small coin purse and I hear the cashier humour her as she offers embarrassingly unnecessary commentary. I want to stop her before she leaves the store and ask, 'When was the last time you were touched — I mean, really touched?' When Leanne says things like 'it's too soon', she says this from the position of someone who knows she will be touched in a few hours and again tomorrow and most probably every day after that. When I think about George I know that it's very much not soon enough.

'OK, tell me more,' says Leanne. 'What's he like?'

I sit up so she can see my face. 'He's perfect.'

'Just perfect, not extraordinary?'

I grab Leanne's arm so she will focus and hear

299

my words. 'No, you don't understand — he's literally perfect.'

'OK, but what's his flaw?'

Leanne and I made an agreement when we were in Year 10 that every guy has a flaw and as a woman you must find it as fast as possible. It happened when she fell deeply in lust with Troy Adeyemi, the new sixth-former transferred from somewhere mysterious and exotic like Kent. He was really quiet, bordering on mute, but Amy Mitchell had told us that she had seen him with his mum in Tesco and that he could definitely speak. What he lacked in conversational skills he made up for in aesthetics; he had impossibly high, almost feminine cheekbones set into a perfectly symmetrical face. He stood a good head above most of the other guys and had arms so strong that, even at fifteen years old, I couldn't look at him without imagining him throwing me on to a bed; not that I would have had any idea what to do when I got there.

Leanne and I plotted for months about how she would secure him. She was allowed to claim him because we had come to an agreement that anyone who said they 'actually, truly' fancied someone would earn the right to pursue that person indefinitely. I was a bit miffed in this case. When Troy started I thought that our shared status of 'token mixed-race kid in class' would propel us together. It didn't. He looked at me the way you would examine a torn cuticle.

Leanne didn't fare much better but had a significant weapon in her arsenal: her grandparents had recently moved to the outskirts of town, into a house ordinary in every way aside from one key detail — an outdoor pool. Leanne's grandfather had been plagued by arthritis for many years and thought a daily swim and the coastal air would heal his ailments. We thought a pool party with amazing bikinis might lure in Troy.

We had to wait until the weather was appropriate to mobilize. Leanne endured eight long months of watching Troy from afar before the longest winter ever ended. She was unwilling to do anything without parental permission, so we had to work within the parameters of what her grandmother was willing to accommodate. That would be no adult supervision for the time it took her to do her big shop and have a slice of cake and a cup of tea in the garden centre. Leanne managed to invite Troy and a few of his friends with the promise of an empty house and perhaps the implication that there would be alcohol; I think this was when I really started to understand how determined Leanne could be. Of course, there was no alcohol; in fact I had to hide the jug of squash left out by Leanne's gran. The boys did not seem too disappointed by the lack of booze or birds — they were happy to raid the fridge and throw each other into the pool. I remember one moment when, stepping out of the house after returning from the loo, I looked at the scene unfolding before me and thought, I will never be happier than this.

As the afternoon drew to a close the lads became restless and Leanne started to worry about her grandmother's return. When Troy told

Leanne that they were leaving to attend another party (our invitation apparently got lost in the post) she told him she had to show him something in the kitchen. Troy's friends deftly ignored me as Leanne went inside to complete her master plan. When they emerged five minutes later Troy looked as handsome as ever and Leanne looked miserable. She was silent the entire time we cleared the garden and mopped the water from the tiles around the pool. She was silent even after her grandparents came home and I had to speak on behalf of both of us when they asked if we had had a nice time with our friends.

Later that evening as we both climbed into her queen-sized bed she let out a long, low moan. 'It was awful,' she said, 'it was so, so awful.' I could feel her body grow tense, simply from the memory of whatever horror she was about to share. 'He just sort of licked me,' she said. 'I mean, he licked my whole face! How can he be so beautiful and such a bad kisser?' It was after this night that we decided that every man, however wonderful he may appear, however beautiful or cool, has a flaw, and as a woman it is your job to find it and find it fast.

'He's gotta have a flaw,' says Leanne now.

'Well, his fiancée died — '

'Oh God!' cries Leanne.

'I know,' I say.

'You can never compete with a dead ex.'

'He seems pretty together about it,' I say.

Leanne looks thoughtful. 'As flaws go, it's not that bad,' she says. 'What did we say Alexander's flaw was?' I don't like that she has changed the subject from George but I have to admit I was thinking the same.

'I think that he's a bit self-absorbed,' I say.

'Sounds about right,' says Leanne. 'That's quite a big one; why did I let you get away with that?'

'I didn't give you a choice. I'd fixed him so firmly in my sights, an articulated tank couldn't have pushed me off course.'

'So what makes it different this time?'

'This time is *so* different,' I say. 'This time I have the list.'

She makes me get it out. 'We were quite drunk, you know,' she says. I pass her the now thin and grubby piece of paper and she carefully examines each point. 'So, he's meeting the criteria?'

'He's more than meeting them; he's surpassing them.'

Leanne nods. 'Well, he's got the looks. Job?'

'He's a freelance researcher working in international development.'

'Nice.'

I point to the next thing on the list. 'He's really in touch with his emotions; he went on a ten-day silent retreat.'

'He's in touch with something,' says Leanne.

'I won't lie,' I say, jabbing at the next point, 'I don't really know what his relationship with his family is like, but I know he lives alone. He wants kids but he doesn't have them because — '

'Dead ex,' says Leanne matter-of-factly.

'Exactly, but it's the rest that's really amazing.

He listens to me, I mean *really* listens, and asks questions afterwards. I don't have to debate with myself about whether he likes me or whether he wants to be with me.'

'That's nice,' says Leanne softly. 'What about the cat, though?'

'He has one! He's called Marley,' I say.

Leanne shrugs. 'Close enough.'

36

As Leanne helps me to unpack, Dad calls to tell me he's bringing Moses over from Alexander's. He adds, 'Can you sort it out with your mum, she's been crying.' Which has as much authenticity as a Louis Vuitton bag on a Hackney market stall.

I choose to ignore him and say, 'I'll see you soon.'

When Dad drops Moses off, Millie is so excited by the impromptu sleepover that her bouncing and shouting prevents him from addressing the issue again. He gives me a big hug instead. I am reminded of being a child and falling asleep in his lap as he watched old, black-and-white films into the early hours of the morning. As he holds me I think, you fucked me up, Dad. You made me think I could find a guy who would always be there.

Once we've managed to sedate the children with snacks and Disney, I suggest to Leanne that we get into our PJs and open a bottle of wine, but Leanne says, 'Let's finish getting you organized.' As we return upstairs she says, 'We should definitely review things. I called Cara the other day. She said to ask you if you'd finished having your tantrum.'

'Review? I'm not a project. I just want to hang out with my friend.'

'What did she mean?' asks Leanne, ignoring

my admonishment. 'I take it you had a falling-out?'

I hand Leanne a pile of clothes and she starts to arrange them in colour-coordinated piles. I shake my head, perhaps too emphatically.

'A disagreement,' I say. 'She can be so up herself sometimes. It's as if she thinks she's superior to everyone.'

'Really?' asks Leanne. She tilts her head, as if examining an object from a different angle. It makes me angry. Leanne always gave me the impression she was keen to have a bitch about Cara.

'I didn't even think you liked her?' I ask, trying and failing to disguise my outrage. *I* didn't like Cara when I first encountered her at work. When we spoke, which was rarely, it was in brief, instructive missives (from her). I told myself, and anyone who might be interested, that she was 'very self-focused' and 'not my kind of girl', which is sort of true but also a lie, the sort of lie we tell to protect ourselves. I was intrigued by her and I was intimidated by her, both much more impressive than being likeable; as soon as she offered me an invitation into her world, I RSVP'd yes.

'I admire Cara's spirit,' says Leanne thoughtfully. I want to know if Leanne admires my spirit but I'm scared to ask.

'You don't need to call a friendervention every time I have a minor crisis,' I say.

'As if I'd have time,' Leanne says under her breath, but not under her breath enough that I don't hear it, which seems careless.

James's voice floats upstairs. 'You've got a Moses coming through!' My son runs in and stands next to the bed.

'Up!' he shouts with his arms raised. I pull him up, scattering Leanne's folding in the process. Moses squishes my face between his small palms and says, 'Bisbik.'

'No biscuits, darling,' I say.

'Bisbik peeeeease.' Leanne smiles at Moses and I think that maybe she believes I've done one thing right.

'Shall we get our wine o'clock on?' I ask her.

'Actually,' she says, 'I was hoping since you're here that James and I could go out.'

It's an affront — I'm a friend in need; I feel like she should offer the evening to me. To leave your newly single mate to go out on a hot date with your husband seems callous, but Leanne's giving me a roof over my head so what can I say but, 'Of course. Of course, I'll do something fun with the kids. We'll bake cakes.'

Leanne gives me a 'like heck you will' glance but she says thank you. With that she's gone to get ready and leaves me to potter around aimlessly. I take Moses downstairs and leave him playing cars with Lucas, who is clearly basing his game on a recently witnessed incident of road rage. I go to the kitchen to make a cup of tea and try to source some biscuits but turn up nothing. Millie wanders into the room and watches me for a few moments.

'What you doing, Auntie Marfa?' she asks. I continue to root around in a cupboard of saucepans.

'I'm looking for biscuits.'

Leanne comes in and stands behind her daughter. Seeing them there together, the same half-quizzical, half-judging expression on their faces, I am struck by how similar they look. Millie has her father's colouring but her mannerisms are pure Leanne. I always think Moses looks nothing like me but in this moment I wonder if it's something you can only see from a distance.

'She's looking for biscuits,' Millie says.

'We had a clear-out,' says Leanne. I look at Millie, who shrugs.

'No worries, we can make them,' I say. 'Wanna make biscuits with Auntie Martha?' Millie whoops.

Leanne gently pushes me aside and gets out baking stuff.

'We won't be long,' she says after she has laid it all out. She gives Millie a kiss on the head. 'Daddy and I are going to get pizza.' The word pizza causes my stomach to growl; all the drama distracted me from dinner.

'Let's start now,' I tell Millie. 'Go get the boys.' Millie runs off.

'Thanks for this,' says Leanne.

'Any time, and thanks for letting us stay — I promise I'll get something sorted soon.'

'No problem.'

Leanne leaves and it's only when I hear the door slam that I realize that she's *gone* gone. The kids run in, hyped up by the promise of sugar. Seeing the three of them there is a little intimidating, but I know I've got this.

When all the children are covered in flour I realize I have no idea how to make biscuits. I've eaten a lot of them though, so I can guess the basics — flour, sugar and loads of butter; what doesn't taste better with loads of butter? I get Millie to be head stirrer and ask the boys to sort the raisins. They dump the entire bag on the floor. Millie is taking her job very seriously; the tip of her tongue pokes out of her mouth as she focuses on not letting anything spill from the mixing bowl. 'Do you ever make biscuits with your mum?' I ask her.

'No,' says Millie, 'she doesn't really like a mess.' I feel a bit smug that I'm introducing her to this quintessential bonding activity. The boys grow bored before the biscuits are ready and I have to abandon the project to build them a den under the dining table. When I return to Millie she has created a dozen mismatched biscuits. She looks so proud and I don't want to take this away from her so I put them in the oven as they are.

It's a little way before bedtime but with three kids to get ready I decide to get started. The boys seem to sense that they are being short-changed and both begin to protest. Lucas begs for his mother and Moses chooses his preferred method of resistance, violence. Every time I try to pick him up he struggles and kicks like a wild animal. 'Millie, can you be a big girl and look after Moses whilst I put Lucas to bed?'

'Yes,' she says confidently. As I carry a

mournful Lucas upstairs I hear her say, 'Moses, do you like jam?'

Lucas bleats pitifully as I get him into his pyjamas. I want to tell him that if he thinks life is bad now, he's got a big shock a-comin'. I carry him to bed, where he lies down but raises the volume on his crying. If he were Moses I would leave him to it and get stuck into wine time but this seems a bit inappropriate with someone else's child. I kneel down beside the bed and stroke his hot little head.

'One day,' I say gently, 'there was a little boy called Lucas. He had a lovely mummy and daddy but what he didn't know was that his mummy was a princess.' Lucas grows quiet. 'When she was little she lived with the king and queen in a little castle in Saltdean.'

'Like Grandma and Grandad?' asks Lucas.

'Of course,' I say. Lucas pops his thumb into his mouth.

'Princess Mummy liked being a princess but she thought it was really boring. Princesses have to wear big, big dresses and really heavy crowns and they can't climb trees or swim in the sea, so one day she went to her daddy and said, 'What do I have to do if I don't want to be a princess any more?' Her daddy said that princesses need to look after the castle so that princes can catch dragons, and that if she didn't want to be a princess any more she needed to go and catch her own dragon. So, one day the princess walked to the scariest, darkest part of Saltdean until she found a massive, scary dragon called Henry. She said, 'I need a favour. Can you come back to my castle?' So, they both went back to the castle and the king and queen told her, 'Well done, you don't have to be a princess any more,' and they all had a big party.'

Lucas has closed his eyes and his breathing is starting to slow; I take the opportunity to slip out. In the kitchen the scene before me makes Mardi Gras look like a tea party. Millie has decided to introduce Moses to a variety of condiments and he is creating food art on the tiled floor. 'OK, both you guys need a bath now!' Millie looks happy but Moses stares at me as if I have committed the deepest of betrayals.

In the bathroom Millie tells me her dad lets her have loads of bubbles and tips about half a bottle of Matey into the water. 'Does your daddy give you a bath every night?' I ask.

'Yes,' says Millie, 'it's 'daddy time'.' As she says this she makes quotation marks in the air with her fingers.

'Do you know what that means?' I ask, imitating her action.

'No,' she says happily. After undressing she leaps into the foam with so much excitement I suspect I might have been had. I take off Moses's clothes and nappy and put him in beside her. He is still scowling. Millie tries to cheer him up by putting bubbles on her head but he is unmoved.

'Why doesn't he like baths?' says Millie. 'Baths are the best!'

'I guess everybody's different, baby,' I say.

*　*　*

After their bath, I tell Millie to go and put on her pyjamas and then I tuck Moses into the bed we will share. Despite his earlier refusal he is obviously knackered and falls asleep almost instantly. I watch him for a couple of minutes; I wonder if all the change is too much for him. Perhaps settling down with someone quickly and providing him with a good male role model is the most important thing I can do right now.

I go to Millie's bedroom, where she is lying in bed with her pale pink duvet pulled up to her chin. As I'm giving her a kiss on the forehead she says, 'I love you staying.' It feels so good to hear it. 'What will we do tomorrow?' Millie asks.

'Whatever you want.'

'Can we make friendship bracelets?'

'Sure,' I say. I pat the duvet around her, making her giggle. 'Millie, what's that smell?'

Millie's eyes stretch open. 'The biscuits,' she whispers.

I race downstairs, which is futile because it's clear from the acrid scent making its way up the stairs that the few seconds I save will not rescue these baked goods. I pull twelve lumps of coal out of the oven. I guess I'll never know if I had the right recipe. I feel more let down by this than I should. In search of something to help me hide from my own disappointment, I find a bottle of red wine. It looks quite nice but I know that Leanne bulk-buys wine from Costco, so it won't be missed.

I sink the first glass quickly, too quickly; the effects of the alcohol are immediately felt in my head and extremities. I pour another glass and then break a big chunk of cheddar from a block in the fridge to line my stomach. I walk round the house nibbling on my cheese, taking in little details that I've never noticed in all the years of coming here, like a small bowl of mints on the kitchen counter and a large vase filled with umbrellas by the door. As I head upstairs I realize there's another reason I'm here. I want to study them — Leanne and James. I might get some insight into what it is that makes a marriage work.

I start in the bathroom; the best questions are answered in the bathroom. The cupboard is full of very expensive cleansers and at least five different moisturizers, so perhaps the secret to a long-lasting relationship is very good skin. The only thing that looks like it might belong to James is a dusty bottle of aftershave. Alexander is metro-sexual when it comes to products. Perhaps the answer is letting your wife have more space in the cabinets.

The half a bottle of wine I've consumed has emboldened me and I decide it's perfectly OK to go into the master bedroom. The room is all soft and creamy and not the sort of place secrets could hide at all. I peek into the cupboards and in the bedside cabinets; not a break-up letter or a sex toy to be found. I start to feel desperate. I look under the bed and deep into the sock drawer, and then under the dresser I find a battered old shoebox. I open it gingerly and as I do a photo slips on to the floor. It's a picture of Leanne and James circa 2014; I know this because Leanne still has a tragically severe crop that she got in a bid to be taken more seriously at work and then spent a year growing out. In the picture James has his face squeezed up against hers; his eyes are closed but his face still bursts with pleasure. Leanne looks irritated by him but if you know her, as I do, you can tell that she's loving it. I start to look through the photos, dozens of terrible, blurred selfies from a time before selfies were a thing; photos of a wet-eyed James holding a tiny, wrinkled Millie. I scoop up the box and take it to the living room, retrieving the rest of the wine on the way. The box is a journey through Leanne's life. Unlike her Facebook it's unedited; photos featuring her with no make-up or with sneaky rolls of flab showing sit right alongside shots of her looking radiant in her youth.

Towards the bottom of the box are a collection of Leanne and me throughout our school days together, including a photo of us standing awkwardly in our school uniforms and looking ridiculously young. I remember feeling like I knew so much and that my troubles were so weighty; looking at the pictures we were clearly babies. There's another picture of us in swimwear, which I'm sure was taken on the day Leanne discovered Troy's fatal flaw. There're photos of trips and events that have long since deserted my memory bank. I would never have kept evidence of a time when I felt so ugly and unfortunate. Looking at the pictures now, I regret this. I don't look ugly, I look wonderful, and between the two of us this past version of me is far more fortunate. The secret, I think, is in this shoebox. The secret is cherishing everything, even the things that feel hideous at the time.

I must fall asleep because light streaming through the window is what wakes me. The photos have gone, and I have been covered with a throw. My mouth feels dry, so I get up and go to the kitchen to find something to drink. Any evidence of last night's carnage has disappeared and on the counter, covered in cling film, is a plate of twelve identical biscuits. I take one and bite into it. It's light but still chewy. It's honeyed and full of fruit and there's also a touch of spice. It's perfect.

37

I go up to the spare room and get into bed beside Moses. Shortly afterwards, Leanne comes to the door in a skirt suit and grey T-shirt. 'See you tonight, I guess,' she says. 'The spare key is on the hook in the kitchen.' She doesn't mention the fact that I trashed her house or went through her personal belongings or got drunk when her children were supposed to be under my care; so I don't either. 'Do you want me to take Moses into nursery when I drop off Lucas?' They don't actually go to the same nursery but it's sort of on the way. I know I should say no — I should tell her that she's done enough — but I nod my head. She leaves the room and I wake Moses and get him ready. This is when I love him most, when his body is warm and uncoordinated.

Leanne comes back up to get him. 'Should I give him a breakfast bar?' she says, looking at him anxiously.

'No, it's OK,' I say, 'they give them breakfast.' Leanne narrows her eyes at me. For once I can't tell what her expression is saying but I think she basically believes I outsource my parenting. I'm too tired to try and challenge this so I let her reach out for Moses's hand.

Millie appears behind her and says, 'Fanks for making the biscuits, they're 'licious.' Leanne and I look at each other but she doesn't say anything. When they're gone I climb back into bed and lie there until my bladder won't let me any longer. I need a plan. My doctor's note from the hospital has a couple more days on it and the hours stretch ahead of me intimidatingly. I need coffee and then a plan. I message George.

Marthashotbod: Good morning x
Undeterred83: How are you? Sorry I've been MIA. Just found out I've got funding for a new project. Been doing some research.
Marthashotbod: No worries. I'm better thanks. Good luck with it.
Undeterred83: Thanks. I'll message you later.
Marthashotbod: OK.

I wish I had some news of my own to share with him. I try and work out how to make coffee in Leanne's fancy machine and end up with a mug of dirty lukewarm water. I find a jar of decaf instant in the cupboard and add loads of sugar. As I drink it I look out to the garden. I've never really understood gardens — they're like a whole extra room to maintain and clean but one that, in this country, you can only use two and a half months of the year. It does look very peaceful out there, though. I remember digging up potatoes on the retreat and I contemplate going outside.

I decide against it because I know it won't be the same doing it alone; I've never felt more alone. I meant to walk away from Alexander leaving everything else intact but it's like ripping him out has frayed the edges of the rest of my life. Despite being an only child, I've always been shit at going it alone — I need someone else to validate my decisions. Leanne has done that for me for almost as long as I remember.

We didn't immediately become friends at school. I'd noticed Leanne but had written her off. I thought she was the kind of girl one would describe as perky, someone who wouldn't have allowed my presence to dull their shine. For the first year of secondary school I hung out with a couple of girls I'd vaguely known at juniors — a mouthy brunette called Janine, who even at that age it was apparent would lead me down a path of destruction and promiscuity; and a meek, mousy girl, Sophia, who had the unfortunate affliction of frequent, unannounced nosebleeds. If I'm honest I wanted an upgrade.

During a geography test I got one. I was stuck on a question on the formation of cliffs. We had attended a field trip to Seven Sisters but I had spent the day worrying about the fact that my new jeans didn't fit right around the crotch. I couldn't remember anything that we had been told and was chewing on my purple gel pen, hoping for divine inspiration, when Leanne, who was sitting next to me, hissed, 'You need to write in black.' She slid a biro across the desk and I quickly exchanged my purple pen for her offering. She finished the test long before me, and left the room before I could return her property. I carried it with me for nearly a week, until I found myself behind her in a long lunch line.

'How did you do?' she asked as I handed her the biro.

'Crap,' I said.

'Me too,' she admitted. I didn't know at the time that Leanne's 'crap' and my 'crap' were entirely distinct entities.

'You wanna study together for the next one?' she asked.

'Yeah,' I said. She grabbed my hand and used the pen I had returned to write her number on it. Even when the most attractive guy I have ever met gave me his number (a Trinidadian basketball player I met in a club in Soho, whom I never saw again because he either typed his number incorrectly or offered it insincerely), the thrill was not matched by the moment Leanne took hold of my hand and extended hers in friendship. From then on, I stopped feeling alone. There was always someone to bounce off and to reassure. We remained that way until after university, when I met Alexander. It's like he was a virus killing off other parts of my life, making me weaker. And somehow, he was still managing to do it.

The ringing doorbell startles me. I try to pull my tunic, crumpled from a night's sleep, down my thighs before I open the door. Behind it is a handsome man, sort of surreally handsome. Blond, windswept hair; slow, sexy smile; and, despite the low temperatures, thick, brown biceps, gripped by the almost-too-tight sleeves of a brilliant, white T-shirt.

'Hi,' I say.

'Hi,' he says absent-mindedly, rubbing his abs

with his hands. 'I'm the window cleaner.' I can't help but think of a really bad porn film Leanne and I once watched after she stole it from her older half brother. This makes me blush and then the fact that I'm embarrassed makes me flush even more.

'Just looking for this month's payment.'

'What is it?'

'Fifteen.'

I run upstairs and grab my purse. When I'm back at the front door I try to count out fifteen pounds but only find eleven pounds sixty-three, a piece of chewing gum and a kirby grip.

'Sorry,' I say. 'Do you want a tenner and then you can get the rest from Leanne later?'

'Don't worry,' he says. 'Give her my card; she can pay me next time or do a transfer.' As he reaches up the step to pass me the card the bottom of his T-shirt rises up to unveil a thick stripe of taut skin. It takes me a few seconds to remember what to do with my arm before I reach out and take it. I watch him walk away. The business card is beautiful. In thick, gorgeous typography it says 'Dean Halpin, Windows' and his contact details. I feel a bit sick. Everything in Leanne's life is aspirational; even her hot window cleaner has his shit together. If I want to be a woman to be reckoned with I can't hang about in gardens, I can't expect anyone to hold my hand. I need to face up to my problems and make things happen and I have to start today. I send a message.

'MEET ME IN BILL'S AT 12 P.M.'

38

She arrives nine minutes late. She's completely bare-faced and when she takes off her leather jacket I see she's wearing a soft grey T-shirt, so lived in that it's evident that what she isn't wearing is a bra. Her look says, 'I try not to be sexy but, God damn it, I just can't help it.'

'Thanks for coming, Poppy,' I say.

'No, no! Thanks for asking! I wanted to message you but Alexander said you'd need some time.' And there he is, casually coming out of her mouth within a minute of meeting. Fortunately, we are interrupted by a waitress.

'Can I get you anything?' she asks.

Poppy flashes her a brilliant smile before asking me, 'Are we drinking?' I want to slap her. My right hand actually itches.

'No,' I say.

'Ooh, OK,' says Poppy. She plays with a lock of hair as she looks at the menu. 'I'll have a hot chocolate, please. Do you have any marshmallows?' She looks back at the waitress.

'No, I don't think so,' she says.

'No worries,' says Poppy. 'You have amazing cheek-bones, by the way.'

The waitress touches her face. 'Thank you,' she says. 'Would you like some cream or something with your hot chocolate?'

'Oh, you're amazing,' says Poppy. The waitress looks at her like she's a little bit in love. When she leaves, Poppy turns her attention to me. She creates a little ledge with her hands and rests her chin on it as she appraises me. 'You're looking really good,' she says.

I fold my arms. 'Let's start by getting one thing clear,' I say. 'We're not gonna be friends.' I feel grateful that I have never liked her. I remember the first time she was introduced to me and stood there with this expression of faux humility, as if silently apologizing for being so attractive.

Alexander, sensing my apprehension, would often try and sell her to me. 'Poppy has started an ironic cross-stitch group for young professionals; you might like it?' The fact that he stopped doing this several months ago should have alerted me to something. From what I understand, Poppy started as an intern, which meant fetching Alexander sushi and tidying up, and then her role stretched and morphed into a PA, which meant the same with the occasional email. She was studying interior design or visual merchandising or something that made me think, yeah, you probably don't have to be able to read to do that. When our paths crossed at the flat she would often try to ingratiate herself with me by offering a macaroon or a used magazine, but I resisted her charm offensive. Today I see that all those little gestures were silent apologies for her betrayal. I take a sip of my water.

'So, when did you start fucking my husband?' I ask. It's a bit soap opera but it feels so good saying it.

Poppy coughs. She leans back and places her

322

hands in her lap. 'It wasn't like that,' she says.

'No? You haven't slept with him?'

Poppy clears her throat. 'Neither of us saw this coming. It wasn't like we planned to . . . It was more of an emotional relationship, I guess.' Make me gag. 'I know things have been hard for you two since Moses was born and so I . . . I just don't think this had anything to do with me, really. Perhaps it made what was already there clearer.'

Did Alexander cheat on me? I don't know and the reason I don't know is because, as many couples fail to, we did not lay down the groundwork and agree with each other, or even ourselves, what cheating actually was. Was it cheating to walk to the expensive coffee shop because the barista has a cute smile? Was it cheating to give up your seat on the train to a perfectly able-bodied woman simply because you want her to think of you as gallant? Was it cheating for your knee to be pushed against your new colleague's thigh when having lunch in a crowded pub and to leave it there just a few seconds too long before moving it? If yes, then I suppose Alexander did cheat, but then so did I.

'Did you ever think that maybe he was just spinning you a line? 'My wife doesn't understand me' — it's like king of the clichés.'

'I don't think so,' says Poppy. 'He wasn't telling me to get anything from me, he just knew I could meet him where he is. Anyway, I had a boyfriend.'

'And he had a wife.'

The tips of Poppy's ears turn red. She is so

young and for the first time I don't think about this with envy. I look at her and I see me ten years ago, seduced by Alexander's insistence that I was the only woman that could save him.

'You know why you can meet him where he is? Because you're not fully formed; you're basically amoebic in your emotional development. You can meet him where he is because you don't know who you are. Let me tell you now — not as his ex or your rival or whatever — as a woman to a, well, almost woman. Get out, don't make the mistake I did. However shiny and pretty he looks now, it's all just an illusion.'

'He said you'd say that,' says Poppy. She looks sad, as if she's disappointed that I'm so predictable. The waitress brings out her drink; I want to stand up, put my hand on the back of her head and push her face into the cream on top of that hot chocolate. Maybe Greg's right; perhaps I do have a problem with violence. 'People grow apart,' she says. 'I can't help that.'

'So when you two grow apart, or more specifically you grow up, it will be OK if some floozy takes him away from you?'

'If that's what he wants,' she says.

'How very big of you,' I say.

'That's the thing: we just give each other what the other wants.'

'I agree,' I say. 'He wants to pretend he's a kid. He wants to act like he has no responsibilities but he does.'

'Oh, he knows that,' says Poppy. 'He adores Moses and so do I.'

'That's cute,' I say, 'but he can't raise *our* child

on adoration alone.'

'Look, Moses has nothing to do with this — he still loves Moses.' Implication received. He no longer loves *me*. I move my chair closer to the table, so that she can see the seriousness in my eyes.

'Tell him from me I want you nowhere near my child.'

'That's not reasonable,' says Poppy.

'It's perfectly reasonable. Moses has been through enough without someone else playing Mummy to him. You'd know that if you had kids.'

Poppy smiles and I am filled with horror. She is smiling because she doesn't have kids but she is thinking, as most women at the start of a relationship do, that she could. She could have a child with the father of my child. We would be linked for the rest of our lives and Alexander would have to parent two children when he does such a sloppy job of parenting one. Poppy glances around before she speaks, as if checking for witnesses.

'I'm in Alexander's life, so I'm in Moses's. I appreciate you might not feel comfortable with that but please accept it. It will be so much easier if we're friends. I'm actually really nice.' I think this is meant to be a joke but nothing about its delivery indicates this. Also, I get the sense that she's loving this; she's soaking up the drama of it all. How exciting to play the role of the measured mistress. I can see her later, recreating the scene for her friends. I know she'll shake her head and say, 'It's insane!'

'I know this is all fun and games for you, your little adventure with an older man, but this is my life; this was a family. You don't know half of what we've been through. You weren't there when his mum passed away or when our dead baby was dragged out of my body. You don't know how devastating it all was.'

'I know,' says Poppy, 'he told me.'

'He told you what?' I ask.

'Everything,' she says. She makes a sweeping gesture with her hand as she says this, a gesture that is meant to represent the beginning and the end of my marriage and all the gruesome bits in between. Alexander never once spoke about the baby after we lost her. Except for one occasion when he mentioned that he had found some 'stuff' in a drawer (baby books and tiny clothes) and put it in a bag to take to the charity shop. Now he's telling this flat-chested woman-child all the gory details. I should be angry, I should be outraged — instead, I cry. If there is a humiliation greater than crying in front of your soon-to-be ex-husband's much younger, much hotter girlfriend in Bill's cafe, I don't want to know what it is. Poppy moves towards me and I look up sharply, giving her a gaze that I hope communicates in no uncertain terms that if she touches me I will remove all her fingers. It clearly reads this way or near enough because she recoils.

'I'm gonna go,' she says, pushing away from the table. She takes a few steps and then looks back and says, 'Take care of yourself.' I picture her and Alexander curling together like vines in bed tonight, expressing artificial concern for my well-being. I didn't even get to slip in any details of George. If anyone was going to walk out it was going to be me, preferably after covering her with milkshake. Instead she gets to glide away like a model, leaving me to pay for her untouched hot chocolate with my eleven pounds sixty-three.

39

'She's such a bitch,' I tell Leanne when she's home from work. Leanne continues to spiralize courgettes. 'I suppose we knew she was a bitch but we didn't know the levels; we didn't understand the depths of her bitchiness.' This doesn't even raise a smirk from Leanne. 'What's wrong? Tough day at work?' Leanne starts to crush garlic without answering me. 'Coz, yunno, I've had a coffee with my husband's mistress and you're supposed to agree she's a bitch. That's like best friend 101.'

Leanne puts down the crusher and says, 'It's a waste of your energy focusing on her. You've had an afternoon to yourself. An afternoon that you could have spent doing something useful.' Leanne gestures to the baking stuff still in the sink. 'Instead you fill your time creating drama.' Leanne and I once made a rule that we would always be honest with each other. It happened the morning after I drank too many blue WKDs and asked a boy on the bus to be my boyfriend; when he refused (repeatedly) I cried and then covered the seat and my new dress in blue vomit. The next morning, I chastised Leanne for not making clear to me that it was a terrible idea to proposition a stranger on the number 5 and we promised we'd offer each other honest counsel from that day forward; we pinky swore on it. But telling the truth doesn't mean spewing negativity all over your friend, especially when that friend is processing the fact that her ex has a hot, young, new girlfriend.

'I already have one mother,' I tell Leanne, 'I don't need another one.' Leanne washes her hands and doesn't comment. I say her name to let her know the conversation is far from over. She stands across from me and places her palms flat on the island.

'Maybe you do. We're not kids any more — we *have* kids. The little scrapes you get yourself into are no longer cute.' Her words sting, as was their intention. She looks at me pityingly and I decide it's time that Leanne heard some truths of my own.

'We can't all be perfect, Leanne, and you know what, some of us don't want to be. You think you've got it all figured out, don't you? Well, here's something you haven't figured out. We can see it, we can all see how hard you're trying and how much you care what people think of you. It doesn't look that perfect, it looks exhausting. It looks sad.'

Leanne curls her hands into fists before leaning forward and saying, 'I'd rather be sad than a mess. I'd rather be someone my daughter can look up to.'

I rise from my stool. 'Are you saying my son shouldn't be proud of me? Are you really saying that?'

'If the shoe fits,' says Leanne.

I jab my forefinger on to the counter. I can feel the tenseness in my jaw as I say, 'My son will be proud of me. Because I may be a mess; I may not have chrome door-knobs and Ocado deliveries and all the other shit you think is so important, but I'm a good person. I care about people. I'm a loyal friend.'

Leanne laughs and the sound shocks me. 'Of course you're a loyal friend!' she cries. 'If you weren't you wouldn't have anyone to clean up your little accidents.'

'Fuck off, Leanne,' I say. 'I've never asked you to fix anything. All I've asked is for you to be there for me, to show a bit of interest. You barely listen to me these days.'

Leanne and I have fought before — there was the time she and Rebecca Grayson from the year above went to see Peter Andre in concert and didn't even ask me; when she ditched my birthday celebrations for a first date with a bloke who only talked about *World of Warcraft*; and when she went to bed on my wedding night, when what I needed her to do was sit with me and hold my hand until I passed out, stone-cold drunk. Leanne covers her face with her hands and when she takes them away her expression is hard and unreadable.

'I listen,' says Leanne, 'but I don't know why I bother because you say the same things over and over again. And you don't seem to want to hear any solutions. I'm here for you, I really am — may I remind you that you're living in my house? — but when are you going to fucking start being there for yourself?'

I shake my head. She's just being cruel. 'What is this about?' I ask. 'It's not all about me. I think it's because, even if I'm fucking everything up,

I'm trying to make changes. I'm moving, I'm not living the same boring life day after day until I die.'

Leanne just looks at me, her bright green eyes shining with anger, and then she starts to cry. I feel panicked. I was angry; I didn't really mean to hurt her.

'Martha,' she says, as she drags her hands across her face. 'James has cancer.'

I wait for the punchline. It doesn't come.

'What?'

'He's been diagnosed with prostate cancer.'

'Oh, honey,' I say. 'Oh no. Oh, Lee . . . I hear that's the best one to have, though.' Leanne looks shocked and then starts to laugh and then I laugh and then we both start to cry. I grab her hands across the island and I don't want to let go.

'It *is* the best kind,' she says eventually. 'Everything should be OK, but it's just the thought, the thought of being without him . . . I don't know if I could do it.'

'It won't happen', I say, 'but if it did, of course you could do it.'

'Yes, I know,' says Leanne, 'but I wouldn't want to.'

★ ★ ★

I force Leanne to abandon the garlicky courgetti concoction and order pizza. When James comes in we are sitting on the bar stools next to the island eating it out of the box. When I see him and his little, smiling eyes, my own fill with tears.

'Aw,' says James, and then to Leanne, 'you told her.'

'I'm so sorry, James,' I say.

'Yes,' says James. 'I'm dying, but then again, aren't we all.' He comes over to me and gives me a hug. I've never noticed before but James is the best hugger. He doesn't just tentatively place his hands on your back; he really squeezes so that the air rushes out of your body and your feet leave the floor. When he releases me, I tell him that I will move out as soon as I can.

'Don't worry,' says James as he lifts a slice of pizza from the box, 'I like your influence.'

'He will be having surgery soon, though,' says Leanne, although she is looking at James.

'I'll be out of your hair as soon as possible,' I say. Then, after a pause: 'When did you find out?'

James takes off his tie. 'Martha, do you mind if we just ... don't. I've been with HR all afternoon. I want to be the man without cancer for a minute.'

'Sure,' I say. 'In fact, why don't you guys go out again tonight? They have sofas at the cinema on London Road; it's so cosy.'

James shrugs. 'That'll probably take my mind off cancer.' He looks at Leanne. 'Fancy it?'

'What's a cinema again?' she asks.

'Dark place, no kids, snogging in the back,' says James.

'Definitely,' says Leanne. 'Thanks, Martha.'

'Any time,' I say, and I really mean it.

★ ★ ★

When James and Leanne have left in a taxi, I gather the children on to the sofa. I am not making the same mistake as last night; I am employing the support of a trusted friend — the television.

'Today, kiddos, we are going to watch the greatest film known to man.'

'*Frozen*?!' shouts Millie.

'No, better than that.'

'*Frozen 2*?!' shouts Millie. I ignore her.

'It's *Mary Poppins*!'

Lucas and Millie stare at me in silence. God, what is Leanne teaching these kids? I put the DVD in. They're bored by the start of it and I have to admit there's a lot of build-up so I fast-forward to when the adventure begins. Moses recognizes 'Jolly Holiday' from his previous exposure to Mary and starts to clap his hands. Lucas and Millie also get into the spirit of things and Millie makes a gallant effort to join in with the songs. I have loved Mary from the moment I met her; so strong and capable, and of course beautiful, but her beauty is the least interesting thing about her. We four snuggle up on the sofa and it seems I am not the only one entranced by her magic, but I forgot how long the film is and halfway through the children are sleeping. I carry them upstairs one by one. I take Millie last and as I lift her she wakes up.

'I'm angry with you,' she says.

'Why, darling?'

'You never did friendship bracelets.'

'Oh, Millie,' I say, 'I'm so sorry. Why didn't you say something?'

'I just 'membered,' Millie says, and smiles.

'You silly sausage,' I say, and tickle her. 'How am I supposed to remember if you forgot?'

Millie curls up her body so that my fingers can't reach her tummy. 'It doesn't matter if *I* didn't 'member — you're supposed to 'member cause you promised,' she says.

I think about my wedding vows and say, 'You know, I think you might be on to something there.'

★　★　★

Downstairs I watch the rest of the film. Usually it makes me really happy but I feel a little overwhelmed when Mary flies away. How can she leave so readily? How can she go like that when Bert is clearly so in love with her? I want a bit of Mary for myself, to be able to leave before everything turns to shit, or better yet, I want my own Mary — someone to work her magic and show me how to make myself happy. And then I realize that maybe I do have one.

40

'It's called 'sorry I'm a defensive, insecure cow who has never appreciated how much you've done for me'' I tell Cara as I put a cocktail down in front of her.

'Interesting name,' she says.

'It's called 'Sorry' for short,' I say.

Cara takes a sip. 'Mmmm, what's in it?' she asks.

'Basically booze.'

'I love it. And I'm sorry too.'

'What for?' I ask.

Cara puts her hand on my forearm. 'If you want to have a fictional boyfriend by all means go ahead.'

I shake her hand off my arm. 'You bitch,' I say.

Cara shrugs and I have to laugh.

'And Leanne told me you weren't well,' Cara says. She drops her head. 'I should have come to the hospital. I can be . . . stubborn.'

I point at her and feign confusion. 'You?'

'Shut up,' says Cara sharply. 'Listen, I had to bite my tongue so much when you were with A-hole pretending to be happy. I'm not good at it and I don't want you to do it again. The idea of you hiding in some virtual love affair makes me fucking angry and I don't get angry about shit I don't care about. I want you to show the world who you are. Open the door, shake those amazing tatas and say, 'Look out, here I come!''

'You think my boobs are amazing?' I ask, grabbing them.

'Come on,' says Cara, 'you know you've got great baps.'

'Well, no actually, I don't. Don't you think you could have mentioned that before?' I look down at my chest. My left boob is definitely bigger than my right but I suppose they are pretty good in a lopsided kind of way.

'They're stuck on the front of your body; I didn't think you'd need it pointed out to you. If you wait for someone to tell you how fabulous you are, you may be waiting for ever. Anyway, that's enough talk about your tits. How are things going?'

'Well, actually . . . ' I take a fortifying inhalation. 'I wanted to ask if I could take up your offer to stay at the flat. If you're still willing to let me and it's still available?'

Cara takes a sip of her drink. 'Of course it is. I was just waiting for you to come to your senses.'

I lean over and kiss her on the cheek. 'How soon can I move in? It's just there's a situation at Leanne's.'

'Too much limescale in the kettle?' asks Cara.

'James has cancer,' I say.

Cara puts down her drink. 'Fuck. Fuuuuck. Fuck that. Fuck cancer. I mean, he's a boring little fucker but he doesn't deserve that.'

'It's pretty shit,' I say.

'Which one is it?' she asks.

'Prostate.'

'That's the best kind,' she says.

'That's what I said.' We both sit in quiet

contemplation. I wonder if Cara's thinking what I'm thinking: that we're too young for our friends' husbands to be dying.

'How's Leanne?' asks Cara.

'She's doing OK. To be honest, she seems a lot less uptight than usual.'

'Well, she couldn't get any more uptight.'

'That's mean,' I say.

'That's honest,' says Cara.

'It's not necessary to be honest all the time.'

'No, it's not, but I am,' says Cara. 'It's my thing. And — honestly — you need to get laid so why are you messin' about with this fantasy guy?'

'He's not a fantasy, he's so real it's untrue. And he's back in about five weeks.'

'What's so real about him?' asks Cara.

'I'm not going to tell you because you will mock me,' I reply sternly.

'I promise I won't mock you,' she says.

I take another deep breath. 'You know the list we wrote, the one to the universe?'

'Vaguely.'

'The universe answered and sent me George.' Cara doesn't react. 'I don't just mean a guy called George, I mean everything on the list. It's him. I mean all the things I asked for in one man. And I know it sounds crazy and it feels crazy but, you know, good crazy. I even tried to ignore it myself because it seemed so mental. You know I went on that date with Tom, and it was awful, and then I thought, what the hell, because George really is everything, *everything* I ever wanted. I've barely thought about Alexander because it's like I let go of what I didn't need and created space for what I did.' Cara sits in silence.

'The thing is, I think it's been better this way because George has been in Africa and we've got to know each other and we haven't let sex or expectations get in the way. We've established that we can trust one another and that's what I was missing the whole time I was married — trust.' Cara remains perfectly still. I look up to the sky. 'Fine, go on then,' I say, and Cara collapses into giggles.

When she has recovered she says, 'Let me get this straight: you're in love with a dude you've never met, who says whatever you want to hear, and he's in *Africa*.'

'Yes.'

'One word — catfish.'

'No, no,' I say. 'He's not African and I think that might be a bit racist, by the way. He's from Brighton, he's just working out there.'

'Fine,' says Cara. 'You've got a boyfriend. You've got a boyfriend that lives in the internet. I'm very happy for you.'

'Thank you,' I say.

'I just want you to have what you want. I get my kicks from flesh-and-blood guys but if virtual is your thing, I'm behind you every step of the way. I will totally attend your Skype wedding.'

'You know I hate you.'

'I do,' says Cara sweetly. 'Look, you can move in whenever you want. I'm going away next week, then I'm back for a few days, and after that I'm in Stockholm.'

'Where are you going next week?'

Cara pauses to have some of her drink. As she does, something very odd happens; a band of colour rises up her neck. It takes a few seconds for me to comprehend that Cara is blushing.

'I'm going to see Rico.'

'In Brazil? But you hate the heat!'

Cara shrugs. 'Sometimes we do crazy things for love.'

I clap my hands over my heart. 'Oh my God, you love him!'

'Jesus Christ, don't wet your pants. I don't know if I love him yet, but I like him a lot and I think it might be worth going out there to, I don't know, investigate some stuff.'

'What stuff?'

'Mainly his penis, granted, but to see if I can handle being with someone for an extended period of time, I guess.' I can't believe that Cara has met a guy she's willing to let her hair frizz for. 'OK, we're done with that. So, the flat.'

I really want to push for more details but I know it's pointless. 'I'll try and sort myself out for next week. How much is the rent?'

'I'll get you the keys. The rent is free for the first three months.'

'No, Car,' I say, 'I can't do that.'

'You can and you will. Your payment to me will be getting on with your life, because I can't always be the one with the stories at cocktail hour — it's exhausting.'

'No, it's not right — '

'What's not right is you pussying about in a shit marriage for years and never doing anything for yourself. What about this business?'

'I kind of put it on hold,' I say.

Cara slams her palm on to the table, causing me to jump and several punters to look over at us. 'Stop putting your life on hold, Martha. It's getting really fucking boring.'

'OK,' I mutter.

'I've got a ticket to this event tomorrow night, it's kind of a networking thing. You'll meet a ton of people and you'll be inspired and then you'll move into my fabulous flat and then you'll take over the world.' She holds up her glass and doesn't move until I join her in her toast.

'OK,' I say. 'OK, fine. What's the event?'

'It's some women's thing.'

'The business I was thinking about was for women, women looking for love.'

'That's cheesy as fuck but this will be perfect for that. I'll text you the details.'

'Thank you, Cara. Thanks for everything,' I say.

'Thank me by living your life,' says Cara.

'Cara, I'm sorry about messing things up between you and Marc,' I say.

'Forget about it, he owes me about a million favours.'

'Why?' I ask.

'You don't know how many Saturdays I sat waiting for him to come and take me to the bloody park.'

'Wait! What?!' I shake my head as if it might lodge the information into place. 'Marc's your —'

'Dad, yeah.'

'Cara,' I say, 'this explains *so* much.'

41

Leanne is happy to babysit so I have no excuse not to go. I'm not sure what to wear to a networking event so, despite the lack of luck it's brought me, I decide on the funeral dress. When I arrive, the other women look like they're dressed to go to a nightclub; one even has a bustier on. It makes me realize how much I have to learn.

We're given a champagne cocktail on arrival and I think I could get used to this being in business malarkey. A lot of the people here seem to know each other; I realize I'm opening myself up to a whole new social circle. I once read that you become who you associate with; if I hang out with these women maybe I can get some of what they have. We're ushered to some seats set up in rows. It takes a few minutes for everyone to settle but finally the crowd falls silent and a woman walks to the front of the room. She's wearing a tight-fitting, black trouser suit and impossibly high heels. She introduces herself as Agnes.

'Thanks for having me back,' she says. The audience gives her a round of applause. 'Today I'm going to be talking about reclaiming your feminine power.' I take my notepad out of my bag. 'How often throughout your day do you honestly feel like a woman?' she says. As she says the word 'woman' she grabs her crotch with her right hand and everyone cheers. I write 'how often do you feel like a woman' on my pad. I can feel the person sitting to my left watching me. She seems amused by my note taking. I look around and no one else is writing so maybe it's not the done thing. I slip the pad under my chair.

'First time?' whispers the woman.

'Yeah, you?'

'I've been coming for years.' She places her hand on my knee. 'Just relax, everyone's great.' I smile a thank you. For years, I've been trying to find somewhere I really belong and perhaps I've finally found it. I don't understand much of the rest of what Agnes says — she spends a lot of time talking about chakras — but I like just being in her presence, feeling her energy and the reaction she elicits from the group.

'Enjoy!' she shouts when she finishes, and everyone cheers again. I guess this is when the networking starts. Most of the women go to get more drinks, and around me ladies greet each other enthusiastically. I see an older woman standing alone and approach her.

'Hi,' I say, and reach my hand out. She looks at it for a few seconds before shaking it. 'What's your business?' I ask. She laughs, and her face, which had previously looked quite serious, softens beautifully.

'Design,' she says.

'Oh, I used to be married to a designer,' I say. I say this lightly, like it was a lifetime ago, which in some way it feels like it was.

'Guy or girl?' asks the woman. I love this, how cosmopolitan my life is becoming. That I'm hobnobbing with the type of people intelligent enough not to assume.

'He was a guy,' I say. 'Still is.'

'Well, I'm sorry he put you off,' she says.

'Designers?'

She laughs again and I feel pleased I'm such a natural at this.

'I'm just going to get us a drink,' she says. 'I'm Moira.'

'Martha,' I say.

'M and M, I like that,' Moira says before walking away. As soon as she's gone a black girl with a big afro grabs my arm.

'Don't let Moira get her teeth into you, she's such a predator. Seriously ruthless. You're far too sweet.' I'm a bit disappointed that my inexperience is so obvious. 'Here, talk to Annie, she's a newbie too.' The woman pulls me towards a girl with a gorgeous head of blonde curls.

'Hey, Annie,' she says to the girl, 'this is . . . '

'Martha,' I say, and offer my hand. The girl shakes it and, satisfied her work is done, the woman with the afro leaves.

'It's Áine, actually,' says the girl with a soft Irish accent. Her skin is flawless and she doesn't have a lick of make-up on.

'You look kind of young to be starting your own business,' I say.

Áine frowns. 'I'm not starting a business, I'm a student. I want to be an animator.' I guess I didn't establish the exact purpose of the event. I suppose it's just a general female empowerment thing.

'So, is this your first time at a sex club?' asks Áine.

'A what? I'm not at a sex club!' I say. Áine giggles and then stops when I don't.

'Excuse me,' I say, and run to the reception. As I do I see so much that I didn't previously. The low lighting and scantily dressed bar staff, all women. It's like one of those optical illusion pictures that looks like a boat or whatever, but then someone points out that if you focus on it in a different way it looks like a fox playing table tennis, and you just can't unsee it.

I step out on to the pavement and call Cara. 'You sent me to a sex club!' I hiss.

'OK, hun,' she says. She sounds distracted.

'This is so inappropriate!'

'You need a new perspective,' she says.

'I feel violated!' I shout.

'OK, darling, talk to you later. Byeeeee!'

I'm fuming. This is the most disrespectful thing that has ever happened to me. I feel a hand on my shoulder and turn to see Áine.

'You're not leaving, are you?' she asks.

'Yeah, I think . . . I don't think . . . '

'Don't go,' she says. 'I'll be honest, you're the only girl I've seen that I like tonight.'

'It's just, I don't . . . I mean, I'm not . . . ' Áine takes my hand; the action silences me.

'I know,' she says, 'but live a little.'

And even though I am livid with Cara, I did promise; so I let her lead me back in.

⋆   ⋆   ⋆

I wake up with Áine's curls covering my face. They smell like almonds. Had you asked me before this morning, I would have told you that it would be weird to wake up next to a woman, but it isn't. It feels a bit like the mornings after I have bunked in with Leanne, safe and cosy; although with Leanne I have never had an orgasm the night before, let alone three. I think Áine is asleep but then she reaches behind and slaps my thigh.

'Morning, beauty face,' she says.

'Good morning,' I say.

'You want eggs?'

'Yeah.'

Áine's place is stunning. She has the penthouse flat in an apartment building; out of the French windows the sea looks close enough to step into.

'Student accommodation has come on,' I say as I sit at the breakfast bar, and Áine places a cup of coffee in front of me.

'My dad's loaded,' she says. 'When I got accepted on my course he bought this place as an investment.'

'Wow,' I say, looking round again, 'lucky for some.'

'Maybe,' says Áine. She returns her attention to the frying pan. 'I'd rather have a dad with no money that wasn't a bigot.' I drink my coffee.

A few minutes later, Áine places a plate of creamy scrambled eggs in front of me.

'Wait,' she says, then picks a sprig of parsley from a pot on the counter top and sprinkles it over the eggs.

'This is brilliant, thank you. You're good at this.'

Áine sits opposite me with her own plate. '*You're* good at this,' she says. She eyes me meaningfully and I fight to hide my smile. 'I can't actually believe this is your first time.'

'Well, it is,' I say. Last night was my first time at many things.

★   ★   ★

When we went back into the club, music was pumping and most people were on the dance floor. The DJ was playing these amazing dance tracks imprinted on my muscle memory from my university days, and even though I was trying to stay angry with Cara, the mood pulled me in. Áine made me go to the centre of the dance floor and it felt like I was being consumed by the music and the crowd. Sweat was dripping down my entire body and I felt my hair sticking to the back of my neck. Ordinarily I would be mortified by this but I barely noticed.

When the intro to Christina Aguilera's 'Dirrty' filled the room, the energy lifted even more. Áine flapped her hands in front of my face to cool me down and I returned the favour. When I did, the woman with the afro spotted me and thought I was waving at her. She waved back and then beckoned me over to the stage where she was standing. No chance, I thought, at the same time as Áine screamed, 'Yes!' She pushed me over and it just felt easier to let her pull me up with the other half a dozen women dancing there. I froze for a couple of seconds, looking out at all the people staring back at me. They were dancing but they also seemed to be encouraging me.

I started to shake my hips and a woman in a cat suit shouted, 'Go, sister!' I raised my arms over my head and let the song work through me. I tried to embody the sassiness of the lyrics, dragging my nails up my thighs and swinging my hair around. Áine started smacking me playfully on the bum and I wiggled it in her direction to calls for more from the crowd. She wrapped an arm round my waist and we rolled our bodies in unison. I've danced with girls like that before but only for boys; this was for me. As the song climaxed we broke apart and I did a series of vigorous chest thrusts, throwing my head back with each one, and at the last line I opened my arms as if receiving an encore and shouted along with Christina, 'It's about time for my arrival!'

Áine asked me if I wanted another drink and I told her that I was actually pretty hungry, and I should be getting home.

'Home! As if. Have you been to Incognito Burrito? It's fantastic!' I had not.

Incognito is a tiny takeaway on a side road near the beach. The place was packed; apparently it was not so Incognito any more. Áine said I had to have the pork — I'd only ever had chicken before so I had to say yes. We found a place to stand in the corner and eat. When I bit into it my teeth glided through the meat like it was marshmallow.

'Right?! Right?!' said Áine with her mouth full. She told me she moved to Brighton not long after coming out. Her family, but her father particularly, had told her it was a phase, a phase he would not tolerate. Up until that point she'd been his golden girl.

'He's such a tool. He didn't realize that all the shite that made me such a good girl, yunno, no interest in the boys and going to the footie with him, was screaming lesbian.' I laughed. 'Brighton seemed like the holy land to me. I like animation enough but to be honest if I didn't study it I couldn't have justified coming here.'

'But your dad must know that Brighton is one of the most gay-friendly places in the UK?' I asked.

'People see what they wanna see,' she said. Áine quizzed me about growing up in Brighton, about the clubs I had been to and if I had ever seen Nick Cave.

'To be honest, I'm not the best Brightonian. I've never even swum in the sea.'

At this point Áine dropped the remainder of her burrito. 'No way!' she said. 'That's not possible. We're going.'

'Going where?' I said.

'The sea, obviously. You can't live by the sea and not go in; it's disrespectful.'

'Áine, can I point out that it's winter and the night,' I said, but I still let her drag me down the narrow street towards the water. As we stood on the pebbles I pulled my coat around me as Áine took hers off.

'We won't swim, just get in the water. Make it official. Come on: are you a man or a mouse?' she said.

'Actually, I'm a woman,' I told her. She stopped then and turned me towards her.

348

'That you are,' she said, and she kissed me. The heat from her mouth contrasted deliciously with the cold air and although it was a very sweet kiss there was just enough pressure to tell me there was much more where that came from. It was a risk kissing me like that, and it made me think I should take one too.

'OK, before I change my mind.' I dropped my coat to the ground and ran into the sea in the funeral dress. I had imagined that it would be cold but it was even colder than I had imagined. I wasn't sure that I would be able to keep moving forward; my breathing had become shallow and my teeth were chattering. I could hear Áine shouting beside me but I was so frigid I couldn't even shout back. As soon as the water had hit my chest, I considered it official and retreated to the shore, where Áine helped me into my coat before putting on her own.

'You poor thing,' she said.

'Why . . . are you . . . OK?' I asked.

'The Irish Sea, I guess,' she said. 'Now, we better get you to my place to dry off.'

'Where's your place?'

Áine smiled and raised her eyebrow before pointing to the building in front of us. 'Right there.'

★ ★ ★

'You're obviously a natural then,' says Áine. She scoops up the last of her eggs and wrinkles her nose at me as she chews them.

'Thanks, I guess. You too,' I say.

349

'Well, no, I've had a lot of practice,' she says.

'How? If you've just come out,' I ask.

'Boarding school,' she says with a smirk. 'And you're sure I can't tempt you away from men?' she asks as she clears up our plates. I shake my head. Last night before we went to bed I made sure that she understood it couldn't be more than a one-off. I didn't want to be responsible for any more hurt in the world. Áine said she would rather be with me once than never at all. All evening I had known that spending the night was a possibility but it was only when she said that, that the coin finally settled on heads. We had a shower, which led naturally to more kissing. Áine moved beyond that very slowly but I still panicked a little.

'Just do what *you* like,' she said, and I simply didn't know. When she noticed my hesitation she said, 'Do what feels good.' And it seems that what felt good to me also felt good to her. Rather than sex seeming like a performance, method acting for a piece entitled 'Skinny, Kinky Girl Satisfies Man', it felt like a game, a shared experience, not two separate ones that happened to be occurring at the same time.

'Thank you though, it was great,' I say.

'It was, wasn't it,' says Áine. Then she asks, 'What do you do?' It should feel weird going back to basics after sleeping together but it doesn't.

'Nothing,' I answer. 'Nothing I want to talk about.'

'What do you want to do?' asks Áine, unfazed by my negativity.

'I don't know any more.'

Áine looks at me as if I haven't finished speaking, so I continue. 'I thought I wanted to be a singer, but it's not me. I don't have the drive or the talent. I don't even know why I let myself believe I could do it for so long. And I kidded myself I could start a business but I can't even run my own life.'

Áine pushes out her bottom lip and then says, 'I'm the queen of fooling myself. I mean, I always knew I wanted to be with women but the idea of having a girlfriend in my backward parish with my idiotic father, it didn't fit. So, I thought I couldn't do it at all. Broke a million boys' hearts being who I didn't want to be. The thing is, you *can* do what you want to do — you just have to get over the fact that it's not gonna look exactly as you thought it would. Who knows, maybe it will look better than you even imagined.'

'Maybe,' I say. 'You never know.' Áine smiles at me encouragingly. 'Look,' I say, 'I better go.'

'So soon?' She says this uncritically; she wants me to stay but she's willing to grant me my freedom.

'Yeah, I'd love to stay longer but I left my kid with my best friend.'

'You have a kid?' Áine looks at me as if she's meeting me again for the first time.

'It's a long story.'

As I leave, Áine gives me a kiss on the cheek and a scrap of paper with her email address written on it. 'In case you need any design work, for your business,' she says.

'I don't think I'll be doing that,' I say, but I put it in my pocket.

Áine leans against her door frame and watches me walk towards the lift. 'Aw, but you never know,' she says. 'You never know.'

42

I know it's time to let go of my dream. It's time to let go of a lot of dreams but this one is overripe and ready to fall from the tree. I return to work and ask Bob to give me a permanent nine-to-five contract because people who are not going to become singers do not need to work shifts. Bob seems mildly impressed by my decision. 'I knew you had a Debenhams voucher in you,' he says. Fairfax gives a Debenhams voucher to anyone who works at the company for ten years or more. I grip the seat of my chair after he says this. I sense I need to physically hold myself on to it. 'I'll get a contract for you ASAP but you can start working the hours now.'

'Thanks,' I say, and get up to leave.

'Welcome to the team,' says Bob.

'I've been working here for months, Bob.'

He leans back and puts his hands behind his head. Two perfectly spherical sweat patches shine at me like headlights.

'Yes,' he says, 'but now you really work here. Now you *work* work here.'

I go back to my desk and stare at the blank monitor. Greg is on a call but he keeps glancing at me between sentences. After he says goodbye he swivels his chair towards me. 'You all right?' he asks.

'Greg,' I say, without looking away from the computer, 'do you want to go out tonight and get very, very drunk?' I look at him; I can tell he's amused. 'I mean excruciatingly, can't see your hand in front of your face drunk.'

'There's nothing I'd like to do more, but I'm taking the girls to the panto. You should come; bring Moses.' In response, I start to cry. 'Shit, sorry mate. I can probably move the pantomime . . . ' He pats me on the back.

'No, no, it's fine. I'm fine.' I try to dry my tears with a Post-it note. Greg hands me a handkerchief and I wipe my face with it before blowing my nose. 'Thanks,' I say, handing it back to him. He takes it gingerly and puts it in his pocket. 'Who has handkerchiefs anyway?'

'Is it divorce stuff?' asks Greg.

'No, not really. It's just . . . do you ever feel like no matter what you do, your life won't get started?'

Greg takes off his headset. 'Let's go for a fag break,' he says.

'You don't smoke,' I say.

'I won't tell anyone.'

★　★　★

We sit on the fire escape and watch the pigeons in the car park fight over a discarded muffin.

'That's what I feel like,' I say.

'Like a pigeon?'

'Like the muffin.'

Greg puts his fingers in his mouth and lets out a long, sharp whistle. The birds quickly disperse. 'Is the nine-to-five life so bad?' he asks.

'It's not the nine-to-five, it's just . . . It's the

giving up. When I separated I thought I was just letting go of my relationship but it really means letting go of everything.'

'Yeah, but giving up stuff is sometimes creating space to let good stuff in. Like, aren't you seeing someone?'

'Yeah . . . how did you know?'

'You're always on your phone under the desk,' says Greg. 'I figured it was a new bloke or a serious addiction to Angry Birds.'

I laugh and say, 'No one plays Angry Birds any more.'

Greg nudges my foot with his toe. 'So what's he like?'

'He's perfect,' I say into the floor.

'Don't sound so happy about it.'

'I'm just worried — ' The words catch in my throat for a second. 'I'm worried I won't be good enough for him.'

'How can you think that? You're great.' I look at Greg to see if his eyes will reveal the lie. 'You're funny and you're clever and you always have Polos.'

'I take fresh breath very seriously,' I say.

'See, funny,' says Greg.

'I don't wanna be funny. I want to be hot. I want to be fascinating.'

'Hot's overrated,' says Greg. 'What are you gonna do with hot when you're in a nursing home?'

'You really know how to flatter a girl.'

'No, I'm not saying you're not hot; of course you're hot. I just mean — '

'Yeah,' I say. 'Moonwalk out of that one.'

'I just think people place too much importance on hot,' says Greg quietly.

'George is hot.'

'Is that your guy?' asks Greg.

'Yeah. I kind of wish he wasn't so hot. Like,
stop me if this is TMI, but I'm scared he's gonna
turn and run the second he sees my saggy mum
tum.' Greg chuckles and shakes his head.
'Thanks for that,' I say, 'that helps.'

'No, it's just that . . . I'll let you into a secret
— and you need to know I'm breaking the bro
code to tell you this — but guys don't care about
that shit.'

'Sure, sure, that's why all those magazines are
filled with girls in polo neck jumpers reading
Joyce.'

Greg ducks down so he can see my face more
clearly. 'Really, we don't. I mean, a lot of the
time we're too busy worrying about our own
shit, but most of the time we're just thinking
about how fucking lucky we are to be there.'

'Is that how you feel about Lisa?' I ask.

'Lisa?' Greg looks a little confused.

'Does she make you think about how lucky
you are?'

'Martha,' says Greg in a serious tone, 'Lisa
would be lucky to have me.'

I laugh. The sensation is like stepping into a
warm bath. 'We better go in,' I say.

'You sure you're OK?'

'Yeah, anyway I'm getting cold.'

'You want my jacket?'

'Nah, you're good.' I stand up and square my
shoulders. 'Come on. I have to get on, I *work*

work here now.' I look down at Greg, still sitting on the escape. 'Move it, this attitude won't get you your voucher.'

Greg jumps up. 'And what a travesty that would be,' he says.

★ ★ ★

Bob meets me at my desk. He's smiling, which is what he does when he's about to sack someone. Only I could go from getting a new contract to getting fired within the space of a few minutes. 'Can I speak with you, Martha?'

'Sure,' I say. He walks briskly towards his office and I have to jog to keep up with him. I turn to look at Greg before I go into Bob's office. He puts his forefinger under his chin and uses it to lift his head a couple of inches.

'Take a seat,' says Bob. I sit on the edge of the chair. 'I want to talk to you about your request earlier today.'

'OK,' I say. I wonder if that mad woman who rang looking for Darren called back and reported me.

'We've had a problem with Carlos.' Carlos is the shift supervisor. His problem is that he's a functioning alcoholic, and everybody knows this, but Bob is implying a new, more recent problem. 'Porn.' Although we're the only people in the room, I look round for help. This seems like a very odd subject change, even for Bob. 'He's been watching a lot of porn. *A lot* of porn.' Bob gets up and walks round to lean against the front of his desk. 'Look, I don't mind — boys will be boys — but some of the girls don't like it. And you know, with all that sexual harassment business out there. We just can't afford a lawsuit.' I nod yes; that sexual harassment business is rather a hassle. 'So, I had to let him go. Shame, great guy,' says Bob. He's silent for a moment, clearly lost in some special memory he and Carlos shared.

'Which is where you come in,' he continues. 'I'm offering you a promotion.' It should be a joyous moment, being offered advancement at your job; a spiritual feast of recognition and validation. Instead I feel like someone's seen me standing on the edge of a cliff face, snuck up behind me and given me a little push. 'Carlos had to go and then you ask for this new contract and I realize it's supercilious.'

'I — I don't think that's what you mean.'

'Yeah it is, love, look it up. Anyway, I'm saying we wanna see your contract and raise you a brand-new contract with one pound forty extra per hour and your own parking space.'

'I don't drive.'

'But you'll know it's there,' says Bob earnestly. When I don't respond he adds, 'You won't get a better offer than this.' I believe him.

'Can I think about it?' I ask. Bob looks at me as if I've been given a winning lottery ticket and used it to wrap up chewed gum.

'Not much to think about in my opinion, but think away,' says Bob. 'Let me know by six.'

I don't even thank him before I stand up. I know I should — even a douche like Bob deserves gratitude — but I can't. I'm afraid that if I open my mouth to speak a scream will escape. When I leave his office I can see Greg staring at me; his eyes are asking a question I'm not ready to answer. I turn and walk out of the floor and I keep walking — down three flights of stairs, past Darryl sat on his chair in the reception area, and I don't stop until my legs ache. Even then I want to keep walking, I want to keep walking until I know where I'm going.

43

The nursery worker looks startled when I arrive to collect Moses. 'Is there a problem?' she asks.

'I felt like getting him early,' I say.

'Sure thing,' she says. She turns to the room and calls, 'Momo!' To my knowledge no one has ever called him that in his life, but he pops out from within a Wendy house and toddles over. It brings home how removed I am from him; these strangers are raising my child. 'He hasn't had his lunch.'

'It's fine,' I say as I pull on his coat. I kneel down in front of him to do up the buttons. 'We're going on an adventure,' I tell him.

★   ★   ★

It feels like the train to London might be enough for Moses. He bounces tirelessly in the seat next to me, shouting 'Thomas!' each time another train passes. I remember taking the same journey with my own mother; she always brought homemade sandwiches, informing me she wouldn't be a victim of London prices. We don't have a picnic, so we create a makeshift one out of two Marks & Spencer sandwiches and a packet of crisps.

'What did you do at nursery today?' I ask Moses.

'Nursery,' he says solemnly.

'I love you,' I say, and for the first time he says back, 'I lull you.'

This was always the sort of stuff I thought we would do as a three. Take the train, share the baby's delight. It's odd how you convince yourself that you will do these things, that you will eat dinner together every evening and create pedestrian, but poignant to you, traditions. Why would you manage as three what you could not do as two? For the first few years we were together, Alexander and I would alternate Christmas at each other's family homes. Well, that was the agreement, but it was only a verbal contract and more often than not we had Christmas at the Rosses'. Initially Alexander convinced me with the undeniable truth that his parents lived further away and therefore could see us less, and then his mother was dying, and then his mother was dead. That year we tried to piece together some semblance of a holiday but every activity was punctuated by her absence and any moment approaching joy was seasoned with guilt.

The following year I convinced Alexander to invite his dad to our flat. Alexander's sister, Meghan (an amiable but nervy secondary school teacher), had just had a baby and I thought it might be helpful for her not to have the stress of cooking for us too. Also, I hoped that it might be an opportunity, perhaps my best opportunity, to win over Eric Ross.

Alexander's parents had always made it clear that I wasn't welcome. They weren't openly hostile; that would probably have been easier, that would have given me something to push against and an excuse to stay at home. No, they just communicated through their demeanour that they were only barely tolerating me. In fairness to Alexander's mother, I'm not sure anyone would be good enough for her darling son; in the case of his father I think he mistrusted any person who wasn't as hateful as him.

I had been preparing for two days — cleaning the flat, securing the goose they always ate, and watching dozens of online videos to learn how to cook it. Eric arrived long faced and empty handed. He removed his stiff suit jacket from his portly frame and positioned himself in the only armchair. I didn't spend much time with the men in the morning; I was standing guard at the oven, determined to get the dinner ready for their immovable 1 p.m. serving time. I paused only to give Eric his present, a cashmere scarf I had bought on credit. He thanked me before placing the gift on the floor beside him, unopened.

At ten minutes to one I emerged from the kitchen, sweaty but triumphant. 'Dinner will be served at one,' I chirped.

Eric took a long slug of his Scotch and said, 'I'm not hungry.' Alexander said nothing. I remember leaning against the kitchen counter, arguing with myself over the benefits of holding in my anger. Eventually I picked up the bird and threw the whole thing in the bin, and instantly regretted it. I told Alexander that Moxie got to it and we ate the veggies on our laps. Since that day, Eric may have said a few hundred words to me, and I like it that way. We learn how to be from our parents, either by emulating them or distancing ourselves. Alexander is charming, sometimes to a fault; he often makes promises he cannot deliver. A boy with excess charm could only be raised by a man with none.

I guess, given these beginnings, it might have been unfair of me to expect Alexander to be able to create traditions for our son. The work of parenting should be split equally but each job description doesn't have to look the same. I kiss the top of Moses's head, the only bit of him that still smells like baby. He nestles into my chest as I do so. I hope this means he has accepted my application as chief parent in charge of new discoveries.

5) <u>Must be close to his family.</u>

Marthashotbod: Are you close to your mother?
Undeterred83: Of course.
Marthashotbod: Why's that?
Undeterred83: Because she's my mother. That's enough.

I agree.

⋆ ⋆ ⋆

'Ooh,' says Moses. We are standing in the entrance hall of the Natural History Museum. The skeleton of a blue whale towers above us. I look at Moses and I know that's what I want, the rush of experiencing something new; excitement so immense it verges on fear. I take his hand and he looks at me and says 'ooh' again. I remember seeing a model of the blue whale in the museum as a child and being unable to accept that something that big could exist in reality. I became obsessed with the creatures; I remember Mum and I spending hours at the library researching them and her getting hold of some obscure documentary on their migration, which I watched until the tape in the video became mangled in the machine one day. I decided that, despite my lack of almost any mathematical skills, I could be a marine biologist. Luckily this was the same year Take That released 'Could It Be Magic', so I ended the year focused on a seventeen-year-old lad from Stoke-on-Trent and not the world's largest mammal. Holding my son's hand, with so much discovery before us, I am immediately taken back to a time when anything was possible.

'Come on, mate,' I say, 'there's so much more.'

We cover the dinosaurs and all the mammals. I'm so impressed by how patient and well behaved Moses is, or perhaps he is often patient and well behaved and I don't take the time to notice. We stop for tea and chocolate cake. I decide there and then that this is a fine tradition. As Moses works away at his slice I think about how much I want to protect him and how outlandish a task that is. 'Moses,' I say, 'I want you to know that, whatever happens, Mummy loves you and Daddy loves you, and, even if it doesn't always seem like it, Mummy and Daddy love each other.'

'Juice!' shouts Moses, pointing at his carton of orange from concentrate.

★ ★ ★

Exhausted by all the sights and sounds of the city, Moses falls asleep almost immediately on the train home. I lean back against the window and let him nestle into me. He fits perfectly, as he always has, no matter what his size. A woman across the aisle watches us and smiles a smile that makes me know she is remembering a small boy that was once in her own life. She catches me watching her, watching us, and her smile widens. I know she sees me as reliable, responsible, loving and loved, and I know that I have to be the person she sees. Careful not to wake Moses, I ease my phone out of my bag and call Bob. It's quarter to six.

'Greg told me your son was vomiting blood,' he says. 'It's not catching, is it?'

'No, it's all good. I'll be in tomorrow. I'm just phoning to say I'll take the job.'

'Course you will.'

44

Even though Moses is still drifting in and out of consciousness I take a bus in the opposite direction to Leanne's house. The skies are black and the probably ecologically sound but basically ineffective street lighting leaves me almost blind. It's OK, though; I would know this walk in my sleep. I paused after every step the last time I made the journey; I don't know what or who I was hoping would intervene. This time I scurry. Moses is growing heavier with each second and I want to arrive before the guilt about keeping him out so late stops me.

I hear something soft and foreign, possibly Indian, playing from inside the house. It's such a blatant indication that someone's real, actual life is happening behind there that my hand hovers for a few seconds before I thump my fist against the door four times. I'm reaching for another round of knocks when it swings open, causing me to lose balance and fall forward a little and making Moses, resting on my left hip, shake his head, as if showing his disapproval before settling back to sleep.

Jacqueline watches this with a blank expression, a kind of therapist magnolia in the paint chart of emotions. Her long blonde bob is tousled in a way that any man observing her would assume was the result of violent lovemaking and any woman would know was the

366

result of at least an hour with a full head of hot rollers. She has on a navy and white striped Breton top and a pair of faded blue jeans. Her feet are bare and perfectly pedicured.

'Martha? Are you OK?' she asks. It comes so readily that it makes me think that maybe I was not the first nor perhaps the last client to turn up unannounced.

'No, no, not really.'

'Have you had thoughts about harming yourself?'

'What?! No! At least I don't think so ... ' Jacqueline seems to relax a little. As long as I don't top myself on her doorstep we're good, I guess. 'I want to know why you told me to end it with Alexander. It's just that everything has got so much worse since then.'

'I'm not sure that I told you to end your relationship, but of course it wasn't a formal session, so I don't have notes.'

'You seemed so sure,' I say, and Moses murmurs so I whisper, 'You seemed so sure that I should end my relationship and since then, my life has been in tatters.'

Jacqueline bites her bottom lip and then ushers me in. 'Get that child in from the cold,' she says. She shows me into her therapy room. I put Moses on one of her squidgy leather armchairs and I sit on the other. She sits on her swivel chair between us. 'You want some water?' she asks.

'No,' I say. I feel ashamed now, now I am in her home, stealing her heat and her time. I really wanted someone to blame and Jacqueline, with her questions to answer questions and her exquisite soft furnishings, seemed like such a great choice.

'I'm going to book you a cab,' she says. 'Will he need a seat?' I shake my head. She picks up her phone and presses a button; obviously she has a cab firm on speed dial. 'Yes,' she says. 'Yes, to . . . ' She looks at me questioningly.

'Windlesham Road,' I say, and she repeats this.

Then she puts the phone on her desk and says, 'Have you been doing any work on yourself?'

'Yes! Loads! I mean, I've been trying to . . . '

'Have you been speaking to someone?'

'Sort of,' I say quietly.

'Well, that's good and, Martha, sometimes progress doesn't look neat and linear; it's like a cut healing — at one stage it's a nasty, ugly scab but that means things are getting better.'

'It doesn't feel like things are getting better.'

'It won't always; you have to look for the good sometimes.' She glances at Moses, nestled in her chair. 'Look for it and if you can't see it, create it, and if you can't do that . . . ' She stops as if remembering something before continuing briskly. 'In any case, there's little in the world that can't be undone. Tell him you were wrong and that you want to make another go of it.' I think about this, about putting back together what has been unpicked, and I think there is quite a lot that can't be undone actually.

A man sticks his head round the door. He is older than Jacqueline but he's attractive; certainly he was very attractive at one stage in his life, and something about the way he carries himself suggests he is still cruising on the fumes of this time.

'Do we have guests, Jac?' he says with a hint of mirth in his voice. Jacqueline excuses herself, which seems excessive given that she didn't really invite me. Even though she shuts the door behind her I can make out the clipped sentences of a whispered argument. Odd words and phrases float into the room. 'No . . . Never stops . . . Outrageous . . . One night . . . You always . . . Absolutely not . . . ' I've been looking to Jacqueline for answers but it seems she's just as messed up as the rest of us.

There's silence and then some shuffling and then Jacqueline opens the door and says, 'Your car's here.' She stands in the doorway and watches me climb in, holding Moses. I look at her before we pull away. Her face seems to say, 'We're not that different.' Either that or, 'Thank God that crazy bitch has gone.'

⋆   ⋆   ⋆

Cara steals another piece of chorizo from the pile on the chopping board and chews it thoughtfully. 'What's this for again?'

'It's a celebration of life,' I say. James is playing with some Lego on the floor with the boys and as I say this he looks up at me and smiles. 'And a chance to say thank you to my beautiful friends. I'm recognizing the good in my life.' I pinch one of Cara's cheeks and she makes a gagging noise.

'If you're going to be pulling out that mushy shit, I'll need to drink a lot more,' she says.

'I promise I will keep the *mushy shit* to the bare minimum,' I say. Cara grabs another piece of chorizo. 'If you stop eating the ingredients,' I add. 'Why don't you make yourself useful and lay the table.' Cara rolls her eyes but she sets about creating a lovely dinner setting, even going into the garden to pick some holly to make a small centrepiece. Only an hour after the anticipated start time, Leanne, James, Cara, the kids and I sit down together to eat.

'This must be when we say grace,' says Cara in a sing-song voice.

'Well, actually,' I say, standing up, 'I do sort of want to offer thanks.' Six pairs of eyes are trained on me; I clear my throat. 'I made this dinner to say thank you to you all. Leanne and James, obviously for putting me up, but all of you for helping me almost keep it together recently.' Leanne smiles and Cara gives me a wink. 'Not long ago,' I continue, 'with the help of my friends I wrote a list. A list of the things I thought I wanted.' James looks at Leanne with furrowed eyebrows and she dismisses his silent question with a quick shake of her head. 'What I failed to realize was all the wonderful things I already have. I have amazing friends, some of whom have beautiful children, and I have a man in my life who lights it up every day.' I bend down and give Moses a kiss in the middle of his curls. 'So, I want to write a new list. I want us to write it together. A list of all the things we're happy to have in our lives. We're not going to say grace; we're going to give gratitude.' I sit down. 'Leanne, can you start?'

'I'm grateful to have this wonderful man beside me,' says Leanne, and James drops his head coyly. 'I'm grateful for every day we've spent together and every day we will spend together going forward.' She looks at James until he looks back at her.

'I'm not going to cry,' he says, and Leanne laughs.

'Your turn, babe,' she says.

'I'm grateful for all the laughter in this home,' he says, 'from my wonderful, crazy children and my wonderful wife and her crazy, wonderful friends.' James looks to Millie.

'I'm happy for Barbie and butterflies and *Star Wars* and pizza and Mummy and Daddy and sometimes Lucas, and I'm happy that Moses and Auntie Marf are having a sleepover and Grandma and sometimes Ruby but sometimes not because sometimes she takes the pink felt tips and — '

'Honey, the food will get cold,' says Leanne.

'I'm happy for all the things,' says Millie with a firm nod of her head.

'Thank you, darling,' I say. After some coaxing, Lucas says he's grateful for his scooter, and when asked what he loves, Moses simply says, 'Horsey.'

Cara says, 'I'm grateful that you lot let me study how the normal live and, you know, it's not so bad.' I blow her a kiss and she points a warning finger at me.

'I am grateful that I have everyone in this room together and for the realization that that may be enough.' I raise my glass and everyone except Moses and Lucas follows suit. 'To love and laughter and Barbie and butterflies and scooting and horses and normality and having enough,' I say. 'Let's eat.' Everyone takes a drink and starts the food.

'Why is the pasta crunchy?' asks Millie.

★   ★   ★

As we're clearing away the dinner plates the doorbell rings. Leanne is picking food out of Lucas's hair and James is debating with Millie about the size of her dessert, so I go and answer it. He's facing away from me when I open the door, so he doesn't see my surprise. Greg turns around and puts his hands in his pockets. 'Hey,' he says casually.

I laugh and ask, 'What are you doing here?'

'Nothing. I mean, I just wanted to see if you were OK. I was driving by your mum's and thought I'd stop in. She said you were here.'

I lean against the door frame. 'Yeah, I needed some space.'

'So, everything's OK?' Greg says this intently, as if to make sure I understand it's not just a platitude.

'I'm really good. Thanks so much for checking, Greg.'

'No problem,' he says, 'anytime.'

'I'm doing a thing,' I say, gesturing behind me.

Greg takes a step back. 'Oh, of course, sorry to interrupt. Better get back. I was just on my way home. See you.'

He starts to walk down the path and I say,

'No! Come in for a drink.'

'Yep, you should totally come in,' says Cara from behind me. She wedges herself in next to me and appraises Greg coolly. A small hand prizes my legs open and Millie's head appears between them.

'Come in! Auntie Marfa's friend, come in!' she shouts.

Greg turns back and looks slightly afraid. 'No, I'll get off. Early start. See you soon, though,' he says, and then gives me a little salute.

I return to the kitchen, where the strawberries and ice cream are on the counter, and Cara follows me, stopping at the island to top up her wine glass.

'Who was that?' she asks.

'Greg, from work,' I say, indicating that she should pour me a glass.

She does so and takes a sip of her own before saying, 'Does that mean that the other boyfriend has been kicked to the kerb?' She smiles into her wine glass and I narrow my eyes at her.

'Nothing's going on with Greg, he's a . . . ' I pause and try to locate the right word. 'Friend. But OK, I accept that I have to meet George, get to know him first before anything can be official. I haven't even sent him a message today because I'm holding back a bit.'

It's kind of true. I want it to be true. Cara nods as one would to a small child who has finally accepted that the stove is hot.

45

In the morning I wake full of the warmth created by an evening earmarked as a great memory, but underneath the joy, anxiety begs for attention like a mosquito bite. Being with Áine was wonderful — maybe even necessary — but I realize that in spending the night with her I have betrayed George. And maybe not — maybe he's the type of guy that might like his girlfriend indulging in that kind of experience — but it's definitely too early to ask. That's the problem with guidelines; no matter how comprehensive, they can never cover every eventuality. You'll never get to, 'If I accidentally have lesbian sex whilst trying to discover who I am, he will react in the following ways . . . ' I don't think George will be keen, though; my list guy wouldn't want to share me, and it just seems so very me to find something perfect and then fuck it up before I even get to experience it properly. I message him to say I want to talk but he doesn't respond. As I wait for him to get back to me, I feel the cold finger of panic tap me on the shoulder. I need to know I can reach him, not just practically but emotionally.

One summer Alexander had gone on a design course in Copenhagen. I remember when he told me he had been accepted, his voice growing more and more excited with each sentence. As his eagerness grew so did my terror; I was utterly convinced he was going to abandon me. My belief wasn't that he would find someone else but something else — something better, more exciting, less me. I really wanted to go with him but he was insistent that if I went it was to be for myself; whichever way I tried to spin it I could not find a way to make that true. When he left I really thought he was leaving me for good and so when he called a few days later to say that he was miserable, perhaps the most miserable he had been in his life, I was moved to tears of unabashed joy.

Alexander started to write me emails — long, meandering missives without purpose. He told me about the silly little occurrences of his days. He wrote a whole message about the museum he went to that had an entire wing dedicated to chairs; he told me that he was desperate for Marmite and related the crazy conversations that ensued when he tried to describe it to supermarket staff; he told me he had a pass to the theme park and that on some mornings it was so quiet he would have a whole roller-coaster to himself. He didn't say much about the course itself; broad strokes about the content (stuff he knew) and the people (polite but boring). I wasn't really interested anyway. I craved the minutiae, the things that if he didn't share with me he would share with no one. They were so intimate that, although his emails contained no expressions of love, I considered them love letters.

I want to write to George but I don't have his email address so I send him a message through

Linger, composing it first in the notes section of my phone.

Marthashotbod: My friend's husband has cancer. Leanne and I have been friends for ever and it's so strange, really scary. I guess you know what that's like. I'm scared for him obviously but it makes everything seem scary. Like you never know when something is going to end or start! I'm just really feeling like I want to hold on to things.

It's early. I'm getting ready for work. I should tell you I work in a call centre. It's not what I wanted to do and it's not what I want to do but it is what I do. It's OK. I can do it. It feeds my kid, that's the important thing. I'm looking for something bigger, not that I know what that is yet. I got a promotion at work and I should be really pleased. Anyone normal would be really pleased but I guess you know by now that I'm not normal. I'm starting to think that might not be a bad thing. I'm weird but I'm me.

Anyway, holding on to things, it's probably good. Like, I don't really want this job but maybe I should hold on to it anyway. Maybe the secret is in the holding on but I held on to my marriage and maybe I shouldn't have . . . I guess everything has a lesson? I suppose you found that out with Cass.

When I was at the retreat they told me that I had to learn to sit with discomfort. I think I get it now: no matter what you do there's gonna be hurt and pain and shit. You've got to love that as much as you love the good stuff. I think there's good stuff here with you and me, I really do, even though we haven't met yet! The other thing is though, you can't really enjoy the good stuff unless you're honest about the crap and I want you to know there's a lot of crap. I've done some stuff I'm not proud of and I want to be able to share that stuff with the person I'm with. That's why I'm writing to say that I really want to share that with you.

I have a confession. Before I met you I wrote a list. On the list I put all the things I want in a man, not things I think I deserve — I promise I'm not a diva — but just the things that I think I might need. It's important that you know that so much of what was on that list I see in you. You are my list and I want to be yours. So, let's meet as soon as we can. Let's start this, let's be perfect for each other; let's be imperfect for each other perfectly.

George responds almost immediately.

Undeterred83: Well, I'm just about to go on safari, so meeting soon might

be hard lol. I'll be in touch.

I stare at the message for some time. I guess I hope if I stare at it long enough it will make me feel what I want to feel, but it doesn't; nothing he says to me ever will. Nothing any man ever says to me will.

I want to break something. I tear through my bag until I find the list and every word on it now seems to be taunting me. I rip it to shreds in a frenzy, making the pieces smaller and smaller until my fingers hurt. The resulting pile of scraps doesn't quell my anger and so I pull them into my cupped hands and carry them downstairs. The only available receptacle is Leanne's huge Le Creuset casserole dish. I throw the pieces in and then drag through the kitchen drawers for a match. I find a packet, procured from an Indian restaurant, light one and throw it in. The pitiful flame it creates is deeply unsatisfying, so I run to the booze cabinet and pull out some brandy to use as an accelerant. It works; it works a little too well. The resulting flames shoot a couple of feet out of the pot and I am engulfed in fear — not of the danger but of Leanne's reaction if I burn her house down. I grab the pot and practically lob it in the sink. Then I throw on the tap as far as it will go. The fire is extinguished and I fall to the floor, sweat and relief pouring from my body. I'm still sitting there when my phone rings, up in the bedroom. I panic that if my accidental bonfire hasn't woken up the whole house, my jarring ringtone will. I fly up the stairs and somehow manage to reach it before the voicemail kicks in.

Unbelievably, after everything, his is the only voice I want to hear.

'Sorry it's so early. Is now an OK time?' asks Alexander.

'It's the perfect time,' I say.

46

'Can we meet today?' Alexander asks.

'Of course.'

'Let's meet tonight at the cafe on the corner. Eight OK?'

I remember how lovely it is to have a cafe on a corner that needs no further specification.

After work I take Moses to Mum's and ask her to have him. I think she may be able to say no to me but she won't be able to resist him. She's steelier than I give her credit for, though. She leads us through to the kitchen in silence and when I ask if she will have Moses overnight she says, 'You can't just waltz back in here and expect me to have him, no questions asked.' I put Moses on the floor and he immediately runs from the room, returning a few seconds later with his little dump truck, which he settles down to play with. I sit at the kitchen table.

'OK, ask away,' I say.

Mum continues to stand by the kitchen counter. 'Where are you going to live?' she asks. 'You can't stay at Leanne's for ever.'

'Cara's given us her flat for a bit while she's out of the country.'

'Money?'

'I've got a new contract at work. And a promotion.'

Mum sits down. It's the first time in my life

I've had answers and I think we're both a little in shock.

'Am I too hard on you?' asks Mum.

I'm stunned. How can she be asking me a question that I've been screaming the answer to my entire life? I sit up in my chair and speak very clearly; I want to make sure that every word I say is heard.

'Mum, you're *absolutely* too hard on me.'

Mum straightens a place mat so that it runs in line with the edge of the table.

'When I was pregnant with you, I ate four oranges every day. I think I read an article somewhere about it. I drove your dad mad, making sure we had them in. It's not like it is now, when you can get whatever you want, whenever. I drank so much water. You know how much you pee when you're pregnant anyway. Those days, you could have a little drink when you were expecting. Not me, not a drop passed my lips.'

'I get it, Mum, you're a saint,' I say, slumping down in my seat.

'No, no,' says Mum, holding out her hand to ask for more time. 'No, not a saint: scared. I had lost two babies — I wasn't going to let you go and I was going to do everything in my power to make sure you were perfect, and you were. They said I mollycoddled you, that you were going to be spoiled. I don't think I put you down for two years. I didn't care.' Mum looks past me, towards the hall. 'I don't mean to push you; I am just so scared for you and you've always been such a timid child. I need to know that you're tough enough to keep yourself safe when I'm not here, when I can't be here.'

I feel like it's all hot air, another lecture whitewashed in sentiment. I really just want her to say she'll take Moses so that I can get on with my life.

'I'm sorry,' she says. So small and so ordinary, I almost miss it. The thing I had been waiting for without knowing I was waiting for it. I don't even know what she's saying sorry for but I am willing to take sorry for anything.

'Thanks, Mum,' I say.

'And thank you. Thank you for letting me support you through this; you never ask for help.' I laugh. I feel like all I do is mess up and flounder and cry for help. 'Of course I'll have him; I'll always have him. He can move in again, if you like. You, I'm not so sure.'

I try to suppress my smile but, as with most things, I'm unsuccessful. 'You'll be happy to know I'm meeting with Alexander this evening.'

Mum chews the inside of her mouth, as if she is actually trying to clamp it closed with her teeth.

'What?' I say.

'I am happy you're meeting him — you need to talk — but I don't want you to rush back into anything.'

I cover my face with my hands and speak through my fingers. 'Jesus, Mum, I can't win with you.'

'No, no,' says Mum. 'Don't get angry again! I just . . . I see how much you've been trying to do since the break-up. You have this, I don't know

. . . energy. Maybe you should be together but maybe not for a while. And it can't hurt to make him stew a little.' She pulls Moses into her lap. 'I know I gave you a bit of stick but maybe I don't know everything.'

I stand up and then lean down and give her a kiss on the head. 'You're a nightmare,' I say, 'but you're my nightmare.'

47

I wonder if the universe has one last coupon for me to cash in. If everything has been a test or a dream and Alexander and I must meet for one final, Technicolor ending. I consider this as I choose my seat in the greasy spoon he has asked me to meet him in. I pick a table by the window; it feels quite romantic with the drizzle running down it. I know that, whatever I've been through over the past few weeks, Alexander has had his own journey. I forgot for a while what I knew from the start: that his journeys before always led back to me. He may not be perfect — he may never be perfect — but maybe he is something much better than that: mine.

It seems Alexander's latest journey didn't involve him getting a new battery for his watch because he is five and then ten and then fifteen minutes late, and then just before I'm about to call it a day and accept that I have been stood up, he pushes through the door along with a gust of cold air. He stands on the entrance mat and runs his hand through his hair, before looking around for me. When he sees me, he assumes an expression of calm, one that I have not seen in months or perhaps even years. He walks purposefully towards me. I stand to meet him and for four, maybe five seconds I think he is going to kiss me and I panic a little about how to react to it. He just says, 'Hi,' though, before sitting down, and I am left standing.

'I'm going to get a coffee,' I say. 'Do you want one?'

'Er . . . yeah.' I go to the counter and ask them to bring two mugs of the stuff they have sitting on the warmer all day and night. As I walk back to the table I watch Alexander biting the skin on the inside of his right thumb, something he only does when he's nervous and that he hates about himself. I never knew whether it was the act itself he hated, or what it represented — his fallibility.

'It's coming,' I tell him.

'Thanks for meeting me,' he says.

'Of course, why wouldn't I . . . ?'

'It's just how things have been . . . It hasn't been the smoothest, for Moses or for us. I was hoping we could be friends.' Friends. This word is meant to be a gift to me but it's like a bucket of water on the very last embers of a dying fire.

'And what would that look like to you?' I ask. I try to hide the anger and humiliation but I'm not sure I do because Alexander tips his head to the right, which is what he does whenever I am being 'unreasonable'.

'You know . . . how we used to be.'

'How we used to be?' I laugh. It's comical how desperately out of touch he is. 'How we used to be was me listening to you bang on and on about what you're doing and what you need, and who I am or what I want to be never being a factor.'

Alexander looks up and I notice the waitress has brought over the coffee. She puts two mugs of grey liquid in front of us before walking away. Alexander smiles cordially until she is back behind the counter, then says, 'Does everything have to be so dramatic?'

Alexander used to hate it when I made displays of emotion in public. He said it made him feel vulnerable, as if feeling vulnerable was an entirely bad thing. We once went to a wedding in Birmingham — some girl he had been at university with — and we were wandering towards the station the next morning when we came upon the Hall of Memory, a memorial to the people of Birmingham who had given their lives in service. Only when I saw it did I remember standing there, clutching my grandfather's left hand as he saluted his fallen compatriots with his right. People would watch him as he stood, stock-still, shoulders back, and it was my first memory of feeling pride. Of course, as an adult, I realized they were probably just trying to piece together how this little brown girl belonged to this old white man, but that knowledge didn't taint the memory. I stopped for a few seconds and the tears rushed to my eyes — not for the ones who hadn't made it, but for the one who survived them all but still didn't survive long enough for me. Alexander, not realizing I had stopped, had gone on ahead and was now doubling back on himself to jimmy me along. 'We have a train to catch,' he said. 'We don't have time for your drama.'

Today there is time. I will make time because my drama deserves as much attention as anything he has to offer. I rest my chin on my right hand.

'You know, I thought for a minute, actually for more than a minute, for quite a while . . . Imagine me brushing my teeth, getting on the bus like a fool . . . Thinking that you were gonna meet me here today and ask me to get back with you!' Alexander doesn't respond, and I clap my hands together like a child with a new toy. 'You know what my biggest fear was, all this time? My fear was that you would show up unannounced on your rented white horse and sweep me off my feet, and even though in the back of my mind I would know it would be the wrong thing, I would go. I would go back to you, only to end up in the same place in two years, five years, ten years, fifty years.'

'I'm pretty sure one or both of us will be dead in fifty years,' says Alexander. I pick up a fork and slam its prongs into the Formica table between us.

'Why the hell did you try and make me feel so bad when you clearly don't give a shit?'

'That's not fair, I — '

'You forget, I've watched you go through break-ups, and you never go out without a fight or at least a last shag. What is it you used to say?' I click my fingers several times. 'Break-up sex is the WD-40 that stops the door creaking as it closes.' Alexander smiles at his own wit and it is with this smile that I understand how self-serving he is. 'So, the only reason you wouldn't have had one last hurrah with me is if you already had someone filling the gap.' We look at each other. I like to think we're having a silent conversation, and obviously I can't read his

387

mind, but I'd like to believe he's saying something along the lines of, 'I'm sorry, I'm a piece of shit. I don't deserve you anyway,' or thereabouts.

'I don't think there's any point in wading through everything.' He sees me open my mouth to protest and holds up his finger. 'I actually asked you here to try and move things forward.' He gets some documents out of the leather portfolio he has brought with him and hands me several pages.

'What is it?' I try to look through what he's given me but the letters seem to float above the page.

'It's my financial statement. Then there's one for you to complete and return to me and there's also a parenting agreement, which I think we should meet again and discuss when you're less . . . well, less . . . heightened.'

I look up from the pages. 'We've hardly spoken, Alexander. Don't you even miss me?'

'I feel like it's easier . . . cleaner . . . if we just get everything sorted. Better for Moses too,' says Alexander, which is not quite answering the question but answering it all the same.

'Better for you and Poppy, more like,' I say, and I mean this to be hurtful but Alexander nods his head.

'It's serious with Poppy, yes. I want to move things forward.'

I ask the question that I didn't have the stomach to ask when I was a girl. 'Why her and not me?'

Alexander looks down at his lap. I think he's

not going to answer but then he speaks quickly, as if he might change his mind. 'She's so open — she accepts me for what I am. I always felt like you were stuck in this fantasy world of what should be or what could be; I could never compete with it.'

'Did you try to, though?'

'Maybe not, but also you didn't give me a chance. You were always lost in the future.' Alexander leans across the table towards me. 'Do you have any idea how hard it is running your own business? Do you know how many nights I was awake with stress and worry?' He sits back in his chair. 'Poppy gets it. She doesn't try and put even more pressure on me.'

'I know — I know what it's like,' I say, 'but I also know there's more to life than work.'

'Spoken like an irresponsible brat,' says Alexander. I couldn't have been more surprised if he had spat in my face.

'What the fuck are you talking about, Alexander? Your girlfriend probably doesn't even have the training wheels off her bike.'

'I'm talking about your bank statements, which still come to the flat because you couldn't even be bothered to change the address. What have you been spending all the money in the savings account on?'

'You've been opening my post?' I ask. Alexander doesn't open post, he just leaves it in a pile on the kitchen table.

'Don't change the subject,' he says. 'That money was for Moses.' He taps the table to emphasize the key words. 'That money' — tap

— 'was for your son' — tap — 'and you've blown it on shit.' Tap.

'It wasn't shit,' I say. 'I bought a business course and — '

'More pie-in-the-sky crap,' says Alexander.

I think about when he was starting his business and I was getting loans to keep the lights on. I think about the MacBook I bought him for his birthday. Spending money was fine when it was for his gain.

'No, you don't get the right to an opinion,' I say. 'What I spend my money on is *my* business.'

'Yes, do what the fuck you want — spend it on ponies and sweeties and whatever it is you think will make you happy — but I want to make sure that my money is well and truly out of it.'

'Fine,' I say.

'It's not just that.' Alexander fixes my gaze and lowers his voice. 'Drugs, Martha?'

I let my head loll back in exasperation. I can imagine Greta gleefully retelling my fall from grace.

'For God's sake, Alexander, it was a bit of weed.'

'I know you've found being a mum hard,' says Alexander, 'but there's a limit, and buying drugs in the middle of the afternoon goes way past it.'

I can't accept what he says; I refuse to. 'What about the time you went to that stag do and took so many mushrooms I had to travel halfway across the country, so I could hold your hand on the train home?'

Alexander doesn't say anything; he knows it's the ultimate weapon against me. I want input, I want emotion, even if it's negative; his silence is another attack. I shove the papers into my bag and tell Alexander I have somewhere to be.

'That's cool,' he says, as if he has not just eviscerated my character. 'Call me when you've gone over it. We'll speak in a few days.'

I can't even respond — the way my life is at the moment, a few days feels like a lifetime away.

48

The Fairfax 'End of Year Tapas Extravaganza' is an event you go to when you have nowhere else to go. I had thought it was called an 'end of year extravaganza' to be non-denominational and inclusive, but Bob told me the directors thought that people would expect less booze if they left out the word 'Christmas'. I'm not sure there is anything sadder than going to an office party actually *at* the office — it just drives home the message that this is all you have — but alcohol is definitely the answer to my encounter with Alexander, and *free* alcohol is always the answer. Walking to the door, I have exactly the same feeling I do before I go on shift. Darryl is sitting in the reception, as he always seems to be. 'Happy End of Year, Darryl,' I say.

'Thanks, love,' he says. He has swapped his security cap for a Santa hat, which seems to have the opposite effect to the one desired in that it just makes him look sadder.

'Darryl, do you have a family?' I ask.

'Oh yes,' says Darryl. 'Missus and three girls.'

'Is it hard being away from them? You work here a lot.'

Darryl's shoulders start to shake and for a terrifying second I think he is crying, before I realize that he is laughing. He leans forward and says to me, 'Hear that?'

I hold my breath and pay attention but all I

can hear is the soft swoosh of traffic outside. 'No, I can't hear anything.'

Darryl leans back and folds his arms, 'I rest my case,' he says.

'Have a good night,' I say.

'Oh, I will,' he says, before chuckling again. I can tell he means it. I suppose it's wrong of me to assume that a place means the same thing to different people.

The party is on the second floor. Usually home to the canteen and several meeting spaces, it has been made into a Christmas fiesta, courtesy of a job lot of maracas and a truckload of cheap tinsel. Tashi is just by the lift entrance and squeals when she sees me. I let myself be swept up into an embrace by her, and even at this point the squealing doesn't stop. 'So, so pleased to see you! How are you?!'

'Better for seeing you,' I say.

'Congrats on your promotion.'

'Ugh, don't,' I say.

'Why would you say that?' Tashi asks. She holds me away from her and examines my face.

I twist away from her hands and her enquiring eyes and say, 'Well, it's not exactly celebratory. Congrats, you've won yourself another five years working here!' I lean against the trestle table set up by the lift. It was a bit ambitious to think I could come to a party at my workplace and not think about work.

'Some people would kill for the opportunity. If someone offers you something you should be grateful. It's a gift, even if it's really hard to see right away. If you're negative about it, the universe will hear that.'

I laugh. 'The universe and I aren't really on speaking terms.'

'Fine,' says Tashi, coming and sitting next to me. 'What about me? Be positive for me. Someone who's a bit lost and wants to know what to do with their life and might be looking to you for some guidance.'

I put my arm round her shoulder. 'You want guidance?'

She nods.

'You've come to the wrong place on so many levels.' I pick up a leaflet resting on the table. It depicts a weary-looking donkey, carrying a load of bricks. 'Is this yours?' I ask.

'Yes!' she says. 'It's to support working horses and donkeys. Make sure they're being cared for properly.'

'You're collecting?'

'Well, it's a raffle. There's a hamper and a trip to a sanctuary in Dorset.'

'Had any interest?'

'Jim from IT gave me a carrot.'

The lift opens and three lads from the post room step on to the floor. They spot Tashi's leaflets.

'Collecting money for your mum, are you!' shouts one, and the others cheer and applaud him.

'Tashi,' I say, 'these aren't your people. That's my guidance: get out whilst you still can.'

'Well, actually,' she says, and she stares at her shoes, 'I was thinking about volunteering with the charity.'

'The donkey people?'

'Yeah, Brett says — '

'Who?!' I suddenly realize why she's being all sheepish.

'Brett, you know — from the retreat.'

'Yes, I know! Lovely, brawny one. Massive, actually.' I try to make a measure of his breadth with my hands. 'Massive!'

'Yes, that one. After you'd gone, we ended up talking loads, and then we kept in touch afterwards and he got me into the Working Horse and Donkey thing, and now a space has come up on this trip he's taking and — '

'Go!' I stand in front of Tashi and hold both her hands. 'Take it from someone withered and cynical; please, just go. Go now.'

'Now?' asks Tashi, looking at her stand.

'Yes, now.'

Tashi grabs her bag and shoves her leaflets and the carrot into it before dashing towards the lift. 'Thanks,' she says as she waits for it to arrive.

'You go get your happy ending,' I say, because who am I to burst her bubble?

★ ★ ★

Bob spots me standing alone and pushes me into the throng with a firm hand against the small of my back. He stops at a group of three women standing near a drinks table. 'Ladies, this is Martha, our latest addition to the senior team.' He then leans uncomfortably close and whispers in my ear, 'Welcome to the inner sanctum; try the punch.' He pats me on the hip and then backs away, telling me he's got babies to kiss.

'Tool,' says one of the three women, a statuesque brunette. 'I'm Hope, HR.' She sticks out her hand and I accept a solid handshake. 'Don't drink the punch — it's laced with some dreadful coconut liqueur. Here, have some fizz.' She pours me a serving into a plastic cup. 'This is Helen and Anekwe.'

'Hi,' I say to both. 'Yeah, we've met,' I say, addressing Anekwe.

'Yes, you're the girl that's always flirting with that boy in the break room.'

'Flirting? Boy?' I say, as if these words have only just been introduced to my lexicon.

'Yeah, this one.' She thrusts her chin forward and I turn to see Greg dancing towards us, a sombrero on his head.

'They've turned the boardroom into a disco and it's carnage in there,' he says. 'I can get you in, though.'

'It's OK,' says Anekwe. Hope and Helen shake their heads.

'It's you and me then, bud,' he says.

I put down my drink as he takes my hand to lead me away. I manage to stop his trajectory towards the boardroom by dragging him behind the giant yucca next to the recycling bin.

'I've had the shittiest day, Greg. I'm not in a disco mood.'

Greg removes his hat. 'What happened? Is Moses OK?'

'Yeah, yeah, it's just . . . ' Greg watches me, his face willing to receive whatever I will say. 'My marriage is over.' I start to cry. I try to blink back the tears because it feels too much to be both 'woman who cries at work' and 'woman who cries at parties' simultaneously. Greg puts his arms round me and he does this kind of scooping thing so that I feel safe and supported, and I stop worrying about being a 'woman who' and focus on what I am, which is really sad.

After a minute or so, Greg releases me. He then holds me at arm's length as if checking for injuries and says, 'My diagnosis is not enough alcohol. I could be wrong but it would be a first.' He leaves me by the plant for a bit and returns with four shots in hot pink, plastic shot glasses.

'What is it?' I ask.

Greg shrugs. 'Dunno.'

'I don't know if I should,' I say. 'Alcohol is a depressant, right?'

Greg hands me two of the shots. 'And that's the beauty of divorce: it feels so shit, the only way is up!'

I can drink to that. We both throw our heads back and inhale the first shot; it's definitely, probably tequila.

'Anyway, there's karaoke starting now — you're gonna need a bit of a buzz on to watch Bob up there.'

'Jesus, yes!' I say, and raise my second tiny shot glass. Greg carefully taps his against mine before we drink. It's definitely, probably vodka.

The boardroom is filling up fast and Greg snags us some space sitting on a table to the right of what I assume is a makeshift stage. An older man I don't recognize is standing at the front, holding a microphone.

397

'That's Pete,' whispers Greg. 'He's one of the accountants. He does karaoke at Paddy's on Tuesdays.'

'Welcome!' says Pete. 'And for your delight and deliberation we have Bob, head of customer caaaaaaare!' Bob appears from somewhere within the crowd and whips the microphone out of Pete's hand.

'Thanks,' he says. 'Can I just say, this has been an awesome year!' Bob raises his arm to encourage audience participation, but the only result is someone in the back shouting, 'Can someone tell my payslip!'

'I, for one,' Bob continues, 'want each and every one of you to know that you have played a vital role in making a good company great!' Bob does a semi-squat and makes a growling sound.

'I don't understand,' I whisper to Greg. 'Is that Tony the Tiger?' Greg claps his hand over his mouth a little too late to stop his laughter escaping.

'Anyway,' says Bob, shooting a dark look in our direction, 'I appreciate all of you. Except for you, Marina. Should you even be here? I mean, are you allowed in the building? Can someone deal with that . . . But for the rest of you, this one's for you . . . ' Bob adopts a wide-legged stance, one that his trousers seem unqualified to accommodate, and bounces unsteadily to the introduction of 'Sex On Fire'. As the song progresses it becomes clear that he has partially choreographed the whole thing; his voice is not too bad but he completely negates the impact of this by constantly thrusting and looking so pleased with himself. I cover my eyes with my hands.

'I can't watch,' I whisper. Greg grabs my wrists from behind and pulls them away from my face. Bob holds his final pose for several seconds. I suspect in the version he had rehearsed in his head there would be applause. I'm not sure how Pete is as an accountant, but when it comes to karaoke he is a pro at covering up; he plays some jolly incidental music to mask the silence and starts some playful banter with the crowd. Bob leaves the stage and the room.

'Damn!' I say.

'Damn indeedy!' says Greg.

'Why would anyone do that?' I ask him, just as Pete is saying, 'Next up, we have Greg from customer care.'

49

Greg doesn't look at me as he bounds towards the stage. Pete continues to read from a clipboard: 'Greg says that he wants to dedicate this to someone he thinks is really hot and who he hopes will appreciate it, but he also says that it's important that you know that he would rather stand in front of a train than do this. He says by the end of this song he will have been to hell and back and feel like he's slayed a dragon. Whatever the heck that means.'

By this point Greg has taken position centre stage. He thanks Pete warmly as he is passed the mic and, whilst he keeps his eyes lowered for the entire introduction to Aerosmith's 'I Don't Want To Miss A Thing', when he sings the first line he looks up and directly at me. He is really, truly awful and he doesn't get better. He literally murders every note of the ballad. Within the audience there is a small enclave of people from customer care who know and love Greg and cheer him on just for being him, but to everyone else he's a dude who's completely tone-deaf. Most of the crowd are laughing and the rest are jeering; the guys from IT start throwing Twiglets at him. The further into the song he gets, the higher and more fervent the notes become, and we all know that approaching is what *should* be a glorious crescendo. I can feel the anticipation in the room and I have to rescue him. Just before he reaches the end of the bridge I storm the stage, grab the microphone and kiss him, and as I do the backing track soars and the crowd erupts into cheers and applause. It's all pretty dramatic.

Everyone is still cheering when we pull apart. I look at them all and they get louder. I lean in and whisper to Greg, 'Shall we get out of here?'

'I thought you'd never ask,' he says.

He guides me through the room; guys whack him on the back as we pass but he doesn't stop or let go of my hand. We ignore the cries from people to stay as the lift doors close behind us, and as soon as it starts to move Greg is kissing me again. His hands feel like they have known my body my whole life; it feels safe and sexy at the same time, very sexy. I'm surprised by how pulled to him I feel, how my body responds so readily when I have only just realized how I feel about him — maybe it knew before me. The lift doors open and we both try to rearrange ourselves.

'Evening,' says Darryl, doing little to hide his amusement.

'Night,' we both mutter, as we scramble past him self-consciously.

Outside Greg tries to hail a taxi but several speed past him. As he raises his arm to try another one, I pull it down. 'Let's walk,' I say. 'We're in no rush, right?'

Greg smiles. I've never noticed the dimple that appears in his left cheek when he does. 'No,' he says, 'we're not.' Greg tells me he lives about fifteen minutes away. He fusses over me, making me reassure him several times that I can walk the distance in my boots.

'These boots were made for walking,' I tell him.

'That was terrible,' he says.

'Not as terrible as your singing,' I say.

'What's a man to do? I had to get your attention,' he says.

I can't really respond to that. I don't know why I had never properly noticed Greg, right beside me all that time. I guess because with him it was easy, too easy. Somewhere in the dark recesses of my soul I had decided that if he accepted me, no questions asked, there must be something wrong with *him*.

Greg's place is on the top floor of a dilapidated building. As we climb the stairs he apologizes for the smell. 'The people downstairs seem to eat the same fish stew every day.' The flat itself is charming, a bachelor pad crossed with a fairy princess castle. The black leather sofa is strewn with fluffy pink pillows and a Bambi snow globe sits in the centre of the glass coffee table.

'It's nice,' I say.

'You don't have to tell me that,' says Greg.

'I know,' I say. After taking off our coats we start kissing again, this time firmer, with more intent.

Greg stops and looks at me seriously and says, 'Do you want a Spanish omelette?' I smile and say yes. It's nice watching him work and so I sit in silence as he chops the potatoes and seasons the eggs. Ten minutes later he places a perfectly browned slice in front of me and the first bite warms my stomach in the way that only true comfort food can.

'This is really good,' I say. 'Who knew you were so good with your hands?'

Greg chuckles and puts a liberal serving of barbecue sauce on his own slice. 'Well, Mum was always in the pub or sleeping off being down the pub; I had to feed the kids and I learned a handful of staples. Most of them are some variation of egg and potato. I didn't even know this was called a Spanish omelette till I met my ex, so she gave me that at least.'

'What about your dad?' I ask. 'Couldn't he help?'

Greg snorts. 'You'd have to find him to ask him, and if you did you'd have done better than me.' He doesn't say it angrily; it's just a truth for him.

'How are you such a good dad when you haven't had one?'

'I don't know that I'm a good dad, I do my best. I do what feels right — what else can you do? And I love it. Don't get me wrong, the girls do my head in sometimes. But even then I feel so lucky it's my head they're doing in.'

After we've filled our bellies, Greg pours us some wine. As we settle on the sofa to drink it he asks, 'What about your fella? The one you're seeing.'

'I don't know how much I'm seeing him.'

'And the ex?' asks Greg. 'I don't want to step on any toes and you seemed quite upset earlier.' I put my legs across his lap and he gently strokes my shins as I speak.

'No, no, it's fine. I don't know if I was upset about him, actually. To be honest he's a bit of a tosser. I think I was upset about losing *it*, not him.'

'It?' asks Greg.

'The knowing someone's there, the having someone to call when you're alone and pissed. Being able to go home and tell someone all the shitty little petty things that happened to you that day and they, like, have to listen, they're contractually obliged. I'm just scared I'm not going to have that again.'

Greg pulls me on to his lap. 'You can have that again,' he says.

'Yeah?'

'You can have that again,' he repeats, and he kisses me. When we stop, Greg says to me, 'I want you to know that I want you to stay the night, and that doesn't mean I want us to do anything — I mean, I do, I really do want us to do stuff — but we don't have to. I mean, I want whatever you want.'

'It's OK,' I say.

'Cool,' says Greg.

'Shall we, then?' I ask. Greg looks surprised. 'Show me where the magic happens.'

Greg takes me to his bedroom. His bed is a mess and he hastily tries to pull up the covers. As he does I notice a photo frame on the table next to his bed, turned to face the wall. I brace myself before I pick it up; I'm prepared to see a picture of his ex and I want to be ready for her beauty. Instead the picture is of Greg and his girls

— they look like they've been caught in the middle of a pile-on. I know it's recent because Charlotte is smiling and I can clearly see the gap where her tooth had been.

Greg sits on the bed. 'You OK?' he asks.

'Yeah,' I say as I join him. 'Why was this turned against the wall?'

He takes the frame from my hand and looks at the photo. 'It's a shit picture,' he says. It is, to be honest; the shot is totally out of focus and they all look sweaty and red. 'I just like to know it's there.'

He puts the photo down on the other side of the bed and he's still looking at it when I say, 'I thought it was going to be a picture of your ex.'

Greg scoots closer to me so that our bodies are side by side and we can't see each other's faces. 'Why would you think that?' He bumps his leg against mine.

'Something you should know — I can be a bit cynical.'

'No!' says Greg. 'I seriously never noticed.'

I hear the smile in his voice and I shimmy down the mattress so I can look up at him. 'So, what's she like?' I ask.

Greg sighs. 'She's a woman.'

I poke him in the leg with my finger. 'Come on, indulge me,' I say.

Greg lies down beside me. 'OK, I don't know . . . She's a woman, she's small. She's really clean, she likes dark chocolate.'

'What made you fall in love with her?'

Greg exhales loudly. 'You know, I can't remember. I'm sorry; that sounds like a cop-out but it's true. I guess she was reliable. I'd never had that. My mum was such a mess and here was this girl, who was . . . She was together. I knew she'd look after any kids we had.'

'And?'

'And she did,' he says. 'I won't lie, I picked a great mother. I just did a shitty job of picking a wife.'

'I'm not sure the guy I picked was a great father or husband,' I say.

Greg props himself up on one elbow and looks down at me. 'That can't be true,' he says. 'Look at you, you're so amazing — there must have been some good in him.' I try to think but I can only recall Alexander's face in the cafe, the way he dismissed me and his obvious eagerness to get back to his new life with his new girl and forget about everything that we had.

'You know, I think you're right,' I say. 'I mean, he's fine, he has his own business, he's clever. I think he probably has a lot of good in him. I think maybe I just wasn't the one to bring it out.'

'Maybe,' says Greg, 'but also that wasn't your job.'

'Oh right, what was my job then?'

'To be you.' He kisses me. 'That's all I'll ever want from you: for you to keep being you, and I want that for as long as you'll let me hang around.'

'Greg,' I say, 'I know you said we didn't have to do anything, but I've got to tell you something . . . ' He watches me, his big brown eyes unblinking. 'I want to.'

It's strange that until this time I hadn't

realized that sex is a conversation. It can say 'I hate you' or 'I need you'; it can be a shout or a whisper. With Greg everything feels so familiar but also really new and exhilarating. I am a little scared by how much I want to have sex with him, and not because I think it will make him like me more; because it will add another dimension to how we like each other. Greg explores every part of my body — the creases behind my knees and the tips of my elbows — and not because he has to, but because he wants to. I feel like what Greg is trying to say is, 'I want to know you, all of you, because I like what I know already.'

Afterwards he pulls my back to him so that we're spooning and every inch of our bodies is touching. I've heard people say that they fit together before and secretly judged them for being so pathetic, for trying to create something where there is nothing. Of course bodies fit together — that's what they were built to do — but I understand now what they meant. The ease with which we lie together . . . it doesn't feel like a compromise to be so close to him. I'm not, as I often have been in the past, biding my time until I can slip away and return to being just me. It feels like, why haven't I been sleeping this way, with this person, the whole time? And so that's what I do.

★   ★   ★

I wake up alone and I'm less disappointed than I thought I would be. What makes life hard is the constant unknowing. If I accept as fact that everyone is going to let me down, maybe things will be a little easier. I sit up in bed and consider whether to get dressed when Greg walks in, still in his boxer shorts. He is holding two mugs in his right hand. He bows gently from the waist as he holds them out so I can take one. 'And the pièce de résistance,' he says, pulling out a packet of chocolate chip cookies from behind his back, 'biscuits, the good kind.' He places them on my lap and then climbs in the bed beside me with his own tea.

'I bet you give these to all the ladies,' I say.

Greg blows on his drink before saying, 'Nah, the last bird only got Rich-Teas.' When I don't respond he adds, 'That was a joke; there was no last bird.'

'I know, Greg,' I say. We both drink our tea and Greg warms his feet on mine under the covers. 'You got work?' I ask him. He shakes his head. 'So, what do you want to do today?'

Greg takes a long intake of breath and strokes his chin as if he is giving the question great thought; then he kisses me and his kiss answers many of my questions: Did he really mean everything he said? Is he happy I'm here? Will he still want me here tomorrow? His kiss tells me this is the beginning of something or the end of something, or perhaps that they are one and the same. I hear my phone offer up a notification from somewhere in the living room; I keep kissing Greg. I'll get to it later, maybe.

Epilogue

One year later

There's a cafe around the corner from our home, a three-bedroom cottage a couple of roads back from the seafront. On Sundays when the girls are staying, Greg will often take the kids there for breakfast, leaving me to enjoy an hour of silence. It's a necessity; I spend my weeks listening to the cute but chaotic compositions of the three-and four-year-olds who take my class, 'Music with Martha'. I love it but even love can become overwhelming. Greg adores these breakfasts and when he gets back later in the day, without fail he tells me he's going to reduce his hours at work and spend more time at home. I just smile and nod because I know he won't.

When I left to start my business, Greg took my job. Then, when Bob was fired after being overheard by a customer calling someone something very much out of line with company policy, Greg took over running the department. He wants to leave the office at six but he's so committed to his team it's always an effort to pull himself away, but it's an effort I know he makes and that's all that matters to me.

Cara returned to Rio for an extended visit and let Moses and I stay on in her flat at very much mates' rates, so I was able to save enough to get together a deposit for the cottage. Mum and

Dad come over for dinner at least once a week. Mum hates my curtains but she thinks Greg's fantastic and he seems to like her too.

James's surgery was successful and Leanne took a sabbatical to spend time with him during his recovery. She was surprised how much she appreciated a slower pace of life, so they're planning a move to rural Sussex. I hate the idea of her not being around the corner but I know how important it can be to move on.

Alexander and I had mediation and he agreed to give me a lump sum, which I used to get the business off the ground. We talk occasionally when he's dropping off Moses or if we bump into each other out and about. We're not friends but we're not *not* friends and that's enough. He and Poppy got engaged a few months ago; I didn't attend the party.

The sun is beckoning me so persuasively through the bedroom window that I decide to abandon my lie-in and join Greg and the kids. When Moses spots me in the cafe doorway he shouts, 'Pancakes, Mummy!' Greg and the girls look up and wave. I mouth 'coffee' and Greg gives me a thumbs up.

I stand at the counter behind a guy shifting impatiently from foot to foot. When he is passed his drink in a cardboard takeaway cup he lifts the lid and peers into it. 'Are you sure this is soya milk?' he asks.

'If that's what you wanted,' says the cafe owner.

'Yes, but people have made mistakes before.'

'Not this time,' says the owner carefully. The

man turns and collides with me. A generous amount of liquid from the still-open cup falls on to my sleeve. Although I am the innocent party, I start to apologize.

'Why don't you look where you're going?' says the man. I look up and into the eyes of George; eyes that are as startlingly blue as I remember from his profile picture, looking back at me from within his list-perfect, redheaded six-foot-something frame.

I smile and say, 'I think I might retract that apology.' I say this to give him an opportunity to start again, to recognize me and be the George I once knew.

He narrows his eyes, I think at first in realization, but then he mumbles, 'Idiot.' He pushes past me and leaves the cafe without looking back.

I return to the counter and the owner asks me if I'm OK. 'Yeah, I'm great thanks,' I say. I order my coffee and a stack of pancakes with extra bacon.

'I'll bring it over,' he says.

When I slide into the booth next to Greg, he pecks me on the lips. 'Morning, buddy,' he says.

'Ew,' says Charlotte, but she's smiling. I poke my tongue out at her and she does the same, spraying toast crumbs in the process.

'What was that about?' asks Greg, nodding in the direction of the counter.

'Nothing. Someone I thought I knew.' I can feel Greg looking at me, waiting for more. When I don't speak he pushes my leg with his knee and I mime elbowing him in response. Greg chuckles and starts rearranging his sandwich; he likes to try and have the perfect ratio of bacon and egg in every bite.

'There's a craft ale festival on at Stanmer House today,' he says. 'Do you wanna go? We could let the kids have a run round and grab a sneaky ale.' I watch as Greg is finally satisfied with his work and sighs happily as he takes a large bite.

I squeeze his thigh under the table and say, 'Yes. Yes, yes, and yes again.'

Acknowledgements

Enormous thanks to everyone involved in the Penguin Random House WriteNow mentoring scheme, particularly Siena Parker for holding my hand and Sarah Rigby for giving me the confidence to jump! To all my WriteNow cohorts, you've made my life brighter. I want to know you and read your work for the rest of my days.

Thank you to all my Transworld teammates, especially, of course, my mentor and editor Francesca Best. Still wanna see more of you on Insta but in every other way you're killing it!

Mum and Dad, thanks always for showing me the benefit hard graft and for only ever wanting me to be happy. Rachel and Shellon, independent studies show you are the best sisters on the planet and, undoubtedly, I couldn't have done this without my much better-looking brother James.

Shout out to my big, beautiful, crazy family who have taught me that there is never an inappropriate time for humour. Special mention to my cuz Nadine, without whom this book would have no ending.

To my amazing, unwavering cheerleaders — Adele, Anna, Ceri, Chloe, Chris, Rhiannon, Gemma, Nicola, Sharon, Troy, Natalie, Varsha and Martin — you all keep me sane, or an approximation of it.

Graham, I'll be forever grateful for your advice, friendship and stellar fathering skills. Indeed, thank you to all the Allcotts. It has been a privilege to start this new chapter of my life with your continued support (and name).

And most of all thank you Roscoe, for giving me a reason to get up and start again, each and every morning.

We do hope that you have enjoyed reading this large print book.

Did you know that all of our titles are available for purchase?

We publish a wide range of high quality large print books including:
Romances, Mysteries, Classics
General Fiction
Non Fiction and Westerns

Special interest titles available in large print are:
The Little Oxford Dictionary
Music Book
Song Book
Hymn Book
Service Book

Also available from us courtesy of Oxford University Press:
Young Readers' Dictionary
(large print edition)
Young Readers' Thesaurus
(large print edition)

For further information or a free brochure, please contact us at:
Ulverscroft Large Print Books Ltd.,
The Green, Bradgate Road, Anstey,
Leicester, LE7 7FU, England.
Tel: (00 44) 0116 236 4325
Fax: (00 44) 0116 234 0205

FOUR

Andy Jones

In the time they've known each other, Sally, Al and Mike have shared — well, almost everything. Sally and Al have been married for seven years, but now their relationship is hanging by a thread. Sally and Mike have been best friends since university. Mike and Al have been friends for many years. Yet with Al poised to become Mike's boss, their relationship is coming under threat. And now there's Mike and Faye. They haven't been together long, but Mike's pretty sure that this time it's the real deal. As the three old friends sit on a train heading towards Brighton to meet Faye, little do they know that after this weekend, the four of them will have shared . . . everything. They all know they have made a mistake. But they could never have imagined the consequences.

THE DROWNED VILLAGE

Kathleen McGurl

It's the summer of 1935, and eleven-year-old Stella Walker is preparing to leave her home forever. Forced to evacuate to make way for a new reservoir, the village of Brackendale Green will soon be lost. But before the water has even reached them, a dreadful event threatens to tear Stella's family apart . . . In the present day, Stella is living with her granddaughter Laura, who helps to care for her as she attempts to leave double heartache behind. A fierce summer has dried up the lake and revealed the remnants of the deserted village, and Stella is sure the place still holds answers for her. With only days until the rain returns, she begs Laura to make the journey for her — and to finally solve the mysteries of the almost forgotten past.

THE AU PAIR

Emma Rous

Seraphine Mayes and her brother Danny are known as the summer-born Summerbournes: the first set of summer twins to be born at Summerbourne House. But on that day, their mother threw herself to her death, their au pair fled, and the village thrilled with whispers of dark-cloaked figures and a stolen baby. Now twenty-five, and mourning the recent death of her father, Seraphine uncovers a family photograph taken on the day she and Danny were born featuring both parents posing with just one baby. Seraphine begins to suspect that they might not be twins after all, and that there was more to her mother's death than she has ever been told. Why did their beloved au pair flee that day? Where is she now? And does she hold the key to what really happened?

Anthony Horowitz may have committed more (fictional) murders than any other living author. As a TV screenwriter he created both *Midsomer Murders* and the BAFTA-winning *Foyle's War*. Other TV work includes *Poirot* and the widely acclaimed mini-series *Collison* and *Injustice*. He is also the author of a string of bestselling children's books, including the Alex Rider series which has sold over 13 million copies worldwide. His first Sherlock Holmes novel, *The House of Silk*, spent seven weeks in the *Sunday Times* Top 10. Horowitz has claimed Sir Arthur Conan Doyle as an inspiration for his work ever since encountering the Holmes canon, aged sixteen. He currently lives in Clerkenwell.

You can discover more about the author at: www.anthonyhorowitz.com
Twitter — @AnthonyHorowitz

MORIARTY

Days after Sherlock Holmes and his arch-
enemy Moriarty fall to their doom at the
Reichenbach Falls, Pinkerton agent Frederick
Chase arrives in Europe from New York. The
death of Moriarty has created a poisonous
vacuum which has been swiftly filled by a
fiendish new criminal mastermind who has
risen to take his place. Ably assisted by
Inspector Athelney Jones of Scotland Yard,
a devoted student of Holmes's methods of
investigation and deduction, Chase must
forge a path through the darkest corners of
the capital to shine a light on this shadowy
figure — a man much feared but seldom
seen; a man determined to engulf London in
a tide of murder and menace.

Books by Anthony Horowitz
Published by Ulverscroft:

THE HOUSE OF SILK

ANTHONY HOROWITZ

MORIARTY

Complete and Unabridged

CHARNWOOD
Leicester

First published in Great Britain in 2014 by
Orion Books
an imprint of
The Orion Publishing Group Ltd.
London

First Charnwood Edition
published 2015
by arrangement with
The Orion Publishing Group Ltd.
An Hachette Livre UK Company
London

The moral right of the author has been asserted

All the characters in this book are fictitious, and any resemblance to actual persons, living or dead, is purely coincidental.

A catalogue record for this book is available from the British Library.

ISBN 978–1–4448–2562–6

Published by
F. A. Thorpe (Publishing)
Anstey, Leicestershire

Set by Words & Graphics Ltd.
Anstey, Leicestershire
Printed and bound in Great Britain by
T. J. International Ltd., Padstow, Cornwall

This book is printed on acid-free paper

For my friend, Matthew Marsh
And in memory of Henry Marsh,
1982–2012

From The Times of London
24th April 1891

HIGHGATE BODY FOUND

Police have no explanation for a peculiarly brutal murder that has come to light close by Merton Lane in the normally pleasant and quiet vicinity of Highgate. The deceased, a man in his twenties, had been shot in the head but of particular interest to the police was the fact that his hands had been tied prior to the killing. Inspector G. Lestrade, who is in charge of the enquiry, inclines to the belief that this dreadful act took the form of an execution and may be related to recent unrest in the streets of London. He has identified the victim as Jonathan Pilgrim, an American who had been staying at a private club in Mayfair and who may have been visiting the metropolis for reasons of business. Scotland Yard has been in contact with the American legation but so far no address has been found for the dead man and it may be some weeks before any relatives come forward. The investigation continues.

1

The Reichenbach Falls

Does anyone really believe what happened at the
Reichenbach Falls? A great many accounts have
been written but it seems to me that all of them
have left something to be desired — which is to
say, the truth. Take the *Journal de Genève* and
Reuters, for example. I read them from start to
finish, not an easy task for they're both written in
that painfully dry manner of most European
publications, as if they're reporting the news
because they have to, not because it's something
they want you to know. And what exactly did
they tell me? That Sherlock Holmes and his
foremost adversary, Professor James Moriarty, of
whose existence the public were only now
learning, had met and that both of them died.
Well, it might as well have been an automobile
accident for all the excitement those two
authorities managed to put into their prose. Even
the headlines were dull.

But what really puzzles me is the narrative of
Dr John Watson. He describes the entire affair in
Strand Magazine, starting with the knock on the
door of his consulting room on the evening of
April 24th 1891 and continuing with his journey
to Switzerland. I yield to no one in my
admiration for the chronicler of the adventures,
exploits, memoirs, casebooks and so on of the

great detective. As I sit at my Remington Number Two improved model typewriter (an American invention, of course) and begin this great labour, I know that I am likely to fall short of the standards of accuracy and entertainment that he maintained to the end. But I have to ask myself — how could he have got it so wrong? How could he have failed to notice inconsistencies that would have struck even the most obtuse police commissioner as glaringly obvious? Robert Pinkerton used to say that a lie was like a dead coyote. The longer you leave it, the more it smells. He'd have been the first to say that everything about the Reichenbach Falls stank.

You must forgive me if I seem a touch overemphatic but my story — *this* story — begins with Reichenbach and what follows will make no sense without a close examination of the facts. And who am I? So that you may know whose company you keep, let me tell you that my name is Frederick Chase, that I am a senior investigator with the Pinkerton Detective Agency in New York and that I was in Europe for the first — and quite possibly the last — time in my life. My appearance? Well, it's never easy for any man to describe himself but I will be honest and say that I could not call myself handsome. My hair was black, my eyes an indifferent shade of brown. I was slender and though only in my forties, I was already too put-upon by the challenges life had thrown my way. I was unmarried and sometimes I worried that it showed in my wardrobe, which was perhaps a little too well worn. If there were a dozen men in the room I would be the last to speak. That was my nature.

I was at Reichenbach five days after the confrontation that the world has come to know as 'The Final Problem'. Well, there was nothing final about it, as we now know, and I guess that just leaves us with the problem.

So. Let's take it from the start.

Sherlock Holmes, the greatest consulting detective who ever lived, flees England in fear of his life. Dr Watson, who knows the man better than anyone and who would never hear a word said against him, is forced to admit that at this time Holmes is at less than his best, utterly worn out by the predicament in which he finds himself and which he cannot control. Can we blame him? He has been attacked no fewer than three times in the space of just one morning. He has come within an inch of being crushed by a two-horse van that rushes past him on Welbeck Street; he has almost been hit by a brick that falls or is thrown from a roof on Vere Street — and, right outside Watson's front door, he finds himself attacked by some good fellow who's been waiting with a bludgeon. Does he have any choice but to flee?

Well, yes. There are so many other choices available to him that I have to wonder what exactly was in Mr Holmes's mind. Not, of course, that he's particularly forthcoming in the stories, all of which I've read (without ever once guessing the solution, for what it's worth). To begin with, what makes him think he will be safer on the Continent than he will be closer to home? London itself is a densely knit, teeming city, which he knows intimately and, as he once confided, he has many rooms ('five small refuges', Watson says) scattered around the place, which are known only to him.

He could disguise himself. In fact he *does* disguise himself. Only the next day, after Watson has arrived at Victoria Station, he notices an aged Italian priest in discussion with a porter and even goes so far as to offer him his assistance. Later, the priest enters his carriage and the two of them sit together face to face for several minutes before Watson recognises his friend. Holmes's disguises were so brilliant that he could have spent the next three years as a Catholic priest without anyone being the wiser. He could have entered an Italian monastery. *Padre Sherlock* . . . that would have thrown his enemies. They might even have let him pursue some of his other interests — beekeeping, for example — on the side.

Instead, Holmes goes haring off on a journey that seems to have nothing that resembles an itinerary and he asks Watson to accompany him. Why? The most incompetent criminal will surely work out that where one goes, the other will quite probably follow. And let's not forget that we are talking here about a criminal like no other, the master of his profession, a man who is equally feared and admired by Holmes himself. I don't believe for a minute that he could possibly have underestimated Moriarty. Common sense tells me that he must have been playing another game.

Sherlock Holmes travels to Canterbury, Newhaven, Brussels and Strasbourg, followed every step of the way. At Strasbourg, he receives a telegram from the London police informing him that all the members of Moriarty's gang have been captured. This is, as it turns out, quite false. One key player has slipped through the net — although I use the term ill-advisedly as the big fat fish that is Colonel Sebastian Moran has never been anywhere near it.

Colonel Moran, the finest sharpshooter in Europe, was well known to Pinkerton's, by the way. Indeed, by the end of his career, he was known to every law enforcement agency on the planet. He had been famous once for bringing down eleven tigers in a single week in Rajasthan, a feat that astonished his fellow hunters as much as it outraged the members of the Royal Geographical Society. Holmes called him the second most dangerous man in London — all the more so in that he was motivated entirely by money. The murder of Mrs Abigail Stewart, for example, an eminently respectable widow shot through the head as she played bridge in Lauder, was committed only so that he could pay off his gambling debts at the Bagatelle Card Club. It is strange to reflect that as Holmes sat reading the telegram, Moran was less than a hundred yards away, sipping herbal tea on a hotel terrace. Well, the two of them would meet soon enough.

From Strasbourg, Holmes continues to Geneva and spends a week exploring the snow-capped hills and pretty villages of the Rhône Valley. Watson describes this interlude as 'charming', which is not the word I would have used in the circumstances but I suppose we can only admire the way these two men, such close friends, can relax in each other's company even at such a time as this. Holmes is still in fear of his life, and there is another incident. Following a path close to the steel-grey water of the Daubensee, he is almost hit by a boulder that comes rolling down from the mountain above. His guide, a local man, assures him that such an event is quite commonplace and I am inclined to believe him. I've looked at the maps and I've worked out the distances. As far as I can see, Holmes's enemy is already well ahead of him, waiting for him to arrive. Even so, Holmes is convinced that once again he has been attacked and spends the rest of the day in a state of extreme anxiety.

At last he reaches the village of Meiringen on the River Aar where he and Watson stay at the Englischer Hof, a guest house run by a former waiter from the Grosvenor Hotel in London. It is this man, Peter Steiler, who suggests that Holmes should visit the Reichenbach Falls, and for a brief time the Swiss police will suspect *him* of having been in Moriarty's pay — which tells you everything you need to know about the investigative techniques of the Swiss police. If you want my view, they'd have been hard pressed to find a snowflake on an Alpine glacier. I stayed at the guest house and I interviewed Steiler myself. He wasn't just innocent. He was simple, barely taking his nose out of his pots and pans (his wife actually ran the place). Until the world came knocking at his door, Steiler wasn't even aware of his famous guest's identity and his first response after the news of Holmes's death had been revealed was to name a fondue after him.

Of course he recommended the Reichenbach Falls. It would have been suspicious if he hadn't. They were already a popular destination for tourists and romantics. In the summer months, you might find half a dozen artists dotted along the mossy path, trying to capture the meltwater of the Rosenlaui Glacier as it plunged three hundred feet down into that ravine. Trying and failing. There was something almost supernatural about that grim place that would have defied the pastels and oils of all but the greatest painters. I've seen works by Charles Parsons and Emanuel Leutze in New York and maybe they would have been able to do something with it. It was as if the world were ending here in a perpetual apocalypse of thundering water and spray rising like steam, the birds frightened away and the sun blocked out. The walls that enclosed this raging deluge were jagged and harsh and as old as Rip van Winkle. Sherlock Holmes had often shown a certain fondness for melodrama but never more so than here. It was a stage like no other to act out a grand finale and one that would resonate, like the falls themselves, for centuries to come.

It's at this point that things begin to get a little murky.

Holmes and Watson stand together for a while and are about to continue on their way when they are surprised by the arrival of a slightly plump, fair-haired fourteen-year-old boy. And with good reason. He is dressed to the nines in traditional Swiss costume with close-fitting trousers tucked into socks that rise up almost to his knees, a white shirt and a loose-fitting red waistcoat. All this strikes me as a touch incongruous. This is Switzerland, not a Palace Theatre vaudeville. I feel the boy is trying too hard.

At any event, he claims to have come from the Englischer Hof. A woman has been taken ill but refuses for some reason to be seen by a Swiss physician. This is what he says. And what would you do if you were Watson? Would you refuse to believe this unlikely story and stay put or would you abandon your friend — at the worst possible time and in a truly infernal place? That's all we ever hear about the Swiss boy, by the way — although you and I will meet him again soon enough. Watson suggests that he may have been working for Moriarty but does not mention him again. As for Watson, he takes his leave and hurries off to his non-existent patient; generous but wrong-headed to the last.

We must now wait three years for Holmes's reappearance — and it is important to remember that, to all intents and purposes, as far as this narrative is concerned, it is believed that he is dead. Only much later does he explain himself (Watson relates it all in 'The Adventure of the Empty House'), and although I have read many written statements in my line of work, few of them have managed to stack up quite so many improbabilities. This is his account, however, and we must, I suppose, take it at face value.

After Watson has left, according to Holmes, Professor James Moriarty makes his appearance, walking along the narrow path that curves halfway around the falls. This path comes to an abrupt end, so there can be no question of Holmes attempting to escape — not that such a course of action would ever have crossed his mind. Give him his due: this is a man who has always faced his fears square on, whether they be a deadly swamp adder, a hideous poison that might drive you to insanity or a hell-hound set loose on the moors. Holmes has done many things that are, frankly, baffling — but he has never run away.

The two men exchange words. Holmes asks permission to leave a note for his old companion and Professor Moriarty agrees. This much at least can be verified for those three sheets of paper are among the most prized possessions of the British Library Reading Room in London where I have seen them displayed. However, once these courtesies have been dispensed with, the two men rush at each other in what seems to be less a fight, more a suicide pact, each determined to drag the other into the roaring torrent of water. And so it might have been. But Holmes still has one trick up his sleeve. He has learned *bartitsu*. I had never heard of it before but apparently it's a martial art invented by a British engineer, which combines boxing and judo, and he puts it to good use.

Moriarty is taken by surprise. He is propelled over the edge and, with a terrible scream, plunges into the abyss. Holmes sees him brush against a rock before he disappears into the water. He himself is safe . . . Forgive me, but is there not something a little unsatisfactory about this encounter? You have to ask yourself why Moriarty allows himself to be challenged in this way. Old-school heroics are all very well (although I've never yet met a criminal who went in for them) but what possible purpose can it have served to endanger himself? To put it bluntly, why didn't he simply take out a revolver and shoot his opponent at close range?

If that is strange, Holmes's behaviour now becomes completely inexplicable. On the spur of the moment, he decides to use what has just occurred to feign his own death. He climbs up the rock face behind the path and hides there until Watson returns. In this way, of course, there will be no second set of footprints to show that he has survived. What's the point? Professor Moriarty is now dead and the British police have announced that the entire gang has been arrested so why does he still believe himself to be in danger? What exactly is there to be gained? If I had been Holmes, I would have hurried back to the Englischer Hof for a nice Wiener schnitzel and a celebratory glass of Neuchâtel.

Meanwhile, Dr Watson, realising he has been tricked, rushes back to the scene, where an abandoned alpenstock and a set of footprints tell their own tale. He summons help and investigates the scene with several men from the hotel and a local police officer by the name of Gessner. Holmes sees them but does not make himself known, even though he must be aware of the distress it will cause his most trusted companion. They find the letter. They read it and, realising there is nothing more to be done, they all leave. Holmes begins to climb down again and it is now that the narrative takes another unexpected and wholly inexplicable turn. It appears that Professor Moriarty has not come to the Reichenbach Falls alone. As Holmes begins his descent — no easy task in itself — a man suddenly appears and attempts to knock him off his perch with a number of boulders. The man is Colonel Sebastian Moran.

What on earth is he doing there? Was he present when Holmes and Moriarty fought, and if so, why didn't he try to help? Where is his gun? Has the greatest marksman in the world accidentally left it on the train? Neither Holmes nor Watson, nor anyone else for that matter, has ever provided reasonable answers to questions which, even as I sit here hammering at the keys, seem inescapable. And once I start asking them, I can't stop. I feel as if I am in a runaway coach, tearing down Fifth Avenue, unable to stop at the lights.

That is about as much as we know of the Reichenbach Falls. The story that I must now tell begins five days later when three men come together in the crypt of St Michael's church in Meiringen. One is a detective inspector from Scotland Yard, the famous command centre of the British police. His name is Athelney Jones. I am the second.

The third man is tall and thin with a prominent forehead and sunken eyes which might view the world with a cold malevolence and cunning were there any life in them at all. But now they are glazed and empty. The man, formally dressed in a suit with a wing collar and a long frock coat, has been fished out of the Reichenbach Brook, some distance from the falls. His left leg is broken and there are other serious injuries to his shoulder and head, but death must surely have been caused by drowning. The local police have attached a label to his wrist, which has been folded across his chest. On it is written the name: James Moriarty.

This is the reason I have come all the way to Switzerland. It appears that I have arrived too late.

2

Inspector Athelney Jones

'Are you sure it is really him?'

'I am as sure of it as I can be, Mr Chase. But setting aside any personal convictions, let us consider the evidence. His appearance and the circumstances of his being here would certainly seem to fit all the facts at our disposal. And if this is not Moriarty, we are obliged to ask ourselves who he actually is, how he came to be killed and, for that matter, what has happened to Moriarty himself.'

'Only one body was recovered.'

'So I understand. Poor Mr Holmes . . . to be deprived of the consolation of a Christian burial, which every man deserves. But of one thing we can be certain. His name will live on. There is some comfort in that.'

This conversation took place in the damp, gloomy basement of the church, a place untouched by the warmth and fragrance of that spring day. Inspector Jones stood next to me, leaning over the drowned man with his hands clasped tightly behind him, as if he were afraid of being contaminated. I watched his dark grey eyes travel the full length of the cadaver, arriving at the feet, one of which had lost its shoe. It appeared that Moriarty had had a fondness for embroidered silk socks.

15

We had met, just a short while ago, at the police station in Meiringen. I was frankly surprised that a tiny village stuck in the middle of the Swiss mountains surrounded by goats and buttercups should have need of one. But, as I've already mentioned, it was a popular tourist destination and what with the recent coming of the railway, there must have been an increasing number of travellers passing through. There were two men on duty, both of them dressed in dark blue uniforms, standing behind the wooden counter that stretched across the front room. One of them was the hapless Sergeant Gessner who had been summoned to the falls — and it was already obvious to me that he would have been much happier dealing with lost passports, train tickets, street directions . . . anything rather than the more serious business of murder.

He and his companion spoke little of my language and I had been forced to explain myself using the images and headlines of an English newspaper, which I had brought with me for that express purpose. I had heard that a body had been dragged out of the water beneath the Reichenbach Falls and had asked to see it, but these Swiss police were obstinate in the way of many a uniformed man given limited power. Speaking over each other, and with a great deal of gesticulation, they had made it clear to me that they were waiting for the arrival of a senior officer who had come all the way from England and that any decision would be his. I told them that I had travelled a great deal further and that my business was quite serious too but that didn't

16

matter. I'm sorry, *mein Herr*. There was nothing they could do to help.

I took out my watch and glanced at it. It was already eleven o'clock with half the morning wasted and I was afraid the rest of it would go the same way, but just then the front door opened and, feeling the breeze on the back of my neck, I turned to see a man standing there, silhouetted against the morning light. He said nothing, but as he moved inside I saw that he was about the same age as me, perhaps a little younger, with dark-coloured hair lying flat on his forehead and soft grey eyes that questioned everything. There was a sort of seriousness about him, and when he stepped into a room, you had to stop and take notice. He was wearing a brown lounge suit with a pale overcoat, which was unbuttoned and hung loosely from his shoulders. It was evident that he had recently been quite ill and had lost weight. I could see it in his clothes, which were a little too large for him, and in the pallor and pinched quality of his face. He carried a walking stick made of rosewood with an odd, complicated silver handle. Having approached the counter, he rested on the stick, using it to support him.

'*Können Sie mir helfen?*' he asked. He spoke German very naturally but with no attempt at a German accent, as if he had studied the words but never actually heard them. '*Ich bin Inspector Athelney Jones von Scotland Yard.*'

He had examined me very briefly, accepting my presence and filing it away for later use, but otherwise he had ignored me. His name,

17

however, had an immediate effect on the two policemen.

'Jones. Inspector Jones,' they repeated, and when he held out his own letter of introduction they took it with much bowing and smiling and, having asked him to wait a few moments while they entered the details in the police log, retired to an inner office, leaving the two of us alone.

It would have been impossible for us to ignore each other and he was the first to break the silence, translating what he had already said.

'My name is Athelney Jones,' he said.

'Did I hear you say you were from Scotland Yard?'

'Indeed.'

'I'm Frederick Chase.'

We shook hands. His grip was curiously loose, as if his hand were barely connected to his wrist.

'This is a beautiful spot,' he went on. 'I have never had the pleasure of travelling in Switzerland. In fact, this is only the third time I have been abroad at all.' He turned his attention briefly to my steamer trunk which, having nowhere to stay, I had been obliged to bring with me. 'You have just arrived?'

'An hour ago,' I said. 'I guess we must have been on the same train.'

'And your business . . . ?'

I hesitated. The assistance of a British police officer was essential to the task that had brought me to Meiringen, but at the same time I did not wish to appear too forward. In America, there had often been conflicts of interest between Pinkerton's and the official government services.

18

Why should it be any different here? 'I am here on a private matter . . . ' I began.

He smiled at this, although at the same time I saw a veil of something in his eyes that might have been pain. 'Then perhaps you will allow me to tell *you*, Mr Chase,' he remarked. He considered for a moment. 'You are a Pinkerton's agent from New York and last week you set off for England in the hope of tracking down Professor James Moriarty. He had received a communication which is important to you and which you hoped to find about his person. You were shocked to hear of his death and came directly here. I see, incidentally, you have a low opinion of the Swiss police — '

'Wait a minute!' I exclaimed. I held up a hand. 'Stop right there! Have you been spying on me, Inspector Jones? Have you spoken to my office? I find it pretty bad that the British police should have gone behind my back and involved themselves in my affairs!'

'You do not need to concern yourself,' Jones returned, again with that same strange smile. 'Everything I have told you I have deduced from my observation of you here, in this room. And I could add more, if you wish.'

'Why not?'

'You live in an old-fashioned apartment block, several floors up. You do not think your company looks after you as well as it might, particularly as you are one of its most successful investigators. You are not married. I am sorry to see that the sea crossing was a particularly disagreeable one — and not just because of the very bad weather

19

on the second or perhaps the third day. You are thinking that your entire trip has been a wild goose chase. I hope, for your sake, it is not.'

He fell silent and I stared at him as if seeing him for the first time. 'You are right in almost everything you say,' I rasped. 'But how the devil you managed it is quite beyond me. Will you explain yourself?'

'It was all very straightforward,' he replied. 'I might almost say elementary.' He chose the last word carefully, as if it had some special significance.

'That's easy enough for you to say.' I glanced at the door that now separated us from the two Swiss policemen. Sergeant Gessner seemed to be on the telephone — I could hear his voice jabbering away on the other side. The empty counter stretched out, a barrier between them and us. 'Please, Inspector Jones. Will you tell me how you reached these conclusions?'

'Very well, although I should warn you that it will all seem painfully obvious once it is explained.' He shifted his weight on the walking stick, trying to find a comfortable position in which to stand. 'That you are American is evident from the way you speak and from your clothes. Your waistcoat in particular, striped and with four pockets, would have been extremely difficult to find in London. I take note of your vocabulary. Just now, you said, 'I guess' where we would have said 'I think'. My knowledge of accents is limited, but yours would suggest the East Coast.'

'My home is in Boston,' I said. 'I now live and

20

work in New York. Please, continue!'

'As I came in, you were examining your watch and although it was partly covered by your fingers, I saw quite clearly the symbol engraved on the casing — an eye with, beneath it, the words 'We Never Sleep'. This is, of course, the legend of the Pinkerton Detective Agency whose principal offices are, as I recall, in New York. That you embarked from there is evident from the New York Port Authority stamp on your luggage.' He glanced a second time at my steamer trunk, which I had stood beneath the photograph of a scowling man, presumably some local ne'er-do-well. 'As for your disdain of the Swiss police — why should you choose to look at your own watch when there is a perfectly good working clock on the wall just to one side? They have, I can see, been less than helpful.'

'You are absolutely right, sir. But how do you know of my connection with Professor Moriarty?'

'What other possible reason could there be for you to have come here to Meiringen? I would wager that, but for the events of the last week, you would never have heard of this unremarkable village.'

'My business could have been with Sherlock Holmes.'

'In which case you would have surely stayed in London and begun your enquiries in Baker Street. There is nothing here but the dead body of a man, and whoever he is, he is certainly not Holmes. No. From New York, your most likely destination would have been Southampton — which is confirmed by the folded copy of the

21

Hampshire Echo protruding from your right-hand jacket pocket. The date on the masthead, I see, is Thursday the seventh of May which would suggest that you purchased it at the dock and were then compelled to travel at once to the Continent. And what was the news that could have brought you here? There was only one story of interest that day. It *had* to be Moriarty.' He smiled. 'I am surprised I did not see you. As you say, we must surely have travelled on the same train.'

'You mentioned a communication.'

'There is nothing Moriarty can say to you. He is dead. It is unlikely you could identify him — very few people have ever seen him face to face. Therefore it must be something he has that interests you, something you hope to find about his person — a letter or a parcel sent from America. I presume that this is what you were discussing with the police when I arrived.'

'I was asking them to let me examine the body.'

'There is a little more to add.'

'The crossing?'

'You were forced to share a cabin — '

'How do you know?' I exclaimed.

'Your fingernails and teeth suggest to me that you do not smoke but I can still detect a strong smell of tobacco about you. This tells me that although your employers must surely have chosen the best man for whatever job this is — they have, after all, sent you halfway across the world — they were not prepared to pay for a single cabin. It cannot have been very pleasant for you, sharing with a smoker.'

'It was not.'

22

'And the weather made it worse.' He lifted a hand, waving away my question before I could ask it. 'That is a nasty cut on the side of your neck. It cannot have been easy shaving at sea, particularly during a storm.'

I laughed out loud. 'Inspector Jones,' I said, 'I am a simple man. I have achieved what I have achieved by diligence and hard work. I have never come across techniques such as these before and had no idea that British police inspectors were trained to use them.'

'Not all of us were,' Jones replied, quietly. 'But you might say that I received special instruction . . . and I learned from the best.'

'There is just one last thing. You still haven't explained to me how you know of my status and my living arrangements in New York.'

'You wear no wedding ring, which might not be conclusive in itself but — you will forgive me — no wife would permit her husband to leave with such stains on his cuffs nor with shoes that cry out to be reheeled. As to the apartment, that is again simply a question of observation and deduction. I notice that the fabric of your jacket — the right sleeve — has been quite worn down. How could this have occurred unless you had become accustomed to climbing several flights of stairs, rubbing your arm against a metal banister? I would imagine your office has an elevator. An old-fashioned apartment block might not.'

He stopped, and I could see that all the talking had tired him for he rested more heavily on his stick. For my part, I was gazing with an admiration that I made no attempt to disguise

23

and might have stood there for a while longer had the door not suddenly opened and the two police officers reappeared. They spoke rapidly in German and although the meaning was unclear, their tone was friendly enough, and I gathered that they were now ready to escort the Scotland Yard man to wherever the body lay. This proved to be the case. Jones straightened up and began to move towards the door.

'Can I have a word?' I said. 'I am sure you have your instructions, Inspector Jones, but it may just turn out that I'm able to help you. Everything you said to me — that extraordinary demonstration just now — was absolutely right. I've followed Moriarty here because of a communication that was made three weeks ago and which may have serious consequences for you and for me. It is true that I cannot identify him, but it is of the utmost importance that I'm at least allowed to see the body.'

The man from Scotland Yard paused, his hand clenched around the top of the walking stick. 'You understand, sir, that I am here following orders given to me by my superiors.'

'You have my word that I will not interfere in any way.'

The two Swiss policemen were waiting for us. Jones came to a decision and nodded. '*Er kommt mit uns.*' He turned to me. 'You can join us.'

'I am truly grateful to you,' I said. 'And I give you my word that you won't regret it.'

We left my luggage at the police station and crossed the village, following the main road past a scattering of houses. All the while Jones and

Gessner spoke in German, keeping their voices low. At length we arrived at the church of St Michael, a queer little building with its bright red roof and rather top-heavy bell tower. The policemen unlocked the door for us and stood back as we stepped inside. I bowed my head in front of the altar but Inspector Jones, I noticed, did not. We came to a flight of steps leading down to the crypt and he indicated that he wished to continue with me alone. Gessner needed little persuasion: even in the coolness of the church with its thick stone walls, the smell of death was already apparent.

The body was as I have described it. When living, the man who lay stretched out in front of us would have been unusually tall though with stooped shoulders. I could imagine him a librarian or perhaps a lecturer in a university, which, of course, James Moriarty had once been. His clothes, black and old-fashioned, clung to him like seaweed — I fancied they were still wet. There are many ways to die but few leave a nastier imprint on the human frame than drowning. His flesh was heavy and foul. Its colour was hideous to describe.

'We cannot be certain that this is Moriarty,' I suggested. 'You were quite correct when you said that I could not identify him. But can you?'

Jones shook his head. 'I never set eyes on him. Nor did any of my colleagues. Moriarty lived in the shadows most of his life and made a virtue of it. It is possible that in due course we will be able to find someone who worked with him in his capacity as a professor of mathematics, and be

25

assured that I will set about just such an investigation on my return. For the present, however, I will say this much. The man in front of us is the right age and the clothes he is wearing are undoubtedly English. You see the pocket watch? It is silver-cased and clearly marked, 'John Myers of London'. He did not come here for the pleasures of the countryside. He died at the same time as Sherlock Holmes. So I ask you again. Who else can he be?'

'Has the body been searched?'

'The Swiss police went through the pockets, yes.'

'And there was nothing?'

'A few coins. A handkerchief. Nothing more. What is it you were hoping to find?'

I had been waiting for the question. I did not hesitate. I knew that everything, certainly my immediate future, hung on my answer. Even now I can see us, standing alone in the dark crypt with the body stretched out before us. 'Moriarty received a letter on the twenty-second or the twenty-third of April,' I explained. 'It was written by a criminal very well known to Pinkerton's, a man in every respect as wicked and as dangerous as Moriarty himself, inviting him to a meeting. Although it would appear that Moriarty is dead, I still hoped I might find it about his person, or if not, then perhaps at his place of residence.'

'It is this man that interests you and not Moriarty?'

'He is the reason I am here.'

Jones shook his head. 'Sergeant Gessner was explaining to me as we came here that the police have already made enquiries and have been unable to discover where Moriarty was staying. He may have established his base in a village nearby but if so he certainly used an assumed name. There is nowhere outside here that we can search. What makes you think he might have this letter on him?'

'Perhaps I'm grasping at straws,' I said. 'No, I'll admit it. I *am* grasping at straws. But the way these people work . . . sometimes they use signs and symbols as a method of identification. The letter itself could become a passport — and if so, Moriarty would have kept it close.'

'If you wish, we can examine him one more time.'

'I think we must.'

It was a grisly task. The body, cold and waterlogged, felt utterly inhuman in our hands and as we turned it, we could almost feel the flesh separating itself from the bones. The clothes were slimy. Reaching into the jacket, I found the shirt had been rucked back and my hand briefly came into contact with dead, white skin. Although there had been no prior arrangement between us, I concentrated on the upper part of the body while Jones busied himself with the lower. Just like the police before us, we found nothing. The pockets were empty. If they had contained anything more than the few items Jones had mentioned, the rushing waters of the Reichenbach Falls must have brutally ripped them away. We worked in silence. Finally, I reeled away, the gorge rising in my throat.

'There is nothing,' I said. 'You were right. It

was a waste of time.'

'One moment.' Jones had seen something. He reached out and took hold of the dead man's jacket, examining the stitching around the breast pocket.

'I've looked,' I said. 'There's nothing there.'

'Not the pocket,' Jones said. 'Look at this seam. This stitching has no business being here. I think it has been added later.' He rubbed the fabric between his fingers. 'There might be something inside the lining.'

I leaned forward. He was right. A line of stitches stretched out a couple of inches below the pocket. 'I have a knife,' I said. I took out the jackknife that I always carried with me and handed it to my new friend.

Jones inserted the point into the seam and gently sliced down. I watched as the stitches were cut through and the material came away. There was a secret pocket in the dead man's jacket — and there was indeed something inside. Jones eased out a folded square of paper. It was still wet and might have disintegrated had he not handled it with the greatest delicacy. Using the flat blade of the knife he laid it on the stone table next to the body. Carefully, he unfolded it, a single page covered in handwriting that could have been a child's.

We leaned over together. This is what we read:

HoLmES WaS CeRtAiNLY NOt A DIFFi-CulT mAn to LiVe WItH. He wAs QuIeT iN HiS WAYs and his hABiTS wErE REgulAr. iT wAs RARE fOR HIm To BE up AfTeR

TEN at nighT aND hE hAD INVariABLY breAKfasteD AND GoNE OUT BeFOrE i RoSe in The morNINg. SOMEtImEs He SPeNt hiS DAy At ThE ChEmiCaL lABoRatORY, SoMeTimes IN THE dIsSeCting ROoms And oCcAsionaLly iN lOnG WALKs whICH ApPeAREd TO taKE HIM INtO THE LOwEsT PORTioNs OF thE CITy. nothINg COuld exCEeD HiS ENErgY WHeN tHE wORk-ING FiT WAs upOn HiM.

If Jones was disappointed, he didn't show it. But this wasn't the letter that I had described. It did not seem to be relevant in any way at all.

'What do you make of it?' he asked.

'I . . . I do not know what to say.' I read the words a second time. 'I know this text,' I continued. 'Of course I know it. This is part of a narrative written by Dr John Watson. It has been copied from *Lippincott's Magazine*!'

'I think you will find it was actually from *Beeton's Christmas Annual*,' Jones corrected me. 'It is from Chapter Three of *A Study in Scarlet*. But that does not make it any the less mysterious. I take it this is not what you expected to find.'

'It was the last thing I expected.'

'It is certainly very puzzling. But I have been here long enough. I suggest we retreat from this grim place and fortify ourselves with a glass of wine.'

I took one last look at the dead man on the slab then turned and together we climbed back up, Jones limping heavily.

3

The Midnight Watch

Athelney Jones had taken a room at the Englischer Hof and suggested that I do the same. We headed there together after we had parted company with the Swiss policemen, walking through the village with the sun brilliant in a cloudless sky and everything silent apart from our own footsteps and the occasional jangle of a bell coming from the sheep or goats that were grazing in the nearby hills. Jones was deep in thought, reflecting on the document we had discovered in the dead man's pocket. What on earth was Moriarty doing with an extract from a Sherlock Holmes story hidden about him as he travelled to Switzerland? Had he perhaps been seeking some insight into his adversary's mind before the two of them met at the Reichenbach Falls? Or was it actually the communication I had described, the reason for my long journey to Switzerland? Could it have some secret meaning unknown to both of us? Jones did not address these questions to me but I could see that they were plainly on his mind.

The hotel was small and charming with shapes cut into the wood and flowers hanging around the windows; the very image of a Swiss chalet that every English traveller might dream of finding. Fortunately, there was room for me, and a boy was dispatched to the police station to collect my luggage. Jones and I parted company at the stairs. He had the page in his hand.

'I would like, with your permission, to hold onto it a while longer,' he said.

'You think you can make some sense of it?'

'I can at least give it my full attention and . . . who knows?' He was tired. The walk from the police station had not been a long one but, combined with the high altitude, it had almost drained him.

'Of course,' I said. 'Will we meet again this evening?'

'We can dine together. Shall we say eight o'clock?'

'That will suit me very well, Inspector Jones. Apart from anything else, it will give me time to walk to the famous Reichenbach Falls. I never thought I'd find myself in Switzerland of all places, and this village — it's quite delightful, like something out of a fairy story.'

'You might perhaps ask about Moriarty. If he didn't stay in a hotel or a guest house, he might have taken a room in a private home. And someone may have seen him before he met up with Holmes.'

'I thought the Swiss police had already made these enquiries.'

'Wachtmeister Gessner? An admirable man doing the best that he can. But it won't hurt to ask again.'

'Very well. I'll see what I can do.'

I did as I was asked and strolled through the village, talking to those inhabitants who spoke

31

my language, not that there were many of them. There were two words though that they all understood: Sherlock Holmes. At the mention of his name, they became serious and animated. That such a man had visited Meiringen was extraordinary; that he had died here beyond belief. They wanted to help. Sadly, though, none of them had seen Moriarty. No stranger had taken a room in their midst. They had nothing to offer me but broken English and sympathy. Eventually, I returned to my own room. On second thoughts, I had no desire to walk to the falls, which were at least two hours away. The truth was that I could not even think of them without shuddering and visiting them would have told me nothing I did not already know.

* * *

Athelney Jones and I dined late that night and I was glad to see that he had recovered his strength. We sat together in the snug hotel restaurant with the tables packed closely together, animal heads on the wall, and a roaring fire quite out of proportion to the size of the room. It was needed though, for with the darkness a torrent of cold air had come twisting through the mountain passes and settled on the village. This was, after all, only May, and we were at an elevation of almost two thousand feet. There were only a few other diners around us and we had chosen a table close to the inglenook so that we could talk together undisturbed.

We were welcomed by a small, round-shouldered

woman wearing an apron dress with puffed-out sleeves and a shawl. She brought us a basket of bread and a pint of red wine served in a pitcher and, setting them down, introduced herself as Greta Steiler, the Swiss wife of our English host. 'We have only soup and roast meat tonight,' she explained. Her English was excellent and I hoped the cooking would be the same. 'My husband is alone in the kitchen today and you are lucky we are only half full. If we had any more guests, I do not know how we would manage.'

'What has happened to your cook?' Jones asked.

'He went to visit his mother in Rosenlaui because she hasn't been well. He was due back almost a week ago but we haven't heard from him — and this after he has been with us five years! And then we have this business with the falls and with all the police and the detectives asking us their questions. I wait for Meiringen to be back as it was. We do not ask for all this excitement.'

She bustled off and I poured myself some wine but Jones refused, helping himself instead to water. 'The document . . . ' I began. From the moment we had sat down, I had wanted to ask what he had made of it.

'I may be able to shed a certain light on the matter,' Jones replied. 'To begin with, it is very likely that it *is* the communication of which you spoke. It certainly seems to have been written by an American.'

'How can you possibly know?'

'I have examined the paper closely and found it to be clay-coated groundwood and therefore

33

very probably American in origin.'

'And the content?'

'We will come to that shortly. But first, I think, we should reach an agreement.' Jones lifted his glass. He swirled it round and I saw the firelight reflecting in the liquid. 'I am here as a representative of the British police. As soon as we heard that Sherlock Holmes was dead, it was felt that one of us should attend upon the scene, if only as a matter of courtesy. He had, as I am sure you are aware, been helpful to us on a number of occasions. And anything relating to the activities of Professor James Moriarty was naturally of interest to us. What happened at the Reichenbach Falls seems straightforward enough but even so there is clearly something afoot, as Mr Holmes was wont to say. Your presence here and your suggestion that Moriarty was in contact with a member of the American underworld — '

'Not just a member, sir. The master.'

'It may well be that we have mutual interests and should work side by side although I must warn you that, generally speaking, Scotland Yard has a certain reticence about dealing with foreign detective agencies, particularly private ones. It may not be helpful, but that's how it is. It follows that, if I am to make the case to my superiors, I need to know more. In short, you must tell me everything about yourself and the events that have brought you here. You can do so in confidence. But it is only on the strength of what you tell me that I can decide what course of action I should take.'

'I will willingly tell you everything, Inspector

Jones,' I said. 'And I'll make no secret of the fact that I am greatly in need of any help you and the British police can provide.' I broke off as Frau Steiler returned to the table with two bowls of steaming soup and *Spätzle* — which was the word she used to describe the little dumplings floating in a murky brown liquid. It smelled better than it looked and, with the scent of boiled chicken and herbs rising in my nostrils, I began my narrative.

'I was, as I have already told you, born in Boston, where my father was the owner of a very highly regarded law practice with offices in Court Square. My childhood memories are of a family that was correct in every detail, with several servants and a black nanny — Tilly — who was very dear to me.'

'You were an only child?'

'No, sir, I was the second of two boys. My brother, Arthur, was quite a few years older than me and we were never close. My father was a member of Boston's Republican Party and spent much of his time surrounded by like-minded gentlemen who prided themselves on the values which they had brought with them from England and which they felt set them apart as a sort of elite. They were members of the Somerset Club and the Myopia Club and many others. My mother, I'm afraid, was fragile in her health and spent much of the time in bed. The result was that I saw very little of either of my parents and that might explain why, in my teens, I became quite rebellious in nature and finally left home in circumstances which I still regret.

35

'My brother had already joined the family firm and it was expected that I would do the same. However, I had no aptitude for the law. I found the textbooks dry and almost indecipherable. Besides, I had other ambitions. I cannot quite say what it was that first interested me in the criminal world . . . it may have been stories that I found in *Merry's Museum*. This was a magazine read by every child in the neighbourhood. But there was also an incident I remember very clearly. We were members of the congregation at the Warren Avenue Baptist Church. We never missed a service and it was the one place we were together as a family. Well, when I was about twenty, it was discovered that the sexton, one Thomas Piper, had committed a series of quite gruesome murders — '

'Piper?' Jones's eyes narrowed. 'I recall the name. His first victim was a young girl . . . '

'That's correct. The story was widely reported outside America. As for me, although my entire community felt nothing but outrage, I must confess that I was thrilled that such a man could have concealed himself in our midst. I had seen him often in his long black cape, always smiling and beneficent. If he could be guilty of such crimes, was there anyone in our community who could genuinely claim to be above suspicion?

'It was at this moment that I found my vocation in life. The dry world of the lawyer was not for me. I wanted to be a detective. I had heard of the Pinkertons. They were already legendary throughout America. Just a few days after the scandal came to light, I told my father that I wanted to travel to New York to join them.'

I fell silent. Jones was watching me with an intensity that I would come to know well and I knew that he was weighing my every word. There was a part of me that did not wish to open myself up to him in this way but at the same time I knew that he would demand nothing less.

'My father was a quiet man and a very cultivated one,' I continued. 'He had never raised his voice to me, not in my entire life, but he did so on that day. To him, with all his sensibilities, the work of the policeman and the detective (for he saw no difference between the two) was lowly, disgusting. He begged me to change my mind. I refused. We quarrelled, and in the end I left with hardly more than a few dollars in my pocket and the growing fear that, as my home slipped away behind me, I was making a terrible mistake.

'I took the train to New York and it is hard to convey to you my first impressions as I left Grand Central Depot. I found myself in a city of extraordinary opulence and abject poverty, of astonishing elegance and extreme depravity, the two living so close by that I only had to turn my head to pass from one to the other. Somehow I made my way to the Lower East Side, a part of the city that put me in mind of the tower of Babel, for here there were Poles, Italians, Jews, Bohemians, all of them speaking their own languages and observing their own customs. Even the smells in the streets were new to me. After my long, protected childhood, it was as if I were seeing the world for the first time.

'It was easy enough to find a room in a

tenement; every door carried an advertisement. I spent that first night in a dark, airless place with no furniture, a tiny stove and a kerosene lamp and I will admit that I was very glad to open my eyes and see the first light of dawn.

'I had considered applying to the police force in New York, thinking that I would need some experience as a guardian of the law before I could apply to the Pinkertons, but I soon discovered that such a course of action would be practically impossible. I had brought with me no letters of recommendation; I had no connections, and without preferment of one sort or another, it would be hard even to get a foot through the door. The police were poorly resourced and corruption was rife. Would the famous detective agency, 'The Eye that Never Sleeps', even consider a rash and inexperienced youth? There was only one way to find out. I went straight to their office and applied.

'I was fortunate. Allan Pinkerton, the most famous detective in America and the founder of the company, and his sons, Robert and William, were actively seeking recruits. It may surprise you to learn that police experience was not a requirement. In fact, it was the other way round. Many senior police officers in America first learned their trade with Pinkerton's. Honesty, integrity, reliability . . . these were the qualities that counted and I found myself being interviewed along with former bootmakers, teachers and wine merchants, all hoping to better themselves in the company. Nor did my youth count against me: I was well presented and

I had a good knowledge of the law. By the end of the day I had been recruited as a special operative, working on a temporary basis for $2.50 a day plus bed and board. The hours were long and it was made clear to me that my employment could be terminated at any time if I was found wanting. I was determined that it should not be.'

Briefly, I stirred my soup with my spoon. A man at a table on the far side of the room suddenly broke into loud laughter, I think at his own joke. It struck me that he laughed in a way that was peculiarly Germanic, although perhaps it was an unworthy thought.

I began again. 'I am moving quickly forward, Mr Jones, because my own life story will be of little interest to you.'

'On the contrary, I am immersed.'

'Well, let me just say that my work was found to be more than satisfactory and that, over the years, I rose up within the ranks. I will mention that I returned to Boston and that I was reunited with my father, although he never completely forgave me. He died a few years ago, leaving his practice to my brother and a small sum to me. It has proved useful for, although I am not complaining, I have never been highly paid.'

'The enforcement of the law has never been particularly well remunerated in any country, to my knowledge,' Jones returned. 'I might add that criminality pays more. However, you must forgive me. I interrupt.'

'I have investigated fraud, murder, counterfeiting, bank robberies and missing persons — all of

39

which are prevalent in New York. I cannot say that I have used the same methods, the same extraordinary intelligence that you demonstrated to me this morning. I am dogged in my approach. I am fastidious. I may read a hundred witness statements before I find the two conflicting remarks that will lead me to the truth. And it is this, more than anything, which has led me frequently to success and brought me to the attention of my superiors. Let me tell you, however, of one investigation that was entrusted to me in the spring of 1889. Although I didn't know it at the time, it was this more than anything that was eventually to bring me here.

'We had a client, a man called William Orton, the president of Western Union. He had come to us because his company's lines had been intercepted and a series of completely false and damaging messages were being sent to the New York stock market with devastating results. Several large companies had been brought to the very edge of bankruptcy, and investors found themselves with losses stretching into the millions. The chairman of a mining company in Colorado, receiving one of these wires, went up to his bedroom and shot himself. Orton thought it must be the work of an extremely malevolent and cold-hearted practical joker. It took me three months and an endless series of interviews to discover the truth. It was, in fact, a remarkable and completely original form of embezzlement. A consortium of brokers, working out of Wall Street, were buying up the stocks of the companies that had been affected — acquiring them, of course, at rock-bottom prices. In this way, they were making a fortune. The operation required nerve, imagination, cunning and the bringing together of a great many criminal talents. At Pinkerton's, we knew at once that we had never encountered anything quite like it. Eventually, we arrested the gang — but the leader, the man who had initiated the whole enterprise, slipped through our fingers. His name was Clarence Devereux.

'You have to understand that America is a young country and as such it is still, in many respects, uncivilised. I was actually shocked by the lawlessness that I found all around me when I first arrived in New York, although I suppose I might have expected it. How else could a company like the Pinkerton Detective Agency have become so successful if it wasn't needed? The tenement where I lived was surrounded by brothels, gaming places and saloons where the criminal classes congregated and boasted quite openly about their exploits. I've already mentioned forgers, counterfeiters and bank robbers. To those I might have added the countless footpads who made it dangerous to venture out at night and the pickpockets who committed their crimes quite brazenly in the day.

'There were criminals everywhere. A thousand thieves; two thousand prostitutes. But — and this, you might say, was the saving grace — they were disparate and disorganised, nearly always acting alone. Of course, there were exceptions. Jim Dunlap and Bob Scott headed an organisation that became known as The Ring and which stole three million dollars, an amazing sum, from banks across the country. Other gangs — the Dead Rabbits and the Bowery Boys — came and went. There were the Plug Uglies over in Baltimore. I read all the files. But Clarence Devereux was the first man to see the advantages of a comprehensive criminal network with its own code of practice and a fully worked-out chain of command. We first heard of him at the time of the Western Union business, but by then he had already established himself as the most brilliant and most successful criminal of his generation.'

'And this man is the reason you are here?' Jones enquired. 'He is the author of the letter sent to the late Professor Moriarty?'

'I believe so, yes.'

'Please, continue.'

I had not even tasted the soup in front of me. Jones was still watching me intently. It was a strange meal, two foreigners in a Swiss restaurant, neither of them eating a thing. I wondered how much time had passed since I had begun my tale. Outside, the night seemed darker than ever and the flames were crackling, leaping at the chimney.

'By now I had been promoted to the role of General Operative,' I continued, 'and Robert Pinkerton made me personally responsible for Devereux's arrest. I was given a special team — three investigators, a cashier, a secretary, two stenographers and an office boy — and together we became known as the Midnight Watch, a reference to the long hours we kept. Our office, tucked away in the basement, was jammed with correspondence and not an inch of our four walls was visible beneath the veritable rogues' gallery that we had pinned into place. Reports from Chicago, Washington and Philadelphia were sent to us and slowly, methodically, we worked our way through hundreds of pages. It was an exhausting business but by the beginning of this year, a face had begun to take shape . . . well, not so much a face, a presence.'

'Clarence Devereux.'

'I cannot even be certain that that is his real name. He has never been seen. No illustration or photograph of him exists. It is said that he is about forty years of age; that he came to America from Europe, from a well-to-do family; that he is charming, highly cultivated and philanthropic. Yes, I see you start. But I know for a fact that he has given substantial sums of money to the New York Foundling Hospital and to the Home for the Friendless. He has endowed a scholarship at Harvard University and he was one of the founding subscribers of the Metropolitan Opera.

'And yet at the same time, I tell you, there is no more evil influence in the whole of America. Clarence Devereux is a criminal like no other, utterly ruthless, as much feared by the villains who work for him as by the victims whose lives he has ruined. There is no form of depravity, no vice that is below him. Indeed, he takes such pleasure in the organisation and execution of his various schemes that we have been led to believe that he commits his crimes as much to amuse himself as to benefit from any profits they might

43

bring. After all, he has already made his fortune. He is a showman, a ringmaster who brings misery to everyone he touches, leaving his bloody fingerprints everywhere he goes.

'I have studied him. I have pursued him. He represents everything that I loathe and find most vile and to bring an end to his activities would be the crowning moment of my career. And yet he remains out of my reach. Sometimes I feel that he knows my every move; that he is toying with me. Clarence Devereux is very careful about the way he operates, hiding behind his false identity. Never once will he expose himself or put himself in any danger. He will plan a crime — a bank robbery, a burglary, a murder; work out the details, recruit the gang, take the spoils — but he himself will not come close. He remains invisible. He has, however, one trait that may one day help me identify him. It is said that he has a strange psychological condition called agoraphobia — which is to say, a morbid fear of open spaces. He remains indoors and travels only in a covered carriage.

'There is something else. As we continued our work, we were able to track down three men who knew his true identity and who almost certainly worked for him: his closest lieutenants and bodyguards. They formed a satellite around him, all three of them vicious criminals in their own right. Two of them are brothers — Edgar and Leland Mortlake. The third started life as a smatterhauler, which is what we call a handkerchief thief, but soon graduated to safe-cracking and grand larceny. His name is Scotchy Lavelle.'

'Can you not arrest them?'

'We have arrested them — many times. They are all three of them graduates of Sing Sing and the Tombs but in recent years they have been careful to keep their hands clean. They pretend to be respectable businessmen now and there is no evidence to prove otherwise. Arresting them again would do no good. The police have questioned them repeatedly but there is nothing in this world that would make them talk. They represent the new breed of gangster, the one that we at Pinkerton's most fear. They are no longer afraid of the law. They think themselves above it.'

'Have you met them?'

'I have observed all three of them from a distance and from behind a wire mesh. I always thought it best that we should remain unacquainted. If Devereux can keep his face a secret from me, it seems only fair to repay the compliment.' Mrs Steiler walked past and placed another log on the fire although her restaurant was already sweltering. I waited until she had left us and then finished my account. 'For two years we investigated Clarence Devereux with little success, but then, just a few months ago, we had a breakthrough. One of my investigators was a young man called Jonathan Pilgrim.'

'I know that name too,' Jones muttered.

'He was only in his twenties when I first met him and in his enthusiasm and basic decency he reminded me of myself at his age. He was a remarkable fellow who'd come to us from the west. A fine cello player and a baseball player too. I once saw him pitch at Bloomingdale Park.

When he was nineteen, he trailed a horse herd a thousand miles across the Texas plains and he'd had experience of ranches, mines — he'd even spent time working the riverboats. He joined the team in New York and, working on his own, managed to get close to Leland Mortlake. Let's just say that the older of the two brothers had always enjoyed the company of a handsome boy and with his straw-coloured hair and bright blue eyes, JP was very handsome indeed. He became Mortlake's secretary and travelling companion. The two of them dined together. They visited the theatre and the opera and hung out at the saloons. Well, in January, Mortlake announced that he was moving to London and he invited JP to go with him.

'It was a brilliant opportunity. We had an agent right inside the gang and although Jonathan never came face to face with Devereux — how much easier it would have made our task if he had! — he did have access to much of Mortlake's correspondence. Although it placed him in the greatest personal danger, he eavesdropped on conversations, kept an eye on everyone who came and went and made extensive notes on the workings of the gang. I used to meet with him secretly on the third Sunday of every month at the Haymarket, a dance hall on Thirtieth Street. He would report everything that he had learned to me.

'From him, I gathered that although Clarence Devereux exerted almost total control over the American underworld, it still was not enough. He was turning his attention to England. He had been in communication with a certain Professor James Moriarty, exploring the possibility of what might be termed a transatlantic alliance. Can you imagine it, Inspector Jones? A criminal fraternity whose tentacles would extend all the way from the west coast of California to the heart of Europe! A worldwide confederation. The coming together of two evil geniuses.'

'You knew of Moriarty?'

'By name and by reputation, most certainly. Although it is unfortunately true that Scotland Yard is not always cooperative in its dealings with Pinkerton's, we still have our contacts within the New York police — and for that matter with the Rijkswacht and the Sûreté. We had always been afraid that one day Moriarty might head west but it now appeared that the exact opposite had occurred.

'Scotchy Lavelle, Leland Mortlake and Edgar Mortlake had all set themselves up in London by the start of the New Year. Jonathan had gone with them and, a few weeks later, he sent us a telegraph to the effect that Clarence Devereux had also joined them. It was exactly what we had been waiting for. There are not so many forty-year-old wealthy Americans in London. His psychological condition, if true, could also help to identify him. At once, the Midnight Watch drew together the passenger lists of every steamship that had made the crossing from America to England in the past month and although it was a huge task — there were hundreds of names — we still thought it possible to narrow them down. Unless Clarence Devereux had somehow found a way to fly, he must be among them and to find him we worked night and day.

'While this was continuing, we received a second telegraph from Jonathan Pilgrim informing us that he had personally delivered a letter to Moriarty, arranging a meeting between him and Devereux. Yes! Our agent had actually met Moriarty. The two of them talked. But the very next day, before he could tell us exactly what had taken place, tragedy struck: Jonathan must have been discovered by the gang. Perhaps that last telegraph was the undoing of him. At any event, he was brutally killed.'

'He was tied up and shot. I remember the report.'

'Yes, Inspector — this was not so much a murder as an execution. It is how New York gangs frequently deal with informers.'

'Even so, you followed him across the Atlantic.'

'I still believed it would be easier to find Devereux in London than it was in New York and it also occurred to me that if I could pinpoint this meeting between Devereux and Moriarty, why, it would be two birds with one stone: the arrest of the two greatest criminals on the planet at one fell swoop.

'So you can imagine my dismay when I disembarked from my vessel, stepping on English soil for the first time, only to see the newspaper headlines . . . Moriarty believed dead. That was May seventh. My immediate thought was to come here to Meiringen, a village I had never heard of in a country I had never visited. Why? Because of the letter; if Moriarty still had it with him, it might lead me to Devereux. It even occurred to me that Devereux might be here and that his presence might be connected in some way to what had occurred at the Reichenbach Falls. At any event, there was nothing to be gained by kicking my heels in Southampton. I took the first train to Paris and then down to Switzerland and I was attempting to prise some sort of co-operation from the Swiss police — without much success — this morning when you and I met.'

I fell silent. It was too late now to attack my soup, which had cooled in the long telling of my tale. I took instead a sip of wine, which tasted sweet and heavy on my lips. Inspector Jones had listened to my long discourse as if the two of us had been alone in the room. I knew that he had absorbed every detail, that he had missed nothing and would — if called upon — be able to set down almost everything I had said. And yet it was not without effort. I had already marked him as the sort of man who sets the very highest standards for himself but who achieves them only through perseverance and fortitude. It was as if he were at war with himself.

'Your informant, Jonathan Pilgrim; do you know where he was staying?'

'He had rooms at a club — the Bostonian. I believe it is in a part of London called Mayfair. If he had one weakness as an agent, it is that he was independently minded. He told us very little and will, I am sure, have left nothing behind.'

'What of the others? The Mortlake brothers and Lavelle?'

'As far as I know, they are still in London.'

'You know them. You know what they look like. Can you not use them to reach Devereux?'

'They are too careful. If they ever meet, it is in secret and behind locked doors. They communicate only through telegrams and secret codes.'

Jones considered what I had told him. I watched the flames devouring the logs in the fireplace and waited for him to speak. 'Your story is of the greatest interest,' he said at length. 'And I would see no reason not to offer you my assistance. However, it may already be too late.'

'Why is that?'

'Now that Moriarty is dead, why should this man, Clarence Devereux, wish to remain in London?'

'Because it may be an opportunity for him; Devereux was suggesting some sort of partnership. With Moriarty gone, everything can be his alone. He can inherit Moriarty's entire organisation.'

Jones sniffed at that. 'We had arrested pretty much the entire gang before Professor Moriarty reached Meiringen,' he remarked. 'And Sherlock Holmes himself had left an envelope containing the identities and the addresses of many of his associates. Clarence Devereux may have come to England in search of a business partner but he will have already discovered that his journey was in vain. The same, I fear, may be true for you.'

'The note that we found in Moriarty's pocket — you said it would shed some light on the affair.'

'And so it does.'

'You have solved it?'

'Yes.'

'Then tell me, for Heaven's sake! Moriarty may be finished but Clarence Devereux most certainly is not and if there is anything you or I can do to rid the world of this evil creature, we must not hesitate.'

Jones had finished his soup. He moved his plate aside, clearing a space, then took out the sheet of paper, unfolded it and laid it in front of me. It seemed to me that the restaurant had suddenly become quieter. The candles were throwing dark, nimble shadows across the tables. The animal heads craned towards us as if trying to listen in.

Once again I read the extract with its jumble of capital and small letters.

'It makes no sense to you?' Jones enquired.

'None at all.'

'Then let me explain.'

4

The Letter

HoLmES WaS CeRtAiNLY NOt A DIFFiCulT mAn to LiVe WItH. He wAs QuIeT iN HiS WAYs and his hABiTS wErE REgulAr. iT wAs RARE fOR Him To BE up AfTeR TEN at nighT aND hE hAD INVariABLY breAKfasteD AND GoNE OUT BeFOrE i RoSe in The morNINg. SOMEtImEs He SPeNt hiS DAy At ThE ChEmiCaL lABoRatORY, SoMeTimes IN THE dIsSeCting ROoms And oCcAsionaLly iN lOnG WALKs whICH ApPeAREd TO taKE HIM INtO THE LOwEsT PORTioNs OF thE CITy. nothINg COuld exCEeD HiS ENErgY WHeN tHE wORkING FiT WAs upOn HiM.

'Do you really believe,' I said, 'that there is some sort of secret message contained on this page?'

'I not only believe it. I know it to be the case.'

I took the paper and held it up to the light. 'Could it be written in invisible ink?'

Jones smiled. He took the page back again and laid it between us on the white tablecloth. For the moment, all thoughts of our dinner had been forgotten. 'You may be aware that Mr Sherlock Holmes wrote a monograph on the subject of codes and secret writings,' he began.

'I was not,' I said.

52

'I have read it, as I have read everything that he has, generously, allowed to come to the public attention. The monograph examines no fewer than one hundred and sixty forms of concealed communication and, more importantly, the methods by which he was able to bring them to light.'

'You will forgive me, Inspector,' I interrupted. 'Whatever the relevance of this letter, it cannot be in code. We both recognise the contents. You said as much yourself. It was written, word for word, by Dr John Watson.'

'That is indeed the case. But there is of course one peculiarity. Why do you think it has been copied in this way? Why has the writer taken such care with his presentation of the text?'

'I'd guess it's obvious, isn't it? To disguise his handwriting!'

'I think not. After all, Moriarty knew who the letter had come from. There was no need for disguise. No. I believe the capital and the small letters go to the very heart of the matter and there is nothing indiscriminate about them. The moment I set eyes on the passage, I saw that it had been written slowly and methodically. You can observe the heavy indentation of the pen on the paper. This is more than an exercise in copying. It is a deliberate attempt to communicate something to Moriarty that will remain secret should it fall into the wrong hands.'

'So there is a code!'

'Exactly.'

'And you were able to crack it!'

'Through trial and error, yes.' Jones nodded. 'I

take no credit for it, mind. Where Holmes has gone, I have merely followed.'

'Then what does it say?' I glanced once again at the page. 'What can it possibly say?'

'I shall explain it to you, Chase. I trust you will forgive the familiarity but I am beginning to think that you and I may be united in a common pursuit.'

'I very much hope so.'

'Very well. As you rightly say, the letters alone cannot mean anything for they are exactly as Dr Watson set them down. We are therefore left with the seemingly random scattering of small and capital letters. But let us suppose it is not random. There are three hundred and ninety letters on the page. That in itself is an interesting number in that it is exactly divisible by five. So let us begin by separating the letters into groups of that length — '

'Wait a minute. It's also divisible by six.'

'Six would create far more combinations than are actually required.' He scowled. 'Anyway, I tried six without success — trial and error. I am no Sherlock Holmes and so it is sometimes necessary to take the long way round.' He took out a second sheet of paper and laid it beside the first. 'We must ignore the spaces between the words. We must ignore everything apart from the question of whether the letter is large or small. And in that event, the text will look like this:

LsLsL LLsLL sLsLs LLLLL sLLLL LsLss LsLss sLsLs LLsLL ssLsL sLsLs LLsLL LLsss sssss LLsLL sLsLL LsssL ssLsL sLLLL sLLLL

sLsLL ssLsL sLLLL sssss sLsLL sLsLL LLLss
sLLLL sssLL sssss LLLLL sLLLL LLsLL sLsLs
LsssL sssss LLLsL LLLsL sLsLs LLsLs ssLLL
sLsLs LLsLs sLsLs LLsLs sLLLL sLsLs sssLL
LLLsL sLsLs sssLL sssLs ssLsL sssss LsssL
sLsLL LLLss sLLLL sLsLL LsLLs sLLLL
LLLsL LLLLL sLsLL LLLss LsLLs sLLLL
sssss LLsLL sssss LLsLL sLLLL ssLLL sLsLL
sLLsL LLLsL LLsss LsLsL

Jones had carefully written the groups of letters across the page. I stared at them. 'It's the electrical telegraph system!' I exclaimed.

'It is something very similar,' the detective agreed. 'Morse code, with each group representing a single letter! And you will see, Chase, that certain groups repeat themselves. 'sLLLL', for example, appears no fewer than eleven times.'

'A vowel?' I suggested.

'Almost certainly, and 'sssss' might be another, appearing seven times. But set out this way, the groups are confusing. My next step was to assign each one of them a number, making it simpler to see what it was in fact we had before us. We are helped by the fact that only nineteen of the twenty-six letters of the alphabet have actually been used.'

He withdrew a third sheet of paper. On this, he had written as follows:

1 2 3 4 5 6 6 3 2 7 3 2 8 9 2 10 11 7 5 5 10 7 5
9 10 10 12 5 13 9 4 5 2 3 11 9 14 14 3 15 16 3 15
3 15 5 3 13 14 3 13 17 7 9 11 10 12 5 10 18 5 14
4 10 12 18 5 9 2 9 2 5 16 10 19 14 8 1

'You understand,' he explained, 'that each number merely stands for a group. So one equals LsLsL, two equals LLsLL and so on . . . '

'I see that. Yes.'

'And what does it tell you?' This was a very different Athelney Jones from the one I had seen earlier, exhausted after the walk from the church. There was no escaping the energy and the sense of excitement that glimmered in his eyes.

'Each number now stands for a single letter,' I said. 'But there are a lot of numbers — nineteen, as you correctly say — and we are not helped by the fact that there are no spaces. We have no way of telling where one word ends and the next begins.'

'That is indeed the case,' Jones agreed. 'However, at the very least we can see now which numbers — 3, 5 and 10, for example — crop up the most frequently. These must be vowels or perhaps the more commonly used letters such as T, R or S. Unfortunately, you are correct in saying that without spaces, we cannot spot the shapes of common English words such as 'the' or 'a'. That is very much to our disadvantage.'

'So how were you able to continue?'

'With a combination of diligence and good luck: I began by asking myself if there might be a single word appearing in this communication which I would be able to recognise simply from its shape. Several came to mind. SHERLOCK HOLMES, for example, was one. PINKERTONS was another. But in the end I settled on MORI-ARTY. If it was he for whom the message was intended, then it was surely not unreasonable to suppose that his name might appear. I therefore searched for a sequence of eight digits in which one — and only one — was repeated in the third and sixth position as is the case with the R in MORIARTY. For example, at the very beginning of the message we come upon 6 6 3 2 7 3 2 8 where the 3 might be an R. But that cannot be MORIARTY because of the double 6 and the repeated 2. Later on in the text we see 5 3 13 14 3 13 17 7 where the figure 13 might stand for R. But this time it is the repeated 3 that defeats us.

'In fact, in the entire message, the correct formulation appears only once — near the beginning of the first line we have 7 3 2 8 9 2 10 11. In this instance, the number 2 stands for R and — as in the name itself — no other letter is repeated. And if we assume that this stands for MORIARTY, something very interesting happens. For if we then examine the letters that appear *before* it, this is what we read . . . '

1 R O 4 5 6 6 O R

'It could be more than one word,' I said.

'But I do not think it is more than one word,' returned he. 'Look at the repeated R, the repeated O — and whatever letter is represented by the repeated 6. As far as I can tell, there is only one word in the English language with a shape like that. And consider also the context. This is a salutation to the receiver of the message.'

'Professor!' I exclaimed.

'Exactly. Professor Moriarty — the first two

words of the communication. And, using that information, many more of the letters contained in the code are revealed.

PROFESSOR MORIARTY — M E E T M E A T T 12 E 13 A F E R O Y A 14 14 O 15 16 O 15 O 15 E O 13 14 O 13 17 M A Y T 12 E T 18 E 14 F T 12 18 E A R A R E 16 T 19 14 I P

' 'Professor Moriarty, meet me at . . . ' ' I began. My voice trailed off. 'There is not very much more after that,' I said.

'I do not agree. 'Meet me at' is followed by 'T 12 E'. What else can that be but 'the'? You will see that the same formulation is repeated in the third line after MAY. And that provides us with another letter. 12 is H! And looking at the second line, you will see the letters ROYA all together. Again, the fifth letter is obvious. It can only be one word.

'Royal?'

'Precisely. Meet me at the something Royal . . . '

'What can that be?'

'It can only be the Café Royal!' Jones explained. I looked blank so he continued. 'It is a famous restaurant in the heart of London. Like yourself, Clarence Devereux might not have heard of it but it would be easy enough to find.'

'And what of the word that follows?' I asked.

'That is not so difficult. We now have the L. So — L O 15 16 O 15. The repeated 15 gives us another clue if we need it.'

'London,' I said. 'The Café Royal, London. It can be nothing else.'

'I agree. That is the meeting place. And now let us see what comes next.'

ONE O C L O C 17 MAY THE T 18 E L FT H

'It is perfectly obvious,' I cried. 'One o'clock, May the twelfth!'

'That is three days from now. You see how quickly the code unravels itself. But let us proceed to the end.'

W E A R A R E 16 T 19 L I P

'We are . . . ' I stopped, confused.

'It is not 'we are'. It is 'wear a'. From what you told me, it is almost certain that Moriarty and Clarence Devereux have never seen each other face to face. Both pride themselves on the fact that nobody knows their appearance. So Moriarty is being instructed to wear something that will identify him. That something is contained in the last eight letters.'

R E 16 T 19 L I P

I said nothing and with a smile, Jones finished his work for me. 'It can only be a red tulip,' he said, 'a buttonhole. And there you have it, Chase . . . '

PROFESSOR MORIARTY. MEET ME AT THE CAFÉ ROYAL, LONDON. ONE O'CLOCK, MAY THE TWELFTH. WEAR A RED TULIP.

'We were lucky. Professor Moriarty was the key to the entire thing. Had the sender omitted the salutation, we would have been stuck.'

'But you are remarkable, Inspector Jones! I cannot express my admiration strongly enough. I wouldn't have known where to begin.'

'Pshaw. It was not so very difficult. I'm sure Mr Holmes would have achieved the same in half the time.'

'This is exactly what I had been hoping for,' I said. 'It's the vindication of my long journey to Europe — and the costs involved, for that matter. Clarence Devereux is coming to this place, the Café Royal, three days from now. He will approach a man wearing a red tulip and in doing so he'll identify himself.'

'If he knows that Moriarty is dead, he will not come.'

'That's true.' I fell silent, then thought again. 'But suppose you were to issue a statement to the effect that you believe Moriarty to be alive? After all, you were sent to enquire into what had taken place at the Reichenbach Falls. You could easily say that you had found fresh evidence that Moriarty had not been involved in the attack.'

'And the body in the crypt?'

I paused. 'Couldn't we pretend that it was somebody else?' At that moment, our hostess approached the table to remove the plates. 'Mrs Steiler,' I said. 'Can you tell me the name of the chef whose mother was ill?'

'Franz Hirzel.' She looked at my soup, barely touched. 'Not good?'

'It was excellent,' I replied. I waited until she

had gone back into the kitchen. 'There's the name for you, if you need one. The dead man can be our wandering chef. He was on his way back, he got drunk and fell into the falls. It's just a coincidence that the two incidents occurred at about the same time. Tell the papers that Moriarty is still alive and let Devereux walk into a trap.' Jones looked down with his lips tightly pursed, so I went on. 'I haven't known you very long and yet I can see you don't like the idea of doing something dishonest. I feel the same. But trust me when I say that you have no idea what sort of disease has arrived in your city. You owe it to your fellow citizens to do everything you can to purge it. Believe me, Inspector. With Moriarty gone, this meeting is our only hope. We *have* to be there. We have to see what comes of it.'

Mrs Steiler returned with the main course, two plates of roast lamb. I picked up my knife and fork, this time determined to eat.

Jones nodded slowly. 'You're right,' he said. 'I will send a telegram to Scotland Yard and we can leave tomorrow. If the trains are kind to us, we will just arrive in time.'

I raised my glass. 'To the capture of Clarence Devereux,' I said. 'And — if I may — to the two of us, Scotland Yard and Pinkerton's, working together.'

We drank and in this way our association began. And yet how bitter that wine might have tasted and how reluctant we might have been to continue if we had only known what lay ahead.

5

At the Café Royal

Not many Americans have the opportunity to travel across Europe and yet I cannot describe very much of what I saw. For much of the time I had my face pressed against the glass, gazing at the little farmhouses dotted over the hills, the rushing streams, the valleys with their early summer flowers, and yet I was ill at ease, unable to concentrate on what I saw. The train journey was a very slow business and, in our second-class carriage, an uncomfortable one. My constant fear was that we would arrive too late for, as Jones had told me, we had a distance of some five hundred miles to cover with four trains and the steam packet from Calais to London Bridge. We couldn't afford to miss even one of our connections. From Meiringen we headed west, crossing Lake Brienz at Interlaken and then continuing up to Bern. It was from here that Jones sent the cable that we'd devised together, stating that Professor Moriarty had miraculously escaped from the catastrophe of the Reichenbach Falls and was believed to have returned to England. The post office was some distance from the station and almost cost us our next train as Jones was unable to walk for any great length of time. He was quite pale and clearly in discomfort as we took our seats in our carriage.

We sat in silence for the first hour or two, each of us absorbed in our own thoughts. However, as we approached the French border near Moutier, we became more talkative. I told Jones something of the history of the Pinkertons — he had a keen interest in the methods of investigation practised by foreign law enforcers, dull though they were compared to his own — and I gave him a detailed account of their involvement in the Burlington and Quincy Railroad strike which had taken place a few years before. The agency had been accused of inciting riots and even murdering strikers, although I assured him that their role had only been to protect property and to keep the peace. That was their story, anyway.

After that, Jones turned away, immersing himself in a printed pamphlet which he had brought with him and which turned out to be a monograph by Sherlock Holmes no less, this one on the subject of ash. Apparently — or so Jones assured me — Holmes was able to differentiate between one hundred and forty different types of ash, from cigars, cigarettes and pipes, although he himself had only mastered ninety of them. To humour him, I made my way to the salon dining room and took a pinch of five different samples from the mystified passengers. Jones was extremely grateful and spent the next hour examining them minutely with a magnifying glass he had extracted from his travelling bag.

'How I would have liked to have encountered Sherlock Holmes!' I exclaimed when he finally cast the ashes aside, dismissing them quite literally with a wave of his hand. 'Did you ever meet him?'

'Yes. I did.' He fell silent and I saw, to my surprise, that my question had in some way offended him. This was strange as so much of what he had said in our brief acquaintance had led me to believe that he was an ardent, even a fanatical, admirer of the famous detective. 'I actually met him on three occasions,' he continued. He paused, as if unsure where to begin. 'The first was not exactly a meeting as I was only there as part of a larger assembly. He gave a lecture to a number of us at Scotland Yard — it led directly to the arrest of the Bishopsgate jewel thief. To this day, I am inclined to think that Mr Holmes relied more on guesswork than strict logic. He could not possibly have known that the man was born with a club foot. The second occasion, however, was quite different and has been made public by Dr John Watson who actually mentions me by name. I cannot say it gives an account of me that is particularly kind.'

'I'm sorry to hear it,' I said.

'You have not read the investigation that came to be known as 'The Sign of the Four'? It was a most unusual case.' Jones took out a cigarette and lit it. I hadn't seen him smoke before and he seemed to have forgotten the conversation we'd had when we first met. At the last moment, he remembered. 'I'm sorry to inflict this on you a second time,' he said. 'I occasionally indulge. You don't mind?'

'Not at all.'

He shook out the match and discarded it. 'I had not been a police inspector for very long at the time,' he explained. 'I had only recently been promoted. Perhaps if Dr Watson had known this, he might have been a little more charitable. At any event, I happened to be in Norwood one evening in September — this was '88 — investigating a trifling matter, a housemaid who had been accused by her mistress of theft. I had just finished interviewing her when a messenger arrived with the news of a murder that had taken place in a house not far away and, being the most senior officer present, it was my duty to attend.

'That was how I came upon Pondicherry Lodge, a great white Aladdin's Cave of a place, standing in its own grounds with a garden that could have been a graveyard, it was filled with so many holes. The owner was one Bartholomew Sholto and I will never forget my first sight of him, sitting in a wooden armchair in a study that was more like a laboratory, up on the third floor, quite dead, with a hideous grin stamped across his face.

'Sherlock Holmes was there. He had broken down the door to get in which by rights he shouldn't have because this was a police matter. It was the first time I had seen the great man at close quarters and in action too, for he had already begun his investigation. What can I tell you, Chase? He was taller than I remembered, with the leanness of an aesthete as if he had deliberately starved himself. This gave prominence to his chin, his cheekbones and above all to his eyes which never seemed to settle on anything without stripping them of all the information they might provide. There was an energy about him, a restlessness that I had never encountered in any other man. His movements were brief and economical. He gave you the sense that there was no time to be wasted. He was wearing a dark frock coat and no hat. When I first saw him, he was holding a tape measure which he folded away.'

'And Dr Watson . . . ?'

'I took less notice of him. He stood in the shadows at the edge of the room, a shorter man, round-faced, genial.

'I do not need to describe the details of the case. You can read them if they are of interest to you. The dead man was, as I said, Bartholomew Sholto. It transpired that he and his twin brother, Thaddeus, had been bequeathed a great treasure by their father. They'd had trouble finding it, mind, hence all the holes in the garden. But the facts of the case seemed quite straightforward to me. The two of them had argued as men often will when confronted by unexpected wealth. Thaddeus had killed his brother using a blowpipe and a poison dart — I should have explained that the house was full of Indian curiosities. I arrested him and also took in his servant, a man called McMurdo, as his accomplice.'

'And were you right?'

'No, sir, as it turned out, I was wrong. I had made a complete fool of myself and although I was not the first to do so — I had colleagues who had been in exactly the same position as I — at the time it was small consolation.'

He fell silent, staring out of the window at the French countryside although, from the look in his eyes, I was sure he saw none of it.

'And the third time?' I asked.

'That was a few months later . . . the curious business of the Abernettys. I will not discuss it now, if you don't mind. It still annoys me. It began with what seemed to be, on the face of it, a burglary — although a very unusual one. All I will say is that once again I missed everything of importance and stood idly by while Mr Holmes made the arrest. It will not happen again, Mr Chase. I promise you that.'

Jones barely spoke to me for the next few hours. We made our connection in Paris quite easily and it was the second time I had crossed the city without so much as glimpsing the Eiffel Tower. But what did it matter? London lay ahead of us and already I was uneasy. I felt that a shadow had fallen over us but to whom it belonged — be it Holmes, Devereux or even Moriarty — I dared not say.

* * *

And so to London.

It has been said that good Americans, when they die, go to Paris. Perhaps the less saintly variety would end up like me, dragging my steamer trunk from Charing Cross Station with the drivers shouting, the beggar boys circling, and the crowds streaming past. For this was where Inspector Jones and I parted company; he to return to his home in Camberwell, I to find a hotel that would suit a general operative travelling on a Pinkerton's budget. I had been surprised to learn that he had a wife and child. He had struck me as a single, even a solitary, man. But he had mentioned them to me in Paris and as we disembarked from our steamship at Dover he was clutching an India rubber ball and a puppet of the French policeman Flagéolet, which he had picked up near the Gare du Nord. The revelation troubled me but I said nothing until we reached the very end of our trip.

'You will forgive me, Inspector,' I remarked, as we were preparing to go our separate ways. 'I know it is not for me to say, but I wonder if you should not reconsider.'

'Reconsider what?'

'This entire adventure — by which I mean the pursuit of Clarence Devereux. I may not have made it clear to you quite how ruthless, how vicious this man is. Trust me when I say that you would not choose to have him as your enemy. He left a trail of bloodshed behind him in New York and if he is in London, as I believe, he will certainly do the same there. Look at what happened to poor Jonathan Pilgrim! It is my task to hunt him down and I have no dependants. The same is not true for you and I feel uncomfortable bringing you into imminent danger.'

'It is not you who has brought me here. I am merely pursuing the enquiry that was given to me by my superiors at Scotland Yard.'

'Devereux will have no respect for Scotland Yard or for you. Your rank and position will not protect you.'

'That makes no difference.' He stopped and looked up at the dull afternoon sky, for London had welcomed us with clouds and drizzle. 'If this man has come to England and plans to continue his criminal activities as you have suggested, then he must be stopped and that is my duty.'

'There are plenty of other detectives.'

'But I was the one who was sent to Meiringen.' He smiled. 'I understand your sentiments, Chase, and I will say that they do you credit. It is true that I have a family. I would not do anything that would threaten their well-being and yet the choice is not mine. For better or for worse, you and I have been thrown together and that is how we shall remain. If it sets your mind at ease, I will add, in confidence, that I would not want Lestrade, Gregson or any of my other friends and colleagues stealing the credit for hunting this man down. But here is a cab approaching. I must be on my way!'

I can still see him hurrying away with the ball in one hand and the blue-uniformed doll hanging limply over his arm. And I wonder now as I wondered then how Dr Watson could have turned him into such a fool in his own account. I have read 'The Sign of the Four' since then and can say that the Athelney Jones in that adventure bears very little similarity to the man I knew and who was, I would have said, unequalled by any at Scotland Yard.

There were several hotels close to the station

in Northumberland Avenue but their very names — the Grand, the Victoria, the Metropole — warned me they would not fit the bill in any sense of those words and in the end I found somewhere on the Embankment, close by the bridge . . . so close, in fact, that the whole place rattled every time a train went past. Hexam's Hotel was grimy and ramshackle. The carpets were threadbare and the chandeliers lopsided. But the sheets were clean, it only cost two shillings a night, and once I had wiped the soot off the window, I was rewarded with a glimpse of the river and a coal ship gliding slowly past. I had dinner in the hotel's restaurant, alone but for a scowling maid and a disgruntled Boots, then sat reading in my room until midnight when I eventually fell into a troubled sleep.

Inspector Jones and I had arranged to meet at twelve o'clock the following day outside the Café Royal on Regent Street, a full hour ahead of the assignation. After much consideration — we had, after all, spent thirty hours together on the train — we had devised a plan that seemed to cover every eventuality. I would wear the red tulip, posing as Moriarty, while Jones would sit at a table, close enough to overhear any conversation that ensued. We had both agreed that it was highly unlikely that Clarence Devereux would appear in person. Apart from the unnecessary risk of his exposing himself to danger, there was the question of his agoraphobia that would make his journey down Regent Street, even in a closed carriage, highly impractical. He would surely send a confederate and that person would expect to find Moriarty alone.

And then? There were three possibilities.

Hopefully, I would be met by someone who would escort me to the house or to the hotel where Devereux was staying. In that event, Jones would follow quietly behind, to ensure my safety and also, of course, to make note of the address. Alternatively, Devereux's accomplice might know what Moriarty looked like. He would see immediately that I was a fake and walk out. In this event, Jones would slip out of the restaurant and follow him to wherever he had come from, which might at least give us a clue as to where Devereux might be found. And finally, there was a chance that nobody would show up at all. However, Moriarty's survival at Reichenbach had been widely reported in the London newspapers and we had every reason to hope that Devereux would suppose him alive.

I had purchased a red tulip from a flower stall outside the station and was wearing it as I approached the Café Royal, located in the very epicentre of the city. Chicago might have its State Street and New York the luxury of Broadway, but neither of them, I venture to say, came close to the elegance and charm of Regent Street with its clean air and handsome classical façades. Carriages rolled past in both directions, sweeping round the curve of the road in an endless stream. The pavements were thronged with loungers and urchins, English gentlemen and foreign visitors but above all with ladies, immaculately dressed, accompanied by servants who struggled under the weight of their many

71

purchases. And what had they been buying? I passed windows displaying perfumes, gloves and jewellery, vanille chocolates and ormolu clocks. It seemed that there was nothing you could find here that was not expensive and very little that was actually necessary.

Jones was waiting for me, dressed in a suit, as ever leaning on his walking stick. 'You found a hotel?' he asked. I gave him the name and the address. 'And you had no trouble finding this address?'

'It was only a short walk and they gave me excellent direction.'

'Good.'

Jones glanced doubtfully in the direction of the Café Royal. 'This is a pretty place for a rendezvous,' he muttered. 'How our man will even find you, I don't know. And following him without being observed is going to be difficult, to say the least.'

He had a point. Even the entrance on Regent Street — three sets of doors set behind three pillars — suggested too many ways in and too many ways out and once we'd entered it was unclear where we were supposed to meet as the building was a warren of corridors and staircases, bars, restaurants and meeting rooms — some of them obstructed by mirrored screens, others partly concealed by great displays of flowers. Nor did it help that half of London seemed to have gathered here for lunch. I had never seen such an assembly of the well-to-do. Clarence Devereux and his entire gang could have already been there, planning their next murder or perhaps an armed assault on the Bank of England and we wouldn't have been able to spot them. There was so much noise, we wouldn't have been able to hear them either.

We chose the café on the ground floor, which, with its high ceilings and bright, public atmosphere, seemed to be the most natural place for a meeting between two strangers. It was a beautiful room with turquoise pillars and gold ornamentation, top hats and billycocks hanging everywhere and people packed together at marble tables while the waiters in their black tailcoats and long white aprons fought their way through like circus performers, their overladen trays almost seeming to float above their shoulders. Somehow we managed to find two tables side by side. Neither Jones nor I had spoken since we came in. To anyone watching, it would appear that we were unaware of each other's existence. I ordered a small glass of wine. Meanwhile, Jones had taken out a French newspaper and called to the waiter for a cup of tea.

We sat side by side, ignoring each other, watching as the minute hand of the clock on the far wall climbed ever higher. I could sense the detective growing more and more tense as the hour approached. He had already persuaded himself that we were going to be disappointed and that our rush across the continent had been to no avail. But at exactly one o'clock, I saw a figure appear at the doorway and scrutinise the room, peering through the crowd. Beside me, Jones stiffened and his eyes — always serious — became suddenly alert.

The new arrival was a child of about fourteen, smartly dressed in the bright blue jacket and shako cap of a telegraph boy. He looked ill at ease, as if he were unused to the clothes that he had been forced to wear and they certainly didn't fit him very well for the uniform was tight and trim and he was the exact opposite. Indeed, with his plump stomach, short legs and round cheeks it struck me that he rather resembled the cupids that ornamented the very room in which we sat.

He saw me — or rather the tulip on my coat — and with a glint of recognition began to make his way through the crowd. He reached me and, without asking permission, sat down opposite me, crossing one foot over his knee. This in itself was a display of arrogance that would have been unbecoming to his station — but now that he was close, it was quite obvious that he had never worked for the telegraph office. He was too knowing. There was something very strange about his eyes, which were moist and empty as if they had never looked on anything that was not evil. At the same time, his eyelashes were fine, his teeth white, his lips full — and the overall effect was that he was both very pretty and very ugly at the same time.

'You waiting for someone?' he asked. His voice was husky, almost that of a man.

'I might be,' I replied.

'Nice tulip. Not something you would see every day, mister, I would say.'

'A red tulip,' I agreed. 'Does it signify something to you?'

74

'It might do. It might not.'

He fell silent.

'What is your name?' I asked.

'Do I need a name?' He winked at me, mischievously. 'I wouldn't say I do, mister. What good is a name when one is 'ardly going to be hac-quainted. But I'll tell you what. If you want to call me something, you can call me Perry.'

Inspector Jones was still pretending to read his newspaper but I knew that he was attending to every word that was spoken. He had lowered the page a little so that he could peek over the top but at the same time his face was blank, showing no interest at all.

'Well, Perry,' I said, 'there was someone I was waiting to meet but I can say without doubt that it's not you.'

'Of course not, mister, my job is to bring you to 'im but first we 'ave to ascertain that you is who you say you is. You got the tulip, sure enough. But do you 'ave a certain letter that was sent to you by my master?'

I did indeed have the torn page with the coded message. It was Jones who had suggested that I might be asked to present it and so I had brought it with me. I drew it out and placed it on the table.

The boy barely glanced at it. 'Are you the professor?' he asked.

'I am,' I said, keeping my voice low.

'Professor Moriarty?'

'Yes.'

'Not drowned in the Reeking-back Falls?'

'Why do you ask these foolish questions?' This

was surely how the real Moriarty would speak. 'It was your master who arranged this meeting. If you persist in wasting my time, I can assure you, you will suffer the consequences.'

But the boy was not to be intimidated. 'Then tell me how many ravens flew out of the Tower of London?'

'What?'

'The ravens. The tower. How many?'

It was the one eventuality we had most feared. Turning over the plan on our long train journey, Jones and I had discussed the likelihood of there being a recognition signal. Two criminals of the magnitude of Clarence Devereux and Professor James Moriarty would not deliver themselves into each other's hands without the certainty that they were safe. And here was the final precaution — a riddle taking the form of an exchange of words which must have been agreed in a separate communication.

I waved the question aside. 'Enough of these stupid games,' I said. 'I have travelled a long way to meet with Clarence Devereux. You know who I'm talking about. Don't pretend! I see it in your eyes.'

'You're mistaken, mister. I've never heard that name.'

'Then why are you here? You know me. You know of the letter. Don't try to pretend otherwise.'

The boy was suddenly anxious to be on his way. I saw him glance at the door and a moment later he pulled away from the table, getting to his feet. But before he could move, I grabbed hold of his arm, pinning him down.

'Tell me where I can find him,' I said. I was keeping my voice low, aware of the other diners all around me, sipping their coffees and their wine, ordering their food, chatting animatedly as they began their lunch. Athelney Jones was still sitting at his table, close to me and yet completely separate. Nobody in the room had noticed us. At that moment, as we played out our little drama, we were quite alone.

'There's no need to get nasty, mister.' Perry's voice was also low but it was ugly, filled with threat.

'I will not let you leave until you tell me what I want to know.'

'You're 'urting me!' Tears sprang to his eyes as if to remind me that he was, after all, only a child. But then, even as I hesitated, he twisted in my grasp and suddenly I felt something pressing against my neck. How he had managed to produce it with just one hand is beyond me but I could feel it cutting through my skin even though he was barely exerting any pressure at all. Looking down, I saw the weapon that he had withdrawn from somewhere inside his jacket. It was a horrible thing — a black-handled surgeon's knife with a blade that must have measured at least five inches. He was holding it very carefully so that only he and I could see it although surely the gentleman at the next table might have caught sight of it had he not, inexplicably, returned to his French newspaper.

'Let me go,' the boy hissed, 'or by God, I'll cut your throat clean through, 'ere and now, and put all these nice people off their dinners, no mistake. I've seen the blood shoot seven feet up when I done it before. Come gushing out, it does. Not the sort of thing you want to 'appen in a posh 'ouse like this.' He pressed with his hand and I felt a trickle of blood run down the side of my neck.

'You're making a mistake,' I whispered. 'I am Moriarty . . . '

'No more fun and games, mister. You been done by them ravens. I'm going to count to three . . . '

'There's no need for this!'

'One — '

'I'm telling you — '

'Two . . . '

He didn't reach three. I let him go. He was a devil-child and he had made it quite clear that he would happily commit murder, even in this public place. Meanwhile, Jones had done nothing, although he must have seen what was happening. Would he have stood by and let the boy murder me in plain sight to achieve his aim? The boy hurried away, weaving through the crowd. I snatched up a napkin and held it against my neck. When I looked up again, Jones was on his feet, moving away.

'Is everything all right, monsieur?' A waiter had appeared, conjuring himself up from nowhere, and hovered over me, his face filled with alarm.

I took away the napkin and saw a smear of bright red blood on the linen. 'It's nothing,' I said. 'A small accident.'

I hurried to the door but by the time I reached the street it was too late. Both Inspector Jones and the boy who called himself Perry had gone.

6

Bladeston House

I didn't see Jones until the following day when he came hurrying into my hotel, full of the same nervous energy that I had witnessed when he was deciphering the message taken from the dead man's pocket. I had just breakfasted when he arrived and sat down opposite me.

'This is where you're staying, Chase?' He looked around him at the shabby wallpaper and the few tables positioned close to one another on the well-trodden carpet. I had been kept awake half the night by a man with a racking cough who, for some reason, had been given the room next to mine. I had expected him to join me in the breakfast room but so far he had not shown himself. Apart from this one mysterious guest, I was alone at Hexam's and frankly I was not surprised. It wasn't the sort of accommodation that Baedeker or Murray would have recommended, unless it was to avoid. Accordingly, we had the breakfast room to ourselves. 'Well, I suppose it will do well enough. Not quite the Clarendon but things are proceeding apace and with luck, it may only be a matter of weeks before you are on your way back to New York.' He rested his stick against the table and suddenly he was more solicitous. 'You were not hurt, I trust. I saw the boy produce the knife and didn't know what to do.'

'You could have stopped him.'

'And given us both away? From the look of him, he wasn't the sort to yield under pressure. If I had arrested him, it would have achieved nothing.'

I ran a finger along the mark that Perry had left on my neck. 'It was a close-run thing,' I said. 'He could have cut my throat.'

'Forgive me, my friend. I had to make a judgement. I had no time to think.'

'Well, I suppose you acted for the best. But you see now what I was trying to tell you, Inspector. These are vicious people, utterly without qualms. A child of no more than fourteen! And in a crowded restaurant! It almost beggars belief. Fortunately, he didn't hurt me. The more important question is, did he lead you to Clarence Devereux?'

'Not to Devereux. No. It was a pretty chase across London, I can tell you. All the way up Regent Street to Oxford Circus and then east to Tottenham Court Road. I would have lost him in the crowd but we were fortunate that he was wearing a bright blue coat. I had to keep my distance though and it was just as well I did for he turned round several times to ensure he was not being followed. Even so, I almost lost him at Tottenham Court Road. He had climbed onto an omnibus and I only just spotted him as he took his place on the knife-board, up on the roof.'

'You were fortunate, again, that he did not sit inside.'

81

'Perhaps. I flagged down a hansom that was heading the right way and we followed. I must say I was glad not to have to walk much further, particularly when we began to climb up towards the northern suburbs.'

'That was where the boy went?'

'Indeed. Perry — if that *was* his name — led me to the Archway Tavern and from there he took the cable tramway up to Highgate Village. I travelled with him, he in the front compartment, I in the back.'

'And then?'

'Well, from the tramway, I followed the boy a short way back down the hill and along Merton Lane. The sight of it caused me some alarm, I will admit, for was it not here that the body of your agent, Jonathan Pilgrim, was discovered? At any event, he continued to a house completely surrounded by a high wall on the edge of the Southampton Estate and it was here that, finally, I lost him. As he approached his destination, he hastened his step. You will have observed, Chase, that I do not enjoy the best of health, and I was still some distance away when I saw the boy disappear behind the wall. I hurried forward but by the time I had turned the corner, he had gone. I did not actually see him go into the house but there could still be no doubt of it. At the back was an empty field with a couple of shrubs. No sign of him there. A few more residences stood close by, but if he had been making for any of them, I would have surely seen him as he moved across. No. Bladeston House it had to be. There was a gate set in the wall in the back. That must have been where he entered. It was locked.

'Bladeston House is not a particularly welcoming place and it is my opinion that the occupants had made it their business to keep it so. A wall surmounted with metal spikes surrounds it. Every window is barred. There was a Chubb patent lock in the garden door, which only the most accomplished burglar would be able to crack. Might the boy come out again? I retreated some distance and kept watch using a device which I have often found useful . . . ' He gestured at the walking stick and for the first time I saw that the cumbersome silver handle I had noticed earlier could unfold to become a pair of binoculars. 'There was no sign of Perry, leading me to conclude that he could not have been delivering another message. He must surely live there.'

'You did not go in?'

'I very much wanted to.' Jones smiled. 'But it seemed to me that we should do so together. This is as much your investigation as mine.'

'You are very considerate.'

'However, I have not been idle,' he continued. 'I have made certain enquiries which I think may be of interest to you. Bladeston House is the property of George Bladeston, the publisher, who died last year. His family is unimpeachable. They rented the property out six months ago to an American businessman who goes by the name of Scott Lavelle.'

'Scotchy Lavelle!' I exclaimed.

'The same. This is undoubtedly Devereux's

lieutenant, the man of whom you spoke.'

'And Devereux himself?'

'Lavelle can lead us to him. I see you have finished your breakfast. Shall we leave straight away? For I tell you, Chase, the game is very much afoot.'

I needed no further encouragement and together we followed the same trail that the child Perry had set down for us the day before, continuing through the heart of the capital, up into the suburbs, finally travelling on the cable tramway which pulled us effortlessly up the hill.

'This is a remarkable device,' I exclaimed.

'It's a shame I cannot show you more of the area. There are some fine views from the Heath, which is nearby. Highgate was once a village in its own right but I fear it has lost much of its charm.'

'That happened the day Scotchy Lavelle arrived,' I said. 'When he and his friends have been dealt with, we will both enjoy the city more.'

We reached the house, which was just as Jones had described only grimmer, more determined to keep its distance from the world outside. It was not a handsome building, taller than it was wide and built out of dull grey bricks, more suited to the city than the countryside. Its architecture was Gothic with an elaborate archway constructed over the front door and pointed windows covered with tracery, gargoyles and all the rest of it. Jones had certainly been right about the security measures. Gates, spikes, bars, shutters . . . the last time I had seen a building like this, I had been looking at a prison. Any casual visitor, or indeed a thief in the night, would have found entrance impossible, but then knowing these people as I did I had expected nothing less.

We were not even able to approach the front door as there was an ornate metal gate set in the wall, separating the entrance from the street, and this too was locked. Jones rang a bell for attention.

'Is there anyone in?' I asked.

'I see a movement behind the window,' he replied. 'We are being watched. Suspicious minds, they must have here. Ah! Their man approaches . . . '

A footman, dressed all in black, walked to us at such a mournful pace that he might have been about to announce that no visit was possible because the master of the house was dead. He reached the gate and spoke to us from the other side of the bars.

'May I help you?'

'We are here to see Mr Lavelle,' Jones said.

'I am afraid Mr Lavelle is not receiving visitors today,' the footman returned.

'I am Inspector Jones of Scotland Yard,' Jones replied. 'He will most certainly receive me. And if you don't open this gate in five seconds, Clayton, you'll be back in Newgate where you belong.'

The servant looked up, startled, and examined my companion more closely. 'Mr Jones!' he exclaimed in quite a different voice. 'Lord, sir, I didn't recognise you.'

'Well, I never forget a face, Clayton, and it

gives me no pleasure to see yours.' As the footman fumbled in his pocket for the keys and opened the gate, Jones turned to me and said, in a low voice, 'Six months for dog-sneaking the last time we met. It seems Mr Lavelle is none too fussy about the company he keeps.'

Clayton opened the gate and led us into the house, struggling to regain his composure with every step. 'What can you tell us of your new master?' Jones demanded.

'I can tell you nothing, sir. He is an American gentleman. He is very private.'

'I'm sure. How long have you worked for him?'

'Since January.'

'I guess he didn't ask for a reference,' I muttered.

'I will tell Mr Lavelle you are here,' Clayton said.

He left us alone in a vast, shadowy entrance hall whose walls, rising high above us, were covered with wooden panelling of the gloomiest sort. A massive staircase, uncarpeted, led up to the second floor which took the form of a galleried walkway open on every side so that we could be observed from any one of a number of upper doorways without knowing it. Even the pictures on the walls were dark and miserable — winter scenes of frozen lakes and trees bereft of leaves. Two wooden chairs had been set on either side of a fireplace but it was hard to imagine anyone wishing to sit in them, even for a moment, in this gloomy place.

Clayton returned. 'Mr Lavelle will see you in his study.'

We were shown into a room filled with books that had never been read — they had a musty, unloved look about them. As we entered, a man glared at us from behind a monstrous Jacobean desk and for a moment, I thought he was about to attack us. His appearance was that of a prizefighter even if he did not dress the part. He was completely bald with an upturned nose and very small eyes that were set deep in his face. He was wearing a boldly patterned suit that fitted him tightly and he wore a ring on almost every finger of both his hands, the gaudy stones fighting with each other. One might have been acceptable but the overall effect was tawdry and strangely unpleasant. The folds of his neck had bunched up as they sought a way to enter his collar and I knew him at once. Scotchy Lavelle. It seemed strange to be meeting him for the first time in the surroundings of a suburban house, thousands of miles from New York.

There were two seats opposite the desk and although he had given us no invitation, we took them. It signalled at least our determination to stay.

'Now what is all this?' he demanded. 'Inspector Jones of Scotland Yard? What are you doing here? What do you want? I've got nothing to say to you.' He noticed me. 'And who's he with you?'

'My name is Frederick Chase,' I replied. 'I'm with the Pinkerton Agency in New York.'

'Pinkerton's! A ragbag of bums and back-stabbers. How far do I have to go to be away from them?' He was using the coarse language of the lower Manhattan streets. 'There's no Pinkerton's over here and I won't speak to you, not in my own crib, thank you very much.' He turned to Jones. 'Scotland Yard, you say! I have no business with you either. I've done nothing wrong.'

'We are looking for an associate of yours,' Jones explained. 'A man called Clarence Devereux.'

'I don't know the name. I never heard it. He's no associate. He's nothing to me.' Lavelle's small, pugnacious eyes dared us to challenge him.

'You did not travel with him to England?'

'Didn't you just hear me? How could I travel with someone I never met?'

'Your accent tells me that you are American,' Jones tried. 'Can you tell me what brings you to England?'

'Can I tell you? Maybe I can — but I don't know why the blazes I should.' He jabbed a single finger towards us. 'All right, all right. I'm a company promoter. Nothing wrong with that! I raise capital. I offer opportunities for investment. You want shares in soap, candles, bootlaces or what have you, I'm your man. Maybe I can interest you in an investment, Mr Jones? Or you, Mr Pinkerton? A nice little gold mine in Sacramento. Or coal and iron in Vermissa. You'll get a better return than a catch-pole's salary, I can promise you.'

Lavelle was taunting us. We both knew the truth of his connection to Devereux and he was well aware of it. But with no evidence of any crime, planned or committed, there was little we could do.

Inspector Jones tried a second time. 'Yesterday I followed a young man — a child — to this house. He was fair-haired, dressed in the uniform of a telegraph boy. Did you meet with him?'

'Why would I have done that?' Lavelle sneered. 'I may have received a telegraph. I may not. I don't know. You'll have to ask Clayton.'

'I saw the boy come into the house. He did not leave.'

'Sitting there with your peeper, were you? Measuring me? Well, there's no squeakers here, telegraph or otherwise.'

'Who resides here?'

'What's it to you? Why should I tell you that? I've already said. I'm a respectable businessman. You can ask about me at the legation, why don't you? They'll vouch for me.'

'If you do not wish to assist us, Mr Lavelle, we can return here with a warrant and a dozen officers. If you are as you say you are, then you will answer my questions.'

Lavelle yawned and scratched the back of his neck. He was still scowling at us but I could see that he had weighed up his options and knew he had no choice but to give us what we demanded.

'There are five of us,' he said. 'No, six. Myself and my woman, Clayton, the cook, the maid and the kitchen boy.'

'You said there were no children here.'

'He's no child. He's nineteen. And he's a ginger.'

89

'We would still like to meet him,' I interposed. 'Where is he?'

'Where do you think you'll find a kitchen boy?' Lavelle snarled. 'He's in the kitchen.' He tapped the fingers of one hand against the desk, making the jewelled rings dance. 'I'll fetch him for you.'

'We will go to him,' I said.

'Want to nosey around, do you? Very well. But after that you can hop the twig. You have no reason to be here, I tell you, and I've had enough of the both of you.'

He rose up from behind the desk, the movement reminding me of a swimmer breaking the surface of the sea. As he revealed himself to us, he seemed to shrink in size, with the huge desk looming over him. At the same time, it seemed to me that the lurid colour and tight fit of his suit along with his surfeit of jewellery only diminished him further.

He was already moving to the door. 'This way!' he commanded.

Like supplicants who had just been interviewed for a menial position in his household, Jones and I followed. We recrossed the hall and this time we were met by a woman coming down the stairs, a great deal younger than Lavelle and, like him, dressed extravagantly, in her case in swathes of crimson silk that hugged her ample form rather too closely. Her neckline was low enough to have caused a commotion had she walked onto the streets of Boston and her arms were bare. A string of diamonds — real or paste, I could not say — hung around her neck.

90

'Who is it, Scotchy?' she asked. She had a Bronx accent. Even at a distance, I could smell soap and lavender water.

'It's no one,' Lavelle snapped, doubtless annoyed that she had betrayed him by using the name by which he was known to myself and to many law enforcers across America.

'I've been waiting for you.' She had the whining voice of a schoolgirl dragged unwillingly to class. 'You said we were going out . . . '

'Shut the potato trap and give the red rag a holiday.'

'Scotchy?'

'Just get upstairs and wait for me, Hen. I'll tell you when I'm ready for you.'

Pouting, the woman hitched up her skirts, turned and ran up the way she had come.

'Your wife?' Jones enquired.

'My convenience. What's it to you? I met her in a goosing slum and brought her with me when I travelled. This way . . . '

He led us across the hall and through a doorway into the kitchen, a cavernous room where three people were busily occupied. Clayton had laid out the silver, which he was polishing, each implement receiving the most careful attention. The ginger-haired kitchen boy, a lanky, pockmarked lad who did not resemble Perry in the least, was sitting in the scullery, peeling vegetables. A rather severe woman with grey hair and an apron was stirring a large pot on the cooking range and the whole room was filled with the smell of curry. Every surface in the kitchen had been scrubbed clean. The floor,

91

black and white tiles, was immaculate. Two large windows and a glass-panelled door looked out into the garden, providing natural light, and yet, even so, I had a sense that this was a gloomy place. As in the rest of the house, the windows were barred, the door locked. It would be easy to believe that these people were being held here against their will.

They stopped what they were doing when we came in. The kitchen boy got to his feet. Lavelle stood in the doorway, his broad shoulders almost touching the frames. 'These men want to talk to you,' he muttered, as if no further explanation was required.

'Thank you, Mr Lavelle,' I said. 'And as we know how busy you are, we will not ask you to stay. Clayton can show us out when we are done.'

He wasn't too pleased about that, but went anyway. Jones said nothing but I could see he was surprised that I had dismissed Lavelle in this manner and it occurred to me that I had behaved, perhaps, a touch impetuously. However, this was my investigation too, and as much as I looked up to Jones, I surely had a right to make my presence felt.

'My name is Inspector Athelney Jones,' my companion began. 'I am making enquiries about a man called Clarence Devereux. Does that name mean anything to you?'

None of them spoke.

'Yesterday, shortly after two o'clock in the afternoon, I saw a boy enter this house. I had followed him here from Regent Street. He was wearing a bright blue coat and a hat. I see that the path leads directly to this room. Were any of you here when he came in?'

'I was here all afternoon,' the cook mumbled. 'There was only me and Thomas and we didn't see no one.'

Thomas, the kitchen boy, nodded in agreement.

'What were you doing?' I asked.

She looked at me insolently. 'Cooking!'

'Luncheon or dinner?'

'Both!'

'And what are you cooking now?'

'Mr and Mrs Lavelle are going out today. This is for tonight. And those vegetables . . . ' she nodded at Thomas, ' . . . is for tomorrow. And then we'll start work on the day after!'

'No one came to the house,' Clayton cut in. 'If they had rung the bell, I would have answered it. And we don't get many callers here. Mr Lavelle don't encourage 'em.'

'The boy didn't come in the front way,' I said. 'He entered through the garden door.'

'That's not possible,' Clayton said. 'It's locked both sides.'

'I would like to see it.'

'To what purpose?'

'I don't think it's your business to ask questions, Clayton. It is simply to do as I say.'

'Very well, sir.'

He put down the fork that he had been polishing and lumbered over to the dresser, an oversized piece of furniture that dominated an entire wall. I had noticed a panel with a dozen

93

keys hanging beside it and he carefully selected one, then used it to open the kitchen door, turning it in yet another of the complicated locks that lent themselves to the security of the house. The three of us — Jones, Clayton and myself — stepped into the garden. A curving path led to the wooden gate at the bottom with lawns and flowerbeds on either side. I suspected these had been planted by the former residents, for they had once been neat and symmetrical but were already in a state of some neglect. I led the way, with Clayton next to me and Jones limping behind. In this way we came to the door that we had observed from outside and saw that, as well as the Chubb lock, there was a metal hasp with a second lock on the inside, securing the door to the frame. It would have been very difficult to scale the wall, which was topped with sharp spikes and which would, furthermore, be in full sight of the house. Nor could anybody have jumped down. They would certainly have left footmarks in the lawn.

'Do you have the key to this lock?' Jones asked, indicating the metal hasp.

'I have it in the house,' Clayton replied. 'But this gate is never used, Mr Jones, despite what you and this other gentleman may say. We're very careful in this house. Nobody comes in except through the front door and the keys are themselves kept in a safe place.' He paused. 'Do you want me to open it?'

'Two locks — one inside, one out. Both of them, I would have said, added recently. What is it your employer fears?' I asked.

'Mr Lavelle does not discuss his affairs with me.' Clayton sneered at me. 'Have you seen enough?' It struck me that his manner was deliberately impertinent. Although he had encountered Athelney Jones in his former life, he had no fear of me.

'I will not tell you what I have or have not seen,' I returned. But he was right. There was no reason to stay any longer.

We went back to the kitchen. Once again, I was the first to enter and I saw that the cook and the kitchen boy had returned to their work as if they had forgotten we had called. Thomas was in the scullery and the old woman had joined him, selecting onions from a shelf one at a time as if she suspected that they might be counterfeit. Finally Jones arrived and the footman once more locked the door behind him and returned the key to its place. It was clear that there was nothing more to be said. We could perhaps have demanded to be allowed to search the house for the missing telegraph boy but what would that achieve? A place like this would have a hundred hiding places and possibly secret panels too. Jones nodded at Clayton and we left.

'I do not think the boy came to the house,' I said as we stood, once more, on the other side of the front gate.

'Why do you believe that?'

'I searched around the garden door. There was no sign of any footprints, man or boy. And he could not have opened the door from the outside as there was a metal hasp within.'

'I saw it myself, Chase. And I agree that, from

the evidence, it would seem impossible for the boy to have entered, unless, of course, the hasp had been unfastened in expectation of his arrival. And yet consider this. I followed him and, unwittingly, he brought me directly to the house of Scotchy Lavelle, a man familiar to you and a known associate of Clarence Devereux. This must have been where he came unless Devereux himself is living somewhere nearby and, as I told you, it is impossible that he went elsewhere. When the evidence leads to only one possible conclusion, the truth of it, no matter how unlikely, cannot be ignored. I believe the boy entered the house and I believe he may still be there.'

'Then what are we to do?'

'We must seek the proper authority and return to make a full search.'

'If the boy knows we are looking for him, he will leave.'

'Maybe so, but I would like to speak to that woman of Lavelle's. Henrietta — was that her name? She may be more nervous of the police than he. As for Clayton, he may be too afraid to talk for the moment, but I will make him see sense. Trust me, Chase. There will be something in the house that will direct us along the next step of the way.'

'To Clarence Devereux!'

'Precisely. If the two men are in communication with one another, which they must be, we will find the link.'

We did return, as it happened, the very next day — but not to make the search that Jones anticipated. For by the time the sun had risen once again over Highgate Hill, Bladeston House would have become the scene of a peculiarly horrible and utterly baffling crime.

7

Blood and Shadows

It was the maid who discovered the bodies and who awoke the neighbourhood with her screams the next morning. Contrary to what her employer had told us, Miss Mary Stagg did not live in the house and it was for that simple reason that she did not die there. Mary shared a small cottage with her sister, who was also in service, in Highgate Village, the two of them having inherited it from their parents. She had not been at Bladeston House when we were there — it happened to be her day off and she and her sister had gone shopping. She had presented herself the following morning, just as the sun was rising, to clear the hearths and to help prepare the breakfast and had been puzzled to find both the front gate and the front door open. Such an unusual lapse of security should have warned her that something was seriously amiss but she had continued forward, doubtless whistling a tune, only to encounter a scene of horror she would remember to the end of her days.

Even I had to steel myself as I climbed down from the barouche which had been sent to collect me. Athelney Jones was waiting at the door and one look at his face — pale and disgusted — warned me that this was a scene of horror which he, with all his experience, had never encountered before.

'What snakepit have we uncovered, Chase?' he demanded, when he saw me. 'To think that you and I were here only yesterday. Was it our visit that in some way, unwittingly, led to this bloodbath?'

'Lavelle . . . ?' I asked.

'All of them! Clayton, the ginger-haired boy, the cook, the mistress . . . they have all been murdered.'

'How?'

'You will see. Four of them died in their beds. Maybe they should be grateful. But Lavelle . . . ' He drew a breath. 'This is as bad as Swallow Gardens or Pinchin Street — the very worst of the worst.'

Together, we went into the house. There were seven or eight police officers present, creeping slowly and silently in the shadows as if they might somehow wish themselves away. The hall, which had seemed dark when I first entered, had become significantly darker and there was the heavy smell of the butcher's shop in the air. I became aware of the buzzing of flies and at the same time saw what might have been a thick pool of tar on the floor.

'Good God!' I exclaimed and brought my hand to my eyes, half covering them whilst unable to avoid staring at the scene that presented itself to me.

Scotchy Lavelle was sitting in one of the heavy wooden chairs that I had noticed the day before and which had been dragged forward expressly for this purpose. He was dressed in a silk nightshirt which reached to his ankles. His feet were bare. He had been positioned so that he faced a mirror. Whoever had done this had wanted him to see what was going to happen.

He had not been tied into place. He had been nailed there. Jagged squares of metal protruded from the backs of his broken hands which even in death still clasped the arms of the chair as if determined not to let go. The hammer that had been used for this evil deed lay in front of the fireplace and there was a china vase, lying on its side. Nearby, I noticed two bright ribbons which must have been brought down from the bedroom and which were also strewn on the floor.

Scotchy Lavelle's throat had been cut cleanly and viciously in a manner that could not help but remind me of the surgeon's knife that Perry had so cheerfully used to threaten me in the Café Royal. I wondered if Jones had already leapt to the same, unavoidable conclusion. This horrific murder could have been committed by a child . . . though not one acting alone. It would have taken at least two people to drag Lavelle into place. And what of the rest of the household?

'They were murdered in their sleep,' Jones muttered, as if looking into my mind. 'The cook, the kitchen boy, the woman whose name was, perhaps, Henrietta. There is not a mark of any struggle on them. Clayton slept in the basement. He has been stabbed through the heart.'

'But did none of them wake up?' I asked. 'Are you really telling me they heard nothing?'

'I believe they were drugged.'

100

I absorbed this information and even as I spoke I knew Jones was ahead of me. 'The curry!' I exclaimed. 'You remember, Jones? I asked the woman what she was cooking and she said that it was for dinner. They must have all eaten it, and whoever came here . . . it would have been easy enough to add some powerful drug, maybe powdered opium. The curry would have disguised the taste.'

'But they would have had to reach the kitchen first,' Jones muttered.

'We should examine the door.'

We both circled the body, keeping our distance, for the blood and the shadows looked very much like one another and we had to be careful where we placed our feet. It was only when we had reached the relative sanctuary of the kitchen that we breathed again. For a second time I found myself examining the spotless cooking range, the tiled floor, the open door of the scullery with the shelves neatly stacked. In the midst of all this, the cooking pot that had held the curry sat dark and empty, like a guilty secret. The one surviving maid was in this room, hunched up in a chair and weeping into her apron, watched over by a uniformed police constable.

'This is bad,' I said. 'This is very bad.'

'But who would do such a thing and why? That must be our first line of investigation.' I could see that Jones, knocked off his feet by the ruthlessness of the murders, was struggling to regain the composure that had been so much part of his nature when we were together in

101

Meiringen. 'We know that Scott Lavelle — or Scotchy Lavelle — was part of a gang headed by Clarence Devereux.'

'Of that there can be no doubt,' I said.

'He arranges to meet with Professor James Moriarty and to that end he sends a boy, Perry, to the Café Royal. A man pretending to be Moriarty is there but the impersonation fails. The boy knows you are not who you say you are . . .'

' . . . because of the ravens in the tower.'

'So that is the end of the matter. The boy makes the long journey to Highgate and reports back to the people who sent him. There will be no meeting. Perhaps Moriarty is dead after all. That is what these people are led to believe.'

'And then we appear.'

'Yes, detectives from two separate nations. We know about the boy. We ask questions — but the truth of it is, Chase, we make little progress. I imagine Lavelle was smiling when we left.'

'He's not doing so now,' I said, although I couldn't help but think of the great red gash in his throat. It had the shape of a demonic smile.

'Why has he been killed? Why now? But here is our first clue, our first indication of what may have taken place. The door is unlocked.'

Athelney Jones was right. The door that led into the garden, that we had seen Clayton fasten and unfasten with a key from beside the dresser, was open. He turned the handle and, grateful for the fresh air, I followed him out onto the ill-trimmed lawn that we had crossed only the day before.

Together we walked down to the wall and saw at once that the far door was also open. The Chubb had been unlocked on the outside. A circular hole had been drilled through the wood, positioned exactly to reveal the inner lock. This had then been cut through and the metal hasp removed. Jones inspected the handiwork.

'The Chubb appears undamaged,' he said. 'If it was picked, then our intruders have shown skills beyond those of any common or garden burglar — not that such a creature was involved, of that we can be sure. It is possible that they were able to lay their hands on a duplicate key. We will see. The other lock, the one holding the hasp, is of particular interest. You will see that they have cut a hole in the door, perhaps using a centre bit with two or three blades. It would have made very little noise. But see where they have placed it!'

'The hole is level with the lock,' I said.

'Exactly. It has been measured to the inch. A second drill has then been used to cut through the casing, exposing the wards. It is a professional job — but it would not have been possible if the intruders had not stood where we are now and made careful note of the exact position of the lock.'

'They could have been helped by someone inside the house.'

'Everyone inside the house is dead, apart from the maid. I am more inclined to think they acted on their own.'

'You speak of intruders, Inspector Jones. You are certain there was more than one?'

'Undoubtedly. There are tracks.' He gestured with his walking stick and, looking down, I was able to make out two sets of footprints, side by side, heading away from the wall and approaching the house. 'A man and a boy,' he continued. 'You can see that the boy is carefree. He almost trips along. The man has left a deeper impression. He is tall, at least six feet in height, and he was wearing unusual boots. You see the square toe? He held back while the boy raced ahead.'

'The boy had been here before.'

'It is true that his stride could suggest a familiarity with his surroundings. Note also that he follows the most direct route to the kitchen. There was a moon, I believe, last night, but he had no fear of being seen.'

'He knew that the household was asleep.'

'Drugged and sound asleep. There still remains the question of how he entered the house, but my guess is that he climbed a drainpipe and entered by the second floor.' Athelney Jones unfolded the binoculars on his walking stick and used them to examine the upper part of the building. There was indeed a slender drainpipe beside the kitchen door which would never have supported the weight of an adult — perhaps it was for this reason that Lavelle had never considered it as a breach in his defences. But for a child, it would have been a different matter entirely, and once he had reached the first floor . . .

'The windows are snibbed,' Jones continued. 'It would be easy enough to slide a knife inside the frame. He would then have come down the stairs and opened the door to allow his accomplice in.'

'The boy of whom we speak . . . it must be the same,' I said.

'Perry? Undoubtedly.' Athelney Jones lowered the walking stick. 'I would not normally associate a child with crimes as gruesome as these, but I saw him with you. I saw the weapon he carried. He came here. I followed him myself. He entered through the garden door, came into the kitchen and saw the curry being prepared. It must have been then that he made his preparations, intending to return at night with his colleague. But there still remains the one question. Why did Lavelle lie to us? Why did they all pretend the boy had not been here? They had sent him to meet us. There could be no other reason for him to have appeared in the Café Royal. But when he returned, alone, what then occurred?'

'And why, if he was working for Lavelle, did he turn on his master and assist in his murder?'

'I hoped you might shed some light on that. Your work in America . . .'

'I can only repeat what I have already told you, Inspector. The American criminal has no discrimination and no sense of loyalty. Until Clarence Devereux came onto the scene, he worked in isolation, with no organisation or structure. Even afterwards, he remained vicious, treacherous and unpredictable. Crime in New York was often as bloody as this and as incomprehensible. Brothers could fall out over the toss of a coin and one of them — both of them — might end up dead. Sisters too. Do you see now? I was trying to warn you. The events here at Bladeston House are only the start, the first warning signs of the poison that has entered the bloodstream of your country. Maybe Devereux was responsible. Maybe our visit here — for you can be sure that he will have received the intelligence — was enough to persuade him that Lavelle had to be silenced. I don't know. It all makes me sick. But I fear a great deal more blood may be shed before we arrive at the truth.'

There was nothing more to be gained by lingering in the garden and reluctantly we re-entered the charnel house, as it had now become. The one survivor of the household, Mary Stagg, was still in the kitchen but she had little to tell us.

'I used to work for Mr and Mrs Bladeston,' she explained, between sobs. 'And I'll be honest with you, gentlemen. I was much happier then. They were a good family. You knew where you were with them. But then Mr Bladeston died and they said they would be putting up the house for rent at the start of the year and Mrs Bladeston persuaded me to stay. She said it would help her, knowing the place was being looked after.

'But I didn't like the American gentleman from the start. He had a wicked temper and you should have heard his language! It wasn't the sort of words a gentleman would use. The cook was the first to go. She wasn't having any of it. And then Mr Sykes decided he'd had enough and he was replaced by Mr Clayton and I didn't very much like him either. And I was saying to

Annie — that's my sister, sir — that I was thinking of handing in my notice too. And now this!'

'Was the garden gate always kept locked?' Jones asked, once the maid had recovered her composure.

'Always, sir. Every gate, every window. The moment Mr Lavelle came here, he was very particular about it. Everything had to be locked and shut down and all the keys in their right place. Nobody ever came to the door, not even the delivery boy, unless Mr Clayton was there to greet them. We used to have such dinners and parties in Mr Bladeston's time. The house was a happy place then. But in just a few months, Mr Lavelle turned it into a sort of prison — with him as the main prisoner for he seldom went out.'

'Mrs Lavelle? Did you have any dealings with her?'

The maid flinched, and despite everything she could not conceal the look of distaste that crept across her face. At that moment I understood how difficult her position must have been since Scotchy and his entourage had arrived.

'Begging your pardon, sir, but I'm not sure she was Mrs Lavelle. We just called her 'madam' and a right proper madam she was too. Nothing was ever right for her — but she did what Mr Lavelle told her. She never went out unless he said.'

'There were no visitors?'

'Two gentlemen used to come from time to time. I didn't see very much of them. They were tall, well-built with dark hair and one of them

107

with a moustache. Otherwise, they were as alike as peas in a pod. Brothers, for sure.'

'Leland and Edgar Mortlake,' I muttered.

'Did you ever hear of a man called Clarence Devereux?' Jones asked.

'No, sir, but there was another man they talked about all the time, not that he ever came here, and when they spoke of him, they did so in a low voice. I heard his name once and I never forgot it.' The maid paused, twisting her handkerchief in her hands. 'I was passing the study and Mr Lavelle was talking to Mr Clayton . . . at least, I think it was he. I couldn't see and it wasn't my place to eavesdrop. But they were deep in conversation. And that was when I heard them. 'We must always be prepared for Moriarty.' That's what Mr Lavelle said. I don't know why it made such an impression on me — only later on, Mr Clayton made a joke of it. 'You shouldn't do that, Mary,' he said to me once, when I left the door open, 'or Professor Moriarty will get you.' It's a horrible name. I sometimes used to think of it when I was trying to get to sleep and it would turn over and over in my head. It seemed the whole house was afraid of this Moriarty, and with good reason, for you can see what's happened now!'

There was nothing more that Mary Stagg could tell us and, after warning her not to reveal what had taken place to anyone, Athelney Jones sent her home in the company of a constable. The good woman clearly could not wait to get out of the house and I rather doubted she would ever return.

108

'Could Moriarty have done this?' I asked.

'Moriarty is dead.'

'He may have had associates, fellow criminals, members of his gang. You saw the way that Lavelle was killed, Inspector Jones. The way I see it, it's nothing less than a message, written in blood, perhaps sent as a warning.'

Jones thought for a moment. 'You told me that Moriarty and Devereux planned to meet, to create a criminal association . . .'

'That's right.'

'But they never did meet. We know that from the coded message that we found in Meiringen. As far as we can tell, they had no business together, so why would one wish to kill the other?'

'Perhaps Devereux had something to do with what happened at the Reichenbach Falls.'

Jones shook his head wearily. 'At the moment, nothing makes sense. I need time to reflect and to clear my thoughts. But that will not happen here. For now, we must search the house and see what secrets, if any, the various rooms may reveal.'

And so we set about our grim task — for it was as if we were exploring a catacomb. Each door opened upon another corpse. We started with the kitchen boy, Thomas, who had closed his eyes one last time in a bare, shabby room beside the scullery. The sight of him lying there, still dressed in the clothes he had worn to work, his bare feet resting on the sheet, clearly affected Jones, and I was reminded that he had a child who might only be a few years younger than this young victim. Thomas had been strangled. The rope was still around his neck. Half a dozen steps led down to a basement room where Clayton had lived and died. A carving knife, perhaps taken from the kitchen, had been plunged into his heart and remained there, almost seeming to pin him, like an insect in a laboratory, to the bed. With heavy hearts, we made our way up to the attic room where the cook — we now knew her name to be Mrs Winters — lay scowling in death as she had in life. She too had been strangled.

'Why did they all have to die?' I asked. 'They may have worked for Lavelle but surely they were blameless.'

'Their assailants could not risk any of them waking up,' Jones muttered. 'And with Lavelle dead, they would have had no reason to hold back what they knew. This way, they are prevented from speaking to us.'

'The boy and the woman were strangled but Clayton was stabbed.'

'He was the strongest of the three of them, and although he had been drugged, he would have been the most likely to wake up. The killers were taking no chances. With him, they used a knife.'

I turned away. I had already seen enough. 'Where next?' I asked.

'The bedroom.'

The flame-haired woman whom Lavelle had addressed as 'Hen' lay sprawling on a goose-feather mattress, wearing a nightdress of pink cambric with ruffles around her neck and sleeves. Death seemed to have aged her ten years. Her left arm was flung out, reaching towards the man who had lain beside her, as if he could still bring her comfort.

'She has been smothered,' Jones said.

'How can you tell?'

'There are lipstick marks on the pillow. That was the murder weapon. And you can see also the bruising around the nose and mouth, where it was held in place.'

'Dear God in Heaven,' I muttered. I looked at the empty space where the bed covers had been thrown back. 'And what of Lavelle?'

'He is the reason for all this.'

We made a quick search of the bedroom but it revealed little. 'Hen' had a fondness for cheap jewellery and expensive dresses, the closets bursting with silk and taffeta. Her bathroom contained more perfumes and toiletries than the entire first floor of Lord & Taylor on Broadway — or so I remarked to Jones. But the truth was that both of us knew that we were only delaying the inevitable and, with a heavy heart, we made our way back downstairs.

Scotchy Lavelle sat waiting for us, a few police officers still lingering around him, wishing they could be anywhere but here. I watched as Jones examined the body, leaning forward on his stick, being careful to keep his distance. I remembered the anger and the hostility with which we had been greeted only the day before. 'Want to nosey around, do you?' Had Scotchy been more obliging, might he have escaped this fate?

'He was carried here, half-conscious,' Jones muttered. 'There are many indications of what

111

took place. First, the chair was moved and he was tied down.'

'The ribbons!'

'There is no other reason for them to be here. The killers must have brought them down from the bedroom for that express purpose. They tied Lavelle to the chair and then, having assured themselves that everything was as they wanted, they dashed water into his face to wake him up. It is hard to see with so much blood but I would have said the collar and sleeves of his nightshirt are damp and anyway we have, as evidence, the upturned vase which was brought in from the kitchen. I saw it there yesterday.'

'And what then?'

'Lavelle awakens. I have no doubt that he recognised his two assailants. Certainly the boy he must have met before.' Jones stopped himself. 'But I am wrong to describe it to you in this way. I am sure you have observed every detail for yourself.'

'Observed, yes,' I replied. 'But I don't have quite your facility for completing the picture, Inspector. Pray, continue.'

'Very well. Lavelle is tied down and helpless. Although he may not know it, his entire household has been killed. And it is now that his own ordeal begins. The man and the boy require information. They begin to torture him.'

'They nail his hands to the chair.'

'They do more than that. I cannot bring myself to examine it too closely but I would say that they used the same hammer to break his knee. Look at the way the fabric of his nightshirt lies. They have also smashed the heel of his left foot.'

'It is disgusting. It's horrific. What was it, I wonder, that they wished to know?'

'Matters relating to the organisation for which he worked.'

'And did he talk?'

Jones considered. 'It is almost impossible to tell but we must assume he did. Had he kept silent, his injuries would surely have been even more extensive.'

'And still they killed him.'

'I would imagine that death would have come as a relief.' Jones sighed. 'I have never encountered a crime like this in England. The Whitechapel Murders, which came straight to mind when I arrived, were barbaric and vile. But even they lacked the cruelty, the cold-blooded calculation that we have witnessed here.'

'Where next?'

'The study. That was where Lavelle greeted us and, if he had letters or documents of any interest, we will probably find them there.'

It was to that room that we returned. The curtains had been drawn back allowing some light from the front to come through but it still seemed dark and abandoned without its owner, as if it belonged to a house that had been deserted long ago. Only one day before, the desk and the chair had been the stage from which our lead actor had played his part. Now they were useless and the unread books seemed more irrelevant than ever. Still, we went through the drawers. We examined the shelves. Jones was quite certain that Scotchy Lavelle would have left something of value behind.

I could have told him otherwise. I knew that any organisation run by a man like Clarence Devereux would take no chances when it came to its own protection. There would be no letters lying conveniently in wastepaper baskets, no addresses scribbled carelessly on the backs of envelopes. This whole house had been designed specifically to guard its own secrets and to keep the world at bay. Lavelle had described himself as a company promoter but there was not a scrap of evidence in the room to support this. He was an invisible man with no background and no foreground, and plans, strategies and conspiracies he would have taken with him to the grave.

Athelney Jones was struggling to conceal his disappointment. All the papers we found were blank. There was a cheque book with no entries, a handful of receipts for trifling domestic matters, some letters of credit and promissory notes that seemed entirely respectable, an invitation to a party at the American legation 'celebrating American and British business enterprise'. It was only when he was thumbing through Lavelle's diary, turning one empty page after another, that he suddenly stopped and drew my attention to a single word and a figure, written in capital letters and encircled.

HORNER 13

'What do you make of that?' he demanded.

'Horner?' I considered. 'Could it be referring

114

to Perry? He was about thirteen.'

'I think he was older.' Jones reached into the back of the drawer and found something there. When he held out his hand, I saw that he was holding a bar of shaving soap, brand new, still wrapped in the paper. 'It seems a strange place to keep such a thing,' he remarked.

'Do you think it has some significance?'

'Perhaps. But I cannot see what.'

'There is nothing,' I said. 'There is nothing here for us. I begin to regret that we ever found this house. It's shrouded in mystery and death and leads us nowhere.'

'Do not give up hope,' Jones replied. 'Our path may be a murky one but our enemy has shown himself. The battle lines are at least engaged.'

He had no sooner spoken than we were interrupted by a commotion from the hall. Someone had come in. The police officers were trying to prevent them moving forward. There were voices raised in anger and, among them, an accent that I recognised as American.

Jones and I hurried out of the study to find a slim, rather languid man with black hair plastered down in an oily wave across his forehead, small eyes and a well cultivated moustache drooping over his lip. If Scotchy Lavelle had exuded violence, this man presented more a sense of considered menace. He would kill you — but he would think about it first. The many years he had spent in prison had left their mark on him, for his skin was unnaturally pale and dead-looking. It was made worse by the fact that he was dressed entirely in black — a tight-fitting frock coat and patent leather shoes — and held a walking stick, also black, which he was brandishing almost like a weapon, holding back the police officers who had rounded on him, pressing him back. He had not come alone. Three young men had entered the house and stood surrounding him, hooligan boys from the look of them, aged about twenty with pale faces, ragged clothes, sticks and heavy boots.

They had all seen what had happened to Scotchy Lavelle. How could they have avoided it? The man was staring at the corpse with horror but also with disgust, as if it were a personal insult that such a thing could be permitted.

'What the devil has happened here?' he was demanding. He looked round as Jones emerged from the study. 'Who are you?'

'My name is Athelney Jones. I am a detective from Scotland Yard.'

'A detective! Well, that's very helpful. A little bit late, don't you think? Do you know who did this?' It was his accent I had heard. Less profane than Lavelle's, it was nonetheless clear that he too had come from New York.

'I arrived only a short while ago,' Jones replied. 'You know this man?'

'I knew him. Yes.'

'And who are you?'

'I'm not sure I'm minded to give you my name.'

'You will not leave this house until you do, sir.' Athelney Jones had drawn himself up to his full height, propping himself on his walking stick. He was looking at the American, eye to eye. 'I am a

British police officer,' he continued. 'You have entered the scene of a violent and inexplicable murder. If you have any information, it is your duty to share it with me and if you refuse, I promise you will find yourself spending the night in Newgate — you and the hoodlums with whom you surround yourself.'

'I know who he is,' I said. 'His name is Edgar Mortlake.'

Mortlake turned his little black eyes on me. 'You know me,' he said, 'but we haven't met.' He sniffed the air. 'Pinkerton's?'

'How did you guess?'

'I'd know that smell anywhere. New York? Chicago? Or maybe Philly? Never mind. A little far away from home either way, aren't you, boy?' The American smiled with a sense of confidence and self-control that was positively chilling. He seemed to be unaware of the smell of blood and the sight of the broken and mutilated corpse sitting in the same room just inches from him.

'And what business brings you here?' Jones demanded.

'My own business.' Mortlake sneered at him. 'And certainly none of yours.'

Jones turned to the nearest police constable, who had been watching this exchange with increasing alarm.

'I want you to arrest this man,' he said. 'The charge is obstruction. I'll have him up before the magistrate this very day.' The constable hesitated. 'Do your duty,' Jones said.

I will never forget that moment. There were Jones and Mortlake, standing face to face, surrounded by perhaps half a dozen police officers but with the hooligan boys in opposition. It was as if a war were about to break out. And in the middle of it all, Scotchy Lavelle sat silently, the unwitting cause of all this and yet, for the moment, almost forgotten.

It was Mortlake who backed down. 'There's no need for this,' he said, forcing the faintest shadow of a smile to his death's-head face. 'Why should I wish to interfere with the British police?' He lifted his cane, gesturing at the corpse. 'Scotchy and I were in business together.'

'He said he was a company promoter.'

'Is that what he said? Well, he was many things. He invested in a little club I have in Mayfair. You could say we were co-founders.'

'Would that be the Bostonian?' I asked. I recalled the name. It had been where Jonathan Pilgrim had stayed when he came to the country.

I had taken Mortlake by surprise, although he tried not to show it. 'That's the one,' he exclaimed. 'I see you've been busy, Pinkerton. Or are you a member? We have a lot of American visitors. But then, I doubt you could afford us.'

I ignored him. 'Is Clarence Devereux another partner in this little enterprise?'

'I don't know any Clarence Devereux.'

'I believe you do.'

'You're mistaken.'

I'd had enough. 'I know who you are, Edgar Mortlake,' I said. 'I have seen your record sheet. Bank burglary. Safe-cracking. A year in the Tombs for armed assault. And that was only the most recent of your convictions.'

118

'You should be careful how you speak to me!' Mortlake took a couple of paces towards me and his entourage circled him nervously, wondering what he was going to do. 'That was all in the past,' he snarled. 'I'm in England now . . . an American citizen with a respectable enterprise, and it would seem that your job is to protect me, not to harass me.' He nodded at the dead man. 'A duty you have signally failed to carry out where my late partner was concerned. Where's the woman?'

'If you are referring to Henrietta, she is upstairs,' Jones said. 'She was also killed.'

'And the rest of them?'

'The entire household has been murdered.'

Mortlake seemed to be thrown for the first time. He took one last look at the blood and his lip curled in disgust. 'There is nothing for me here,' he said. 'I will leave the two of you gentlemen to sniff around.'

Before anyone could stop him, he had swept out again, as brazenly as he had come in. The three hooligan boys closed in on him and I saw that their primary concern was to protect him, to provide a living wall between him and his enemies in the outside world.

'Edgar Mortlake,' I said. 'The gang is making itself known.'

'And that may be helpful to us.' Jones glanced at the open door.

Mortlake had reached the bottom of the garden and passed through the gate. Even as we watched, he climbed into the carriage that was waiting for him, followed by his three protectors, and with the cracking of a whip he was off, back towards Highgate Hill. It occurred to me that if the murder of Scotchy Lavelle and his household had been designed to send a message then it was one that had most definitely been received.

8

Scotland Yard

If Hexam's had anything to recommend it — and the list was not a long one — it was its close proximity to the centre of London. The breakfast room was once again empty and, after finishing my meal, I left the maid and the Boots behind me and set off, intending to follow the Embankment, something that Jones had recommended the day before.

The Thames was glistening on the other side of a long row of trees that graced the boulevard. There was a fresh spring breeze blowing and as I stepped out of the hotel, a black-hulled river steam ship chuffed past on its way to the Port of London. I stopped and watched it pass and it was at that moment that I had the strange feeling that I was being watched. It was still early and there were few people around: a woman, pushing a pram, a man in a bowler hat walking with a dog. I turned and looked back at the hotel. And it was then that I saw him, standing behind a window on the second floor, gazing out into the street. It took me only a second to work out that he occupied the room next to mine. This was the man whom I had heard coughing throughout the night. He was too far away — and the windows were too grimy — for me to see him clearly. He had dark hair and wore dark clothes. He was almost unnaturally still. It might have been my imagination but I would have said his eyes were fixed on me. Then he reached out with one hand and drew the curtain across. I tried to put him out of my mind and continued on my way. But I could no longer enjoy the walk as much as I had hoped. I was uneasy without knowing why.

Another fifteen minutes brought me to my destination. Scotland Yard, as it was already known (although in fact it was situated in Whitehall Place), was an impressive building that straddled the ground between Victoria Embankment and Westminster. It was also a pretty ugly one, or so it seemed to me as I crossed the boulevard and looked for the main entrance. It was as if the architect had changed his mind after construction had begun. Two floors of austere granite suddenly yielded to red and white brickwork, ornate casements and Flemish-style tourelles, giving the impression of two quite separate buildings squashed one on top of the other. There was something of a prison about the place too. Its four wings enclosed a courtyard barely touched by the sun. The inmates of Newgate would probably enjoy their exercise more than the unfortunate police officials penned up here.

Athelney Jones was waiting for me and raised a hand in greeting. 'You got my message! Excellent. The meeting is to start very soon. It is quite remarkable. In all my time here, I would say it is almost unique. No fewer than fourteen of the most senior detective inspectors have come together in response to the Highgate murders. We won't have it, Chase. It is simply beyond the pale.'

'And I am to be permitted to attend?'

'It wasn't easy. I won't pretend otherwise. Lestrade was against it — and Gregson too. I told you when we first met, there are many here who believe we should have no dealings with a commercial detective agency such as Pinkerton's. In my view, it is foolish, this lack of co-operation when we have the same aims. Still, this time I have been able to persuade them of the importance of your presence. Come — we should go in.'

We climbed a set of wide steps and entered a hall where several uniformed constables stood behind tall desks, examining the letters of introduction and passports of those who wished to enter. Jones had already prepared the way for me and together we fought our way up a crowded staircase with uniformed men, clerks and messengers pushing past each other in both directions.

'The building's already too small for us,' he complained. 'And we have barely been here a year! They found a murdered woman in the basement during the construction.'

'Who killed her?'

'We don't know. No one has any idea who she was or how she came to be there. Do you not find it strange, Chase, that the finest police force in Europe should have chosen to locate itself at the scene of an unsolved crime?' We reached the third floor and passed a series of doors, evenly spaced. Jones nodded as we passed one of them.

'My office. The best rooms have a view over the river.'

'And yours?'

'I look into the quadrangle.' He smiled. 'Perhaps when you and I get to the end of this business, they'll think to move me. At least I am close to the records office and the telegraph room!'

We had passed an open door and, sure enough, there were about a dozen men dressed in dark suits, sitting at tables or along a high counter, crouched over their telegraph sets with papers and printed tape all around them.

'How quickly can you contact America?' I asked.

'The actual message can be sent in a matter of minutes,' Jones replied. 'The printing takes a while longer and if there is too much traffic it can be days. Do you wish to communicate with your office?'

'I should send them a report,' I said. 'They've heard nothing from me since I left.'

'In truth, you'd do better to apply to the Central Telegraph Office in Newgate Street. You may find them more obliging.'

We continued through a set of doors and into a large, airless room, the windows recessed in such a way that they seemed to hold back the light. A vast table, curved at both ends, took up all the available space and seemed to have been fashioned not so much to bring people together as to keep them apart. I had never seen such a great expanse of polished wood. There were already nine or ten men in the room, one or two smoking pipes, talking amongst themselves in low voices. Their ages ranged, I would have said, from about twenty-five to about fifty. Their clothes were by no means uniform. Although the majority were smartly dressed in frock coats, one man wore a tweed suit while another presented himself in the unusual attire of a green pea-jacket and cravat.

It was this man who first saw us as we came in and strode hastily towards us as if about to make an arrest. My first impression was that it would be hard to imagine him as anything other than a police officer. He was lean and businesslike with dark, inquisitive eyes that examined me as if I — and everyone else he met — must surely have something to hide. His voice, when he spoke, had an edge to it that was almost deliberately unfriendly.

'Well, well, Jones,' he exclaimed. 'I take it this is the gentleman of whom you spoke.'

'I am Frederick Chase,' I said, extending a hand.

He shook it briefly. 'Lestrade,' he said and his eyes glinted. 'I would welcome you to our little gathering, Mr Chase, but I'm not sure welcome is the right word. These are queer times. This business at Bladeston House . . . very, very bad. I am not sure what it portends.'

'I am here to give you any help I can,' I said, heartily.

'And who is it that most needs help, I wonder? Well, we shall see.'

Several more inspectors had entered the room and finally the door was closed. Jones gestured at me to sit next to him. 'Say nothing for a while,' he said, quietly. 'And watch out for Lestrade and Gregson.'

'Why?'

'You cannot agree with one without antagonising the other. Youghal over there is a good man but he is still finding his feet. And next to him . . . ' He glanced at a man with a high-domed forehead and intense eyes who was sitting at the head of the table. Although he was not one of the most physically impressive men in the room, there was still something about him that suggested great inner strength. 'Alec MacDonald. I believe him to have the best brain in the business and if anyone can steer this enquiry in the right direction, it is he.'

A large, breathless man lowered himself into the seat on the other side of me. He was wearing a frogged jacket which was stretched tight across his chest. 'Bradstreet,' he muttered.

'Frederick Chase.'

'Delighted.' He took out an empty pipe and tapped it on the table in front of him.

Inspector Lestrade began the meeting with a natural authority that seemed to outrank the others in the room. 'Gentlemen,' he said. 'Before we get down to the very serious business that brings us here today, it's fitting that we pay our respects to a good friend and colleague whom we have recently lost. I refer, of course, to Mr Sherlock Holmes, who was known to many of us here and, by reputation, to the public at large. He helped me in no small way on one or two occasions, I will admit, starting with that business at Lauriston Gardens some years ago. It is true that he had a queer way about him, spinning those fine theories of his like gossamer out of thin air — and although some of it may have been no more than guesswork, none of us here would deny that he was often successful and I'm sure we'll all miss him following his unfortunate demise at the Reichenbach Falls.'

'Is there no chance that he could have survived?' The speaker was young and smartly dressed, about halfway down the table. 'After all, his body has never been found.'

'That much is true, Forrester,' Lestrade agreed. 'But we have all read the letter.'

'I was at that dreadful place,' Jones said. 'If he fought Moriarty and fell, I am afraid there is very little chance that he could have been saved.'

Lestrade shook his head solemnly. 'I'll admit that I've been wrong about one or two things in the past,' he said. 'Particularly where Sherlock Holmes was concerned. But this time I have looked at the evidence and I can tell you without any doubt at all that he is dead. I would stake my reputation on it.'

'We should not pretend that the loss of Sherlock Holmes is anything short of a catastrophe,' the man sitting opposite me said. He was tall with fair hair and as he spoke, Jones whispered to me, 'Gregson.' He continued: 'You mentioned the Lauriston Gardens affair, Lestrade. Without Holmes, it would have gone nowhere. Why, you were about to search the whole of London for a girl called Rachel when in fact it was *Rache*, the German for revenge, that the victim had left as a final clue.' There were quite a few smiles around the table at that and one or two of the detectives laughed out loud.

'There is one silver lining to the cloud,' Inspector Youghal said. 'At least we'll no longer find ourselves being caricatured by his associate, Dr Watson. I was of the view that his scribblings did our reputations no good at all.'

'Holmes was a damned odd fellow,' a fifth man exclaimed. As he spoke, he rubbed his eyeglass between finger and thumb as if he were adjusting it to better see the others in the room. 'I worked with him, you know, on that business with the missing horse. Silver Blaze. A very strange individual. Sherlock Holmes, not the horse. He had a habit of speaking in riddles. Dogs that bark in the night, indeed! I admired him. I liked him. But I'm not at all sure I will miss him.'

'I was always suspicious of his methods,' Forrester concurred. 'He made it all sound easy enough and we took him at his word. But is it really possible to tell a man's age from his handwriting? Or his height from the length of his stride? Much of what he said was unsound, unscientific and occasionally preposterous. We believed him because he got results, but it was not a sound platform for modern detective work.'

'He made fools of all of us,' exclaimed yet another inspector. 'It's true that I also benefited on one occasion from his expertise. But is it not the case, perhaps, that we were becoming too dependent on Mr Holmes? Did we ever solve anything without him?' He turned to the colleagues on his left and right. 'As hard as it is and as ungrateful as it may sound, perhaps we should embrace his going as an opportunity for us to achieve results on our own two feet.'

'Well said, Inspector Lanner.' It was Mac-Donald who had spoken and now all eyes were on him. 'I never met Mr Holmes myself,' he continued in his thick Scottish accent. 'But I think we are agreed that we owe him our thanks and our respect and it's now time to move on. For better or for worse he has left us on our own and, having acknowledged as much, let us consider the matter at hand.' He picked up a sheet of paper that had been lying in front of him and read from it. 'Mr Scott Lavelle, tortured and his throat cut. Henrietta Barlowe, smothered. Peter Clayton, a petty criminal who was known to us, stabbed. Thomas Jerrold and Lucy Winters strangled. An entire household in a respectable suburb wiped out in the course of one night. We cannot have it, gentlemen. It cannot be allowed.'

Everyone in the room murmured their agreement.

'And as I understand it, these are not the first atrocities that have taken place recently in Highgate. Lestrade?'

'You are right. There was a death not one month ago, a young man by the name of Jonathan Pilgrim. Hands tied, shot in the head.' Lestrade gazed at me as if I had been the one responsible and for a moment I felt the anger rise within me. I had been close to Pilgrim. It was his death, more than anything, which drove me on in my pursuit of Clarence Devereux. But I understood this was simply Lestrade's manner. He meant nothing by it. 'Pilgrim carried papers that showed him to be an American only recently arrived in the country,' he continued. 'He must have had an interest in Lavelle as his body was found only a short distance from Bladeston House.'

I felt it was time for me to speak out and so I did.

'Pilgrim was investigating Clarence Devereux,' I said. 'I myself sent him to this country for that purpose. Devereux and Lavelle were working in collaboration and must have somehow discovered my agent. It was they who killed him.'

'But in that case, who killed Lavelle?' Bradstreet asked.

MacDonald held up a hand. 'Mr Chase,' he said, 'we have been given a full explanation of your presence in London by Inspector Jones and I must say that it is only due to the exceptional circumstances of this case that you find yourself here today.'

'I'm grateful for it.'

'Well, you have him to thank. We will hear from you shortly. But it seems to me that if we are going to get to the bottom of these appalling murders, we need to go back to the very start . . . even to the Reichenbach Falls.' He turned to an inspector who had not so far spoken. This was a slight, grey-haired individual who had been nervously picking his nails and who looked like someone who never wanted to be noticed. 'Inspector Patterson,' he said, 'you were responsible for the apprehension of Moriarty's gang. You helped to drive him abroad. I think you should share with us exactly what occurred.'

'Certainly.' Patterson did not look up as he spoke, as if his report were engraved in the tabletop. 'You are all aware that Mr Holmes approached me last February although it had been his intention, I think, to meet with Lestrade.'

'I was on another case,' Lestrade explained with a scowl.

'In Woking, I believe. Well, yes, in your absence, Mr Holmes came to me and asked for my co-operation in the identification and arrest of a gang that had been operating in London for some time — or so he said — and in particular, one man.'

'Professor Moriarty,' Jones muttered.

'The very same. I have to say that at the time the name was unknown to me and when Holmes explained that he was famous throughout Europe for some theory he had devised and, moreover, that he had held the Chair of Mathematics at one of our most prestigious universities, I thought he was making fun of me. But he was of the utmost seriousness. He referred to Moriarty in the very darkest terms and went on to furnish me with evidence that could leave no doubt of what he said.

'By the beginning of last month, assisted by Inspector Barton here, I had drawn together a schematic — you might say a map — of London that showed an extraordinary, interlinking network of criminality.'

'With Moriarty at the centre,' Barton added,

131

puffing on his pipe.

'Indeed. I might add that we were assisted by a great number of informers who suddenly chose to come forward. It was as if, sensing Moriarty's weakness, they seized this moment to get their revenge, for there was no doubt that he had ruled by intimidation and threat. We received anonymous letters. Evidence of his past crimes — about which we had no knowledge whatsoever — suddenly came to light. Moriarty's journey from obscurity to centre stage was a very short one and, at a given signal from Holmes, for he was most particular about the timing, we pounced. In the course of a single weekend, we made arrests in Holborn, Clerkenwell, Islington, Westminster and Piccadilly. We entered houses as far afield as Ruislip and Norbury. Men of the utmost respectability — teachers, stockbrokers, even an archdeacon — were taken into custody. On the Monday, I was able to telegraph Holmes who was by this time in Strasbourg and inform him that we had the entire gang.'

'All but the leader himself,' Barton agreed and, around the table, the inspectors, who had been listening intently, nodded their heads in sombre silence.

'We now know that Moriarty had taken off after Holmes,' Patterson concluded. 'I hold myself at least in part responsible for what ensued, but at the same time I cannot believe Holmes had not expected it. Why else would he have left the country so abruptly? At any event, there you have it. Barton and I are preparing the charges even now and the cases will come to court soon enough.'

'Excellent work,' MacDonald said. He paused for a moment and frowned. 'But am I alone in finding a disparity here? In February of this year, you and Sherlock Holmes begin to close in on Moriarty and at around about the same time an American criminal by the name of Clarence Devereux arrives in London, seeking an alliance with that same Moriarty. How can it be?'

'Devereux did not know that Moriarty was finished,' another inspector said. 'We've all seen the letter, sent in code. It was only in April that they agreed to meet.'

'Devereux could have been very useful to Moriarty,' Gregson suggested. 'His arrival couldn't have been better timed. Moriarty was on the run. Devereux could have helped him rebuild his empire.'

'I disagree!' Lestrade pounded his fist on the table and looked around him peevishly. 'Clarence Devereux! Clarence Devereux! This is all the merest moonshine. We know *nothing* about Clarence Devereux. Who is he? Where does he live? Is he still in London? Does he even exist?'

'We knew nothing about Moriarty until Sherlock Holmes drew him to our attention.'

'Moriarty was real enough. But I suggest we address ourselves to the Pinkerton Agency in New York. I would like to see every scrap of evidence that they have concerning this man.'

'There is no need,' I said. 'I brought copies of all the files with me and I will happily make them available to you.'

'You left America three weeks ago,' Lestrade

responded. 'Much can have happened in that time. And with respect, Mr Chase, you are a junior agent in this business. I wouldn't talk to a police constable if I wished to be brought up to date. I would prefer to deal with the people who sent you here.'

'I am, sir, a senior investigator. But I will not argue with you.' I could see there was no point antagonising the man. 'You must address yourself to Mr Robert Pinkerton himself. It was he who assigned me to this case and he takes the closest interest in every development.'

'We will do that.' MacDonald scribbled a note in front of him.

'Clarence Devereux is here in London. I am certain of it. I have heard his name mentioned and I have felt his presence.'

The speaker was, by some margin, the youngest person in the room. I had noticed him sitting upright in his chair throughout the lengthy speeches, as if he could barely prevent himself from breaking in. He had fair hair, cut very short, and a keen, boyish face. He could not have been more than twenty-five or twenty-six years old. 'My name is Stanley Hopkins,' he said, introducing himself to me. 'And although I never had the honour of meeting Mr Sherlock Holmes, I very much wish he was still with us for I believe we face a challenge such as none of us in this room has ever encountered. I am in close contact with the criminal fraternity. Being new to this profession and even newer to this rank, I make it my business to maintain a presence in the streets of London — in Friars Mount, in Nichols Row, in Bluegate Fields . . .

'In the past few weeks, I have become aware of a silence, an emptiness — a sense of fear. None of the auction gangs are active. Nor are the pawners, nor the cardsharps. The young women in the Haymarket and on Waterloo Bridge have been absent from their trade.' He blushed slightly. 'I speak to them sometimes because they can be useful to me, but now even they have gone. Of course it may be the case that the superlative work of Mr Barton and Mr Patterson has been rewarded with the state of affairs we have all wished for, if only in our dreams: a London free of crime, that with Moriarty finished, his followers have become disheartened and crept back into the sewer from which they came. Sadly, I know that is not true. As the philosopher puts it, nature abhors a vacuum. It may be that Devereux came here to ally himself with Moriarty. But finding Moriarty gone, he has simply taken his place.'

'I believe it too,' someone — I think Lanner — said. 'The evidence is there, in the streets.'

'Outbursts of violence,' Bradstreet muttered. 'That business at the White Swan.'

'And the fire on the Harrow Road. Six people died . . . '

'Pimlico . . . '

'What are you talking about?' Lestrade cut in, addressing himself to Hopkins. 'Why should we believe that anything has changed? Where's the proof?'

'I had one informer who was prepared to speak to me and I have to say that in a way I had a certain liking for him. He had been in trouble from the day he climbed out of the cradle. Petty stuff. Fare dodging, thimble-rigging — but lately he had graduated in the school of crime. He had fallen in with a bad lot and I saw him less and less. Well, one week ago, I met him by arrangement in a rookery near Dean Street. I could see at once that he did not want to be there, that he had only come for old times' sake for I had helped him once or twice in the past. 'I can't see you, Mr Hopkins,' he said to me. 'It's all changed now. We can't meet any more.' 'What is it, Charlie?' I demanded. I could see that he was pale, his whole body shaking. 'You don't understand . . . ' he began.

'There was a movement in the alleyway. A man was standing there, silhouetted against the gas lamp. I could not see who he was and anyway he was already moving away. I cannot even be sure he had been observing us. But for Charlie, it was enough. He did not dare to speak the name but this is what he said. 'The American,' he said. 'He's here now and that's the end of it.' 'What do you mean? What American?' 'I've told you all I can, Mr Hopkins. I shouldn't have come. They'll know!' And before I could stop him, he hurried away, disappearing into the shadows. That was the last I saw of him.' Hopkins paused. 'Two days later, Charlie was pulled out of the Thames. His hands were tied and death was due to drowning. I will not describe his other injuries, but I will say only this: I have no doubt at all that what Mr Chase tells us is the truth. An evil tide has come our way. We must fight it before it overwhelms us all.'

There was a long silence after this. Then Inspector MacDonald once again turned to Athelney Jones. 'What did you find at Bladeston House?' he asked. 'Are there any lines of enquiry you can pursue?'

'There are two,' Jones replied. 'Although I will be honest and say that there is a great deal about these murders that still remains unclear. The evidence takes me in one direction. Common sense takes me in quite another. Still . . . I found a name and a number in Lavelle's diary: HORNER 13. It was written in capitals and circled. There was nothing else on the page. It struck me at the time as very strange.'

'I arrested a man called Horner,' Bradstreet announced, rolling his pipe in his hands. 'John Horner. He was a plumber at the Hotel Cosmopolitan. Of course, I'd got completely the wrong man. Holmes put me right.'

'There is a tea shop in Crouch End,' Youghal added. 'It was run by a Mrs Horner, I believe. But it closed long ago.'

'There was a block of shaving soap in the same drawer,' I recalled. 'I wondered if that might be significant?' Nobody spoke so I continued. 'Could Horner perhaps be a druggist or a chemist's shop?'

Again, this elicited no reply.

'What else, Inspector Jones?' MacDonald asked.

'We met a man, an unpleasant character by the name of Edgar Mortlake. Mr Chase knew him from New York and identified him as one of

Devereux's associates. It seems that he is the proprietor of a club in Mayfair, a place called the Bostonian.'

That name caused a stir around the table.

'I know it,' Inspector Gregson said. 'Expensive, trashy. It opened only recently.'

'I visited the place,' Lestrade said. 'Pilgrim had a room there at the time of his death. I looked through his things but I found nothing of any interest.'

'He wrote to me from there,' I concurred. 'It was thanks to him that I knew about the letter that Devereux had sent to Moriarty.'

'The Bostonian is the home of almost every wealthy American in London,' Gregson continued. 'It's owned by two brothers — Leland and Edgar Mortlake. They have their own chef and they create their own cocktails. There are two floors, the upper one of which is used for gaming.'

'Is it not obvious?' Bradstreet exclaimed. 'If Clarence Devereux is anywhere in London, surely that is where he is to be found. An American club with an American name, run by a known felon.'

'I would have thought, in that case, it would be the last place he would present himself,' Hopkins said, quietly. 'Surely, the whole point is that he doesn't want to make himself known.'

'We should raid the building,' Lestrade said, ignoring him. 'I myself will arrange it. A surprise visit with a dozen or more officers this very day.'

'I would suggest the early evening,' Gregson said. 'For that is when it will be busiest.'

'Perhaps we will find this Clarence Devereux at the card table. If so, we will make short work of him. We are not going to be colonised by criminals from foreign countries. This gangster-ish violence must stop.'

Soon afterwards, the meeting came to an end. Jones and I left together and as we made our way down the stairs, he turned to me.

'Well, it's agreed,' he said. 'We intend to mount a raid on a club which has but a tenuous link with the man we are seeking and a man whose existence several of my colleagues are inclined to doubt. Even if Clarence Devereux happens to be there, we will be unable to recognise him and going there will only tell him that we are on his tail. What do you say, Chase? Would you not call it a complete waste of time?'

'I would not be so bold,' I replied.

'Your reticence does you credit. But I must return to my office. You can spend the afternoon seeing something of the city. I will send a note to your hotel and the two of us will meet again tonight.'

9

The Bostonian

In fact, Jones was wrong. As things turned out, the raid on the Bostonian did prove useful in one small but significant respect.

It was already dark when I left my room at the hotel and as I stepped into the corridor I was aware of the door next to mine swinging shut. Once again I did not see the occupant beyond a shadowy figure who vanished immediately as the door closed but it occurred to me that I had not heard him go past, which I should surely have done as the carpet was threadbare. Had he been waiting outside as I made my preparations? Had he left when he heard me approach? I was tempted to challenge him but decided against it. Jones had been precise about the hour of our meeting. There might be a perfectly innocent explanation for the behaviour of my mysterious neighbour. At any event, he could wait.

And so we found ourselves, an hour later, standing beneath a gas lamp on the corner of Trebeck Street, waiting for the signal — the scream of a whistle and the tramp of a dozen leather boots — which would announce that the adventure had begun. The club was in front of us: a narrow, quite ordinary white-fronted building on a corner. But for the heavy curtains drawn across the windows and the occasional snatch of piano music jingling into the night, it could have been a bank. Jones was in a strange mood. He had been virtually silent since I had joined him and appeared to be deep in thought. It was unseasonably cold and damp — it seemed as if the summer was never going to arrive — and we were both wearing heavy coats. I wondered if the weather was accentuating the pain in his leg. But suddenly he turned to me and asked, 'Did you not find Lestrade's testimony to be of particular interest?'

The question had taken me by surprise. 'Which part of it?'

'How did he know that your agent, Jonathan Pilgrim, had a room at the Bostonian?'

I thought for a moment. 'I have no idea. It could be that Pilgrim was carrying the key to his room. Or I suppose he could have had the address written down.'

'Was he a careless man?'

'He was headstrong. He could be reckless. But he was very aware of the danger of discovery.'

'My point exactly: it's almost as if he wanted us to come here. I hope we are not making a grave mistake.'

He lapsed once again into silence and I took out my watch. There were another five minutes until the raid began and I wished we hadn't arrived so early. It seemed to me that my companion was avoiding my eye. He always stood awkwardly and I knew that he was in fairly constant discomfort and needed his walking stick. But as we waited there, he was more awkward than ever.

'Is there something the matter, Jones?' I asked at length.

'No. Not at all,' he replied. Then: 'As a matter of fact, there was something I wished to ask you.'

'Please!'

'I hope you will not find it presumptuous but my wife wondered if you might like to join us for dinner tomorrow night.' I was amazed that something so trivial should have caused him so much difficulty but before I could answer, he continued quickly, 'I have of course described you to her and she is most keen to meet you and to hear something of your life in America.'

'I would be delighted to come,' I said.

'Elspeth does worry about me a great deal,' he went on. 'Between ourselves, she would be much happier if I were to find another occupation and she has often said as much. Needless to say, she knows almost nothing of the events at Bladeston House. I have told her that I am engaged on a murder investigation but I have given her none of the details and would ask you to do the same. Fortunately, she does not often read the newspapers. Elspeth has a very delicate nature and if she had any idea of the sort of people we were up against, she would be greatly troubled.'

'I am very glad to be invited,' I said. 'For what it's worth, the food at Hexam's Hotel is atrocious. Please don't worry yourself, Inspector. I'll take my lead from you and will answer any questions that Mrs Jones poses with the utmost discretion.' I looked up briefly into the gaslight. 'My dearest mother never once discussed my work with me. I know it caused her discomfort.

If only for that reason, I'll take the greatest care.'

'Then it's agreed.' Jones looked relieved. 'We can meet at Scotland Yard and travel together to Camberwell. You will also meet my daughter, Beatrice. She is six years old and as eager to know about my business as my wife is to avoid it.'

I already knew that there was a child involved. Beatrice was doubtless the recipient of the French puppet that Jones had brought back from Paris. 'Dress?' I asked.

'Come as you are. There is no need for formality.'

Our discussion was interrupted by the shrill scream of a whistle and at once the quiet street was filled with uniformed men running towards a single door. Jones and I were here as onlookers — Lestrade had taken charge of the operation and he was the first to climb the steps and grab hold of the handle. The door was locked. We watched him step back, search for the doorbell, and ring it impatiently. Eventually, the door was opened. He and the police constables piled in. We followed.

I had not expected the interior of the Bostonian to be quite so lavish, despite what Inspector Gregson had told us. Trebeck Street was narrow and poorly lit but the front door took us into a glittering world of mirrors and chandeliers, marble floors and ornate ceilings. Paintings in gilt frames covered every inch of the walls, many of them by well-known American artists . . . Albert Pinkham Ryder, Thomas Cole. Anyone who had ever visited the Union Club in

Park Avenue or the Metropolitan on 60th Street would have felt themselves at home, and that was surely the point. A rack of newspapers by the entrance contained only American publications. The dozens of bottles set out on the brightly polished glass shelves were largely American brands — Jim Beam and Old Fitzgerald bourbon, Fleischmann Extra Dry Gin. There were at least fifty people in the front room and I heard accents from the East Coast, from Texas, from Milwaukee. A young man in a tailcoat had been playing a piano, the front panel removed to show its inner workings. He had stopped the moment we came in and sat there, his eyes fixed on the keys.

Police officers were already moving through the room and I could feel the indignation of the crowd as the men and women, all in their finest evening wear, separated to allow them to pass. Lestrade had marched straight up to the bar as if demanding a drink and the barman was staring at him, open-mouthed. Jones and I hung back. Neither of us had been sure of the wisdom of this enterprise and we were both wondering where to begin. Two policemen were already climbing the stairs to the second floor. The rest of them were covering the doors so that nobody could enter or leave the club without being challenged. I will admit that I was greatly impressed by the Metropolitan Police. They were well-organised and disciplined even if, as far as I could tell, they had no idea why they were here.

Lestrade was still haranguing the barman when a door at the side opened and two men came out. I recognised them both at once. Edgar Mortlake we had already met. This time, his brother was with him. Just as the maid at Bladeston House had told us, the two of them were very much alike (they were both dressed in black tie) and yet they were nonetheless curiously different, as if some artist or sculptor had been at work and deliberately created from one a more brutal and hot-blooded representation in the other. Leland Mortlake had the same black hair and small eyes as his brother but no moustache. He was a few years older and they weighed heavily on him: his face was fleshier, his lips thicker, his whole expression one of contempt. He was several inches shorter than Edgar but even before he spoke I could see that he was the more dominant of the two. Edgar was standing a few steps behind him. It was his natural position.

They had not seen Lestrade — or if they had, had chosen to ignore him. However, Edgar recognised both Jones and myself and, nudging his brother, led him over to us.

'What's this?' Leland demanded. His voice was hoarse and he breathed heavily as if the act of speaking exhausted him.

'I know them,' Edgar explained. 'This one is a Pinkerton's man. He didn't trouble to give me his name. The other is Alan Jones or something of the sort. Scotland Yard. They were at Bladeston House.'

'What do you want?'

The question was aimed at Jones and he replied. 'We are searching for a man named

Clarence Devereux.'

'I don't know him. He's not here.'

'I told you I was unacquainted with him,' Edgar added. 'So why have you come here? If you wanted membership, you could have asked when we met in Highgate. Although I think you may find our annual fees a little beyond your means.'

By now, Lestrade had noticed the exchange and came striding over. 'You are Leland Mortlake?' he demanded.

'I am Edgar Mortlake. That's my brother, if you wish to speak to him.'

'We're looking for —'

'I know who you're looking for. I've already said. He's not here.'

'Nobody is leaving here tonight until they have given me proof of their identity,' Lestrade said. 'I wish to see the register of your guests — their names and addresses. I intend to search this club from the top floor to the basement.'

'You cannot.'

'I very much think I can, Mr Mortlake. And I will.'

'You had a man staying here at the beginning of the year,' I said. 'He was here until the end of April. His name was Jonathan Pilgrim.'

'What of him?'

'You remember him?'

Leland Mortlake stared vacantly, his small eyes still filled with resentment. But it was his brother who answered my question. 'Yes. I believe we did have a guest with that name.'

'What room?'

'The Revere. On the second floor.' The information was given reluctantly.

'Has it been occupied since?'

'No. It's empty.'

'I'd like to see it.'

Leland turned to his brother and for a moment I thought the two of them were going to protest. But before either of them could speak, Jones stepped forward. 'Mr Chase is with me and he has the authorisation of Scotland Yard. Take us to the room.'

'Whatever you say.' Edgar Mortlake looked at us with controlled fury and had we not been in London, surrounded by the British police, I cannot say what might have ensued. 'But this is the second time you have bossed me about and I can tell you, Mr Jones, that I don't like it. There won't be a third time, of that I can assure you.'

'Are you threatening us?' I demanded. 'Are you forgetting who we are?'

'I'm just saying that I won't stand for it.' Edgar lifted a finger. 'And it is you, perhaps, who has forgotten who you're dealing with, Mr Pinkerton. You may rue the day that you chose to interfere.'

'Dry up, Edgar!' Leland muttered.

'Whatever you say, Leland,' Edgar returned.

'This is an outrage,' the older brother continued. 'But you must do as you want. We have nothing to hide.'

We left Lestrade with them, the police already beginning the long process of interviewing each and every one of the guests, painstakingly noting down their details. Together, we climbed the stairs, arriving at a narrow corridor running left and right. On one side, there was another large room lit by candelabra and with several tables covered with green baize. Evidently, this was where the gaming took place. We did not enter it, following the corridor in the other direction past several bedrooms, each one named after a famous Bostonian. Revere was about halfway down. The door was unlocked.

'I cannot imagine what it is that you hope to find,' Jones muttered as we went in.

'I'm not sure I expect to find anything,' I replied. 'Inspector Lestrade said that he had already been here. And yet Pilgrim was a clever man. If he thought himself to be in danger, there's a chance he might have tried to leave something behind.'

'One thing is certain. There is nothing to be discovered downstairs.'

'I quite agree.'

At first glance, the room was unpromising. There was a bed, freshly made, and a closet, empty. Another door led into a bathroom with both a water closet and a gas-heated bath. The Bostonian certainly knew how to look after its guests and I could not help feeling envious, remembering my own shabby hotel. The wallpaper, curtains and furnishings were all of the highest quality. We began a search, opening the drawers, pulling up the mattress, even turning the pictures, but it was clear that once Jonathan Pilgrim had left, the room had been stripped and cleaned.

'This is a waste of time,' I said.

'So it would seem. And yet . . . what have we here?' As Jones spoke, he leafed through a pile of magazines that stood on an occasional table at the foot of the bed.

'There is nothing,' I said. 'I've already looked.'

It was true. I had quickly thumbed through the magazines — *The Century, The Atlantic Monthly, The North American Review*. But it was not the publications that interested Jones. He had pulled out a small advertising card from one of them and showed it to me. I read:

POSITIVELY THE BEST HAIR TONIC HORNER'S 'LUXURIANT'

The world-renowned remedy for baldness, grey hair and weak or thin moustaches.

Physicians and Analysts pronounce it to be perfectly safe and devoid of any Metallic or other injurious Ingredients.

Manufactured only by Albert Horner 13 Chancery Lane, London El.

'Jonathan Pilgrim was not bald,' I said. 'He had a fine head of hair.'

Jones smiled. 'You see but you do not observe. Look at the name — Horner. And the address: number thirteen!'

'Horner 13!' I exclaimed. They were the words we had found in the diary in Scotchy Lavelle's desk.

149

'Exactly. And if your agent was as capable as you suggest, it is quite possible that he left this here on purpose in the hope that it would be found. It would, of course, mean nothing to anyone cleaning the room.'

'It means nothing to me either! What can a hair tonic possibly have to do with Clarence Devereux or with the murders at Bladeston House?'

'We shall see. It seems that for once, and despite his best efforts, Lestrade has actually helped our investigation. It makes a change.' Jones slipped the advertisement into his pocket. 'We will say nothing of this, Chase. Agreed?'

'Of course.'

We left the room, closing the door behind us, and made our way back downstairs.

10

Horner's of Chancery Lane

It was just as well that Horner's advertised itself with a red and white barber's pole for otherwise we might not have found it. To begin with, it wasn't actually on Chancery Lane. There was a narrow, muddy thoroughfare that ran down to Staples Inn Garden with a haberdasher's — Reilly & Son — and the Chancery Lane Safe Deposit Company on the corner and a little row of very shabby houses opposite. The barber shop occupied the front parlour of one of these with a sign above the door and a further advertisement in the window: *Shaving 1d; haircut 2d*. On one side was a tobacconist that had closed down. The house on the other side looked fairly abandoned too.

A hurdy-gurdy man was playing in the street, perched on a stool and wearing a ragged top hat and a worn-out, shapeless coat. He was not very accomplished. Indeed, had I been working in the vicinity, he would have driven me quite mad with the almost tuneless howling and tinkling of his instrument. The moment he saw us, he stood and called out: 'Hair tonic in the ha'porths and pen'orths. Try Horner's special hair tonic! Get your cut or your shave here!' He was an odd fellow, very thin and unsteady on his feet. As we approached, he stopped playing and handed us a card from a satchel slung over his shoulder. It was identical to the one we had found at the Bostonian.

We entered the building and found ourselves in a small, uncomfortable room with a single barber's chair facing a mirror so cracked and dusty that it barely showed any reflection at all. There were two shelves lined with bottles of Horner's Luxuriant as well as other hair restorers and cantharides lotions. The floor hadn't been swept and tufts of old hair were still strewn across it — as unsavoury a sight as one could wish to see, though not as bad as the soap bowl, a congealed mess which still carried the spiky fragments of men's beards. I was already beginning to think that this was the last place in London I would wish to come for a haircut when the barber himself arrived.

He had climbed up a staircase in the back parlour and tottered towards us, wiping his hands on a handkerchief. It was hard to determine his age — he was both old and young at the same time with a round, quite pleasant face, clean-shaven and smiling. But he had a terrible haircut. Indeed, it was as if he had been attacked by a cat. His hair was long on one side, short on the other with patches missing altogether, exposing his skull. Nor had it been washed for some time, leaving it with both a colour and a texture that was disagreeable to say the least.

He was, however, amiable enough. 'Good morning, gentlemen,' he exclaimed. 'Although this cursed weather refuses to change! Have you ever known London so wet and so miserable and here we are in May! What can I do for you? One haircut? Two haircuts? You are fortunate in that I am very quiet today.'

This was true in every sense. Outside, the hurdy-gurdy player had at last chosen to take a rest.

'We are not here for a haircut,' Jones replied. He picked up one of the bottles and smelled the contents. 'Do I take it you are Albert Horner?'

'No, sir. Bless you! Mr Horner died long ago. But this was his business and I took it over.'

'Quite recently, by the look of it,' Jones remarked. I glanced at him, wondering how he could have come to such a conclusion for, to my eye, both the man and the shop could have been here for years. 'The barber's pole is old,' Jones continued, for my benefit. 'But I could not help noticing that the screws fastening it to the wall are new. The shelves may be dusty, but the bottles are not. That tells the same tale.'

'You're absolutely right!' the barber exclaimed. 'We've been here less than three months and we kept the old name. And why not? Old Mr Horner was well known and much admired. We're already popular among the lawyers and the judges who work in this area — even if many of them insist on wearing wigs.'

'So what is your name?' I asked.

'Silas Beckett, sir, at your service.'

Jones produced the advertisement. 'We found this in a club called the Bostonian. I take it that name means nothing to you, or the man who was staying there. An American gentleman called Jonathan Pilgrim.'

153

'American, sir? I don't believe I've ever had an American in here.' He gestured at me. 'Apart from yourself.'

Beckett was no detective. It was my accent that had given me away.

'And the name Scotchy Lavelle — have you heard it?'

'I speak to my customers, sir. But it's not often they tell me their name. Was he another American?'

'And Clarence Devereux?'

'You're running ahead of me, sir. So many names! Can I interest you in a bottle of our hair tonic?' He asked this almost impertinently, as if he were anxious to bring the interview to an end.

'Do you know him?'

'Clarence Devereux? No, sir. Perhaps you might try across the road, at the haberdasher's. I am very sorry that I cannot be of assistance. In short, it would seem we are wasting each other's time.'

'That may be so, Mr Beckett, but there is just one thing you can tell me that would interest me.' I saw Jones examining the barber carefully. 'Are you a religious man?'

The question was so unexpected that I'm not sure who was more surprised — Beckett or I. 'I'm sorry?' He blinked.

'Religious. Do you go to church?'

'Why do you ask?' Jones said nothing and Beckett sighed, clearly anxious to be rid of us. 'No, sir, for my sins, I am not a regular churchgoer.'

'It is just as I thought,' Jones muttered. 'You

154

have made it quite clear that you cannot help us, Mr Beckett. I will wish you a good day.'

We left the barber's shop and walked back up to Chancery Lane. Behind us, the hurdy-gurdy player struck up again. As soon as we turned the corner, Jones stopped and laughed. 'We have stumbled onto something quite remarkable here, my boy. Holmes himself would have been entertained by this: a barber who cannot cut hair, a hurdy-gurdy player who cannot play, and a hair tonic that contains large quantities of benzoin. Hardly a three-pipe problem, but not without interest.'

'But what is the meaning of it?' I exclaimed. 'And why did you ask Mr Beckett about his religious beliefs?'

'Is it not obvious to you?'

'Not at all.'

'Well, it will be made clear soon enough. We are having dinner together tonight. Why not come to Scotland Yard at three o'clock? We can meet outside, as we did before, and then everything will be explained.'

★   ★   ★

Three o'clock.

I was there exactly on time, stepping out of my hansom on Whitehall with Big Ben chiming the hour. We had stopped on the far side of the road, which is to say, the one opposite Scotland Yard. I paid the driver. It was a bright, cloudless afternoon, though still a little chilly.

I must set down exactly what happened.

Ahead of me, crossing the road, I saw a boy whom I recognised instantly. It was Perry, who had sat next to me in the Café Royal and who had held a knife to my neck. I stood there and it seemed to me that everything had become very still, as if an artist had taken the scene and captured it on a canvas. Even at a distance, Perry was enveloped in what I can only describe as an aura of menace. This time, he was dressed as a naval cadet. He had a cap, a dark blue double-fronted jacket with two lines of buttons, and a leather pouch hanging diagonally across his chest. As before, he seemed to be squeezed into the uniform he was wearing, his stomach pressing against the waistband, his neck too large for the collar. His hair looked even more yellow in the afternoon sun.

Why was he here? What was he doing?

Athelney Jones appeared, walking out of Scotland Yard, looking for me, and I raised a hand in alarm. Jones saw me and I pointed in the direction of the boy, who was walking briskly down the pavement, his plump little legs carrying him ever further away.

Jones recognised him but he was too far away to do anything.

There was a brougham waiting for Perry, barely fifty yards from where I was standing. As he approached it, a door opened. There was a man inside, half hidden in the shadows. He was tall, thin, dressed entirely in black. It was impossible to make out his face but I thought I heard him cough. Had Jones seen him? It was unlikely for he was quite a distance ahead and on the wrong side of the road. The boy climbed into the brougham. The door closed behind him.

Without any further thought, I ran towards it. I saw the driver whip up the horse and the carriage jolted forward — but even so I might have been able to reach it. Jones was on the edge of my vision. He had begun to move too, using his walking stick to lever himself forward. The brougham continued down Whitehall, picking up speed, heading for Parliament Square. I was running as fast as I could but I wasn't getting any nearer. To reach it, I had to cross Whitehall but there was a great deal of traffic. Already, the brougham was disappearing around the corner.

I veered to one side. I had left the pavement and I was in the road.

Athelney Jones cried out a warning. I didn't hear him but I saw him calling to me, his hand raised.

Suddenly, there was an omnibus bearing down on me. At first, I did not see it for two horses filled my vision: huge, monstrous, with staring eyes. They could have been joined together, a single creature drawn from Greek mythology. Then I became aware of the vehicle being hauled behind them, the driver pulling at the reins, the half a dozen people crowded together on the roof, trapped there, horrified witnesses to the unfolding drama.

Somebody screamed. The driver was still struggling with the reins and I was aware of hooves pounding down, the wheels grinding against the hard surface, that same surface rushing up at me as I threw myself forward. The whole world tilted and the sky swept across my vision.

I might have been killed, but in fact the omnibus missed me by inches, veering away and then drawing to a halt a short distance ahead. I had cracked my head and my knee but I was unaware of the pain. I twisted round, looking for the brougham, but it had already gone. The boy and his travelling companion had made their escape.

Jones reached me. To this day, I am not sure how he managed to cover the distance so quickly. 'Chase!' he exclaimed. 'My dear fellow! Are you all right? You were almost crushed . . . '

'Did you see them?' I demanded. 'Perry! The boy from the Café Royal! He was here. And there was a man with him . . . '

'Yes.'

'Did you see his face?'

'No. A man in his forties or fifties, perhaps, tall and thin. But he was concealed, inside the carriage.'

'Help me . . . '

Jones was leaning down, helping me to my feet. I was aware of a little blood trickling past my eye and wiped it away. 'What was it all about, Jones?' I asked. 'Why were they here?'

My question was answered seconds later.

The explosion was so close that we felt it as well as heard it, a blast of wind and dust rushing to us where we stood. All around us, horses whinnied and carriages veered out of control as the drivers fought with the reins. I saw two hansoms collide with each other and one tilted and crashed to the ground. Men and women who had been walking past stopped, clutching onto each other, turning in alarm. Pieces of brick and glass rained down on us and a smell of burning pervaded the air. I looked round. A huge plume of smoke was rising up from within Scotland Yard. Of course! What else could have been the target?

'The devils!' Jones exclaimed.

Together, we hurried across the road. By now the traffic had come to a standstill. Without even thinking that there might be a second device, we plunged into the building, fighting our way past the clerks, the constables and the visitors who were desperately trying to find their way out. The lower floor at least seemed undamaged but, as we stood there, a uniformed policeman appeared, coming down the stairs, his face blackened and blood streaming from a wound in his head. Jones grabbed hold of him.

'What happened?' he demanded. 'What floor?'

'The third floor,' the man replied. 'I was there! It was so close . . . '

We wasted no time. We ran over to the stairs and began the long climb up, both of us aware that we had made the same journey together only the day before. We passed many more police officers and assistants, making their way down, many of them hurt, clutching onto each other. One or two of them urged us not to continue but we ignored them. As we climbed higher, we smelled burning and there was so much smoke in the air it became hard to breathe. Finally, we reached the third floor and almost at once bumped into a man whom I recognised from the conference. It was Inspector Gregson. His fair hair was awry and he was in a state of shock but he did not seem to have been hurt.

'It was in the telegraph room,' he cried. 'A package brought by a messenger boy was placed against the wall of your office, Jones. Had you been at your desk . . . ' Gregson broke off, his eyes filled with horror. 'I fear Stevens has been killed.'

Jones's face showed his dismay. 'How many others?'

'I can't say. We've been ordered to evacuate the building.'

We had no intention of doing so. We pressed forward, ignoring the casualties who were limping past, some of them with their clothes torn, others streaming blood. There was an uncanny silence on the third floor. Nobody was screaming but I thought I could hear the crackle of flames. I followed Jones, the two of us finally reaching the door of his office. Now it was open. I looked inside, into a scene of horror.

The office was not a large one. A single window looked out over the inner quadrangle, as Jones had told me. The room was filled with debris for the entire wall on the left had been shattered. There was a wooden desk covered with dust and brickwork and I could see at once that Gregson had been right. Had Jones been sitting there, he would have been killed. As it was, a young man lay on the floor with a police constable — dazed and helpless — crouching over him. Jones hurried in and knelt beside the

160

body. It was obvious that he was dead. There was a dreadful wound in the side of his head and his hand was outstretched, the fingers still.

'Stevens!' he exclaimed. 'He was my secretary . . . my assistant.'

Smoke was pouring in through the hole in the wall and I saw that the damage in the telegraph room had been even worse. The room was on fire, the flames licking at the ceiling, reaching up to the roof. There were two more figures lying amongst the wreckage. It was hard to be sure if they were men or boys as they had been horribly injured, both of them disfigured by the blast. There was paper everywhere. Some of the pages seemed to be floating in the air. It must have been the heat. The fire was rapidly spreading.

I went over to Jones. 'There's nothing we can do!' I cried. 'We must do as we've been told and leave the building. Go now!' I told the young constable.

He left and Jones turned to me; there were tears in his eyes — though whether from grief or due to the smoke, I could not say. 'Was this meant for me?' he asked.

I nodded. 'I very much think so.'

I took hold of him and led him out of the office. It could not have been more than a few minutes since the detonation, but already we were alone on the third floor. I knew that if the fire spread, or if the smoke overwhelmed us, we might die here — and although Jones was unwilling, I forced him to accompany me to the staircase and back down. Behind us, I heard part of the ceiling collapse in the telegraph office. We should perhaps have carried the dead secretary with us or at least covered the body as a mark of respect, but right then, it seemed to me, our own safety was paramount.

Several steam fire engines had arrived by the time we burst out into the open air. The firemen were already running forward, trailing their hoses across the pavement. All the other traffic had disappeared. The road, which had been normal and busy just a short while ago, was eerily empty. I helped Jones walk away from the building and, finding an unoccupied bench, set him down. He was leaning heavily on his stick and there were still tears in his eyes.

'Stevens,' he muttered. 'He had been with me three years — and recently married! I was talking to him only half an hour ago.'

'I'm sorry.' I didn't know what else to say.

'This happened before. A bomb in Scotland Yard, six or seven years ago. It was the Fenians and I wasn't in London. But this time . . . ' He seemed dazed. 'You really believe I was the target?'

'I warned you,' I said. 'These people are ruthless and it was only yesterday that Edgar Mortlake threatened you.'

'Revenge for our raid on the Bostonian!'

'You cannot prove it, but I cannot see any other reason for this attack.' I broke off. 'Had you not come out to greet me, you would have been sitting in your office. Do you not see that, Jones? You escaped by a matter of seconds.'

He grabbed my arm. 'You have been the saving of me.'

'I am very glad of it.'

We looked across the road, at the firemen operating the steam pumps while others raised the ladders. Smoke was still pouring out of the building, thicker now, blanketing the sky.

'What now?' I asked.

Jones shook his head wearily. There were black streaks on his cheekbones and across his forehead. I guessed I must look the same. 'I don't know,' he replied. 'But whatever you do, don't tell Elspeth!'

11

Dinner in Camberwell

We took a much later train than we had intended, leaving Holborn Viaduct just as night fell and the crowds seemed to blend into the sudden darkness like ink spattered on a page. Jones was in a sombre mood. He had met Lestrade, Gregson and some of the other detective inspectors in the hours following the explosion but there were to be no decisions made until the next day. The conclusion that he had narrowly escaped an attempt on his life seemed inescapable. We had the words spoken by Edgar Mortlake as the proof of it and surely the timing of the attack could not have been coincidental. Lestrade was in favour of arresting both the brothers immediately but in the end it had been Jones himself who had urged caution. He had no evidence beyond a brief conversation that they might deny had ever taken place. He had, he said, already devised a better strategy — although he was not yet prepared to say what it was. I agreed. Clarence Devereux and his gang had run circles around Pinkerton's for many years and would surely do the same with the British police. If we were going to reel them in, we would need to take the utmost care.

'It is unlikely that Elspeth will have heard about the bomb,' Jones said, as our train drew into an area of London known as Camberwell and we prepared to climb down, 'and I will have to tell her for it is inconceivable that I should withhold such information from her. But the position of it! The possibility that I might have been the intended target . . . '

'We will say nothing of that,' I said.

'She will somehow discern it. She has a way of homing in on the truth.' He sighed. 'And yet still I do not understand these adversaries of ours. What was it they hoped to achieve? Had I been killed, there are any number of inspectors who could have taken my place. You have met many of them yourself. And if they had really wanted me dead, there are many easier ways they could have achieved their aim. Here we are now, on a station platform. An assassin with a knife or a garrotte could do the job in the blink of an eye.'

'It is possible that their intention was never to kill you,' I said.

'That is not what you said before.'

'I said that you were the target and I still believe that to be the case. The truth is that it would not have mattered to Clarence Devereux if you lived or died. It was no more than a demonstration of his power, his immunity from prosecution. He laughs in the face of the British police and at the same time he warns them: do not come close, do not interfere with my business.'

'Then he misunderstands us. After this, we will redouble our efforts.' He said no more until we had left the station. 'There is no logic, Chase, I tell you,' he continued. 'Who was the man in the brougham? What are we to make of the meeting between Moriarty and Devereux, the role of this boy Perry, the murder of Lavelle, even Horner's of Chancery Lane? Separately, I have an understanding of them. But when I try to bring them together, they defy common sense. It is like reading a book in which the chapters have been published in the wrong order or where the writer has deliberately set out to confuse.'

'We will only find out the meaning of it when we find Clarence Devereux,' I said.

'I begin to wonder if we ever will. Lestrade was right. He seems to be a phantom. He has no presence.'

'Was not Moriarty the same?'

'That is true. Moriarty was a name, a presence — an entity unknown to me until the very end. That was his power. It may well be that Devereux has learned from his example.' Jones was beginning to limp, resting heavily on his stick. 'I am tired. Forgive me if we talk no further. I must compose myself for whatever awaits me at home.'

'Would you rather I did not come?'

'No, no, my friend, to postpone would only make Elspeth fear that events have taken a worse turn than they have. We will dine together as planned.'

It had been but a short distance from Holborn to Camberwell and yet the journey seemed to have taken us ever further into the night. By the time we arrived, a thick fog was rolling through the streets, deadening the air and turning the last commuters into ghosts. A growler lumbered past. I heard the clatter of the horse's hooves and the creak of the wheels but the carriage itself was little more than a dark shadow, vanishing around a corner.

Jones lived close to the station. I have to say that his property was very much as I had imagined it might be: a handsome terraced house with bay windows and white stucco pillars in front of a solid, black-painted door. The style was typically English, the effect one of calm and security. Three steps led up from the street and in climbing them I had a strange sense that I was leaving all the perils of the day behind. Perhaps it was the warm glow of light that I could discern, leaking through the edges of the curtained windows. Or maybe it was the smell of meat and vegetables that wafted up from the kitchen somewhere below. But I was already glad to be here. We entered a narrow hallway with a carpeted staircase opposite and Jones led me through a doorway and into the front room. In fact the room ran the full length of the house, with a folding screen pulled back to reveal a dining table set for three at the front, a library and a piano at the back. There was a fire burning in the hearth but it was hardly needed. With the abundant furniture, the embroidered boxes and baskets, the dark red wallpaper and the heavy curtains, the room was already cosy enough.

Mrs Jones was sitting in a plush armchair with a strikingly pretty six-year-old girl leaning against her, the policeman puppet dangling over her arm. Her mother had been reading to her but as we came in she closed the book and the little girl turned, delighted to see us. She had none of her father's looks. With her light brown hair, tumbling in ringlets, her bright green eyes and smile, she was much more her mother's daughter, for Elspeth Jones clearly reflected her across the years.

'Not in bed yet, Beatrice?' Jones asked.

'No, Papa. Mama said I could stay up.'

'Well, this is the gentleman I imagine you wish to meet; my friend, Mr Frederick Chase.'

'Good evening, sir,' the girl said. She showed me the doll. 'This came from Paris. My papa gave him to me.'

'He seems a fine fellow,' I said. I always felt uncomfortable around children and tried not to show it.

'I have never met an American before.'

'I hope you will not find me very different from yourself. It was not so many years ago that my ancestors left this country. My great-grandfather came from London. A place called Bow.'

'Is New York very loud?'

'Loud?' I smiled. It was such an odd choice of word. 'Well, it's certainly very busy. And the buildings are very tall. Some of them are so tall that we call them skyscrapers.'

'Because they scrape the sky?'

'Because they seem to.'

'That's enough now, Beatrice. Nanny is waiting for you upstairs.' Mrs Jones turned to me. 'She is so inquisitive that one day I'm sure she'll be a detective, just like her father.'

'I fear it will be some time before the Metropolitan Police are prepared to admit

168

women to their ranks,' Jones remarked.

'Then she can be a lady detective, like Mrs Gladden in those excellent books of Mr Forrester's.' She smiled at her daughter. 'You may say good night to Mr Chase.'

'Good night, Mr Chase.' Obediently, the little girl hurried out of the room.

I turned my attention to Elspeth Jones. She was, as I had at once perceived, very similar in looks to her daughter although her hair had been cut short over her forehead and gathered up in the Grecian style. She struck me somehow as a very caring woman, one who would bring a quiet intelligence to everything she did. She was simply dressed in a shade of dusty pink with a belt and a high collar and no jewellery that I could see. Now that Beatrice had gone, she gave me her full attention.

'Mr Chase,' she said. 'I am very pleased to meet you.'

'And you, ma'am,' I returned.

'Will you have some grog?' She gestured and I saw a jug and three glasses had been set out on a brass table beside the fire. 'It seems these wintery nights will never end and I like to have something warm waiting when my husband returns home.'

She poured three glasses of the tincture and we sat together in that slightly awkward silence that comes when people meet each other for the first time and none of them is quite sure how to proceed. But then the maid appeared to say that dinner was ready and once we had taken our places at the table, the company became more at ease.

The maid brought a pretty decent stew, boiled neck of mutton with carrots and mashed turnips, certainly far superior to anything I had been offered at Hexam's, and while Athelney Jones poured the wine, his wife carefully steered the conversation in the direction that she preferred. Indeed, her skill was that she seemed natural and uncalculating but I was aware that during the next hour we never once touched on anything to do with the police. She asked me many questions about America: the food, the culture, the nature of the people. She wanted to know if I had yet seen Thomas Edison's Kinetoscope, a device that had been much discussed in the British press but which had yet to be exhibited. Sadly, I had not.

'How do you find England?' she asked.

'I like London very much,' I replied. 'It reminds me more of Boston than New York, certainly in the number of art galleries and museums, the handsome architecture, the shops. Of course, you have so much history here. I envy you that. Would that I had more time for leisure. Every time I walk in the streets I find all manner of diversions.'

'Perhaps you might be tempted to remain here longer.'

'It is not such a wild supposition, Mrs Jones. It has long been my desire to travel in Europe ... something that is true of many of my countrymen. Most of us came from here, after all. If I am successful in this current investigation with your husband, perhaps I might persuade my superiors to allow me a sabbatical.'

It was my first reference to the business that had brought Athelney Jones and myself together and, as a steaming bread and butter pudding was brought to the table by the little maid who seemed to pop up from nowhere and disappear just as abruptly, our conversation turned to darker things.

'I must tell you something, my dear, that will concern you,' Jones began. 'But you will learn about it from the newspapers soon enough, rarely though you read them . . .' With that, he described the events of the afternoon, the attack on Scotland Yard and my own part in what had happened. As agreed, he mentioned neither the position of the bomb nor the death of his secretary, Stevens.

Elspeth Jones listened in silence until he had finished. 'Were many people killed?' she asked.

'Three, but there were a great many injured,' Jones replied.

'It seems incredible that such an attack on the Metropolitan Police could be considered, let alone carried out,' she said. 'And this so soon after the unspeakable events in Highgate!' She turned to me, fixing me with her bright, inquisitive eyes. 'You will forgive me, Mr Chase, if I say that some very dark forces have followed you from America.'

'I must disagree with you on one major point, Mrs Jones. It was I who followed them.'

'And yet you have arrived at the same time.'

'Mr Chase is not to blame,' Jones muttered, reproachfully.

'I know that, Athelney. And if I suggested otherwise, I apologise. But I begin to wonder if

171

this should even be a police matter. Perhaps it is time for higher authorities to become involved.'

'It may well be that they already are.'

' 'It may well be' is not enough. Police officers have been killed!' She paused. 'Was the bomb very close to your office?'

Jones hesitated. 'It was on the same floor.'

'Were you the intended target?'

I saw him consider before he answered. 'It is too early to say. Several inspectors have offices close to where the bomb was placed. It could have been intended for any one of us. I implore you, my dear, let us speak no more of it.' Fortunately, the maid chose that moment to appear with the coffee. 'Shall we remove to the other room?'

We left the table and returned to the back parlour where the fire was now burning low. At the last moment, the maid had handed Mrs Jones a parcel wrapped in brown paper and, as we sat down, she passed it to her husband. 'I am sorry to trouble you, Athelney, but I wonder if you would mind walking up the road to Mrs Mills?'

'Now?'

'It is her laundry and some books for her to read.' She turned to me and continued in the same breath, 'Mrs Mills is a member of our congregation and recently widowed. To add to her misfortunes, she has not been very well and we do what we can to be good neighbours.'

'Is it not rather late?' Jones asked, still holding the parcel.

'Not at all. She does not sleep very much and

172

I told her you would be looking in. She was delighted to hear it. You know how fond she is of you. Anyway, a stroll will do you good before bed.'

'Very well. Perhaps Chase will accompany me . . . ?'

'Mr Chase has not finished his coffee. He will keep me company while you are gone.'

Her strategy was obvious. She wanted to speak to me on my own and had arranged things to that effect. Throughout the evening, I had been amused to watch my friend, Athelney Jones, in the privacy of his home. So forceful and single-minded when pursuing his investigation, he was altogether quieter and less demonstrative in the company of his wife. Their closeness was indisputable. They filled each other's silences and anticipated the other's demands. And yet I would have said that she was by far the stronger of the two. In her company, Jones lost much of his authority and it made me think that even Sherlock Holmes might have been a lesser detective had he chosen to marry.

Her husband stood up. He took the parcel, kissed her gently on the forehead, and left the room. She waited until she had heard the front door open and close. Then she looked at me in a quite different way, no longer the hostess, and I realised that she was assessing me, deciding whether to draw me into some inner circle of confidence.

'My husband tells me that you have been a detective with Pinkerton's for some time,' she began.

173

'For longer than I care to remember, Mrs Jones,' I replied, 'although strictly speaking, I am an investigator, not a detective. It is not quite the same thing.'

'In what way?'

'We are more straightforward in our methods. A crime is committed. We investigate it. But in most cases it is simply a matter of procedure, which is to say that, unlike the British, we do not go in so much for duplicity and deception.'

'Do you enjoy the work?'

I thought for a moment. 'Yes. There are people in this world who are very bad, who bring nothing but misery to others, and I think it is right to bring them down.'

'You are not married?'

'No.'

'You have never been tempted?'

'You are very forthright.'

'I hope I do not offend you. I only wish to know you a little better. It is important to me.'

'Then I will answer your question. Of course I have been tempted. But I have been of a solitary nature ever since I was a child and in recent years I have allowed my work to consume me. I like the idea of matrimony but I am not sure that for me it would be ideal.' I was uncomfortable with the way the conversation was turning and tried to change the subject. 'You have a beautiful home, Mrs Jones, and a charming family.'

'My husband is very taken with you, Mr Chase.'

'For that I am grateful.'

'And what, I wonder, do you make of him?'

I put down my coffee cup. 'I'm not sure I know what you mean.'

'Do you like him?'

'Do you really want me to answer that?'

'I would not have asked you if I did not.'

'I like him very much. He has welcomed me as a stranger to this country and he has been singularly kind to me when others, I am sure, would have been obstructive. He is also, if I may say so, a brilliant man. In fact, I would go further and add that I have never met a detective quite like him. His methods are extraordinary.'

'Does he remind you of anyone?'

I paused. 'He reminds me of Sherlock Holmes.'

'Yes.' Suddenly her voice was cold. 'Sherlock Holmes.'

'Mrs Jones — that you have deliberately arranged for your husband to leave is obvious. But I don't know why, and I feel it is discourteous to discuss him in his absence. So why don't you tell me. What is it that is on your mind?'

She said nothing but examined me carefully and, sitting there with the firelight reflecting softly on her face, I suddenly thought her very beautiful. Eventually she spoke. 'My husband keeps an office upstairs,' she said. 'He uses it sometimes as a retreat, when he is involved in a case. Would you care to see it?'

'Very much.'

'And I would very much like to show it to you. You need have no concern, by the way. I am permitted to enter when I wish and we will only be there for a minute or two.'

I followed her out of the room and up the stairs past watercolours — mainly birds and butterflies — hanging in plain wooden frames on the striped paper. We reached the first landing and entered a small, uncarpeted room that looked out onto the back garden. I knew at once that this was where Jones worked. And yet it was not he who dominated the room.

The first thing I saw, sitting on a table, was a neat pile of *Strand Magazines*, each one so well preserved as to appear brand new. I did not need to open them to know what I would find inside. They all carried accounts of the adventures of Sherlock Holmes as narrated by Dr John H. Watson and the great detective was present all over the room in photographs, daguerreotypes and newspaper headlines which had been tacked to the wall: BLUE CARBUNCLE RECOVERED, COBURG SQUARE BANK ROBBERY FOILED. On studying the books and monographs on the shelves, I saw that a great many of them had been written by Holmes. Among them was a sizeable volume on the scientific analysis of bloodstains, another (*One Hundred and Sixty Ciphers Examined*) on codes and a third, which reminded me of the train journey from Meiringen, on different types of tobacco ash. There were other books by Winwood Reade, Wendell Holmes, Emile Gaboriau and Edgar Allen Poe, several encyclopedias and gazetteers and a copy of the *Anthropological Journal* lying open at an article concerning the shape of the human ear. Though austere in its general appearance — apart from the bookshelves, the only furniture was a desk, a chair and two small tables — the room was cluttered, with every inch of every surface holding one strange object or another. I saw a magnifying glass, a Bunsen burner, glass phials filled with chemicals, a stuffed snake — a swamp adder, I think — a number of bones, a map of Upper Norwood, what might have been a mandrake root and a Turkish slipper.

I had been hovering in the doorway. Elspeth Jones had gone in ahead of me and now twisted round. 'This is where my husband works,' she said. 'He spends more time here than any other room in the house. I am sure I do not need to tell you who has been his inspiration.'

'It is very evident.'

'We have already spoken his name.' She drew herself up. 'There are times when I wish I had never heard it!' She was angry and her anger made her quite different from the mother who had read to her child and the wife who had sat with me at the dinner table. 'This is what I want to tell you, Mr Chase. If you are to work with my husband, it is vital that you understand. My husband first met Sherlock Holmes following the murder of one Bartholomew Sholto, an investigation that concluded with the loss of the great treasure of Agra. As it happens, he came out of it with some credit, although he never saw it that way, and the account published by Dr Watson portrayed him in a particularly unflattering light.'

Jones had already alluded to it. But I said nothing.

'The two of them met again on a rather less spectacular business, a break-in in North London and the strange theft of three porcelain figures.'

'The Abernettys.'

'He has told you?'

'He has alluded to it. I know none of the details.'

'He doesn't speak of that affair very often — and with good reason.' She paused, composing herself. 'Once again he failed. Once again Dr Watson will have turned him into a laughing stock although, fortunately, he has yet to publish this particular tale. After it was all over, my husband spent weeks torturing himself. Why had he not realised that the dead man had been in prison? There was oakum under his fingernails — a fairly obvious clue when you think about it. Why had he been so blind to the significance of the three identical figurines when it had been so immediately obvious to Mr Holmes? He had missed every single clue of any importance ... the footprints, the sleeping neighbour, even the fold in the dead man's sock. How could he even call himself a detective when he had been shown up as a bumbling amateur?'

'You are too hard on him.'

'He was too hard on himself! I must speak to you in confidence, Mr Chase, hoping with all my heart that you are indeed the friend that you profess to be. Following the Abernetty business, my husband became very ill. He complained of tiredness, toothache, a sense of weakness in his bones. His wrists and his ankles swelled up. At first, I thought he had overworked himself, that all he needed was rest and a little sunshine. However, the doctor soon diagnosed something much more serious. He was afflicted with the rickets, a disease that had actually touched him briefly when he was a child but which had returned in a much more serious and vengeful form.

'He was forced to take a year off work and during that time, I nursed him day and night. To begin with, all I looked for was his recovery but as the months passed and he became a little stronger, I began to hope that he might put his police career behind him. His brother, Peter, is an inspector. His father had risen to become a superintendent. There was, I knew, a sense of family tradition. But even so, with a young child and a wife who feared for him almost daily and with the knowledge that he would never recover his former strength, I allowed myself to believe that he might choose to begin a new life elsewhere.

'I was deceived. My husband dedicated the year of his hiatus to the betterment of his career as a detective. He had met Sherlock Holmes twice. He had been beaten by him twice. He was determined that, should they meet again, history would not repeat itself a third time. In short, Inspector Athelney Jones would make himself the equal of the world's most famous consulting detective and to that end he threw himself into his work with a vigour that belied the disease that had crippled him. You see some of the evidence around you but believe me when I say that this is but a small part of it. He has read everything that Mr Holmes has ever written. He has studied his methods and replicated his experiments. He has consulted with every inspector who ever worked with him. He has, in short, made Sherlock Holmes the very paradigm of his own life.'

Everything she said made sense to me. From the moment I had met Athelney Jones I had been aware of his interest in the great detective. But I had not appreciated how much it went to the heart and soul of who he was.

'My husband returned to his office a few months ago,' Elspeth Jones concluded. 'He thinks he has fully recovered from the worst of his illness — but what actually sustains him is his knowledge of Holmes's work and his belief that he is now Holmes's equal.' There was a terrible pause and then, faltering, she continued. 'I do not share that belief. God forgive me for saying it. I love my husband. I admire him. But more than anything, if he remains blinded by this cruel self-belief, I fear for him.'

'You are wrong — ' I began.

'Do not try to be kind to me. Look around you. Here is the evidence. Heaven knows where this obsession will take him.'

'What do you want me to do?'

'Protect him. I do not know these people he is up against, but I am terribly afraid for him. They would seem to be ruthless. He, in his own way, is so lacking in guile. Is it wrong of me to speak to you in this way? I do not know how I would live without him and these dreadful murders, the attempt today . . . '

She broke off. The whole house was silent.

'Mrs Jones,' I said. 'You have my word that I will do everything I can to guide us both through to safety. It is true that we find ourselves up against a formidable enemy but I do not share your misgivings. Your husband has already demonstrated to me, time and again, his extraordinary intelligence. I am perhaps a few years older than he, but even so I recognise the fact that I am the junior partner in this enterprise. That said, I promise you with all my heart that I will look out for him. I will stand by him. And should we find ourselves in danger, I will do everything in my power to protect him.'

'You are very kind, Mr Chase. I can ask no more.'

'He will be back very soon,' I said. 'We should go downstairs.'

She took my arm and we went back down together. Shortly afterwards, Jones returned and found us sitting before the fire, discussing the five boroughs of New York. He did not see that anything was amiss and I said nothing.

But as I returned to Camberwell station, I was deep in thought. The night was still black, the fog rolling across the pavement. Somewhere far away, a dog howled in the darkness, warning me of things I did not want to know.

12

Foreign Soil

Jones was in a more ebullient mood when we met the next day, exhibiting that strange alacrity of spirit which, I now knew, had found its inspiration in the example set by the greatest detective of all.

'You will be relieved to hear that, finally, we make progress!' he announced as we met outside my hotel.

'You have been back to Chancery Lane?' I asked.

'Silas Beckett and his associates can wait. I would say that it will be at least a week before they slip away into the night.'

'How can you be so sure if you have not returned?'

'I knew it before we left, my dear Chase. Did you not remark upon the position of the hurdy-gurdy player? He was standing precisely eight paces from the front door of the barber's shop.'

'I'm afraid I do not follow you at all.'

'I begin to think that you and I might have a future together. You shall leave Pinkerton's and I shall resign from Scotland Yard. You will enjoy living in London. No! I am quite serious. The city has need of a new consulting detective. We might even take rooms on Baker Street! What do you say?'

'I am not sure what to say.'

'Well, we have more pressing matters at hand. First, our friend Perry. We have now learned that he entered Scotland Yard at twenty minutes to three and claimed to be carrying a package for me, a large box wrapped in brown paper. He was directed to my office on the third floor.'

'Why didn't he leave it in your office?'

'He could not have done so. I was behind my desk and would have been sure to recognise him. Instead, he placed it as near as he could, which was on the other side of the wall in the telegraph office. They are used to seeing messenger boys, apprentices and cadets coming in and going out and one more would have made no difference.'

'But you left.'

'I left to meet you, as we had arranged. Perry must have been just a minute or two ahead of me. That's how close it was! You saw him enter the carriage. Have you had any further thoughts as to the identity of his companion?'

'I have no idea.'

'No matter. Our adversaries may have made their first serious error, Chase. Had they chosen a hansom for their adventure, it might have been impossible to find them. The streets of London are littered with hansoms, licensed and unlicensed, and the driver might never have come forward. The brougham is an altogether rarer beast and its driver is even now in our hands.'

'How did you find him?'

'We have had three divisions on the streets, almost a hundred men. Did you really think that we would allow such an outrage as took place yesterday to go unpunished? Not an inn, not an alley, not a coach house or stable has been overlooked. All night they have been out and now, finally, we have a man who remembers carrying a fare to Whitehall, who heard the explosion and picked up a second passenger shortly afterwards.'

'And where did they go?'

'I have yet to speak to the driver. But if he can tell us where he took them, or where this man came from, then our task will have been accomplished and Devereux may yet fall into our hands.'

Jones had arrived in a cab, which was still waiting for us, and we travelled across London, battling our way through the interminable traffic, without speaking. I was grateful for the silence. It allowed me to reflect on what Elspeth Jones had said to me the night before and to wonder if she had some intuition about what lay ahead. For his part, Jones had not referred to the dinner, although he must have been aware that his wife had arranged things so as to speak privately with me for half an hour. Did he know that we had entered his study? In retrospect, I had found the encounter strangely disturbing. I wished that she and I had spoken a little more . . . or perhaps less.

We finally drew in to a cabstand near Piccadilly Circus, the very heart of the western end of the city, the equivalent, if you like, of Times Square. I saw at once a well-maintained, brightly polished brougham parked with a uniformed police constable standing beside it.

The driver, a huge man in a topcoat that seemed to billow out like a tent, was sitting in his place with the reins across his knees and a scowl on his face.

We climbed down. 'Mr Guthrie?' Jones asked, striding forward.

'Aye, that's me,' the driver responded. 'And I bin 'ere an hour or more. What's it to be when a honest man is kept from 'is livelihood like this?'

He had not moved, staring down at us as if he were as firmly tied into his seat as the horse in its harness. He really was a vast man, with rolling cheeks, side whiskers and crimson-coloured skin that had come either from long exposure to the air in all weathers or, more likely, from sclerosis.

'I am sure we can recompense you for your time,' Jones remarked.

'I don't want your recompents, guv'nor. I want to be paid!'

'You will receive all the money that is due to you — but you must first tell me everything I wish to know. Yesterday you picked up a man.'

'Yesterday I picked up several men.'

'But one of them you took to Whitehall, close to Scotland Yard. It was about three o'clock in the afternoon.'

'I know nothing of the hour. What's an hour to me?' He shook his huge head before Jones could interrupt and it seemed to me that the horse, in sympathy, did the same. 'All right, all right. I know what man you speak of. A tall gentleman. I can tell you that because 'e 'ad to fold 'imself over to get in. Queer customer — that's what I thought.'

185

'What age?'

'Thirty or forty.' He thought for a minute. 'Or maybe fifty. I can't say. Older than he was young — that's all. Nasty eyes. Not the sort of eyes you'd want to have looking your way.'

'And where did you pick him up?'

'At the Strand.'

Jones turned to me. 'That is of no help to us,' he said, quietly. 'The Strand is one of the busiest cabstands in London. It is close to one of the main railway stations and all the drivers use it because it is clear of many of the omnibus routes.'

'So our mysterious passenger could have arrived from anywhere.'

'Precisely. Tell me, Mr Guthrie. You took him directly to Whitehall?'

'I took him as direct as the traffic would allow.'

'He was alone?'

'Alone as alone can be. He kept 'imself to 'imself, wrapped up in the corner with 'is 'at over 'is eyes and 'is eyes turned down to 'is collar. He coughed a few times but not one word did he say to me.'

'He must have informed you of the destination.'

''Whitehall,' he said when he got in. And 'Stop!' when he wanted to get out. Well, there's two words for you. But nothing else. Not so much as a please or a thank you.'

'You took him to Whitehall. What then?'

'He told me to wait.' The driver sniffed, realising his error. 'A third word, guv'nor. That was all it was. 'Wait!' I've 'ad more communication from the 'orse.'

186

'What happened?'

'You know what 'appened! All London knows what 'appened. There was a bang as loud as a Japanese mortar in Vauxhall Gardens. What in 'eaven's name is that, thinks I. But the cove, 'e don't even move. 'E just sits there, looking out, and I get the idea 'e's waiting for someone. And then the boy comes running over and climbs in. A messenger boy. What's going on 'ere, I ask? Only I don't ask because it's clear that neither of 'em's going to say.'

'Did they speak to each other, the man and the boy?'

'They spoke. But I didn't 'ear them. Not with me up front and the doors and the windows closed.'

'Where did you take them?' I asked.

'Not so very far. Through Parliament Square and over to Victoria.'

'To a private house?'

'I don't know what it was. But I can tell you the number. I wouldn't normally remember. I've got no 'ead for numbers. My 'ead is full of numbers so why should I remember one above another? But this one was as easy as one two three. It was one two three. One hundred and twenty-three Victoria Street and if there's nothing else, guv'nor, I've got some more numbers for you. Sixpence the quarter hour waiting time and I've been here two hours at the least. What do you say to that?'

Jones gave the man some money and we hurried away together, striding along the pavement past Fortnum & Mason and up to

Green Park. We hailed another cab and Jones gave the driver the address. 'We have them!' he said to me. 'Even if they do not actually reside in Victoria Street, the house will lead us to them.'

'The man in the brougham,' I muttered. 'He could not have been Clarence Devereux. He would never have ventured out in a coach without first covering the windows.'

'The driver said that he was withdrawn, his face buried in his collar.'

'Not enough, I think, for someone suffering as he does from agoraphobia. There is something else, Jones. It is very strange but I feel that the address, 123 Victoria Street, is known to me.'

'How can that be?'

'I cannot say. I have seen it somewhere, read it . . . I don't know.' I broke off and once again we travelled in silence until we finally arrived in Victoria Street, a wide and well-populated thoroughfare with the crowds drifting in and out of the elegant shops and arcades. We found the house we were looking for, a solid, not very handsome building, recently constructed and clearly too large to be a private home. It immediately put me in mind of Bladeston House and I saw that it had the same sense of impregnability, with barred windows, a gate, and a narrow path leading to an imposing front door. I noticed Jones looking upwards and followed his eyes to the American flag that fluttered on the roof, then down to the plaque set beside the main gate.

'It is the legation of the United States of America!' I exclaimed. 'Of course. We have had many communications with the envoy's staff and Robert Pinkerton stayed here when he was in London. That's how I know the address.'

'The legation . . . ' Jones repeated the word in a voice that was suddenly strained. He paused for a moment, allowing its significance to sink in, and I understood that our coachman might as well have taken his two passengers to the moon for all the good it would do us. 'It is prohibited to us. No officer of the law can enter a legation.'

'But this is where they came,' I exclaimed, 'Perry and his associate. Can it be possible?' I reached out and grabbed hold of the railing as if I could prise it apart. 'Has Clarence Devereux taken sanctuary within his own country's legation? We must go in!'

'It is not possible, I tell you,' Jones insisted. 'We will have to address ourselves to the department of the Foreign Secretary — '

'Then that is what we must do!'

'I do not believe we have enough evidence to support such a request. We have only the word of Mr Guthrie that he brought his passengers here and we cannot be sure that they even entered. It's exactly what happened at Highgate. I followed the boy to Bladeston House but we still cannot say with any certainty that he ever went into the place.'

'Bladeston House! You may remember — Scotchy Lavelle boasted that he enjoyed the protection of the legation.'

'It was my first thought, Chase. At the time, it struck me as very singular.'

'And there was an invitation in his desk. He

189

and that woman had been summoned to this very place.'

'I have it in my office . . . or what remains of it.' Jones had removed anything of interest from Bladeston House, including the diary and the block of soap that had led us to Horner's of Chancery Lane. 'A party to celebrate business enterprise.'

'Can you remember the date?'

Jones glanced at me. He could see at once what I had in mind. 'I believe it was for tomorrow night,' he replied.

'Well, of one thing we can be certain,' I said. 'Scotchy Lavelle won't be attending.'

'For either of us to go in his place would be an extremely serious matter.'

'For you, perhaps, but not for me. I am, after all, an American citizen.'

'I will not let you enter on your own.'

'There can be no possible danger. It is a reception for English and American business-men . . . ' I smiled. 'Is that really how Scotchy thought of himself? I suppose criminal enterprise passes as business of a sort.' I turned to Athelney Jones and he could surely see I was determined. 'We cannot let this opportunity pass us by. If we apply to the Foreign Secretary, it will only warn Clarence Devereux of our intentions.'

'You assume he is here.'

'Does not the evidence suggest it? We can at least take a look inside,' I continued, quickly. 'And surely the risk is small. We will be two guests among many.'

Jones stood, supporting himself on his stick,

gazing at the gate and the door that remained fastened in front of him. The wind had dropped and the flag had fallen, as if ashamed to show its colours.

'Very well,' he said. 'We'll go.'

13

The Third Secretary

The American legation had been transformed for the minister's reception. The gate stood open and torches had been arranged in two lines, blazing the way to the front door. There were half a dozen footmen, equally brilliant in their bright red coats and old-fashioned wigs, bowing to the guests as they climbed down from the phaetons and landaus which had assembled outside. With the lights glowing behind the windows, the piano music playing on the other side of the front door and the flames throwing dark orange shadows across the brickwork, it really was easy to forget that this was a rather drab building and that we were in London, not New York. Even the flag was flying.

Athelney Jones and I had arrived together, both of us in tailcoats and white tie. I noticed that he had exchanged his usual walking stick for another with an ivory handle and wondered if he had one for every occasion. He looked nervous, for once unsure of himself — and I had to remind myself how much of a risk he was taking, coming here. For a British police officer to enter a foreign legation under false pretences and in pursuit of a criminal investigation could be the end of his career. I saw him hesitate, contemplating the open doorway. Our eyes met.

He nodded and we moved forward.

He had retrieved the invitation that he had taken from Bladeston House. Fortunately it had survived both the explosion and the fire although, on close inspection, it was slightly singed. 'The Envoy Extraordinary and Minister Plenipotentiary, Mr Robert T. Lincoln, requests the pleasure of the company of . . . ' The words were written in perfect copperplate and to this had been added: ' . . . Mr Scotland Lavelle and guest.' We were fortunate that the woman whom we had known, all too briefly, as Hen had not been named. We had decided that if we were questioned, I would claim to be Scott, Scotchy or Mr Scotland, as he now seemed to be. Jones would be the anonymous guest and if asked would give his own name.

But in fact, neither of us was examined in any way. A footman glanced at our invitation and waved us through to a wide entrance hall, lined with books that were obviously artificial — they did not pretend to be otherwise — as well as two plaster replicas of classical Greek goddesses, one at each end. The party was taking place on the second floor. It was from here that the piano music was coming. A thickly carpeted staircase led up, but in order to begin the climb, the guests had to pass a line of four men and a woman who had positioned themselves purposefully so as to be able to greet each and every one of them.

The first man I barely noticed for he was standing with his back to the door. He had grey hair and drooping eyelids and there was something so dull and self-effacing about him that he seemed completely unsuited to be part of a welcoming committee. He was also the shortest of the four of them — even the woman towered over him.

It was clear that this lady was the wife of the envoy. Though in no way beautiful, with a prominent nose, pale skin and hair packed too tightly into curls, she was still undeniably regal, greeting all those who approached her as if she alone were the reason they had come. She was severely dressed in brown wool twill with puffed-out gigot sleeves and a ribbon around her neck. As I took her hand and bowed, I smelled lavender water.

'Scotland Lavelle,' I murmured.

'You are very welcome, Mr Lavelle.' The monarch herself could not have said it with less enthusiasm.

Her husband, standing next to her, was more genial, a large, square-shouldered man with deep black hair which swept across his head in two contradictory waves. The smile on his face was fighting a losing battle with the seriousness in his eyes and his every movement seemed formal to the point of being stilted. His cheeks and indeed his mouth were obliterated by a huge beard and moustache which stretched all the way to his ears and which I might almost have described as lopsided and even unkempt. I had seen him addressing the people at the front of the line and it occurred to me that both he and his wife were concealing something, with greater or lesser success. They had been touched quite recently by some sort of sadness and it was still with them, here in the room.

I found myself standing in front of him and once again repeated my false name. By now I was getting used to it. He seized my hand in a powerful grip. 'I am Robert Lincoln,' he said.

'Mr Lincoln . . . ' The name was of course well known to me.

'It is a great pleasure to welcome you to my London home, Mr Lavelle. May I present to you my councillor, Mr White?' This was the third man in the line, also bearded, about ten years younger than the envoy. That gentleman bowed. 'I hope the evening is both enjoyable and useful to you.'

I waited until Athelney Jones had made his introductions and together the two of us climbed the stairs.

'Lincoln . . . ?' he asked.

'The son of Abraham Lincoln,' I replied. How could I have forgotten that this descendant of one of America's most famous families had been sent to the court of King James? A seat had actually been reserved for Robert Lincoln at the Ford Theatre on the night his father had been assassinated and the sympathy that many people felt for him had been translated into enthusiastic support. It was said that Lincoln might himself run for president at the time of the next election.

'This imposture will be the undoing of me,' Jones muttered, half seriously.

'We are in,' I replied. 'And, so far, without any difficulty.'

'I cannot find it in my heart to believe that a

195

criminal organisation could be hiding itself in the sanctuary of an international legation. Such an idea does not bear thinking about.'

'They invited Scotchy,' I reminded him. 'Let's see if we can find the fat boy and the man from the brougham.'

We passed through an archway and into a room that stretched the entire length of the building with floor-to-ceiling windows that might have provided views over the gardens at the back had they not been heavily curtained. There was a crowd of some hundred people already gathered together with a young man at the piano playing the syncopated rhythms which, I imagined, would have been unfamiliar to Athelney Jones but which I recognised as originating from the streets of New Orleans. A long table stood with glasses and what looked like bowls of fruit punch, and waiters were already circulating with plates of food . . . raw oysters with cucumbers and radishes, fishballs, vol-au-vents and so on. It amused me to see that many of the dishes carried labels advertising the ingredients; among them were E. C. Hazard's tomato ketchup, Baltimore vinegar and Colburn's Philadelphia Mustard. Later on, one of the tables would be displaying Chase and Sanborn's finest coffee. But then this was a business gathering and so perhaps the legation staff considered these notices to be part of the etiquette.

There was not a great deal we could do. This was the room in which the reception was to take place and there was no question of our creeping around the legation in search of Clarence

Devereux. If he was here, there was a chance we might stumble across him — or at least across somebody who knew him. If not, we had wasted our time.

We drank some mint julep (*Bourbon from Four Roses, Kentucky*, the label read) and mingled with the other guests. There were soon a couple of hundred people present, all of them in their finest evening dress, and I noticed the little man from the door among them. He was angrily dismissing a waiter who had approached him with a plate of curried sausages. 'I do not eat meat!' The words, expressed in a high-pitched voice, seemed somehow ungracious and out of keeping with the affair. Then, finally, the envoy, his wife and his councillor came up from the entrance hall, signalling that the assembly was complete. From that moment on, wherever Robert Lincoln placed himself, a small crowd gathered round him, and such was his command of the room that Jones and I were unable to escape being drawn into one such circle.

'What is to be done with this business of seal hunting?' someone asked him. With his whiskers and beady eyes, it struck me that there was something seal-like about the interlocutor himself. 'Will we go to war over the Bering Sea?'

'I think not, sir,' Lincoln replied in his quiet way. 'I am quite confident that we will be able to negotiate a settlement.'

'But they are American seals!'

'I am not convinced the seals think of themselves as American, Canadian or anything else. Particularly when they end up as somebody's handbag.' The envoy's eyes twinkled for a moment. Then he turned and suddenly he and I were face to face. 'And what brings you to London, Mr Lavelle?' he asked.

I was so impressed that he had remembered my name — or, at least, the name I had given him — that I faltered and Jones had to answer for me. 'We are in business together, sir. Company promoters.'

'And you are?'

'My name is Jones.'

'I am delighted to see you here.' He nodded at the younger man standing next to him. 'My friend, Mr White, believes that we should look to Central and South America as our natural trading partners. But it is my belief that Europe is the future. If I or my staff can be of any assistance in your enterprise . . . '

He was about to move on but before he could so do, I suddenly blurted out: 'You could indeed help us in one respect, sir.'

He swayed on his foot. 'And how is that?'

'We are seeking an introduction to Clarence Devereux.'

I had spoken the words deliberately loudly and was it my imagination or did a certain hush descend on the room?

The envoy looked at me, puzzled. 'Clarence Devereux? I cannot say I know the name. Who is he?'

'He is a businessman from New York,' I replied.

'In what sort of business?'

But before I could answer, the councillor

stepped in. 'If this gentleman has registered his address with the legation, I am sure one of the secretaries will be able to assist you,' he said. 'You can call at any time.' Gently, without seeming to do so, he led the envoy away.

Jones and I were left alone.

'Mr Jones! Mr Pinkerton!'

My heart sank, hearing myself addressed in this way. I turned and found myself facing Edgar and Leland Mortlake. Although dressed more formally in white tie, as the occasion demanded, the two men presented exactly the same appearance that they had at the Bostonian and it was as if no time had passed between then and now.

'Perhaps I am mistaken,' Edgar Mortlake began, 'but I am sure I just heard the envoy addressing you as Scotland Lavelle. I knew it couldn't be right when I heard the name as poor Scotchy is in no state to attend.'

'An outrage!' Leland Mortlake rasped, his thick lips curling in a scowl.

'It seems to me that you have no right to be here. You were not invited. And if you are present it is only by theft — you stole the invitation, did you not? — and by lying to the envoy of the United States of America.'

'We came in pursuit of our enquiries and following an attack on my office that led to the death of two police officers,' Jones replied. 'You will, of course, pretend you know nothing of that. But we can discuss this at another time. We will leave.'

'I don't think so.' Edgar raised a hand and a

younger, rather pompous-looking man, one I had not seen downstairs, came hurrying over, as if he sensed trouble. 'These two gentlemen are detectives. One is a Pinkerton's agent. The other is from Scotland Yard. They have entered the legation under false pretences and have interrogated the envoy himself.'

The official stared at us. 'Is this true?' he asked.

'It is true that I am a police officer,' Jones replied. 'And I did speak just now with Mr Lincoln. But it was not my intention to meet him and I certainly did not interrogate him.'

'You must have them removed,' Edgar snapped.

'Arrested,' Leland added. As always, one word seemed to be all he could manage.

The official was clearly uncomfortable, aware that this conversation was taking place in a crowded room with the envoy and his wife no more than a few feet away. Jones had maintained his equanimity but I could see that he was deeply troubled. Meanwhile, the two brothers were gloating, enjoying our predicament. 'Gentlemen, you had better come with me,' the official said, at length.

'Gladly.' Jones and I followed him out of the room, leaving the party behind. Neither of us spoke until we had reached the corridor and the doors had been closed. But finding ourselves alone, Jones turned to our escort. 'I do not deny that we should not be here and that, at the very least, this is a most serious breach of protocol. For that I can only apologise. But I can assure you that you will find redress with my superiors and now, with your permission, my friend and I will leave.'

'I am very sorry,' the official replied. 'I do not have the authority to make that decision. I must speak to my own superiors before I can permit you to depart.' He gestured. 'There is a room just down here. If you will wait a few minutes, you will not be detained for long.'

We could not argue. The official showed us into an office where, I presumed, visiting members of the public might find themselves, for it was sparsely furnished with a table and three chairs. A picture of Benjamin Harrison, the twenty-third President of the United States, hung on one wall and a large window looked out onto Victoria Street with the beacons still alight below. The door closed and we were left on our own.

Jones sat down heavily. 'This is a bad business,' he remarked.

'And one that is entirely my fault,' I said, adding quickly, 'I cannot tell you how much I regret the impulse that brought us here tonight.'

'All in all it was probably futile. But I will not blame you, Chase. It was my own decision and there is some significance in the fact that the brothers Mortlake were both here.' He shook his head. 'That said, I do not care to think what may ensue.'

'They will not fire you.'

'They may have no choice.'

'Well, what does it matter?' I exclaimed. 'You have the most remarkable mind I have ever encountered. From the moment we met in Meiringen, I saw that you stood apart from Lestrade and the rest of them. In all my years with the Pinkertons, I have never met an agent like you. Scotland Yard may choose to dispense with you, but let me assure you, my dear Jones, that they will come searching for you, wherever you are. London needs a new consulting detective. You were saying the same only yesterday.'

'It was in my mind, it is true.'

'Then you should make it an actuality. And maybe I will stay here a little longer myself, just as your wife suggested. Yes — why not? I can become your very own Watson, but I can promise you I will cast you in a more flattering light!' He smiled at that. I went over to the window, looking out at the footmen and the waiting coaches. 'Why must we wait here?' I asked. 'The devil with it, Jones, let us be on our way. We can face the consequences tomorrow.'

But before Jones could reply, the door opened and the official returned. He walked towards me and drew the curtain, deliberately blocking the view.

'Are we to be allowed to leave?' I demanded.

'No, sir. The third secretary wishes to meet with you in private.'

'Where is he?'

'He will be here presently.'

No sooner had he spoken than there was a movement at the door and the secretary walked in. I recognised at once the short, grey-haired man I had seen in the entrance hall. Now that we were in close proximity, he seemed even smaller than I had first thought, putting me in mind of the puppet that Jones had purchased for his daughter. He had a very round face with the eyes, nose and mouth grouped tightly — almost too tightly — together. His hair was thin and wispy, showing through to a skull that was peppered with liver spots. Most peculiar of all were his fingers, which, though perfectly formed, were too small for his hands, perhaps half the length they should have been.

'Thank you, Mr Isham,' he said, dismissing the official in the queer, high-pitched voice I had noted earlier. 'Shall we sit down, gentlemen? This is an unfortunate business and we need to be brief.'

We sat down.

'Let me introduce myself. My name is Coleman De Vriess and I hold the position of third secretary here at the legation. You are Inspector Athelney Jones of Scotland Yard?' Jones nodded and he turned to me. 'And you . . . ?'

'My name is Frederick Chase. I am an American citizen, an agent with the Pinkerton Agency in New York.'

'Why are you here?'

It was Jones who replied. 'You will be aware of the outrage that took place two days ago at Scotland Yard. I believe that I was the target of an attack that left three men dead and many more wounded.'

'And your enquiries brought you here?'

'We believe that the man responsible may be

203

hiding behind the protection of the legation, yes.'

'And who might that man be?'

'His name is Clarence Devereux.'

De Vriess shook his head. 'Apart from the envoy and his wife, this legation has only twelve permanent members of staff,' he said. 'I can assure you I have never met the man of whom you speak. And of course we are aware of what happened at Scotland Yard. How could you think otherwise? Mr Lincoln himself sent a message of condolence to your Commissioner and I can understand your desire to apprehend the perpetrator by any means at your disposal. At the same time, however, I cannot stress too highly the impropriety of what you have done, coming here tonight. You are aware, sir, of the principal of extraterritoriality, that the residence of the envoy is protected from British law and that for a police officer to come here in this manner is a flagrant abuse of international protocol.'

'Wait a minute!' I cried. 'We have seen two men in this building tonight, Edgar and Leland Mortlake, and we know them to be gangsters of the very worst kind. I have seen their files at Pinkerton's. I know them for what they are. Yes, Inspector Jones and I may have stepped outside the niceties of the law, but are you going to sit there protecting them and obstructing us, particularly in light of what has occurred?'

'It is the responsibility of this legation to protect American citizens,' De Vriess returned. His voice had not changed but there was anger in his eyes. 'To the best of my knowledge, the two gentlemen of whom you speak are

204

businessmen, nothing more. Do you have evidence of any crime they have committed in this country? Is there any good reason to request their extradition? No. I thought not. And if I may say so, there is nothing to be gained by adding slander to the list of charges which will be brought against you.'

'What is it you plan to do?' Jones asked.

'You have my sympathy, Inspector Jones.' From the look on the third secretary's face, he had anything but. He folded his hands on his lap, lacing his fingers together. The tips barely reached his knuckles. 'It is my intention to lodge a formal complaint with your superiors first thing tomorrow and I will accept nothing less than your dismissal from the force. As to your friend, there is little we can do to rein in Mr Pinkerton's agents. They are well known for their excesses and for their irresponsible behaviour. I will have you removed from this country, Mr Chase, and you may well find yourself being prosecuted in an American court. And that, gentlemen, is all. I have a party to return to. You will be shown to the door.'

Jones stood up. 'I have one question,' he said.

'And what is that?'

'When you came into this room, you addressed me, correctly, as Athelney Jones. I wonder how you came by that information as neither of the Mortlake brothers were fully acquainted with my first name?'

'I do not see the relevance — '

'But I do!' To my astonishment, Jones strode across the room and, using his walking stick,

205

hooked the edge of the curtain and threw it back, revealing the scene outside. For a moment I thought there was something he wanted us to see but then I realised he had quite another aim in mind. The effect on the third secretary was extraordinary. It was as if he had been struck in the face. For a moment, he sat in the chair, staring wildly, gasping for breath. Then he twisted round, unable to look outside for one minute longer.

'I would advise you against reporting me to anyone, Clarence Devereux!' exclaimed Jones.

'Devereux . . . ?' I got to my feet, staring at the cowering figure.

'Now everything is explained,' Jones went on. 'The connections between Lavelle, the Mortlakes and the legation; the reasons why the carriage came to this place and why you can never be found. Is Mr Lincoln aware, I wonder, of the sort of man he employs as his third secretary?'

'The drapes!' the man who had called himself Coleman De Vriess muttered in a high-pitched whisper. 'Close them, damn you!'

'I will do no such thing. Admit who you are!'

'You have no right to be here. Get out!'

'We are leaving, of our own volition. But let me tell you, Devereux. We know who you are now. We know where you are. And although you may hide in the legation for a while to come, you can no longer rely on its protection. We have found you and we will not let you go!'

'You will die before you come close.'

'I think not!'

'You cannot touch me. And I swear to you — you will regret this day!'

Jones was ready to leave but I was not. 'You are Devereux?' I exclaimed, looming over this small, trembling man. 'You are the criminal mastermind we have so long feared? It was you who came to London believing that you could yoke the entire underworld to your desires? I would not believe it but for the evidence of my own eyes and what I see is beneath contempt.'

With an animal snarl, Devereux lunged at me and might have grabbed hold of me had Jones not pulled me back.

'Can we not arrest him?' I cried. 'I have travelled halfway around the world to find this man. We can't just leave him.'

'There is nothing we can do. We have no authority here.'

'Jones . . . '

'Forgive me, Chase. I know your feelings. But we have no choice. We must leave now. We cannot be found here.'

Still I wanted to fall upon Devereux, De Vriess, whatever he called himself. The man was trembling, his eyes half-closed. I thought of the trail of blood that had brought us here, the fate of Jonathan Pilgrim, who had been so mercilessly put to death by this creature or his cohorts. I remembered all the suffering he had caused. I believe, had I not left my jackknife at the hotel when I changed, I would have plunged it into him with no second thought but Jones had seized hold of me. 'Come!'

'We can't!'

'We must! We have no evidence against him, nothing but the strange psychological condition that has reduced him to this state.'

'You will die for this,' Devereux hissed. He was half-covering his eyes, his whole body contorted. 'And it will be slow. I will make you pay.'

I wanted to reply but Jones dragged me out of the room. The corridor was empty and nobody tried to apprehend us as we continued down the stairs and back out into the street. Only once we were in the open, away from the legation gates, did I free myself from my friend's grip and spin round, sucking in the evening air. 'That was Devereux! Clarence Devereux!'

'None other. Was it not obvious? When we first entered the hall, he had his back to the door. It was his agoraphobia. He did not dare look out! And before he came into the room, he sent his lackey in to draw the curtains for the same reason.' Jones laughed. 'And his name! There's vanity for you. Coleman De Vriess. CD. He chooses to hide behind the same initials.'

'But did we really have to leave him? For Heaven's sake, Jones, we have just discovered the greatest criminal of his generation and we walk out without apprehending him, without saying another word!'

'If we had tried to apprehend him, all would have been lost. Our own position was tenuous for we were there under false pretences. I have no doubt that Mr Lincoln and his friends are unaware of the sort of man they are protecting but even so their natural instinct would have been to come to his defence, to support one of their own.' Jones smiled grimly. 'Well, the game has changed. Now we are at liberty, we can regroup and plan our next move.'

'To arrest him!'

'Of course.'

I looked back at the legation — at the coaches, the footmen, the flickering lights. It was true. We had found Clarence Devereux. There was only one problem. How in Heaven's name were we going to draw him out?

14

Setting the Trap

I slept fitfully that night. My rest was once again disturbed by my troublesome neighbour who had never once left his room but who seemed to haunt the hotel with his presence. He seemed to eat neither breakfast nor dinner. He had arrived at the same time as me — or so the maid told me — but he never went out. I thought of confronting him but decided against it. For all I knew, he might be a perfectly innocent traveller, transformed into a threat only by my imagination. Indeed, had it not been for the noise of his coughing and that one, brief glimpse at the window, I would not even be aware of his existence.

Far more disturbing were my weird, distorted dreams of Clarence Devereux. I saw his face, his malevolent eyes, those ridiculous fingers of his, too small for any man. 'I do not eat meat!' I heard him cry, but then I found myself lying on an oversized plate with a knife on one side, a fork on the other, and I was certain he was about to eat me. I was back at the legation with Robert Lincoln and his wife. I was at Bladeston House with blood pooling around my feet. Finally, I was at the Reichenbach Falls, plunging down for an eternity with the water crashing around me only to open my eyes and find myself in bed, the sheets crumpled and a rainstorm lashing against the windows.

I had no appetite and ate little breakfast for I was anxious to hear from Jones as to what, if anything, had ensued as a result of our evening's adventure. The news, when we met, was not good. Contrary to my expectations, an official complaint had already been made by the American legation, naming Jones and addressed to the Commissioner.

'Our friend Coleman De Vriess had the temerity to sign it himself,' Jones said as we sat together in another cab, splashing through the puddles that the brief storm had left behind. 'It was delivered at nine o'clock this morning. Fast work, would you not say?'

'What will happen?' I asked.

'I will almost certainly lose my position.'

'This is my doing . . .'

'Tut, man, it is of no importance. My beloved Elspeth will be delighted for one and anyway we have several days before any action will be taken. First there will have to be an interrogation, then a committee, then a report, a review and finally a recommendation. This is how the British police force works. A great deal can happen in that time.'

'But what can we do?'

'We have a dilemma, it is true. We cannot arrest Clarence Devereux. It will be difficult even to interview him without the permission of his envoy and I suspect that will not be forthcoming, particularly in the light of last night's events. What proof do we have that he is involved in any nefarious activity?'

'You have seen the files that I brought from

New York. And you heard what your colleague Stanley Hopkins had to say. Devereux's name is known all over London.'

'But the name of Coleman De Vriess is not. I have to say, it is an ingenious idea for a criminal to hide behind the curtain of diplomatic immunity.' Jones chuckled. He did not appear remotely put out. 'No. There is only one way we can lay our hands on Mr Devereux and that is to capture him red-handed. We must set a trap. The moment he makes an appearance outside the legation, we will have him.'

'Where will we begin?'

'The answer is perfectly obvious. Indeed . . . Slow down, driver! I believe we have arrived.'

We had driven but a short distance and, looking around me, I saw that we had returned to the top of Chancery Lane. I had almost forgotten Silas Beckett and his unpleasant barber's shop, such had been the pace of events. But as we climbed down, I saw that a group of police constables were waiting for us, out of sight of both the shop and the hurdy-gurdy man whose lamentable playing could be heard around the corner. 'Stay close to me,' Jones commanded. Then, to the nearest of the officers: 'You know what to do?'

'Yes, sir.'

'Do not on any account show yourselves until we are in the shop.'

This was something else that Jones had inherited from Sherlock Holmes; the maddening habit of not explaining himself until the last minute — and not even then, it would seem, for he did not say a word as we turned the corner and began to walk down the rutted track that led to Staples Inn Gardens. The moment we appeared, the hurdy-gurdy man stopped playing and I recalled that he had behaved in exactly the same way the last time we had come here. It would have been natural for Jones to make straight for the barber's shop — was that not why we were here? — but instead he walked up to the silent musician.

'Hair tonic, sir?' the man asked. 'Cut or shave?'

'Not today, thank you,' Jones replied. 'But since you mention it, I would be interested to see the style of your own hair.' And before the man could stop him, he had reached out and plucked the top hat off his head, revealing a shock of bright red hair. 'It is just as I thought.'

'What do you mean?' I asked.

'Red hair!'

'What can the colour of his hair possibly have to do with the matter?'

'It has everything to do with it.' He turned to the indignant musician. 'I believe I am addressing Mr Duncan Ross — at least, that is the name you were using two years ago. Your true name, however, is Archie Cooke and this is not the first time you have been engaged on an enterprise such as this!' The other man started and would have fled but for the weight of the musical instrument which held him down. Jones grabbed his arm. 'You and I are going to enter the barber's shop together. Let me advise you against making any trouble. It may go easier for you in the end.'

'I am an honest man!' Cooke protested. 'I play music. I'm paid to advertise the shop. I know nothing more.'

'That's enough of that, Archie. I know everything. Disown your partner if you must, but waste no more of my time.'

The three of us crossed the road and re-entered the dingy parlour where we had first met Silas Beckett. I noticed that Archie was limping heavily. As the door closed behind us, the barber appeared, once again climbing up from the basement. He was astonished to see the hurdy-gurdy player and one look at Jones told him that his game — whatever it was — was up. I thought he would turn and run. There might be another way out of the building. But Jones had anticipated him.

'Stay where you are, John Clay!' he commanded, releasing the other man and propelling him into the well-worn leather chair. 'Yes! I know your true name. I know exactly what you are doing here. Do not attempt to run. I have officers at both ends of the street. But if you will trust me and play fair with me, there is still a chance that this may not end too badly for you.'

The barber considered. Then I saw him slump and it was as if he had allowed a coat to slip from his shoulders. He had visibly changed into an older, wiser man and when he spoke his voice had altered too. 'I prefer *Mr* Clay,' he said.

'I am surprised to see you out of jail so soon.'

'The judge, a very civilised gentleman, recognised the damage that a lengthy sentence would have on a delicate constitution such as

214

mine.' It was hard to believe that it was the same man speaking. 'It may also have helped that we had, by coincidence, both gone to the same school.'

'What . . . ?' I began.

'Let me introduce you to Mr John Clay, the well-known murderer, thief, smasher and forger — or so Sherlock Holmes described him. He is a criminal of the utmost ingenuity, Chase, the inventor of the so-called Red-Headed League.'

'The robbery at Coburg Square!' I exclaimed. Had I not seen a newspaper article about the very same, pinned to the wall in Jones's study?

'The failed robbery. When I first came here, I found it hard to believe that I was encountering the very same John Clay and that he had once again returned to his favourite *modus operandi*. And yet I quickly perceived it had to be the case. You will permit me to explain, Mr Clay?'

'You can do what you like, sir. It is a matter of indifference to me.'

'Very well. What we were presented with here was a barber's shop that had been expressly designed to put off customers. Not only was the room filthy, but the barber's own hair has been quite hideously cut. It would be a foolish soul who would allow the razor to come anywhere near their head in such a place or, for that matter, to purchase a hair tonic whose principal ingredient would appear to be glue. Why, I would be more comfortable at Sweeney Todd's! But that, of course, was the idea. For Mr Clay had more pressing matters to attend to. Just across the road is the Chancery Lane Safe Deposit

Company. For five years or more it has provided strongrooms for London's wealthiest families.'

'Six thousand safes,' Clay muttered, sadly.

'Mr Clay has been tunnelling beneath the road, intending to break into the vault. His associate, Archie Cooke, was a necessary part of the operation, providing two services. First, the appalling noise of his playing would cover the sound of the digging taking place beneath his feet. I was able to work out how far the tunnel extended by his position in the street. You are, I believe, almost there.'

'Another few days and we will be done.'

'He also provided a warning should anyone approach the shop.'

'He stopped playing!' I said.

'Precisely. The silence would alert Mr Clay and give him time to climb back up to the surface. He could not, however, change his trousers. I saw at once that the knees were very creased — the very same clue that Holmes noticed last time, by the way.'

'You asked if he was religious.'

'He had clearly been kneeling. Had he been at prayer, the result might have been the same. As soon as he told me that he did not attend church, I knew that my conclusion was correct. On the last occasion, Mr Clay used an ingenious fabrication to persuade a London pawnbroker to absent himself from his premises. This present ruse shows that he has lost none of his inventiveness.'

John Clay bowed. There was something close to a smile on that strange, boyish face. 'I have to say, sir, that it gives me some consolation to be arrested by the best. Sherlock Holmes last time and now you! Permit me to say, though, that I have never actually murdered anyone. There was a death, it is true, but we had both been drinking and the person in question fell. He was not pushed.'

'I have no interest in your past, Mr Clay. It may be that you can escape arrest — or at least ameliorate your situation by assisting me. Can I trust you to be honest?'

'You are speaking, sir, to a distant relative of Her Majesty the Queen — albeit one who has long been ignored. If it is possible to come to some sort of arrangement that will help me in my current difficulties, I will be true to my word.'

'It is as I hoped. Let me tell you then how I found my way to Chancery Lane in the first place. My friend and I visited the scene of a number of vicious murders, Bladeston House in Highgate. The owner, one Scott or Scotchy Lavelle, had written the name of this establishment, and part of its address, in his diary.'

'I knew Lavelle. I didn't kill him. But I can't say I was too sorry to hear of his demise.'

'Is the name Jonathan Pilgrim familiar to you?'

'No.'

'He was an agent of Pinkerton's, the American law-enforcement agency, and he also knew of your scheme. He was himself murdered but he left behind one of your advertising cards which also brought us here.'

There was a brief silence. Then Clay drew

himself up. 'Archie, old pal, make some tea. Gentlemen, can I invite you into my back parlour? I never thought I would be glad to meet two officers of the law, nor to have the bracelets snapped on my wrists, but I am glad to see you. Have tea with me and I will tell you my story. You have my word, on my royal blood, that it is my overwhelming desire to help!'

We repaired to the back room and sat on rickety chairs at a bare wooden table while Archie poked among the coals. Following Jones's revelations, Clay seemed to have regained so much of his composure that the three of us could have been three old friends, discussing something that we had been planning from the start.

'I came out of Holloway,' Clay began. 'Not a pleasant place. To a gentleman of breeding, something like a pigsty and I couldn't even pay chummage to get a room of my own. Never mind. The judge, a charming man as I may have mentioned, had at least been lenient — and I cast about me, wondering what I might do next. The failure of my red-headed scheme had been something of a shock to me. What do you say, Archie? It had required a great deal of preparation. It was a shame that Holmes got involved. Another few days and we'd have got away with it.

'This was in February and the moment I stepped outside, I knew that something was wrong. All my old chums were lying low and the pubs of Shoreditch could have been funeral parlours for all the fun that was to be had. It was as if the Ripper himself had come back to haunt the streets of London . . . that or something worse.

'It was worse, as I found out soon enough. A new mob had arrived. Americans, it was said. I have never been very partial to Americans myself, present company excepted. In my view, it was a great shame that my ancestor, King George the Third, allowed the colonies to slip through his fingers. But I digress . . . These people had come over from New York and, having planted themselves in the city, they had spread like syphilis. I have lost many friends, many colleagues. They didn't play by our rules and for six weeks the streets and alleyways had been running with blood and I can assure you that I'm not employing a metaphor in this particular instance. I mean it. These people were vicious.'

The kettle had boiled. Archie filled the teapot and brought it to the table. He was still moving with difficulty and I saw that he was in pain.

'Where was Moriarty?' I asked.

'Moriarty? I never met him myself, although I knew of him, of course. We all did. There was a man to be feared if ever there was one. And he took his cut too! There was no crime committed in London that he didn't take his share of and we all used to complain about it — in whispers — although to be fair he was always there when you needed him. I'll say that for him. But he'd gone, disappeared. This fellow, Clarence Devereux, had taken his place. And Devereux made Moriarty look like a fairy godmother though he too never showed himself, sending his lieutenants to do his dirty work.

'Archie and I were sitting in our little lodging house owned by a Jew in Petticoat Lane when they came calling, Scotchy Lavelle, a nasty, pig-eyed man, surrounded by a bunch of hooligan boys. They were English, to their eternal shame and damnation, for that was how these newcomers worked. They recruited straight from the gutter. That gave them the muscle for an army drawn from the rookeries and the opium dens who would do anything for half a crown. No loyalty. No patriotism. And they were well informed. They knew everything about the city and the professionals who worked it — the busters and the screwmen, the skittle-sharps and the rest of them. And they knew about me.

'They bust in while we were having breakfast and tied Archie to a chair. Scotchy did nothing himself. He stood there, strutting, while his boys did the dirty work for him. Then, finally, he laid out his proposition. Why do I call it that? It was a demand and it would be death if I refused, no doubt of that.

'There was an empty shop just off Chancery Lane, opposite the Safe Deposit Company. They reckoned it would take me a few weeks to tunnel underneath the road and break in. The place was filled with gold and silver, jewellery and cash. They would pay the rent for the premises but Archie and me, we would do all the filthy work, squatting underground. We'd take all the risk. And what did they want in return for their kindness? Mr Devereux would take half of everything, they told me. Half! Even Moriarty never demanded more than twenty per cent.'

'And you agreed?' Jones asked.

'When you're surrounded by five cutthroats and the bacon's gone cold, it's best not to argue. Even so, I have my dignity. I protested in no uncertain terms. And that was when that devil turned to poor Archie. 'Hurt him!' he said. The words were spoken. There was nothing I could do.'

'You could have stopped them,' Archie mumbled.

'It all happened too quickly. It was horrible. They pulled his shoe off and right in front of me . . . ' Clay stopped. 'Show them, Archie.'

The red-haired boy leaned down and took his shoe off. And now I understood why he had been limping when we brought him into the barber's shop. He had lost the nail from his big toe, which was still swollen and bloody.

'They did this to me!' he whispered, and there were tears in his eyes.

'They used a pair of pliers,' Clay continued. 'There was a lot of screaming and it quite put me off my breakfast, I can tell you. And I knew it could be worse. If I refused, they might start on me! I had never seen such wanton savagery and of course I knew at that point I had no choice.

'We moved in here. It was my idea to reopen the barber's shop and — you've got it in one — to do everything in my power to prevent customers from entering. In the entire time we've been here, I've only had to give half a dozen haircuts — and didn't do too bad a job, though I say so myself. I've been underground

221

with Archie as my lookout and it's been the devil's own work, I can tell you. Mudstone, limestone, chalk! Whatever happened to good old-fashioned London clay?'

'After the murder of Scott Lavelle, did you hear from Clarence Devereux?' Jones asked.

Clay shook his head. 'Not from Devereux. I read about the death in the newspapers and Archie and I went out and celebrated with a bottle of gin. I thought it was too good to be true. The next day we had a visit from an even nastier piece of work. I've never been a nark, but I'll make an exception for these fine fellows. His name was Edgar Mortlake. He was tall, well-dressed with oily black hair.'

'We know him.'

'You don't want to know him! He gave us another two weeks to get into the vault. After that, he said, we'd lose another toenail.'

'*You* didn't lose a toenail!'

'You know what I mean, Archie. That was what he said and we've been working night and day ever since.'

'And what was the arrangement to be, once you had broken into the vault?'

'Mr Mortlake said he would communicate with us personally.'

'You are to hand over the proceeds to him?'

'Oh yes. He wants to see it all for himself. They trust no one, these Americans. You can forget your honour among thieves. Archie and I even wondered if they would be content with half. They might draw us into a trap and cut both our throats.'

'There will be a trap,' Jones muttered. 'But it will not be you who falls into it. And now, I would very much like to see this tunnel of yours. It must be quite a feat of engineering. And I would be interested to know how you intended to break through the walls of the vault itself.'

'It is only London brick. There is steel plating on the first floor but the safes are less well protected below. Mr Devereux had made the necessary enquiries, I'll at least give him that.'

We got up from the table, leaving the tea unpoured, and made our way down a steep and narrow staircase that brought us into a cellar beneath the shop. There was barely enough room for the four of us as most of the floor was taken up by mounds of soil and broken brickwork. One of the walls had been battered through and, crouching down, I saw a circular tunnel disappearing into the distance, lit by oil lamps and held up by rough planks of wood. It amazed me that John Clay would have been able to breathe in there. Even in the cellar, the air was warm and dank. He would only have been able to progress on his knees, with his body bent forward, passing the loose soil behind him as he went.

'You have been more than forthright with me, Mr Clay,' Jones remarked, the oil lamps casting dark shadows across his face. 'And whatever crimes you may have committed in the past, they are not, for the time being, under consideration. A great evil has come to this country, just as I was warned, and here is the opportunity to be rid of it once and for all. Come, Chase. Let us return to the surface. We have been in the dark for far too long and little time remains.'

We climbed the stairs and left the barber's shop. I had never seen Jones more determined nor more confident, leaving me in no doubt whatsoever that although he seemed to hold all London in his grip, Devereux's time would soon be done.

15

Blackwall Basin

From *The Times* of London
20th May 1891

A DARING ROBBERY IN LONDON

The whole of London has been outraged by a crime that took place in the small hours of the morning when thieves broke into the Chancery Lane Safe Deposit, which has been a place of security for businesses and families for the past six years. Boasting six thousand safes and strongrooms with armed night watchmen on constant patrol, this highly regarded institution might have seemed impregnable. However, the thieves, with extraordinary fortitude, had burrowed underneath the street and broke in through the walls of one of the lower vestibules. They then proceeded to ransack many of the strongboxes, seizing goods valued at several hundred pounds. Their audacity might have been rewarded with even greater returns but for the quick-wittedness of Mr Fitzroy Smith, the night supervisor, who became aware of a strange draught in the corridor and went downstairs to investigate. However, clients of the Chancery Lane Safe

Deposit have besieged the building since the break-in was discovered, clamouring to know if their own valuables have been removed. The case is being investigated by Inspector A. MacDonald of Scotland Yard, but so far no arrests have been made.

I have no idea how Jones had persuaded *The Times* to fall in with his plans but this was the story that appeared twenty-four hours after our meeting with John Clay. It led, inevitably, to a panic, a mob of the well-to-do besieging Chancery Lane, and I cannot say for sure how he managed them, either. I would imagine that officials at the Safe Deposit were suitably emollient: 'No, sir, *your* strongbox was not interfered with. Sadly, we cannot let you inside today. The police are still pursuing their enquiries.'

To close a major business for forty-eight hours as a result of a robbery that had never taken place was certainly quite an achievement, but then the stakes were high and, the fact was, Jones was running out of time. The Commissioner had read the letter from Coleman De Vriess and had called an enquiry to take place at the first opportunity and, as Jones had made clear to me, a Scotland Yard enquiry was akin to a formal dismissal.

It was a Wednesday when the newspaper story broke. I did not see Jones then but he sent a note to the hotel and we met the following day at an address in Chiltern Street, just south of Baker Street Station. The building in question turned out to be very small and narrow, though well lit, with a sitting room on the first floor and a bedroom above. It had been empty for some time although it had been dusted and kept clean. Jones was as self-assured as I had ever seen him, standing in front of the fireplace with his walking stick in front of him.

At first, I was puzzled. What part could this address possibly play in our investigation? Was it in some way connected with John Clay? Jones soon enlightened me. 'Mr Clay is safe at his lodgings in Petticoat Lane. I have two men keeping watch on him and his associate, Archie Cooke. But I do not think they will attempt to fly the coop. The truth is that they are both as fond of Mr Devereux as we are and will be happy to see him brought to justice, particularly if, by helping us, they are able to escape it themselves.'

'They have made contact with him?'

'He understands that they are holding several hundred pounds' worth of articles stolen from the Chancery Lane Safe Deposit, of which he believes himself to be entitled to half. The article in *The Times* was particularly well phrased, I thought — but will it be enough to entice him out of the legation? Who knows? Perhaps he will decide to send his agents, but even that may be enough to provide us with the evidence we need to make an arrest. We must just hope that he moves quickly. Mr Clay has made it clear to them that he needs to leave London urgently. That was of course my doing. Let us see what unfolds.'

'And what of this place? Why are we here?'

'Is it not obvious, my dear Chase?' Jones

smiled and it occurred to me that I was seeing him as he might once have been, before his illness had struck him down. 'Whatever may happen in the next few days, it is clear to me that my career with Scotland Yard is finished. This is a conversation we have already begun. But we have spoken before, you and I, of working together. Why should we not make it a reality? Do you not think it might work?'

'And these rooms . . . ?'

' . . . are for rent on very reasonable terms. There is one bedroom — for you. I will, of course, continue to live with my dear Elspeth and Beatrice. But would not this be an ideal consulting room? Twelve steps from the street and just round the corner from . . . well, it's of no matter. Would you consider it, my dear fellow? You have already told me that you are unmarried and have no family ties. Does America hold so very much for you that you would wish to return?'

'And how would I live?'

'It would be an equal partnership. The money we would make as consulting detectives would, I am sure, be more than enough.'

For a moment, I was unsure how to reply. 'Inspector Jones,' I said at length, 'you never cease to surprise me and meeting you has certainly been one of the most remarkable experiences of my life. Will you forgive me if I ask for a little more time to consider your proposal?'

'Of course.' If he was disappointed by my reticence, he tried not to show it.

'What you say is true,' I continued. 'I have led

a somewhat solitary life in New York and I have allowed my work to consume me. I know that my time with the Pinkerton Agency is coming to an end and it might be good for me to consider new horizons. Even so, I must give the matter more thought. What say we leave any decision until our work is done and Clarence Devereux is brought to justice? From the way things are proceeding, that cannot be too long.'

'I utterly concur. But shall I tell the landlord that we are interested? I am sure he can be persuaded to keep the rooms for a week or two. And after that, if you are in agreement, we will have to set about finding a Mrs Hudson to look after us. That is of the foremost importance. As to the future and our ability to sustain ourselves, I have many friends within Scotland Yard. Business will be forthcoming, I assure you.'

'Your Holmes to my Watson? Maybe it's not such a bad idea. They have, after all, left a gap that must be filled.'

He stepped forward and held out a hand. I took it. And in that moment, I think we were as close as we would ever be. I was still quite dazed by the suggestion but I could tell that my friend Jones was fired with enthusiasm, as if he were about to achieve something that he had been searching for his entire life.

That same evening, John Clay received a message from Clarence Devereux, delivered by a street urchin who had been paid sixpence for his pains. He was to present himself — along with the entire proceeds of the Chancery Lane Safe Deposit robbery — at Warehouse 17, Blackwall

Basin. The meeting would take place at five o'clock in the afternoon, the following day. There was no signature on the note. The words, written in capital letters, were short and simple. Jones examined both the ink and the paper with his usual forensic eye but there was nothing that connected it with America or with the legation. Even so, neither of us had any doubt as to the identity of the sender.

The trap was set.

And so to the Friday. I had barely finished breakfast when the Boots informed me that I had a visitor. 'Show him in,' I said. There was still tea in the pot for two.

'He's outside,' Boots returned, with a scowl. 'He's not the sort to be seen in a respectable establishment. He's in the hall.'

Intrigued, I set down my napkin and left the room to find the most reprehensible-looking fellow waiting for me by the front door. I saw at once that he was dressed as a sailor, though one who would have disgraced any ship that would choose to have him as part of its crew. His red flannel shirt hung out of his canvas trousers and he had an ill-fitting pilot's coat whose sleeves barely reached halfway down his arms. He was unshaven, his face stained with indigo, and there was a filthy bandage wrapped around his ankle. He had a crutch tucked under his arm and if it were not for the absence of a parrot, the picture of piracy and dissolution could not have been more complete.

'Who are you?' I demanded. 'What is it you want?'

'Beg pardon, sir.' The man touched a dirty finger to his forelock. 'I come from Blackwall Basin.'

'And what is your business with me?'

'To bring you to Mr Clay.'

'I'll be damned if I'll go anywhere with you. Are you telling me that Clay sent you here? How did he know this address?'

'It was given to him by that policeman. What's his name? Jones! He's waiting for you even now.'

'Waiting for me where?'

'I'm right in front of you, Chase. And the two of us should be on our way!'

'Jones!' I stared at him and as I did so, the detective moved forward, leaving the chimera of the sailor behind. 'Is it really you?' I exclaimed. 'Well, I'll be damned! You had me completely fooled. But why are you dressed like this? Why are you here?'

'We must set out at once,' Jones replied, and his voice was completely serious. 'Our friend Mr Clay will be at the warehouse later but we must be there ahead of him. Devereux will not suspect that anything is amiss. He will have read the newspaper and he knows that Clay lives in fear of him. Even so, we can take no chances. Everything must be prepared.'

'And the disguise?'

'A necessary addition — and not just for me.' He leaned down and picked up a cloth bag which he threw at me. 'A sailor's jacket and trousers — they came from the slop-house but they are less filthy than they appear. How quickly can you get changed? I have a cab waiting outside.'

Jones had suggested to me that I might one day recount our adventures — in the new *Strand*, perhaps — and it was as if, in taking me to the London docks, he had set me my first, impossible task. For how can I begin to describe the extraordinary panorama, the sprawling metropolis on the edge of the city, that now presented itself to me? My first impression was of a darkening sky but it was only smoke, vomiting out of the chimneys and reflecting drearily in the water below. Against this were silhouetted a hundred cranes and a thousand masts, a fleet of sailing ships, steamboats, barges, coasters and lighters, few of them moving, the majority of them frozen together in a grey tableau. I had never seen so many different flags. It seemed that the whole world had gathered here and as I drew nearer I saw negroes, lascars, Poles and Germans all shouting in different languages as if the tower of Babel had just fallen and they were fighting their way out of the debris.

The river itself ran black and indifferent to the chaos it had propagated. A network of canals had been cut inland, giving berth to Russian brigs, to hoys laden with straw, to luggers and sloops, while the cranes swung round with sacks of grain and great lengths of timber still smelling of turpentine, and the scene was as much an assault on the nose as on the eyes with spices, tea, cigars and, above all, rum, making their presence known long before they were seen. After a while, it became impossible to progress any faster than walking pace. Our way was blocked by a tangle of sailors and stevedores, horses, vans and wagons and even the widest passageways proved unequal to the task of processing this great mass of humanity.

Eventually, we climbed down. We were surrounded by shops — a carpenter's, a wheelwright's, a blacksmith's, a plumber's — vague figures going about their business behind dirty windows. A butcher in a blue apron strode past carrying a fat, squealing pig in a tiny cage, the whole thing balanced on his shoulder. A crowd of ragamuffin children — chasing each other or being chased — scattered on each side. There was a cry of warning and something foul and odorous splashed down from an open doorway above. Jones grabbed hold of me and we continued past a chandler and the inevitable pawnbroker, an old Jew sitting in the doorway, examining a pocket watch with an oversized magnifying glass. Ahead of us, I saw the first of the warehouses, a construction of woodwork, iron and brick, mouldering in the damp and half-sinking into the ground, which seemed unable to bear its weight. There were derricks jutting out in every direction and barrels of wine, boxes of hardware and all manner of sacks and hogsheads being lifted on ropes and pulleys, unloaded onto platforms and then swallowed up inside.

We continued, leaving some of the crowds behind us. The warehouses appeared to be numbered without rhyme or reason and we quickly came upon number seventeen which was square and solid, four storeys high, located on the corner where a canal met the river with large doorways open front and back. Jones led us to a pile of old nets strewn on the towpath and threw himself down, inviting me to do the same. A couple of crates and a rusting cannon completed our *fête champêtre*. Jones took out a bottle of gin and I opened it and took a cautious sip. It contained only water. I understood his purpose. We had several hours to wait until the rendezvous. Dressed as we were — for I was now in the attire of an itinerant dockworker — we would give no cause for suspicion, easily blending in with the scenery. We might be two dissolute labourers, waiting for the foreman to take pity on us and give us a day's work.

Fortunately, it was a warm day and I must confess I quite enjoyed lying there in silent companionship with the constant activity going on all around us. I did not dare take out my watch — there was always the possibility that we were being observed — but from the movement of the clouds I could tell how the afternoon was passing and I was confident that Athelney Jones would be aware of any movement or anything that might suggest that Clarence Devereux was on his way.

In fact it was John Clay and Archie Cooke who arrived first, the two of them sitting next to each other on a light cart with a great pile of merchandise covered by a tarpaulin behind them. Clay, in his vanity, had cut his hair short, ridding himself of the strange appearance he had adopted when he was pretending to be a barber. I expected the two of them to stop but they drove straight into the warehouse without noticing us.

'Now it begins,' Chase muttered, barely glancing at me.

Another hour passed. There were still crowds of people in the dock, for labour would continue until night fell and perhaps even beyond. Behind us, a barge laden with corn and oil-cake was slowly pulling out, churning through the sluggish water, on its way to who knew where. Clay had disappeared inside the building. I could just make out the back of the vehicle that had brought him here but the rest of it was lost in the shadows. The sun must surely be setting but the sky remained the same miserable shade of grey.

Another carriage approached, this one a brougham with the windows curtained and two grim-faced attendants behind the horse. They could have been undertakers on their way to the cemetery and the sight of the window, covered by a heavy black curtain, made me wonder if we might have achieved our aim and drawn Clarence Devereux out of the legation. Could he have come to assess the stolen property for himself? Jones nudged me and we shuffled forward, watching as the carriage came to a halt just in the shadow of the entrance. All our hopes rested on the opening of the door. Next to me, Jones was still, watchful, and I remembered that, for him, it was his entire career that was at stake.

We were both to be disappointed. It was Edgar Mortlake, the younger of the two brothers, who stepped out and surveyed his surroundings with distaste. Two hooligan boys had travelled with him — these people never went anywhere alone — and they stood either side of him, providing the same protection that had been in evidence when we first met him at Bladeston House. Jones and I moved closer still, keeping to the shadows and remaining out of sight. It was quite possible that Mortlake had agents outside the building but the two of us posed no obvious threat — or so I hoped. At least we now had a better view of what was happening inside.

The setting reminded me of a theatre of Shakespeare's time with the four tiers surrounding a central stage and providing an excellent vantage point for an audience that had failed to appear. The building was as tall as it was wide, dominated by a circular stained-glass window which might have been stolen from a chapel. There were wooden beams criss-crossing each other, dangling ropes — some of them connected to hooks and counterweights to lift goods to the upper floor — slanting platforms and, hidden away here and there, tiny offices. The ground floor, where the drama was to take place, was open and almost empty with a light scattering of sawdust. It seemed that I had watched the entire cast arrive.

The cart was parked to one side, the horse snorting and shifting its head impatiently. A pair of trestle tables had been set up and John Clay and Archie Cooke were standing in front of them, rather in the manner of two shopkeepers with a difficult customer. There were about fifty different objects on display: silver cutlery and candlesticks, jewellery, several oil paintings, glassware and china, banknotes and coins. I had no idea where they had all come from

— Chancery Lane Safe Deposit had, of course, not been touched — but supposed Jones must have supplied them, perhaps from the evidence room in Scotland Yard.

From where we were standing, we were able to hear the conversation that ensued. Mortlake strode the full length of the tables, his hands clasped behind his back. He was wearing the dark frock coat that he seemed to favour but he had left his walking stick behind. He stopped opposite John Clay, his eyes glinting with hostility. 'A poor haul, Mr Clay,' he muttered, 'quite miserable. Not at all what we had expected.'

'We were unlucky, Mr Mortlake,' Clay replied. 'The tunnel worked well enough — although it was the devil's own work, you have no idea! But we were disturbed before we could open too many of the boxes.'

'This is all of it?' Mortlake stepped closer so that he towered over the smaller man. 'You haven't thought to hold something back?'

'This is all of it, sir. You have my word as a gentleman.'

'Upon our lives!' Archie croaked.

'It is indeed your lives that will be forfeit if I find you are lying to me.'

'There's a thousand pounds here,' Clay insisted.

'That's not what I read in the newspapers.'

'The newspapers lied. The Safe Deposit Company would not want to alarm their customers. A thousand pounds, Mr Mortlake! Five hundred each. Not so bad for a few weeks' labour, the labour in question being Archie's and mine. You and your friends come out of it handsomely.'

'My friends are of a different opinion. In fact, I must inform you that Mr Devereux is far from satisfied. He had expected more and feels that you have disappointed him; that you are, in effect, in breach of contract. He has therefore instructed me to take all of it.'

'All of it?'

'You may keep this.' Mortlake leaned forward and plucked out a silver eggcup. 'A souvenir of your work.'

'An eggcup?'

'An eggcup and your life. And the next time Mr Devereux has need of your services, you will perhaps come up with a strategy that leads to a decent return. There is a bank in Russell Square that has come to our attention and I would advise you against leaving — or trying to leave — London. We will see you in due course.'

Mortlake nodded at the hooligan boys who produced sacks that they proceeded to fill, sweeping the goods off the tables. Athelney Jones had seen enough. I saw him stride into full view, at the same time producing a whistle from his pocket. He blew a single, long blast and suddenly a dozen policemen in full uniform appeared at both ends of the warehouse, blocking the exits. To this day I am not sure where they had been concealed. Could they have come off one of the boats that had been moored nearby? Had they been tucked away in one of the offices? Wherever they had come from, they had been well drilled and closed in around us as Jones and I walked purposefully towards the little group.

238

'Stand where you are, Mr Mortlake,' Jones announced. 'I have witnessed everything that has taken place here and I have heard you name your accomplice. I am arresting you for conspiracy to commit burglary and for receiving stolen goods. You are exposed as part of a criminal network that has brought terror and bloodshed to the streets of London but this is the end of it. You, your brother and Clarence Devereux will answer to the courts.'

Throughout this lengthy speech, Edgar Mortlake had stood there, showing no expression at all. When Jones had finished he turned not to the detective but to the thief, John Clay, who was blinking uncomfortably. 'You knew of this,' he said, simply.

'They gave me no choice. But I will tell you that, in actual fact, I don't give a jot. I've had enough of your threats, your violence, your greed and I cannot forgive you for what you did to my friend Archie. You give crime a bad name. London will be better off once it's seen the back of you.'

'You have betrayed us.'

'Wait . . . ' Clay began.

I saw Mortlake's hand swing through the air and thought he had slapped the other man across the face although it was strange, for there was no sound of any contact. Clay looked puzzled too. Then I realised it was far, far worse. Mortlake had something concealed in his sleeve, a viciously sharp blade on some sort of mechanism which had sprung out like a snake's tongue. He had used it to cut Clay's throat. For just one moment, I entertained the hope that he had missed, that Clay had not been harmed, but then a thin line of red appeared above the thief's collar. Clay stood there, gasping for air, looking to us for explanation. Then the wound opened and a torrent of blood poured out. Clay fell to his knees and Archie screamed and covered his eyes. I could only watch as the nightmare continued before me.

The hooligan boys had dropped the sacks that they had been carrying and produced guns. Moving almost mechanically, they spread out and began to blast at the policemen, killing two or three of them in the first volley. Even as the bodies fell to the ground, one of them picked up a machete — it was lying on a crate — and swung it through the air, severing a rope just a few feet away. Mortlake had reached out and taken hold of a second rope: the two of them were connected and there must have been a counterweight for he was suddenly lifted high into the air like a magician performing a trick or perhaps an acrobat at the circus. In seconds, even as the noise of the gunfire and the smoke from the revolvers billowed out, he had become a tiny figure four storeys up, swinging himself onto a platform and disappearing from sight.

'Get after him!' Jones shouted.

Most of the policemen were armed and returned fire. Hopelessly outnumbered, Mortlake's protectors continued to empty their pistols but were quickly shot down, one of them spinning onto a trestle table, which collapsed beneath him. I could only wonder at the sense of loyalty or fear that had persuaded them to sacrifice their lives for their master who had simply abandoned them to their fate.

I had not stayed to watch any more of the shoot-out. Ducking down, afraid for my own safety, I had obeyed Jones's command and had already reached a wooden staircase that zig-zagged from floor to floor. There was a second, similar set of stairs at the far end and, as I watched, three policemen peeled off to cover them. Mortlake might have made a dramatic escape from the area of combat but he must still be trapped within the building.

I climbed the stairs, which creaked and bent beneath my weight. Dust and the smell of gunpowder filled my nostrils. Finally, I reached the top and — breathless, my heart pounding — I found myself in a narrow passageway with a wooden wall on one side of me and an unprotected drop on the other. Glancing back down, I saw Athelney Jones had taken charge of the situation. He was not physically able to follow me. Clay lay spreadeagled in a widening pool of blood which seemed even more shocking from this height, like a vast red ink blot. There were casks, crates, hogsheads and bulging sacks scattered all around me and I proceeded slowly, suddenly remembering that although I was unarmed, Mortlake carried a dreadful weapon and could leap out from any of a hundred hiding places. The three police officers had also reached the top but were some distance away, silhouetted against the round window, proceeding slowly towards me.

I came to an opening. It was as if part of the wall had been folded back — not exactly a door nor a window but something in between. I saw the grey of the evening and the rushing clouds. The Thames was before me, a couple of tugs making their way east but otherwise still and silent. In front of me was a long platform connected to the warehouse by two rusting chains with a complicated winch system constructed beside it. Perhaps Mortlake had hoped to use it to lower himself back down, but either it wasn't working or I had arrived too quickly for there suddenly he was, in front of me, his coat flapping in the breeze and his dead eyes fixed on mine.

I remained where I was, not daring to move forward. The knife, now stained with blood, was still jutting from his sleeve. Standing there on the platform, with his oily black hair and moustache, he reminded me more than ever of an actor on the stage. I'm sure the Kiralfy brothers of New York never presented a character more vengeful nor more dangerous.

'Well, well, well,' he exclaimed. 'Pinkerton, you surprise me. I have come upon your sort before, Bob Pinkerton's boys, and they are not usually so astute. You seem to have outplayed me.'

'You have nowhere to go, Mortlake!' I returned. I did not dare move any closer forward. I was still afraid that he would rush at me and use that hideous weapon. He stood where he was. The sluggish water of the river was below him but if he tried to jump he would surely drown, if the fall did not kill him first. 'Put down your weapon. Give yourself up.'

His reply was a profanity of the worst sort. I felt the presence of the police officers nearby and saw them out of the corner of my eye, gathering uncertainly in the doorway behind me. Not exactly the cavalry, but I was relieved that I was no longer on my own.

'Give us Devereux!' I said. 'He is the one we want. Turn him in and it will go easier for you.'

'I will give you nothing but this: the promise that you will regret this until the end of your days. But trust me, Pinkerton, there won't be many of them. You and I will have our reckoning.'

In a single movement, without hesitating, Mortlake turned and jumped. I saw him fall through the air, his coat flapping up behind him, and watched as he plunged feet first into the river, disappearing beneath the surface. I ran forward, the wood tilting beneath me and suddenly I was dizzy and might have fallen myself had not one of the constables grabbed hold of me.

'It's too late, sir!' I heard a voice shouting. 'He's finished.'

I was being held and I was grateful for it. I stared down at the water but there was nothing more to see, not even a ripple.

Edgar Mortlake had gone.

16

We Make an Arrest

That evening, we raided the Bostonian for a second time.

Inspector Jones had instructed me to meet him at eight o'clock and, accompanied by an impressive entourage of uniformed constables, we marched in at exactly that hour, once again silencing the pianist as we made our way past the gilded mirrors and marble panels, in front of the bar with all its glittering crystal and glass, ignoring the muttered protests of the largely American assembly, many of whom were having their evening interrupted for a second time. This time we knew exactly where we were going. We had seen the Mortlakes emerge from a door on the other side of the bar. This must be where their private office was to be found.

We entered without knocking. Leland Mortlake was sitting behind a desk, framed by two windows with red velvet curtains. There was a glass of whisky in front of him and a fat cigar, smouldering in an ashtray. At first, we thought he was alone but then a youth of about eighteen with oily hair and a pinched, narrow face got to his feet, rising up from the place where he had been kneeling next to Mortlake. I had seen his type many times before and felt revolted. For a moment neither of us spoke. The boy stood there, sullen, unsure what to do.

'Get out of here, Robbie,' Mortlake said.

'Whatever you say, sir.' The boy hurried past us, anxious to be on his way.

Leland Mortlake waited until the door had closed, then turned to us, coldly furious. 'What is it?' he snarled. 'Don't you ever knock?' His tongue, moist and grey, flickered briefly between his bulbous lips. He was wearing evening clothes and his hands, curled into fists, rested on the desk.

'Where is your brother?' Jones demanded.

'Edgar? I haven't seen him.'

'Do you know where he was this afternoon?'

'No.'

'You are lying. Your brother was at a warehouse in the Blackwall Basin. He was taking receipt of a collection of items, stolen from the Chancery Lane Safe Deposit. We surprised him there and would have seized him had he not committed murder in front of our eyes. He is now a wanted man. We know that you and he organised the theft in collaboration with a third man, Clarence Devereux. Do not deny it! You were with him only the other night at the American legation.'

'I do deny it. I told you the last time you came. I know no Clarence Devereux.'

'He also calls himself Coleman De Vriess.'

'I don't know that name either.'

'Your brother may have slipped through our fingers but you have not. You will come with me now for questioning at Scotland Yard and you will not leave until you have informed us of his whereabouts.'

'I will do no such thing.'

'If you will not come of your own volition, I will have no choice but to place you under arrest.'

'On what charge?'

'Obstruction and as an accessory to murder.'

'Ridiculous!'

'I do not think so.'

There was a long silence. Mortlake was sitting there, fighting for breath, his shoulders rising and falling while the rest of his body remained still. I had never thought it possible for the human face to display such intense hatred but the very blood was swelling in his cheeks and I was worried that if he had some weapon — a gun — close at hand, perhaps in one of the drawers of his bureau, he would not hesitate to use it and to hell with the consequences.

Finally he spoke. 'I am an American citizen, a visitor to your country. Your accusations are false and scandalous. I wish to telephone my legation.'

'You can telephone them from my office,' Jones replied.

'You have no right — '

'I have every right. Enough of this! Will you accompany us or must I call my men into the room?'

Scowling horribly, Mortlake rose from his seat. His shirt was hanging out of his trousers and, with a slow, deliberate movement, he tucked it back in. 'You are wasting your time,' he murmured. 'I have nothing to tell you. I have not seen my brother. I know nothing of his affairs.'

'We shall see.'

We stood there, the three of us, each waiting for the other to make a move. Finally, Leland Mortlake smashed out the cigar, then walked to the door, his bulky frame passing between us. I was glad that there were two policemen waiting outside for, with every moment that we stood in the Bostonian, I felt myself to be in enemy territory. As we made our way back past the bar, Mortlake turned to the barman and called out: 'Inform Mr White at the legation.'

'Yes, sir.'

Henry White had been the councillor, introduced to us by Robert Lincoln himself. I had a suspicion that Mortlake was bluffing, attempting to intimidate us. Jones ignored him anyway.

We continued through the silent, indignant crowd, some of them jostling against us as if they were unwilling to let us leave. A waiter reached out as if to take hold of Mortlake and, imposing myself between them, I pushed them apart. I was quite relieved when we passed through the door and found ourselves in Trebeck Street. There were two growlers waiting for us. I had already noticed that Jones had decided to spare his prisoner the indignity of a Black Maria, the famous coach used by Scotland Yard. A lackey at the door handed Mortlake a cape and a walking stick but Jones took hold of the latter. 'I will keep this, if you don't mind. You never know what you might find in such a device.'

'It is a walking stick, nothing more. But you must do as you must.' Mortlake's eyes blazed. 'You will pay for this. I promise you.'

We stepped onto the pavement. It seemed to me that the street was darker than ever, the gas lamps unequal to their struggle against the night sky and the thin drizzle that was falling constantly. The cobblestones with their oily reflections provided more illumination. One of the horses snorted and Mortlake stumbled. I was close by and reached out to steady him, for it appeared that he had lost his footing. But one glance in his direction showed that something much worse had occurred. All the colour had left his face. His eyes were wide and he was gasping for breath, grinding his jaw as if he were trying to say something but could no longer speak. He seemed to be terrified . . . frightened to death was the thought that crossed my mind.

'Jones . . . ' I began.

Inspector Jones had already seen what was happening and had taken hold of his prisoner, one arm stretched across his back. Mortlake was making the most horrible sound and I saw some sort of foam appear on his lower lip. His body began to convulse.

'A doctor!' Jones shouted.

There was no doctor to be found; certainly not in the empty street and nor, it would seem, in the club itself. Mortlake fell to his knees, his shoulders heaving, his face distorted.

'What is happening?' I cried. 'Is it his heart?'

'I don't know. Lay him down. Surely a doctor can be found, for Heaven's sake?'

It was already too late. Mortlake pitched forward onto the pavement and lay still. It was only then that we saw it, illuminated by the street lamp; a slender reed protruding from the side of his neck. 'Do not touch it!' Jones commanded.

'What is it? It looks like a thorn.'

'It is a thorn! It is poisoned. I have seen this before but I cannot believe . . . I *will not* believe . . . that it has happened a second time.'

'What are you talking about?'

'Pondicherry Lodge!' Jones knelt beside the prostrate form of Leland Mortlake. He had stopped breathing and his face was utterly white. 'He is dead.'

'How? I don't understand! What has happened?'

'He has been the victim of a blowpipe. Someone has fired a dart into his neck as we attempted to get him out of the club and we allowed it to happen even while he was in our hands. It is strychnine or some such poison. It has taken immediate effect.'

'But why?'

'To silence him.' Jones looked up at me with anguish in his eyes. 'And yet it cannot be. Once again, Chase, I tell you, nothing is as it seems. Who could have known we were coming tonight?'

'Nobody could have known. I swear that I told no one!'

'Then this attack must have been planned whether we were here or not. The blowpipe, the dart, they were already prepared. It had been decided that Leland Mortlake must die long before we arrived.'

'Who would want to kill him?' I stood there, all sorts of thoughts rushing through my mind.

'It must have been Clarence Devereux! He is playing some devilish game. He killed Lavelle. He tried to kill you . . . for who else could it have been in the brougham that was parked nearby? Now he has killed Mortlake.'

'It could not have been Devereux at Scotland Yard.'

'Why not?'

'Because the driver dropped him in the street — had it been Devereux, he would surely have been unable to step out into the open.'

'Then if it was not him, who was it?' I gazed helplessly. 'Was it Moriarty?'

'No! That cannot be possible.'

We were both of us attenuated, drenched through by the drizzle, close to exhaustion. It seemed that an eternity had passed since we had ridden out together to the London docks and that expedition too had not worked out as we had planned. We stood facing each other, helpless, while around us the police officers crept forward, staring at the corpse with dismay. The door of the club suddenly slammed shut, cutting off the light. It was as if the people who worked there wanted nothing more to do with us.

'Deal with this, Sergeant!' Jones called to one of the policemen, although I could not tell which. All the life seemed to have gone out of him. His face was drawn and there was nothing in his eyes. 'Have the body removed and then take down the details of everyone in the club. I know we have done it once before but we must do it again! Allow no one to leave until you have their statements.' He turned to me and spoke more quietly. 'They will find nothing. The killer will have already left. Come with me, Chase. Let us get out of this damned place.'

We walked down the street and into Shepherd's Market. There we found a public house on a corner — the Grapes. We went inside, into the warmth, and Jones ordered half a pint of red wine which we shared between us. He had also produced a cigarette, which he lit. It was only the second time I had seen him smoke. At length, he began to talk, choosing his words carefully.

'Moriarty cannot be alive. I will not believe it! You must remember the letter . . . the coded letter that began all this. It was addressed to Moriarty and it was found in the pocket of the dead man. It follows, therefore, that the dead man must in all probability have been Moriarty. As always, the logic is inescapable. It was only because he was killed that Devereux and his cohorts were able to take his place, fully establishing themselves in London. And it is only because of the letter that we have been able to proceed thus far.'

'Then if it is not Moriarty taking revenge, it must be his former associates. Even before he set out for Meiringen, he could have left them instructions . . .'

'There you may be right. Inspector Patterson said that he had arrested them all but he may have been mistaken. Certainly, we seem to have stumbled onto two opposing factions. On the one side, Lavelle, the Mortlakes, Clarence Devereux. And on the other . . .'

251

'. . . the fair-haired boy and the man in the brougham.'

'Perhaps.'

'I am wasting my time!' I said. I could feel my clothes, damp against my skin. I drank the wine but it tasted of nothing and barely warmed me at all. 'I have come all the way from America in pursuit of Clarence Devereux and I have found him but you say I cannot touch him. I have Edgar Mortlake in front of me but he escapes. Scotchy Lavelle, John Clay, Leland Mortlake . . . all of them dead. And my young agent, Jonathan Pilgrim . . . I sent him here and that cost him his life. I feel the shadow of Moriarty hanging over us at every turn and frankly, Jones, I have had enough. Without you, I would have got nowhere but even with your help I have failed. I should return home, hand in my notice and find some other way to spend my days.'

'I will not hear of it,' Jones returned. 'You say we are making no progress but that is far from true. We have found Devereux and know his true identity. At the same time his own forces have been decimated, his latest scheme — the robbery at Chancery Lane — undone. He cannot escape. I will have men at every port in the country . . . '

'Three days from now, you may no longer have the authority.'

'And much can happen in three days.' Jones laid a hand on my shoulder. 'Do not be dispirited. The picture is a murky one, I grant you. But still it begins to take shape. Devereux is a rat in a hole but even now he must be fearful. He will have to strike out. It may be that he will finally make the mistake that allows us to capture him. But believe me, he will act soon.'

'You think so?'

'I am sure of it.'

Athelney Jones was right. Our enemy did indeed act — but not in a way that either of us could have foreseen.

17

Dead Man's Walk

I knew that something terrible and unexpected had happened the moment I set eyes on Athelney Jones at Hexam's Hotel the next day. His features, in which the long history of his illness was always written, were more drawn and haggard than ever and he was so pale that I felt obliged to lead him to a chair, for I was certain he was about to faint. I did not let him speak but ordered hot tea and lemon and sat with him until it arrived. My first thought was that his meeting with the Commissioner had already taken place and that he had lost his position with the Metropolitan Police, but knowing him as I now did and recalling our conversation in the rooms in Chiltern Street, I knew that such an event would hardly matter to him and that whatever had happened was much, much worse.

His first words proved me right. 'They have taken Beatrice.'

'What?'

'My daughter — they are holding her ransom.'

'How do you know? How can it be possible?'

'My wife sent me a telegram. It was brought by a messenger for it will be weeks before our own telegraph room has been repaired. I received it in my office, this morning; an urgent summons telling me to come home at once. Of course I did as I was instructed. When I arrived, Elspeth was in such distress that she could barely make herself understood and I was obliged to give her a few drops of sal volatile to calm her down. Poor woman! What must have been going through her thoughts as she waited for me to return — alone and with no one to console her?

'Beatrice disappeared this morning. She had gone out with her nanny, Miss Jackson, a good reliable woman who has been with us these past five years. It was their custom always to stroll together on Myatt's Fields, quite close to the house. This morning, Miss Jackson's attention was briefly diverted by an elderly woman, asking her for directions. I have interviewed her and I have no doubt that this old woman, whose face was hidden by a veil, was part of the conspiracy and served as a distraction. When Miss Jackson next turned round, Beatrice had gone.'

'Could she not have simply strayed?'

'It would not have been in her character, but even so the nanny tried to persuade herself of exactly that. It is human nature to cling onto one's hopes, no matter how far-fetched they may be. She made a thorough search of the park and the surrounding area before she called for assistance. Nobody had seen our daughter. It was as if she had vanished from the face of the earth and, not wishing to delay any further, Miss Jackson hurried home in considerable distress. Elspeth was waiting for her. She did not need to be told what had happened for a note had already been slipped through the door. I have it here.'

Jones unfolded a sheet of paper and handed it to me. There were but a few words, written in block capitals, all the more menacing for their stark simplicity.

WE HAVE YOUR DAUHTER. REMAIN AT HOME. TELL NO ONE. WE WILL CONTACT YOU BEFORE DAY'S END.

'This tells us almost nothing,' I said.

'It tells us a great deal,' Jones replied, irritably. 'It is from an educated man pretending to be an uneducated one. He is left-handed. He works in, or has access to, a library, though one that is seldom visited. He is single-minded and ruthless but at the same time he is acting under stress, which makes him impetuous. The letter was written in the heat of the moment. Almost certainly, I am describing Clarence Devereux for I believe him to be the author of this letter.'

'How can you know so much?'

'Is it not obvious? He pretends to misspell 'daughter' but his spelling is correct in every other respect, even to the extent of including the apostrophe in 'day's'. Searching for a piece of paper, he has reached for a book on a shelf and torn out one of the flyleaves. You can see that two sides of the page are machine-cut while the outer edge is deckled. The book has not been read. Observe the dust and the discolouration — caused by sunlight — along the top. He used his left hand to tear it from the binding. His thumb, slanting outwards, has left a clear impression. It was an act of vandalism, the mark of a man in a hurry, and it would have been noticed if the book had been frequently used.' Jones buried his head in his hands. 'Why is it that my skills can tell me all this but could not forewarn me that my own child might be in danger?'

'Do not distress yourself,' I said. 'Nobody could have foreseen this. In all my years as an agent I never encountered anything like it. For Devereux to have targeted you in this way . . . it's an outrage! Have you informed your colleagues at Scotland Yard?'

'I dare not.'

'I think you should.'

'No. I cannot put her at risk.'

I thought for a moment. 'You should not be here. The note commands you to remain at home.'

'Elspeth is there now. But I had to come. If they have set upon me in this manner, it is almost certain that they will try something similar with you. She agreed with me. We had to warn you.'

'I have seen nobody.'

'Have you been out of the hotel?'

'Not yet. No. I spent the morning in my room, writing my report for Robert Pinkerton.'

'Then I found you in time. You must return with me to Camberwell. Is it too much to ask of you? Whatever occurs, we must face it together.'

'All that matters is the return of your daughter.'

'Thank you.'

I reached out and briefly laid a hand on his

arm. 'They will not harm her, Jones. It is you and me that they want.'

'But why?'

'I cannot say, but we must prepare for the worst.' I stood up. 'I will return to my room and fetch my coat. I wish I had brought my gun with me from New York. Finish the tea and rest a little. You may have need of your strength.'

We travelled together on the train back to Camberwell, neither of us speaking as we made our way through the outer reaches of London. Jones sat with his eyes half-closed, deep in thought. For my part, I could not help but reflect on the much larger journey that we had undertaken together, the one that had started in Meiringen. Were we about to reach its end? Right now it might seem that Clarence Devereux had the upper hand but I consoled myself with the thought that he might finally have out-reached himself and that, by striking at the detective's family, he had made his first false move. It was the action of a desperate man and perhaps one that we might be able to turn against him.

The train seemed almost deliberately slow, but at last we reached our destination and hurried back to the house where I had been a guest, at dinner, only a week before. Elspeth Jones was waiting for us in the room where she and I had first met. She was standing with one hand resting on a chair. It was the same chair where I had found her sitting, reading to her daughter. She saw me and made no effort to conceal the anger in her eyes. Perhaps I deserved it. She had asked me for my protection and I had promised her that all would be well. How vain those words now seemed.

'You have heard nothing?'

'No. And there is nothing here?'

'Not a word. Maria is upstairs. She is inconsolable although I have told her she cannot be blamed.' Maria, I assumed, was Miss Jackson, the nanny. 'Did you see Lestrade?'

'No.' Jones lowered his head. 'God forgive me if I am making the wrong decision, but I cannot disobey their instructions.'

'I will not allow you to face them alone.'

'I am not alone. Mr Chase is with me.'

'I do not trust Mr Chase.'

'Elspeth!' Jones was offended.

'You are unkind, Mrs Jones,' I began. 'Throughout this business, I have done everything I can — '

'You will forgive me if I speak openly.' The woman turned to her husband. 'In the circumstances, I cannot be expected to do otherwise. From the very start, when you left for Switzerland, I was afraid of something like this. I have had a sense of approaching evil, Athelney. No — do not shake your head at me like that. Do we not learn in the church that evil has a physical presence, that we may feel it like a cold winter or a coming storm? 'Deliver us from evil!' We say it every night. And now it is here. Maybe you invited it. Maybe it was coming anyway. I do not care who I offend. I will not lose you to it.'

'I have no choice but to do as they ask.'

'And if they kill you?'

'I don't believe they want to kill us,' I said. 'It would do them no good. To begin with, other officers would take our place soon enough. And although the murder of a Pinkerton's man might be received with a certain indifference, the death of a Scotland Yard inspector would be quite another matter. There is no way our enemy would wish to bring such trouble upon himself.'

'Then what is his intention?'

'I have no idea. To warn us, to frighten us — perhaps to show us the extent of his power.'

'He will kill Beatrice.'

'Again, I don't think so. He is using her to reach us. You have the letter as proof of that. I know these people. I know the way they work. These are New York methods. Extortion. Intimidation. But I swear to God, they will not harm your child — simply because they have nothing to gain.'

Elspeth nodded very slightly but did not look at me again. The three of us sat at the table and so began what I can honestly describe as the longest afternoon of my life with the clock on the mantelpiece sonorously marking every second that passed. We could do nothing but wait. Conversation between us was impossible and although the little maid came up with tea and sandwiches, none of us ate. I was aware of the traffic moving outside and the sky already darkening but I must have slipped into a reverie because I was suddenly aware of a loud knock on the door, jerking me awake.

'It is she!' Elspeth exclaimed.

'Let us pray . . . ' Jones was already on his feet

although the long time spent sitting had locked his muscles together and he moved awkwardly.

We all followed him to the front door but when he threw it open there was no sign of his daughter. A man in a cap stood there, holding out a second message. Jones snatched it from him. 'Where did you receive this?' he demanded.

The messenger looked indignant. 'I was in the pub. The Camberwell Arms. A man gave me a bob to deliver this.'

'Describe him to me! I am a police officer and if you hold anything back it will go the worse for you.'

'I've done nothing wrong. I'm a carpenter by trade and I hardly saw him. He was a dark fellow with a hat and a scarf drawn over his chin. He asked me if I wanted to earn a shilling and he gave me this. He said there was two men in the house and I was to give it to either of them. That's all I know.'

Jones took the letter and we returned to the sitting room where he opened it. It was written in the same hand as the first but this time the language was even terser.

DEAD MAN'S WALK. BOTH OF YOU. NO POLICE.

'Dead Man's Walk!' Elspeth said, with a shudder. 'What a horrible name. What is it?' Jones did not answer her question. 'Tell me!'

'I do not know. But I can look it up in my index. Give me but a minute . . . '

Elspeth Jones and I stood there together as

Jones clumped upstairs to his study. We waited while he searched through the various paragraphs he had brought together over the years — Holmes, of course, had done the same. And I am sure we both counted every one of his steps as he made his way back down.

'It is in Southwark,' he explained, as he entered the room.

'Do you know what it is?'

'I do, my dear, and you must not concern yourself. It is a cemetery — one that has fallen into disuse. It was closed down years ago.'

'Why a cemetery? Are they telling you that our daughter . . . '

'No. They have chosen somewhere quiet and out of the way for whatever business it is that they wish to conduct. This is as good a place as any.'

'You must not leave!' Elspeth seized the note as if she could find further clues in its brief message. 'If they have Beatrice there, you can now go to the police. You *must* go to the police. I will not allow you to put yourself in danger.'

'If we do not obey their instructions, I think it very unlikely that we will find our girl there, my love. These people are cunning and give every indication that they know what they are doing. It may be that they are watching us even as we speak.'

'How is that possible? Why do you think that?'

'The first note was addressed to me alone. This one refers to both of us. The messenger was told there are two men in this house. They know that Chase is here.'

'I will not let you do this!' Elspeth Jones spoke quietly but her voice was filled with passion. 'Please listen to me, my dearest one. Let me go instead of you. Surely these people cannot be so wicked that they will ignore a mother's pleas. I will exchange myself for her — '

'That is not their desire. It is Chase and I who have to go. We are the ones they wish to speak with. But you do not have to be afraid. What Chase said was right. They have nothing to gain from harming us. It is my belief that Clarence Devereux wishes to strike some sort of deal with us. That is all. At any event, there is no point in this speculation when Beatrice's life is at stake. If we refuse to obey their instructions, they will do their worst. Of that there can be no doubt.'

'They do not say what time they want you.'

'Then we must leave immediately.'

Elspeth did not argue. Instead, she took her husband in her arms, embracing him as if for the last time. I will confess that I had my doubts about what Jones had just said. If Clarence Devereux had merely wished to speak to us, he would not have kidnapped a six-year-old girl and used her to drag us to a disused cemetery. He might have nothing to gain by harming us but that wouldn't stop him doing so. I knew him. I knew how he operated. We might as well have argued with the scarlet fever as with him and once we were in his hands he would destroy us simply because it was in his nature.

We left the house. It seemed to me that the night was unseasonably cold although there was not the slightest breeze. Jones held his wife at the

263

door, the two of them gazing into each other's eyes, and then, suddenly, we were alone in the seemingly empty street. And yet I knew that we were being watched.

'We are leaving, damn you!' I cried. 'We are alone. We will come to Dead Man's Walk and you can do with us as you please!'

'They cannot hear us,' Jones said.

'They are nearby,' I replied. 'You said as much yourself. They know we are on our way.'

We were not a great distance from Southwark and made our way there by cab. Jones wore a greatcoat and I noticed that he had brought with him a new walking stick, this one with a handle carved in the shape of a raven's head. It was a suitable accessory for a cemetery. He was unusually tense and silent and it struck me that he hadn't believed a word of what he had said to his wife either. We were heading into mortal peril and he knew it. He had known it when he invited me along.

Dead Man's Walk has long since disappeared. It was one of those cemeteries built in the first part of the century when nobody understood how many people would live in London and therefore, inevitably, die there. All too quickly it had become oversubscribed with so many bodies crammed in next to one another that the tombstones and memorials, rather than providing the solace and remembrance that had been intended, had become a hideous spectacle, slanting at strange angles, leaning on each other, locked in an eternal struggle for space. For many years, a foul and putrid smell had hung over the place. The later graves were desperately shallow, unequal to the task, and it would not be uncommon to find rotting pieces of coffin wood or even shards of human bone poking through the soil. Inevitably, the cemetery had been abandoned. Other cemeteries had been sold off and some had become parks. But Dead Man's Walk had been left behind, a long irregular space between a railway line and an old workhouse, with rusting gates at each end, a few mouldy trees and a sense that it belonged neither to this world nor to the next but existed in a dark, dismal province of its own.

The cab dropped us as the church bells were striking eight o'clock, the hollow chimes echoing in the dark. I saw at once that we were expected and my spirits sank. There were a dozen roughs waiting for us, so dirty and ragged that they could themselves have been summoned from the graves that surrounded them. They were dressed, for the most part, in close-fitting coatees, greasy corduroys and boots. Some of them were bareheaded, others wore billycocks and carried cudgels which they balanced on their shoulders or on the crooks of their arms. Torches had been lit, throwing red light across the gravestones as if they were determined to make the scene even more hellish. How long they had been there, I could not say, but it seemed incredible to me that we were simply going to deliver ourselves to them. I had to remind myself that there was no alternative, that we had made our choice.

Still, we lingered at the gate.

'Where is my daughter?' Jones called out.

'You came alone?' The speaker was a bearded man with long, tangled hair and a broken nose that threw uneven shadows across his face.

'Yes. Where is she?'

There was a pause. A sudden breeze whispered through the cemetery and the flames bowed in recognition. Then a figure appeared, stepping out from behind a monument with a stone angel perched above. For a moment, I thought it might be Clarence Devereux but then I remembered that his condition would not allow him to show himself in this open space. It was Edgar Mortlake. I had last seen him plunging into the river and to my eyes he now seemed more dead than alive, moving slowly, as if the impact of the water had broken several of his bones. He was not alone. Beatrice Jones, pale and tearful, was holding his hand. Her hair was unbrushed and there were smuts on her face. Her dress was torn and soiled. But she looked unharmed.

'We don't give a damn about your dear little daughter!' Mortlake shouted. 'It's you we want. You and your infernal friend.'

'We're here.'

'Come closer. Come and join us! We have nothing to gain by keeping her. We have a carriage waiting to send her home. But if you do not do as I say, you will see something you might rather not.' He had lifted his other hand, revealing a long-bladed knife, which glinted in the flames as it hung over the little girl. Mercifully, she could not see it. I had no doubt at all that he would use it if we did not obey his instructions. He would cut the girl's throat where she stood. Jones and I exchanged a glance. Together, we moved forward.

At once we were surrounded, the hooligan boys moving behind us, cutting off any means of escape. Mortlake stepped towards us, still holding onto Beatrice. She had recognised her father but was too terrified to speak. 'Take the girl back home.' He handed her to one of the younger men, a curly-haired rogue with a smile and a stye in one eye. The two of them walked off together. 'You see, Inspector Jones? I am true to my word.'

Jones waited until his daughter had left the cemetery. 'You are a coward — a man who steals a child and uses her for his own evil ends. You are beneath contempt.'

'And you are the cripple who killed my brother.' Mortlake was very close to Jones now, his face inches away, staring at him with eyes on the edge of madness. 'You will suffer for that, I assure you. But first there are some questions you must answer. And answer them you will!'

Mortlake nodded and I saw one of the roughs step forward with a shillelagh, which he swung viciously through the air, hammering it into the back of Jones's head. Jones fell without another word and I realised that I was now alone with the enemy, that they were all around me, and that Mortlake had already turned to me. I knew what was coming. I expected it. But I was still unprepared for the explosion of pain that sent me hurtling forward into a tunnel of darkness and certain death.

18

The Meat Rack

I was almost afraid to open my eyes for I was quite convinced that I must be dying. How else could I be so cold?

As consciousness returned, I found myself lying on a stone floor with a light flickering somewhere close by. I had no idea how long I had been here nor how badly I had been hurt, although my head was still pounding from the blow I had received. I wondered if I had been removed from London. The chill had penetrated right through to my bones and my body was shuddering involuntarily. There was no feeling whatsoever in my hands and my very teeth were aching. It was as if I had been transported to the frozen north and left to perish on an ice floe. But no. I was indoors. It was concrete, not ice, beneath me. I pulled myself into a sitting position and wrapped my hands around me, partly to conserve what little bodily warmth remained, partly to hold myself together. I saw Athelney Jones. He had already regained consciousness but he looked quite close to death. He was sitting slumped against a brick wall with his walking stick next to him. There were sparkles of ice on his shoulders, his collar and his lips.

'Jones . . . ?'

'Chase! Thank God you are awake.'

'Where are we?' A cloud of white vapour emerged from my mouth as I spoke.

'Smithfield, I think. Or somewhere similar.'

'Smithfield? What is that?'

My question answered itself. We were in a meat market. There were a hundred carcasses in the room. I had seen them but, with my senses returning to me only slowly, I had been unable to grasp what they were. Now I examined them; whole sheep, stripped bare, missing their heads, their fleeces or anything that would have identified them as God's creatures, lying with their limbs stretched out, stacked up in piles that reached almost to the ceiling. Small pools of blood had trickled out and then frozen solid, the colour more mauve than red. I looked around me. The chamber was square with two ladders attached to rails so that they could slide from one end to the other. It reminded me of the cargo hold of a ship. A steel door provided the only possible way out, but I was certain it was locked and to touch it would have torn the skin from my fingertips. Two tallow candles had been placed on the floor. Otherwise, we would have been left in the pitch dark.

'How long have we been here?' I asked. It was as much as I could do to enunciate the words. My teeth were locked together.

'Not long. It cannot be long.'

'Are you hurt?'

'No. No more than you.'

'Your daughter . . . ?'

'Safe . . . or so I believe. We can at least give thanks for that.' Jones reached out and took hold

269

of his stick, dragging it towards him. 'Chase, I am sorry.'

'Why?'

'It was I who brought you here. This is my doing. I would have done anything — anything — to get Beatrice back. But it was not fair to bring you into this.' His words were breathless, staccato, as stripped of warmth as the butchered sheep that surrounded us. It could not be otherwise. Every word, even as it was uttered, had to fight against the biting cold.

And yet I replied: 'Do not blame yourself. We began together and together we will end. It is as it should be.'

We retreated into silence, conserving our strength, both of us aware that our lives were slipping away from us. Was this to be our fate, to be left here until the blood had frozen in our veins? Jones was almost certainly correct. This had to be a major meat market — and one that was surrounded by cold rooms. The walls that contained us would be packed with charcoal and somewhere nearby a compression refrigerating machine would be grinding away, pumping glaciated — and lethal — air into the chamber. The mechanism was fairly new and we might be the first to be killed by it — not that I could find a great deal of consolation in the thought.

I still refused to believe that they intended to kill us — not immediately, at any rate — and it was this thought that made me determined not to slip back into unconsciousness. Edgar Mortlake had said that there were questions for us to answer. Our suffering now must surely be no more than a prelude to that interrogation. It would end soon enough. With fingers that could barely move, I fumbled in my pockets only to discover that my trusty jackknife, the one weapon that I always carried with me, had gone. It barely mattered. I would have been in no state to use it.

I cannot say how many minutes passed. I was aware that I was falling into a deep sleep, which had stretched out like a chasm beneath me. I knew that if I closed my eyes I would never open them again but still I could not stop myself. I had stopped shivering. I had reached some strange condition beyond cold and hypothermia. But even as I felt myself drifting away, the door opened and a man appeared, barely more than a silhouette in the flickering light. It was Mortlake. He looked down at us with contempt.

'Still with us?' he asked. 'You'll have cooled down a little, I suppose. Well, come this way, gentlemen. Everything has been made ready for you. On your feet, I say! There is someone I believe you wish to see.'

We could not stand. Three men came into the room and pulled us to our feet, handling us with as much care as if we had become carcasses ourselves. It was strange to have their hands on me but to feel nothing. However, even opening the door had raised the temperature a little and the movement seemed to restore my almost frozen blood. I found that I could walk. I watched Jones stand with all his weight resting on his walking stick, attempting to regain at least something of his dignity before he was propelled towards the door. Neither of us spoke to Edgar Mortlake. Why waste our words? He had already made it clear that he intended to enjoy our pain and humiliation. He had us completely in his power and anything we said would only give him the excuse to torment us more. Helped by the ruffians who had surely accompanied us from the cemetery, we made our way out of the storage room and into a vaulted corridor, the rough stonework like that of a tomb. Walking was difficult on feet that had no sensation and we stumbled forward until we came to a flight of stairs, leading down, the way now lit by gas lamps. We had to be half-carried or otherwise we would have fallen. But the air was warmer. My breath no longer frosted. I could feel the movement returning to my limbs.

A second corridor stretched out at the bottom of the stairs. I had the impression we were some distance underground. I could feel it in the heaviness of the air and the strange silence that pressed upon my ears. I was already walking unaided but Jones made tortuous progress, relying on his stick. Mortlake was somewhere behind us, doubtless relishing what was to come. We turned a corner and stumbled to a halt in a remarkable place, a long subterranean chamber whose existence might never be suspected by those who walked above.

It was formed of brick walls and vaulted ceilings with arches, dozens of them, arranged opposite each other in two lines. Steel girders had been fixed in place above our heads with hooks suspended on the ends of rusting chains.

The floor consisted of cobblestones, centuries old and heavily worn, with tramlines swerving and criss-crossing each other on their way into the bowels of the earth. Everything was gaslit, the lamps throwing a luminescent haze that hung suspended in mid-air, like a winter's fog. The air was damp and putrid. A pair of trestle tables had been set up in front of us with a number of implements which I could not bring myself to examine and there were two rickety wooden chairs; one for Jones, one for myself. Another three men, making six in total, awaited us. They presented an even grimmer spectacle than they had at Dead Man's Walk for we were their prisoners, entirely in their hands. It was we who were the dead men now.

None of them was speaking and yet I heard echoes . . . voices, far away and out of sight. There was the clang of steel striking steel. The complex must be vast and we were in but one secluded corner of it. I thought of shouting out, calling for help but knew it would be pointless. It would be impossible for any rescuer to tell where the sound had come from and I would surely be struck down before I could utter two words.

'Sit down!' Mortlake had given the order and we had no choice. We sat on the chairs and, even as we did so, I heard an extraordinary sound: the crack of a whip, the rattle of wheels turning on the cobbles, the clatter of horses' hooves. I turned my head and saw a sight I will never forget: a glistening black carriage, pulled by two black horses, hurtling towards us with a black-clad coachman at the reins. It seemed to form itself out of the darkness, like something from a tale by the Brothers Grimm. Finally, it drew to a halt. The door opened and Clarence Devereux stepped out.

Such an elaborate entrance for so small a man! And all for an audience of just two! Slowly, deliberately he walked towards us, dressed in a top hat and cape with a brightly coloured silk waistcoat visible beneath and what could have been a child's gloves on his tiny hands. He stopped a few feet away, his face pale, examining us through heavy-lidded eyes. It was only here, of course, that he could feel at ease. For a man with his strange condition, to be buried underground might come as a relief.

'Are you cold?' he asked, his thin voice filled with mock concern. He blinked twice. 'Warm them up!'

I felt my arms and shoulders seized and saw the same thing happening to Jones. All six men closed in on us and while Devereux and Mortlake watched, they began to beat us, taking it in turns to pound us with their fists. There was nothing I could do but sit there and take it, brilliant lights exploding in my eyes each time my face was struck. When they had finished I could feel blood streaming from my nose. I tasted it in my mouth. Jones was bowed over, one eye closed, his cheek swollen. He had not uttered a sound while the punishment was administered but then nor, for that matter, had I.

'That's better,' Devereux muttered once the men had finished and stepped back and we were sitting panting in our chairs. 'I want to make it quite clear to you that I dislike this. I will add that I abhor the methods that brought you here. The kidnap of a little girl is not something I would normally have suggested and if it is any consolation to you, Inspector Jones, I can assure you that she is now back with her mother. I could have used her more. I could have tortured her in front of you. But whatever you may think of me, I am not that sort of man. I am sorry that she will never set eyes on her father again and that her last memories of you will not have been pleasant ones. But I dare say she will forget you in time. Children are very resilient. We can, I think, dismiss her from our thoughts.

'Nor do I usually make it my business to kill police officers and lawmen. It creates too many aggravations. Pinkerton's is one thing but Scotland Yard quite another and it may well be that one day I will regret this. But for too long now the two of you have been causing me difficulties. What really bothers me is that I do not quite understand how you have managed to achieve so much. That is why you are here and the pain you have just suffered is only a foretaste of what is to come. I see that you are both shivering, by the way. I will do you the favour of supposing that it is through exhaustion and cold rather than fear. Give them a little wine!'

He gave the order with exactly the same tone that he had used to initiate the beating. At once a cup of red wine was pressed into my hand. Jones was given the same. He did not drink but I did, the dark red liquid wiping away the taste of my own blood.

'In just a few weeks you have reached the very heart of my organisation and you have left a trail of destruction in your wake. My friend Scotchy Lavelle was tortured and killed and, quite inexplicably, his entire household was murdered with him. Now, Scotchy was a very careful man. He had plenty of enemies in New York and he knew how to keep his head down. He had rented a quiet house in a quiet neighbourhood and it makes me wonder: how did you ever find him? Who told you where he lived? He was, I admit, known to Pinkerton's and I have no doubt that you, Mr Chase, would have recognised him. But you had been in England less than forty-eight hours and yet you went directly to Highgate, and for the life of me, I cannot work out how you did it.'

I thought that Jones would explain that we had followed the messenger boy Perry from the Café Royal but he remained silent. Devereux, however, wanted a reply and it struck me that our situation, already bad, might become considerably worse if he didn't get one.

'It was Pilgrim,' I said.

'Pilgrim?'

'He was an agent. He worked for me.'

'Jonathan Pilgrim,' Mortlake growled. 'My brother's secretary.'

Devereux looked puzzled. 'He was a Pinkerton? We knew that he was an informer — we discovered he was telling tales and we made him pay for it. But I was of the understanding that he worked for Professor Moriarty.'

'Then you were mistaken,' I said. 'He was working for me.'

'He was English.'

'He was American.'

'And he gave you Scotchy's address? It is possible he was working for you, I suppose, although it's a shame we never thought to ask him ourselves. I did tell Leland that he had been in too much haste to be rid of him. Still, I wonder if you are trying to deceive me, Mr Chase, and would warn you most sincerely not to do so. It may be that you have underestimated me for you have seen me at my weakest. But if you lie to me, I will know and you will pay. You have nothing to add? Well, let us move on. Pilgrim told you the address. You came to Bladeston House. And that very same night Scotchy and his entire household were killed in their sleep. How did that happen? Why did it happen?'

'That is not for us to answer.'

'We shall see. Scotchy said nothing to you. Of that I am sure. He would have said nothing to the police and I am equally certain that he would have left no incriminating papers, no letters, no clues. He was, as I say, a careful man. And yet, the very next day you turned up at my club.'

'Jonathan Pilgrim had written to me from that address. And the police knew that he had a room there.'

'How could they have known? How did they even discover Pilgrim's identity? Do you take us for amateurs, Mr Chase? Do you really think we would have abandoned the body without emptying its pockets first? There was no way the police could have connected Pilgrim with us but they did — and that in itself tells me that something is wrong.'

'Perhaps you should invite Inspector Lestrade to this little gathering of yours. I'm sure he'll be glad to give his side of the tale.'

'We do not need Lestrade. We have you.' Devereux thought for a moment, then continued. 'And then, just twenty-four hours later, we find you in Chancery Lane at the scene of a robbery that has been weeks in preparation and which I expect to return many thousands of pounds in profit — not just the property of London's wealthier classes, but their secrets too. Once again, I am trying to place myself in your shoes. How did you know? Who told you? Was it John Clay? I do not think so. He wouldn't have had the nerve. Was it Scotchy? Unthinkable! How did you find your way there?'

'Your friend Lavelle had left a note in his diary.' This time it was Jones who had replied, speaking through broken teeth and lips that were stained with blood. He still had not touched his wine.

'No! I will not accept that, Inspector Jones. Scotchy would never have been so stupid.'

'And yet I assure you it is the case.'

'Will you still assure me in half an hour's time? We shall see. You were responsible for the failure of that particular enterprise and at the time I was prepared to accept it. It was, after all, just one of many. But what I cannot accept, what must be answered tonight, is your intrusion into the legation. How did you come to be there? What led you to me? For the sake of my future safety in this country, I must know. Do you hear what I am telling you, Inspector Jones? This is why I have taken such pains to bring you here. You came face to face with me in my own home. Taking advantage of my affliction, you humiliated me. I am not saying that I intend to punish you for this, but I must take steps to ensure that it never happens again.'

'You have too great a belief in your own abilities,' Jones said. 'Finding you was simple. The trail from Meiringen to Highgate to Mayfair and to the legation was obvious. Anyone could have followed it.'

'And if you think we're going to tell you our methods, you can go to the devil!' I added. 'Why should we talk to you, Devereux? You plan to kill us anyway. Why not just get it over with and be done with it?'

There was a lengthy silence. Throughout all this, Edgar Mortlake had been staring at us with a silent, smouldering hatred, while the other men stood around, barely interested in what was being discussed.

'All right. So be it.' Devereux had been twisting the middle finger of his glove. Now his hands fell to his sides. He seemed almost saddened by what he had to say.

'Do you know where you are? You are underneath Smithfield, one of the greatest meat markets in the world. This city is a ravenous beast that feeds on more flesh than you can begin to imagine. Every day, it arrives from all over the world — oxen, pigs, lambs, rabbits, cocks, hens, pigeons, turkeys, geese. They travel thousands of miles from Spain and Holland and much further afield, from America, Australia and New Zealand. We are on the very edge of the market here. We cannot be heard and we will not be disturbed. But not so far from where you are sitting, the butchers in their half-sleeves and aprons have arrived. Their carts and wicker baskets are waiting to be filled. Snow Hill is around the next corner. Yes. The market has its own underground station and soon the first train will draw in, direct from Deptford docks. It will be unloaded here . . . five hundred tons a day. All that life reduced to tongues and tails, kidneys, hearts, hindquarters, flanks and endless casks of tripe.

'Why am I telling you this? I have a personal interest which I will share with you, before I leave you to your fate. My parents came originally from Europe but, as a child, I was brought up in the Packinghouse District of Chicago and remember it well. My house was on Madison Street, close to the Bull's Head Market and stockyards. I see it all even now . . . the steam hoists and the refrigerator cars, the great herds being driven in, their eyes wide with fear. How could I forget? The meat market pervaded my life. The smoke and the smells were everywhere. In the summer heat, the flies came in their tens of thousands and the local river ran red with blood — the butchers were not too delicate when it came to the disposal of offal. Enough meat to feed an army! I say it quite literally for much of the produce was sent to feed the Union troops who were still fighting the Civil War.

'Will it surprise you to learn that I grew up with the strongest disinclination ever to eat meat myself? From the moment I was able to make my own decisions, I became what has come to be called a vegetarian — a word that originated here in England, you might like to know. The lifelong condition from which I have suffered I also blame on my childhood. I used to have nightmares about the animals trapped in their pens, awaiting the horrors of the slaughterhouse. I saw their eyes staring at me through the bars. And somehow their fear transmitted itself to me. In my young mind, it occurred to me that the animals were safe only while they remained locked up, that once they were removed from their cages they would be butchered. And so I in turn became afraid of open spaces, the outside world. As a child, I drew the covers over my head before I could sleep. In a way, those covers have remained in place ever since.

'I ask you both for a moment to consider the suffering and cruelty inflicted on animals simply to sate our appetite. I mean this quite seriously, for it has a bearing on your immediate future. Let me show you . . . ' He walked over to the tables and gestured at the objects on display.

I could not help myself. For the first time, I examined the saws, the knives, the hooks, the steel rods and the branding irons that had been laid out for our benefit.

'Animals are beaten. They are whipped. They are branded. They are castrated. They are skinned and thrown into boiling water and I do not believe that they are always dead when this is done. They are blinded and they are brutalised and at the very end, they are hung upside down and their throats are cut. All of this will happen to you if you do not tell me what I wish to know. How did you find me? How do you know so much about my business? Who do you actually work for?' He held up a hand. 'You, Inspector Jones, are with Scotland Yard. And you, Mr Chase, are with Pinkerton's. But I have dealt with both these organisations in the past and I know their methods. The two of you are different. You break international conventions by entering the sanctity of a legation and I begin to wonder which side of the law you are actually on. You interview Scotchy Lavelle and the next day he is murdered. You arrest Leland Mortlake and seconds later he dies with a poisoned dart in his neck.

'I take a great deal of risk in dealing with you in this manner and, believe me, I wish it could be otherwise. I am above all a pragmatist and I know that the forces of the law — both in England and America — will redouble their efforts after your deaths. But I have no alternative. I must know. The one thing I can offer you, if you will co-operate and tell me the truth — is a fast and painless end. The smallest blade, inserted into the spine of a bull, will kill it instantly. The same can be done for you. There is no need for violence. Tell me what I want to know and it will be much easier for you.'

There was a lengthy silence. Far away, I heard the sound of metal striking metal but it could have been a mile away, above or beneath the surface of the road. We were utterly alone, surrounded by the six men who were preparing to do unspeakable things to us. And our screams would do us no good. If anyone did chance to hear us, we would simply be mistaken for animals being slaughtered.

'We cannot tell you what you want to know,' Jones replied, 'because your assertions are based on a false premise. I am a British police officer. Chase has spent the last twenty years working with the Pinkertons. We followed a trail, albeit a strange one, that led us to the legation and to Chancery Lane. It is possible that you have enemies of whom you are ignorant. Those enemies led us to you. And you yourself were careless. Had you not communicated with Professor Moriarty in the first place, our investigation would never have begun.'

'I did not communicate with him.'

'I read the letter with my own eyes.'

'You are lying.'

'Why would I lie? You have made my situation perfectly clear to me. What do I have to gain by deceit?'

'The letter may have been written by Edgar or Leland Mortlake,' I cut in. 'Perhaps it came from Scotchy Lavelle. But it was just one of many mistakes that you made. You have the upper hand, but do what you will with us, others will come after us. Your time is over. Why do you pretend otherwise?'

Devereux looked at me curiously, then turned back to Jones. 'You are protecting someone, Inspector Jones. I do not know who they are, nor why you are prepared to suffer so much on their account, but I am telling you that I know it. How do you think I have survived so long, untouched by the law and unhindered by those rivals who would gladly see my downfall? I have an instinct. You are playing me false.'

'You are wrong!' I shouted, and at the same time I launched myself out of my chair. I had taken Mortlake and the other men unawares. They had been lulled by Devereux's long speech and our own seeming lethargy. Now, before anyone could stop me, I threw myself onto Devereux, one hand grabbing his silk waistcoat, the other around his throat. Would that I could have reached one of the knives set out on the table! Still, I brought him crashing to the ground and was half-strangling him when several hands seized hold of me and I was pulled free. I felt a cosh strike against the side of my head, not hard enough to knock me unconscious, and a moment later someone's fist crashed into the side of my face. Dazed, and with fresh blood streaming from my nose, I was thrown back into my chair.

Clarence Devereux stood up, his face pale with anger. I knew that he had never been attacked in this way — certainly not in front of his own men. 'We are finished,' he rasped. 'I had hoped we might conduct ourselves as gentlemen but the business between us is over and I will not stay to watch you being torn apart. Mortlake! You know what to do. Do not let them die until you have heard the truth — then report back to me.'

'Wait . . . ' Jones cried.

But Devereux ignored him. He climbed back into the coach. The driver pulled hard on the reins, turning the horses round. Then he whipped them on and the whole contraption disappeared down the tunnel, the way they had come.

Mortlake walked over to the table. He took his time, running his hand over the implements. Finally he chose what looked like a barber's razor. He flicked it open to reveal a curious notched blade which he held up to the light. The six men from the cemetery closed in on us.

'All right,' Mortlake said. 'Let's begin.'

19

A Return to Light

After the beating I had received, I was too weak to move. I could only sit there watching as Mortlake balanced the razor at his fingertips, holding it out before him as if to admire its beauty. Never before had I felt so helpless. At that moment, I accepted that I had set too much store by my own capabilities and that all my plans and aspirations were about to come to this bloody end. Clarence Devereux had beaten me. Small consolation that he had briefly felt my fingers around his throat. Their impression would have faded long before he reached the safety of the legation and by then I would be lost in a vortex of pain. I felt hands fall, heavy, on my shoulders. Two of Mortlake's men had approached and stood either side of me, one of them holding a length of rope. The other grabbed hold of my wrist, preparing to tie me down.

But then Inspector Jones spoke. 'Hold off!' he said, and I was astonished to hear him sound so calm. 'You are wasting your time, Mortlake.'

'You believe so?'

'We will tell you everything your master wishes to know. There is no need for this squalid and inhuman behaviour. It has been made clear to us that we are to die in this place so what is to be gained by remaining silent? I will describe to you, step by step, the journey that brought us here and my friend, Mr Chase, will corroborate every word I say. But you will find it of little value. Let me assure you of that now.' Jones had drawn up his walking stick across his lap as if it might provide a barrier between himself and his tormentors. 'We have no secrets and no matter how much you debase yourself in God's eyes, you will discover nothing that will be of any use.'

Mortlake considered, but only briefly. 'You don't seem to understand, Inspector Jones,' he replied. 'You have information and I am sure you will provide it. But that is no longer the point. My brother Leland died in your custody and even if his killer was completely unknown to you, I hold you responsible and will make you pay. I might start by removing your tongue. That is how indifferent I am about what you have to say.'

'In that case, I'm afraid you leave me no choice.' Jones swung the stick round so that the tip faced towards Mortlake and at the same moment I saw that he had unscrewed the raven's head to reveal a hollow interior. Holding the stick with one hand, he inserted the index finger of the other and twisted. At once there was an explosion, deafening in the confined space, and a great red chasm appeared in Mortlake's stomach even as gobbets of blood and bone erupted out of his back. The blast had almost torn him in half. He stood there, the knife falling away, his arms thrown forward, his shoulders hunched. A wisp of smoke curled up from the bottom of the walking stick which, I now understood, had concealed an ingenious gun. Mortlake groaned.

Fresh blood poured over his lip. He fell to the ground and lay still.

The gun had one bullet only.

'Now!' Jones shouted and the two of us rose up from our chairs together, even as the six remaining hoodlums stared in wonderment at what had occurred. With remarkable speed — I would never have expected him to be so vigorous — Jones lashed out with the stick and although it was now useless as a firearm, it struck the man nearest to him in the face, sending him reeling back with blood spouting from his nose. For my part, I seized hold of the rope which would have been used to bind me and pulled it towards me, then swung my elbow into the throat of my assailant who, losing his balance, was unable to defend himself and fell, gurgling, to his knees.

For just one brief instant, I thought that we had succeeded and that against all the odds we were going to make good our escape. But I had allowed my imagination and the sudden reversal of fortune to get the better of me. There were still four thugs who had not been harmed and two of them had produced revolvers. The man whose face Jones had struck was also armed and I could see that he was in no mood for reasoned debate. They had formed a semi-circle around us and were about to fire. We could not reach them. There was nothing to prevent them gunning us down.

And then the lights went out.

The gas lamps, long lines of them stretching in every direction, simply flickered and died as if extinguished by a sudden rush of air. One moment we were trapped, about to die. The next we were plunged into a darkness that was all-encompassing, absolute. I think there might have been a part of me that wondered if I had not indeed been killed, for surely death would not be so very different from this. But I was alive and breathing and my heart was most certainly pounding. At the same time, I was utterly disconnected from everything around me, unable to see even my own hands.

'Chase!'

I heard Jones call out my name and felt his hand on my sleeve, pulling me down. The truth is that by doing so he saved my life. Even as I dropped to the ground, Mortlake's gang opened fire. I saw the blaze of the muzzles and felt the bullets as they fanned out over my head and shoulders, smashing into the wall behind me. Had I remained standing, I would have been torn apart. As it was, I was fortunate to avoid any ricochets.

'This way!' Jones whispered. He was crouching beside me and, still holding onto my arm, he pulled me with him, away from the men, away from the torture implements spread over the tables, further into the great nothingness that our world had become. There was a second blast of guns but this time I felt that the bullets came less close and I knew that with every inch that we shuffled away, the chances of our being hit were diminishing. My hand felt something. It was the wall of the passageway that had been behind us when Devereux was making his speech and through which we had first entered.

Following Jones's lead I stood up, pressing my hands against the brickwork. I was still blind. But if I stayed close to the wall, it would surely lead me out.

Or so I thought. Before we could take another step, a yellow light glimmered, spreading over the floor and illuminating the whole area around us. With a sense of dread, I turned and saw Mortlake spread out on the ground and, next to him, the man with the beard and the broken nose who had first addressed us at the cemetery. He was holding up an oil lamp that he had somehow managed to light. Despite all our efforts, we had moved only a short distance from the group. Not far enough. Once again, we were in plain sight.

'There they are!' he shouted. 'Kill them!'

I saw the guns turned on me once more and with a sense of resignation, I waited for the end. But we were not the ones who died.

Something invisible punched the man in the head. The side of his skull exploded and a spurt of red liquid burst out over his shoulder. As he tumbled sideways, still clutching the oil lamp, distorted shadows fell over the other five men. They had not yet had a chance to shoot and by the time their companion crashed to the floor, it was too late. The light had gone out again. He had been shot — but by whom? And why? We could not answer these questions now. In the dark or in the light, we were still in mortal danger and would be until we reached the surface and the safety of the street.

Taking advantage of the confusion behind us

— our assailants were still not certain what had occurred — we broke into a stumbling run. I was aware of two contradictory impulses warring in my mind. I wanted to be away as quickly as I could but, being quite blind in the pitch dark, I was also afraid of crashing into some obstacle. I could hear Jones somewhere beside me but I was no longer sure if he was near or far. Was it my imagination or was the ground rising slightly beneath my feet? That was the crucial test. The higher we climbed, the more likely we were to reach street level where we might be safe.

And then I saw a light flickering about fifty yards away, a candle lit by a match. How could it be? Who had lit it? I staggered to a halt and called out to Jones, a single word. 'There!' It was directly in front of us, a tiny beacon surely designed to draw us out of danger. I had no sense of distance, not knowing even where I stood. I was certain that the candle had been placed there deliberately to help us, but even if it had been lit by the devil himself, what choice did we have? Moving faster, hearing the footsteps of our pursuers close behind, we pressed forward. Another gunshot. Again the bullet rebounded off the wall and I felt brick dust stinging my eyes. A shouted profanity. And then something else, still far away, but coming rapidly closer — a huge sound, a heavy panting, the grinding of metal, and I smelled burning. The air around me became warm and moist.

There was an underground steam train heading towards us, making for Snow Hill, the station that Devereux had mentioned. I could not see it but the sound of it was becoming more thunderous with every second that passed. The darkness had become a curtain in front of my eyes and I was desperate to tear it free. I had a sudden terror that I might have strayed onto the railway tracks, that I would set eyes on the locomotive only when it bore me down. But then it turned a corner and although I still could not see it — I was aware only of its immense bulk — a beam of light suddenly engulfed me, illuminating the arches and the vaulted ceiling in such a way as to make them fantastical, not part of a London meat market but some sort of supernatural kingdom inhabited by ghosts and monsters.

Jones stood beside me and we both knew that the train would have revealed us to our pursuers. It was on a track parallel to the passage where we stood, separated by a series of archways, and as it moved forward the light cut in and out, creating a strange effect in which any movement was reduced to a series of still images such as one might see in a Coney Island entertainment machine. At the same time, smoke was belching out of its chimney and steam billowing out of its cylinders, the two swirling together and embracing each other like two phantom lovers. The train itself was a fantastic thing: the closer it came, the more dreadful it seemed and if this were a kingdom then here, surely, was the dragon.

I looked round; I could not help myself. Four men stood behind me and they were very close, having made faster progress than either Jones or I could manage. They were making use of the sudden illumination that had been given to them. The train would pass by in less than half a minute and it was only while its light was pinning us down that they could finish us. I saw them running forward, there one second, invisible the next, in this terrible black and white world with the beam finding its way intermittently through the gaps in the brickwork and the fumes threatening to smother us all.

Jones shouted something at me but I no longer heard the words. Four men suddenly became three. Another had thrown himself forward, impossibly, a fountain of blood erupting from his shoulders. The train was almost upon us. And then a figure stepped out from behind a mouldering brick column. It was the boy Perry, his face lit up in a demonic smile and his eyes ablaze. He ran towards me, lifting a huge butcher's knife in his right hand. I fell back. But I was not his target. One of Mortlake's men had crept up on me, had been inches away from me. The boy plunged the blade into his throat, jerked it out and thrust it in again. Blood curtained down, splashing onto his arms. He was close enough for me to hear his high-pitched laughter. His mouth was stretched open, showing bright white teeth. The roar of the locomotive filled my ears and I was no longer breathing air, only carbon and steam. My throat was on fire.

Darkness. The train had rushed by, leaving only the carriages clanking past, one after another.

'Chase!' It was Jones calling my name. 'Where are you?'

'Here!'

'We must get out of this charnel house.'

The candle was still flickering. We made for it, unsure what we were leaving in our wake. I thought I heard the soft thud of a bullet finding its target, not a revolver but some sort of airgun. And the boy was there too. I heard a scream followed by a terrible gurgle as his blade cut through flesh. Somehow, Jones and I linked arms and, choking, with tears streaming from our eyes, we ran forward, aware that the ground was indeed sloping upwards, and more steeply with every step. We reached the candle and saw that it had been deliberately placed at a corner. Looking round it, we saw the moonlit sky. A flight of metal stairs led to an opening. With the last of our strength, we staggered forward and climbed into the faint light of dawn.

Nobody followed us. We had left the horrors of that subterranean world behind. It was quite possible that Devereux's men had all perished, but even if some of them had appeared there would have been little they could do for we were now surrounded by other people: butchers and delivery boys, market clerks and inspectors, buyers and sellers, creeping in silence to their work. We saw a policeman and rushed towards him.

'I am Detective Inspector Athelney Jones of Scotland Yard,' Jones gasped. 'I have been the victim of a murderous attack. Call for reinforcements. I must have your protection.'

God knows what we must have looked like, drawn and desperate, bruised and covered in blood, our clothes dishevelled, our skin streaked with dirt and soot. The policeman looked at us with equanimity. 'Now, now, sir,' he said. 'What's all this about?'

★　★　★

The sky was already turning pink when we made our way back to Camberwell. I had travelled with Jones — I could not return to my hotel until we had seen the conclusion of the night's work together. We had spoken little but as we reached Denmark Hill, seated together in the carriage that the policeman had eventually been persuaded to provide, he turned to me.

'You saw him.'

'You mean Perry, the child who led us to Bladeston House?'

'Yes. He was there.'

'He was.'

'I still do not understand it, Chase . . . '

'Nor I, Jones. First he tries to murder you at Scotland Yard. Now it is as if he wished to save you.'

'He and the man who was with him. But who were they and how did they find us?' Jones closed his eyes, deep in thought. He was close to exhaustion and would have slept but for the uncertainty of what lay ahead. We only had Devereux's word that Beatrice had been returned and we had no reason to trust anything he said. 'You did not tell them about Perry,' he continued. 'When Devereux asked you how we found our way to Highgate, you did not say that

295

we had followed the child from the Café Royal.'

'Why should I have told him the truth?' I said. 'It seemed better to leave him uncertain. And it was more important for me to hear him freely admit to the murder of Jonathan Pilgrim. He did so. Of course, we always knew he was responsible, but now we have heard it with our own ears and can testify to it in a court of law.'

'If we can ever drag him before it.'

'We will, Jones. After tonight, he cannot be safe anywhere.'

We reached the front door of Jones's house but we had no need to open it. Seeing our carriage pull up, Elspeth came flying out, her hair loose and a shawl around her shoulders. She fell into her husband's arms.

'Where is Beatrice?' Jones asked.

'She is upstairs, asleep. I have been worrying myself to death about you.'

'I am here. We are safe.'

'But you are hurt. Your poor face! What has happened to you?'

'It is nothing. We are alive. That is all that matters.'

The three of us went into the house. The fire was blazing and breakfast was already being cooked but I was asleep, in an armchair, long before it was served.

20

Diplomatic Immunity

It seemed strange that, in the end, the entire affair — my long and painful search for the greatest criminal who ever came out of America — should come down to the formality of a meeting with three men in a room. We went back to the legation in Victoria Street, this time using our own names and with the full knowledge of the Chief Commissioner. Indeed, permission had been sought as far up as the office of the Foreign Secretary, Lord Salisbury himself. And so we found ourselves sitting in front of the envoy, Robert T. Lincoln, and his councillor, Henry White, both of whom had greeted us on the night of the party. The third man was Charles Isham, Lincoln's secretary, a rather wayward young man now wearing a mauve jacket and a floppy cravat. It was he who had arrested us at the behest of Edgar and Leland Mortlake.

We were in a room that must surely be used as a library; two entire walls being lined with books, hefty legal tomes which had surely never been read. The walls opposite were painted an anaemic shade of grey, covered with portraits of former envoys, the earliest of them in high collars and stocks. Wire screens had been drawn over the windows, blocking the view into Victoria

Street, and I wondered if this might presage a visit from Devereux himself. He had not been there when we arrived, nor had his name yet been mentioned. We were at least certain that he must be somewhere in the building, assuming, that is, that he had returned there after his appearance at Smithfield market. Inspector Jones had positioned police constables around the building, all of them out of uniform. They had been discreetly watching everyone who came and went during the day.

Robert Lincoln I have already described. Large and ungainly though he was, I had found him an impressive person when he had been the host at his reception, graciously acknowledging the many guests who wished to speak to him while ensuring that any conversation took place on his own terms. He was the same now, sitting in a high-backed chair with an antique table beside him. Even in this quieter and more confidential setting, he commanded the room. He did not need to speak. He thought long and hard before he made any pronouncement and his sentences were brief and to the point. White seemed to be the more worried of the three, sitting to one side and examining us with ever watchful eyes. It was he who had begun the conversation.

'I must ask you, Inspector Jones, quite what you had in mind when you came here a few days ago, masquerading under a false name and carrying an invitation which you had purloined. Were you unaware of the seriousness of your conduct?'

'It has been made very clear to me and I can only extend my apologies to you and to the envoy. Let me say, though, that the situation was a desperate one. I was in pursuit of a dangerous gang of criminals. There had been much bloodshed. They attempted to kill me . . . an explosion that claimed more than one life.'

'How can you be sure that they were responsible?' Lincoln asked.

'I cannot, sir. All I can say is that Chase and I pursued them to this address. A brougham driver brought them here directly from Scotland Yard immediately following the outrage.'

'He could have been mistaken.'

'It is possible, but I do not believe it. Mr Guthrie seemed quite certain of himself. Otherwise, I would not have entered in the manner that I did.'

'That was my suggestion,' I said. I was not feeling well and knew that I presented a disagreeable sight. The ill treatment that I had received at the hands of Mortlake's thugs had been more serious than I had thought: the whole side of my face was swollen, my eye blackened, my lip cracked so that I spoke with difficulty. Jones looked little better. Smartly presented though we both were, I was aware that we must resemble the victims of a train wreck. 'I was responsible,' I continued. 'I persuaded Inspector Jones to come.'

'We are well aware of the methods of the Pinkerton Agency,' Isham muttered. He had been unsympathetic from the start. 'Inciting riots. Attempting to incriminate hard-working men because they had chosen, quite legitimately, to go on strike — '

'As far as I am aware, we have been guilty of none of those things. Certainly, I was not involved in the Chicago railway strikes or any others.'

'That's not in question now, Charlie,' Lincoln said, quietly.

'We acted unlawfully,' Jones continued. 'I admit it. But as things turned out, we were . . . I will not say justified, but at least we were proven right. The criminal known as Clarence Devereux was indeed seeking refuge within these walls, using the assumed name of Coleman De Vriess. Or perhaps that is his real name and Devereux is his alias. Either way, we discovered him here. And that was what led him to strike back at us in a way that was unparalleled in all my years as an officer of the law.'

'He kidnapped your daughter.'

'Yes, Minister,' Jones said, addressing the envoy formally. 'His men took my six-year-old child and used her as bait to capture Chase and myself.'

'I have two daughters,' Lincoln muttered. 'And only recently I lost a son to sickness. I understand your anguish.'

'Last night, in the catacombs beneath Smithfield meat market, Clarence Devereux threatened us with torture and death. We are only here thanks to a miraculous escape, which we are still hard-pressed to explain. Well, that is for another time. But right now, sir, I can swear that the man who assaulted us and who is responsible for a catalogue of crimes in both your country and mine is the same man whom you call your third secretary. I am here to request — even to demand — that we be allowed to question him and, in due course, bring him to face justice in a court of law.'

There was a lengthy silence after this. Everyone was waiting for Lincoln to speak but instead he nodded at his councillor who stroked his beard pensively and then addressed us thus: 'I regret that it is not quite as simple and as straightforward as you would like, Inspector Jones. Let us set aside, for a moment, your personal testimony and whether or not it is to be believed.'

'Wait!' I began, already outraged by the position he had chosen to take. But Jones raised a hand, cautioning me to stay silent.

'I am not saying that I doubt your word even though I will admit that your methods, your intrusion here, leave much to be desired. I can also see for myself the injuries sustained by you and by your associate, Mr Chase. No. What is of the essence here is the principle of extraterritoriality. An envoy is the representative of those who sent him and almost a century ago, Thomas McKean, the Chief Justice of Pennsylvania, set down that the person of the public minister serving abroad is both sacred and inviolable and that to suggest otherwise would be a direct attack on the sanctity of the nation state. I must add that this protection extends to all who serve under the envoy. How could it be otherwise? To deny his servants the same privilege of diplomatic immunity would cause all manner of difficulties and would eventually undermine the independence of the envoy himself.'

'Forgive me, sir. But surely the envoy has the right to waive that immunity if he deems it appropriate?'

'That has never been the practice of the United States. Our view is that the legation remains outside the civil law of the country in which it finds itself. It is, you might say, an island. I am afraid that these premises are protected from criminal process. Mr De Vriess, like Mr Isham and myself, can refuse to testify in both civil and criminal proceedings. Indeed, even were he to choose otherwise, he would still require authorisation from the envoy himself.'

'You are saying, then, that we cannot prosecute him?'

'That is exactly what I am saying.'

'But you would surely agree that natural law, basic humanity, demands that all crimes must be punished.'

'You have given us no evidence,' Isham cut in. 'Mr Chase has been injured. You have been forced to endure the temporary loss of your daughter. But nothing that you say fits the character of Mr De Vriess as we know him.'

'And what if I am telling the truth? What if I tell you that, unbeknownst to you, Coleman De Vriess has taken advantage of the system that you describe? Will you gentlemen sit here and protect a man who has come to London only to inflict terror on its population?'

'It is not we who protect him!'

'But still he is protected. His associate, Edgar Mortlake, was sipping cocktails within these very walls. With my own eyes I saw Mortlake cut the throat of a man who had crossed him. It was he who took my girl, and his brother, Leland, the cold-blooded partner in his schemes, was responsible for the murder of the Pinkerton agent, Jonathan Pilgrim. Would you stand up for them if they were still alive? When my friend Chase came to England, he brought with him files that were filled with the vile activities of this gang, carried out all over America. I have seen them. I can show them to you. Murders, thefts, blackmail, extortion . . . Clarence Devereux was the chief architect of all this misery, the same Clarence Devereux who only last night threatened to torture us to death, like cattle. I know that you are honourable men; I refuse to believe that you will stand in the way of due process and continue to live with this viper among you.'

'The evidence!' Isham insisted. 'It is all very well for you to speak of process. I myself have studied the law. *Probatio vincit praesumptionem*. There! What do you say to that?'

'You speak in Latin, sir. I speak of a daughter stolen from my arms.'

'If we cannot prosecute him, can we at least not question him?' I asked. 'Surely we have the right to interview him, inside Scotland Yard and with any counsel that you wish to provide. We will prove to you the truth of our allegations and then, if we cannot prosecute him here, at least we can see him sent home to face justice in America. Inspector Jones is right. He should be anathema to you. Do you really doubt us? You see the injuries we have both suffered. From where do you think they came?'

Charles Isham still looked doubtful but Henry White glanced at Lincoln who came to a decision. 'Where is Mr De Vriess?' he asked.

'He is waiting in the next room.'

'Then perhaps you might ask him to step in.'

It was progress of sorts. Isham, the secretary, stood up and went to a pair of adjoining doors and opened them — and a second later, after a brief, murmured exchange, Clarence Devereux stepped into the room. I cannot quite express the strange thrill that I felt to see him, to know that he could do me no further harm. Certainly, he was meek enough, affecting that same self-deprecation that he had displayed when we first set eyes on him, barely noticing him, that night at the legation. He pretended to be startled to be in such grand company, blinking nervously in front of the envoy and his advisors. Nor did he seem to recognise Jones and myself, looking at us as if we were complete strangers. He was wearing the same coloured silk waistcoat that he had worn the night before but in every other respect he could have been a quite different man.

'Minister?' he queried, as Isham closed the door.

'Please take a seat, Mr De Vriess.'

Another chair was made available and Devereux sat down, keeping a distance between himself and us. 'May I ask why I have been summoned here, sir?' He looked at us a second time. 'I know these gentlemen! They were here on the night of the Anglo-American trade celebration. One of the guests recognised them as imposters and I was forced to eject them. Why are they here?'

'They have made some very serious allegations about you,' White explained.

'Allegations? About me?'

'May I ask where you were last night, Mr De Vriess?'

'I was here, Mr White. Where else could I have been? You know that I am unable to venture out unless it is a matter of urgency and even then I can only do so with the most careful preparation.'

'They claim they met you at Smithfield market.'

'I will not call it a lie, sir. I will not say that they are seeking revenge for what took place here a week ago. It would be quite wrong to make such assertions in front of His Excellency. I will say only that it is the most dreadful error. That this is a case of mistaken identity. They have confused me with someone else.'

'You do not know the name Clarence Devereux?'

'Clarence Devereux? Clarence Devereux?' His eyes brightened. 'CD! There you have it. We share the same initials! Is this the cause of the misunderstanding? But no, I have never heard the name.'

Lincoln turned to Jones, inviting him to speak.

'You deny that you imprisoned us last night, that you and your men abused us and would have put us to death if we had not managed to get away? Did you not tell us of your childhood in Chicago, your hatred of meat, the fear that led to your agoraphobia?'

'I was born in Chicago. That is true. But the rest of it is fantasy. Minister, I assure you . . . '

'If you were not there, then undo your collar,' I exclaimed. 'Explain to us the marks around your neck. I placed them there with my own hands and I'm glad I did it. Will you tell us how you came by them?'

'It is true that you attacked me,' Devereux replied. 'You seized me by the neck. But it was not in any meat market. It was here, in this legation. You came here under false pretences and became violent when it fell upon me to eject you.'

'Perhaps that is the motive for all this,' Isham remarked. He was so fervent in his defence of Devereux that I began to wonder if he had not been in some way bribed or coerced. 'There is clearly enmity between these three gentlemen. I will not impugn their motives but it seems very likely to me that a mistake has been made. And I would point out, Minister, that Mr De Vriess has been a good and loyal servant of the American government both in Washington for the past six or seven years and here. Certainly, there can be no doubt about his affliction. Is it likely, given his illness, that he could be the mastermind of an international criminal network? Looking at him now, is that what you see?'

Lincoln sat in gloomy silence, then slowly shook his head. 'Gentlemen,' he said. 'It grieves me to say that you have not made your case. I

306

will not doubt your word, for you are both honourable men, I am sure. But Isham is right. Without physical evidence, it is impossible for me to proceed and although I can promise you we will investigate this matter further, it must be done within the grounds of this legation and in keeping with its rules.'

The meeting was over. But suddenly Jones got to his feet and I recognised at once the energy and the determination that I knew so well. 'You want evidence?' he asked. 'Then perhaps I can give it to you.' He took out of his pocket a piece of paper with a jagged edge and a few words written in block capitals. He laid it on the table beside Lincoln. I saw the words: WE HAVE YOUR DAUHTER. 'This was the note that was sent to me to entice me into the cemetery known as Dead Man's Walk,' Jones explained. 'It was the means by which Devereux was able to capture both Chase and myself.'

'What of it?' Isham asked.

'It has been torn from a book and the moment I saw it I knew it had been taken from a library just such as this.' Jones turned to the bookshelves. 'The sun hits these windows at a strange angle,' he continued. 'As a result, it falls onto very few of your books but I remarked, the moment I came in here, that a few volumes at the very end have been allowed to fade. The top of this page, as you can see, has also been damaged.' Without asking permission, he went over to the shelves and examined them. 'These books have not been read for some time,' he continued. 'They are all perfectly aligned ... all except one which has been recently removed and which has not been replaced in its exact position.' He took out the offending volume and brought it over to Lincoln. 'Let us see . . . ' He opened it.

The frontispiece had been torn out. The jagged edge was there for all to see and it was obvious — indeed, it was unarguable — that it matched the edge of the page on which the kidnapper had written his note.

The open book was greeted by a silence that was profound and it occurred to me then that great trials have turned on less. Though Lincoln and his advisors gave nothing away, they stared at it as if they read in it all the mysteries of life, and even Devereux visibly shrank into himself, recognising that the game might, after all, be lost.

'There can be no doubt that this page was taken from this library,' Lincoln said at last. 'How do you explain this, Mr De Vriess?'

'I cannot. It is a trick!'

'It would seem to me that you might, after all, have a case to answer.'

'Anyone could have removed that book. They could have done so themselves when they were here!'

'They did not come to the library,' Isham muttered. These were the first words he had spoken on our side.

Devereux was becoming desperate. 'Minister, you yourself argued just moments ago that I am protected from the criminal process.'

'So you are and so you must be. And yet I

cannot stand by and do nothing. Two officers of the law have identified you. It cannot be denied that grave events have taken place. And now they have evidence . . . '

Another long silence was interrupted by the councillor of the legation. 'It would not be without precedent for a member of the diplomatic corps to be questioned by the police,' White said. Even I was surprised by the speed with which these gentlemen were shifting ground — but then, of course, they were politicians. 'If there is a case to be made against you, it is only reasonable that you should, at the very least, co-operate, for how else will we clear your name?'

'Even outside the legation, you will still enjoy its full protection,' Isham added. 'We can extend to you the right of innocent passage — *ius transitus innoxii*. It will allow our friends in the British police the right to interview you whilst still placing you outside their jurisdiction.'

'And then?'

'You will be returned here. If you have been unable to explain yourself satisfactorily, it will be for the minister to decide what will be done next.'

'But I cannot leave! You know I cannot venture outside.'

'I have a closed wagon waiting for you,' Jones said. 'A Black Maria might strike fear into the heart of ordinary criminals but for you it will be a place of refuge. It has no windows and a door that will remain securely fastened — I can assure you of that. It will transport you directly to Scotland Yard.'

'No! I will not go!' Devereux turned to

Lincoln and for the first time I saw real fear in his eyes. 'This is a trick, sir. These men do not intend to interview me. They mean to kill me. The two of them are not what they seem.' The words tripped out, faster and faster. 'First there was Lavelle. They saw him and the very next day he was murdered in his own home, along with his entire household. Then Leland Mortlake, a respected businessman! Your Excellency will remember meeting him. He was no sooner arrested than he was poisoned. And now they have come for me. If you force me to leave with them, I will never reach Scotland Yard — or if I do I will die there. They will kill me before I step into this Black Maria of theirs! I have nothing to answer for. I am an innocent man. I am not well. You know that. I will answer any questions you put to me and allow you a complete examination of my life but I swear to you, you are sending me to my death. Do not make me go!'

He sounded so pathetic and so frightened that I would have been inclined to believe him myself had I not known that it was all an act. I wondered if Lincoln might not take pity on him but the envoy cast his eyes down and said nothing.

'We mean him no harm,' Jones said. 'You have my word on it. We will speak with him. There are many, many questions that remain unanswered. Once we have satisfied ourselves on these — and have a full confession — we will return him to you according to diplomatic law. Lord Salisbury himself has agreed. It is indifferent to us whether this man faces justice in Britain or in the United States. Our only concern is that he should not escape the consequences of what he has done.'

'Then it is agreed,' Lincoln said. He got to his feet, suddenly tired. 'Henry — I want you to send an envoy to Scotland Yard. He is to be present throughout the cross-examination — which will not begin until he arrives. I wish to see Mr De Vriess back at the legation before nightfall.'

'It may take more than one day to arrive at the truth.'

'I am aware of that, Inspector Jones. In that event, he will be returned to you tomorrow. But he is not to spend even one night behind bars.'

'Very well, sir . . . '

Without another word, and without even glancing at Devereux, Lincoln left the room.

'I must not go! I will not leave!' Devereux grabbed hold of the arms of the chair like a child, tears welling in his eyes, and the next few minutes were as strange and as undignified as any I can remember. We had to call more officials into the room and prise him away by force. While White and Isham watched in dismay, he was dragged downstairs, a whimpering wretch who began to screech the moment he saw the open door. Only the night before, this same man had stood, surrounded by his cronies, sentencing us to a painful death. It was almost impossible to compare that man with the creature he had become.

A cover was found and thrown over his head and we were able to escort him out to the gate where the Black Maria was waiting. White had come with us. 'You are not to begin your questioning until my representative arrives.'

'I understand.'

311

'And you will accord Mr De Vriess the respect due to the third secretary of this legation.'

'You have my word on it.'

'I will see you again this evening. Is it too much to hope that this business will be concluded by then?'

'We will do what we can.'

These were the arrangements that Jones had made for the transfer of Clarence Devereux from the legation. Five police constables had come from Scotland Yard, all of them hand-picked by Jones himself. Nobody else was to be allowed to come close. There was to be no chance of a second poison dart being fired from somewhere in the crowd. Nor was the mysterious sniper who had come to our rescue at Smithfield market going to be presented with a target. Devereux himself was blind and unable to resist and we made sure that he was surrounded, protected by a human shield until he reached the Black Maria, which had been parked directly beside the gate. The vehicle — in fact it was dark blue — was a solid box on four wheels and it had been thoroughly searched before it set out: once Devereux was inside, Jones was fairly certain that he would be safe. The doors were already open and, with utmost care, we bundled him in. The interior was dark, with two benches facing each other, one on either side. To any ordinary criminal, it might have seemed a dreadful mode of transport but the irony was that, given his condition, Devereux would find it almost homely. We closed and locked the doors. One of the constables climbed onto the footplate at the back and would remain standing there for the entire journey. So far, everything had gone according to plan.

We prepared to leave. Two more police officers took their places next to each other, sitting behind the horses at the front of the Black Maria. Meanwhile, Jones and I climbed into a curricle that had been parked behind, Jones taking hold of the reins. The other two constables would walk ahead in the road ensuring that the way was clear. Our progress would be slow but the distance was not great. More policemen, the same men who had been watching the legation, would be waiting for us at every corner. It struck me that we resembled nothing so much as a funeral procession. There were no mourners standing in respectful silence, but we set off with almost as much solemnity.

The legation disappeared behind us. Henry White was standing on the pavement, watching us go, his countenance grave. Then he turned and went back the way he had come. 'We've done it!' I said. I could not disguise my sense of relief. 'The bloodiest criminal who ever came to this country is in our custody and it is all thanks to you and your genius with that book! Finally, it is over.'

'I am not so sure.'

'My dear Athelney — can you not rest for one moment? I tell you, we have succeeded. *You* have succeeded! See — we are already well on our way.'

'And yet, I wonder — '

'What? You have your doubts even now?'

'They are more than doubts. It does not work. None of it works. Unless . . . '

He stopped. Ahead of us, the police constable was pulling at the reins. A boy pushing a barrow laden with vegetables had turned across the street, blocking our path because one of the wheels seemed to have got stuck in a rut. Another policeman walked ahead to help clear the path.

The boy looked up. It was Perry, dressed now in a ragged tunic and belt. A moment before, his hands had been empty but suddenly he lifted them and the surgeon's knife with which he had once threatened me was already there, glinting in the sun. Without a word he brought it swinging round. The second policeman fell in a welter of blood. At the same moment, there was a shot — it sounded like a piece of paper being torn — and the officer who had been holding the reins of the Black Maria was hurled sideways, crashing down into the road. A second shot and his companion followed. One of the horses reared up, knocking into the other. A woman emerging from a shop began to scream and scream. A carriage coming the other way veered onto the pavement, almost hitting her, and crashed into a fence.

Athelney Jones had produced a gun. Against all the rules, he must have carried it into the legation and it had been in his pocket all along. He brought it up and aimed at the child.

I took out my own gun. Jones looked at me and I think I saw shock, dismay and finally resignation pass through his eyes.

'I'm sorry,' I said, and shot him in the head.

21

The Truth of the Matter

It would appear, my dear reader, that I have deceived you — although, in truth, you are not very dear to me and anyway, I have taken the greatest pains to avoid any deception at all. That is to say, I have not lied. At least, I have not lied to *you*. It is perhaps a matter of interpretation but there is all the difference in the world, for example, between 'I am Frederick Chase' and 'Let me tell you that my name is Frederick Chase' which I remember typing on the very first page. Did I say that the body on the slab in Meiringen was James Moriarty? No. I merely stated, quite accurately, that it was the name written on the label attached to the dead man's wrist. It should not have escaped your attention, by now, that I, your narrator, am Professor James Moriarty. Frederick Chase existed only in my imagination ... and perhaps in yours. You should not be surprised. Which of the two names appeared on the front cover?

All along, I have been scrupulously fair, if only for my own amusement. I have never described an emotion that I did not feel. Even my dreams I have made available to you. (Would Frederick Chase have dreamed of drowning in the Reichenbach Falls? I don't think so.) I have presented my thoughts and opinions exactly as they were. I *did* like Athelney Jones and even tried to prevent him pursuing the case when I learned he was married. I did think him a capable man — though obviously with limitations. His attempts at disguise, for example, were ridiculous. When he presented himself dressed as a pirate or a fisherman on the day we set out for Blackwall Basin, I not only recognised him, I had to work hard to prevent myself laughing out loud. I have faithfully recorded every spoken word, mine and others. I may have been forced to withhold certain details from time to time, but I have added nothing extraneous. An elaborate game, you might think, but I have found the business of writing a curiously tedious one — all those hours spent pummelling away at a machine that has proved unequal to the task of eighty thousand two hundred and forty-six words (a peculiarity of mine, the ability to count and to recall the number of every word as I go). Several of the keys have jammed and the letter e is so faded as to be indecipherable. One day, someone will have to type the whole thing again. My old adversary, Sherlock Holmes, was fortunate indeed to have his Watson, the faithful chronicler of his adventures, but I could afford no such luxury. I know that this will not be published in my lifetime, if at all. Such is the nature of my profession.

I must explain myself. We have travelled thus far together and we must come to an understanding before we go our separate ways. I am tired. I feel I have written enough already but even so it is necessary to go back to the start

— indeed, even further than that — to put everything into perspective. I am reminded of the Gestalt theory proposed by Christian von Ehrenfels in his fascinating volume, *Über Gestaltqualitäten* — I was reading it, as it happens, on the train to Meiringen — which questions the relationship between the brain and the eye. There is an optical illusion that has become popular. You think you are seeing a candlestick. Then, on closer examination, you perceive that it is in fact two people facing each other. This has, in some ways, been a similar exercise though hardly quite so trivial.

Why was I in Meiringen? Why was it necessary to fake my own death? Why did I meet with Inspector Athelney Jones and become his travelling companion and friend? Well, let me turn on the electric light and pour another brandy. Now. I am ready.

I was the Napoleon of crime. It was Sherlock Holmes who first called me that and I will be immodest enough to admit that I was rather pleased by the description. Unfortunately, as the year of 1890 drew to its close I had no idea that my exile on St Helena was about to begin. The few scant details that he relates about my life are essentially correct and it is not my intention to expand on them very much here. I was indeed one of two boys — twins — born to a respectable family in the town of Ballinasloe, County Galway. My father was a barrister but when I was eleven or twelve years old he became involved with the Irish Republican Brotherhood and, knowing the danger into which this might

317

place him, determined that my brother and I should be sent to England to complete our education. I found myself at Hall's Academy in Waddington where I excelled at astronomy and mathematics. From there I went to Queen's College, Cork, where I studied under the great George Boole and it was with his guidance that, at the age of twenty-one, I published the treatise on Binomial Theorem which, I am proud to say, caused quite a stir across Europe. As a result, I was offered the Mathematical Chair of a university which was the scene of a great scandal that was to change the course of my life. I do not intend to elucidate on the precise nature of that scandal, but I will admit that I am not proud of what took place. Although my brother stood by me, neither of my parents ever spoke to me again.

But the man had hereditary tendencies of the most diabolical kind. A criminal strain ran in his blood...

That was what Holmes — or Watson — wrote but they were quite wrong and my parents would have been mortified had they read it. They were, as I have said, respectable people, and there was never a hint of misconduct in my long family tree. My readers may find it hard to accept that an ordinary teacher might decide, quite deliberately, to break out into a criminal career, but such I assure you was the case. At the time, I was working as a private tutor in Woolwich, and although it is true that a number of my students were cadets from the Royal Military Academy which was close by, I was not quite the 'army coach' that has been stated. One of these, a pleasant, hard-working man by the name of Roger Pilgrim, had first accrued gambling debts and had thence fallen in with a group of swells. He came to me one evening in great distress. It was not the police that he feared — his own gang had turned on him over a small sum of money which they believed he owed and Pilgrim quite seriously believed he would be torn limb from limb. I agreed, somewhat reluctantly, to intercede on his behalf.

It was then that I made the discovery that was to change my life a second time, viz., that the criminal underclass — the thieves, burglars, counterfeiters and conmen who were the plague of London — were all unremittingly stupid. I thought I would be afraid of them. As things turned out, I would have felt more anxiety walking through a field of sheep. I saw at once that what they lacked, crucially, was organisation and that as a mathematician I was ideally suited to the task. If I could bring the same discipline to their nefarious activities that I could to binomial coefficients, I would create a force that could take on the world. I will confess that although it was the intellectual challenge that first interested me, I was already thinking of personal profit for I was growing tired of living hand to mouth.

It took me a little over three years to achieve my goals and perhaps one day I will describe that process, although it is, frankly, unlikely. Apart from any other considerations, I have never been one to blow my own trumpet. Anonymity has always been my watchword — after all, how could the police pursue a man whose very existence was unknown to them? I will merely say that Roger Pilgrim stayed with me and provided the physical support — which is to say, the persuasion — that was occasionally required although we very seldom resorted to violence. Not for us the heavy-handed methods of Clarence Devereux and his gang. We became close friends. I was the best man at his wedding and still remember the day his wife gave birth to their first child, Jonathan. And so, we arrive at the beginning.

As the year 1890 drew to a close, I was very comfortable and confident that my career would continue to thrive. There was not a felon in London who did not work for me. There had, inevitably, been bloodshed along the way but things had settled down and all that was behind me. Even the meanest and most feeble-minded criminals had come to appreciate that they were better off working under my protection. Yes, I took a goodly share of their profits but I was always there when circumstances turned against them, readily paying for their bail or defence. I could also be very useful. A cracksman searching for a fence? A swindler desirous of a false referee? I brought them together, opening doors in more than one sense.

There was, of course, Sherlock Holmes. The world's greatest consultant detective could not fail to come to my attention but curiously I never gave him much thought. Did I have anything to do with the absurd Musgrave ritual or the equally unlikely Sign of Four? What did I care about the marriage of Lord St Simon or that trivial scandal in Bohemia? I know Watson would have you think that we were great adversaries. Well, it helped his sales. But the fact was that we were operating in quite separate fields of activity and, but for a single occurrence, we might never have met.

That occurrence was the arrival of Clarence Devereux and his entourage — Edgar and Leland Mortlake and Scotchy Lavelle. Everything that I told Athelney Jones about them was true. They were vicious criminals who had enjoyed spectacular success in America. What was not true, however, was my assertion that they intended to join forces with me. Quite the contrary, they came to England to stamp me out, to take over my criminal empire, and in the months that followed, they acted with a speed and violence that took me quite by surprise. Using the foulest methods, they turned my followers against me. Anyone who protested, they killed — always bloodily, as a warning to everyone else. They also used police informers against me, feeding information both to Scotland Yard and to Holmes so that I found myself fighting a war on three fronts. So much for honour among thieves! Perhaps I had become over-confident. Certainly I was unprepared. But I will say this much in my own defence: they were not gentlemen. They were Americans. They paid not the slightest attention to the rules of sportsmanship and civility to which I had always deferred.

Well, I have already said that criminals are

stupid. To that I should have added that they are also self-serving. Very quickly, my associates realised which way the wind was blowing and 'fell in line', as I believe the saying goes. One by one, my closest advisors abandoned me. I cannot blame them. I think, had I been in their shoes, I would have done the same. At any event, by the start of April I found myself, unbelievably, a fugitive. My one advantage was that Devereux had no idea what I looked like and could not find me. He would have killed me if he had.

At this point, I had just three close allies. All of them have already appeared in this narrative.

Peregrine, Percy or Perry was perhaps the most remarkable of the three. Although almost impossible to believe, he had begun life as the youngest son of the Duke of Lomond and would have been entitled to a comfortable, even a cosseted, life had he not taken violent exception to the private school in Edinburgh where he had been sent at the age of seven. The place was run by Jesuits who gave their students the Bible and the birch in equal measure and, after one week, Perry ran away and came south to London. His despairing parents began a nationwide search and offered a huge reward for information as to his whereabouts, but a boy who is determined not to be found will not be, and Perry disappeared cheerfully into the metropolis, sleeping under arches and in doorways in the company of the thousands of other children who somehow managed to scratch a living in the capital. For a short while — and there is a certain irony in this — he was a member of the

Baker Street Irregulars, the gang of street urchins who attended upon Sherlock Holmes, but the wages were derisory and anyway, Perry had quickly discovered that he preferred crime. I am deeply fond of him but I will admit that there is something quite disturbing about him, perhaps a result of cross-breeding within the Lomond family. By the time I met him, he was eleven years old and had already, to my knowledge, killed at least twice. He killed more frequently after I had taken him into my service — there was no preventing it — and I must add, somewhat regretfully, that his bizarre bloodlust could occasionally be useful to me. Nobody ever noticed Perry. He seemed to be nothing more than a blond, rather plump child, and with his fondness for disguises and theatricality he could inveigle himself into any room, any situation. He found his métier with me. I will not say that I became a second father to him — it would have been far too dangerous as Perry had a loathing of authority figures and would gladly have murdered the first. But we were, in our own way, close.

I need write less about Colonel Sebastian Moran. I have described him already and Dr Watson will provide any further information you may require. Educated at Eton and Oxford, a soldier, gambler, big-game hunter and, above all, sniper, Moran was my first lieutenant for many years. We were never friends. That simply was not his way. Gruff in manner and prone to almost uncontrollable fits of rage, the wonder is that he stayed with me for as long as he did and, in truth, he only did so because I paid him handsomely. He would never have joined Devereux for he had a strong antipathy towards Americans — indeed, to many foreigners — and that marked him out from the start. If I remind you that his weapon of choice was a silenced airgun, invented by the German mechanic Leopold Von Herder, you will perhaps be able to work out his role in this tale.

Finally, I come to Jonathan Pilgrim, the son of my old student, Roger. His father and I had gone our separate ways — he to an early retirement in Brighton. He had become a wealthy man during his time with me and his wife had been afraid for him from the start, so I was hardly surprised and only a little saddened when he begged leave to part from me. There are all too few friends in the life of a master criminal, too few people one can trust, and he was both. However, we corresponded occasionally and sixteen years later he sent me his son who had grown up as wayward as his father had once been. Quite what his mother made of this strange apprenticeship I will never know but Roger had recognised that Jonathan would turn to crime with or without me and had decided that with me was the better option. He was an extraordinarily good-looking boy with a freshness and an openness that one could not help but like, and to this day I regret the fact that, in my desperation, I allowed him to infiltrate Devereux's inner circle. Everything that you have read in this narrative, everything I have done, began with his murder.

Never has a man felt more alone than I, when

I came across Jonathan's body in Highgate, where we had arranged to meet so that he could provide me with whatever fresh information he had gathered. The manner of his death, the way he had been bound and then executed, disgusted me. As I knelt beside him, with tears streaming from my eyes, I knew that Clarence Devereux had outmanoeuvred me and that this was as low as my fortunes could fall. I was finished. I could flee the country. I could do away with myself. I could not endure any more.

I gave way to this foolishness for perhaps five seconds. It was replaced by a fury and a thirst for revenge that entirely consumed me — and it was at that exact moment that a plan formed in my head so daring and unexpected that I was certain it must succeed. You must remember my circumstances. I had Colonel Moran and I had the boy, but apart from them there was nobody I could call upon for help and the three of us were hopelessly outnumbered. All my former associates had been turned against me. Worse still, I had no way of finding Clarence Devereux for, like me, he had never revealed himself. Thanks to Pilgrim, I had learned about the Mortlakes and their club, the Bostonian. I knew, however, that none of the gang would ever betray their leader to me. Pilgrim had also directed me to Scotchy Lavelle who lived close to where the body had been found but he was an extremely cautious man. His house was like a fortress. It might be possible to kill him but I needed to reach him, to get from him the information that would allow me to bring down the rest of the gang.

Suppose, then, that I were to draw Scotland Yard and all its resources to my cause? Was it possible that I could somehow use them to defeat my enemy, working as it were from inside with neither party aware of who I was? The greatest mathematical insights — the diagonal argument, for example, or the theory of ordinary points — have always come in a flash. So it was with my idea. I would have to die in a way that was memorable and unarguable but then I would return, in another guise. I would both use the Metropolitan Police to do my work for me and conceal myself within them, seizing any opportunity that came my way. Clearly I could not pretend to be a detective myself. It would be too easy to check my credentials. But suppose I had come from far away? Almost at once my thoughts turned to the Pinkerton Agency in New York. It made complete sense that they would have followed Devereux and the others to England. At the same time, the well-known lack of co-operation between the two agencies would play into my hands. If I presented myself with the right documents and files, surely no one would suspect me or question my right to be there?

First, I placed certain papers — including the address of the Bostonian — in Jonathan Pilgrim's pockets. They were there for the police to find. Next, I prepared to die. It almost amused me to rope Sherlock Holmes into my scheme but who better to help me take my last bow on the stage? Holmes was almost certainly unaware that he had been helped in his

326

investigations by Clarence Devereux. Three times — in January, February and March — he had crossed my path and had, I knew, prepared extensive notes on my affairs which he would eventually deliver to the police. At the end of April, I called on him at his rooms in Baker Street. My one fear was that he would have learned how desperate things had become for me and how little power I really had, but fortunately this was not the case. He accepted me for what I pretended to be, a vengeful and dangerous foe, determined to have him removed from the scene.

I should also mention that I had taken some elementary precautions before I risked meeting Holmes face to face and I am surprised that he did not perceive this for he knew how important to me my anonymity had always been. A wig, a little whitening, hunched shoulders and shoes designed to give me extra height . . . Holmes was not the only master of disguise and it delights me that the description of me which he gave to Watson — 'extremely tall and thin, his forehead domes out in a white curve' — was entirely inaccurate. I could not know then how things would play out and it has always been my habit to prepare for every eventuality.

I do not need to repeat our words. Dr Watson has got there first. I will simply say that, by the end of our conversation, Holmes was in fear of his life and that I followed it up with several attacks upon him — all of them designed to frighten, not to kill.

Holmes did exactly as I hoped. He sent Inspector Patterson a list of my former colleagues, not knowing that they were all, by now, employed by Devereux, then fled to the Continent. Along with Perry and Colonel Moran, I followed, waiting for the opportunity to put the first climax of my scheme into action. It came at Meiringen, at the Reichenbach Falls.

I guessed that Holmes would have to visit that dreadful place. It was in his nature. No tourist, not even a man in fear of his life, could pass by without gazing down at the rushing waters. I made my way there ahead of him, walked the narrow path and knew at once that I had the setting I required. It would be perilous. Of that there could be no doubt. But I like to think that only a mathematician could survive what might seem to be a suicidal plunge into the rapids. Who else could so carefully calculate all the necessary angles, the volume of the water plunging down, the exact speed of descent and the odds of not drowning or being smashed to pieces?

The next day, when Holmes and Watson set out from the Englischer Hof, everything was in place. Colonel Moran was concealed, high above the falls, a necessary safeguard should anything go amiss. Perry, who had perhaps thrown himself too strenuously into the part, was disguised as a Swiss lad. I myself was waiting on the shoulder of the hill nearby. Holmes and Watson arrived and Perry produced the letter, supposedly written by the landlord, summoning Watson back to the hotel. Holmes was left alone. It was at this point that I presented myself and the rest, one might say, is history.

The two of us exchanged words. We prepared

for the end. Do not think for a minute that I was entirely sanguine about the chances of my success. The water was pouring down ferociously and there were jagged rocks all around. Had there been any alternative, I would gladly have considered it. But I must seem dead, and with that in mind I naturally permitted Holmes to write his letter of farewell. I was a little surprised that he felt a need to record what was going to happen but then I had no idea that we were both, in fact, preparing to fake our own deaths, a situation which in retrospect strikes me as slightly bizarre. However, it was his testimony that I most needed and I watched him leave the note close to his alpenstock before we squared off and began to grapple like a pair of wrestlers at the London Athletic. This was, for me, the most disagreeable part of the experience for I have never been fond of human contact and Holmes reeked of tobacco. I was really quite grateful when he brought his *bartitsu* skills to the fore and threw me over the edge.

It nearly killed me. Such a strange and horrible experience to be plummeting endlessly as if out of the sky and yet to be surrounded by water, barely able to breathe. I was blind. The howl of the water was in my ears. Although I had worked out exactly how many seconds it would take me to reach the bottom, I seemed to hang there for an eternity. I was vaguely aware of the rocks rushing towards me and actually touched them with one leg, although very lightly, for otherwise I would have shattered the bone. Finally, I plunged into the freezing water, all the air was punched out of me and I was swirling, turning, almost being reborn in a sort of life after death. Somewhere within me I realised that I had survived but could not break surface in case Holmes was watching. I had instructed Colonel Moran to keep him busy, to distract his attention by hurling small boulders in his direction, and it was while this was happening that I swam to the shore and crawled out, shivering and exhausted, into a place of concealment.

How strange — indeed, how almost laughable — it is that both Holmes and I used the same incident to make our disappearance from the world; I, for the reasons I have described, and he . . . ? Well, there is no satisfactory answer to that. It is clear though that Holmes had an agenda of his own, that he wished to hide away for the three years that came to be known as 'the great hiatus', and it was a constant worry to me that he would turn up again for I, almost alone in the world, knew that he had survived. I even suspected for a while that he might have taken the room next to mine at Hexam's Hotel and that it was he whom I heard coughing in the darkness. Where did he go during this time and what did he do when he got there? I neither know nor care. The important thing was that he did not interfere with my plans and I was very relieved not to see him again.

All that was required now was a body to take my place, the final proof of what had occurred. I had already prepared one. That very morning I had come across a local man returning from the village of Rosenlaui. I had taken him for a labourer or a shepherd but in fact he turned out to be Franz Hirzel, the chef of the Englischer Hof. He vaguely resembled me in age and in his general physical appearance and it was with some regret that I murdered him. I have never enjoyed taking a life, particularly when the person concerned is an innocent bystander, as Hirzel undoubtedly was. My needs, however, were too great for any scruples. Perry and I dressed him in clothes similar to the ones I was wearing, complete with a silver pocket watch. I had myself sewn the secret pocket containing the coded letter which I had written in London. Now I dumped him in the water and hurried away.

If Athelney Jones had thought about it for one moment, it would have been extremely unlikely that Clarence Devereux would write a formal letter inviting Professor James Moriarty to a meeting. Word of mouth would have been safer — and why go to the trouble of inventing such a peculiar code? He might also have asked why Moriarty should have felt compelled to carry the letter with him all the way to Switzerland, why he had bothered sewing it into his jacket. It was all extremely unlikely, but it was the first of a series of clues that I was laying for the British police, to draw them into my scheme.

From the moment I met Inspector Jones, I knew that providence, which had for so long turned against me, was finally on my side. It would have been impossible for Scotland Yard to have chosen a better representative for the task I had in mind. Jones was so brilliant in so many ways, so obtuse in others, so trusting, so naïve. When his wife told me his story, his strange obsession with Sherlock Holmes, I could hardly believe my luck. To the very end he was completely malleable — and that was his misfortune. He was as much a puppet in my hands as the toy policeman he had purchased for his daughter on the way home.

Take that first meeting in the police station at Meiringen. He picked up every clue that I had deliberately laid out for whatever detective might arrive: the Pinkerton's watch (purchased, in fact, from a pawnbroker in Shoreditch), the false American accent, the waistcoat, the newspaper brought from Southampton and prominently displayed, the labels on my case. As to the rest of it, he was hopelessly wrong. I had cut myself shaving in the poor light of a Paris hotel, not on a transatlantic crossing. The clothes I was wearing had been purchased deliberately for the masquerade and did not in fact belong to me, so the smell of cigarettes and the worn-out sleeve were completely irrelevant. But he made his deductions and I was suitably impressed. For him to believe in me, I had to make him think that I believed in him.

I told him about the letter and urged him on until he examined the chef's body for a second time and found it. Using an extract from *A Study in Scarlet* was perhaps over-theatrical but at the time it amused me and I thought it might distract from the other improbabilities I have already described. I was impressed by the speed with which Jones deciphered the letter — of course I would have been ready to help had he not been up to the task — but in fact the code had been constructed in a way that made it fairly simple to crack: the quite unnecessary insertion of the word MORIARTY made the process straightforward.

And so to the Café Royal. It was as if I had set out a series of stepping stones — the letter, the meeting, Bladeston House — each one leading to the next, and it was my task only to make the necessary connections. Perry arrived, dressed as a telegraph boy and pretending to be an emissary of Clarence Devereux. We acted out a scene that we had already rehearsed and he hurried out, but not too quickly, allowing Jones to follow. The bright blue jacket was quite deliberate, by the way. It ensured that Perry did not get lost in the crowd. For the same reason, he sat on the roof of the omnibus to Highgate rather than inside it. He did not enter Bladeston House. At the last moment, he hurried round the back, stripped off his blue jacket and lay on it, concealed behind a nearby shrub. Having lost sight of him, Jones assumed he must have gone in through the garden gate. Why would he have done otherwise?

Scotchy Lavelle would never have invited me into his home but the following day, confronted by a detective from Scotland Yard, he had no choice. We got past the manservant, Clayton, and met with Lavelle himself and though the two of us, Jones and I, seemed to have a common purpose, in fact we were diametrically opposed. He was enquiring about crimes of the recent past. I was preparing a crime that would take place in the immediate future. For, being inside Bladeston House, I was able to take stock of its defences.

'Want to nosey around, do you?' Lavelle asked.

I most certainly did. It was I who insisted on visiting the kitchen and continued from there down to the garden gate. I needed to see the metal hasp. Again, how fortunate to be a mathematician with a precise eye for measurements. I made a mental image of the position of the second lock so I would know where to drill when I returned. And once again, I played fair with you, my reader. I stated that I was the first to re-enter the kitchen and that I was briefly alone. What I failed to mention was that it gave me time to slip a strong opiate into the curry that would be served for dinner. Everything was now set for the next stage of my plan.

I returned just after eleven o'clock with Perry, who loved this sort of adventure. We picked the lock and drilled through the gate, then Perry climbed up to the second floor. Jones was right about that. We made no noise but we were reasonably confident that we would not be disturbed. Perry let me in through the kitchen door — I had told him where he would find the key — and then we set to work.

I am not proud of what took place that night. I am not a monster, but circumstances had compelled me to do monstrous things. First we silenced Clayton, the kitchen boy, the cook and the American mistress of Scotchy Lavelle. Why did they have to die? Simply because, had they been interrogated the following day, they would all have sworn that the telegraph boy never entered the house and, with nothing to lose, they might have been believed. If so, the entire scheme would have unravelled and I could not afford to take the chance. Perry committed three of the murders and I rather fear that he enjoyed them. I myself smothered Henrietta and then carried Lavelle downstairs, still deeply asleep. I tied him to a chair and woke him with cold water. Then I inflicted a great deal of pain on him. It was a disagreeable business but at that stage I did not know where Clarence Devereux could be found. Nor did I know what he was planning. To give him his due, Lavelle was courageous and resisted for quite some time, but no man can withstand the torment of a smashed knee when it is manipulated and from him I learned of the robbery that was about to take place in Chancery Lane. Lavelle also told me that Devereux was to be found in the American legation, but he did so with a certain bravado, for in his mind his master was out of my reach. I could not break into the legation and Devereux never emerged. I saw at once that, with his agoraphobia, my enemy was a true snail within a shell. How could I possibly winkle him out?

I let Perry cut Lavelle's throat — give the boy a treat — and we left together. But first I wrote the entry in the diary for Jones to find the next day: HORNER 13. Just in case the clue was not obvious enough, I placed a bar of shaving soap in the same drawer; an odd item for a man to have in his desk, you might think, but I hoped it would put Jones in mind of barber's shops. I also left the invitation to the party at the American legation somewhere he would see it.

The horrible murders at Bladeston House were enough to galvanise Scotland Yard into action. With all the single-minded determination that I had come to recognise in the British police, they decided to set up a meeting and talk about it. Even so, I was pleased when Jones told me that I was to be included. My one great concern was that Jones, or one of his colleagues, would decide to contact the Pinkerton Agency in New York, in which event I would be exposed at once as a fraud. It was for this reason that I asked about the telegraph room. It would take days to send a message abroad and perhaps days for the reply but that still left me with a sense of unease and little enough time to bring my plans to fruition. Then, when Inspector Lestrade insisted on contacting the agency personally, I decided I would have to take action. Before I left the building, I knew exactly what I had to do.

It was I, of course, who ordered the attack on Scotland Yard the following day. Although everything I subsequently said was designed to make Jones believe that he was the intended victim of the explosion, it was in fact the telegraph room — a fortunate coincidence that it was next to his office — that was the real target, ensuring that Lestrade's irritating message would not be sent for some time to come. Perry carried the bomb into the building while Colonel Moran waited for him in a brougham. Just before the explosion, I went through the charade of drawing attention to them, even risking my life beneath the wheels of an omnibus. It was important that Jones should see that they had come in a brougham — I had chosen that type of carriage on purpose — for I knew that he would use every means at his disposal to track it down. Perry and Moran told the driver to take them to the American legation but, just as at Bladeston House, they did not in fact go in. It was enough that they had been close by.

I was quite surprised that Jones so readily agreed to ignore the sanctity of diplomatic immunity and to place his career at risk by entering the legation in disguise, but by this time we were such close friends and he was so determined to find Clarence Devereux — particularly following the loss of life at Scotland Yard — that he would have done anything and it was he who unmasked Coleman De Vriess. I expressed the necessary amazement but in fact had very quickly guessed as much myself.

From this point on, Jones took charge of the investigation and I had little to do but to follow, dutifully playing Watson to his Holmes. We had visited the Bostonian together and it had been interesting for me to meet Leland Mortlake for the first time. However, the real advantage of the raid was that it had allowed me to plant yet another clue. The Scotland Yard detectives had been singularly incapable of working out what HORNER 13 meant, even when I had reminded them of the shaving soap and had suggested that it might refer to a druggist or some similar establishment. No wonder Holmes so frequently walked all over them! I had therefore picked up an advertisement for the barber's shop which I slipped amongst the magazines in Pilgrim's room, even as I pretended to examine them. Jones found it and once again the game, as he would have put it, was afoot.

His unravelling of the Chancery Lane business was, I have to say, quite masterly, worthy of the great detective himself, and I had no argument with the trap that he devised at the Blackwall Basin. If only Devereux himself had come to inspect the plunder that John Clay had supposedly removed from the Safe Deposit Company, how much more easily the whole thing would have ended. But he did not. Edgar Mortlake slipped through our fingers and Devereux remained out of our reach; I realised that he would need further goading, another setback, before he would deliver himself into my hands.

The arrest of Leland Mortlake provided exactly that. It was a little sad, but not surprising, that Jones should leap to the conclusion that a blowpipe had been used, when the poisoned dart was discovered in the back of Leland's neck. He had, of course, been witness to a similar death, described by Watson in 'The Sign of the Four'. In fact, I had been carrying the dart all the time and simply slid it into my victim's flesh as I steered him away from an overzealous waiter when we were leaving the club. The tip was covered with anaesthetic ether as well as strychnine, so he would have felt nothing. I would have liked him to suffer more. This was, after all, the man whose loathsome

338

company Jonathan Pilgrim had been forced to endure. But his death was a provocation, nothing more. And it most certainly worked.

I could not have foreseen that Devereux would respond by kidnapping Jones's daughter. Even I would never have stooped so low, but then, as I have said, we played by different rules. What was I to do when Jones came to my hotel with the news? I saw at once that to accompany him would place me in the gravest danger but at the same time it was clear that the game was reaching its climax. I had to be there. Once again, luck was on my side. Perry happened to be in my hotel room. The two of us had been in conference when Jones arrived. I was able to tell him of this latest development and to make arrangements for my protection.

Both Perry and Colonel Moran were outside the Joneses' home, waiting in a hansom, when we left that night. You may recall that when I stepped into the street, I called out, as if I were addressing the kidnappers. In fact, my words were intended for Moran, letting him know our destination and giving him time to reach it ahead of us. So when we came to Dead Man's Walk, he was already there. He saw us knocked unconscious. He and Perry followed us to Smithfield meat market and, although it was a close call, they managed to find us just when it mattered most. It was when I was face to face with Devereux, by the way, that I came closest to being unmasked. He had guessed that Jonathan Pilgrim had been working for me and that he was not a Pinkerton's man at all. He began to deny that he had ever written the coded letter that had begun all this and, had I not interrupted, the truth would surely have come out. I threw myself at Devereux for that simple reason — to bring any further discussion to an end — even though it cost me the injuries that I subsequently received.

I am almost finished. Another drop of brandy and we will get there. Now . . . where was I?

All my efforts had been directed towards extracting Clarence Devereux from the legation and when we arrived for our interview with Robert Lincoln, both Colonel Moran and Perry were already in place, one on a nearby rooftop, the other in the street, now disguised as a costermonger. They have, all along, been superbly efficient. It is true that Moran is interested only in the money that I pay him, while Perry is highly disreputable, an underage sadist, but even so I could not have chosen two better companions.

And Jones! I think by the end he had actually guessed — perhaps not who I was, but certainly who I was not. All along he had been aware that something was wrong. His problem was, he simply couldn't work out what it was. His wife had been right about him. He was not as clever as he thought and that was to be the undoing of him. Ironically, she had been the wiser of the two for she had mistrusted me from our first meeting and even, at the very end, voiced her suspicions out loud. I feel sorry for her and for her daughter, but there could be no alternative. Jones had to die. I pulled the trigger, but I wish

340

even now that it could have ended another way.

He was a good man. I admired him. And although in the end I was forced to kill him, I will always think of him as my friend.

22

A Fresh Start

I took out my own gun. Jones looked at me and I think I saw shock, dismay and finally resignation pass through his eyes.

'I'm sorry,' I said, and shot him in the head.

He was killed instantly, his body falling sideways as his walking stick tumbled to the ground one last time, rattling against the paving stones. Everything had to happen very quickly for I knew that there were many Scotland Yard men nearby. I climbed down from the curricle and walked the few steps to the Black Maria which had stopped in the middle of the road. Both the driver and his companion were dead. The constable who had been positioned at the rear was still clinging onto the door as if it was his duty to keep it shut. I shot him in the back and watched him crumple. At the same moment, Colonel Moran fired a third time and the policeman standing next to Perry spun round and fell. I saw Perry scowl. It was one less person for him to kill.

I climbed onto the Black Maria, pushing one of the dead men out of the way. I was vaguely aware of pedestrians pointing and screaming but of course none of them approached. They would have been mad to try and I had counted on their fear and panic to give me time to make my escape. Perry hurried over, wiping his knife on a rag, and climbed up next to me.

'Can I drive?' he asked.

'Later,' I said.

I whipped on the horses. They had already calmed down — but then the police would have trained them to make their way through noisy protests and hostile crowds. With Perry beside me, I directed them a few yards up Victoria Street, then pulled on the reins to force them into a tight turn. This was another mistake that Athelney Jones had made. He had deployed his men along the route that would take us to Scotland Yard, but I had no intention of going that way. As we completed the turn, Colonel Moran appeared in a doorway, his face flushed, the Von Herder airgun already returned to the golfing bag that he carried over his shoulder. He climbed onto the back of the Black Maria, as we had agreed.

Another crack of the whip and we were hurtling past Victoria Station and down towards Chelsea. There were more crowds at this end of the street and they were aware that something had happened but could not tell what it was. Nobody tried to stand in our way. We rattled over a pothole and I heard Moran swear. Part of me wondered if he would still be there when we reached our destination and I have to say it rather amused me to think of him being hurled off in one of the suburbs. At the same time, I wondered what our passenger must be thinking. He would have heard the shots. He would have felt the carriage turn. It was quite likely that he had guessed what had occurred but the doors were locked and there would be nothing he could do.

We passed through Chelsea and into Fulham — or West Kensington as its residents insisted it be called. When we reached the hospital, I handed the reins to Perry who guided the horses with a happy smile on his face. We were proceeding more slowly now. It would be hours before the gaggle of inspectors at Scotland Yard could mount anything that resembled a search and there was no point drawing attention to ourselves. I called out to Colonel Moran and received a grunt by way of reply. It seemed he was still hanging on.

It took us the best part of an hour to reach Richmond Park, entering through Bishop's Gate which I had chosen as it was not actually intended for public use. I wanted an open space and the park seemed ideal for what I had in mind. We drove into the largest field we could find with views all around us, the river concealed by the rise of the hill but the village clearly visible and the city far beyond. It was a glorious day, the spring sun finally shining and only a few puffs of cloud floating above the horizon. At last we stopped. Colonel Moran climbed down and walked round to the horses, at the same time stretching his arms.

'Did you have to go so damned far?' he demanded.

Ignoring him, I went to the back and opened the door. Clarence Devereux knew what his fate was to be. Even as the glare of the sunlight burst into the interior, he huddled away, hiding in a corner, covering his eyes. I did not speak to him. I climbed inside and dragged him out. I was certain that he carried no weapon and once he was in the open, he would be helpless, no better than a fish on dry land. Finally, I signalled to Perry who led the horses over to a clump of trees where a second carriage stood waiting. I had, of course, concealed it there earlier. It would now be his task to unhitch the horses and then to reconnect them. We had a long journey ahead of us, all the way to the south coast.

I stood there with my enemy grovelling on his knees. I knew that he could feel the breeze upon his cheeks. He could hear birdsong and understood well enough where he was even if he didn't open his eyes. I still had the gun that I had used to kill Athelney Jones. Perry, too, was armed. There was little chance that we would be disturbed by strollers for the park was huge — two thousand three hundred and sixty acres, to be precise — and I had deliberately chosen an area that was remote. Nor did I intend to be here long.

Moran stood beside me, examining our prisoner with his usual blend of cruelty and contempt. With his bald forehead and huge moustache he did rather unfortunately resemble a villain out of a pantomime, but he was quite unaware of his appearance or perhaps indifferent to it. It struck me that although he had not been a pleasant man when we first met, he was getting worse, more irascible, as he grew older.

'So what now, Professor?' he asked. 'I imagine

you must be quite pleased with yourself.'

'It all worked out very much as I expected,' I admitted. 'There was a moment when, despite everything, I thought the minister was not going to give his secretary over to us. Why do these people have to be so officious? Fortunately, the late Inspector Jones was able to circumvent this with one last display of genius. I will be forever grateful to him.'

'I take it . . . this nasty little man . . . you're going to kill him?'

'Of course not! Do you really believe I would have gone to such extremes had that been my intention? I need him very much alive. I have *always* needed him alive. Otherwise my task would have been a great deal easier.'

'Why?'

'It will be some years before I can operate again in England, Colonel. First, I have to rebuild my organisation and that will take time. But even when that is done, I have a problem . . . '

'Sherlock Holmes?'

'No. He seems to have left the stage. But as surprised as I am to admit it, I must learn to beware of the police.'

'They know who you are.'

'Precisely. It won't take them very long to work out what happened — even Lestrade might be able to bring the pieces together. And they've all seen me.'

'You've sat amongst 'em and they've seen your face. You've killed one of their own. They'll search for you, high and low.'

'Which is why I must leave the country. The *Vandalia* leaves the port of Le Havre for New York in three days' time. Perry and I will be on board and Mr Devereux will come with us.'

'And then?'

I looked down at Devereux. 'Open your eyes,' I said.

'No!' He was a criminal mastermind, the greatest evil to have emerged from America. He had almost destroyed me. But at that moment he sounded like a child. His hands were pressed against his face and he was rocking back and forth, moaning to himself.

'Open your eyes,' I repeated. 'If you wish to live, you will do it now.' Very slowly, Devereux did as I said but he remained still, staring at the grass, too afraid to lift his head. 'Look at me!'

It took him a huge effort but he obeyed and it occurred to me that he would continue obeying me for what remained of his life. He was crying. The tears were streaming from both his eyes and his nose. His skin was completely white. I had read certain papers about agoraphobia, a condition that had only been recognised quite recently, but I was fascinated to see its effect at such close quarters. Had I handed Devereux my revolver, I am not sure he would have been able to use it. He was paralysed with fear. At the same time, Perry reappeared from behind the trees, dragging with him a large steamer trunk. It was in this that Devereux would be making his journey.

'Is he going in?' he asked.

'Not yet, Perry.' I turned to Devereux. 'Why

did you have to come here?' I asked him. 'You had wealth and success in America. The forces of law, both public and private, were unable to reach you. You had your world and I mine. What made you think that by bringing them into collision you would cause anything but harm?' Devereux tried to speak but could no longer formulate the words. 'And what has been the result? So much bloodshed, so much pain. You have caused the deaths of my closest friends.' I was thinking of Jonathan Pilgrim but also of Athelney Jones. 'Worst of all, you have forced me to descend to your level, using methods which frankly I found distasteful. That is why I feel nothing but hatred for you and why one day you must die. But not today.'

'What do you want?'

'You wished to take over my organisation. Now I will take over yours. You leave me with no choice for, thanks to you, I am finished here. I therefore need to know the names of all your associates in America, all the people you have worked with, the street criminals and their masters. You will tell me everything you know about the crooked politicians, the lawyers, the judges, the press, the police — and about the Pinkertons too. England is a closed door for me for the time being but America is most certainly not. The new world! That is where I intend to re-establish myself. We have many days of travel ahead of us. By the end of it, you will have given me all the information I need.'

'You are a devil!'

'No. I am a criminal. The two are not at all the

same . . . or so I thought, until I met you.'

'Now?' Perry asked.

I nodded. 'Yes, Perry, I am already sick of the sight of him.'

Perry fell on Devereux with glee, binding and gagging him, then bundling him into the steamer trunk and closing the lid. Meanwhile, I spoke again with Moran.

'I trust that you will come with us, Colonel,' I said. 'I am aware that you do not hold the country that is our destination in particularly high regard, but even so I will have need of your services.'

'Will you pay?'

'Of course.'

'My fees will be doubled, if I'm to work abroad.'

'They will be good value even at that price.'

Moran nodded. 'I'll join you in a month or two. Before that, I'm slipping out to India, to the mangrove forests of the Sundarbans. I've heard there are plenty of tigers at this time of the year. You'll leave a message for me in the usual place? Once I'm back, I'll wait to hear from you.'

'Excellent.'

We shook hands. Then the three of us lifted the steamer trunk, now well secured, and placed it in the carriage. Finally, Perry and I climbed up together and, with the boy holding the reins, we set off down the hillside, heading for the River Thames. The sun was shining. I could smell the meadows all around and at that moment I was not thinking of crime, nor of the many triumphs that surely awaited me in America. No. For some unfathomable reason, my attention had turned to something quite different. I was considering the different solutions applicable to the Korteweg de Vries equation, a mathematical model I had long been intending to examine but for which I'd never had the time.

We bumped over the grass and came to a track. Perry was sitting happily beside me. Our guest, in his trunk, was in the back. And there was the river; a crystalline twist of blue in the soft green fields. With the different variables — x, t and $\emptyset$ — spinning in my head, I made my way down towards it.

THE
STRAND
MAGAZINE

THE THREE
MONARCHS

DR. JOHN H. WATSON

EDITED By Geo: Newnes — OFFICES

SOUTHAMPTON
STREET

AN·ILLUSTRATED·MONTHLY

It has never been my desire to write very much about my own affairs for I am well aware that it is only my long and intimate acquaintance with Mr Sherlock Holmes and the many insights that I have been afforded into his deductive methods that are of interest to the public at large. Indeed, it has often struck me that, but for our chance introduction, when I was looking for inexpensive lodgings in London, I would simply have followed my calling as a doctor of medicine and might never have set pen to paper at all.

And yet some aspects of what might be called my private life have, necessarily, appeared in these pages. Readers will, for example, be aware of the wound that I received at the decisive Battle of Maiwand and the frequent troubles that it caused me in my career. I believe I have had reason to mention my older brother, Henry, who having disappointed everyone in his life, none more so than himself, took to drink and died young. On a happier note, my marriage to Miss Mary Morstan, as she was when I met her, has been central to at least one of my narratives for I would never have met her had she not first presented herself as a client of Sherlock Holmes. I loved her from the very start and made no attempt to disguise the fact from my readers — and why should I have? We were married soon afterwards and, although our union was not to be a long one, we were as close to each other as it is possible for a man and a woman to be.

Our first home was in a quiet street close by Paddington Station: not perhaps the most elegant part of town, but one that was conducive to my return to civil practice. It was a pleasant house with a large, airy consulting room at street level and two further floors above, which my new wife decorated with both modesty and good taste. And yet I will confess that to find myself surrounded by all the hallmarks of domesticity, with everything in its right place and almost nothing surplus to requirement, caused me at first an uneasiness which was hard to define. Even the maid, a neat little creature who seemed determined to avoid me, inspired in me a vague sense of threat. It was a strange sensation. On the one hand I was completely happy, but at the same time I was uncomfortable, missing something without knowing exactly what it was.

It embarrasses me that I was not able to diagnose more quickly the source of my disquiet. The many months that I had spent at 221b Baker Street had of course left their mark on me. Quite simply, I was missing my old rooms. I might have complained often enough about Holmes's abominable habits; his refusal to throw away a single document so that every surface was piled high with papers of one sort or another, his extraordinary untidiness with cigars in the coal scuttle, test tubes and flasks scattered amongst the breakfast things, bullets lined up along the window sill and tobacco stored in the toe of a Persian slipper. Well, I missed them now. How often had I gone to bed with the sound of Holmes's Stradivarius winding its way up the stairs, or risen to the scent of his first morning pipe? And added to this was the bizarre array of visitors who beat a path to our front door — the grand duke from Bohemia, the typist, the school-teacher, or, of course, the harassed inspector from Scotland Yard.

I had seen little of Sherlock Holmes in the year following my marriage. I had stayed away perhaps purposefully for there was a part of me that worried that my new wife might take it amiss if I went in search of a life I had left behind. I was also, I will admit, concerned that Sherlock Holmes himself might have moved on. There was a part of me that dreaded to find a new lodger in my place, although Holmes's finances were such that he would have had no need to continue such an arrangement. I said nothing of this, but my dear Mary already knew me better than I thought for one evening she broke off from her needlework and said, 'You really must visit Mr Holmes.'

'What on earth makes you think of him?' I asked.

'Why, you do!' she laughed. 'I could see that he was on your mind a moment ago. Do not deny it! Just now, your eye settled on the drawer where you keep your service revolver and I noticed you smile at the recollection of some adventure you had together.'

'You are very much the detective, my dear. Holmes would be proud of you.'

'And he will, I am sure, be delighted to see

you. You must visit him tomorrow.'

I needed no further prompting and, having dealt with the few patients who had come to my door, I set off the following afternoon, planning to arrive in time for tea. The summer of '89 was a particularly warm one and the sun was beating down as I made my way along Baker Street. Approaching my old lodgings I was surprised to hear music, and moments later came upon a small crowd gathered round a dancing dog that was performing tricks for its master who was accompanying it on the trumpet. Such entertainers could be found all over the capital although this one had strayed some distance from the station. I was forced to step off the pavement and make my way round in order to enter the familiar front door where I was greeted by the boy in buttons who led me upstairs.

Sherlock Holmes was languishing in an armchair with the blinds half drawn and a shadow across his forehead reaching almost to his eyes. He was evidently pleased to see me, for he greeted me as if nothing had changed and as if I had never really been away. Slightly to my regret, however, I saw that he was not alone. My old chair on the other side of the fireplace was taken by a burly, sweating figure whom I recognised at once as Inspector Athelney Jones of Scotland Yard, the detective whose wrong-footed assumptions and subsequent actions had caused us both irritation and amusement when we were investigating the murder of Bartholomew Sholto at Pondicherry Lodge. Seeing me, he sprang up as if to leave but Holmes hastily reassured him. 'You have timed your visit quite perfectly, my dear Watson,' he said. 'I have no doubt you will remember our friend, Inspector Jones. He arrived just a few moments before you and was about to consult me on a matter of the greatest delicacy — or so he assured me.'

'I am quite happy to come back if it is not, after all, convenient,' Jones demurred.

'Not at all. I confess that I have found it increasingly difficult to rouse myself without the friendship and good counsel of my own Boswell. Take the Trepoff murder, for example, or the strange behaviour of Dr Moore Agar — in both instances it was only through purest chance that I prevailed. You have no objection, Watson, to hearing what the inspector has to say?'

'Not at all.'

'Then it is agreed.'

But before Jones could begin, the door opened and Mrs Hudson bustled in carrying a tray laden with tea, scones, a small plate of butter and a seed and currant cake. The pageboy must have informed her of my arrival, for I noticed that she had included a third cup but, casting his eye over the spread, Holmes came to a very different conclusion.

'I see, Mrs Hudson, that you were unable to resist the charms of the street entertainer who has chosen our doorstep for his performance.'

'It is true, Mr Holmes,' the good woman replied, blushing. 'I heard the music and did watch for a while from an upstairs window. I was going to call out to them to move on but the dog was so amusing and the crowd so good-natured that I thought better of it.' She scowled. 'But I cannot see what it is on my tea tray that could possibly have given you any information concerning my movements.'

'It is of no great importance,' Holmes laughed. 'The tea looks excellent and, as you can see, our good friend Watson is here to enjoy it.'

'And a great pleasure it is to see you again, Dr Watson. The house isn't the same without you.'

I waited for Mrs Hudson to leave before turning to my friend. 'You will forgive me, Holmes,' I said. 'But I cannot see how you could have drawn such a conclusion from a plate of scones and a seed cake.'

'Neither of them told me anything,' Holmes replied. 'It was in fact the parsley that Mrs Hudson has placed on top of the butter.'

'The parsley?'

'It has been placed there only a minute ago. But the butter has been out of the pantry and in the sun. You will see that it has melted in this warm weather.'

I looked down. It was indeed the case.

'The parsley has not sunk into the butter, which suggests an interval of time during which Mrs Hudson was interrupted in her duties. Apart from the arrival of my two visitors, the only distraction has been the music and the applause of the crowd outside.'

'Astonishing!' Jones exclaimed.

'Elementary,' Holmes returned. 'The greater part of my work is founded upon just such observations as these. But we have more serious business at hand. You must tell us, Inspector, what it is that brings you here. And meanwhile, Watson, might I inveigle upon you to pour the tea?'

I was happy to oblige and, while I set about my work, Athelney Jones began his narrative, which I set down as follows.

'Early this morning, I was called out to a house in Hamworth Hill, in North London. The business that had brought me there was a death by misadventure, not a murder — that had been made clear to me from the start. The house was owned by an elderly couple, a Mr and Mrs Abernetty, who lived there alone, for they had never had children. They had been woken up at night by the sound of breaking wood and had come downstairs to discover a young man, darkly dressed, rifling through their possessions. The man was a burglar. There can be no doubt of that for, as I would soon discover, he had broken into two other houses in the same terrace. Seeing Harold Abernetty standing at the doorway in his dressing gown, the intruder rushed at him and might well have done him serious harm. But as it happened, Abernetty had brought down with him a revolver, which he always kept close by, fearing just this eventuality. He fired a single shot, killing this young man at once.

'All this I learned from Mr Abernetty. He struck me as an elderly, completely harmless fellow. His wife, a few years his junior, sat in an armchair and sobbed almost the entire time I was there. I learned that they had inherited the house from its former owner, a Mrs Matilda

Briggs. She had given it to them, quite freely, to thank them for their long service. They had lived there for the past six years, quietly and without incident. They were retired and devout members of the local church and it would be hard to imagine a more respectable couple.

'So much for the owners. Let me now describe to you the victim. He was, I would have said, about thirty years of age, pale of complexion and hollow-eyed. He was wearing a suit and a pair of leather shoes which were spattered with mud. These were of particular interest to me as it had rained two nights before the break-in and, venturing into the Abernettys' garden — they had a small square of land behind the house — I had quickly found footprints made by the dead man. He had evidently come round the side and broken in through the back door. I also discovered the jemmy he had used. It was in the bag which he had brought with him and which also contained the proceeds of the robbery.'

'And what was it that this young man had stolen from the elderly and harmless Abernettys?' Holmes asked.

'Mr Holmes, you hit the mark! It is exactly the reason I am here.'

Jones had brought with him a portmanteau bag which, I assumed, had belonged to the dead man. He opened it and, deliberately, with no attempt at a drama, produced three china figures that he stood in front of us, side by side. They were identical, crude and vulgar representations of our monarch, Queen Victoria, the Empress of India herself. Each one was about nine inches high and brightly coloured. They showed her in ceremonial dress with a small diamond crown, a lace veil and a sash across her chest. Holmes examined them, turning each one briefly in his hands.

'Souvenirs of the Golden Jubilee,' he muttered. 'There is barely an arcade in London that does not sell them and I believe they are of little value. These have been taken from three different houses. The first belongs to a hectic and disorganised family with at least one small child. The second, I would say, was the property of an artist or a jeweller who attended the jubilee celebrations with his wife. The third must therefore have come from the Abernettys themselves.'

'You are absolutely right, Mr Holmes,' Jones exclaimed. 'The Abernettys live at number six, at the end of a short terrace. My investigation led me to discover that two of their neighbours, the Dunstables at number five and a lady by the name of Mrs Webster at number one, had been burgled during the same night. Mrs Webster is now a widow but her husband was a watchmaker while the house next door is indeed occupied by a family with two small children. They're currently away. But all three figurines are identical. How could you possibly have known?'

'It is simplicity itself,' Holmes replied. 'You will observe that the first figurine has not been dusted for some time and carries the small, sticky fingermarks that can only belong to a child — and one who has used our monarch as a plaything. The second has been broken and very skilfully repaired — I will presume by the owner and he, surely, would not have undertaken such a task unless the day of the jubilee did not have some special significance for him. It is quite likely he was there with his wife — or, as she now is, his widow. Are you telling me that nothing else was taken, Inspector?'

'That is precisely why I am here, Mr Holmes. When I first visited the house on Hamworth Hill, I thought I would be investigating a straightforward burglary, though one that had gone tragically awry. Instead, what I found was an unfathomable mystery. Why should any young man risk his liberty and end up losing his life for the sake of three statuettes that, you rightly say, he could have bought for a few shillings anywhere in London? I have to know the answer — and recalling my acquaintance with you I took the liberty of coming here in the hope that you might be able to help.'

Holmes fell silent and I wondered how he was going to respond to the Scotland Yard man. It was part of his mercurial character that a case with no obvious interest might set him alight while a mystery such as might have come from the pen of Poe himself would leave him languidly reclining in his chair. At last he spoke.

'Your problem does present a few features of interest,' he began. 'At the same time, though, it would seem that no crime has been committed. This man, Abernetty, was defending himself and his wife and, on the face of it, there is no doubt that he was confronted by a desperate and dangerous young man. Where is the body, by the way?'

'I have had it removed to the mortuary at St Thomas's Hospital.'

'That is a shame. You will doubtless have removed many of the clues with it. I have one more question, Inspector Jones. How well acquainted were the three neighbours — which is to say, the Abernettys, the Dunstables and Mrs Webster?'

'They all seem to be on the very best of terms, Mr Holmes, although, as I have explained, I have been unable to speak to Mr Dunstable. He is a stockbroker's clerk and is currently away.'

'It is much as I expected.'

'Do I take it then that, as you show an interest in the matter, you are prepared to help me with my investigation?'

Once again, Holmes said nothing but I saw him glance at the tea tray and saw the twinkle in his eyes that I knew so well.

'Hamworth Hill is not so very far from here but, that said, I have no desire to make the trek up in this unseasonal weather,' he began. 'I would be inclined to leave the matter in your own capable hands, Inspector. However, there is still the question of the parsley in the butter which, though immaterial in itself, would nonetheless seem to have a bearing on the case.' I thought he was in some way joking, toying with his hapless visitor, but everything about his demeanour was perfectly serious. 'I will look into this for you. It is too late to do anything today but shall we meet tomorrow at, say, ten o'clock?'

'At Hamworth Hill?'

'At the mortuary. And you, Watson, having

heard this tale, must come with us. I insist on it. Your practice can, I am sure, manage for a few hours without you.'

'How can I refuse you, Holmes?' I asked, although the truth was that my curiosity had been piqued. The three monarchs still stood in front of me and I was keen to know what secret they might conceal.

And so we met the following day in the frigid, white-tiled interior of the mortuary where the body of the unfortunate burglar was presented to us. He was, in appearance, exactly as Inspector Jones had described him. The bullet had struck him just above the heart and I have no doubt that his death would have been instantaneous. Such considerations, however, did not seem to be of interest to Holmes, who had barely glanced at the wound before he turned to the silent inspector, one hand resting beneath his chin.

'I would be interested to know what you were able to construe from the body,' he said.

'No more than I have already said,' Jones replied. 'He is young, perhaps thirty. He looks English . . . '

'Nothing more?'

'I'm afraid not. Is there something I've missed?'

'Only that he has very recently been released from prison. I would say, in the last few days. He served a long sentence. He was drinking sherry before he died. This is a bloodstain, here. But this most certainly is not. That is most curious.'

'How can you tell that he has been in prison?'

'I would have thought that would be obvious

to you. You must have seen men with the pallor that comes of being denied sunshine for a length of time. His hair has been cut in a terrier crop and what are these fibres beneath his fingernails? I detect the smell of pine tar. He has undoubtedly been picking oakum. His shoes are brand new and yet they are out of fashion. Could it be that they were taken from him at the time of his arrest and returned to him on his departure from jail? Ha! There is a fold in his left sock. I find that to be of the greatest significance.'

'I see no significance at all.'

'That is because you are not looking for it, my dear Inspector Jones. You ignore whatever seems irrelevant to your investigation without appreciating that it is in the smallest and most insignificant details that the truth can be found. But there is nothing more to be done here. Let us continue to Hamworth Hill.'

Inspector Jones sat morose and silent as we travelled together by coach to North London. We finally arrived at a quiet road containing a row of six houses, all of them very similar, built in the classical style — brick and white stucco — with the entrance set back from the road and two pillars framing the front door. The Abernettys lived at the far end, as Jones had told us, and it was immediately apparent to me that their house was in a state of some decay, with the paint flaking off the front walls, a few cracks in the plasterwork and the windows tarnished and in need of repair.

'It is strange, do you not think, Watson,' Holmes remarked, 'that our burglar should have considered this house worthy of his attention.'

'You took the very thought out of my mind. It would seem obvious to me that the occupants were not wealthy.'

'You have to remember that it was night,' Jones muttered. He was leaning against the coach and his face was flushed as if the exertion of returning here had worn him out. 'This is a well-to-do street in a fashionable suburb and it might well be that, with the cover of darkness, the house would have looked as enticing as its neighbours. Moreover, the burglar broke into numbers one and five as well as number six.'

'I believe you said that a Mrs Webster lives at number one. I think we shall begin with her.'

'Not with the Abernettys?'

'The pleasure of meeting the Abernettys will be all the greater for the anticipation.'

It was, therefore, to the home of the elderly widow, Cordelia Webster, that we next repaired. She was a short, stout woman who greeted us effusively and never once seemed to stop moving from the moment she opened her door and led us into her cosy front room. It was clear that, since the death of her husband, she had lived a somewhat solitary life and that the break-in, and even the death a few doors away, had provided her with considerable excitement.

'I could not believe at first that anything was amiss,' she explained. 'For I heard nothing during the night and, when the police officer called on me the following day, I was sure he must be mistaken.'

'The door at the back had been broken open,'

Jones explained. 'I found footprints in the back garden, identical to those I had already observed at the Abernettys.'

'I assumed at once that it was my jewellery he was after,' Mrs Webster continued. 'I have a strongbox in my bedroom. But nothing had been touched. It was only the little statue of Queen Victoria that was missing from its place on the pianoforte.'

'You would have been sorry to lose it, I am sure.'

'Indeed so, Mr Holmes. My husband and I travelled to St Paul's on the day of the jubilee and watched the procession with Her Majesty as it arrived. What an example she is to us all! I have to say that I bear my own loss more easily knowing that we share the pain of widowhood.'

'Your husband died recently?'

'Last year. It was tuberculosis. But I must tell you that Mrs Abernetty could not have been kinder to me. In the days following the funeral, she was here constantly. I was beside myself — I'm sure you can imagine — and she looked after me. She cooked for me, she kept me company . . . nothing was too much trouble. But then she and her husband did exactly the same for old Mrs Briggs. I swear you would not find two more caring people in the world.'

'Mrs Briggs, I understand, was your erstwhile neighbour.'

'Indeed so. It was she who employed the Abernettys. Mrs Abernetty was her nurse and Mr Abernetty was her general servant. That was how the two of them came to live there. She and

I were very close and many times she told me how grateful she was to them. Matilda Briggs was not wealthy. Her husband had been a solicitor, a prominent member of the Law Society. He died at the age of eighty-three or -four and left her quite on her own.'

'There were no children?'

'They had none of their own. There was a sister and she had a son but he was shot dead in Afghanistan. He was a soldier.'

'And how old was the nephew?'

'He could have been no more than twenty when he died. I never met him and poor Matilda would never speak of him without becoming quite upset. The boy was all the family that she had, but she could not even bring herself to have his photograph near her. At the end of her life, she had no one to whom she could leave the house and so she gave it to the Abernettys to thank them for their long service. It was a very generous thing to do.'

'Were you surprised?'

'Not at all. She mentioned to me that they had discussed it with her and she made it clear to me that this was what she had decided. She left the rest of her money to the church but the house she gave to them.'

'You have been most lucid and helpful, Mrs Webster,' Holmes said. He held out a hand and Jones gave him the figurine that he had brought with him. 'You are quite certain, incidentally, that this is the correct one? They are, after all, practically identical.'

'No, no, no. It is mine, most certainly. I

managed to drop it while I was doing the cleaning and it was quite badly broken. But my husband took great pains to repair it for he knew how fond I was of it.'

'He could have purchased another one.'

'It would not have been the same. He enjoyed mending it for me.'

There only remained to examine the back door where the break-in had taken place and this we did. Jones showed us the footprints that he had found and which were still clearly visible in the flower bed. Holmes examined them, then turned his attention to the lock that had been forced open.

'This must have made a great deal of noise,' he said. He turned to Mrs Webster who was standing close by in the expectation and, indeed, the hope of further interrogation. 'You really heard nothing?'

'I do sleep very heavily,' that lady admitted. 'On some nights I take a little laudanum and a few months ago Mrs Abernetty recommended pillows stuffed with camel hair. She was absolutely right. Since then I have had no trouble at all.'

We took our leave and walked together to the far end of the terrace, passing the house owned by the Dunstables who were still absent.

'It is a shame we cannot interview them,' I said to Holmes.

'I doubt that they would have very much to tell us, Watson — and I suspect that the same will be true of the Abernettys. However, we shall see. This is the front door . . . in need of fresh paint. The whole house appears neglected. Still, it came to them as a bequest, and a most generous one it must be said. Will you ring, Watson? Ah — I think I hear someone approach.'

The door was opened by Harold Abernetty, a tall, slow-moving man with stooped shoulders, deeply lined features and long silver hair. He was about sixty years old and reminded me, I must confess, of an undertaker. His expression was certainly very mournful and he was wearing a morning coat, which was sober and a little threadbare.

'Inspector Jones!' he exclaimed, recognising our companion. 'Do you have any news? I am glad to see you. But who are these gentlemen whom you have brought with you?'

'This is Mr Sherlock Holmes, the famous detective,' Jones replied. 'And this is his companion, Dr Watson.'

'Mr Holmes! But of course I know the name. I must say to you, sir, that I am amazed that so trifling a matter should be of interest to one such as you.'

'The death of a man is never trifling,' Holmes retorted.

'Indeed so. I was referring to the theft of the statues. But it was quite wrong of me. Will you please come in?'

The house shared the same proportions as Mrs Webster's, but it had a clammy, quite sombre feel. Even though it was still inhabited, it was as if it had been abandoned. Mrs Abernetty was waiting for us in the parlour. She was a very small woman, almost swallowed up by the arm-chair in which she sat, dabbing at her eyes with a handkerchief and still barely able to speak.

'This is a terrible business, Mr Holmes,' Abernetty began. 'I have already explained everything to the inspector but I am of course willing to help you in any way I can.'

'This is my fault,' Mrs Abernetty sobbed. 'Harold shot that young man for my sake.'

'It was my wife who woke me,' Abernetty continued. 'She had heard a door being broken open and sent me downstairs to investigate. I took the gun with me, although I never intended to use it. When the man saw me and came rushing towards me . . . even then, I didn't know what I was doing. I fired the shot and saw him fall — and wish with all my heart that I could have wounded him and not brought an end to his young life.'

'What did you do after he had fallen?'

'I hurried to my wife and told her that I was unharmed. Then I got dressed. My intention was to find the nearest police officer but first I noticed the bag that the young man had brought with him and, although I knew I should not tamper with the evidence, I took a look inside. That was when I saw the three china figures, lying next to each other. I recognised one of them as being our own. I had bought it for my wife as a souvenir of the Golden Jubilee and I saw at once that it was missing from its place on the sideboard. As you can imagine, I was completely astounded by the presence of the other two — but then I remembered that I had seen one in Mrs Webster's front room.'

'It was on her piano,' Mrs Abernetty said.

'I realised then that we might not be the only victims of burglary that night, something that was soon confirmed when Inspector Jones began his enquiry.'

'You cannot blame my husband. He did nothing wrong. He never intended to hurt anyone.'

'You do not need to distress yourself, Mrs Abernetty,' Holmes assured her. 'I have seen your neighbour, Mrs Webster. She speaks very highly of you.'

'She is a good woman,' Abernetty said, 'still much distressed by the loss of her husband last August. But we are all advancing in years. These things are to be expected.'

'She told us about Matilda Briggs.'

Abernetty nodded. 'Then you know how much we owe her. Mrs Briggs employed us for many years. Emilia . . . ' here he turned to his wife, 'nursed her through a long illness and, out of gratitude, having no immediate family of her own, she bequeathed us this house in her will.'

'There was, I believe, a nephew.'

'He was a colour sergeant with the 92nd Highlanders. He was killed at the Battle of Kandahar in southern Afghanistan.'

'It must have been a great blow to her.'

'She was upset, certainly. But the two of them had never been close.'

'And the rest of the money?'

'She gave it to the local church, for the relief of the poor,' Mrs Abernetty said. 'Mrs Briggs was a very devout person and a member of the Royal Maternity Charity, the Temperance Society, the

Society for the Rescue of Young Women and many others.'

Holmes nodded then got his feet, signalling that the interview was over. I was surprised that he had no further questions and that in this instance he chose not to examine the back door or the garden, but then he had already said that he had not expected to learn very much from this encounter. It was only as we left that he turned back to the elderly couple.

'One last question,' he said. 'Where are your neighbours, the stockbroker's clerk and his family?'

'They are in Torquay,' Mrs Abernetty replied. 'They are visiting Mr Dunstable's mother.'

Holmes smiled. 'Mrs Abernetty, you have told me exactly what I wanted to know and your answer was exactly what I had expected. I congratulate you and wish you a good day.'

We walked a short way down the hill in silence but at last the man from Scotland Yard could bear it no more.

'Do you have any answer to this riddle, Mr Holmes?' he burst out. 'Three little statues of almost no value at all are stolen from three adjoining houses. What was the purpose of the theft? It seems to me that you have asked no questions that I have not already asked and seen nothing that I had not already noted. I fear I have wasted your time bringing you here.'

'Far from it, Inspector Jones, I have a few enquiries to make but otherwise the affair could not be more clear. Shall we meet at my rooms in Baker Street tomorrow morning? Would ten o'clock be convenient?'

'I can certainly be there.'

'Then let us part company for the time being. Watson, will you walk with me to the station? I find the air a little fresher up here. Good day to you, Inspector Jones. This has indeed been a quite singular case and I thank you for bringing it to my attention.'

This was all he would say and Jones returned to the waiting coach with a look of complete bafflement on his face. I will admit that I was no wiser myself but knew better than to ask questions to which no answers would yet be forthcoming. I also knew that I would have to absent myself from my practice for a third day in succession as it would be inconceivable for me to miss the solution to such a pretty puzzle as the three monarchs had presented.

The next day, I returned to Baker Street at ten o'clock precisely, meeting Inspector Jones at the door. We climbed the stairs together and were met by Holmes who was wearing his dressing gown and just finishing his breakfast.

'Well, Inspector Jones,' he began, when he saw us, 'we have a name for the dead man. It is Michael Snowden. He was released from Pentonville Prison just three days ago.'

'What was his offence?'

'Blackmail, assault, larceny — I fear Master Snowden led a life that was as dissolute as it was short. Well, at least he never went as far as murder. There is some solace in that.'

'But what brought such a man to Hamworth Hill?'

'He came to claim what was rightfully his.'

'Three china figurines?'

Holmes smiled and lit his pipe, tossing the spent match into the fireplace. 'He came to claim the house that had been left to him by his aunt, Mrs Briggs.'

'Are you saying that he was her nephew? Mr Holmes — you cannot possibly know that!' the inspector cried.

'I do not need to know it, Inspector Jones. I deduced it. When all the evidence points in only one possible direction, then you can be fairly certain that as you move forward you must arrive at the truth. Michael Snowden was never a soldier and he did not die in Afghanistan. This was made clear to me from what Mrs Webster told us. She said that Matilda Briggs was so upset by the death of her nephew that she never kept a picture of him in the house. But that did not strike me as even slightly credible. Had he died in the army, serving his country, she would surely have done the exact opposite. She would have been proud to keep his memory alive. However, a churchgoing woman, a member of the temperance society, were she to have a nephew who was a rake and a criminal — '

'She would pretend that he had died abroad!' I exclaimed.

'As a soldier, or something like that. Precisely, Watson! That was why she would not have his image near her.'

'But she still left the house to the Abernettys,' Jones insisted.

'So they say. But again, Mrs Webster — an

excellent witness, by the way, with an astonishing grasp of detail — made a most interesting remark. The Abernettys, she said, had discussed the will with their employer, Mrs Briggs. Not the other way round! I saw at once what might have happened. An elderly, sick woman, left on her own with a scheming manservant and a wife who is also her nurse, is persuaded to change her will in their favour. They want the house and they take it, cutting the nephew out.

'However, this is a lady with a conscience. At the last moment, she has a change of heart and writes to her nephew, telling him what has happened and expressing a desire that he should inherit after all. I have spoken to the prison warder, incidentally, and he has confirmed that Snowden did indeed receive a letter a few months ago. As the saying goes, blood is thicker than water and perhaps his aunt believes that even at this late stage he will reform. There is little that Michael Snowden can do about the situation. He is still in jail, serving a lengthy sentence. But the moment he is released, he comes to his aunt's house and confronts the two extortionists.'

'They murder him!' Suddenly, I could see it all.

'I am sure they tried to reason with him. They gave him a glass of sherry and it was when he proved adamant — doubtless he threatened them — that Mr Abernetty took out his revolver and shot him. Snowden dropped the sherry, spilling it on his shirt, but much of the stain was, of course, concealed by his blood.'

Jones had listened to all this with something close to distress etched on his features. 'It all seems quite clear to me, Mr Holmes,' he said. 'But I still cannot see how you worked it out.'

'It was the three monarchs that gave the game away. Mr Abernetty needed a reason to kill a young man who — he could at least pretend — was a complete stranger to him. Simple enough to say that he was a burglar. But why would any burglar choose a house that was in such disrepair and which would clearly contain nothing very much of value? That was his dilemma.

'His solution was ingenious. He would rob two more houses in the same terrace and he would do so in such a way that the police could not fail to assume that mere larceny was the motive. Why did he choose number one and number five? He knew that the Dunstables were away in Torquay — that much Mrs Abernetty told us herself. And he was also aware that Mrs Webster, with her laudanum and camel-hair pillows, was a heavy sleeper and unlikely to wake up.'

'But why the three figurines?'

'He had no choice. There was nothing worth stealing in his own house and he did not have the necessary skills to open Mrs Webster's strong-box. He knew, however, that all three houses happened to contain the same jubilee souvenir and that created a perfect diversion. You may recall that my housekeeper, Mrs Hudson, abandoned the tea because she was distracted by a dancing dog, and very much the same principle applied here. Mr Abernetty correctly assumed that you would worry so much about these wholly inoffensive objects that you would never question whether a real burglary had taken place. He was just unfortunate that on this occasion you chose to bring the matter to me.'

'I presume he left the footprints on purpose.'

'Indeed so. I did wonder why we had a burglar who was so keen to mark out his method of entry. It was, of course, Mr Abernetty, wearing Michael Snowden's shoes, who took care to leave footprints in the flower beds. However, he unwittingly left a fold in the dead man's sock as he dragged one of them off. I remarked upon it in the mortuary.'

'Mr Holmes . . . I am beyond words.' Jones got to his feet but it seemed to me that he did so only with an effort and I was reminded that he had displayed the same infirmity when we were at Hamworth Hill. 'You will forgive me if I leave you,' he continued. 'I must make an arrest.'

'Two arrests, Inspector, for Mrs Abernetty was clearly an accessory to the crime.'

'Indeed so.' Jones examined Holmes one last time. 'Your methods are extraordinary,' he muttered. 'I will learn from them. I *must* learn from them. To have missed so much and to have seen so little — I will not let it happen again.'

A short while later, I learned that Athelney Jones had become ill and taken leave from the police force. It was Holmes's opinion that the dreadful business of the Abernettys might have played a part in his decline and so, out of respect to the poor man, I made the decision not to publish my account but instead to place it with certain other papers in the vaults of Cox & Co. in Charing Cross, affording him the same confidence that I would to any of my own patients. Let it be made public at some time in the future, when the events I have described have been forgotten, allowing the inspector's reputation to remain intact.

We do hope that you have enjoyed reading this large print book.

Did you know that all of our titles are available for purchase?

We publish a wide range of high quality large print books including:
Romances, Mysteries, Classics
General Fiction
Non Fiction and Westerns

Special interest titles available in large print are:
The Little Oxford Dictionary
Music Book
Song Book
Hymn Book
Service Book

Also available from us courtesy of Oxford University Press:
Young Readers' Dictionary
(large print edition)
Young Readers' Thesaurus
(large print edition)

For further information or a free brochure, please contact us at:
Ulverscroft Large Print Books Ltd.,
The Green, Bradgate Road, Anstey,
Leicester, LE7 7FU, England.
Tel: (00 44) 0116 236 4325
Fax: (00 44) 0116 234 0205

THE HOUSE OF SILK

Anthony Horowitz

It is November 1890 and London is gripped by a merciless winter. Sherlock Holmes and Dr Watson are enjoying tea by the fire when a gentleman arrives at 221B Baker Street. He begs Holmes for help, telling the unnerving story of a scar-faced man who has been stalking him. Intrigued, Holmes and Watson find themselves swiftly drawn into a series of puzzling and sinister events, stretching from the gas-lit streets of London to the teeming criminal underworld of Boston. As the pair delve deeper into the case, they stumble across a whispered phrase — 'The House of Silk': a mysterious entity and foe, more deadly than any Holmes has encountered, and a conspiracy that threatens to tear apart the very fabric of society itself . . .

THE MONOGRAM MURDERS

Sophie Hannah

Hercule Poirot's quiet supper in a London coffee house is interrupted when a young woman confides to him that she is about to be murdered. She is terrified, but begs Poirot not to find and punish her killer. Once she is dead, she insists, justice will have been done. Later that night, Poirot learns that three guests at the fashionable Bloxham Hotel have been murdered, and a cufflink has been placed in each one's mouth. Could there be a connection with the frightened woman? While Poirot struggles to put together the bizarre pieces of the puzzle, the murderer prepares another hotel bedroom for a fourth victim . . .

THE DROP

Dennis Lehane

Bob Saginowski is a quiet, lonely man working in a Boston bar ostensibly owned by his cousin Marv — though the real owners are a Chechen gang who use it, along with other places around the city, as a 'drop' for their illicit gains. Two days after Christmas Bob rescues an abused puppy from a trash can and meets Nadia, a damaged woman looking for something to believe in. Then he finds himself at the centre of a robbery gone awry, and suddenly a cop named Torres is asking about a decade-old murder; the Chechens who own the bar want their $5,000 back; and a lowlife named Eddie Deeds wants $10,000 for the dog Bob found in the trash. What's a friendless bartender to do?

MIDNIGHT AT MARBLE ARCH

Anne Perry

It is 1896, and Thomas Pitt is in charge of Special Branch. During a lavish party at the Spanish Embassy, a policeman interrupts Pitt's conversation with investor Rawdon Quixwood to break the terrible news that Quixwood's wife Catherine has been viciously assaulted and murdered at their home. At the same party, Pitt's wife Charlotte sees Angeles Castelbranco, an ambassador's daughter, flinch in fear at the teasing of some young men. A few days later, Angeles flees from the same group and, in her terror, falls from a window — what could have caused her to take that fatal step? Pitt and his friend Victor Narraway vow to uncover the unspoken truth behind the deaths of the two women. But as they investigate, danger is only ever one step away . . .